Out Where the Brolgas Dance

Sara Powter

Copyright © Sara Powter 2021

Bible Quotes from the King James Version

ISBN: 978-0-9945782-4-2
Paperback edition

Pacific Wanderland Publications
ABN 99 768 734 831
Kincumber NSW 2251

saragpowter@gmail.com
www.sarapowter.com.au

1st Edition 2021 - Amazon/Kindle
Revised 2025
2nd Edition 2021 - Pacific Wanderland Publications
Revised 2025
1st Edition 2021 - Hard Cover Revised 2025
1st Edition 2023 - Large Print Edition Revised 2025

Psalm 19:7–10
King James Version

The law of the Lord is perfect, converting the soul:
The testimony of the Lord is sure, making wise the simple.
The statutes of the Lord are right, rejoicing the heart:
The commandment of the Lord is pure,
enlightening the eyes.
The fear of the Lord is clean,
enduring forever:
The judgments of the Lord
are true and righteous altogether.
More to be desired are they than gold,
yea, than much fine gold:
Sweeter also than honey and the honeycomb.

Australian Historical Novels
(All stand-alone books)

A First Fleet Stories (1788+)
Gentle Annie Soames
The Emancipated Potter
Paternity Unknown

The Hunter to Macquarie Collection (1795-1822)
When Upon Life's Billows
The Saddler's Song (2025)
Tuppence to Pass (2025)
His Majesty's Pageboy (2026)
A Fist Full of Holey Dollars (2026)
Far From the Whispering Sheoaks (2026)
Bound Down in Iron Chains (2026)

Unlikely Convict Ladies Trilogy (1792-1840s)
Dancing to Her Own Tune
(co-authored by Sheila Hunter & Sara Powter)
Amelia's Tears
A Lady in Irons

The Lockleys of Parramatta (1800-1901)
Unshackled Lives - *Prequel novella - free with newsletter signup*
Hands Upon the Anvil
Out Where the Brolgas Dance
Diamonds in the Dirt
The Earl's Shadow
Once a Jolly Swagman
Jonty's Journey

The Convict Birthstain Collection (1820-1840s)
No More, My Love
The Vine Weaver
Scotch at The Rocks
Waiting at the Sliprails
Convict Shadows of the Past
In Defence of Her Honour
I Can't Stop Tomorrow
Madeline's Boy
Jam or Marmalade for Tea

Sheila Hunter's
Australian Colonial Trilogy (1840-1850s)
Mattie
Ricky
The Heather to the Hawkesbury

Cover Painting
https://www.sl.nsw.gov.au/collection-items/west-view-parramatta
Joseph Lycett, 1819 West View of Parramatta ML53

Thanks to
My Dad, Norman McLean Hunter,
who first took me to the shaker deck in his silica sand works
and showed me how fine gold was separated.

And to both my parents, who showed the faith of our Lord.
Thanks for setting a fabulous example for me.
We often stopped on our travels
to watch the brolgas dance.
It is truly a majestic sight.

To my patient and ever-loving husband, Stephen.
Thanks for doing the initial read.

And thanks, Roby Aiken,
my Grammar angel.
And Noreen Robertson for the final read-through.
And Anna Leffew for her PR work and BETA reading.

It would not have made it in print without you all.
Thank you.

Table of Contents

Chapter 1   Go West, Young Man   5
Chapter 2   Smell of the Eucalypts   15
Chapter 3   Hunting for Treasure   23
Chapter 4   Find the Dancing Birds   47
Chapter 5   Turning Things Around   65
Chapter 6   Eastward Bound   83
Chapter 7   Chilled   111
Chapter 8   Fun Things   127
Chapter 9   Shipmates   163
Chapter 10   Tea with the Governor   189
Chapter 11   For Eternity   205
Chapter 12   Loss and Gain   219
Chapter 13   The Building Begins   241
Chapter 14   Turning the First Sod   259
Chapter 15   Then There Were Four   283
Chapter 16   And Baby Makes More   309
Chapter 17   A Melancholy Day   327
Chapter 18   A Letter Arrives   337
Chapter 19   It's Time   353
The Duke/Earl Tree   377
Main Characters   378
Real People and Places   379
Author's Historical Note   380
Bibliography   382

The grammar and language in this book are
Australian English spelling.

KEY
~ - Time passing in the same locality

- Different locality/country

His Grace, the Duke of Gracemere,
Gracemere Castle,
Maidstone England

Dear Uncle Ned,

Greetings from the other side of the world. I hope this letter finds you all well. As I write, I have two little blonde munchkins playing at my feet. I hope your two ragamuffins are equally active. Jenna particularly sends greetings to Aunt Christina. We still miss you. It's hard to believe they are now two years and four months old and walking everywhere. Both call me "Poppa" and Jenna "Mum Mum". Although they are brother and sister, and they look very similar, Tina is still smaller but is far more agile.

My darling Jenna is again heavy with child and is due around Easter next year. She is nowhere near the size she was last time, so we're hoping for only one babe this time. She is breezing through this confinement. She has taken to motherhood amazingly. Martha and Jack come and go with great regularity and have left spare clothing here for such visits. Marc has taken on much of the responsibility of running the Inn at Emu Plains, therefore freeing them up. Marc and Milly had a baby girl on 4th September, Charlotte Amelia, so they are kept busy. Tim and Anna followed them with William Charles, born on the 6th. Then Charlie and Grace followed the family tradition of twins. Grace had twin boys born early on Sept 26th, Edward William and John Charles. So the Earldom's succession is safe. (Thank goodness). They look different from each other, so I'm glad to say I don't get them confused. Edward (Teddy) is fair-haired, and John has light brown hair (I do hope they stay like this). I am sure Dar has filled you in on all this news. I am merely procrastinating.

Uncle Ned, when you see Mama and Dar, send our love and greetings and tell them all is well here at the Inn and Shop. There have been no problems that Charlie has not handled brilliantly, except for one, which I shall explain later. It's been a very wet year; however, we haven't had any floods. This means that the bushy undergrowth is thick, and I expect next summer to be bad for fires.

Now for the problem

Uncle Ned, Wills has left town and gone to Bathurst and beyond. He said he had not technically run away, as he was officially offered a job as a record keeper. However, he had left, leaving only a letter for me (not Charlie). However, I do feel this was a ruse and that he has, in reality, run away. As you know, both boys have been living with us while Mama and Dar are with you.

Wills finished school this week and was at a loose end. Luke still has two more years to go at The King's School. Wills has not got the academic bent; he's, like me, hands-on. I was sure he loved the work at the Forge, but it was not enough to keep him interested.

Luke, however, wishes there were more time for him at the school. He loves studying. I was thinking that I would sponsor him to attend Sydney College. Mr Cape is sadly no longer there. Mr Braim is now the headmaster and has extended the study facilities.

William Wentworth was talking to Charlie and me last week and is interested in forming a University. I hope this will be done in time for Luke. We told him we support him in this venture, and Luke would hopefully be one of the first students. Wills was listening as he knew Mr Wentworth had crossed the mountains. He later pumped him for information on what it looks like over there. He's always been the lad's hero, as he was named after him. Major Mitchell is another such hero for him.

Uncle Ned, Wills got talking to some men I have mentioned before at the Shop last week, and they were heading West, and I fear it was they who offered the job, over the mountains and far beyond. He briefly mentioned it to me, but I was preoccupied with the children and wasn't fully listening. When I arrived home today, there was a letter on my desk. I am grief-stricken! Charlie and Jenna are also deeply grieved. I went down and showed Charlie Wills' letter. Wills had said nothing to him nor to Luke.

I feel I have failed him!

I believe that the group he has gone with are just exploring. They are not planning on settling or farming; this is even more worrying to me, as I will have no way of contacting him. He did say he would keep me apprised of his direction. Oh, I am so worried.

I know he has also been listening to the Reverend Mr Clarke talk of his gold finds out on a farm near Hartley. (He's been a lecturer at King's this year.) Mr Clarke sadly told Wills in April this year, just as he returned. Mr Clarke reported his findings to Sir George Gipps, and the Governor directed him to "Put it away, Mr Clarke, or we shall all have our throats cut." I fear the idea of his leaving has been festering since then. If this is the case, then I do not wish to think about it. If he has gone to seek a fortune in gold, then I hope he does not get carried away. However, I think Wills has gone to find out the extent of the finds. Wealth has never held much meaning to Wills, hence my puzzlement.

He has said to me more than once, "Ed, I want to go out where the Brolgas dance, to see beyond the hills. To know what is out there. I need to know." He looked so in earnest. He has always had itchy feet. He's been the one to want to explore new things well and new horizons, too. He speaks with such passion.

I can do no more than pray and worry until I hear from him. There is regular traffic along the mountain road. Larger and larger vehicles are now traversing the mountains. Once word gets out about Reverend Clarke's find, I think Governor Gipps may be right. All hell will let loose. It would also change the entire settlement.

I just do not know how to tell Dar and Mama. I feared to write, but I knew I must. I may wait a week or so in case I hear from Wills. Please prepare them; I shall not send the letter at the same time as this, so you will get this missal first.

I will write of homely things in another letter. Please pray for Wills on his venture and us in our worry.

Your loving honorary nephew

Eddie (Edward Lockley)

Main Characters

Wills Lockley, Charles and Sal's 3rd Son
John Saunders, The Hon. (Sir John, Baron's son) CO Harry's cousin
Harry Harlow, The Hon. 2IC - bro. Viscount Anthony Winchester
Edmund Hunt, (Lord) Christina's brother - Viscount Eames
Phillip Corsairs, (Sir) Annabella's cousin
Lewis Bland, Duke's mother's cousin from Scotland
Aidan O'Keefe, cousin to Sal - from Ireland

More at the back of the book

Chapter 1   Go West, Young Man

"*G*eorge, quick, hand me the duffel bag. I've got my things sorted and have to hurry before Ed returns." Wills quickly stuffed his clothing in the long duffel bag. Followed by a parcel wrapped in oilcloth, a leather pouch and spare boots. He added various journals, pads of paper, a roll of pencils, quills, a bottle of ink, a knife and his small Bible.

"Done yet?" George stuck his head out of the bedroom door. "They are still in the kitchen. Can't you hurry?"

"Yes, I'm done." He grabbed his hat and coat. He stuffed his overcoat in the top of the bag, tattered and worn though it was, then pulled the drawstring. He took a look around his bedroom. He sighed, then took a letter from under his pillow. Both boys walked out of the room. Wills closed the door behind him, taking one last look as he did so. He sighed as though in pain and whispered, "Sorry, Ed."

They crept downstairs and towards the front door. Wills quietly opened the door to Eddie's office, propped a letter on the lamp and left.

George had the front door open, and they crept out without making a noise, closing it gently behind them.

Once outside, they moved from the verandah and out onto Phillip Street. Now was the most dangerous part of the escape, and George had taken the duffel bag from Wills in case they were seen. Luck was on their side, and they cut through the building opposite and made it into George Street without being seen.

They both sighed. They had made it so far without being caught. Once in George Street, they collected a second duffel bag that they had placed there earlier. These were George's clothes.

As both were well-known in town, particularly Wills, they stuck to the shadows and shortcuts through town until they reached St. John's cemetery. They'd made arrangements to be collected from there.

After half an hour dodging various carriages and carts, they made it to the meeting place at the cemetery gate. They had a little time to wait but stood watching for the cart that would take them west. Soon, the rumble of three carts caught the boys' attention. As they drew closer, they ducked out of their hiding place and scrambled up onto the back of one of the wagons. They stowed their bags under the canopy and stayed hidden. Both were perspiring with fear. They had made their escape.

George's parents, Fred and Violet Allan, had taken over the Union Hotel last year and had cleaned up the patronage substantially. George was nineteen, and Wills, seventeen. One would think that Wills had been talked into this escapade; however, it was the other way around. George was not particularly keen to leave home and hearth, as for the first time in his life, he not only had a room to himself but was comfortable. He was not an adventurous lad, and it had taken some talking by Wills to persuade him to come with him. George could draw brilliantly, and this skill would be needed as they headed west.

Wills' secret dream had always been to see the inside of this country, but he hoped to 'find his niche.' Wills lived in the shadow of his two older brothers, Charlie and Eddie, as well as his younger brother, Luke, who was an academic. He was destined to study some form of science, particularly since receiving the news from Uncle Ned last year. Wills thought back to the night he'd found out who the Major was. "All my life, I've known him as The Major. He bounced me on his lap, played with me, joked with me and shared many a Sunday meal with the family." Wills thought, still in wonderment.

When he told them who he was, they all felt winded. A Duke! A real live Duke. Then he goes off and marries Mrs Meadows, and it turns out she's a Lady, too. The Honourable Christina, humph. And if that's not bad enough, last year, the news arrived that Dar is an Earl, had been one for most of his life and never knew it. Which meant Charlie was now a Viscount. He, along with the rest of the family, was also now known as "The Honourable". Well, he wanted to 'do' something more than live in the shadow of his older brothers. Eddie and Jenna were busy having babies, running the store and building up the forge. He had enjoyed working there and making stuff, but he wanted more.

The boys crawled out from under the covers once they left town and perched themselves on the seat beside John, the driver. They were both silent, and John tried to draw them out with questions. After some time, he gave up and sat in silence for a while.

After an hour, he said, "Now listen here, lads, this is an adventure. We're heading west, and we don't know what we're going to find. If we're going to stick together on this trip, we have to know something more about each other than our names. So, as neither of you wishes to talk - yet, I shall tell you a bit about myself."

"My name is John Saunders. We've come from England after spending some time in India. On the other wagons are Phillip Corsairs and Aidan O'Keefe on the second wagon, and Edmund Hunt, Harry

Harlow and Lewis Bland on the third. All are financing the exploration with me. I put you two on my vehicle as I want to know more about you. Now, unless you wish to walk home, spill."

Neither boy spoke.

John looked over at the two lads, betting they had both run away, hence their fear. "I presume by your silence that neither told your folks you were coming?"

The boys looked at each other sheepishly, and both nodded.

John's reaction was not what they expected. He threw his head back and laughed. "Well, I figured that was the case. I'll make you a deal: you can still come, but I want you to send regular letters home to let your family know where you are and what you are doing. All right? Let's ensure they understand what we're doing. You can deal with the repercussions when you return home. But the more often you write, and especially if the letters are full of adventures, the less trouble you will be in. Savvy?"

Relief flooded through them. Wills spoke, "Sir, do you mean it - we can still come?"

John looked at him. "Lad, I was about your age when I went on my first adventure. I came back as a grown man. I learnt so much and saw incredible things, as well as having a fabulous experience. Sure, there will be dangers, and we have to be careful, but I do plan to have an adventure. It should take us no more than a year and hopefully less. We'll see how far we get and what we find. And where God leads. I hope to have you home by Christmas next year."

George slumped in his seat. Christmas! He would miss Christmas with his folks. He'd miss the carols and the singing, the food and all the family.

John looked at him. "George, lad, are you all right?"

George nodded. "Yes, sir, it's just I've never been away from home so long. I do want to come, sir; really, I do; at least, I think I do."

John looked concerned. "Lad, once we cross the mountains, there's no turning back. You have until we reach Emu Plains to make your final decision." He looked to Wills, "And you lad?" he asked. "I suppose you're homesick too?"

Wills shook his head. "No, sir, you see, my parents are in England and have been for a year or more. I've been living with my older brother, Ed, even though I suppose my eldest brother, Charlie, is my guardian while my folks are away. I've been at The King's School and have just finished last week. I've been working at the forge with Ed on and off for a few years now. Although I love the work and do eventually plan to return, I want to see some of this vast country first. Ed knows this. He would love to have come, but he and his wife have twins and another one on the way. We used to talk about heading west before he got married, but when he met Jenna, everything changed." He looked sadder rather than sullen. "Ed doesn't spend as much time with me now that he has his children. I miss that. Luke was always reading some book or other, usually it was a science book. Charlie was always busy at the Inn or with his Viceroy duties."

John glanced at him. "Blacksmith, Inn, Lockley, so you're Earl Coxheath's youngin', eh? The Hon Wills." John heard Wills groan. He chuckled. "Never mind, lad, we won't hold it against you. There are a few titles in this mob, but I'm not letting on who. Swallow the pride and enjoy the trip."

Wills brightened. "Oh, sir, so it's all right? Really. I'll work hard. I can keep great journals, and George can paint and sketch as well. We will need to buy some books and journals before we leave Penrith, if that's all right. We can stop the night at Jenna's folks' Inn at Emu Plains. I've been that far, often even ridden up a bit of the road up to Ellison's Pinch, but never much further."

George still looked a little concerned but was determined to stick with Wills. Head west, they would.

~

"Hello, darling love," Eddie said as Jenna met him at the door. She had a toddler in each hand and looked tired.

He swooped and picked up both children, then bent and kissed her. "Mmmm, I like that," he said. So she wrapped an arm around his neck and kissed him again. "No wonder I enjoy coming home. With a welcome like this, who could complain?"

Both children giggled and started wriggling to be put down. He did so, then slid his arm along Jenna's shoulder as they walked into the kitchen.

"Kettle is on, love. How was work? Did you get the Governor's iron gates finished?" she asked.

He nodded. "Finally, Yes."

Cara Connor was just finishing making tea as they entered. Unlike most big houses, they preferred the homeliness of a mug of tea in the kitchen. Cara and Paddy often joined them. If they had visitors, they would use the front Sitting Room. Ed may have a new status, but he had not let it change him.

Jenna sat looking lovingly at her beloved husband. They had been married two years and five days. She was more in love with him now than when they made their vows. Her eyes drank in his form.

His drifted over her face, resting on her lips. He licked his own lips and swallowed. Their eyes locked. While they drank their tea, both children were attempting to climb onto his lap. He knew they would not leave him alone until he had given his full attention to each one. Neddie always demanded it first, and Tina was always willing to oblige. With both children on his knees, Jenna looked on, chin resting on her hands.

Neddie chattered away in a baby talk which no one could understand, save Tina. Ed nodded and tried to make sense of what he was saying. Jenna translated, and Ned grinned up at him. Four large, bright blue eyes stared adoringly at their blonde father.

Tina gently touched his prickly cheek and giggled. She then had a turn, only she translated what her older brother had said, "Cara gave us a cookie. It was nummy. Poppa and Mum Mum have some now?" She spoke so well. Neddie was too lazy to bother.

Moira Connor came in. "Would you like me to take the littlies outside for a romp?"

Ed handed his two precious squirming bundles over to the young Irish lass.

Moira had come to live with her parents after they were "assigned" to Ed's family. They were "lifers" with no hope of parole or Ticket of Leave, but that didn't mean they had to have a tough life. Although their parents were assigned like servants, their children, however, were free. Eddie and Jenna's parents had arrived as convicts. They both knew how tough it was. He'd rescued them when Maryanne had told them how hard it was for her Mam to do the work required of her at her current placement.

Before Major Grace, now the Duke of Gracemere, left, he'd employed Maryanne as a maid for his soon-to-be wife, Christina. Ed had come to know the Irish family and had grown to like them all. He applied for a transfer of indenture for the Connors. Soon, Paddy and Cara, with their two youngest daughters, had moved into a covered cart on the land. Ed had a timber cottage erected for them, and they lived in it while the new house was being built in front. Their cabin was now incorporated into the stables as part of the new staff quarters that were built adjacent to the house.

Paddy had a way with the garden, and from the hard, virgin ground, it soon became a thriving vegetable patch that produced so much it kept the tea house shop buckets filled.

Robbie and Maryanne Ellis ran the Emporium and Tea Rooms that Ed had built. Uncle Ned had given Ed and Jenna a wedding gift of £1000, and with this, he had not only to build their nice new house but also a store in town, a tea room, and a residence adjoining it. With all the building work, they still had over half left. It was now invested at the bank as the Emporium was rolling in money. All the main tradesmen now sold their products from the Emporium. It has become a hub of activity since its opening last year. The saddler, Mr Ellis, Bertie and Robbie's father, was one of the first to request including his items, then the cooper, carpenter, sign-writer and so on, until the shop size had to be doubled. Maryanne persuaded them that the ladies needed somewhere to wait, so they built a small tearoom adjoining. This was already far too small, as perishable goods were also sold from here, including honey, preserves, eggs, vegetables, and fruit, among other things. A commission was taken from each sale, which paid the wages, profit, and bonuses. The turnover was such that the stores were generating a substantial profit, prompting an extension to be already planned.

Moira took the toddlers outside to her papa, and Jenna motioned for Eddie to join her. They, too, left the kitchen.

Cara collected the mugs and set about preparing dinner.

Jenna held her hand out to Eddie and just said, "Come."

He grinned. He'd discovered her 'appetite' during confinement was not just for food. He willingly followed her up to their bedroom before sweeping her into his arms.

"Hush, love, they can hear us downstairs," she whispered, giggling. Her growing belly had not yet impeded their lovemaking nor quenched their desire for each other.

Eddie took her gently in his arms and lifted her onto the bed. She greeted him thus every day. To be without each other, even for a few short hours, was a trial. He so enjoyed the love that his wonderful lady willingly shared, more so while expecting. He closed the door, locked it, and joined her on the bed.

Sometime later, they could hear the children being brought inside. Ed leaned over Jenna and stroked her cheek. "I love you more and more each day, you know, love." She reached up and pulled his head down to hers. Eddie brushed his lips over hers but did not take up the unspoken invitation, as he could hear little footsteps coming up the steps. He groaned and rolled off the bed, and she did, too. He had quickly removed his work clothing, donned a clean outfit and unlocked the door.

The doorknob rattled from the outside. He turned to check Jenna was decently attired and opened it carefully, saying, "I wonder who could be knocking on my door?" Whoops of giggles, and he took them in his arms and walked back down the stairs with them. The love he had for these two blonde munchkins of theirs was overwhelming. He just wanted to have Jenna and them within his reach at all times, protecting them and loving them. They were now to be blessed with another one in a few months. Jenna had thankfully been well throughout much of this confinement, a stark contrast to the last one. At this time, six months, she had been able to sit a teacup on her distended belly. The babes had been impatient and came nearly a month early, only eight months after they were married; by then, Jenna was in constant pain. Just sitting became a trial. They had moved to Sydney a month before the due date and had only been there about ten days before they arrived. That was on August 15, 1842.

Martha, Jenna's mother, attended the birth at the hospital. Jenna has insisted she was allowed in the room.

Eddie and Jack, her father, had to wait outside. He could hear Jenna's screams of pain and Martha's soothing words, but he could not see her. His stomach turned when he thought back to that day. His anxiety knew no bounds.

Jack could say nothing more than, "She's strong" or "She'll be fine," but it gave him no comfort to know he had inflicted this upon her so early in their marriage. They had been married only a week before she realised she'd missed her menses. A week of married bliss, where they had certainly given nature every chance of making a baby.

His mind flicked back; their innocence before marriage made the honeymoon more special. The joys of discovering each other's bodies and the beauty of their frequent joining bonded them. It was on the return trip on their honeymoon that the realisation had hit Jenna like she'd been punched. She had missed her menses. Their shock and joy were confirmed when, in the weeks afterwards, the morning sickness began. Sal, Eddie's mother, was a mine of information and spoke openly with them both. She had six pregnancies and told them what to expect. She also told Eddie how to assist over the following months. This he could understand; he was good at doing things, just not at sitting and waiting. When the Major's friend, Gerry, who was Doctor Gerald Winslow-Smythe, told them that both Jenna and the Major's wife might be expecting twins, he was shocked. They had gone for a walk along the waterfront at Sydney Cove. The ladies were left talking to the Doctor, and he and the Major had gone for a walk together. Uncle Ned and he were in shock, both feeling guilty that what the Major termed 'his base desires' had caused this situation. He was as white with shock and worried as Eddie was. As they leaned on the railing of the Cove, they prayed together. *"Dear Lord, your will be done. Give us both strength to help where needed."* This helped somewhat.

The Major, now Duke, and both the Doctor and Christina were leaving for England the following day. So Eddie had to cope on his own. He had learnt to trust God many years ago, and his faith did not waver, but his understanding was small. Together, he and Jenna prayed. Every day, they prayed. Things had worked out that they had moved into the Major's old cottage that he'd given to Ed's parents, Charles and Sal Lockley. Christina's Cottage was also gifted to them, and his parents moved into that just two doors up. It was nice to have them nearby. Maryanne stayed in the spare room with Ed and Jenna, and the boys moved in with Dar and Mama. Then the letter arrived that would change everything.

Dar was an Earl, and he had no idea. Dar's father, John, had died when he was five; he had been a rebel at home. A fatherless child, living with his mother and little sister. Admittedly, he was in a nice cottage, but he hung around with a crowd of boys who were troublemakers. When a stray sheep had been found in the front yard of their cottage, he'd automatically been found guilty, even though he'd been at work and could not have taken it. He'd been found guilty and transported. On the ship out, he'd been chained to Jack Turner. He discovered that he was a praying man. Charles rediscovered his faith, and over those months, first in the hulks and later on the ship, his faith grew. Jack and he prayed daily, if not even more often. One night, while Jack was praying quietly, he overheard plans for a mutiny on board and woke Charles. They didn't know what to do. They were sailing down the west coast of Africa at the time. He'd noticed one of the battalion majors watching him with interest. He had no idea why, but thought, "I could attract his attention and let him know the plans."

The next time, they were let out on deck for a walk and some air. He nodded, mouthed, "Hello," and mouthed "Help" softly as he passed him. Then he tripped and pulled Jack over, too. He saw the Major understood, and shortly afterwards, he was unshackled and summoned to his cabin.

"You wanted a word?" the Major said abruptly.

"Thank you, sir. I have been wondering how to approach you. Jack and I have been praying daily, and in one of our times of quiet prayer, we overheard a conversation in the next cell." Charles drew a breath. He was reporting on his fellow prisoners, and if this got out, his and Jack's lives would be hell. "Sir, they are planning a mutiny just before we land in Cape Town. I could not let this happen. I am innocent of my charge, but I know all prisoners say that. I am an honest man and wish no harm to occur to anyone, but I cannot, in all good conscience, allow this to occur. Jack Turner agrees with me, and we agreed to let you know somehow." He paused before continuing. "Sir, I have noticed you've been watching me. I do not know why, but I feel I can trust you." He dropped his head in subservience and waited.

"Thank you, man. Your name is… Lockley, is this correct? And your friend's name is Turner?" asked the Major. He was surprised that this convict's voice was well-spoken, even educated.

Charles was astounded that his name was known to him. He said respectfully, "Yes, sir. Both are correct."

"I shall take this information to the other two majors and the ship's captain. We shall prepare. I shall keep you two out of it somehow. Expect a transfer to washing duties or a similar role. I'll call it a mild punishment for insubordination. Your names will not be released. I will not even record this until we dock in Sydney." The Major stood and put out his hand to shake Charles's hand. "Thank you again, Lockley, this shall not go unrewarded. But be assured, your identities will be secured."

Ed knew the story. The Major had kept his word. The two men were transferred from the cell for day duty on the upper decks. He kept watch on them, and when the time came, they were safely secured in an upstairs room with the Major. From that first meeting, they had trusted each other and later became firm friends. Charles, a convict, and Ned, a Major, only to find they were, in fact, an Earl and a Duke and were third cousins. Familial similarity was why the Major had watched Charles so intently - he reminded him of his youngest brother, Douglas, amazingly so. On board, their upstairs duties also meant no stench, a place to sleep, and the opportunity to be clean. So, the bond between the two prospective fathers was already strong, even though, at that stage, they had not discovered the family connections. Ned suspected something, as did Gerry, but Ed had known nothing. Now, the probability of twins drew them even closer.

Eddie was a second-born child, born on Major Ned's birthday, to Charles and the Major's part-time maid, Sal. Eddie had been named after Ned. The Major loved him like his own, so he decided to further his education in secret. He did this with the aid of the blacksmith, Mr Thomas Tindale. They hatched a plan for the lad to attend the best school the colony could offer. Eddie spent five years learning all he could. He left a boy aged ten and returned a man anyone would be proud of.

Eddie returned to the forge and worked hard with Mr Tindale, eventually going into partnership with him. Then he met Jenna. Oh, what a day that was. He's seen the same look on Charles' face the day he saw Sally. He knew Jenna was the one God had planned for Eddie, and it was a shock to learn that she was Jack Turner's daughter. They met before they realised each other's identity. It was meant to be. A God-incidence!

Much of this was revealed to Eddie that day on the waterfront while the girls talked to the Doctor. Some he already knew, but to hear it from the Major himself and his side of the story made it all the more real.

Soon after he went to school in Sydney, the Major had started coming for a family meal on Sunday after church. When he retired, he moved just a few doors up from the inn. Two doors up from him was a recent widow. Mrs Meadows was so beautiful, even to a young lad, and she was a widow. Ed knew that the Major would walk her home from church, but he never saw them together at any other time. Then Doctor Gerry arrived. Eddie thought back to the attack on him by highwaymen and the Doctor's arrival. Things moved at a pace; it was the week of his wedding. He was returning from Emu Plains and had been accosted by highwaymen. It turned out that Doctor Gerry, Gerald Winslow-Smythe, was the Major's best friend from England. He'd come to look for him in New South Wales to tell him that he was needed at home. The Major was now a Duke, as his father and elder brother, David, had died, without leaving any children.

Only hours after his inheritance was revealed, the Major proposed to Mrs Meadows, marrying only three weeks later on Christmas Day.

Four months on, she, too, was possibly expecting twins.

All this went through Eddie's mind as he played with his children on the office floor. They were happily occupied with the alphabet blocks Wills had made for them, so he left them there and sat at his desk to start some work that needed his attention. As he sat, he saw a note leaning on the lamp. Puzzled that Jenna had said nothing about any letters, he opened the sheet of paper and read. It was from Wills. He pushed back his chair and called for Moira to attend to the babes while he went to find Charlie. He tucked the letter in his pocket. He called for Jenna and asked her to come along as well.

They left to find Charlie. He was officially his guardian, although left in Eddie's care. Eddie filled her in on the way down to the Inn.

His heart was in his mouth.

Chapter 2 Smell of the Eucalypts

*T*he small caravan of wagons wended its way out towards the
Blue Mountains. In the December heat, the smell of the eucalyptus oil hit
the nostrils the closer you came to the trees. Although it had been a wet
year, the creeks, although running, were not overflowing. The
undergrowth and scrub were lush and green, as were the fields of grasses
and orchards they passed. For luncheon, they stopped at Rooty Hill, at the
tree with the horse trough hewn out of a log. This was a regular spot for
travellers now. Someone had even left a bucket so the trough could be
refilled from the nearby creek. It was near the Government Farm at Rooty
Hill.

After they left this spot, he dug out his journal and started to
write. It was a bit bumpy on stretches of the road, but he managed to put
down a few thoughts. He'd have to buy a stack of journals in Penrith. He
would also try to keep a personal diary, as well as a working journal, and
he mustn't forget writing paper, wax, and other writing supplies.

Ed had told Wills that this was where the Doctor had let him
sleep on the day he'd been beaten up by highwaymen. They had travelled
this road a few times together. Wills shuddered each time, as he did again.
*Poor Eddie, I know I've disappointed him. I did try to tell him that I
wanted to go, but he didn't listen.* Wills still felt guilty. He loved Eddie and
did not want to upset him or Charlie either, but his bond with Ed was
stronger.

Thankfully, he had not spent any of his allowances over the past
year and therefore had ample funds. He had that safely stashed in three
separate purses. Something else he'd learnt from Eddie's attack. Always
have some small change on hand to give away, but keep the rest hidden.
One pouch was wrapped in his smalls. One tucked in the toe of a shoe,
and the other on his person with a smaller amount. Also, he had some

loose coins in his other pocket.

The trip west proceeded without mishap. Towards late afternoon, they pulled up to the newly opened Post Office in Penrith. Wills had been at the opening with Charlie only last month. He knew he could obtain the paper, journals and writing materials he required. He took the time to scratch another note to Eddie, informing him of who his travelling companions were and that he had promised to write as often as possible. Again, he wrote his apology for why he had left. He also mentioned that the trip was to last up to a year, and they should be home by Christmas next year, if not earlier.

Thus posted, he proceeded to fill his shopping list. He also purchased painting paper for George, some watercolour paints, charcoal, and special pads for his drawings.

George accompanied John to the local store and helped load some pre-ordered goods. Wills would join them later.

The wagon, duly loaded, set off for Emu Plains. They pulled into the now-familiar yard about an hour before dusk. Marc greeted them. Wills hopped off and asked if it would be all right to stay for the night, paid, of course.

Marc nodded, "Sure - but it's only hammocks in the shed. We're full these days. Milly and I have one room, Pa and Maa, another and the girls the third, although they are away tonight. The boys are sleeping on the floor of the sitting room. So all visitors have to sleep rough." Wills had warned the group of this. This was normal at any wayside Inn, so it was to be expected. The benefits, though, included a home-cooked hot dinner, a well with plenty of water, and a privy.

Martha welcomed Wills warmly. He looked guiltily at her but introduced the rest of the group.

"May I have a word with you later, please, Mrs Turner?" Wills said. "With Mama and Dar away, Ed and Jenna are busy, as is Charlie; I need to tell someone why I'm here. I would have talked it over with Dar before I left, but he wasn't there."

Martha said, "Of course, Wills. How about you help with dinner, and we can chat? Cathy and Vicky are staying with Mary tonight as it's her birthday. Milly is working in her leather room at the back of the stables. So you can peel the vegetables." Wills nodded. His heart sank; he wouldn't get to see them.

He poured his heart out to her. "I didn't think I'd miss Mama and Dar so much. We had so much fun as kids, but now everyone is busy except me. Luke always has his nose in books and doesn't even want to swim anymore, let alone fish or go bushwalking. Ed and Charlie have not only their lovely wives but also babies, too. I just don't fit in any more. Oh, don't get me wrong, I know they love me, and I love them, too; that's not the problem. I, well, I'm lonely, I suppose, Mrs Turner." He swallowed, holding back both pride and tears. There was nothing more overwhelming than admitting a weakness, and that's how he saw it.

Martha turned to him. "Oh, Wills, it's so hard. You're at that awkward age of seventeen, being too young for marriage and too old to be a child. Luke, as we know, is a scholar, and his nose is always in books. He's found his passion. Wills, I think this trip is a good idea. Go on it and enjoy yourself. Learn to know yourself. That's a hard thing to think about, but I'm serious. You must know yourself, your innermost self, before you can settle into life. Many people drift through their lives, living on the surface. Not thinking about anything more than what the next meal is. You're a deep thinker. You're like my Alex, he is too, but thankfully, he found his niche early." She picked up a vegetable knife, handed it to Wills, and pointed to a pile of potatoes. "Diced with the skins on, please, in half-inch cubes."

He nodded. He had done this hundreds of times for Mama for stews. His mind still jumbled, and his heart racked with guilt; her words were like a balm. He went about his job mechanically.

"So, Mrs Turner, you're not angry with me?" he asked plaintively.

"Oh, no, lad. I do wish you'd done things differently, but now you've spoken to me, I will let Ed know how things are. I do understand." Martha then asked Wills, "What is your favourite dessert?"

"Mama used to make 'Steamed Spotted Dick' with custard." I haven't had it since she left," he replied.

"Jack and Marc both love it, but I'll make three small ones as they will cook quicker. You finish the vegetables and plonk them in the pot with the meat. I'll get on with puddings." Martha wiped her hands on her apron. She washed up the board she'd cut the kangaroo tail on, and then she washed the knife, too. Then she finely diced the meat, and it was now sizzling in butter on the stove. She stirred it and threw in some onions.

Wills's mouth watered. Even Mama's stew didn't smell this good. He'd had enough of Mrs Turner's cooking to know she was a fabulous cook and had taught Jenna well, too. Ed's kitchen help, Cara Connor, could do amazing things with potatoes, but the rest was, well, ho-hum. He would rather Jenna cook.

After the smells wafted around him again, he couldn't resist saying, "That smells so good. Why doesn't Mama's stew smell like this?"

Martha smiled. "Butter, not dripping, you have to sear the meat in a hot pan with butter, then add onions and pepper and let them cook. Only then you add the vegetables and a little water or stock to remove all the juices. Once the pan is clean, add the rest of the water. Cover and cook. If you skip that first bit of butter, the taste is bland. Simple." She could see Wills taking this all in. "Also, dice the meat finely. As fine as you can, and it cooks quicker, which we need tonight. Chop in big chunks if you can leave it to simmer for some time, like an hour or even four, then they get tender. Big chunks take much longer, and we don't have time to cook them tonight, so fine ones cook quickly. It's like making more small puddings rather than one big one. They cook quicker." She moved around the kitchen with speed and grace, whisking the batter for the puddings and adding currants and spices to the mix. She grabbed three pudding ceramic bowls and poured the batter evenly into each. She then placed a dampened cloth over the top and tied a string around the lip of the bowl. These were then placed in a pot of boiling water and then covered with a lid. They would cook while the main course was being eaten.

"Next thing to make was the custard. With so many people to feed, a large one will be needed. Wills, six eggs to a pint of milk. Remember that. Work out the ratios, but for your lot, that's what you'd need. I'll double it." She broke a dozen eggs into a bowl and whisked them with a fork. She set them aside and ladled two pints of milk into a saucepan, and added two teaspoons of runny light honey. "Taste that," she said. Handing him the spoon to lick.

"Oh, delicious, why it's sweet and light, not like the honey we get. It has a bitterness to it," said Wills.

"It's why we buy Mrs Walker's honey. Hers is 'White Box' honey. It's not normal bitter gum, honey. Sometimes, we also get native honey; it's different again. I prefer to cook with this," Martha said.

"I never knew honey could taste so different." Wills was genuinely interested. "There's more to this cooking caper than I thought," he said. He'd relaxed by now and was his bright, cheerful self.

Martha laughed. "Ingredients can make a huge difference, as can the way you cook things. Think of eggs. You can boil them hard or soft, scramble them, fry, or poach them or use them in cakes or custards. Each way, they taste different. So it is with life, Wills. You can sit at home and be a blacksmith. Nothing wrong with that, mind you, and you may well go back to it. Alternatively, you can embark on this adventure and learn everything you can from it. Your life is like that egg. It's what you *do* with it that counts. Your attitude to life is the most important thing." She continued to prepare food while talking. "Think about Charlie; he was a convict's child who's now a Viscount, but he is still a convict child in his brain. Look at Ed now, also a convict's boy, but he's a blacksmith and a darned good one. He has built an incredible future, not just for himself, his wife, and children, but for the entire community. He thinks beyond himself. He thinks of the greater good. Wills, it's why you love him so." Martha was stirring the milk and feeling the pan. She took it off the stove and placed it on the table; she picked up the egg mix and poured it quickly into the milk, stirring constantly. In the warm milk, the mixture thickened, and she poured it into another ceramic bowl, setting it aside to cool. She went and took a small jar from the cupboard. "Jenna gave me some of these. Caroline Evans gave them to her. It's called nutmeg, I think, but oh, it adds a delicious flavour to the custard. I only use a tiny bit as I can't get any more. I only have six of them. Captain Evans used to get them for Caro." She grated a tiny amount on top of the custard and covered it with a muslin cloth to keep the flies away.

All the time, Wills was dicing potatoes and other vegetables. Soon, the pile was ready to add to the stew. He watched Martha pour in half a cup of dark ale, and his eyes grew. "Ale! Why ale?"

"Again, flavour, I did say water or stock, didn't I? Well, this is Jack's version of stock. Dark ale is best in a beef stew, too," she laughed again. She stirred the pot until all the sticky juices from the bottom of the pan were stirred in. Then she added the vegetables. More stirring, then three jugs of water. "Add the salt last, Wills." She put the lid on tightly and pushed it onto the hot hob. She lifted the lid off the boiling puddings to check them and nodded to herself. "Rising nicely," was all she said.

"Come on, young Wills, let's go find the others." She put a motherly hand on his shoulder and joined the others outside.

~

Although it was hot, as December in Australia was wont to be, the brazier was boiling away outside with a pot of hot water on it. All the men, including Jack, Marc, and Alex, who had joined them, were each with a tankard in hand.

Jack handed Martha a cider and asked Wills, "What'll it be, lad?"

"Cider, thanks, Mr Turner." Jack's homemade cider had a kick to it. Much more than Dar's "I need the Dutch courage your stuff will give me." Everyone roared with laughter except George.

"You'd better fill mine again, Mr Turner. I'll need an army of courage if I go ahead with this. I'm not sure yet how Wills talked me into it." His voice was a little unsteady.

"George, if you need a strong drink to give you courage, you shouldn't go. There'll be another traveller past some time to take you home if you want to go. Wills will be fine with these men. So don't think he'll be in danger," Jack said comfortingly.

Wills spoke up. "George, I didn't think I could go alone, but after talking to Mrs Turner tonight, I know that I can. This is to be my voyage of discovery. I *need* to do this. I need to answer the questions burning in my heart. I'd love to have you come, but don't think you have to." Wills realised he'd spoken the truth. "I really need to do this, and I won't think any less of you. You will always be my friend; distance won't change that." Wills felt like a weight had rolled off him. He sat up straight. "I'm ready for this adventure, but I've been planning it for a long time. Ever since Reverend Clarke first told me of what's out there. I've sprung this on you, and it's not fair."

"Wills, I feel like I'm letting you down, but even being here is far enough for me. Are you sure? I'll come, and I'll cope, but I think I really should leave it a while longer before I venture west. Maybe one day." George swallowed with huge relief. He didn't have to go. He never really wanted to in the first place.

John Saunders said, "Don't get me wrong, lad, I would have loved to have you along, but I need a team that is fully committed. I realised that you were, shall I say, half-hearted at best. We'll not think less of you if you join our next trip. We'd be honoured to have you on board. How about that?"

"Really, sir, you'd want me along next time?" asked George. "That would give me time to get my head around some things. I think I'd like that. Thank you, sir."

"Righty oh, then, my good people, let's get hammocks organised and ready for the night before the light completely goes." John drained his tankard and placed it on the tray beside Jack. The others followed suit, and they walked over to the unhitched wagon.

Phil offered to help hang hammocks, and Wills, Marc, Jack, and he went off to the loft to prepare the evening's sleeping arrangements.

Bramblemere Close
Phillip Street
Parramatta
15 December 1844

His Grace Duke of Gracemere,
Gracemere Castle,
Maidstone England
Dear Uncle Ned,

I hope you are all well. I will get straight to it.

I have had news of Wills. I have received a letter from him, well, four actually, and he said he will regularly update me whenever he can. This seems to be holding true if four in one week is any sign. He is sorry he left without farewells, but nothing would have stopped him from going, and he knows I would have tried.

He's joined an expedition West with a "John Saunders, Gentleman". George Allen accompanied him, but Wills sent him home from Emu Plains. Apparently, he had a long talk with Martha while there, and I didn't realise he was feeling so alone. With Charlie and me being married, each with twins, Liza and Anna also with children, and not living at home, and Luke with his head in books all the time, I did not see the situation for what it was. He felt alone in a house full of people. How did I miss this? How remiss I now feel. I wrote to him at the proposed Bathurst stop and told him he has my blessing (Charlie's, too, by the way.) And to stay safe. I'm sure God will open many a door for him.

He writes: "Our group consists of The Honourable, Sir John Saunders, group leader; Sir Phillip Corsairs; Mr Aidan O'Keefe (an Irishman); Lord Edmund Hunt (A Viscount), The Honourable Harry Harlow and Mr Lewis Bland (from Scotland). We plan to head West across the mountains and see what the grazing lands are like."

Uncle Ned, I'm not sure if you know anything about any of these men.

Sir John made Wills promise that he would write often and tell us of their travels as much as possible. This was the condition for him to be allowed to stay with the convoy. He has confessed all to John. Sir John would have sent them both home otherwise. Wills mentioned that the trip is planned to take about a year. Sir John also wrote and conveyed his apologies, not knowing that neither lad had permission to come with him. Having said that, he's happy to have Wills' skills on his journey. George has now returned home, and I've chatted to him, and all details match, but Wills will continue his journey to adventure in the footsteps of his namesake, William Wentworth.

On to other topics...

The Emporium is going well, with nearly every nook and cranny in both shops stuffed full of one product or another. Maryanne and Robbie live at the back of the shop with their daughter, Olivia (Livvi) Cara. She's a happy baby, born in April. Livvi has become an attention seeker as most who come into the Tea Shop pick her up and cuddle her. She has a mop of red curly hair and large green eyes. She is the image of Maryanne's mother, Cara. We have had to draw up plans to extend the Tea Shop, as it has seriously outgrown the building. Buildings are popping up around us, and we have had to purchase extra land for any future building, just so we never get built out.

Charlie and Grace moved back to the Inn while Mama and Dar are over with you. Teddy is the image of our Ned. Seems the Lockley likeness is still strong. These two look more alike than Ted and John.

Mrs Jenkins, from the church, is now running the ladies' group in the 'Coxheath', the centre Cottage. She has become a remarkably changed person and has blossomed into a good role model for younger women. Amazing how one gesture can make such a difference. Molly, Maryanne, Jenna and Grace all assist with at least two others, watching the children in the backyard at all times. Liza and Anna both bring their children, and this brings more young women in as well. They frequently will have twelve children under five, often more. I'm glad I'm not there. The two in our household make enough noise.

I heard from Dar last week. It's wonderful that they finally found Mama's mother, but it's sad that it took so long. I'm glad they were able to be with her in her final month. I know Mama will be excited to know that she has family who still remembers her. I hope they were not put off by her newly found status of Countess. It makes me wonder if they have told them about that. How do the O'Keefes fit in, though?

I will post this brief screed and write again when I hear more from Wills.

Please pass on my regards to Aunt Christina and your two cherubs.

Eddie

Edward Lockley

Chapter 3   Hunting for Treasure

*T*he caravan of wagons slowly proceeded up the rough dirt and rocky track. The wagons were heavily laden, and the horses were pulling hard. They were planning to travel on Major Mitchell's new road. It cut off many of the steep sections of the old road up the mountains.

Speed was not an issue as they had no schedule. They would get as far as they could each day. On the mountain trek, they planned to stop at the convict stockades along the route. These stockades were used by the road repair crews, although many were now available for overnight travellers. Wherever they chose to stop, it would be early, as this would be the first stop where they would be self-sufficient.

Most exploration trips were weighed down by numerous livestock, convicts serving as carriers, and, in general, too much of everything. This trip was not going into uncharted areas, as basic amenities would be available along the route. They planned to stop at Ellison's Pinch for the first night; then, the next destination would be, hopefully, Victoria Stockade. They planned to be there before nightfall. Wills was again sitting up next to Sir John.

"Sir John, since I was able to buy extra supplies at Penrith Post Office, I now have too much, as I bought extras for George. I'm not good at watercolours, but I did learn how. Perhaps we could all give it a try? I'm much better at writing than drawing, although I can do it, as I have to for work. I'm even better at making stuff."

"Firstly, lad, on this trip, we're first names only, all right? There will be no sirs or lords, just names. So I'm John." He laid out the rules in a gentle way. "Now, what do you mean, 'making stuff?' I thought you were just out of school," John asked.

"Sir, sorry John, as you know a bit about my family, the Earl bit and stuff, but my second oldest brother Eddie is a blacksmith, has been since he was about six, and I've been working with him on and off since I was about twelve. Luke, my little brother, too, but mostly me. I found out

I'm really good at it—especially all the fiddly stuff and welding. I love the work, but I want a bit of adventure. Ed had taught me how to do repairs so I can be of use if a wheel breaks and stuff." He stopped breathless. He so wanted to be able to pull his weight on this trip rather than just be a passenger.

"Well, I'll be blown. I didn't see that in you, lad," said John. "I should have guessed by your physique, and you're somewhat stronger than most seventeen-year-olds." He stood over six feet tall and was of equal build to the six army men.

Up ahead, they could see the other two wagons stopped. They were bringing up the rear as they were the lightest of the three. Their supplies included dry goods, canvases, and clothing for the group.

They had made good time.

Phillip Corsairs, driving the lead wagon, felt the horses needed a rest. It was a flat section that was wide enough for another vehicle to pass, so he pulled over to the side and stopped. There was a marvellous view over the valley below.

Edmund had stopped behind the lead wagon.

John pulled up behind them both.

Wills, Aidan, and Harry went to the horses' heads and tied them to branches. They chocked the wheels and brought water in canvas bags to the horses. Once watered, each man stretched their legs.

Wills grabbed a drawing pad and charcoal stick and sketched the outline of the view. John came over and glanced at his work.

"Who said you can't draw? That's amazing," John said admiringly. "You have captured in a few strokes the depth of the valley and the gum mist. Look, down there, at the fern trees and those rock cliffs."

John pointed out some of the things Wills had not seen. He was busy looking at the structure of the valley rather than what was growing in it. With a flick of the charcoal, he added the tree ferns. In a few minutes, the sketch was done.

John stood in awe of this lad's skill. For someone who said he couldn't draw, he was good, very good. "If this is not being able to draw, what the heck was George like?" he asked.

Wills said, "Oh, Sir, sorry, John; he could glimpse a scene and, in a few coloured strokes, could capture the whole and make it alive. I'm okay with charcoal but not that good with colour. I have to design the ironworks I make before I set out to make them. So I knew how to sketch." He put down the pad and set it against a rock, then walked away to look at it from a distance. He walked over again and added a few strokes and a smear of mist. "John, where are we?"

John said, "We're close to the Mt Victoria stop."

Wills wrote "Mt Victoria Valley" on the bottom in small flowing writing, then signed with 'WJL '44'. "That's the first one done, then," he said.

The other men had drifted over to look at what he had done. They were all friends, and Wills felt a little out of the group. That soon changed. "I thought you said you couldn't draw?" said Aidan. He took the pad from Wills and showed it to the others.

John stood back and said nothing. He smiled. This lad was going to be so valuable. Recording the journey, even if it were only in charcoal. They could be copied and coloured later.

Aidan held up the drawing. "The perspective is good. You've caught it in just a few lines." He had captured what was important but showed the whole.

Harry took it from Aidan, "Dammed, good work, lad. Good work. You have captured the depth and essence. I like it."

Wills later discovered just how honouring this accolade was. Harry turned out to be a noted art critic. Embarrassed, Wills folded the pad and stowed the drawing tools back into his bag.

Phil, Edmund, and John turned back to the wagons. "Come on, folks, we cannot sit here all day. On to find a camp spot for the night."

The three wagons slowly moved on again. Wills sighed with a new joy in his heart. He had a role; he would not be useless after all. He hated being deadwood. He also hated being overlooked.

They stopped again shortly afterwards at a small creek that ran alongside the roadway. Wills scrambled up the embankment to look at a white rock outcrop he could see. Reverend Mr Clarke said to look out for white quartz. He wanted to see if this was some. He had a little hammer with him that he'd bought in Penrith and chipped away some of the overhanging rock. Nothing. No gold in this lot, but at least he'd seen quartz. Now he knew what to look for. It certainly was white, though. Not hard to miss.

Harry quizzed him on his return. "What are you up to, lad?"

Wills showed him the chunk of white rock he had knocked off. Lewis joined them. They stood inspecting the rock, then walked over to the tiny creek. They could see that the quartz ran in a cleft of the hill, top to bottom. Wills pointed this out. "See here, where there are pools? Reverend Clarke said that is where fine gold gets stuck. Only there seems to be none here."

Harry asked, "Gold? What gold?"

Wills told Harry of his school lesson from Reverend Clarke. Then he mentioned that Reverend Clarke had found traces on his trip east. They returned to the vehicles and headed off again, hoping to reach their stop before dark. The moon would be shining as it was already beyond the horizon. Edmund and Harry were, however, wary.

"John," they called back, "Surely we can stop along this stretch for the night. Must we journey further?"

"Edmund, I thought you had more backbone than that. All right. We're nearly at One Tree Hill. How about we stop the night near the Mt Victoria Tollgate?" conceded John.

They continued. The sun was now off the road, and the cool of the evening, even though it was December, had descended.

The wagon caravan rolled up to the Tollgate. The building appeared as though it would collapse at any moment. They were waved through the Tollgate with no charge, as they were all unsprung vehicles. The same thing had happened as they passed the last Toll Gate at Ellison's Pinch.

"Good, sir, is there a spot we could camp for the night?" asked John politely.

The gruff voice said, "Pull 'em around the back, and there are a yard for them hosses. The Inn has a stew worth eatin'. So you can chow down there. Wot about sleepin'? You'se gonna sleep out? Can get cold out, even in December," the old-timer said. "Inn's got hammocks in its barn; you'd do to stay there. Only costs a penny. Leave room for more carts, too." Without waiting for an answer, he walked away.

Edmund led the vehicles to the rear of the Toll Bar. They unhitched, and each grabbed their bags for a night at the Inn.

John wondered how safe they would be, but he had no choice but to leave the gear on the wagons. He'd return after their meal and tie up the load more securely. They wandered over to the nearby Inn and were shown the barn. It was closed in and had a roaring brazier. Considering it was December, it was still chilly. Two other travellers were already inside.

There was a pitcher of water and a basin on a stand inside the door. This was obviously for both washing and drinking, as next to this was a stack of upturned mugs.

Wills took one and tasted the water. It was fresh, so he took a long drink.

Dusk passed quickly, as it did in this country, and the evening cooled. They sat around the brazier, talking with the other two travellers. Eventually, the innkeeper called them in for their evening meal. The nine hungry men soon demolished the large stew and damper that was served. It was followed by a huge golden syrup dumpling dish with thick cream. Wills loved it so much he went back for a second, then a third helping. Cider was served with the meal, but hot tea was offered too. Hunger finally sated, and they filed back to the barn.

John and Harry went to check the wagons, only to find that someone had already rifled through them for valuables. Nothing, however, seemed to have been taken. He'd made sure everything of value was on their persons. John had his spare money tied in a special belt around his waist, but no one knew about this but himself. He'd have to check that Wills' finances were also safe.

With the wagons checked. No others had appeared before darkness claimed the night; they headed off to sleep.

John stoked the brazier before climbing up to his hammock. It gave the barn a warm glow. As he lay listening to the crickets and night sounds, he thought of his rooms at home in England. His own bedroom was almost the size of this barn, and his bed was far more comfortable than this hammock. "Ah, but what an adventure this will be," he sighed and closed his eyes. *"Dear God, please keep us all safe."* That's all he asked as he closed his eyes for the night.

Wills was asleep before John had returned. Wills' anxiety had evaporated after his conversation with Martha Turner. He was at peace and slept the dreamless, deep sleep of youth.

They were awoken just before dawn by a chorus of kookaburras sitting overhead in a gum tree. The Englishmen were still unfamiliar with their joyful chorus and were awakened as they sang. Wills slept on. It took Lewis to shake him before he, too, awoke. "Come on, lazy bones. Up and out. We have a long way to travel," said Lew.

Wills yawned. "I was having a nice dream about finding a chunk of quartz with gold in it. I hope we find some more seams I can check out."

Lew put his fingers to his lip; he said quietly, "Don't mention the G word, lad. That stuff sends people crazy."

"Okay," said Wills.

The others were already packed and had their bags ready before Wills woke. He hurriedly stuffed his items in his bag and dropped it from the loft to the barn floor. He shinnied down the rickety ladder and washed his face in the cold water.

He then grabbed his bag and followed the others to breakfast. Hot porridge with salt and cream, accompanied by fried eggs and toast, was followed by a hot mug or two of strong tea. They each left their pennies on the counter and left. John purchased two cob loaves and a newly woven basket full of eggs in straw from the landlady. She was none too happy until she saw a nice shiny coin.

"Gimme that," she said as she shoved the food at him.

He carefully wrapped the loaves and placed the goods in his wagon.

As the sun rose over the valley, they harnessed up the horses. The wagons had not been raided again. John was pleased. The person who had ransacked them last night had not bothered to return. The three wagons pulled out of the Toll Bar yard and set off on the next leg of the journey.

The innkeeper had been talking to John and Harry the night before and told them that business had picked up in the last two years since the murder. No one wanted to be near the bridge at night. It took some coaching, but John had finally got the full story from him. Seems to have been a love quadrangle rather than a triangle. One of them ended up murdered, and she was said to haunt the bridge. The story, told so convincingly, seemed more to be good for business than real. However, the Toll Keeper confirmed it as they were harnessing the horses.

Harry had a glint in his eye. John knew he had something in mind. As they pulled onto the road, John called out, "Be brave, lads; we may not see the spectre. She does not always appear."

Wills turned to John, "What spectre? What are they talking about?"

"First, let me ask, do you believe in ghosts?" questioned John.

"I don't know, sir. I've never thought much about them, but I believe in the afterlife," answered Wills.

"Hmm, well, that's a start. Sit back, and I'll tell you the story." John, however, held the reins a little more firmly. "I read this story in a newspaper. I didn't know if it was true until I spoke to the innkeeper this morning. Let me see if I can remember how it went."

"After this new road was built, it is said that as vehicles approached the bridge, their horses would become restless and flighty. Even ones who had never travelled the route before." He swallowed and continued. He'd not driven across this bridge himself and hoped the horses would behave. "Well, as the carriage would come around the corner, a young woman would appear. She would be dressed in black, with her long hair streaming behind her and her arms always held out as if pleading for help. Some even reported that her eyes shone, but that doesn't fit, as others say she appeared headless." He took a look at Wills.

Eyes wide, Wills said nothing.

John continued. "The lady was apparently Caroline James, or Mrs William Collits was her married name. There was some issue with her marriage, and she had moved in with her sister and her husband. I can't remember all the details, but it was a messy affair." He swallowed, not wanting to reveal the explicit information to the young lad. Messy was correct; a *Ménage à trois,* at least. "After some time, the four met at an inn nearby, I don't remember which, possibly the one we just stayed in, but later that evening, her dead body was found on this bridge. Her head was smashed by a rock. It only happened about two or three years ago, but she has been seen in and around the bridge several times. I do not believe in ghosts. I also believe in God. I will, however, take no chances and hold the reins tighter."

Within minutes, they rounded the corner to the bridge. The wagons paused, Phillip and his wagon still in the lead. Phillip asked Aidan to walk the horses across. Edmund and his covered wagons followed close behind, with Lewis at the bridle of his horses. John was about to ask Wills to step down when Harry jumped out from behind a rock and went "Boo".

John and Wills both jumped.

"You dirty rotten scoundrel. I've just been telling Wills of the haunted bridge," said John.

Harry was doubled over laughing. "You told me you don't believe in ghosts, though, John." He smiled so innocently up at John. "I thought I'd join you two for a bit. Get to know the young lad we have collected. What do you say?"

"Fine," said John a little sulkily, "But you can walk the horses over the bridge first."

Wills was all eyes. Not looking for a ghost, but he was amazed at the bridge. He was constantly looking around him, and as they approached the bridge, he whipped back into the wagon and reached for his drawing pad. He roughly divided the page into quarters and sketched the outline of the bridge as they crossed it, then repeated it, but with a headless lady floating over the top of it. With a minimum of strokes and the power of charcoal, the drawings were finished before they had walked the length of the bridge. Wills was adding a few more lines to each picture. Buttresses of the bridge curve and the outcrops of rocks on either side. Even the long shadows cast by the rising sun.

Harry crawled up beside him and watched as Wills sketched. The three vehicles paused beside each other, at the top of the cutting and looked back. No spectres, but what a view.

John yelled for Edmund to take the lead.

Lewis hopped back up next to Edmund, and they plodded up the rest of the hill.

Aidan took the reins from Phillip and followed.

Wills finished his pictures and put the book and charcoal down behind him, but within reach. As he looked up, he pointed out some stone steps. "I wonder where they lead?" Sadly, they didn't have time to stop. Hopefully, they could check them out on the return trip.

A while later, they had traversed only a little distance. They had kept pausing to either rest the horses or admire the views. A wide-open space with some buildings surrounded the roadway.

Aidan said, "Eh, John, let's give the horses a break before we hit the next section. I know we have not been travelling long, but I really need to find a tree." They decided on a quick stop. Each used various trees and bushes, and Wills, always with keen eyes, noted many bits of rubbish on the ground. There were broken clay pipes, buttons, smashed bottles, a few odd bits of metal and other rubbish. He picked up two coins he saw and pocketed them. They were old and dirty, but would buy a bed for a night somewhere.

They set off on the long leg to Hartley. Wills hoped they would have a bit of time in this area, as it was where Reverend Clarke said he'd thought there may be gold in the quartz. He'd found some dust in the creek near there.

"John, are we in any hurry to cross the mountains? Is it possible we could stop near the creek in Hartley for a night, possibly even two?" asked Wills.

Harry said, "Is this something to do with your dream?"

Wills nodded.

John said, "Eh? Spill! I presume something to do with why you've been checking each creek?"

Wills nodded again. He told them of Reverend Mr Clarke's discovery of gold flecks in Hartley in April and how the governor had instructed him to keep it quiet. "John, Mr Clarke was one of my teachers at school." He had mentored Wills, as they had shared an interest in adventure and even in gold. "Mr Clarke said that there is a lot of gold and other minerals everywhere, but it's not easy to find or dig, as the gold is in the quartz reefs."

He grabbed his pad and quickly drew a sketch of a gold reef and how fine dust ends up in the creeks. "This is what I'll be looking for."

"So that's why you were climbing the cliff yesterday?" Harry asked.

"Yes, it's not that I want to dig it, but I have an idea." He paused and looked at both men. "You know my brother Eddie had the Lockleys' Emporium shop in Parramatta. I know you know because that's where I met you, John. Well, *if*, and I say *if* any amount of gold is found in this area, and as Mr Clarke thinks, it will be further west in Bathurst and the surrounds. Then many, many people will come out here and want stores and tools and stuff. What I want to consider is acquiring some land now, before the rush, and building a second Emporium in the area. This would give me something that was my own and yet help Ed as well. I would run this one for a percentage of profits rather than a wage."

John and Harry looked at each other. "Lad, is there no end to your depth?" said Harry.

Wills grinned at them both.

John laughed, "And here I was helping a lad look for adventure when, in reality, here's a lad with his life mapped out already. What a fabulous idea! All right, let us have a few days around this Hartley area; we'll have a hunt for some gold. Do you know where Mr Clarke found it?"

Wills nodded. "Yes, sir, I mean John, he drew me a map. No one else would believe him, so he was happy to show me where it was. It's up here." Tapping his head.

They travelled along Mitchell's Road, stopping occasionally to water the horses, investigate some interesting feature or find or use a tree. Much of the trip was easier for travelling. By mid-afternoon, they reached Hartley. There was much to see; the area was so beautiful, and the group had no time limit other than to find a good spot for their first real camp.

They drove into the tiny hamlet of Hartley. The Farmers Inn, The Shamrock Inn, a Catholic Church, Courthouse, and a few other timber structures built in and around other larger buildings were all that were there. No one was much interested in any of these dwellings but seeking someone to ask directions. Finally, a grey-bearded chap appeared. Harry hopped down with Wills and asked about camping areas along a creek or river. He directed them to take the road through town. He then said, "Turn right just before the river. You follow it up a little way and camp on the grass point." The old-timer then added, "Eh, don't be tempted to camp near the river. It comes up in a flash. Camp above the debris line." He nodded good day and watched them drive off.

They headed further down the road and found his directions easy to follow. There was a nice grassy area that was large enough for all three vehicles. The six horses were all hobbled and left to roam on the creek edge. Wills and Lew took some large rounded creek rocks back to camp and started to make a circle of them. Edmund joined them for the second trip. Lew dug out an iron tripod for over the fire and a camp oven.

"John, okay, I have this now; what do I do with it?" Lew stood scratching his head. "I've never cooked in my life." He gave John a broad grin.

John laughed. "I've not done much myself, but it can't be that hard."

Harry appeared and said, "What's for dinner, Lew?"

"Damn. Don't ask me, I just bought the stuff. I have no idea how to use it," said Lew.

Aidan and Edmund looked at each other, horrified.

"Can you cook, Aidan?" Edmund asked.

"No! Can't you?" came the reply.

"Phil, can you? Or Wills, is this another of your skills?"

Phil shook his head. "Never had the need."

They all looked at Wills. "Well, I've never actually cooked myself, but I've helped Mama enough to know what I should do. Mrs Turner gave me a quick lesson when we stayed with her."

They all looked at him, astonished, but smiled at each other.

Wills rubbed his head. What had he got himself in for with these men? "All right, what do we have?"

John and Lewis took him to the food supply. He noted another cooking pot and two billy's, amongst other things.

Wills scratched his head and stood thinking. What could he cook with potatoes, flour, eggs and some vegetables? No meat, seven hungry bellies.

"I wonder if there are any fish in the river. Has anyone ever tickled trout before? Or has anyone brought a fishing line?" asked Wills hopefully. All shook their head.

"Fine, then we're going to make a fish trap. I've seen these before, made by the local people near home. They work brilliantly. That is, unless you want potatoes and eggs for dinner. It should be worth it if we're here for a couple of days." This is not how he'd planned the trip, but that's what an adventure is.

They set the fire but didn't light it. There were hours before dark, and they had work to do. They all headed down to the river and found a shallow section. Wills soon described his idea. They had to build up a semi-circle of rocks to make a pool. Then, they had to work out a way to scare the fish downstream into the trap. That was the easy bit. They somehow then had to grab them.

It took over an hour to make the small fish trap just before the waterfall. They had dragged some small logs to make a diversion so the fish would be directed into the new area.

Wills was worried. "I don't even know if there are fish in this river. John, this may not work."

John laughed. "Well, lad, if it doesn't, we'll have eggs and bread for dinner. We're all learning together. Don't stress, lad. We all needed some activity after sitting for so long." They lifted and threw rocks in a row until the trap was done.

Wills looked down into the murky, shallow water. A glint caught his eye. He bent down to pick it up. "Harry, look at this." He passed over the rock.

"Where did you find this, lad?" Harry asked

"Right here, in the water. Look, there's another one." He bent down and picked it up. He kicked a few more rocks. "Look, another one. Harry, could they be, you know? Really?"

John saw them and walked over. "What have you found? Not fish for sure."

Harry didn't answer but held out his hand. Sitting in it were three large lumps of white quartz. Each was glinting with yellow sparkles.

John looked from Harry to Wills. "Did you just find these?"

Wills nodded. He looked down again. "John, can you move your foot, please?" He did, and Wills dug into the water where he'd been standing. There was a fourth and larger lump.

Wills blanched. "Is it?" he asked Harry.

"If weight is anything to go by, then it's certainly gold. I can't believe it's just sitting there." Harry started looking himself. "Look, here's another piece and another. It looks like your Reverend Clarke was right, but this is reef gold, not river gold. It shouldn't be here like this; these look like freshly broken rocks. There must have been a recent rockfall upstream. Pocket these, and we'll all go have a look later."

Wills pocketed his four rocks, and Harry did likewise with his two.

"Hey, chaps," said Harry, "let's head upstream for a bit, then walk down in the water to see if we can scare the fish. We'll see if this trap of William's works. Oh, and keep an eye open for any white rocks. We'll tell you why later; just collect any you see."

They all headed upstream, walking along the side of the river. They had just passed a rocky outcrop when Wills looked up. "Harry, look. It's from there." He scrambled up the small cliff. "John, Harry, come here. Quick!" He'd plonked himself down on a boulder.

The others soon followed him. They couldn't all fit on the platform. Four could stand looking at the fallen rocks with two near Wills. All amazed at what he'd found. It shouldn't be this easy. Gold was hard to find. Wasn't it? Here, he was knee-deep in gold-filled quartz rocks. Thick veins of gold ran through each rock. His face was fixed on the rubble at his feet. He was sheet white.

Edmund looked at his face. "Lad, what have you found? Is it really gold? Is this what you were talking about?"

Wills nodded. "Edmund, I never dreamed... never guessed that I'd find the mother load. I was hoping for a few specks, that's all. Reverend Clarke said it would be here. I tried to learn about gold. There was no way I could do any research. Nothing was written in any books I could find. So I studied a bit of geology." All stood gazing, speechless.

John tussled Wills' hair. "You've done it, lad. Do you realise you are now rich?"

Wills looked at him. Mouth open. "What? Yes, I suppose I am. How do I get it out of here?"

"We'll help, won't we, lads?" Harry took over. "Okay, Phil, Lew, can you head back and get some sacks or the sheet of canvas, anything you can carry stuff in, and bring a horse, oh, and a bucket. Aidan, Ed, can you head back down the rocks? We'll start throwing them down to you. Stack them in piles. John, can you reach any of the bits still loose and hand them to us? We'll get a bucket brigade going and get this stuff down from here. Come on, Wills lad, your team of workers are ready. Start passing."

Phil, Lew, Aidan and Edmund slid back down the rocky outcrop. The two left for the camp, and Aidan and Ed stood waiting for the first rocks to head their way.

Wills started passing rocks to Harry, who threw them to the waiting men. John reached up the cliff and prized out some of the remaining gold rocks. The vein was clearly visible.

"I can't get many more out, Harry. I'll need a hammer or something. So we'll grab the loose stuff today and come back tomorrow," said John.

It took about thirty minutes for the pile to be stacked up at the bottom. Phil had brought two horses and a pile of bags, buckets and a sheet of sailcloth. Wills climbed down and helped load them on the horses. John and Harry each took a large rock and hit the rock face with them. Another fall of smaller pebbles fell; no gold was visible in them. "Pass a bucket up, chaps. We'll take this too," said Harry.

They scooped up the fine pebbles and carefully handed the full bucket down. John and Harry followed it down.

They finished tying all the rocks to the horses and then started congratulating Wills. "But, sirs, we'll share this. I could not have got it without your help. Equal shares. John, if you had not let me come, well, I never would have got here." He was overwhelmed.

Phil finished tying the load. "Now, didn't we come for fish? Let's walk the horses back down in the river and scare what's in the water to the trap."

Aidan said, "Wills, with your luck, the trap will be full by the time we get there."

Wills laughed weakly. "I hope so. I'm famished. Rich and famished. Reminds me of Esau." John looked at him, puzzled. "In the Bible, Esau sold his birthright to Jacob for food," Wills said to John.

John looked at him with one eyebrow raised but said nothing.

Lew and Phil walked the horses into the river. They spread out across the shallows. They could see some fish darting away from them, but could not see how big or what sort they were. The water was now somewhat murky. As long as there were some to eat, it didn't matter what sort they were.

They slowly walked back down the river until they arrived back at camp. Lew walked down to the trap.

"Are you kidding? Look, it's full." Lew stood on the riverbank looking at the fish splashing in the trap. "How do we catch them?"

Wills stood looking at them, hands on his hips. "Hey, I got them here; you have to catch them," he laughed with relief. "We don't want them all, but let's block the way in so they don't escape. Try using your hands." He had recovered from his shock and was chuckling quietly to himself.

Phil took the horses back to camp and tied them up. He collected another hessian bag from his wagon, then picked up a knife and headed back down to the river. He could hear the others laughing and shrieking as one or the other fell over in the cold water. He had not seen his friends this carefree since they were boys together. They were finally beginning to relax.

By the time Phil arrived, twelve large fish were flapping on the riverbank. He picked them up and stuffed them in the sack.

His friends were all drenched, but laughing. Wills was in the thick of it. "I think these are some sort of fish called perch. They are good for eating. There's certainly enough for a meal, then some. We need two more."

Harry said, "Here, Phil, catch." He threw a large one to Phil. Phil, of course, missed it but gathered it off the ground and stuffed it in the bag with the rest.

"Last one," said Lew, tossing it on the riverbank.

Phil picked it up and stowed it with the rest. Sitting the bag on the bank, he reached to help Lew out of the river; the next thing he, too, was sitting on the water with his friends amongst a pool of splashing fish. Harry and Ed were laughing at Phil's astonished face. Seven wet and bedraggled men hauled themselves out of the cold water and headed back to camp.

Phil and Lew carried the bag full of fish. Wills' teeth were chattering by the time he got to the wagon. He stripped off his sopping clothes and put on dry ones. After laying his wet clothes on the side of the cart to dry, he went to the bag of fish. He looked at them and had to work out how to cook them. He stood scratching his head.

He had forgotten about the gold, but Harry and John had worked out that they were going to lay it under the stores in the covered wagon. Wills turned as the others walked towards him.

"Baked, stew, spit, fried; how do you want them?" Wills asked John and Ed.

John laughed and slapped him on the back. "Oh, Wills, did you really think we can't cook? We wanted to see what you'd do. You are a champ, young sir. We'll fry them." They each produced a frying pan and some dripping.

"We've got a few things to tell you, lad." John and Ed put a dot of dripping in each pan and set it in the coals. "We've all sold out of the army after serving in some rough battles together. We all just put in four years in Afghanistan, then India as well. Four very rough years. After returning home, we all could not settle. The short story is that Harry heard about the new road cut across the mountains here and thought it could be an adventure for him and me. The others came by coincidence or God-incidence." As he sat talking, Edmund and Lew joined them to deal with the fish, scaling and filleting them like professionals.

Wills sighed with relief; he didn't have to cook. He would have tried. He would have done anything to help these men. Now, to hear they were all war heroes.

John continued. "Lad, have you ever heard of a thing called the 'Great Game'?"

"Oh yes, sir, sorry, um, John, my great grandfather was given his Earldom after serving in Poonah in India. Something he did was the reason it started. His name was Charles Lockley."

"You know about the 'Game'?" said Edmund. "Really? Most have never heard of it."

"Charles Lockley, why does that sound familiar?" said Aidan.

"I know, he's Number One," said Harry with awe.

"What?" They all chorused.

"Huh," said Wills. "Number One, what? I've heard a bit about it, though I don't know much. He lived nearly a hundred years ago."

John said, "Lad, you have just become our hero, well, the great-grandson of our hero anyway. It's only with each other that we can discuss 'The Great Game'. As you have a tie, we will tell you a bit about it, but just the basics." John nodded to Harry.

Harry continued. "It started with your Charles Lockley in 1760; at least what he did inspired the 'Great Game' years later. He went undercover as a spy in India and was able to gain such amazing information that the war was turned." Harry flipped the fish. "Seventy years later, in 1830, the situation was again dire in India. Neither side trusted the other, and the only way to get the needed information was for some soldiers to go undercover and infiltrate the locals. They would dye their skin and hair and infiltrate the areas where they needed information. This was initially about trade wars. Money. The 'Game' started then, but it continues. We have all had our identities revealed, so we each had to get out. We were only known to each other as numbers. More to protect our friends than ourselves. In England, we tried returning to our normal lives, but after the adventure of the 'Game', well, we could not find ourselves." He flicked out both fish onto a plate and handed them to Aidan. He added another dob of dripping and put the pan back on the fire. Two more were put on to cook. Ed placed the two from his pan on Aidan's plate, too, and placed two more in to cook.

Lewis sliced one of the cob loaves he'd bought at the Mt Victoria stop and liberally spread the slices with butter. More food appeared from various nooks in the wagon, and soon, a full meal was ready for eating.

John picked up the story. "Harry saw an advertisement for travel to Sydney. He contacted me and asked to meet me at Whites. That's a men's club we all belong to in London. I went." John paused, thinking back. "When I arrived, I saw Ed, Lew and Phil at another table. I greeted them and turned to find Harry. I saw him on the other side of the room with Aidan. What was everyone doing there? I thought, 'What's Harry up to this time'?"

Harry laughed. "I had actually only asked John, and then Aidan turned up. I didn't know the others were there. God led us all there on the same night."

Wills started. "They believe in God too?" He smiled.

"Harry called the others over to join us. He still had not told us what he wanted." He turned to Edmund. "Say thanks, please, Ed."

Edmund bowed his head. "*Thank you, God, for this food and the bond of lifelong friends and discovering new ones, too. Amen."*

John took a bite of his fish. "Well, we took a table in the corner so we wouldn't be disturbed. We were all sitting, looking at Harry. He sat silently. Eventually, he just asked how we'd all settled into our lives again. No one spoke. We all looked at our drinks." John fell silent.

Harry took up the story again. "I knew what their silence meant. It meant 'no,' they had not. Neither had I. My parents had also died that year, and things at home were now different. When you've lived a life full of adventure, returning to the everyday round of balls, parties, and opera is *not* conducive to a happy life. I saw a passage to New South Wales was advertised. Four months or more in a dangerous ship, then the unknown, snakes, spiders and storms. It sounded like the perfect 'holiday' for my friends and me. John was our CO; I was his 2IC. These four were our trusted contacts in 'The Game'. We four had grown up together in and around Tunbridge Wells." He pointed to Ed, John and Phil.

As soon as Harry said Tunbridge Wells, Wills sat up, his eyes swung to Edmund. "You're Edmund Hunt and from Tunbridge Wells. Are you related to the Earl of Riverdell?"

Edmund returned his gaze. "Err, yes, I am. He's my father. How do you know him? He's never been here."

Conversation and eating were suspended. All eyes were now on Wills. "Then Christina is your sister?" he asked.

"Yes, she's my older sister, but..." Edmund looked at the lad. "Oh, you're that Lockley family?"

Wills nodded, dumbfounded.

"Are you serious? I came halfway around the world and met my brother-in-law's cousin?" He roared with laughter.

Ed finally spoke. "Gentlemen," he addressed his friends, "you know my sister has recently returned from the Antipodes with a husband in tow and not the one she left with. His Grace, the Duke of Gracemere, was out here as Major Grace, I believe." He looked at Wills for confirmation.

Wills nodded in reply.

Edmund then continued, "But by rights, he should have been Major Edward Lockley. I'm not sure why, but he never used his real name. Something to do with a brother, I believe. He didn't want to be found." He looked at Wills, who nodded again in agreement.

It seemed he was not the only one with a title after all. "Edmund, I've tried to understand how it works. Are you then a Viscount?" Wills asked.

"Yes, Viscount Eames, but here, I am Edmund Hunt," he said.

"Well, nice to have a family reunion, but to get back to the story," said Harry. "We had drinks in the club, as I was saying. None of us had settled. I proposed the trip here. I would not take their answers that night, but suggested we meet again and have further discussions. I received a note the next morning from John, it just said: "I'm in."

"I wrote that afternoon with similar," said Aidan. "Phil, Ed and Lew all replied the next day. It seemed that we were all disheartened and unsatisfied with our lives."

John took over the conversation again. He'd been cooking fish the entire time, and they were now all eating. Aidan passed the sliced cob loaf around, and they all took some. "Harry had hit on an adventure that should hold enough danger, but without us being shot at. Within weeks, we were bound for Sydney and arrived here three weeks ago. It's so different from what we were told to expect. We'd been told of tent cities, wooden buildings with convicts everywhere. So, rather than staying in town, we heard about the new road that Major Mitchell had built, and it could take us west. So we decided to come for a look. We were told of 'Lockley's Emporium' and that it was a must-see stop in Parramatta, and they could help with our needs. So we stocked up there and met you. It never occurred to me that you were Edmund's sister's Lockley family until we were leaving town. You let it slip, but I still didn't put one and one together." John fell silent for a while. "We still can't tell you much about the 'Game', as it's ongoing, but you know enough to understand that none of us are the sort of chaps to sit back and twiddle our thumbs. So here we are. On the other side of the world and set for an adventure to wherever God will lead." John looked intently at Wills. "Something you said earlier makes me think you might believe too?"

"Yes, John, I do. My entire family does. I so wish you could meet my folks, but they are currently in Ireland. Mama made it there in time to see her mother, Shannon McCarthy, before she died. They have been staying at the Castle with Uncle Ned, the Duke, that is, and Dar's mother is only a few miles away. Last I heard, she was moving in with the Dowager Duchess when Aunt Lilabet married Annabella's brother Matthew."

Aidan and Phillip now looked at him.

Aidan asked, "Was your mother an O'Shane by any chance?"

"Mama wasn't, but her mother was, I believe, Eamon and Nioiclín O'Shane. I think they lived in Cork. I haven't been there, so I don't know the area." Wills was racking his brain to remember the details. "Why, Aidan?"

Aidan laughed. "My mother was also an O'Shane and from Cork, probably the same family. Shannon is a family name. My sister is named after one Shannon McCarthy, who lives with us." He grinned at Wills. "We call her Aunt Shannon."

Phillip said, "My turn. You said Matthew is Annabella's brother. Would that be Annabella Derbyshire, who's now married to a Doctor?"

"If you mean Doctor Gerry, um, Gerald Winslow-Smythe, then

possibly, I've never met her. They met on the ship home and married on board, but yes. Matthew is going to marry my aunt. Why?" asked Wills.

"Oh, nothing, except they are my cousins. I didn't think there would be too many Annabella's in the area. Can you believe God's interweaving? It's taken a trip across the world to find a jigsaw bit that knits us together. John, you found the lad, so that leaves you, Lew," said Phil.

"What about me, Phil?" Harry said.

Phil chuckled. "Oh, Harry, have you never heard Annabella's name before she married? It was Watkins-Harlow. There's some aunt that married a Watkins and hyphenated the name."

Harry sat stunned. "You're a cousin, too?"

Phil nodded, "Distant, but yes."

"I'm not left out. Don't you worry," said Lewis. "Ned Gracemere's mother was Susanna Bland before she married. She was Scottish. Didn't you know?" Lewis was lying back, hands behind his head, chuckling.

"Well, I'm John's cousin too; bet you all didn't know that, did you?" said Harry. "So he can claim Wills through me." Pausing, he then added, "And, of course, through Charles Lockley. We all have a link to your great-grandfather."

John looked over the group of friends, now all linked distantly by blood or marriage, and included Wills among them. Thinking to himself, "What is the purpose of all this?" He said to Wills, "Lad, you seem to be a lynchpin for us. Who knew? Well, other than God, of course. Makes me wonder what He has in store for us next."

After finishing their meal, they cleaned up the plates and pans and relaxed around the fire, continuing to discuss the coincidence, or as Harry said, God-incidence, that had brought them together. Lew put another log on and added a full billy to the hook. "I could do with some tea."

John looked over to Wills, "Forgotten anything, lad?" he asked.

"No, I don't think so, John, why?" replied Wills.

"What about the rocks? Did you forget about them?" John smiled as he spoke.

"Oh, those! Well, not exactly. I saw you and Harry unloading them, and as we're going to share the proceeds, I trust you to stow them properly. At the moment, they are just rocks." He looked up, grinning. "Admittedly, very pretty and valuable rocks."

Harry looked at him, amazed. "Lad, have you any idea how many people would almost kill you for them? They are worth a fortune or ten."

Wills poked at the fire before replying. "Harry, I have food and a roof over my head, a family who loves me, even though I left them without warning. I know I will always be welcomed home." He poked the coals again without looking at Harry, watching the sparks rise from the coals. "My parents arrived as convicts with nothing but the clothes on their backs. I am already rich in the things that truly matter. All the rest of the things that have happened to us are, well, really, God's blessings."

Harry said, "So you're not wedded to finding more gold?"

"Oh no, Harry," Wills said honestly. "That's not to say I'm not happy that I have found it. It's just one step in the adventure. Something deep within me felt I needed to come with you. I don't know why or where it will lead." He paused and smiled. "I would like to see if there is more of it up there, though. Are you all up for a bit of hammering and digging tomorrow?" He grinned as he looked around the faces.

Lew made tea and handed the mugs around.

Phil and Aidan both nodded, "Oh yes, we're in."

"A few days in this beautiful spot, fish on tap and lots of water. This is good for our hearts and souls," Phil said.

Aidan said, "Well, I'm betting there was once a rainbow that hit this spot, and we're going to dig that pot of gold. It's the Irish in me, of course. If only there were leprechauns to help dig it."

"They did their bit, Aidan. And then left it on the shelf for Wills to find," Lewis said, laughing.

John said, "If we're all going digging tomorrow, then we'd better get some sleep. I think this trip may well be the healing balm we're all looking for."

Wills didn't move. "John, before we go, can I ask a question?"

"Sure, lad. Ask away…" John said.

"Well, what do you all do? Do you all have work or have jobs? You've obviously left the army, and I don't understand what your club is, but do you all teach or work in schools? What do you do well, um, to help people?" Wills was obviously puzzled.

They all looked at him. None answered. It was as though they had not heard his question.

Christina looked out of her sitting room window. A carriage and four were stopping up to the front door. "They're here," she said to Annabella.

Ned walked in a few minutes later, followed by the Earl and Countess of Coxheath. Both were fashionably attired but looked tired due to a few days of travel. Sal acknowledged the occupants of the room with a beaming smile. Christina greeted them and threw her arms around the Countess. "Sally, it's so good to see you again. I'm so sorry about your mother, though."

They walked into the sitting room and made themselves comfortable. Sally was still somewhat overwhelmed by the fact that she was greeted thus by the Duchess of Gracemere. "Oh, Christina, just to see her again before she died was a blessing in itself." She wiped away a tear as it trickled down her cheek. "It's as though she hung on all these years, and now she's gone. In a way, I feel cheated, but also blessed. I thought she would have died years ago. So to think I had some time with her is a miracle." They were seated together on a settee, Christina still holding her hands.

She looked over to Annabella and explained some more of the story to them both. "I found out that her parents had died some years after my conviction. My mother had written to her father when I was arrested. He sent his cousin to collect her and bring her home to Ireland. So all these years I was worrying about her, she was actually being well looked after." She went on to fill in the rest of the story. "Shéamus O'Keefe had been living in London and had written to say he was returning home to marry. Grandpapa asked if he'd collect and escort Mother home. He did willingly. Shéamus' wife, Erin, was an O'Shane, Mama's cousin, and had grown up with her mother. They did the trip in easy stages as Mother was still not well. They took her to her parents' house, and she regained her health. After some two years, her parents both died. Once again, she was alone. Shéamus and Erin took her in when her cousin inherited the family home. They had three children, but all were grown. A son, Aidan, who has apparently jaunted off to New South Wales of all places, and two daughters, another Shannon and Caraline, both of whom are married." She looked over to Ned, who'd looked up when he said the name of Aidan. "What is it, Edward?"

"Oh, just something I have to tell you both, but first, finish your story, please," he replied.

"Mother never married again. There was a friend, but nothing developed. So, she stayed with them until she died." Sally sighed. "I can't believe God was so good to let me find her. It has been lovely staying with them for the past two months and discovering family I did not know existed," concluded Sal.

Christina squeezed her hand.

"Would you mind if I went and freshened up before we have tea?" Sal asked. Charles offered his arm to her and escorted her to their rooms. She was still sad.

As soon as the door closed behind them. Gerry, who'd followed them in with them as they arrived, turned to the Duke. "Ned, could there be two Aidan O'Keefe's in Australia? Is this another of God's machinations?"

"I don't know," replied Ned.

"I wonder if she knows who he went with," said Annabella, "if they do, well, that would help." They seated themselves, relaxing until their friends returned. They discussed the forthcoming wedding of Charles's sister Elizabeth, known as Lilabet, to Annabella's brother

Matthew. Neither had previously married, and both were just shy of forty.

The three ladies, Christina, Lilabet, and Elle, had planned a quiet wedding in the Castle Chapel. They had only postponed as they were waiting for Sal and Charles, Lilabet's brother, to arrive back so he could give her away.

Some thirty minutes later, Sal and Charles returned refreshed. Both had changed. Tea was served, and the wedding plans were discussed. Lilabet, Matthew, and Ned's mother, Suze, the Dowager Duchess, and Charles' mother, Elle, the Dowager Countess, were arriving at four o'clock.

Once the staff withdrew, the four friends sat drinking their tea and eating tiny cakes. Gerry and Annabella joined them.

Ned said, "Charles, I have had news from home. I have had a few letters, actually, and Eddie has been keeping me informed with matters of some importance." Charles sat upright and looked worried. "No, nothing's really wrong, but something has arisen," he looked at Christina, who gave him an encouraging look. "Eddie wrote to me in December last to say that Wills has gone off on an adventure. He was initially somewhat distraught, as Wills had tried to gain his attention to discuss something with him, but he was distracted by the children and did not give the conversation his full attention. The upshot, Wills left a letter on his desk as he departed in the morning. Ed only found it after they had well gone."

Sal's hand had flown to her mouth. "Oh, Charles!" She reached out and grasped her husband's hand.

Ned smiled. "There's more, so please don't worry. In the same post, I received two more letters from Eddie." Ned said. "The second was written four days later, they all came on the same ship, so I received them all at once, which I must say was very comforting. Wills wrote from the Turners, where the group had stayed the night. He poured his heart out to Martha, who counselled him wisely." He sipped his tea. "Martha and Jack also wrote to Ed. Wills had finished school and felt somewhat at a loose end. Luke was still deeply engrossed in his studies, while Ed and Charlie were preoccupied with work and their children. He felt alone in a house full of people. I can understand this, as I felt the same in a battalion full of soldiers. Then I met you both and finally Christina." He looked lovingly over to her. "The upshot in this case, both Martha and Jack spoke to Wills and gave him their blessing. They both liked the look of these English chaps he'd met up with. Jack questioned the leader, a John Saunders." Charles looked concerned until Ned said, "Wills writes regularly to Ed. He wrote four letters in the first week, and more get sent whenever he reaches a town. It turns out these six men were soldiers who returned from the Afghanistan war and also served in India. They had all sold out. John Saunders, 'Sir John' as it happens, was CO. His 2IC was Harry Harlow, his cousin." He lifted his eyes to Sal, and he smiled. "The next name was an Aidan O'Keefe."

Sal gasped. "No! That's amazing!"

Ned continued, "Oh, there's more! Lewis Bland is another, and he's my cousin from Scotland. Next is a person whom we know quite well, my love." He looked over to Christina. "Edmund is amongst them, so now we know where your little brother is. He's travelling under the name of Edmund Hunt and Sir Phillip Corsairs; your cousin, Annabella, is the final member of the group."

Gasps of astonishment circled the assembled group as names were mentioned.

Gerry said, "Why, I know most of these men. They served together. I had reason to see them shortly before my departure to Sydney. They had each sold out for various reasons. Mostly because a friend, Christopher, was revealed and then killed. I'll tell you about that later. I can tell you all, but it must not leave this room. They were involved in a thing called, 'The Great Game'. Something you know about Charles, as your Grandfather Charles, in some way, was the number One. They had each had their identity revealed and had to quit the service. Inactivity did not sit well with them, and many others. Trust me, Wills is in safe hands with these men."

Charles finally spoke. "Wills is keeping in touch?"

"Oh yes, and so does Eddie. Every ship that arrives brings more news. I have kept them all so you can read them for yourselves. It's about three weeks since the last letter, so I'm expecting one on the next ship. Maybe even today."

As he spoke, the butler knocked and was invited to enter. "The letter you were awaiting has arrived, Your Grace." He had a silver platter with a letter on it. Ned took it. He smiled as he picked up. "Thank you, Frederick," and nodded a dismissal.

"Speak of the devil. Guess who it's from?" He flicked the seal open and spread out the sheet on his knee.

His eyes quickly perused the script and widened. "I had better read this one out to you all."

> *Bramblemere Close*
> *Phillip Street*
> *Parramatta*
> *20 January 1845*

His Grace Duke of Gracemere,
Gracemere Castle,
Maidstone England

Dear Uncle Ned,

> *I hope this letter finds you all well.*
> *I trust Dar and Mama have returned from Ireland, and Wedding*

plans for Aunt Lilabet and Matthew are well underway, if not already completed. Please send my love to them all.

We are all well. We hear from our wandering brother regularly. They finally reached Bathurst after spending nearly two weeks camped by a creek in Hartley. Wills had always wanted to get there since his conversations with Reverend Clarke in April and his minute gold finds.

The afternoon they arrived, they set up camp near the river. After building a fish trap and, in the process, finding some interesting-looking rocks, they all walked upstream to herd the fish into the trap. However, they were somewhat waylaid by an interesting find. There had been a small rockfall on a low cliff overlooking the river. It had been some of these rocks Wills had found downstream. The rockfall was a quartz outcrop, and it was heavy with gold. They collected all they could carry that night, then over the next week, carried much of this back to their camp. They loaded their booty in the bottom of the wagons. When they arrived in the next town, Lithgow, they had Wills apply for a grant of land that covered this area. It is now his. The gold he has already found will make him a very wealthy man. He insisted on sharing it equally with his new friends, typical Wills. As they did not wish to carry their bounty with them, they sent it back to me by the carrier, concealed in a barrel as 'grain', and 'it' is safely stowed in our cellar, where it will remain until his return. It seems that this trip was 'meant to be'.

I believe Wills shall return a changed man. His letters have already changed. He has new confidence, even in his style of writing. He still has hopes of seeing a Dancing Brolga or two, but apparently, for this, they must head far west and hope that there is water in the wetlands. He hopes that his friends will pander to this wish. I believe he learnt of these dancing cranes from reading both Oxley's and Mitchell's journals. I do not think Reverend Clarke got out this far. It seems the group have no other purpose than to explore. Wills seems to be the one to set their direction. They are happy to follow. I wonder if they will turn back once this quest is completed. Whatever their quest is. I dare say we shall see. Letters will become fewer as they journey, as there will be no way to post them. They should have taken some pigeons.

My paper is full. I draw this epistle to a close. Again, be assured of my love for you all. Hugs to your munchkins. Our third child should have arrived by the time the next letter is posted.

Congratulations to you and Aunt Christina on your impending parenthood again; it seems our dates are again in unison. Hopefully, there is *only one this time for you, too.*

Yours, etc., etc.

Ed

Ned finished reading the letter. "Well, it seems young Wills is rich. If I know the lad, it won't change him in the least. He has a head on his shoulders, that one. It's why I was so surprised that he left the way he did," Ned said.

Charles and Sal looked at each other. Charles finally spoke, "I can't get my head around all of this. I'm so glad we didn't have to wait for months for each letter. Ed had our direction, so why didn't he write to me directly?"

Ned answered, "Ah, the first letter explains all that. Here they are. Keep them." He handed over a sheaf of pages. "You were dealing with enough. I knew Wills was safe. So I made the decision not to tell you."

Charles took them and quickly perused them, then folded them and tucked them in his coat pocket. "Later, but thank you, Ned."

Sal started giggling, hand over her mouth. Soon, tears were flowing down her cheeks. "This is really just too good." She daintily wiped her tears away on a wisp of lace-trimmed lawn. "First, I'm an honest working girl, then a convict. Next, you two rescue me, and I get married to Charles. We become friends, Ned, good friends. God blessed Charles and me with more than we could dream. We have six wonderful children."

Charles agreed. "He certainly did that!" He reached out and held her hand.

Sal continued, "Then Doctor Gerry arrives, and our lives become, well, conflicted, to put it mildly. Christina, you then come into the picture. Ned, you turn out to be a Duke; Charles, an Earl, and then we find you two are cousins. Throw in a wife or two, and here we are today. We are three extremely happy couples, and our lives have created their own tapestry. Only God could have done all this. In Ireland, Erin said to me, "I don't believe in coincidences; I call them 'God-incidences' because when I stop praying, they stop happening.' Oh! I do believe her." Sal wiped her eyes again, still laughing. "And now we hear Wills ran away and fell on his feet with your brother and his friends." Looking at Annabella. "And now they have found gold. If it were not so funny, it would be, oh, I don't know, but almost a comedy or tragedy. Yes, I'm pleased we did not have to wait between letters either, Charles." At that moment, very young voices were heard approaching. Three small children burst into the room. Viscount Lockley, Charles Edward John, known as Chip, arrived first, closely followed by The Lady Sarah Christina Lockley and Miss Annabella 'Bella' Jennifer Winslow-Smythe.

Their nanny followed closely. "I am so sorry, Your Grace, Your Grace, M'Lord, M'Lady, Sir, Ma'am. They got away from me. They heard you were all here." She bobbed a curtsy and tried to gather the three imps and remove them.

"Never mind, Nanny, we always love having them here; I'll ring for you later. Thank you," said Ned. He bent down and picked up his small son. "Well, Chippy. You've landed me in it again. I can command a battalion of soldiers and a gaol full of convicts, but you two have me under your thumbs and firmly twisted around your fingers." He chuckled.

The little lad beamed, wrapped his arms around his father's neck and laid his fair head on his shoulder. "I love you, Dadda."

Ned's heart was full. He, too, was so blessed; first his beloved Christina, then a double blessing of Chip and Sarah. He hugged this warm armful of happiness. "I love you too, Chippy," he said, looking over to his other little child, sitting on her mother's expanding lap. "And yes, you too, my Sarah joy."

"Thank you, Dadda. I wuv you too and Mummy too."

Annabella was sitting with little Bella on her lap. Gerry is standing beside her, his finger absentmindedly stroking her neck.

"How could we all not be happy? We are all so very blessed, Edward. All of us." She kissed her daughter.

Gerry bent and whispered something to Annabella, and she nodded. He cleared his throat. "Friends…"

"Oh, here we go," said Ned, "an announcement."

"Yes, an announcement. Tina and Ned, we know your next bundle of joy is due in about April; well, it, too, will have a playmate a few months later. A happy occurrence for us will occur about July or August," Gerry beamed.

Sal was first to congratulate them, with everyone following.

Ned shook Gerry's hand, as did Charles.

Bella Winslow-Smythe then turned to her father. "Papa, what's everyone happy about?"

Gerry then crouched down to her. "Bella, how would you like to be a big sister, too?"

She wrinkled her nose and said, "I s'pose so, but not if it's a brovver. Can I choose?"

Annabella laughed and said, "No, darling, we can't choose because God already has."

Bella, in her innocence, simply replied, "Oh, that's all right then 'cause He always knows best."

Everyone laughed. "Out of the mouths of babes." Annabella hugged her daughter and said, "Yes, sweetheart, God always knows best. He never misses."

She reached up for Gerry's hand and held it to her cheek. "Always!"

Chapter 4   Find the Dancing Birds

"*J*ohn, how can I ever thank you enough? I know you all had no intention of coming this far west. Getting to Bathurst was amazing," said Wills enthusiastically.

"Why, lad, why Bathurst in particular? There's nothing there but a few small buildings. Oh, and a place to send off another letter, of course," asked John.

They were driving through open grasslands, still heading west on the quest to see the dancing brolgas. The drivers and passengers often swapped places, so it was nice to be back with John for a while.

The others were fun, but it was only with John or Harry that Wills could voice his deep thoughts. He guessed that he would be about thirty, but he dared not ask. They had stocked up on potatoes, oranges, onions, carrots, and a variety of other longer-lasting foods and dry goods.

"Why? Well, it's as far west as my namesake got, William Wentworth. Only when he travelled through were there no buildings at all. He met some local Aboriginals, but his guide could not communicate much with them. Reverend Clarke said that he checked the creeks around here, and nearly everyone had some gold. Now I have seen it, I'm happy. John, you know how I now have the land in Hartley?" asked Wills.

"No, lad. You really bought the land in Hartley?" smiled John. "Is that what you were doing in Lithgow?"

Wills nodded. "And posting a letter or three as well." Looking John in the eye, he said, "Yes, well, I would like to buy some land in Bathurst too. A large flat block and build an Emporium like Eddie's. I have the funds now or will have when we process the quartz, and I can see that in the next few years, word will spread of gold in the area, and it will be a place everyone will need to buy goods." He paused, thinking back on what the small country town was like. "Once we return, if we go through there again, can you help me select a large block and mark it out? I was thinking near the corner of Durham and William Streets. What do you think?"

John turned and looked at his earnest face. "You've really thought about this, haven't you? This is not a mere whim, is it?"

"No, sir, this is sort of what I had planned when I came. I just never expected to find gold on the first night camping. This just enables my dreams to become a reality. It's well beyond comprehension. I keep thinking, 'Why me, Lord'?"

Wills fell into silence for a while. "I want to bring Eddie in on a partnership, John, and work it the same way their store is run, with a few changes." He paused, thinking again. "In Eddie's store, everything is behind counters. I want most things on the floor, and only the small items behind the main counter, with the cash register near the entry door. People can then wander and touch without having to ask for things to be pulled down for them. Saddles can be displayed on a log, so you can even sit on them. You could have a row of different sorts. What do you think?"

John looked over at this boy, no, young man. He'd matured in the past three months. "I suppose you have even sketched exactly what you want to be done?"

"Yes, John, I have. They are at home, but I can show you what I mean." He twisted around and grabbed his sketch pad. With a minimum of lines, he'd made the store interior come to life. John watched as he etched and rubbed. For a lad who said he could not draw. Well, he shook his head in wonderment.

The drawing showed John what was in Wills's heart. The strokes were sure and true. Yes, the lad had thought this out well.

"All right, Wills. Upon our return, we will stake out some land and apply for the title, but it will be in your name alone. Ed can go into business with the shop, but you must own the land outright. Your father named you correctly after an adventurer." John was increasingly intrigued by this young man's skill and knowledge.

"Dar was rather enamoured with Mr Wentworth when I was born. His parents were convicts, too, and he was not accepted by the toffs in the Parliament. It's funny, really, as Dar turned out to be a toff himself. Anyway, that's why I was named William." Wills laughed. "Aptly named because it means to 'want' or 'desire'. Reverend William Clarke told me that when we were studying William the Conqueror. He had his mind fixed on one thing and followed his dream. I'm a bit like that."

Wills had his feet up on the front of the cart, and they hit a large hole. "Ouch! My butt," he yelped.

John laughed. "I think from here, we nearly have to make our own tracks." He added, "We have enough stores for six weeks. So we travel west for three more weeks, then turn back. Dancing birdies or not, I will not risk our lives. Somehow, I do not think land is always as lush as it is now. I believe you've had much rain this past year, but if you look over at that stand of trees, they are all dead. There are also trees and bushes growing in the creeks and rivers, which means they are not used to being this wet."

With this in mind, Wills identified many more signs of drought and death. He even started counting the dead kangaroos and other animals they saw.

In front of them were wide open plains with some rolling hills covered in scrub. John, now in the lead, followed a track westward. He had no idea where it led, only that someone had traversed it before and in a cart of some sort. And they did it quite often. Reverend Clarke had just told Wills, "I followed the tracks". So that's what they were doing.

John cast his eyes around. Some would say "nothing to be seen." But to John, he was in awe of all he saw. Large bouncing animals, some with babies in a pocket on the front.

Wills pointed out the difference between the big male red kangaroo and the smaller female ones. One big male stood with his arms out. He looked like a prizefighter. Wills also pointed out differences in the species as they passed through different areas. "John, as a rule, we call the small ones wallabies and the big ones kangaroos. It's not strictly true, but close enough. There are many different sorts. When we are talking about any of them, we just call them all 'roos'."

Phil yelled across from the wagon. "Wouldn't want to go one round with him, let alone ten in Gentleman Jackson's Boxing ring."

There were laughs and guffaws from the others.

Wills called back. "Phil, they'd rip your stomach open with their back feet before you could get within arm's reach. Do not approach the big ones, and be careful of the little ones."

They saw huge brown birds, like a hawk, but with a wedge-shaped tail. Wills explained that they were called 'Wedge Tail Eagles'. Wills also pointed out the emus. He knew about them, too, and loved them. Reverend Clarke was a fount of information via this young man. He had soaked up every scrap of knowledge imparted to him by this Reverend Gentleman. Around the fireside at night, Wills would tell stories about the animals they saw when he knew something about them. "The emu is a peculiar one; it is a large, flightless bird. The male hatches the eggs while the female just takes off once she had done her bit of laying from five to twenty eggs. The babies are stripy and can easily hide in the grass. You can often see ten or more chicks. We see them around Emu Plains, so if we don't see any out here, I'll show you some when we get back. Oh, and the eggs taste great. Just like a chook egg, only richer. One emu egg equals twelve chook eggs."

"What's a chook?" Ed asked.

"Huh? It's a chicken. You know, normally laying eggs on a farm and stuff," Wills said laughingly.

John sat thinking, then said, "Wills, in England, if we go a mile without seeing someone, it's a miracle. Here, you could go days or weeks without seeing a soul; black or white. The verses from Psalm 23 came to my mind; this place just gets to your heart. It restores my soul.

'The Lord is my shepherd;
I shall not want.
He maketh me to lie down in green pastures:
He leadeth me beside the still waters.
He restoreth my soul:
He leadeth me in the paths of righteousness for his name's sake'."

John noticed a change in the others, as well. He'd sometimes hear laughter, something unknown to him for many a year.

Around the fireside that night, Wills talked of other animals in this country. To him, they were normal, but to these Englishmen, unheard of. He told them about the platypus, a strange water animal with a beak like a duck, but larger. The male ones had a big spur on the back legs, and they could make you very sick. He spoke of wombats, gentle, solid creatures that were known to make a track and stick to it. If you built a building in their path, they'd been known to walk through houses. Thankfully, he didn't need to describe echidnas. They saw one waddling along the road. They stopped and investigated this intriguing creature. It curled into a tight ball and looked like a dangerous football. His descriptions of these other beasts not only stirred questions but had all laughing.

Wills again asked more about England.

They had told him of hunting foxes, called riding to hounds, of steeplechases, pheasant shoots, salmon fishing and other leisure activities.

Wills looked puzzled, then asked, "But what other things do you do? Are there schools? Who teaches the children to read and write? Are children apprenticed too young? Are any of you interested in politics? How do you help people?" He had broached this subject first in Hartley but had let it drop when no one answered him. So he asked again.

All answered again with silence. Nothing! Not one of them was interested in helping anyone but themselves; they each just wished to enjoy their lives. They were each struck dumb. During the war, each had been contributing to the war effort.

Harry looked at the shocked, guilty looks on his friend's faces, knowing that in his heart, he felt the same. He said quietly, "Wills, it's taken a trip across the world and a four-month trip with a colonial lad to jolt the six of us back to reality. You first asked us in Hartley. I know I'm still in denial. I don't wish to answer this, as it's just too challenging to face the reality of the answer." He looked at his friends. "I know we all have faith in the one who made those stars up there, but it's so easy to get caught up in the social whirl that we've all lost track of the important things in life. When you asked us this before, we ignored you. Thinking you didn't mean what you'd asked. But now that we know you better, we understand. Wills, now we know you were serious, weren't you?"

Wills nodded.

Harry said, "I, for one, will use some of the gold money to build a school in our town and teach the children in our village to read and write."

"Hear, hear," said Phil and Ed.

Phil turned to Edmund. "How about we do the same but pool ours and add a foundling school, too? Interested?"

"Phil, you're on," replied Edmund. "I bet Annabella will be the first to support us. Bell is good with that sort of thing."

John said, "Well, I know there is a school in our village, but I bet it's short of funds, teachers and equipment. So I'm in, too."

Aidan then spoke. "Well, it's all very well to teach them to read and write. But they can't do that on an empty belly, so I think some of these schools should have a farm garden. If we can also teach the children some new gardening skills, it could save the entire family, let alone villages, something other than potatoes."

Wills looked at Lewis. He said, "We already have a school, but I know the clothing for these children is threadbare. I've seen it all too often. It's often concerned me that the children would be cold. But I did nothing, leaving it for others to do. As soon as they are out of sight, they are out of mind. The ideas fly away like a butterfly. It's always been someone else doing things, never me. I've been far too busy enjoying myself rather than thinking about anyone else but my own pleasure. I won't let that happen again," he said regretfully. He fell silent for a long time. Absent in mind from the group. He looked sad and guilty. John looked at him, worried. It seemed to go far deeper than his comments reflected.

After some time, Harry looked at Wills. "What is it about you, lad, that has seen through us like an eagle? We have each been soul-searching, but for what we did not know. We just knew we were discontented and empty. On the whole, it's why we came."

The firelight flickered on his face as he looked intently into the flames. Harry, too, was searching his soul, something he had not done for a long time. "Wills, we intentionally ignored you in Hartley the last time you asked us this. I am sorry."

Lew stood up and walked away to be alone with his thoughts.

Each was silent.

Wills looked from face to face. Each solemn and deep in thought. "I find it helps if I write my ideas down. Then, let God develop them until they are moulded into His plan. I feel terrible saying this to you, but Dar suggested this when I was first at school, and it helped me to see things more clearly."

Aidan asked for one of the spare journals.

Wills brought some from the wagon, along with six sticks of charcoal. He handed the bundle to Aidan, who then distributed them. Each wrote in the firelight.

One sat on a rock, waiting for Lew. However, he did not return for hours. When he did, his journal sat untouched.

Phil and Edmund worked with their heads together.

John sat up and laughed. "We're all doing our homework like good children."

It broke the ice. The idea had been firmly planted in their hearts.

Wills was writing, too, both in his personal journal and a letter to Ed. Time to let him know of his dreams.

> Somewhere west of Bathurst,
> About Mid March, (I think.) 1845

Bramblemere Close
Phillip Street
Parramatta

Dear Ed,

I do hope you are all well. I miss you, but not enough to return home yet. I have no idea exactly what date it is, but it's about mid-March.

We still plan to head west and will do so for the next three weeks. By then our supplies will be running low and we'll need to return as I doubt if there is anywhere we could stock up. I hope to see my dancing Brolgas at last. I pray we find a wetland.

Ed, my friends are well, and all send their regards. We have had many interesting discussions around the fireside. The most illuminating was tonight. I again asked what they 'did' with their time. They all spieled off a list of leisure activities, but nothing to help or work in the community. Are we really all that different? It is such a part of our lives that I never even thought about the correctness of asking. God, however, needed the question asked. In my innocence, I put both my foot IN it and my finger ON it. I had asked before, and the question was met with silence, but they must have been thinking about it. Tonight, after much discussion, I think they now have a direction for their lives. As I write, each has a journal, and they are writing about how they can change areas of their lives upon their return home.

Schools are a priority, but so are community gardens, housing, and warm clothing. If these areas alone get some of what has been discussed, then those villages will change. All of this is being funded by the rocks I found. They have insisted that I get half, and the other half is shared between themselves. They each already have some funds; I have none whatsoever. They also said that if I had not asked them to stay by the creek, they would have passed straight by.

Ed, I have applied for the land this outcrop is on. We have hidden it with moss, branches and dirt. Hopefully, no one will come looking.

I didn't wish to take more until I owned it. I did not mind taking the loose rocks, as they would have eventually washed away.

Ed, there is another block of land I'm interested in. We shall be returning by Bathurst again on our way home. On the corner of William and Durham Streets, there is a large site that would be perfect for a second Emporium. I am going to buy it.

Eddie, I would love for you to come in partnership with me on the same terms *80/20* as you are with Mr Tindale. We have checked each creek and river we have passed since Hartley, and very few do not have the desired finds in them. This WILL take off, and every person arriving will need equipment. I would like to be already here and set up before they arrive. What do you think?

I have mentioned it to John and even shown him my ideas.

If you go to my room, you will find a pile of drawings under my large bible. Have a look. I shall buy the land regardless, and it will be a good investment. Farming here is also developing. A new town is planned. I shall have ample funds to build and stock if you do not wish to go partners, but I would be honoured if you would. I would concentrate on just the Emporium Items for the moment, as there is already a farmers' market across the road. There is no other store in town where building supplies, ironmongery or tools are available. Harry wondered why I walked through the town looking, but I wanted to see what was there.

I come to the end of my paper.

I do not know how I will send it, but I trust that God will again provide.

We shall all return as better men.

Your loving brother

Wills

~

Jenna was in labour. This time, Eddie was with her through the birth. Martha delivered the child. There was no time to call a doctor. Jenna had been having back pain all day and told no one. When the real pains started, she still stayed silent. This time, she wanted Ed to be with her.

Martha knew.

By the time her pains were a few minutes apart, Eddie was home from the forge.

Martha made him scrub; he was then taken into their bedroom.

He had thought himself a strong person until he saw the exquisite pain Jenna was suffering. With each contraction, she squeezed his hand so much he thought his fingers would pop. He did not care. He mopped her brow, kissed her forehead, and prayed. She was in her nightgown and in great discomfort.

Martha said, "Come on, love, we're going for a walk."

"*What?*" said Eddie, "How? She can't."

Martha laid a gentle, loving hand on his shoulder. "Trust me, son, she needs to get the baby moving. Walking helps. I have had seven. Sometimes, the baby needs to move into the right position. She's had twins; she can do this, but this baby will be larger as it's a full-term baby. Encourage her and be there for her. I may ask you to get into some unusual positions, such as sitting behind her. This will rest her back. Just do it."

Eddie nodded. He was so anxious; his Jenna was in pain. With each moan or yell, his heart twisted.

Martha and he had her up and walking around the room. She had a contraction while walking, and Martha stood behind her while she leaned against Eddie. She screamed into his shoulder, and he could do nothing to help but hold her.

Martha stood behind her, rubbing her lower back.

"Oh, Maa, that feels so good," she said wearily. "Here comes another one." Again, she clung to Eddie. She was so tired.

A tear rolled down his cheek. Why did he do this to her?

Martha saw and frowned. She shook her head at him and frowned. She said, "Remember your deep breathing, Jenna. In, out, In…"

Eddie swallowed and kissed Jenna's forehead again, and he encouraged her to be strong and bear up.

Between pains, they walked around the room. On the third circuit, she said, "Basin quick." She threw up.

"Good," said Martha. "We're there. Now, Ed, I want you on your knees in the middle of the bed so you can hold her. Wrap your arms around her, under her arms."

Ed hopped up on the bed.

"Now, love," Martha said to Jenna, "Sit on the end here and lean against Ed." She arranged Jenna and said to Ed, "I used to find this was easier."

Cara walked in with towels, a bowl and some more hot water. "Ready yet?"

"Yes," said Martha. "Should be a few minutes. Ed, now you'll have to support her, but don't squeeze her too hard. All right?"

He merely nodded fearfully.

Jenna moaned.

"Okay, here we go. Push love," Martha said.

She did.

"Good girl, now breathe; deep breath," said Martha.

Jenna relaxed against Ed.

"You're doing great, love. I love you," he whispered.

She moaned again, "It's coming."

Martha was on her knees. "Deep breath, then push!"

Jenna did.

"Head is out. One more push, Jen. Deep breath, push!"

Eddie, still holding her, saw one of the most amazing sights he could imagine. A small, pinkish, slippery bundle slithered into Martha's hands. "It's a girl." A wail pierced the air. "A very lusty, healthy girl."

Cara handed Martha a towel, which wrapped the wiggling bundle. Cara wiped her face. She was still attached to Jenna.

Martha said to Ed, "Watch her colour change, Ed, it's coming from the cord. We still have another push to go. It could take a few minutes."

Ed watched his daughter. He watched the cord pulsing, then it went limp. The baby was squirming, pink and healthy.

He saw Cara cut some string and she tied the cord in two sections, and Martha handed Ed some scissors. "Cut the cord there, lad."

Even more horrified, he did as Martha told him to. Snip.

Jenna said, "Maa, now," then screamed.

Ed grasped her, horrified; he saw the gooey lump that Jenna expelled.

"That's it, love, all done." Martha had a sloppy, bloody mess in her hands.

Cara was holding the baby while Ed and Martha helped Jenna back to bed. Once she was settled, Cara handed the baby to her.

Eddie was sitting next to her, still awestruck. "Sweets, are you all right?" he said, concerned.

"Fine, honey, just tired. Honestly!" She gave him a beaming smile. "Look what we made, love. She's beautiful. So beautiful." She could see that she had very pale hair like her older siblings. "She's beautiful, like a little lily, Ed." She ran her finger over the baby's cheek. "I'm in love again, sweetheart; I want lots more. Just so you know."

Eddie was flabbergasted. "But…" He looked at Martha, who just smiled.

"Ed, trust me, the pain is worthwhile, and it's gone until next time. Jenna will bounce back from this one much quicker," said Martha with a laugh. To Jenna, she said, "Feed the babe a bit, then sleep, love."

While they were talking, Cara took the basin with the afterbirth and walked out to bury it.

Eddie took the wrapped tiny bundle for Jenna. Cuddling his new daughter while Jenna prepared herself to feed the baby. He handed his daughter back to her mother and kissed his wife. "I'm so proud of you, love! And in absolute awe. Just in awe."

She beamed back at him. "I love you too, and yes, I want more."

Eddie walked out, shaking his head. "I'll be back in a bit." He blew her a kiss. He was overcome with emotion and overflowing with love.

Paddy had been growing some roses, and he wanted to see if there was one ready to pick for her. A pink one, for love. She needed a huge bunch of them. He needed to collect his thoughts.

~

Two days later, Jenna came downstairs for the first time since Lily's birth. Eddie fussed and fidgeted. How could she even walk after "laying a baby"? Ed did not think Jenna should be downstairs yet.

Martha overruled him. "If Jenna feels well enough to dress, let her."

Jenna was recovering from her lying in and was sitting with the new baby on her lap in their drawing room. She said, "Although she will be named Jennifer Annabella Elizabeth, rather than Lilabet. She is the image of her older sister, Tina." The babe had fair hair and big blue eyes. "However, she is like a lily, Ed. I shall call her Lily."

They were sitting together when there was a knock on the front door. Moira answered the door and received a letter from the postman.

"It's from Mr Wills, ma'am," the postman said, smiling. It was crushed and dirty but unopened.

She took it straight into the sitting room to Ed. "Sir, another letter has come." She passed this missive over to him, and he flicked open the damaged seal.

It was now the 15th of April, and it had taken over three weeks to arrive. On the back of the letter was scrawled...

Ed

A squatter named Mr Barry, from a farm called 'Condobolin', is heading to Bathurst. He said he'll post this. I have given him a shilling.

See, God did provide - again.

Wills L

Eddie read the letter, then handed it to Jenna. Without a word, he walked out, and she heard his footsteps on the stairs. Jenna looked puzzled. She read the letter and then understood. He had gone to find Wills' big Bible. This one would have been too large for him to pack, so he left it beside his bed.

Ed returned with a sheaf of papers.

He ran his fingers through his blonde locks. "Why didn't I know about this? Have I neglected him that much? I should have listened to him." He ran his hands through his thick blonde locks.

"Show them to me, love," Jenna said.

Ed moved to sit next to her. Together, they looked through the drawings and were astounded by the details he'd included.

"Oh Jenna, they are good, very good. His ideas are sound and innovative." He sheafed through them again, slowly digesting each one. "I like it, I really do. I might even try some of these ideas in our shop. I'll talk to Robert tomorrow." Ed stroked the furry blonde hair of his daughter. He felt so close to her as he'd been there at her birth. They eventually decided on Jennifer Annabella Elizabeth, but she was already being called Lily, short for Lilabet, as they had planned after Dar's sister, Elizabeth.

Shauna, Moira's little sister, had finished school and was looking after the toddlers. This gave everyone a break from their antics.

Ed let the twins into the sitting room but told them not to wake their sister. They were nearly three and, on the whole, well-behaved, considering their age. Neddie took control of all infantile activities. Tina was a willing co-conspirator in all his plans. She was thrilled she had a little sister; Ned wasn't. Ed tried to explain that she would grow and be able to play with them both, but it would take time. His response was to poke out his tongue. "Neddie, that's rude. Please apologise to your sister."

"Sorry Rilly," was the best he could manage.

Ed groaned; he hoped that didn't stick. "Lily, not Rilly."

"Lirry, Rilly," Neddie tried again. He shrugged and ran out, Moira hard on his heels.

"It'll come," Jenna said hopefully.

Tina was perched next to Jenna. "Well, I'se glad I got a bubby sister. She's nice. I like her. Can I keep her?" Her big blue eyes looked up lovingly at her mother. "Prease? Can we?"

Jenna's heart melted. "Yes, darling, we'll keep her. But we might have to try to get a brother for Neddie later."

"Awlright, Mama, as long as we can keep this one for me." She bent and kissed the baby's head, then slipped down and followed Neddie's path out the door at top toddler speed. Ed laughed.

The three covered wagons were pulled up along side a swampy area. Mr Barry, the squatter from the farm 'Condobolin', said that sometimes the brolgas could be seen dancing from this spot. They were 'due in' soon. They hoped to see them in the week they had allowed before they had to turn around to head home.

The squatter also told them to watch out for snakes. There were some nasty ones in the area. This was enough to make the Englishmen sleep in the wagons. Even Wills slept across the front seat of John's vehicle.

Wills's eyes were on the sky, looking out for large birds on the wings. Breeding season was about to start, and Reverend Clarke told him that they would dance before the season. They had arrived at the perfect time. John had said it must be about the second week in April.

On the first morning at the waterhole, Wills woke early to the sound of strange noises. He sat up and rubbed his eyes. In the gloom, he could see some large birds flying into the waterway. "They are here," he whispered, not so quietly, to himself.

Phil also heard the same noises and stuck his head out of the canopy. "What's that noise, lad?" he asked quietly.

"They're here, Phil. Some must have flown in last night. We timed it perfectly. They have arrived. Look." Wills pointed to more birds landing near the wetlands.

Along with the brolgas, there were black swans, ducks, magpie geese, jacanas, and various waterfowl, including different types of ducks, grebes, pelicans, cormorants, ibises, spoonbills, egrets, and herons. Then there were all sorts of parrots, hundreds and thousands of them, so many colours. The cacophony of noise had woken the others, and soon, all were sitting in silence on the seats, watching as more and more birds arrived. The sky was dotted with birds of all shapes and sizes. Flying V's of black swans, black and white pelicans, ducks of various shapes and colours.

Wills quietly pointed out different sorts to the watchers. "Reverend Clarke calls the flying birds a 'murmuration'. Isn't it a beautiful word? They fly and sweep and swerve and never hit each other," Wills spoke softly to John and Harry, who had moved to sit next to him. "I think it's mostly about starlings, but it's a fabulous word."

The sun crept over the horizon, and the noise settled down for a while as the birds fed and drank.

Harry rose first and lit the fire. The billys were soon boiling, and the men washed and made tea.

The mist rose from the water in the cool morning air. No one had mentioned the birds. All moved quietly without making much noise. While preparing breakfast, the first of the comments came.

"Wills, now I can see why you wanted to see the birds, but tell me more about these birds. Brolga's, you call them?" Edmund asked.

They were all listening. Wills said, "Reverend Clarke told me about them. It's astounding. I wanted to see all this for myself. He told me about the local legend of the brolgas. A young girl was turned into a beautiful, graceful bird because she was always dancing. He said that the dance is so amazing that the birds prance and jump over a yard high. Then he said they bounce and bow with their wings spread out. As they dance, they throw things, like sticks and twigs, all the while trumpeting."

Wills drank some tea. "The way he spoke, well, it caught my imagination. I hope we shall get to see them dance today." He dragged out his sketch pad. He sat drawing for about half an hour. The birds took shape as he flicked the charcoal across the page. Soon, the dawn flight covered the page. He put the pad down, totally drained.

He was still sitting on the wagon seat. From this elevated site, he could see into the wetlands. There was a dry section a short distance over. He could see two brolgas standing on the short grass. He gasped, standing and watching, he said, "Look."

They all stood and looked to where he pointed. Each climbed silently up onto the wagon seats and watched. Awestruck at the sight, they stood in silence and watched.

The majestic dancing grey cranes rose and fell with wings flapping, their red heads bobbing and bowing. They danced, and they danced.

Wills saw Harry's face. For the first time, the stress lines were gone. The reverence and majesty of the dance, the simple beauty, spoke to their hearts and souls. The seven men stood without moving.

John noticed Lew wipe his eyes.

One of the birds landed close to them, and they could see how large it was. Standing just shy of four feet tall, the shiny black legs and soft velvety light-grey feathers made these remarkable birds look majestic. The crown of red on their heads gave the exalted birds a regal aura. The single ghost-like bird hunted around for food for a while, then flew back to join its friends.

Wills did not realise how long he'd been holding his breath, but he released it and sighed with delight.

John quietly said, "Wills, that was a sight to calm the soul. I can understand Reverend Clarke's obsession. I could stay for a month and see that every day. Oh, Wills, I'm so glad we came." John said thoughtfully. "Sadly, we have only a few days left, but let's make the most of them." John looked down and saw what Wills had drawn. He took the pad from Wills knee and gazed at the sketches he'd done. He had captured the moment when the head of the bird is thrown back, one leg up, and wings outstretched. The colour of the birds was done by smudging the charcoal. It was a splendid work. "This is perfect. You've captured the moment exactly." John called Harry. "Harry, come look at this."

"Wills, lad, these are astonishing," Harry said

"And these too," said John, flicking over the pages.

Phil came over and peered over their shoulders. He could see the movement of the bird captured in the strokes.

Harry looked around for Lew, but he'd gone off on his own again. He was worried for his friend.

Wills blushed. "They are okay, but I wish there was some way I could capture them in colour. Not so much the brolgas, but the vivid colours of all the others. I have some water colour paints that I bought for George. I might have a try later. Maybe we all could try. I could do outlines."

The sun was well up by now and the fire had burned down to coals, and it was ready to cook some food. Lew eventually returned, silent and morose. He picked up his plate without a word and bit into the delicious food.

They sat eating something Edmund called French Toast. He had soaked some soda bread slices, or damper as Wills called it, in beaten egg and fried them in dripping.

"Yum," said Wills

The day was spent around camp while watching the birdlife. Wills had warned everyone to be wary of snakes, and they didn't need a second telling.

On one of the sojourns in the lagoon surrounds, they came across an area you could call a waterhole. They were all hot, so they stripped off and went in for a dip.

It was a quick dip, for as soon as Harry splashed in, he yelled, "Leeches."

"Don't pull them off. Put salt on them," Wills said. He returned to his pants and dug into a pocket. "Here." He pulled a twist of paper from his pocket and sprinkled it on the leeches. The six blighters fell off. "See if we can find some milk thistles of some sort, or um, dandelions. Carefully rub the sap on the bites. It helps."

"Why do you carry salt like that, Wills? Harry asked him, puzzled.

"Oh, Luke and I loved boiled eggs with salt, and we often had a few with us when on an adventure. Easy to carry and didn't need wrapping, eggs were a convenient and portable food. Most of our clothes had twists of salt like this somewhere in the pockets."

Poor Harry had blood pouring down his legs. "Damn things," he muttered.

With much laughter, they retrieved their clothing and headed further along the edge of the wetland. They lost count of the number of different-looking species of feather friends, but certainly more than thirty.

Wills tried listing them, but there were so many that he did not know what they were. He was looking out for the pink Major Mitchell cockatoo and saw some high in a dead tree. Pointing and yelling "Yes," in his excitement, he scared the others, and they took off.

Finally arriving back at camp, he collected his journal and wrote a list of the birds he knew; brolgas, of course, came first; then other cranes and ibis; spoonbills, a funny sort of stork. There were hundreds of black swans, black and white pelicans, and a smaller version of a black and white bird that looked like a goose. So many different sorts of ducks, they counted at least five different varieties, but didn't know the male and female colour differences.

Harry stood on the seat next to him. "Look. They look a bit like farm hens," he said, pointing out some birds walking on the edges. Eagles soared overhead looking for a meal, as did some hawks and other carrion birds.

Lew quietly pointed out an iridescent blue bird with a beak like a tiny kookaburra.

Wills said, "That's a kingfisher."

As they gazed, they saw more and more darting in and out of the water. There was a scurry in the grass, and a small brown bird, like a quail, emerged from the reeds and darted back in again when it saw them.

During the afternoons, each had a try at drawing or painting. They had all been taught when children, but none had excelled. Some tried capturing the landscape, while others worked on the bird outlines that Wills had sketched for them. By late afternoon, they had a picture gallery of the area. Each was pleased with the combined effort.

They sat working on their plans for how they could change their own outlook on life and how to put it into action. Wills' simple question weeks ago had inspired each to look beyond themselves. During their work in India and the neighbouring countries, they saw extreme poverty. It was as though their eyes were closed to it at home. They had shut out the ugliness, thinking only of self. Each felt the raw emotion of guilt falling away from their lives and realised that through their positions in society and the bounteous gift of gold, they could now change things, even if only in their local areas. It would be a start.

Harry thought back to the few days they had been there. On that first evening by the wetland, after they prepared their campsite, Wills had them sitting upon the seats of the carts just before dusk, warning them to stay both still and quiet. They did not know why, but they sat and waited, watching the sky.

Wills had pointed, and they saw what looked like a black patch floating towards them. Then another larger one, and soon the sky was alive with the raucous chorus of millions of parrots and birds coming to drink and spend the night in safety. They dipped and dived and frolicked in the water before settling in the various trees, some dead, around the vibrant waterhole.

The night party of the birds lasted for about an hour. They could still hear the noises of birds talking to each other, but darkness had descended, and they could no longer see them.

Not a word had been spoken. The sight was just too amazing. Each man was deep in thought, wondering at the awesomeness of God, caring for each little thing. Harry could not get the sight from his mind.

Finally, Wills said, "I think that's all we can see for today. I'm hungry."

With that, the camp got moving, and the evening meal of stew was served and eaten. Their hunger sated, they lay around the campfire looking up. The stars seemed so close. They each felt they could reach out and almost touch them.

All these star were unfamiliar to the Englishmen.

Wills pointed out the Southern Cross and the two-pointer stars. The spray of stars splattered in a long grey cloud named the Milky Way.

He told them the Romans had named it. At least, that's what Reverend Clarke had told him.

Tomorrow they needed to leave. Their time at the waterhole had finally come to an end. Harry prepared for bed.

As the birds finally settled in for the evening, silence reigned. They men lay watching the sky in the crisp, clear evening. The stars themselves then started to dance. A meteor shower sent shooting stars across the sky, first one, then another, followed by streams of more. A fireworks display of stupendous size. Trail after trail, tracking across the vastness of space. None could believe what they were seeing. Wills lay with a lump in his throat, unable to speak. He fell asleep on the ground near the fire while watching God's magnificent handiwork displayed.

What a day! Each felt their smallness in the universe.

The six turned in for the night, knowing the dawn chorus from the birds would awaken them again. Wills, still asleep on the ground, could stay where he was. Harry closed his eyes and knew he would sleep peacefully tonight.

~

The next morning, Wills was once again up at dawn. He had slept well by the warmth of the fire. He knew it would be the last time he'd get to see the magical display of the exotic birds. He was soon joined by the others on the wagon seats. They sat wrapped in their blankets, keeping the chill of the morning at bay.

The cacophony of noise started, and soon, the birds began feeding and taking flight.

Wills suggested that they try to list as many types of birds as possible. He had his journal on hand and started listing as many as he could. He had no idea of the various species, but could tell from the shapes of most what types they were. Sometimes, he would write things like black and white goose or brown duck that whistled.

The brolgas were there, but not dancing.

After an hour, the chill had permeated into their bones, and they were all shivering.

Lewis quietly climbed off his wagon, stoked the coals of the fire and put the billys on to heat.

They knew they had to break camp that day, and each was sad that not a single brolga was in sight. They had yet to see them dance up close.

Wills was determined that no sign of their presence would be left. They knew that the fire also must be fully quenched.

Finally, after some hours, the horses were harnessed, and everything stowed into the wagons.

They were about to leave the campsite, and Aidan said, "Look, two have just landed over there." He pointed to a large cleared area, "Over it that clear spot."

The three wagons moved slowly towards the area that Aidan saw. It took ten minutes to move slowly before they finally gazed upon a love display.

They pulled up next to each other. The horses were willing to stand and nibble the knee-high native grasses.

Minutes after they arrived, the dance started. The larger bird bowed first, with the other mimicking; they did this a few times, then started billing and cooing. The large male flapped his wings outstretched as wide as possible, and the smaller female bowed, and then, with her head thrown back, she bowed again. They repeated this often, then they swapped roles, and the dance continued. The male followed the female and hopped and bowed. She did the same, copying his movements. The inspiring dance continued, and the seven watched in awe filled silence. Then, the male brolga presented her with gifts of sticks, throwing them in the air for the morning breezes to catch.

The jumps got higher, and the kicks and displays got bolder and more flamboyant. The closeness of the birds showed the size of the wingspan, something they had not realised before. They were huge; the fully open wings were over eight feet across.

The majestic dancing cranes seemed to be dancing in the air. They bowed to each other, jumped again, dipped their beaks into the shallow water, threw sparkling droplets into the air that caught the early sun with rainbows of colour. They bowed again and then walked off into the head-high grasses. The Brolgas were hidden from view.

Each man released a deep sigh.

"They're gone," whispered Wills.

Chapter 5   Turning Things Around

With a final screech from the stunning pink Major Mitchell cockatoos, the birds farewelled the departing wagons.

The past few days had been the highlight of the trip so far. Outweighing even the gold find, the travelling through the vastness of the country and the creeks and rivers running through pristine valleys were spirit cleansing. Reverend Clarke had been right. There were far more important things in life than gold: people. Wills looked around at his six new friends. Connected now by faith and a purpose, these seven lives all now had direction. No one was sad the journey's end had been reached, as it meant another had started. Each felt they had left the past behind at the leech-infested waterhole. Six men in their early thirties, and one is just two years off twenty, each now driven by new ideas, ideals, and a purpose.

Wills was already planning how to build his Emporium. He knew what it would look like, even to the vents on the roof to let out the summer heat. How would he persuade Eddie to come into partnership? He did not want to cut family ties, and this way, he didn't have to.

The wagons trundled on through mile after mile of hills, grasslands, planes and scrub. Often taking new tracks, they saw heading off into the scrub. Each a new adventure. Overnight stops were often near waterways if one was close by. A swim was always nice to clear off the day's dust and grime. Leeches often found Harry, but occasionally the others, too. Lew's bites turned into big welts when they bit him. He'd laugh and say, "There's not enough whisky in my system."

None had drunk any alcohol for nearly three months, and no one had even missed it. Tea, hot and strong, was the usual tipple, occasionally with some honey if they found a hive of native bees. The keg of honey they had brought was empty of the sweet, sticky goop.

The next planned stop was back in Bathurst to sort out the land Wills wanted. There was an area where they could camp and wander around the creeks and waterways, looking for finds. If their suppositions of the quantity of gold in these were correct, they knew Wills' project would succeed. However, they met Mr Barry, the squatter on the road heading back to his claim 'Condobolin', and he suggested some nice camp spots a little to the north. "Just up the road a bit, lad." He told Wills he'd posted his letter. They bought a few supplies from him. He needed the cash and could get more food later. This meant they could extend their time until Bathurst. Wills thanked him. Mr Barry gave the directions to Phil and John. "It's down that road a bit; you turn at the fork in the road, at the dead tree with a tin nailed to it. Then, continue for about half a day, and there's a creek in the distance. Nice spot for a swim if I say so myself."

It took them to the north of the road they'd taken before, but eventually, it would still lead to Bathurst. They did not need to hurry back, so they decided to go and take a look.

"Wills, exactly how far is 'a bit' in this country?" John asked one day.

"Well, it can be anything from literally 'just around the corner' to 'over the hills and travel for a week'. There is no set distance." Wills laughed. "I've never really thought about it, you know. We just have to check every dead tree at a fork in the road and look for a tin nailed to it."

They also checked each creek they passed. Panning for gold, it was not long before they started finding specks of gold.

At one place they found, they later worked out was some twenty miles from Blackman's Swamp, the squatter had said it was soon to be renamed Orange. They camped by a creek and wandered up and down the waterways. They were using a basin to wash some creek gravel, and saw in pan after pan there was fine gold dust. Lots of it! It did not take too long before the billy had an inch in it. Not chunks like in Hartley, but so much that you could pull back the dirt from a rock and see specks in the gravel. In some areas, they only had to scoop up the fine dust and pour it into the billy. Once they had a cup or so, they would wash out all the muck and gravel, leaving the heavy gold at the bottom with very little black sand left mixed in it.

They stayed a week. There was ample fresh water, and catching fish was fun as they had made a little trap similar to the one in Hartley.

Many of their supplies had been finished at the brolga wetlands, which included butter and tea. Mr Barry had thankfully sold them some flour, tea and butter. So they were content. The rest they could do without. They would have loved some eggs, but he didn't have any with him.

The next day, Aidan came back from one of his wanders. "I found a nest of seven huge dark green eggs; come and look."

He led everyone back to the nest and saw two emus nearby. Wills knew how dangerous these birds could be and kept them all at a safe distance. "They were not sitting on them yet, so the female must still be laying them." An idea formed in Wills's head. "Anyone want French toast for dinner?" he asked.

Edmund's eyes lit up, "Yes, please, but you can't eat them. Can you?" He questioned.

"Oh yes, you can! They are delicious. Like a hen egg but huge. One emu egg to about a dozen chicken eggs. I told you before, Edmund. We'd only need two. Who wants to play chicken, or should I say, Emu dodge? It could be a bit dangerous. They can run blooming fast." Wills said with a smile on his face. "How hungry are you all?"

"Very," said John. "I'm in."

The others all agreed. Lew, Harry, Phil and John volunteered as the runners. They had to distract the emus, and Aidan and Wills would swipe some eggs.

'Project emu' was put into action, and within an hour, the group came back to camp with four warm eggs. Two for tonight's dinner as scrambled eggs on damper toast. One for breakfast as French toast damper and one for tomorrow night. They felt a bit sorry for the birds, but Wills knew they could lay up to sixteen eggs in a clutch, but mostly about ten. They would still have babies. Their timing was good.

They all enjoyed the first fresh egg meal for a few weeks.

John lay patting his full tummy. "Fresh fish, eggs and tea. Who would have thought such good food could come from the land? These plains would grow good crops, too. There are good creeks to water them and not too many dry seasons, as there aren't many dead trees here, like out around that waterhole."

Phillip groaned. "I've eaten too much. I haven't enjoyed food for such a long time. Better than a banquet at Bella's Castle."

Later that evening, they were in the waterhole in the creek, having a swim, when some ducks landed at the other end. Wills saw them and motioned for everyone to be quiet. They were. He duck-dived underwater. Before anyone knew it, two of the ducks disappeared under the water, then a third. His face momentarily surfaced some distance away; then they saw a fourth duck go under.

All watched, none realising they, too, were holding their breath as though to help him.

Wills finally stood up. "Duck for dinner tomorrow, anyone?"

"Where the hell did you learn to do that, lad?" said Aidan.

Wills chuckled. "It's how the Aboriginals do it. They don't have guns, and they have to eat. I've seen them do it on the river banks at home, but have never tried it myself." He was still a bit out of breath. The ducks had all drowned. "I'll show you how they cook them, too. And we don't need to pluck them." He carried two, and Aidan took two. They walked back to camp with the fresh booty.

Wills plonked the ducks on the grass and took a bucket and a spade to the creek bank. He had noticed a clay outcrop earlier when they were looking for gold. Wills scooped out a few big chunks and put them in the bucket with some water. He added a bit more water until the stuff was thick and gloopy. The six men watched what would come next. He placed a few sprigs of lemon myrtle next to each bird's breast section. Without plucking them, Wills encased the whole bird in a clay covering, about an inch thick, then he set it aside and repeated this on the next bird. Finally, all the birds looked like giant brown eggs. As he was doing this, he explained that this way, they cooked in their own juices and when you broke them open, all the feathers stuck to the clay.

As they had already eaten that night, Wills placed the clay encased birds to sit overnight to harden a bit. "We'll cook them tomorrow. The clay needs to firm up a bit, as I've made it a bit wet."

With a cloth thrown over them to keep ants off them. They settled down for the night. Most woke with the usual screech of the pink and grey galahs and cockies. Wills slept on. The Englishmen laughed at the depth of sleep of the youth. He stirred but did not wake. Finally, about an hour after dawn, Edmund woke him with a mug of hot, sweet lemon myrtle tea. "What are you dreaming about this time, lad?" questioned Edmund. "Last time it was about gold, then you found it."

"Well, I won't find this," Wills said sleepily. He didn't elaborate. He merely grimaced. "What time is it? Did I miss the dawn chorus?"

"Yep," said Harry while munching. "And the French toast." He popped the last bit in his mouth. "You're right. The emu eggs were good."

Wills' mouth dropped open.

"Only kidding," Harry said. "It's just cooked. Thought you'd like it hot. Here's yours." He handed Wills a plate of hot French toast. "It really should be Australian toast. Emu eggs and damper," Harry chuckled again. "Tastes great, though."

Wills nodded thanks; he chomped his down, then crawled off the seat and headed to the creek for a quick wash. Sometimes, his dreams would seem so real. One day, he'd find his own Jenna or Gracie or a girl like them; if only Cathy looked at him that way. He wished it were Cathy, but he didn't think she was interested. He splashed in the cold water, the chill easing the heat of his dreams.

"Something's eating the lad this morning," said John. "He's not his normal cheerful self."

"I think it's time we moved on," said Lew. "Every day is a new adventure; who knows what we're missing?" Lew would often still go off by himself. However, he didn't seem quite as morose as before.

John was surprised at Lew's abrupt comment. He knew something was weighing him down.

Edmund agreed. "Fine, but not until tomorrow. We have clay pot roast ducks for dinner tonight if we can wait that long."

Wills arrived back and had brightened somewhat. He had never really been a morning person. Luke was, and it irritated him no end. He needed more tea. John handed him a mug full of hot, black, sweet tea on his arrival back at camp. Just what he needed. "Thanks, John," was all he said. "I need this today."

"You all right, lad?" he probed.

"Mmm," said Wills, "Just a rough night. Too much running around in my mind. Didn't sleep too well."

"Seven men together and all feel that way sometimes," he empathised.

Wills looked him in the eye. "John, do you have someone special at home? A lady, someone?" He regretted the words as soon as they came out. "Sorry, I shouldn't have asked."

"I thought I did, lad. However, she thought differently. We were engaged when I went to India. I thought she'd wait. She didn't. So no, no one is waiting at home anymore. It's why I'm here, I suppose." He looked sad. John had twigged what was eating at Wills. "There comes a time when we have to learn to trust God's timing. Out here, well, there is no temptation. Just let me say, though, do not jump at the first one. Wait until you are sure she's God's chosen one for you."

"Eddie said the same, John. I see him and Jenna, his wife, together. They have been married for over four years. They are as happy today as when they got engaged. I want that. I want the companionship they have, the special someone. It's hard living with them. Even harder when Cathy comes to visit."

John's eyebrows raised. He merely said, "Cathy?"

"One of Jenna's sisters, the youngest; we're the same age. She doesn't look at me that way. She treats me like another brother. I wish she didn't. I've liked her since the day we met."

"We didn't meet her when we stayed?" said John.

"No, they were staying with the Parkers. Mr Parker is Alex's boss. It was Mary's birthday, Alex's girl." Wills said wistfully. "I was looking forward to seeing her, too. But they had stayed over at the Parkers. Alex, of course, couldn't."

"Ahh, the problem becomes clear. Have you spoken to her about your feelings?" John watched his face.

"No way!" exclaimed Wills, looking horrified. "I couldn't."

"Maybe you could mention it to Mrs Turner? I'm betting she knows how the wind blows. Cathy may have said something to her mother. At least you could find out if her feelings are engaged elsewhere," John suggested.

"Do you think so?" said Wills hopefully. They sat drinking their tea.

"What brought this on, lad?" It had seemed to come out of the blue. Something must have happened, something more than just dreams.

"Well, it's the date, John." He fiddled with a stick, then broke it in half. "The squatter told us what day it was, so I figured tomorrow would be the twentieth of April. It's my eighteenth birthday. Eddie met Jenna when he was nearly twenty, but Charlie first spoke to Grace when he was about my age." He sighed. "Birthdays are special family time at home. The Turners always come in for them. This year will be different."

After travelling together for over four months, it was the first time John had seen Wills not on top of things. He was sad, but his last comments explained much. Eddie was his favourite brother. He had figured that much out. Not that Luke and Charlie weren't special; it was that Eddie held a special place in his heart. He had known that when they all met at the store. Unaware they were brothers, he hadn't realised the connection between the Lockley men back then. John felt as though he now knew the family well. There was an odd familiarity about them all, and he'd had an immediate camaraderie with Wills, like he were a little brother. He finally replied, "If Cathy has waited this long, you say she's your age, then have you thought she might be waiting for someone to say something to her? I think you might find that things are not as they seem." He hoped these were the right words. They certainly made Wills brighten.

"Oh, I hope so, John, I hope so. No use sitting here pining, though, is it? What are we going to do today? More gold?"

John's words seemed to have reached deep. Let's hope they were true. "Well, lad, first things first. Show us how to cook these birds. That was a really clever trick you used to catch them. I'll have to try that myself one day." John smiled, "Come on."

Edmund had made another damper and put it on to cook.

The fire had died down after breakfast. It was a lovely lot of hot coals. Wills showed how to scrape the coals back and put the clay balls with the birds inside, around the fire. Then he heaped more coals around them. "Okay, that's them done. What now, chaps? More gold?" He was back to his bright self.

John smiled at Harry, who'd first noticed Wills mood.

Harry smiled back, glad to see the mood had passed. "Sounds good to me," said Harry. "We'll need a bigger bucket soon." He emptied the now-dried gold dust into an empty flour bag, and he tucked it under a mattress. He chuckled as he saw how much of the precious stuff was there on top of what they'd already sent back to Eddie from Lithgow. The poor horses could have had a heavy load to tug over the mountains otherwise. At least they no longer needed to carry so much water, as there were creeks more regularly, and the water in them all was good to drink. Thank goodness it had been a wet season.

Lew, Phil, and Edmund tidied up the campsite while Aidan, John, Harry, and Wills prepared the equipment for gathering more gold.

They would break camp tonight and set off tomorrow. The next leg would be Bathurst again unless they came across something else like this.

Wills was whistling, and soon, the mood of the group was jovial.

John had been astounded that all seven had not had an angry word the entire trip. Wills' attitude this morning had been the first show of emotion from any of them, save Lew, although he kept it to himself. Wills was setting the tone again for them all.

They dug and washed for some hours, and all were hot and sweaty. Lew tripped and fell face-first into the creek. Drenched and spluttering, he sat in the cold water, laughing; it was as if a dam had burst. He laughed and laughed, and then Phil started too. These two were the hardest affected by their time in India and afterwards, and it seemed to have been hardest for them to settle back into life. To see them sitting in a cold creek, frolicking like children, was healing for them and the others. John and Harry wondered if there was much more to their story than either had let on.

"Stuff the gold," said Aidan as he stripped off his shirt and joined in. The water was only knee-deep. Even Harry, who for once was not attacked by leeches, lay in the cold water. "Let's go up to the pool," he said. They left all the tools and buckets on the creek bank and walked upstream to the waterhole.

All the ducks from the night before had flown off. They would return at dusk again. John and Harry both wanted to try to catch one and practised swimming underwater as Wills did. The other four also decided to have a go, and after a few hours, each was able to swim underwater the length of the waterhole. The sun was overhead when they decided to go and check on the cooking ducks. They had worked hard for some hours and were all hungry.

They arrived at camp to see a couple of wild dog-like animals. They were sniffing at the fire.

Wills raced ahead, frightening them off. "Damned dingoes. They'll eat everything if you're not careful. I've never seen one before, but I've heard about them. Fearful of nothing, brazen as hell. We'd better check they haven't got into the food box."

His six friends stood beside him. "What's a ding-go? Is that what you called them?" asked Aidan.

"They are a native dog. The Aborigines have tamed some, but many run wild. Don't get close to a wild one. Nasty creatures with just as nasty tempers. They are a bit timid if there is just one, but even then, I would not trust it." Wills checked the birds while the others checked the safety of the food stores.

Edmund lifted the camp oven from the triangle hook. He poured the now cold coals on the lid back into the fire, and they caught alight again. He lifted the lid, and the smell of fresh damper filled the air. "Perfectly cooked. Not even black around the edges. I'm getting the hang of this," he said proudly. "Nicer than chapatis too. More filling as well, and you can't make French emu egg toast from chapatis either."

Harry chortled. "They won't believe this at home, will they?"

Wills had pulled all four birds from their earth oven. They looked like small brown melons.

"I can't wait to see how they turn out," said Phil.

John could see the hungry dingoes hiding amongst the trees. He was about to throw some crusts to them from the morning's damper when Wills stopped him. "Don't, John," he yelled. "If you feed them, or they find food, they get nasty. We'll have to bury everything as we go from now on. No food left around, nothing. They will follow us otherwise." He looked at the four duck balls. "These are going to be a big temptation for them."

Wills took a big knife and was about to crack one open. "I know," he said. "What we can do is when we're catching ducks tonight is leave them a few to eat. That's if we catch enough for ourselves. I was thinking eight for us and some for them?"

"Sounds like an idea, lad, now crack that duck. I'm ravenous," said Lewis.

"And I'm *gorta*," said Aidan

Wills looked at him and said, "Huh, what's that?"

"It's Irish. It means it means famished or dying of hunger. You've worked us all hard today, lad. Harder than any of us has worked for a few years. Now feed us." He laughed.

Wills chuckled. "Okay, okay, I get it." Wills took the large knife and gently tapped the hard oval clay coating along the top, holding it over a plate. It cracked open, and he tipped it on its side. Some juices dripped into the plate. The perfectly cooked bird sat nestled in the clay bowl. All the feathers were stuck in the clay that had hardened in the fire. He tipped the cooked bird out of the case and onto a plate. John and Phil cut into it, and Phil pulled off a bit to try. His eyes opened wide. "This is delicious, and not just because I'm hungry either." He took another chunk. "Gamey but lemony too; delicious."

Wills handed the next one over, and John cleaved it in half. All the insides had shrivelled to a ball. They threw these into the fire.

Harry reached for the third, and Aidan held the plate for the last one. All had cooked to perfection, bar the last one which had got a bit overcooked on one side. That still meant they would have half a duck each. They sat picking off the flesh until there were just bones.

They used Edmund's damper to sop up the juices.

Aidan took a spade and walked a distance away from camp. He dug a hole in the softened bank of the creek, about two feet deep. Wills brought over the scraps and threw them in. Aidan covered them with a bit of dirt, then set a big stone on top. They knew the wild dogs were still there, but couldn't see them. By the time they were finished and returned to camp, Edmund had made the next damper and set it to cook. They drank their tea; then everyone lay back to digest their meal.

The sun was warm, their tummies full, and soon everyone was asleep in the warm Autumn sun. They woke with a start when Lewis shouted. One of the dingoes, braver than the rest, had padded into the camp area to sniff out some food. It had licked his face. It was this that had woken him. He froze. Inches from his face was a salivating, snarling wild dog.

Wills reached out for a small rock near his head. He had lain on it and moved it just as he fell asleep. He slowly sat up and threw it at the dingo's rump. It took off with a yelp. "Normally, I keep a stick with me when they are near."

"Good shot, Wills," said Edmund.

"You okay, Lew?" Harry enquired.

"Yeah, but I need to change my trews, I'm thinking," replied Lewis.

This brought chortles and laughs.

John checked his watch. "It's three; what time should we head to the waterhole, Wills?"

"Well, we were there about an hour before dusk last night, so about two hours, and we should head off. With those rascals around, we'll need to lock everything down, as dingoes can tear open bags and boxes.

They set to packing up camp, stashing the gold bag well under one of the mattresses, leaving out only what they'd need to eat that night. They planned to have the last egg and add some onion and potato. Aidan just said, "Too hard to explain; leave it with me. I'll whip you up a gourmet dinner." As all were still full from their duck lunch, they weren't too worried. He planned to make a potato pastry with an egg filling, similar to a pie.

They repacked the wagons, ensuring that all the food was properly stored in barrels or boxes. There was no way any dog could get to the food. Once done, they were all hot and sweaty again.

"Swim, anyone? We can then stay around until the birds arrive?" said Phillip.

"I'm all for that," said Lew, his face was bright red.

"Lew, are you all right? I think you're sunburnt," said Wills.

"Nah, lad, I've had my hat on all day," he replied.

"Err, no, Lew, not while you were asleep," John said. "I think Wills is right. And he's not the only one. Aidan, you're very red too." He looked at each of them. "I think we all have a touch of the sun," John said. "The sooner we all get ourselves in the cold water, the better. Even you, Wills."

Lew sat up and then shivered. "Hmm, I think you may be right. Not feeling that great now!"

"Here, drink." John handed him a mug of cool, boiled water, "All of it."

Having spent a lot of time in India, they all knew what to do for heatstroke. Get cool and drink water. Lew was looking wobbly. Phil and Edmund each took an arm and walked him into the creek in the shade. They walked him up to the waterhole and sat with him until the others arrived.

Lew sat submerged up to his neck. His poor face was still burned, but his body was cooling down. Aidan was also beginning to feel the effects of too much sun. They all made it to the creek, sinking into the water with relief. Seven hot bodies cooled themselves. Hopefully, they would all be all right, but Lew and Aidan were very burned.

"Come on, lads, hydration, hydration, hydration. You know the drill." John passed around mugs and the boiled water from the billy he carried.

"Yes, sir!" they all laughingly replied with a salute.

They sat in the shade in the waterhole. Even Wills, with his fair hair, was a little burned. They recovered quickly so that when the ducks arrived, they were keen to try and catch some. The men settled into the pool and sat still. Forty or so ducks landed on the pool. They grouped at the far end as they had before, but they were not particularly worried about the men.

Edmund went first. He swam underwater, snatching two ducks. He made it halfway back, then surfaced slowly so as not to scare the rest away. He took a breath and then went under again. Aidan and Phil went together; each got one, followed by Lew, who grabbed two, John one, and Harry managed three. Wills decided that the dingos would leave them alone if they had lots of food. He went last and grabbed another three. That was thirteen ducks: eight for them, five for the dingoes. Hopefully, that would keep them away from camp.

As they emerged from the pool, they sorted through the ducks and picked out the five smallest ones, throwing them a considerable distance from the pool. The dingoes were watching as they pounced on the first one almost as it hit the ground. The others, they scattered a little further afield, but well away from camp.

They stopped at the clay lump on the way back and filled a bucket with clay and water. Wills mixed this up to a firmer consistency. This time, he was going to get the others to each do a duck. He plucked some tender lemon myrtle twigs from the tree near the creek and popped them in the bucket with the clay.

Aidan and Lew were sitting with wet shirts tied around their heads and necks. Both were still burned but were now feeling a bit better.

John kept handing them fluid; tea, cold, hot, whatever was near at hand. He made them all hydrate. They drained the mugs. Each made three trips to the trees to empty their bladders, and probably more would follow as John kept them drinking. They each felt much better.

It was dark by the time they had finished the clay wrapping the ducks. The bird balls were placed into the coals to cook.

No one felt much like eating. They ate some damper with duck dripping, then ate the last of the oranges and went to bed.

Lew and Aidan didn't sleep too well, but still awoke feeling better. They had turned the bird about midnight. They were all woken by the dawn chorus of wildlife. John made them hydrate more before they broke camp, removed the cooked birds, then stoked the fire, boiled the billy, made breakfast and packed up. The cooked bird balls were carefully placed in the wagon. They should travel beautifully. The night before, they had dismantled the fish trap as they had at Hartley. They returned the fire stones to the river before they had lit it that morning, and they cleaned up the campsite, burying the remainder of the rubbish and food scraps. They had the last mug of tea each and quenched the fire with a large bucket of water. Leaving the site, Wills looked back and saw only the blackened circle and wheel tracks. He smiled. Dar would be pleased. "Duck Creek," he thought. One day, he'd return. He wished he could show Cathy.

John said, "Wills, happy birthday, lad. Sorry, we don't have a cake or anything, but we'll celebrate tonight."

"Thanks, John. No need to do that," said Wills shyly.

They were heading into the rolling foothills of the western slopes of the Blue Mountains. The next weeks would not only get colder, but hillier too. Wills had three letters written and ready to post as soon as they hit the town. They had more gold on board, and they planned to head straight back to Parramatta. They planned to spend a week or so in Bathurst and, of course, a night at least in Emu Plains, so certain issues could hopefully be sorted. Even having an understanding with Cathy would be wonderful. They had some business with some land in both towns.

Wills was excited. He was sitting between John and Harry. "John, I've just had an idea," Wills said excitedly. "With all the gold, you know, we could build two Emporiums. People won't go to Bathurst if they are only heading to Hartley, so they will stop at Emu Plains. They all have to pass through there, so if I build one there, at the foothills, they can stock up there first, then top up at Bathurst. Things will be more expensive in Bathurst because we'll have transport costs. What do you think?"

"Wills, lad, you're thinking so far ahead, but I love it," John said,

"At this rate, you will have a chain of stores."

Wills looked startled.

"Oh," exclaimed John, looking at him. "I've just sown another seed, haven't I?" He grinned at his young friend.

Wills nodded. "Wonderful idea though, John, absolutely wonderful! Parramatta, Emu Plains, Bathurst, and, I think, a warehouse. Ooh, a stockpile of merchandise accessible to all three stores at Parramatta as Ed doesn't have much of a storeroom for stock. John, that's fabulous. There would be no delay in getting produce to any store then. We should start building it first. Then build up the Bathurst one and finally the Emu Plains one." He sat thinking. "I'll stock the Bathurst store with just building equipment first, but have some secret supplies for gold mining and exploration in a basement, for when the rush starts."

John laughed. "So I'm guessing that we're now staying in Emu for more than the night?"

Wills grinned. "Hmm, yes, maybe Bathurst too." He looked sheepish. "Okay, maybe more than one in Emu Plains, too. I'll see how Cathy feels first." He swallowed, "Yes, we'll see."

Wills was sitting in such a way that John could tell the unsure feelings of the last week had gone.

It took four days to reach Bathurst. They had dawdled, checking each creek they passed. They would not send anything back to Eddie from there this time, other than the mail. A rider was often heading back; he would take the letters. One letter for the Turners from John to expect them in a week or two for a few days at least, and four from Wills to Eddie, written over the last few months.

The land purchase in Bathurst took a little more than a week to complete, but the land was finally sorted and only needed to be filed in Sydney and then paid for in Parramatta. The Courthouse would register the paperwork. Their timing could not have been better. The land had only recently been subdivided and placed up for sale. Wills had his pick of the sites. He ended up purchasing two large blocks rather than one. He put a hold on the one next to the store. The streets were nice and wide, allowing for carriage parking. He also wanted lots of room for storage. He planned an excess stock shed there. He thought he might add another floor as well as two basements. Make the floor space larger. Excess bulky stock could be stored upstairs. His mind was constantly returning to various ideas. His mind whirled.

He did not have to pay for the land until the paperwork was done and filed. He planned to pay Mr Moffatt in Parramatta in gold. He knew from Eddie that gold had a fixed price of £10 per ounce. He had already sent Mr Moffatt a note to explain. He, too, could be trusted to keep the gold secret. Mr Moffatt, therefore, needed to be brought in on the finds, as he too needed to prepare for a gold rush. Wills had worked out a way to smelt the gold without letting on where it came from. He wasn't a blacksmith for nothing. Smelting was something he knew about, and gold had a much lower melting point than iron. He could get the help of all his friends, as well as Eddie and Mr Tindale. An ingot could come from anywhere. It would also make it easier to divide the booty and make it easier to carry. Crushing the rock would be the most difficult part of the procedure.

They camped on the new blocks of land. On their last night in Bathurst, he ran the idea by the others. "I was thinking... we could do the crushing of the rock, then smelting the gold at the smithy forge, as well as melting and pouring it into lots of small ingots. What do you think? Easy to carry and hide, but also much easier to break and spend too. But we'd all need to help, and it will be hard work." He looked at his friends.

It had never occurred to them how to divide up their finds. "Wills, that's a fabulous idea. I know I have not even thought that far ahead," Harry said.

"I forgot you were a smithy," said Lew. He was still subdued.

"You never cease to amaze with everything you can do. For such a young man, you have many, many skills," said Edmund. "I would have no idea how even to work out where to go to melt this stuff, let alone how to get it out of the rock. You tell me you can do it all yourself. I'm certainly *in* with helping you."

"Me too," said Harry.

John chipped in, "Lad, I was wondering if you'd know somewhere six English chaps could doss down for, say, a month or so in your Parramatta? I know I, for one, would like to get to know your family better. Maybe help with the beginnings of the Bathurst building as well."

One by one, the others all agreed. "Yes, please. No hurry to head home, and we'd love to see this started. We did say we'd planned for a year. Well, this part of the journey is only halfway there."

Wills smiled, "Oh, yes. I'm sure both the cottages are vacant at the moment, and I'm sure if you don't wish to share rooms, two could also stay with Eddie and me."

"Wonderful," said John, "Wonderful news."

They stopped in at Hartley on the return trip. When they arrived, they closed the fish trap, hoping to catch some for dinner. Then they walked upstream to check on the quartz outcrop. They had only planned on an overnight stop, but on seeing the rock spur, they realised that more than one day would be needed to remove the gold-bearing rock. They had bought a couple of hammers and chisels in Bathurst. Another rockfall had occurred, and a new large seam of gold was visible. This was even thicker than the first one. The protruding rock John had worked on before finally gave way and fell. It revealed that the gold went deep into the cliff. They gasped in awe at the richness of this seam.

They certainly were not going to leave it sitting there, so they brought the horses and loaded up the first of the loose rocks. There was no hurry to remove it all at once. The men had already set up their camp. It was now too cold to swim, as it was mid-May, and mornings were now frosty in the valley. So they didn't walk back into the creek. They were not sure if there would be any fish in the trap. None were particularly worried. They had restocked the stores again in Bathurst. They would not go hungry, but some fresh fish would be a nice addition. They could hear splashing as they walked closer and, after taking the bags of rock back to camp, headed down to the trap. Sure enough, a few were in there. Edmund and Wills braved the cold, taking off their boots and wading in. They had created a narrow channel and herded them in there, making catching easy. They threw seven onto the bank, then removed the rocks to make an opening and released the rest. They could close it as easily if required, but the fish could swim through.

The last time they were here, it was only a few days after they had met. They were still unsure of Wills. The nearly six months of travel had bonded these seven men. Their adventures, misadventures and incidents had drawn them close. Thankfully, even though they saw many snakes, none invaded either their camps or wagons. There had been splinters and a few cuts, but no major injuries other than leech bites and sunburn. Wills smiled at his friends friends. He hoped they would stay for a long time before returning to England.

A chill descended in the valley, and a frost was likely again tonight. The land around Bathurst had been drying out as they left the area. They had no rain the entire trip, but it was obvious that this valley had experienced a flash flood in their absence. Their previous campsite was littered with flood debris. It took a little time to clear a spot. It did, however, mean they did not have to collect firewood as it was scattered over the flattened grass. They pulled the wagons further up on the grassy embankment, above the debris line, just in case there was another storm.

Phil and Lew had a roaring fire going by the time the fishermen returned with their bounty. The billy was boiling, and the pans were ready for the fish. Tonight, they all sat close to the fire. Edmund and Wills were still warming their feet. Both were glad they did not have to brave the icy water again. They ate the fish and retired to bed.

Martha flicked open the seal on the letter. Her eyes opened wide. "Jack, Cathy," she called. "They're on the way back. They should be here in a week or so."

"Who, Maa?" asked Cathy.

"Why, Wills pet, and his friends of course, who else did you think I'd call for you, my love?" Martha knew Cathy's feelings for Wills. Even though so far nothing had been said by him, she knew they were reciprocated. She'd seen how disappointed he was when they found Cathy away from home on his last visit. She had grown to know and love the lad, seeing him regularly on her stays with Jenna and Eddie. He was a quiet but likeable young man.

"Oh, Maa. Is he really?" Cathy sighed. "Oh, I've missed his visits."

"I know, lass, but he'll be here soon." Martha patted her hand.

Cathy returned to her chores outside. Skipping on the way out.

Jack entered, "You called, love?"

"Yes, Jack. Wills and his friends are returning. This was posted from Bathurst about three days ago. It says they will be here in two weeks, so that's next week." Martha continued, "Mr Saunders writes that they'd like to stay a few days if this would be convenient and thought he would give us notice. He also states that Wills is particularly keen to see all of the family. Oh, Jack, I wonder if he's ready to declare himself. Make time to talk for him, will you, please?"

Jack sighed, "Yes, of course, love."

Martha kept reading. Then, re-read it again. She sighed. "Looking at them both mooning around eyeing each other is becoming annoying. They are too young to get married, but there is no reason they cannot start dating. He's eighteen now, Jack."

"I agree, my love; I might have a word to him myself if he says nothing." He bent over and kissed his wife on the cheek. "You are the best of caring mothers, love." Then he walked out to the stable yard. He had better prepare a place for the three wagons.

Martha returned to the vegetables.

Moira answered the knock at the door. She took the handful of letters and placed them on Eddie's desk.

She went and sought out Jenna. "More letters have arrived from Wills, Mrs Jenna. I've left them on Mr Ed's desk. There's a fistful this time. Seems like he's posted them all at once."

Two hours later, Eddie returned from work, and Jenna met him with the news letters had arrived from Wills.

After greeting and kissing his wife, they walked into the office. She sat on the arm of the couch next to him. He opened each one and shuffled them into date order. A small drawing fluttered out of one and landed on the floor. Jenna bent and picked it up. She gasped. He read them to her. They followed his journey out to the West and were amazed at his visual descriptions of the dancing brolgas.

Jenna touched his sleeve and showed him the drawing. It was the first one Wills had drawn with the brolga in full dance flight.

Eddie looked at the effortless strokes and beauty of the small drawing. He looked at Jenna, amazed, and then continued to read. He followed their journey on a map he had obtained. It was a copy of Major Mitchell's map. His descriptions of the paths and roads taken were such that they could see exactly their route. The only section missing was the detour from the West Road to the north of Blackmans' Swamp. This didn't appear on the map.

Eddie read of the finds in the creek, the bag full of booty and the sunburn. They laughed at the duck hunting and gasped at the dingoes.

The fourth letter was different, more business-like. This letter was written from Bathurst. Wills had purchased two blocks of land and had an option on a third in the newly planned town, and would pay on arrival at Parramatta. He wrote, "Could Ed please inform Mr Moffatt that the paperwork will soon arrive, and also for more land he wants to buy in Emu Plains?" He added, "Read on for more about that."

Eddie was intrigued.

Read on, they did.

Wills went on to outline his plans for building his dreams.

The Bathurst building was to be done in two stages. An initial timber shed with stock for the building. This would be built quickly and would eventually be used for a stockroom. Stage two would be a more permanent building, preferably of stone. No tools were yet available in town. With the new subdivision, a great deal would be required in a short time. This would therefore be done first. Later, would follow an expansion onto the second block, with a double-story building. All the gold equipment would then be added to the inventory. The third stage would be a lean-to awning, allowing you to load in all weather conditions. The heat in summer was as deadly as the cold in winter. The awning would give protection so loads could be waterproofed.

Eddie sighed. "Trust Wills to think of people's comfort, even in this," Eddie said as he read. They would be stopping at Emu Plains on the return journey. They would stay at Turners for a few days or so, and he'd look for some suitable land near the west road over the mountains. Here, he would build a third Emporium. Eddie continued to read aloud, "Sweetie, he writes…"

"I have finances in our finds to cover all costs and then some. More booty has come our way, such as you could not believe. We shall call back via Hartley and may stay some days there to see if we can extract more from the cliff. I have purchased this land already and now do not feel so bad about taking it. It's mine. However, as I said before, I have agreed to split this 50/50 with my friends. I wanted to do 7th shares, but they would not hear of it. So, I will take half, and the remaining half will be divided into six. As word of our finds has yet to be kept secret, we will have to smelt the ore and minerals ourselves. I hope you don't mind. Mr Tindale will need to be informed about the project, and we can share some information with him in exchange for the use of the Forge. You can work that out with him.

If all can be fully constructed before the word reaches the masses, this would work in our favour. We have a lot of work ahead of us. This, of course, is presuming you are willing to assist me in this endeavour."

"Oh, Jen, I think we will find our Wills a changed and grown man on his return," Eddie said. "I can see the change from his first letters. His confidence has grown, and he's matured."

Jenna said, "And with some days at Emu with Maa, I hope he finally declared himself to Cathy. She's waited patiently enough for him."

"What do you mean, love?" Eddie looked puzzled.

"Oh, Eddie! Don't tell me you haven't noticed. They sit moodily, looking at each other across the room, never daring to even talk to each other. It's as plain as day that they are mooning for each other."

Eddie's mouth dropped open.

Jenna laughed. "Have you really never noticed? Oh, Ed, I do love you so." She reached over and drew his head down for a kiss. "Mama used to say, 'Marry a man who does not notice what you wear', and I would laugh and ask her why. 'Because, love, he'll not notice what any other woman wears either.' Ed, I love you just the way you are. Just never change." He returned her kiss with passion. He pulled her down from the arm of the couch onto his lap. He was about to place the unfinished letter on the desk, but Jenna said, "No, let's finish it first." He groaned and settled back to reading.

"We are planning to be in Parramatta by about 17th of June. My friends have asked if they could find accommodation for at least a month, possibly longer. They would like to help with the beginnings of the plans, and I think they would be a boon to us. I foresee many trips to and fro across this new road in the future, but now I know what to expect. It can be traversed in a vastly quicker time. We have dawdled through the country, exploring. None of them have any practical experience, but all are to be trusted.

Ed, I feel God's hand in these plans. For the mineral to literally fall in our laps. And YES, I mean Literally! For me to meet these men, and the timing of our trip; everything. Just everything, Ed. We have prayed much, nearly every night. Each day's travel started with a prayer, and each night, their talk often turned to our Bibles. We have all grown in our faith, study and belief. Our Bibles have had a workout. We each had packed one.

I look forward to returning home. I do hope you are not still angry with me. I received your letter sent to Bathurst, so I know you do understand. I love you dearly and look forward to a close working relationship with you.

Your loving brother, hopefully soon to be a business partner. Wills"

"Well, love, it looks like we're going to get to know Wills' new friends." He re-read the section again. "I'll send Moira and Shauna to clean the cottages, and we'll prepare the two upstairs rooms too. They can work out where they want to sleep."

Jenna sat back in her seat. "Ed, I think that this will mean your dream of the foundry may need to be accelerated, too. Not only that, but there will be a huge need for all the tools."

Ed also sat back with her and looked on in amazement. "Jen, can this be happening? Truly?"

He had finished reading the letters but could not remove his eyes from them. In the four and a half years they had been married, so much had already come to fruition. The proposed smithy shop had grown into a huge Emporium in town. Now, this was to grow again. Would Ed be interested in going into partnership with this little brother? Of course he would! As he had with Mr Tindale, it would all be by the book. There would be no legal troubles later. He had seen other families torn apart by money. "Jen, love, we have much thinking to do before they arrive. We'll need to find managers for both new stores, which will involve travel between the three. Jen, this will open up jobs, too, for others." He ran his hand through his fair locks.

She could see his mind was distracted. She sighed and traced her fingers around his neckline, then down to his chest.

"Mmmm." He bent and kissed her. The letters fluttered to the floor, forgotten.

Chapter 6   Eastward Bound

On the second day in Hartley, they realised there was no way they could leave the deep vein of gold so visible. They had stayed for the extra days to remove what they could. Each day, they caught more fish. However, the water was now too cold to swim, so a hot wash was all that they were brave enough to do.

They had to crack the ice in the puddles each morning, and all would be glad to sleep in real beds next week or soon afterwards. Even a spot on the floor in front of a fire would be heaven.

No one had shaved for some months while on the road, but they each had their hair cut and were shaved in Bathurst.

Wills had been looking bedraggled as his beard was both fair and sparse. With icy water, they left the shaving until they arrived at the Mt Victoria stockade. Wills wanted to make himself look very presentable. He had even washed his clothing in the icy water and set it out to dry. He had not realised how much they smelled not to mention how filthy their clothing was. The others did the same, and soon, the grassy area was covered in drying clothes.

The newest rockfall had brought down so much quartz that Phil and Lew were on a continuous trip of returning to camp and unloading, then returning. They had bought extra sacks in Bathurst, and six of these were already filled and placed at the wagons for loading. Phil grabbed the remaining two empty bags and headed back with one horse. Lew stayed in camp.

John and Wills finished throwing the last of the rockfall from the escarpment. They placed more branches on the ledge and smeared mud over the rock face, hopefully hiding the rest of the white quartz outcrop. They finished scooping up the last of the fine pebbles, all still flecked with gold.

Wills lowered these down to Edmund, and they were tied to the saddles.

They had just climbed down when they heard voices. They grabbed some sticks for the fire and put them on the horses, hopefully covering the full sacks. All stood looking at the creek rather than the cliff.

The six of them were together, so any voices could only mean someone had arrived and was possibly talking to Lew.

Thankfully, Lew had stayed at the camp. They hoped he was all right.

Two rough-looking men were walking down the track from camp. They were as surprised to see the six men, who were still standing looking into the creek, as the six were to see them. They hoped their subterfuge had worked.

It seemed that it had. The newcomers greeted them with "g'day" from one. "Wot ya doin' all the way up here?" from the other.

John replied, "We're going to walk the horse downstream to scare the fish into the trap we've made, getting some wood while we're at it." He proceeded to walk the horse to the creek, and they all turned to head back to camp.

Wills looked back to see that the newcomers had continued to walk along the creek bank. They had believed them. He sighed. "They fell for it," he whispered to himself.

They continued back to camp.

John's feet were blue with cold. They had to get him warm.

Wills and Aidan decided to brave the cold and collect some fish for dinner. They left the trap intact in case the wanderers returned. They could give them some. If not, they would take some for tomorrow night's dinner.

Lew greeted their return with concern. He had only just managed to lug the bags into the wagon before the two strangers walked into camp. Thankfully, there had been nothing for them to see. He was sitting tending the fire as they appeared, but this, too, was subterfuge. He had managed to hang an empty camp oven and shove the billy in the coals. He made himself look busy.

Thankfully, their voices had carried, and he had a few minutes of grace.

Lew removed the empty camp oven and stoked the fire. It was soon blazing, and John was sitting warming his feet.

Wills and Aidan soon joined him as they thawed their toes.

"We left the trap closed in case they come back," Aidan said quietly. He knew that if Lew had heard them coming, then they, too, could hear the group chatting.

"Thankfully, we had just finished when the two disreputable

looking men arrived," said John. "We were standing looking in the creek as they walked down the path."

"I looked back as we left, and they had just kept walking," Wills said. "I'd like to check the site before we leave tomorrow, but leave soon after that. Just in case."

Edmund replied softly. "Good idea, lad. We also need to get this back to town as soon as possible. Don't want to be held up either."

"I think a quick trip to Emu is called for," said John, whose teeth were still chattering. "I want to be warm."

Edmund grabbed another blanket and wrapped it around John.

Their clothing was now dry. Edmund gathered it all, and folded it carefully. Sorting into piles.

"Very domesticated, Edmund." Laughed Lew.

They soon had fish frying and Lew sliced a damper. They still had some apples left from the box they had bought in Bathurst. They had cooked some and were eating them as the two men returned.

Wills and John walked down to their trap with them and told them to help themselves. There was no way they were going to get wet again.

The strangers felt the water and decided to pass on the offer. However, they discovered they could reach in and grab a couple from the end of the trap without entering the water. They managed to catch two sizeable ones and were invited to cook them over their fire.

The gold would be safe as they'd be sleeping on it.

They smirked to themselves. Beds of kings; if only these two rogues knew.

The group did not extend an offer for the men to sleep at the camp, and soon after they had eaten, the visitors moved off up the road from whence they had arrived. It was mid-afternoon.

Edmund made another damper and set it to cook.

As the afternoon progressed, four stayed at camp while the other three went back and checked the outcrop. Arriving back half-hour later, they reported the site was untouched. Much relieved, they broke camp and cleared up the site, ready to move on the next morning.

In their absence, the eighteen full bags had been carefully distributed under the mattresses, so the wagons were balanced and the horses not overtaxed with weight.

Wills went to the trap with the spade and broke open the end of the trap to release the remaining fish. He pushed over the few rocks at the end and released them to the stream.

He stood watching until they all swam through and walked back to camp. He stood alone on the creek. This was his first land. His own, and yet it was the means to an end. He had no intention of constructing a building here, well, not a house, possibly a cottage for holidays. He would visit with his brothers one day and get some more of the gold. He raised his eyes heavenward and thanked God. One day, he'd love to bring Cathy, too.

Leaving their camping ground, the wagons left the valley.

The three wagons trundled down the Blue Mountains road. They had decided not to stay at the inn where they stayed on that first night on the road; instead, they stopped at the government Stockade. A contingent of soldiers and convicts remained for road repairs.

They followed the road eastwards and rejoined Mitchell's Road to Mt Victoria Stockade. They would overnight there before the descent into Emu the day after tomorrow.

The heavily laden wagons would be able to be guarded overnight. They had added hundreds of pounds of rocks under the mattresses.

John and Edmund were concerned that there was no way they could secure the new load from Hartley, not to mention the bag of loose river gold.

It was June, and the possibility of snow. It was far too cold to stay on the wagons overnight. They had left Hartley after they cleared out as much gold as they could access, and the last night, they decided to sleep out. They had frozen.

It had also snowed lightly, and although still cold, the sun was out. Because of the chill, Wills slept between John and Harry, but it was oh-so cold. Their stay in Hartley had blown out to much longer.

John had stopped in to the Mt Victoria Stockade on the way west and introduced himself to Major Johnson. They had been invited to break their journey on the return trip, and this time, they would accept the offer. A hot fire and stew would hit the spot. The night watch would keep the gold safe.

John had sent a note through from Hassan's Walls Stockade a few days ago. Although they would be a day or so later than he said, he was sure that this would not be a problem.

Their arrival coincided with a troop of soldiers arriving. Evidently, two convicts had escaped into goodness knows where.

John directed them to the camp area at Hartley and told them they were in that area. He thought they would stay around there as they knew the fish trap made easy pickings.

The troops headed off almost immediately, heading directly to that area. They would block off the access routes into the valley and hopefully corral them until caught or shot. Sadly, that was the lot of escaped convicts.

Lew broke out in a cold sweat when he heard who they were. He had offered them tea. They could have killed him and taken what they wanted.

Harry looked at him and raised an eyebrow, then smiled. This brave Scotsman would not have turned a hair in India, but now he had something to look forward to at home.

After a hot meal and a long sleep in a warm room, the seven men awoke ready for the final descent. Tonight, they'd stop at Ellison Pinch in Linden.

As the horses were so overloaded. It would be a slow trip taken at walking pace down the incline, then into Emu Plains the following day. Wills shaved and even washed his hair, then put on clean clothes, even though they were un-ironed. The others did likewise. Wills looked anxious yet excited. By tomorrow night, he may know if Cathy really thought of him as just a brother or if she felt more for him.

John tousled his neatly combed, clean hair. "All will be well, lad, trust me. I have a feeling." He touched his heart.

He looked into his worried eyes. He was sure that Wills had grown in the months since they had met. He was now at eye level.

The horses, too, felt the men's anticipation and were snorted to get going. The heat was rising from them in the cold, frosty morning. Every breath swirled in a cloud. Ice covered the pavement under the snow, and the road was slippery. It had lightly snowed overnight, and some white flakes still sat on the horses shaggy backs as they were harnessed into the wagons.

As a 'thanks', John left some unused horseshoes at the barracks. This would compensate the officers for the food they had consumed.

Wills had changed quite a few on the trip, but there was still a box of nails and more than a dozen shoes. They left ten with them and most of the nails, keeping a few, just in case for the final legs of the trip.

It was winding and undulating, but overall it was downhill for the majority of this leg of the journey. The going was slow. As planned, they stopped in Linden, at Ellison's Pinch, for the night.

Although the horses were fresh, the load was extremely heavy, and the passengers would have been happy to up the pace somewhat if they could, but the horses were straining as it was. As they didn't have to make camp, they possibly could continue until dusk, but it would be better to send word through and turn up tomorrow. John decided he'd do this. A rider was heading down with Battalion messages, and John sent one to Linden and the Turners.

It turned out that they had to walk the horses over some ice patches, which delayed them quite a bit. They arrived at Linden just before dusk, cold, hungry, and tired. They were greeted warmly. The messenger had told them they were to be expected. He had stopped for an ale. On arrival, Mr Thomas Ellison greeted them warmly, and he led them to the stables at the back. The wagons were placed in a barn, and the doors shut after the men collected their things for the night. They would be sleeping inside on the floor. They didn't care. It was warm.

Mr Ellison's wife, Betsy, had a stew, roast potatoes and real bread.

She also served a huge apple pie with thickened cream.

Aidan was in seventh heaven. Potatoes, cooked in any form, were his favourite. Any food, if it were hot, would satisfy Wills. His stomach may have been satisfied, but his anxiety was building.

John had asked Betsy Ellison to iron Wills's shirt. When he explained why, she laughed.

"So this is Wills Lockley, eh? I've heard Martha speak of him. Apparently, he's keeping young Cathy on tenterhooks." Betsy didn't know Wills was standing close by. When she saw John look past her, she turned.

"Whoops. Am I speaking out of turn?" she asked. She saw him blanch, then smile.

"No, Mrs Ellison, only I thought she saw me as a brother. Are you sure?" He brightened considerably.

"Sure as I can be, my lad. Positively pining for you, said Martha when I saw her last month," Betsy said.

John saw the grin spread across Wills's face. He punched the air with joy behind her back. John had not noticed that Wills had dimples before. He smiled, too.

"Don't mind me; I mouth off when I should be quiet." Betsy took his shirt and put an iron to heat on the stove.

Departing Linden the next morning, Wills wished he could whip up the horses and gallop down the remaining miles, but he would see Cathy tonight. He stayed quiet most of the day, answering politely but without elaborating on his answers. He had been travelling with Phil and Edmund for the last few days, but John took him up for this last leg. Again, they were bringing up the rear. At Mitchell's Pass, Harry joined them. They would soon see the town. Wills was almost on the edge of his seat. John and Harry smiled at his anxiety.

John pulled up the wagon to a slow walk. The other two wagons continued.

"Wills, we're going to pray, lad. You're wound up so tightly you'll bounce like a spring. You need to settle down," Harry said.

"I can't! You're right, though; I'm wound up like a cockatoo screeching in the morning." Wills knew they were not wrong. He'd tried deep breathing, but that hadn't worked. "I think a prayer might just help; thanks, John." He took a deep breath again. He would know in mere minutes. He could feel his heart pounding.

John prayed. "Lord, we ask that you give young Wills the peace and confidence that he needs, whatever the outcome. Amen."

The three each said "Amen" as they drove into the outskirts of Emu Plains. Wills directed them again, and they turned onto the road towards the Inn. John saw that the other two wagons had already arrived, and Cathy was outside waiting, and not so patiently, either. She was almost hopping from one foot to the other.

Harry prompted Wills to hop down. "Go to her, Wills."

At his instigation, he started walking to her. She was in tears. He put his arms out, and soon, she was in them. They stood embracing at the front of the house.

"Oh, Wills, I've missed you so much," said Cathy.

"I've missed you too," He asked if he could kiss her.

She nodded consent, lifting her face to his.

He bent his head and gently touched his lips to hers. She wrapped her arms around his neck and held him close. Their kiss deepened until Jack cleared his throat.

He and Martha were standing at the front door. "Something you need to ask me, lad?" he asked with a smile on his face.

Wills walked over to them with his arm still around her shoulder. "Yes, sir, there is; I'd like to court Cathy, please," he asked with confidence.

Jack replied. "About time, lad. She's been mooning around since you left. She was so upset she'd missed you. Mind you, you're only eighteen, so it's only courting. "

"Oh, Pa, I haven't. I was just upset I had missed him," she said.

"Cathy! Admit it. If that is how you greet a friend, I'll have to watch you harder," Martha laughed.

"Oh, all right. Fine. I missed you. I missed you a lot." She snuggled under his arm and gazed lovingly into his face.

He squeezed her arm. "I missed you as well, but I wasn't sure how you felt about me. I thought you only felt like I was a brother. I hoped, oh, how I hoped. It wasn't until I reached Linden last night that I really had any confidence. Mrs Ellison said you might be really glad to see me."

Jack and Martha smiled at each other and turned to walk into the house.

Wills bent and kissed Cathy again as soon as their backs were turned. He whispered, "I love you, do you know that? I have, for a long time."

"Enough of that, you two, come along," said Jack over his shoulder.

Cathy pulled his head down for another quick kiss, and they walked inside hand in hand. "Yes, I do, but I did wonder; you never said anything."

"I couldn't, I wasn't eighteen. I am now." He was all smiles when he walked through the house and out the back door, Cathy still holding his hand. Wills was still grinning as he walked over to his friends. He introduced Cathy to them. Shyly, she greeted them, bobbing a curtsy to each one. She turned to Wills. "I have to help Mama."

She turned to go, but he pulled her back and gave her a quick kiss. "Just because I can, love," he whispered.

She skipped inside, obviously very happy.

Harry and John smiled at each other.

"Congratulations, lad! I knew things would work out. She's nice too. All that worry for nothing," said John.

"Oh, not for nothing, sir," he turned to watch her. "I'm going to marry that young lady, and soon." He smiled to himself. "Remember, they don't know about our booty yet. However, I don't think anyone will argue with this. Talking of which, I'll lock up the bag of dust."

John handed the flour bag to him.

Marc, Cathy's brother, appeared to help unharness the horses. They led the six horses into the holding yard beside the stables. Marc forked some feed-in for them, and then together, they pushed the wagons to the other side of the barn.

"Cor, they are heavy, Wills, what do you have in them? Rocks or something?" Marc asked.

"Yes, Marc, rocks and lots of 'or something'," he chuckled.

Edmund looked over at John. He shook his head, while grinning.

They unloaded the clothing they needed and the remaining food, all of which they carried into the kitchen. Wills grabbed the flour bag of gold dust that he'd set on the end of the wagon as they moved it. He carried it tucked into his shirt. As the men were friends, Martha had told them they could doss-down inside the sitting room. Nick and Calum slept on the floor near the fire, and they could join them. After so many nights on the road in the cold, this would be a luxury. Any further visitors would have to sleep in hammocks in the barn. As the outside temperature often dropped below freezing, they would not envy them.

Wills had asked Jack and Martha if he could talk to them privately. As the kitchen was a thoroughfare, Jack walked into their bedroom.

Martha sat on the bed as Wills shut the door.

Jack cocked his eyebrows, intrigued. "Lad, you already have our permission to court Cathy."

"Yes, sir, and thank you, but what I have to ask is something that, as yet, I don't want Cathy and your other children to know about. My friends already know, though." Wills pulled the flour bag from inside his jacket. "Sir, we've been blessed on our trip, and I need you to put this somewhere safe. Eddie told us you had a strong box in here." He handed over the bag, which, although small, weighed just under ten pounds.

He held his hand under it, and Jack set it on the bed, opening it to show Martha. Both gasped and turned to stare at him.

"Is this gold?" Martha asked, reaching in to touch it.

Wills nodded. "The other thing I want to say is that I wish to marry Cathy. I always have. I would have liked to wait for a little while.

However, I would like to ask her before she knows about this. Do I have your permission? I'm happy for a long engagement."

He looked at Cathy's parents. "As you can see, I can support her. Only I don't want her to know about the gold until I have asked her. I want to hold off this knowledge for as long as possible. I don't want any of the others to know either. Ed and Jenna don't even know about this lot. There's more than this, too. We have to divide it, of course, but there is more than enough for us. In the meantime, can you lock this away for me, please?"

Jack was stunned. Less than an hour before he'd given this lad permission to court his daughter. An hour later, he was asking for their blessing to marry her. "Lad, I have to talk to Martha about this. I'll lock this away, though, then leave us to talk, please."

Wills nodded assent and watched as Jack lifted the carpet, then the floorboards, to access his strongbox. Once it was replaced, Wills left them to talk. He closed the door quietly behind him as he left. He leaned against the wall, emotionally drained and anxious. It's not as if they didn't know him. He wasn't going to need to wait for their answer. He trusted them enough to know they would seriously consider his request. He walked outside and took a stroll along the riverbank. He sat praying, "Lord, am I doing the right thing? If I am, please give me peace and show me the way forward." He sat for a while until the sun went behind the mountains.

Chilled, he walked inside to rejoin his friends. They were still unloading food into the kitchen.

Cathy was helping fill containers and store the rest of the potatoes, fruit and tea.

Black tea was still hard to get, and Martha didn't really like the green tea that was all they could afford. She had not long finished the last of her supply that Sal had given her before she left for England. She walked in as they had just filled her tea canister. The little metal tin was overflowing.

Edmund asked if she had a billy with a lid or some other metal tin.

Martha found an empty cake tin and Edmund filled that too. What bounty! What a day! "Are you sure you don't want this, lad?" she asked Edmund.

Martha looked over at Wills. He was standing, watching Cathy with a huge grin plastered on his face. Martha motioned for him to go to Jack, and wordlessly, he left the room.

He knocked quietly, and Jack said, "Come in."

He was sitting on the bed. "William, I am stunned at all of this. Of course, we've known Cathy's feelings for some time, but we have been unsure of you." He paused, looking for a reaction.

Wills gave none. He stood awaiting the verdict.

"We've talked. Of course, we talked." Jack was watching Wills's face. He relaxed, releasing his held breath. Wills had hidden his anxiety. Jack said, "The answer is yes, lad."

"Thank you so much, sir. I did not want to speak to her before, to tell her how I felt, as I was under eighteen. I honestly thought she only wanted me as a brother. I was happy about that if that's all she wanted. I just needed to be near her. I love her so much and have for a long time." Wills stated in a matter-of-fact manner. "If I have to give away my share to keep her, I would not hesitate. I think you know me well enough to know I will never hurt her." He swallowed; he hadn't expected to be this nervous. He was praying. "Please, God, give me strength and patience." He took another deep breath and tried to relax.

After some minutes, Jack said, "Oh, Wills. Of course, you can ask her. I'm pretty sure she will say yes. However, I want you to tell her about the gold in our presence; that's the condition."

Wills beamed. "You mean that, sir? Really? Oh, for a while, I was worried. It's so fast, but I thought you would understand once you knew my reason for the speed. It would be extremely difficult for her if she discovered the gold first. I know Cathy well enough that she'd think she was not good enough for me. But, sir, she's the only girl I've ever wanted; since I met her four years ago, I've only wanted her." Wills shook his hand. "Sir, there is more to my story, but I'd like to tell all of you together if that's all right. Maybe we could get some time together over the next day or so, preferably tomorrow. My friends already know my plans, so I don't mind if they are there," Wills said.

Again, he shook Jack's hand and left. Cathy had no idea of the happenings, of course, but she'd noticed that Wills had disappeared. She'd been looking for him outside. She was chilled when she came inside. Wills led her to the sitting room fire and warmed her. He held her in his arms, and he rubbed her back.

She rested on his chest. "Wills, I'd like to stay here forever."

"That's just what I intend, love," Wills said

The comment was not fully understood by her. Time enough for that. She was warming, though. He was still rubbing her back.

Vicky walked in and saw her little sister in Wills's arms. "Oh," was all Vicky could say. She stood staring. "Wills, Pa will see," she said quietly.

Wills looked up. "He knows, Vicks. They both do."

"Oh, that's all right then, I think." She left quietly. She followed the voices originating from the kitchen. She walked into her kitchen, and there were six of the most handsome men she'd ever seen in her life, and she stood still, mouth slightly open.

Harry's eyes caught the graceful swish of a tall, elegant, dignified lady entering the room. Poise and confidence oozed from her. She stood framed by the doorway with sunlight shining from behind her. She looked like she was glowing. She was the most beautiful woman he had ever seen. Their eyes met, and they each smiled at the other.

Marc beckoned her in to join them. "Vicky, come and meet Wills's friends. Harry Harlow, John Saunders, Phillip Corsairs, Aidan O'Keefe, Edmund Hunt, and Lewis Bland." Marc introduced his sister. She tore her eyes from Harry's, and she bobbed a curtsy as they were introduced.

They each bowed in reply.

She glanced again at Harry, only to discover his eyes still on her. She smiled again and dropped her eyes modestly. Her heart was racing.

Marc noticed that Harry's eyes had hardly left Vicky since she walked in.

John noticed, too.

Marc looked at Vicky. She had blushed, and he watched as she raised her eyes to Harry's again. She had never shown interest in any man before. He watched, amazed.

They stood talking for some minutes before Harry excused himself, turned and walked outside. Once outside in the cold, he blanched. He felt ill. She was a convict's daughter. He walked over to the wagon and slid into the straw on the far side. He groaned. "Oh God, help me." Hopefully, she would already be engaged or promised. He had heard of falling in love at first sight but never believed in it. Before today, that was. Now he knew it was true. But why him? Why now? And why her?

John walked outside, looking for him. He saw him sitting on the far side of the wagon. He reached into the wagon and grabbed a couple of blankets. If he had not seen this himself, he wouldn't have believed it. He knew Harry. He had never seen him like this.

"John, did you see her? I couldn't rip my eyes from her. What am I going to do?" Harry's head sank into his hands.

What could he say? John just put his hand on his cousin's shoulder, but gave no reply.

"Now I know what Wills felt. Gutted with anxiety," Harry muttered. "John, we're staying for a week, right?" Harry said.

"Yes," replied John.

"What are my choices? Give me the pros and cons. If I stay, I'm a goner. Ten minutes, and I'm already putty. She's a convict's child, John. I can't take her home."

"Then don't, Harry. Stay here. Make your new life here, not there," said John quietly. "I'm about the only family you have there. You can't call Anthony family any more. He's your brother, but you will have no welcome there. You no longer even have a home." John knew Harry's full story. He also knew Anthony. "Harry, it's only a few months' trip between countries. No reason you can't come back often, but live here. Grow with this new country." He paused. "I'm almost jealous."

"But, John! Could I?" He looked pleadingly.

"Well, what I suggest is you see how it goes. Ask permission to walk out with her first and see if it works out. If it does, you're a lucky devil; if it doesn't, you won't get Wills as a brother-in-law." He laughed, and it broke the ice.

"She may already be taken, John. I have no idea. I've never been hit like that before," said Harry, "She took my breath away."

"Harry, we need to pray about this."

Harry nodded and bowed his head. He felt like weeping.

John prayed, "Dear Lord, we ask that, at this time, you give Harry wisdom. You will lead him in the path You want him to walk. If this is the right path, give him peace. Let him know and accept Your will. Amen."

Strangely, Harry felt better. He shouldn't have been surprised, but he was. It was getting colder, and he said, "Let's go face my future, eh?" He pulled himself up. "Felled by a look, John. Just one blooming honey-gold look and the smile of a princess. Victoria, eh?" He smiled wanly. "No, she was a queen amongst women," he said softly.

John folded the blankets and reached into the cart for something to carry inside as an excuse. He found an overcoat and under it a half-bag of flour he'd forgotten. He handed the blankets to Harry, and he took the overcoat and flour. They walked back inside. Harry walked through into the sitting room and put the blankets down.

John took the flour into the kitchen. He stayed talking to the ladies for some time, helping with the meal preparation. He watched Vicky as they worked. At one stage, she walked out into the cellar. He took his opportunity. John asked, "Is she spoken for, Mrs Turner?"

Martha laughed. "She's like her older sister and now younger one, it seems. She's waiting for the one right man to catch her eye. It hasn't happened yet. She'll know when it does, and nothing will stop her. One day, she'll meet her Eddie. One day, he'll meet his Victoria."

John smiled to himself. "I think she may have," he thought. This would be an interesting week. He walked back into the sitting room and joined his friends. He smiled at Harry, winked and then nodded.

Harry smiled back, deep in thought. "Decisions, decisions! What do I have at home? Nothing, I don't even have one. Isn't it why I'm here anyway?" He swallowed. "Okay, no real decision then, is it?" He was arguing with himself.

Martha put the dinner on to cook.

Wills put out his hand and asked Cathy to come with him.

Martha smiled to herself.

Wills opened the front door and ushered her outside. He grabbed the two overcoats he'd hung next to the door. He placed one around her shoulders and put the other one on. She was surprised but was happy to be allowed to go with him.

Wills closed the door and took her hand. They walked no further than the end of the verandah, farthest from the sitting room. Wills took her hand and pulled her to him.

"Cathy, darling Cathy…" Hell, he had all this thought out a hundred times in his head. He swallowed. "I want to ask you something. Take as long as you want to answer, days if you want, but I want to ask you anyway."

She stood looking him in the eye. "Wills, what's wrong? Have I done something?" Frightened, a tear slid down her cheek.

Wills wiped it away with his thumb. "No, love, of course, you haven't. The thing I want to ask is…" he dropped to his knee. "Will you marry me, Cathy? Please, please say yes."

"Oh, Wills, do you mean it? Really? Yes, yes, yes, of course, I will. But Pa and Maa, you have to ask them," she said excitedly.

"Already done, love. I spoke to them this afternoon. I have their permission. All I needed was an answer from you, my love," he said.

"You have it, Wills, and my heart too, but you've always had that." She walked into his arms and snuggled.

"Sweetheart, your Pa has said we have to have at least a six-month betrothal," Wills said apologetically.

"Mmmm, if we must. Now kiss me." She pulled his head down to hers and silenced his reply.

She was wrapped in his arms, and he was content. Soon, she would be his. He lay his cheek on her head, enjoying her closeness. "I love you so much. I can't believe I've waited so long to say something, but I was so scared. You never encouraged me, and I was so unsure," he said softly.

"Wills, I am still only seventeen. I don't turn eighteen until June twenty-fourth. You've been gone for seven months, two weeks, and four days. Not that I was counting or anything." She looked up with a grin on her face, "…Wasn't counting at all, my William the adventurer."

"Maybe that's why your mother spoke to Mrs Ellison," Wills said with a laugh in his voice.

"My idea, actually. Well, I had to know. I couldn't see you without you knowing how you felt," She looked up coyly. "So it worked?"

"Yes, love, it worked, but I was going to say something anyway. I am eighteen now and can marry you." He lifted her chin and looked adoringly at her. He brushed her lips with his, then crushed her to him. The fire of their passion kept them warm for a while, but the chill took its hold. They stood embracing for a while until she shivered.

"Oh, Cathy, I'm sorry, let's go inside and tell everyone. I didn't realise you were cold. Come on, let us go spread the news." He wrapped her coat around her. "Come on, my love."

They walked back to the door. They stopped for a quick kiss

before he opened the door behind her. A rush of hot air met them, and he ushered her inside.

Neither could wipe the smile from their faces.

"Eh, lad, you look happy," said John.

"I should. Cathy just said, 'Yes'," he swung her around. "Yeah! She said yes." He kissed her in front of everyone.

"Wills, shh. Not in public." She hid her head on his chest.

Marc, Milly and Vicky had not been let into the relationship and were stunned.

Marc said, "Wills, you're a dark horse. When did all this happen?"

Wills laughed. "Oh, the feelings have been there for years. At least mine have. I only recently found she felt the same."

"But you only arrived back today," said Marc's wife, Milly.

"Whirlwind romance," Cathy said, and they laughed as they looked at each other. "Three hours, wasn't it, love, since you asked Pa if you could court me?"

Wills nodded. "Mmm, 'bout that," he replied.

Vicky's eyes lifted and caught Harry's. Neither looked away.

Harry thought, "Three hours; it took me a minute." Less actually. He wanted to stay with her.

Martha drew a breath. She'd seen that look before. The day she met Jack. She looked at him. Jack was standing next to the fire, leaning on the mantelpiece. He still made her catch her breath when she looked at him, even after seven children and a wonderful life.

Harry was talking to Jack, who nodded. "Come help me get some cider, lad," he said to Harry.

Harry followed Jack into the kitchen, then down into the cellar.

"Now, lad, what did you wish to say?" Jack asked.

Harry swallowed. "Well, sir, I do not know if Miss Victoria is spoken for, but I was wondering if I have your permission to ask her for a walk tomorrow and if she's interested in maybe a few rides as well? With your permission, of course."

"Well, now, lad, this is unexpected. You've only met her for the first time today," Jack stated.

"Yes, sir, I realise," said Harry. He swallowed. How do I explain this? He thought. "Sir, would you understand if I said I was interested the moment our eyes met?" Harry looked anxiously at the concerned father.

"Before I say yes, where do you expect this to go? You're heading back to England. I will not have her heartbroken. She is like her mother and sister; it only took a look with them, too." Jack was worried. "Lad, Vicky is a convict's daughter. That can't change, you do realise that? Both Martha and I were convicts."

"Yes, sir, I know. Wills told me. Sir, I'm a free agent. By that, I mean I have few, if any, ties in England. If things go as I'd wish, I would stay and make a home for us here." Harry paused, thinking. "Sir, she may not even be interested, but be assured, I have thought through this. At the moment, I have not even spoken to her at all. I wished to seek your approval before I did."

Jack stood scratching his head. "Oh, lad, I don't know. Before you do, I think I'd like to speak to her myself. Then I shall give you an answer. I shall see how the wind blows."

Harry nodded, releasing his breath. He expected the answer to be an absolute "No." He tried, and now it was up to her.

Jack passed him a small keg of cider, and he knew he had been dismissed. He carried it upstairs and placed it on the kitchen bench.

John saw his return and joined him in the kitchen. He asked, "How did it go?"

"He's withholding his permission until he's spoken to her." Harry sighed. "I suppose that is wise," he said mournfully.

"All's not lost yet, Harry. Trust God. If He's led you to her, God will make a way forward."

Martha walked in and saw them talking. "Have you seen Jack, sir?"

"Yes, Mrs Turner, he was in the cellar. I think he may still be there," Harry said.

Martha merely said, "Oh." She looked puzzled.

The two men walked back into the warm sitting room. She waited until they left, and she walked out to find Jack. She thought, "Not like him to leave guests alone." She walked down the narrow stairs and found him sitting on a cask, deep in thought.

"Ah, Martha love, just who I needed to come." He slipped off the cask and held out his arms.

She walked straight into them. "Jack, what's wrong?"

"I have just had one of the most interesting conversations of my life. Harry wants to walk out with Vicky."

"What?" She gasped. "To my knowledge, they have not even spoken."

"No, they haven't, and he won't without permission." Jack looked at her, concerned. "Am I right to hold him away from her? What if he's God's chosen mate for her? Love, what do we do? He even said that if things work out, he would stay here."

"Oh, Jack, does he know we're convicts or were?"

"Yes, love, I laid our cards on the table. Seems he's thought a lot, though, in a short time." He drew her to him, and she rested her head on his shoulder; both deep in thought.

"Martha, love, I think I need to speak to Vicky before we make a decision." He paused. "She may be dead against this."

Martha agreed. She reached up on tiptoe and kissed him. "I'll send her down." She walked up the steps and went to find her only unattached daughter.

Vicky was watching for her mother's return. Her heart was racing. Oh, she hoped. "Please, God, let him be interested," she prayed quickly.

Martha beckoned, and she went straight over. "Your Pa wants you in the cellar."

Vicky nodded and fled down there as fast as she could without running. She arrived and asked, "Yes, Pa, you wanted me?"

"Take a seat, my girl." Jack settled himself on a cask. She did the same.

"Yes, Pa," she said, and sat down to wait.

"Vicks, I want to know if your heart is engaged with some local lad that I don't know about?" he asked awkwardly.

"No, Papa, no one." She released a silent sigh.

"I've had a request for you to be allowed to accompany someone on a walk tomorrow."

"Oh, Pa, truly?" she asked with her eyes twinkling, her heart skipping a beat.

"Yes, truly, love, but I'm not sure I'll allow it. He's one of the Englishmen; however, I'm not sure if he will stay around. What if he wants to return to England? Love, you're a convict's daughter." He watched her slump on the barrel.

"I know, Pa, I know." She paused before asking, "Pa, who is it?" She had her fingers crossed that it would be Harry.

"Mr Harlow, my dear, it's Harry Harlow who has asked. You could have your heart broken, you know. I don't want that to happen, my sweet girl. I do not want you hurt."

"Pa, could I just go for a walk and take each day as it comes? Nothing may happen after all." She was dancing for joy inside. "Harry," she thought dreamily. She thought back to earlier in the day. She sighed. "Pa, I'd really like to go with him, just to talk. May I?"

"As long as you know, this could get complicated, my girl. I do not want you hurt at all," Jack said.

She smiled and went upstairs, holding her skirts up with a graceful exit. Jack's eyes followed her. She was so different from her older, wild sister, Jenna. Victoria, aptly named after the Queen, had never caused him a day's worry in her life. She had her mother's poise, grace and beauty; oh, what beauty.

Vicky walked up the steps, and before she walked inside, she gave a jump of joy, then lifted her eyes Heavenward and gave thanks to God. Her breath pooled in the cold air. She turned and walked inside, still smiling.

Martha was in the kitchen as she entered. She raised an eyebrow questioningly.

Vicky gave a small nod and a huge smile. She looked into the sitting room and caught Harry's eye. She dropped her eyes, then lifted them again and returned his gaze with a long, lingering smile.

Harry could not believe it; she wanted him too. Jack had obviously approved. His heart soared.

She asked for some help setting the long dinner table. He was up before the others realised she had spoken.

"How can I help, Miss Turner?" His heart nearly turned somersaults.

"Thank you, Mr Harlow. Can you place these on the table?" She handed him some knives and forks. As she did so, their hands brushed against each other. She drew a breath quickly, and her eyes flew to his face. She looked away, but he took her hand.

"Miss Turner, may I have a word?" he asked, his heart now in his mouth.

She didn't answer but nodded.

"I was wondering if you would care for a walk tomorrow sometime?" he enquired hopefully.

"Oh, Mr Harlow, I would like that," her eyes fluttered. "I'd like that a lot, sir." She smiled up at him.

He bowed over her hand. "I look forward to tomorrow then. At your convenience, of course."

She drew a breath; she was scared, but she wanted to give him some encouragement. "Have you ever milked a cow, sir?" she asked. "I have to do ours each morning if you'd like to learn." Her heart was now in her mouth. She felt so forward.

"I'd be honoured to be taught. If you're willing to try." He was in awe; she was reaching out to him. Oh my heart, she was wonderful.

They finished setting the dinner table as Cathy and Martha brought the first course of their meal. A board of sliced bread was placed at each end of the table. Roast meat, potatoes and fresh vegetables were placed on the sideboard.

Jack had come in and called everyone to silence while they said, "Thanks to the Lord" for their food.

"Thank you, good Lord, for the Blessings of today, especially for the Betrothal of Wills and Cathy. We also thank you for the provision of our wonderful food."

Everyone joined in with "Amen."

Jack carved the meat and left the slices on the platter on the sideboard. Each person filed past and filled their plates. They each took a place along with the long table on the trestle seats. Vicky was last, and the only seat left was next to Harry.

He moved aside so she could fit more comfortably. His heart soared again. This girl could hold her own in a palace or in a simple colonial inn. To call her breathtaking was an understatement. The conversation around the table floated over his head. He kept glancing over at her. She seemed not so immune to his presence either. He looked over at first Jack, then Martha. Both gave a nod of acknowledgement, then smiled. The smile swept deep into his soul, peaceful for the first time in years.

John caught his passing glance and returned with a wink. He was beaming.

Lily woke Jenna for her midnight feed. She sat in the rocking chair Sal had given her to feed this little cherub. Her cooing noises melted Jenna's heart every time she saw her, this little blue-eyed bundle of love that she and Eddie had made. Lily's hand was either wrapped around Jenna's finger or was lying on her breast. Her big blue eyes would hold her mother's as she drank.

Jenna could not believe how easy she was. She ate and slept; when she woke, she would lie in her cot, cooing or gurgling. After twins from her first confinement and the double stresses for two, this little mite was so delightful. Every whimper or gurgle was answered by either her big brother or sister if they were awake, or one of the two wonderful Irish lasses who had made their home with them.

Eddie turned over and noticed the bed was empty and cold. He shivered. He pulled back the covers and walked over to the fireplace, pushing another log onto it.

As the bed was cold, Jenna had been up for some time. "Hope she's all right." He padded down the wooden floor of the corridor. She would be in the children's rooms somewhere. Which one had she been attending to this time? Probably Lily.

He found her asleep with the baby still on her breast. Lily was also sleeping. He bent and took the child from her sleeping mother's arms and placed her back in her cot.

He stood looking down at his wife. His heart pounded with pride and awe. She was wonderful, and he was blessed. He bent down and picked her up.

She stirred as he carried her back to bed. She snuggled into his shoulder, and he could feel she was cold.

He laid her gently on the bed and pulled up the blankets. He crawled in gently on his side and took her in his arms. He needed to warm her up. She turned, and he gently pulled her to him, curling up with her, cocooned in his arms.

Thus entwined, they fell asleep again, warm in the other's embrace.

The dawn chorus called them to a new day. Jenna woke still in

Eddie's arms.

Jenna lay looking at this wondrous man in her bed, the father of her three beautiful children. As he had done so many times before, he must have brought her back to bed after she'd fallen asleep with Lily. A lock of his long, fair hair had fallen over his eye. She carefully reached for it and moved it back.

The action was enough to stir him from his slumbers.

His blue eyes looked into her honey ones.

"Sorry, love, I didn't mean to wake you," she said softly.

"It's never a bad thing to wake up with the one person in the world whom you love most." He greeted her with a long morning kiss.

She wrapped her arms around his neck and returned it with passion. "Ed, it's seven weeks since Lily was born."

"Yes," he said. "It is… and?" he murmured as he continued to kiss her.

"…And, well, I want you. I'm much better this time than after the twins. Like all better." She ran her fingers around the neckline of his nightshirt. Twirling his blonde chest hairs around her fingers.

The last seven weeks had been hard for him. But after what he'd seen her go through during the birth of Lily and what she went through last time, he'd learnt to bide his time. She would let him know when she was ready.

"Are you sure, love? It's not too early yet?" Just the thought of her suggestion made his body surge with desire.

"No, Ed and the children are all asleep, and the house is quiet; if you don't take the opportunity now, we may not get one until tonight."

He needed no further prompting. His mind raced. 'Gently,' Dar said, 'gently'. He remembered his father's words before his wedding.

This apparently wasn't what Jenna had in mind. He grinned and added, "Gently, love, remember I'm delicate."

She giggled as her six-foot-plus giant of a blonde husband was enticed lovingly to cool her ardour.

Half an hour later, both lying contentedly in each other's arms, the first cry from the children was heard.

Both groaned with delight.

A new day had started. It was June, and it was cold. The stone house was warmer than the inn or the cottage, but the condensation from their breath swirled in the air around them as they rose.

Eddie bent and kissed her with "Thank you, love."

She replied, "No, thank you," and sighed as she flopped back on her pillows.

He stood naked while stoking the fire.

"Oh, what a body," she thought, desire flooding through her afresh. "Just as well you're already my husband," she said as she watched him dress.

He chuckled.

She wanted to hide away her own stretched body. She had put on so much weight during this confinement. Her tummy still had some stretch marks from the twins. She could still satisfy Ed, but she was embarrassed when he wanted to look at her. He, on the other hand, was even more stunning as he aged. At twenty-five, he was as perfect a male specimen as God could make, as well as good, kind and humble. He was a wonderful father, a fabulous husband and lover, a great brother, a good provider, as well as everything else. No wonder she had fallen for this man as soon as they had met. Literally fallen for him into a horse trough. She gave a laugh as she remembered. He turned and said, "Something amusing you, my darling love?"

"No, sweeting, just remembering the day we met." She smiled. "The goats, remember them? I didn't hear them coming, and you rescued me, and we ended up in the horse trough outside the Union Inn. I still chuckle about it." Jenna laughed at him.

Lily could now be heard crying. Jenna crossed her arms and said, "Oh, damn."

"Jen, it's not like you to swear," Ed exclaimed.

"Fine, then, botheration, bluebells and buttercups." She chuckled. "No, but look." She lifted her crossed arms. "My milk comes as soon as I hear her." Her nightgown had two wet patches on it. She frowned.

"I'll get her; you stay there." Ed pulled a shirt on over his work trousers. "I'll change her first. She'll be wet."

Jenna sank back again and pulled the blankets up to keep warm.

About ten minutes later, he arrived back with not just Lily but all three children. "They want to help," he said meekly.

Both could twist him as they wished. Nearly three, Ned and Tina climbed into bed with their mother. They knew not to disturb her while Lily was feeding. This was talk time, not playtime.

The *why* questions had already begun, and Eddie smiled as Jenna negotiated her way through them. He put more wood on the fire and poked it until it caught.

The room soon warmed, and he bent and kissed her, then left his little family to get on with the morning. Moira and Cara were already in the kitchen, and the kettle was boiling.

Luke appeared, too, and hoped that the kettle would be hot. Cara made them both tea and shooed them away from the stove.

Paddy banged the door as he came inside. "Top o' de marnin' Mr Ed. She be a cold un this marnin'." He shivered. "Heavy frost on the groun' there be. Had to break the ice for the horses."

"Cara, Paddy, how's your place out the back? Is it warm enough for you? I know the timber buildings get much colder."

"Oh, be gone with ye, Mr Ed, we be warm enough. Why, I remember three years ago we spent winter in a covered wagon. Why a cottage of our own with bedrooms and a fire is heav'n on eart'," Paddy replied. "True, she be a bit chilly, but nothing that a visit here won't fix. I can always make the fire out there hotter."

Cara smiled and looked a Paddy, shaking her head and laughing. Eddie looked at them both. Red noses and ruddy cheeks. The girls were the same.

He'd talk to Charlie and get some new blankets for them from Government Stores; one of the benefits of them still being convicts was the things stores could supply for them. The government blankets were surprisingly warm. At least two for each bed. That would help a bit. There was a huge pile of firewood that they knew was free to use. Everything else was nearly new.

He could hear movement upstairs and knew Shauna would be upstairs making the children's beds.

The girls each had work elsewhere. But in payment for them living with their parents, they helped around the house with the children. This was a double blessing as they loved the children and were always happy to play with them at any time they were free.

The back cottage also had a room for their young brothers, Shéamus and Liam, who occasionally got time off from their jobs, and they would come to stay a few days, too.

Tina had heard Shauna walking up the stairs, and as she liked being dressed first hopped off the bed and scooted back to her room. Shauna had just finished making the beds when Tina raced in.

"Morning, Shonna," Tina said. She couldn't quite get her tongue around her name. "Me's first again."

She washed and dressed the little blonde curly-haired cherub, and she walked off to find her brother.

Neddie walked in sedately. Shauna told him to strip off his nightshirt, and he did; she quickly washed and dressed him, and he was soon ready for his porridge.

Lily had fallen asleep again, and Jenna placed her in their bed as she washed and dressed. Once done, she took her sleeping angel to her cot and wrapped her warmly, putting her back to bed. She didn't stir. Jenna returned to her room to find both Irish girls had beaten her to their bed.

It was already made, and they were opening the curtains on the big window. "Thank you, girls. I'd be lost without you both," she said

"Oh, Mrs Jenna, it works both ways. We're all so happy we can be here we'd do anything we can to stay, honest we would," said Moira.

Shauna nodded. "True, Mrs, we would."

"I might be able to do something about that, girls," Jenna said.

The room was tidied, and the three girls walked downstairs. Really, Jenna, at twenty-two, was still only a girl, even though she had three children.

They walked into the warm kitchen, which was the normal hive of activity in the mornings. Unlike most fancy houses, the family ate their breakfast of porridge and eggs with Cara, Paddy and the girls. They did have a dining room, but it was so rarely used that it could be shut up for weeks without anyone entering.

Moira heard a knock on the door and went to investigate. She returned with a letter. She handed it to Eddie.

Realising it was from Wills, he opened the seal and read aloud.

15 June 1845

Emu Plains

Bramblemere Close
Phillip St,
Parramatta

Hi, Ed and everyone else too,

I have a bit of news for you. Cathy and I are to be married. Mr Turner says we have to wait six months, or at least until she is eighteen (which is next week anyway).

It may have come as a surprise to you, but I'm sure Jenna guessed. She sees things.

Mrs Turner also guessed my feelings.

Well, I was only here for three hours before I proposed and she accepted. Yes, I spoke to Mr Turner first and did everything the right way. Cathy had no idea beforehand, other than that I loved her.

Like you, I have a reason, but I'll tell you about that later. It has a lot to do with the barrel in your cellar. There's more to tell, but I can't write it.

We've been here for a week already but decided to stay a few more days and will be with you by about the 17th. I hope you don't mind, but both Cathy and Vicky are coming too, so that's nine of us. I will explain all on arrival.

Jenna, your parents send their love.

Wills

"Jen, he posted this on Sunday, yesterday, so they will be here tomorrow." He looked at Cara. "Did you really know about Cathy? I'm stunned."

"Oh, Mr Ed," said Cara, "'Twas as plain as day, it was. Why every time the lass spoke, or her name was mentioned, his face would light up. She was the same," the Irish lady nodded all knowingly.

Both girls agreed with Jenna when she said, "Ed, I can't believe you missed it. Truly, you had no idea? Cara and I were only discussing it yesterday."

"None, until you said something about him last time." He shook his head. "Wills is all grown up. Well, wouldn't you know it? We'd better get the cottages ready for the men. Stock up some food for them, too."

Jenna smiled at Cara.

"Love, it's all done. Only fresh food is needed. We did it on Saturday while you went fishing with Luke and Charlie," Jenna said.

"All didd'd, Poppa," said Neddie "Uncle Wills is weally coming home?"

"Yes, Ned, Uncle Wills will be here tomorrow, and Aunty Cathy is going to marry him." He tousled his son's hair

"Good," said Tina. "I wike Aunty Caffy, she'd always be watching him. So good!"

He stood looking at his young daughter. Even she had realised. He shook his head with sadness. How could he have missed it?

Cara piped up, "Mr Eddie, the girls and I have been in weekly and flicking the duster over everything while your folks are away. We made the beds on Saturday. With the girls coming, we may have to have two men here, but they can work out who will sleep where once they arrive."

"Thank you so much, Cara, girls. You are all wonderful." Ed said. "I'd better head off to work, but I'll see you all tonight and sort out any more details. Otherwise, I'll leave everything in your capable hands, my love." He bent and gave Jenna a kiss, then bent for a second one. "Paddy, can I have a word, please?" He walked out of the back kitchen door, glancing back to Jenna.

Paddy followed.

They walked down to the vegetable garden. "Paddy, I wanted to have a chat. You know we really appreciate the girls' help. I was wondering if you'd like to talk to them about, well, um, maybe a bit more permanent solution. I'd like both girls to be employed by us and work either here or at the shop, whatever they prefer. But, I also would like them to get some more schooling. Not just the charity school either. Particularly for them to learn to both read and write well. If they do, then the jobs that would open for them both are, well, endless. Have a chat with Cara first; if she's happy, then, by all means, ask the girls. I don't want or need an answer now. Just think about it. Would you do that?" Ed asked.

Paddy stood stunned. "Oh, Mr Ed, ooh, now yer got me. Floored me, you have. Oooh, Mr Ed, I'd love to have me girls under my eye, but schoolin' well, ah done know, they's already at the charity school, 'n I thoughts that be enough." His grin said it all.

Ed looked at Paddy, "Remember, Paddy, Jenna, and I were both educated as convict's children; look at us now. Would you stop your girls from bettering themselves? This is a country where the hard workers *are* rewarded. Don't hold them back, Paddy. Let us do this for them. I had a sponsor paying for my education. Let me pay it forward."

Paddy gazed at him in wonderment.

He laid a hand on his gardener's shoulder. "Talk to Cara. I must go." Eddie walked down the driveway and off to work. He walked via the inn and told Charlie that Wills would be home tomorrow. "I have a surprise for you, too. He's asked Cathy to marry him."

"What?" Charlie spun around. "Why didn't you tell me? I didn't know they were courting."

"They weren't," said Ed. "It all only happened last week, but if I know Wills, I think he wanted to propose before she found out about what's in my cellar."

"Ohh, that makes sense," Charlie said, nodding. Eddie had mentioned he had some gold from Wills, but not how much.

Ed moaned. "Jenna said it was as plain as the nose on my face, but I didn't see it. Even Tina knew, but neither missed much. Jenna certainly never has."

Grace came out onto the verandah with their twins.

"Wuncle Weddie, Wuncle Weddie, did papa tell you we're going to be big brovvers?" said Teddy Lockley, heir to the Earldom.

John said, "It's for Cwritmas, mama said."

Eddie hefted his two-year-old nephews into his arms. He kissed both their cheeks and handed them back to their mother.

"Congratulations to you both! Wonderful news! May I tell Jenna, or does she know already?" he was talking to Gracie.

"She guessed a few weeks ago, Ed, but I swore her to secrecy." Grace laughed.

"Typical, always the last to know everything. Just as well, I don't mind." Ed roared with laughter.

"I'll expect you all for dinner tomorrow night; we'll finally get to hear the rest of the story. All right?" He looked to Charlie, who nodded assent. "Charlie, I was thinking about moving Sunday dinners to our dining room. It's huge and warm. Have a think about it; it's a tight fit at home now."

"Fine by me. We'll be over the mid-afternoon. The children can play for a while," Charlie said.

"Oh, and both Cathy and Vicky are coming too. I smell more to the story, but Wills didn't explain. Tomorrow should be interesting. I have to go. See you tomorrow…and again, congratulations." He walked off quickly but with good reason. He thought about asking the Tindales to dinner, but he might leave that until Sunday. Tomorrow would just be family and Wills's friends.

"Mr Turner, may we have a word, please?" Harry asked.

"As long as you don't mind talking while we work. Grab a fork and help with the hay. Marc, give him yours and clear out."

Marc turned and grinned at Harry. He liked him a lot. He had intentionally spent a considerable amount of time with him over the last week. The more he saw of Harry, the more he liked. Marc handed him the fork and went to Milly's workshop. "Good luck," he whispered. He slapped him on the back as he walked off.

"That pile goes up in the loft. Can you talk while forking?"

"Yes, sir, I can," Harry said. "As you may gather, it's about Miss Vicky."

Jack tried to hide his smile. "I figured it was, lad. Okay, we're alone. What would you like to ask?"

"Well, sir, this week has been an eye-opener to this English lad. I had already learnt to love Wills. He's a lad and a half, that one. However, I never expected this amazing country to be full of young people in his mould. William's Cathy, your Cathy, sir, is another such case; then there's Miss Victoria." He stopped shovelling. "Oh, sir, she's so special," he stopped to think of her.

"Fork, lad," laughed Jack.

"Yes, sir," Harry grinned and shovelled into the pile. "Sorry, sir! I would like to ask if I can officially court her, please. But before you answer, Wills and I have talked. Do you know about his plans for the Emporiums? He wants me to run one as a manager."

Harry never saw his life leading this way, but there was really nothing for him in England. "I don't want a partnership; I'm flush enough, sir. I have £5000 a year income as it is, and there's my share of the booty, too. Sir, I must inform you that my brother is a Viscount. He has told me to find somewhere else to live. If or when we marry, she will have a bit of a title, and we will be flush for funds, sir. I have no reason to return home." Harry shovelled up a few more fork-loads as he waited for Jack to reply.

"So you're really serious, lad? This isn't something you will run out on at some later date?" Jack asked.

"Sir, I have never even looked at a lady before, let alone asked to court one. I am serious. Sir, also, as she's not a convict, I would hope to take her on various trips to England, but our home would be here. This country is amazing, I love it. It's everything I hoped to find in England, but warmer. I'm the reason we are all here. I was discontented and unsettled. God was unsettling me, and I needed a change." He paused, thinking back to the night at 'Whites' in London.

Jack let him talk.

"Sir, I had asked to meet John at the White's Club." Harry started to explain the story.

"I know it," said Jack. Jack had never volunteered anything about his background. Not even to Charles. It was best forgotten.

Harry had forgotten Jack was from London. He knew that from his accent. "I had arranged to meet John there. We're cousins, sir. When I walked in, Aidan was already there, so I asked him to join us. As John arrived, he saw our other three friends sitting at another table in a different part of the room. We all served together in India. God called us together from all corners of the country and beyond, to be in the same place at the same time."

Harry shovelled a few more scoops up in the loft.

"Well, to cut it short, we were all in the same boat. Bored out of our brains, and with no purpose to our lives, some of us had money but no homes. We decided on an extended holiday here. I had seen an advertisement for travel to Sydney Cove. I was intrigued. In the end, we all came. All for much the same reason. To see what was here, nothing more, nothing less. We just knew God wanted us here and together. So here we are. John met Wills in Parramatta and... well, you know that bit too." He took a deep breath, remembering the hollowness of his life in London.

Jack smiled as he worked, but remained quiet.

Harry continued. "God challenged us all. Wills was often the tool He used. One particular night I will remember forever. I was shamed by a boy, sir; a mere lad, and it was done in pure innocence." Harry shook his head as if to shake off some bad memories. "Sir, I have served in the military for years, as I'm the second son. I thought myself both honourable and brave. That was stripped from me in an instant with a simple question from Wills. We were all lying around the fire one night. Wills asked what we all did. We spieled off the list of frivolous things we enjoyed; balls, riding to hounds, shooting, gaming, hunting and all usual sorts of things rich boys get up to in London, as well as other frivolous activities."

Jack still remained silent.

Harry paused and swallowed. "I'll never forget his next question, sir. He asked us what we each did for others or for our communities. It was answered by us all with dead silence."

Even now, the thought stuck in his throat. "Not one of us did a thing for anyone but ourselves. We were all shamed into silence. Mr Turner, I want to tell you this happened a few nights after we left you.

Wills didn't get an answer that night, but a couple of months later, he asked again. After six months in the company of this amazing lad, we are all humbled, changed men. This first question occurred after we found the first of our booty."

Harry looked around to make sure no one was there. "Sir, there is ten times more in there." He pointed to the wagons, "And also in the bag you have locked up, and more up there waiting. And yet, we wanted Wills to keep it all. It meant nothing to him. Do you know what he said?"

Jack shook his head. This is not the conversation he expected to have with the titled English gentleman. "No, lad, tell me all." He had met many in his youth and respected few.

Harry continued. "Sir, he insisted that we each take our share and go home and build village schools, educate the children, feed the hungry, and clothe the poor." Harry wiped his eyes, "Sir, we were so ashamed, embarrassed and remorseful. We are each rich in our own right. He had nothing. Without his prompting, we have each promised to do this. John and I were going to do it together. As I said, we're cousins and live in the same town. He will take half of my share and build that school. The other half, I plan to do the same here. Emu Plains and Bathurst both need schools for all children. I'm the man for that, and I'll help Wills get established as well. Sir, I believe Miss Vicky would be a blessing in this and in the life we could build together, here in Emu Plains." He paused and shot up a pile of hay.

The heap was nearly gone, and Jack picked up a yard broom and swept the last of it into a pile.

Harry scooped it up and waited until the last of it was done.

Jack took his fork and walked up the steps to the loft. "We have to stow it now, lad. Continue, I'm interested in your story."

"Yes, sir," Harry said. "Well, in the time away, we have tweaked and planned. Wills has already made investments, and yesterday, I applied for a land grant here on the Nepean River, a forty-acre block. I'm hoping to build a house for her here and plant an orchard. I want the home base to be as nearby as I can learn much from you." As he finished speaking, he flicked the last load of hay into the corner of the loft.

Jack stood up and leaned on his fork. "Lad, when you approached me last week, honestly, I wanted nothing to do with you. I doubted you from the first, thinking you would not deal honestly with my lass. Wills vouched for you. He is not one to be diddled, and on that strength, I gave permission for you to at least walk out with her. Since then, I have watched you, listened to your friends and pumped them for information. Harry, you have not just my permission, but my blessing. If you are half the man your friends say you are, then I will consider us blessed, too. Just don't you ever hurt my girl."

"Thank you, sir; I really appreciate it." Harry sighed with relief.

"Go and tell her, lad. She's waiting in the kitchen with her mother."

"I will, sir, if I may." Harry took Jack's pitchfork and took them downstairs.

Jack swept the last of the loft before descending the steps, too.

Harry was already knocking on the kitchen door by the time he came down from the loft.

Vicky came to the door holding her bonnet. Harry simply put his hand out to her and asked her for a walk. She smiled up into his face. Nodding, she took his hand and gently squeezed his fingers. He offered her his arm, and they walked off toward the river edge. He had his hand over hers as she held his arm.

Martha sighed. She stood alone in her kitchen. Once her girls were gone, only the four boys would remain with them. All the girls would be married to men with titles. A long sigh of resignation escaped her lips.

Chapter 7   Chilled

*F*our days later, on June 17th, the three wagons rumbled down the road to Parramatta. There were seven men and two ladies aboard them.

Cathy sat squeezed next to Wills. She had sat tucked under his arm for most of the trip. Vicky sat next to Harry, and they were holding hands under a blanket he had wrapped around her. They often smiled at each other but found it awkward to talk with others within earshot. The lunchtime stop was at Rooty Hill. They did not want to stay longer than possible, as days were short, and they expected the night to be cold.

They pushed on to Parramatta and were at the outskirts of the area by late afternoon. They had all had an early morning. The girls had swapped carts at the lunch stop, with Harry and Vicky now on John's cart, Wills and Cathy moving on to the rear seat of Edmund's wagon. Wills liked this as he could kiss Cathy occasionally. Both girls had been let into the secret of the find, but neither knew exactly how much. No one actually knew how much was in the rocks. Wills and Jack retrieved the bag of gold, and Cathy was shown it in the presence of her parents. Vicky knew they had found some, but not the extent of it. Harry wanted to wait until he met Charlie and Eddie and had talked to them first. All Vicky knew were the absolute basics.

Cathy, Martha, and Jack had sat on the side of the big bed at the Turners inn, and Wills revealed to them the find, although still not the quantity as he wasn't sure how much there was, so he just said, "A lot." He mentioned that there was enough for them never to have to worry about her again. All so stunned. They ask no more about their discovery.

It was so cold now that they were all sitting under blankets to keep warm. There was a freezing, westerly wind following them, and the horses were enjoying the good road surface.

Harry had hold of Vicky's hand, gently stroking her palm with his thumb. He hadn't kissed her yet; he probably wouldn't until they were engaged. He was not sure of the procedures here in the new colony, but he felt he was taking advantage of her even holding her hand. He was now absolutely sure he would ask her to marry him. In England, he may have be allowed to have taken her driving a few times with a maid, but no way he could have sat holding her hand under a blanket. Here, all the rules were different. He was learning as they went, but he would not hurt her. He could never hurt her. He looked down at her; he caught his breath. He loved her; oh, how he loved her, and he had only known her a week.

She beamed up at him lovingly. Under the blanket, she had now threaded her fingers into his. They had held hands tightly for most of the afternoon. The wagons stopped for a 'tree run' mid-afternoon. He lifted her down, and she slid down him as she slid to the ground. She lifted her face to his, hoping he'd kiss her. He would only kiss her forehead.

"Not yet, my dear," was all he said. "But soon," he whispered.

She nodded and walked off with Cathy to a clump of shrubs.

Wills shouted, "Check for snakes, girls. It should be too cold for them, but you never can tell."

The men walked off in the other direction. Ten minutes later, they were back on the road. Sitting still for so long didn't help. Hours later, they could see the first smoke spirals from the house fires as they neared a town. Wills said they should pick up the pace as nightfall would make the roads icy and slippery. They were already all chilled from sitting in the cold wind for so long. Both Harry and Wills were holding both of their girls' hands in an attempt to warm them. All the blankets and anything else warm or that could cut the wind were put to use. They were still all chilled.

John, Phil, and Edmund flicked the reins, and the six horses picked up their speed. It was more uncomfortable, and the wind chill was greater, but it was nice knowing they could all get warm within an hour. Vicky shivered, and Harry asked if he could put his arm around her to warm her up.

She nodded. "So cold, Harry!" Her teeth were chattering, and her lips were blue. She was sitting between John and Harry, and although they were all under a blanket, they were all cold. Her dress was thin, and her coat nearly threadbare.

He wrapped his overcoat around her and drew her close to him. She snuggled against him and lay her head on his chest. "I'll have to sit up when we get to town, but this is nice," she whispered up to him.

"Much more than nice," he said so softly she barely heard. Her closeness almost overpowered him. His musky sandalwood scent was a delight for her. "Very nice, Vicky. Very, very nice," he whispered to her. He laid his cheek on her hair and held her tighter. Her hair smelled lemony. He breathed in her scent deeply as she had with his. Clean and pure, just like her.

She was beginning to feel her hands again and had stopped shivering.

John looked over at his cousin over her head. They smiled at each other. Harry was beaming.

Wills, too, was holding Cathy the same way. Her teeth were also chattering, but he didn't have a big overcoat to wrap her in. He held her closer, sharing what cover he had, trying to share his body warmth, and she wrapped her arms around him. He found a sailcloth section in the wagon and wrapped that around their shoulders. That cut the wind and helped those in the front seat as well. She snuggled closer. He lifted her chin and kissed her quietly. "Not long, love."

Edmund chuckled. "Enough, you two; we're entering town. You'll have to behave. Give me directions, Wills."

"Just keep going, Edmund, and leave off. She's so cold. You'll see the Church Street sign; turn left into that." He sat up but pulled the blanket and sailcloth closer around Cathy. He asked her if she was all right.

She replied weakly, still shivering. "Hope so," then slumped against him. She had passed out.

"Cathy, Cathy love, are you all right?" he asked, concerned.

She did not reply.

"Hurry, Edmund. She's passed out." Wills pleaded.

Edmund gee'd up the tired horses. The three wagons trundled down Church Street as the sun tipped the horizon. They had just made it. Wills directed Edmund to turn onto Phillip Street. He urged him to hurry. Edmund pulled into the front yard of Eddie's house. The Englishmen were expecting a cabin-like building, but they had arrived at the stately two-story stone building with a verandah surrounding the top story. Eddie was waiting for them on the front porch. He had dressed in one of his good outfits; he looked for all the world like an English gentleman, only taller and broader. Edmund gasped.

Jenna appeared on the top verandah. Vicky was waving to her. They had not seen each other for some months, as Jenna had not been able to visit while heavily expectant. By the time all three wagons had drawn to a halt, Jenna had come downstairs.

Wills had said to Edmund, "Stop at the front for me to take Cathy straight inside." He stopped and let him down. Cathy, still non-responsive, fell into his arms. "Eddie, quick, she's passed out. She's so cold I couldn't keep her warm."

Eddie heard the panic in his voice. He came over and said to Edmund, "Pull into the stables at the back, sir. Paddy will be there waiting."

"Jenna, open the door quickly, I have to warm her up," Wills said.

Cathy was in his arms, slumped against his shoulder.

Harry had lifted Vicky down and told her to go directly inside to her sisters.

She nodded and went straight to Jenna, who was holding the door open for them. Jenna took her directly to the fireplace. She hugged Vicky, and they both followed Wills as he took his precious bundle to the fire.

Wills had laid Cathy on the floor in front of the roaring fire. She was half propped in his lap and was slowly stirring. Vicky and Jenna were rubbing her legs and hands.

Cathy's eyes flickered open. She saw Wills' concerned face and lifted her hand to stroke his cheek. "I'm all right, love. Truly, I am just cold, really cold." Her teeth were still chattering.

Cara stood back when they had first walked in, then reappeared with a feather quilt and suggested, "Wills, sit her on the settee and sit her close while wrapping her in the quilt. Your body heat will warm her quickly," she said, concerned.

Wills knew the wisdom of this. He lifted her off the floor, carried her to the settee, and sat her on his lap under the cover.

Cara wrapped the quilt around her. "That's not exactly what I had in mind, lad," she said to Wills.

He grinned back. "Cara, did Eddie tell you that we're betrothed?"

"Ah, lad, yes. That's wonderful news," she said. "Nary a whisper beforehand, though, lad," then she chuckled and smiled.

Cathy had wrapped her arms around his waist and was no longer shivering. "Can I stay like this always, love?" she whispered so only he could hear.

He tucked her in and pulled her close. "Forever, love, forever and always," he whispered back.

Vicky and Jenna were still rubbing her feet, which were sticking out from under the blanket. She looked down at them and smiled contentedly. She loved both her sisters.

"I've missed you both so much," Jenna said, "Once you're warm, you have to come and meet Lily. She's beautiful. Now I know you have news, Cathy, but Vicks, who's that handsome man who lifted you down?" Jenna asked.

"That's Harry Harlow, Jenna." She sighed, dreamily. Just saying his name was enough to tell Jenna there was something in this.

"Oh,…and that tells me a lot, doesn't it?" Her eyes sparkled.

"Remember you telling me how you just knew when you met Eddie? Well, I felt the same with Harry. He did too. Jen, he's asked Pa if he can court me. Pa said yes. Wills wanted Cathy to come and spend some time here, but she couldn't come alone, even though they are betrothed. They wanted to be together for when she turns eighteen next week. So I got to come too," she said dreamily. "I got to sit next to Harry all the way here," she sighed.

Jenna, with her hands on her hips, looked from Cathy to Vicky and back again. "So my two little sisters have grown up, eh?"

They both nodded. Then giggled.

"Happy?" she then asked.

Both cooed, "Oh, yes!" in unison.

Cathy wiggled and lifted her hand to Wills's face. She put her hand on his cheek. "So very happy."

He bent and kissed her, warming her lips. They were no longer blue; he was content. He relaxed, and she felt the tension drain from him.

"I'm all right now, love," she said.

"You may well be, but stay there for a bit just to be sure," he said. His stomach was turning somersaults. Although he was worried, she would soon start to feel certain changes in his anatomy if she stayed much longer.

Cara and her girls had fires alight in all the rooms. The house was toasty. The children were in bed.

Luke, at seventeen, had put his overcoat on and had gone to help unload the wagons. He wasn't going to be left out of things.

Gracie came down from the nursery where she had just settled her twins. She walked in and looked over at Wills and Cathy, but said nothing. Her eyes widened. The news that they were betrothed had not filtered to her. Charlie had forgotten to tell her.

Jenna and Vicky seemed to be oblivious to them sitting so close. A short time later, Cathy said, "Wills, I'm getting hot." She struggled to move off the top of the quilt.

"So am I, sweetheart. But I'll hold you forever." He eased her off his lap and onto the settee, still wrapped up warmly. "I'll go and help the others, sweeting." He bent and gave her a long, slow kiss, then walked out to the kitchen and then to the back door.

Her eyes followed him out the door.

By the time the two girls were fully warmed, the men were coming inside. Harry and John were to stay in the big house, and the other four would stay a few doors up the road at the cottages. Cara had fires going in both cottages, and they would walk into a warm, comfortable accommodation with good food supplies.

Wills walked in first, and Cathy ran to him. "Come and get warm, love," she said, leading him to the fire. He was now chilled, as his coat was not one of the thick and warm ones that the others had, military caped coats with multiple layers.

"I'm going to buy myself a big, thick coat like my friends. Theirs are so thick and warm. The biggest, thickest one I can buy," Wills said. He stood warming himself at the fire. Cathy hugged him and rubbed his arms and back as he had done for her shortly before. "And I want to buy you one too, love."

"Oh, Wills, now you're chilled through." She drew him into her arms. "My turn to warm you up, now."

Jenna shook her head. "This is going to take some getting used to," she said to Eddie, and he walked over to her.

Charlie had followed them all into the room.

Harry led the men into the room and over to the fire. They, too, stood warming themselves.

Eddie spoke to Wills. "Are you going to introduce us, Wills?"

Vicky had gone to Harry's side and slipped her hand into his. He took no more advantage of her. Their look spoke volumes.

Eddie and Charlie looked at each other, then at Wills. He only replied with a shy smile and a shrug in reply to their silent question. After a few minutes, the men were somewhat warmed. It was extremely cold outside now, with a heavy frost on the ground. They had only brought in their clothing bags and the flour sack of gold. Everything else would be unloaded tomorrow. They had left most of the food with the Turners. The horses had taken some time to be unharnessed and be rubbed down, then put into stalls in the stables and fed.

Wills went to Eddie. "Ed, I'm sorry I left as I did. I hope you will forgive me."

Eddie put his hand out as though to shake it and instead pulled Wills into his arms. "Always, little brother. Always," he said while embracing him in a bear hug. "I'm sorry I was blind to your needs, lad."

Charlie came to his side and patted his shoulder then also gave him a hug of forgiveness, too.

They drew apart, and Wills knew all was well. "Charlie, Gracie, Ed, Jenna ..." he looked around. "Where's Luke?"

"Here, Wills, I was wondering if I were forgotten," He stepped out from behind the tall figure of John.

"Never, little brother. You're my special kid brother." He gave him a huge smile.

"Please let me introduce you. First, let me explain. They all served together in India; the Honourable Sir John Saunders is, or was their C.O. in India."

John bowed in acknowledgement.

"Henry 'Harry' Harlow was or is his 2IC and the reason they are here, but more of that later. Harry is John's cousin and some sort of cousin to Annabella Winslow-Smythe, about fourth, I think."

Harry bowed.

Wills continued, "Sir Phillip Corsairs, also Annabella Winslow-Smyth's cousin, therefore related to Harry too."

Phil bowed.

"Viscount Eames, known here as Edmund Hunt, he's Aunt

Christina's brother." Wills grinned.

Charlie's jaw dropped. "Why wasn't I told?" he said.

"Forgot, sorry, Charlie," Eddie grinned.

"You knew?" Charlie exclaimed.

Eddie shrugged, grinning. "Had a lot on my mind."

"Mr Lewis Bland; Uncle Ned's mother was Susanna Bland before her marriage, so also we can claim him as family too."

Lew gave acknowledgement, too, with a bow.

The introductions continued, "And finally, but not least, Mr Aidan O'Keefe, from County Cork in Ireland."

"Ireland, eh," Eddie said.

"Yes, sir, I believe your grandmother to have been Shannon O'Shane before her marriage. Her mother was an O'Keefe. Aunt Shannon had been living with us for many years. So, other than John, we're all distant family or as close as can be. And by the look of it, Harry will be more closely related soon, too."

Harry now had his arm firmly around Vicky's tiny waist and had drawn her close. He had the goodness to look embarrassed. All eyes turned to them. He merely smiled but didn't drop his hand.

Vicky, however, moved slightly closer into his embrace.

Charlie stepped forward. "Welcome to Parramatta, good sirs. Eames, eh, seems we have some things in common. I might need to pump you for some information. Still have to get my head around some things." He gave a laugh. "Who's for a drink? We do not stand on formality here, and by the looks of it," looking to Harry, "neither do you," he chuckled. "Let us celebrate the return of the prodigal, Wills. Welcome home, and congratulations too, lad, you too, Cathy."

Cara had handed around glasses of hot mulled wine. The spicy scent of the cinnamon and orange wafted into the air.

Each took a sip and then exclaimed on the quality and flavour of home-brew hooch, as Harry called it. He took a mouthful and coughed. His eyes opened. "Whoa, this has a kick." He opened his mouth as if breathing fire, then chuckled.

Cara was beaming, explaining, "It t'wer me mother's recipe, good sir. Got a good slosh o' quality rum in it, too. T'will warm the cockles of yer heart, from your toes to your ears. Fright away the chill. Dinner will be in fifteen minutes if you'd all like to wash up."

Eddie warned them not to get too close to the fire after they had drunk it. "Has a kick like a mule, but it works."

They all laughed and slowly moved from the fire.

This broke the group up, and Eddie took John and Harry to their rooms. Wills grabbed his bag and headed up to his room. Luke was hard on his heels. Their greeting was to be held in the more private setting of Wills' bedroom.

Wills dumped his bag on his bed and turned to Luke. "I'm sorry I ran off without a word, Luke. I just needed to get away."

"Wills, I came to say I'm sorry for avoiding you and always having my nose in a book. I forgot the important things in life: family. I've missed you, Wills," Luke said apologetically.

They clasped each other in a loving, brotherly hug.

Wills was forgiven, as was Luke. They had always been close.

Luke left him to change, and Wills stripped off the clothing he'd worn for over six months. Moira had placed a jug of hot water in his room, and he poured some into the basin, scrubbing everything he could. Home. Warm, comfortable and forgiven, and now Cathy, too. Utter contentment.

Bramblemere Close
Phillip Street
Parramatta
8 June 1845

c/- His Grace Duke of Gracemere,
Gracemere Castle,
Maidstone England

Dear Dar and Mama, et al,

I do hope you are all well. Lily is growing fast. She can now return a smile and poke out her tongue.

I have good news.

Wills is coming home. I had a quick note and three letters from him, all sent from Bathurst. They said they are due back in Parramatta mid-year, which means soon. He sounds like a changed man. Wonderfully changed. This trip had been both healing and growing for him. He is unable to write much about their finds around the area except to say they are more than ample for them all and sufficient to share. He has sent me amazing plans for his future.

Dar, I do so wish we could consult with you about the developments he has planned. I also wish Uncle Ned were here, too. We could do with your combined wisdom. As yet, we have not told Mr Tindale anything about the finds, but he will have to be let into the secret, as we have to use the forge for processing the ore, and Mr Moffatt will need to know.

Wills has already purchased land in both Hartley and Bathurst. I wonder what more he has planned? ...

I will finish this letter after his arrival home.

Eddie

20 June

Dear all,

Wills is home. But... he is not alone. He has brought his betrothed. Cathy Turner. I am amazed, but Jenna said she's known 'for ages, darling.' She said it was written all over their faces. I must be blind. Charlie did not guess either. Grace, Cara and even little Tina did. Am I really that unobservant?

Jack has said they must not marry for at least six months. They are now planning a January wedding or soon afterwards.

As Cathy was not allowed to travel alone with Wills and his six English friends, Vicky is here too. She is forever under or on the arm of one Henry Harlow. Harry to his friends. I expect another announcement there soon as well. Harry is planning to stay in the colony. His older brother is Viscount Anthony Winchester, who apparently lives near Uncle Ned, and they do not get along. Annabella may know him as he, too, is from Tunbridge Wells, along with Phil, Edmund and John. Four are childhood friends. Lew and Aidan are friends from school, and then the war came, and they all enlisted together. All the connections are too much to take in.

Dar, Wills has applied for another land grant in Emu Plains. They certainly have sufficient funds if the bag I saw is anything to go on. Ten pounds of dust in one flour bag, and that's just the start of it.

The future plans include 'Emporiums' numbers two and three in Emu Plains and Bathurst, with a Warehouse for stock for all three stores in Parramatta. We aim for mostly local products, but with the storehouse, Wills can purchase goods from overseas and store them until needed. Items that cannot be made here yet. Foundry-made tools and, well, you know, the sort of things.

We will be in partnership, with an 80/20 split in his favour, as he'll be footing the bills for the costs. Harry wants to manage one of the stores, but he said he'd float where required. The other five are all keen to help. All six friends have taken a year's lease on Roseneath in O'Connell Street, so they will be on hand. I am so excited about this, Dar and Uncle Ned, but....

I will say little more than, oh, you should see what they have returned with. My jaw dropped. Charlie knows some but not all - yet.

Love to you all.

Eddie.

PS   Please congratulate Aunt Lilabet and Uncle Matthew on their exciting news.

Eddie L

~

A week later

"Ned, I need to have a word with you." Charles Lockley, Earl of Coxheath, said to his cousin. He was standing outside at the balustrade of

Gracemere Castle.

Ned was next to him. He knew what was coming. The letter received last week from Eddie sounded a death knell for this trip.

The friendship between these two men had been forged in a time of adversity nearly thirty years before. They had not realised they were related, let alone the closeness of the ties.

"Ned, we have to head home." Charles looked across to his cousin and saw the wave of sadness wash over his face.

"I know, Charles. As soon as Eddie's last letter arrived, I knew that your time here was drawing to a close. Christina and I were talking about this last night." He paused and looked Charles in the face, "We were wondering if you'd like some company on the trip back?" He looked at his cousin with a smile on his face. "Little Liam is now six months old, and a trip at this time would be convenient before he starts walking. It also means we would miss winter here. Gerry will take over the running of the Estate in my absence. Don't forget that my younger brothers, Paul and Douglas, are both nearby if he needs help. He'll be fine."

Charles swung around to him. "Ned, are you sure? Oh, that would be so wonderful. Oh, Ned, you have made my day." Charles' face had undergone a change, and joy was now visible. "You are serious? You'll come?"

Ned laughed. "Yes, we are coming. But it won't be a simple trip like last time. Travelling with three small children means we're going to take some staff. They will be cooped up in cabins for some time, months even, and I'm not looking forward to that part of the trip."

Sally joined the men on the porch.

Charles reached out his hand to her. "Did you tell him, love?" she asked Charles.

"Yes, Sal, he did," replied Ned, "but we have something to tell you. You're not returning alone. Christina, the children, and I are coming with you. What do you say?"

"Oh, Ned, do you mean it? I spent the night in tears, thinking I would not see you both again." She hugged him. "I have to go and find Christina. Oh, this is wonderful. Absolutely wonderful!" She skipped as she left them.

Charles chuckled. "I think that answers your question, Ned."

"Christina is with Annabella; she's due any day now." Ned looked over the extensive lawns. "Charles, I overheard them talking a week or so ago, and Gerry wants to leave. I think they were wondering if they were overstaying their welcome here. However, I spoke to Gerry and asked if he would run things for me for at least the next eighteen months. You should have seen his face. He's overwhelmed. He gave me an overwhelming yes. He's at a loose end as he doesn't have a home, and his brother George doesn't want him living there. George only has three daughters, so Gerry's now officially the heir. He knows he has to learn to run an Estate. I've been teaching him, so this will be good for him."

"Oh, that's wonderful, Ned," Charles exclaimed.

"I was thinking of staying until Annabella is back on her feet and leaving in September, if not earlier, but certainly before the cold sets in. We'll spend next year in Parramatta with you getting Wills sorted, and we'll return after Christmas in '46 or early '47."

"Ned, really? You'd come for that long?" Charles asked.

"I have another thing to tell you. When I told Mother our plans, she stunned me." Ned looked down at his feet, thinking. Finally, he said, "Charles, she and your mother have been talking, and they both want to come."

"What?" Charles gasped. "Are you serious?"

"Yes, I tried to tell them of the difficulties and what the trip was like. Both were adamant. They have been discussing it for some time. I think we'll be needing the full complement of first-class cabins on the next crossing." Ned chuckled, and it turned into a full belly laugh. "Oh, Charles, these two women are going to set Sydney alight." Ned leaned his head on the balustrade, his shoulders shaking.

Charles, too, started laughing.

Before long, both men were sitting on the ground, wiping tears of laughter from their eyes.

Gerry walked outside to see what was going on. When he heard what had set them off, he, too, sat on the top step of the stairway descending to the garden, laughing. "You are kidding, aren't you, Ned?"

Ned shook his head and said, "I'm perfectly serious. Mother wishes to see the Antipodes, and Elizabeth wishes to come too."

"Oh, *Les Grande Dames* in Sydney," Gerry was stunned. "Gipps will have a heart attack if he's still alive. No wonder you're both in stitches."

The Dowager Duchess of Gracemere was an awe-inspiring sight to behold. She did not merely walk; she flowed. Her presence preceded her. Her gown always had a train of sorts. The air of authority oozed from her. However, since her best friend, Elizabeth, Dowager Countess of Coxheath, had moved in with her after her daughter's marriage, the two had become known as *Les Grande Dames*. It's not that they actually flaunted themselves, but their arrival anywhere, in the crested carriage, outlined in gold, with six liveried footmen and four matching white horses, was enough to give anyone apoplexy. At sixty-five and sixty-four, these two women were still young enough to create a stir, and they managed to achieve that with every outing they undertook. Their friendship had given both ladies a new lease on life. Both were in full health and fit as fiddles. When out of public view, they simply inspired awe. Privately, they also took pleasure in a good laugh over their impact on people.

Ned's children were the only ones not in absolute subservience to them. On their numerous visits to the castle to see their children, supposedly Ned and Charles, they would normally be found in the Nursery, sitting on the floor playing with the three adorable tots, or now sitting, cuddling the newest one, William.

Ned had stated categorically, "Mother, you may call him Liam, but under no circumstances are you to name him Willy. Is that understood?" So, Liam, Ned's second son, became.

Ned was rarely able to control his beloved mother, but on this occasion, he stood firm.

She nodded meekly, chuckling later to Elizabeth, "I already was calling him Liam anyway."

Annabella was delivered of a son, Edward Gerald Charles. Both were well. He had been born on August 15th, the third birthday of Eddie's twins and Liza's son, and so the family were gathered for tea.

Gerry still could not get over the fact that he had a son. More so, now that the child was the heir to the heir. Edward Winslow-Smythe would one day be the Earl. Gerry kept saying to Ned, "I have a son, Ned. And Annabella is fine and Bella is beautiful and God is good and... oh, I could keep going on and on."

Ned smiled. "Oh, yes, God is good, Gerry."

~

A week later, the two grand ladies came for tea.

Ned turned to his gathered family. "I'm glad everyone is here, as I have some news. I have heard back from the shipping company, and a few ships are heading to Sydney. So, dear ones, we set sail in mid-October. The '*Eagle*' is a three-mast barque and has the available cabin space that we require. I have already booked passage and reserved all the cabins, bar two, which were already taken. That leaves us eight cabins. Mother, you and Aunt Elizabeth will each have one, Charles and Sal another, Christina and I, a fourth. The children will have a fifth plus a spare for a playroom. One shall be for our luggage and one for a dining room. The staff will travel in the lower deck, although two can sleep in the children's playroom if they wish."

"Neddie! Seven weeks, you expect me to be ready in that time?" bewailed his mother. "How can I, no, we, be ready in that time?"

"Well, Mother, you do not have to come." He smiled, knowing she had made the decision and nothing would stop her.

"Elle, we must away and bring in the dressmaker. Cool clothing, you say? How cool?" the Dowager Susanna asked her son.

"Mother, Parramatta is hot in summer; imagine the hottest day here, then more, and cold in winter, frozen water and frost. There is no snow, though. You will need clothing for both. Little fashion is available, so take fabrics to have your clothing made."

"Elizabeth, we're going to the Antipodes. Can you imagine that?" she said excitedly. She sat and plonked her hands in her lap. "We'll be ready, son."

Charles looked over to his mother. "Mother, are you sure this will not be too much for you?"

Elizabeth shot him a glance. "Son, I missed twenty-five years with you already. What makes you think I will miss more? With Lilabet now in London..." She huffed. "Well, I need to see where you live and also to meet my grandchildren and great-grandchildren. Try and stop me, my boy." She folded her arms in defiance.

Ned had to turn his back. His shoulders were shaking. Charles watched as he wiped the tears of laughter from his eyes. Oh, yes, he was going to enjoy this trip thoroughly. They all were. It's a pity they had to return eventually. But they must; it was his duty. He thanked God for Gerry. He would hold the fort beautifully.

Gracemere Castle,
Maidstone England
15 August 1845

Bramblemere Close
Phillip Street
Parramatta

My Dearest Eddie,
I hope this letter finds you well. Congratulations on the birth of little Lily. Lilabet is overjoyed to have a great-niece named after her. I added a postscript to your father's letter last week when I wrote. It is always a delight to hear from you. We are all gathered here on the anniversary of your twins' birthday, celebrating the event. Annabella has just gone into labour, so I am writing to you while we wait.

However, I thought I should give you a warning. Your parents are returning... but with us in tow. Our three youngsters should all get on with yours. It's nice that they are all the same age. We shall be a party of six, plus children, and a staff of three. Your grandmother is coming, as is my Mother. This is sure to be an interesting trip. They are now known as 'Les Grande Dames'. Be warned, for they will take the town by storm. I do feel sorry for Governor Gipps.

As for your plans, your father and I have decided that you need some combined wisdom and advice from abroad, so we are returning post-haste. Ha - this is funny. You have far more experience than either of us in this sort of project. However, having said that, we are both so keen to supply any assistance we can.

I would not miss this for anything.

Gerry is taking over here for the next eighteen months at least. . . (we may extend, but I have not mentioned this to your father. Gerry knows, as do my brothers.) Now, re Gerry, his brother George has named him as heir, as he only has daughters.

(I break into this missive to announce Annabella has just safely delivered a son. They have named him Edward Gerald Charles.)

So, Gerry has a son; therefore, even the heir has an heir. Gerry will need to learn to run an Estate, so he can learn on mine with Paul and Douglas to assist.

Ed, I miss life in the colony so much. I shall be glad to drop the formality of here. We are booked on the 'Eagle', which is scheduled to depart in mid-to-late October.

It's nice to hear that you will be able to accommodate us all. However, as Mother insists on bringing her maid and one other maid, we will also have Nanny with us for the children. We may need to arrange alternative accommodation for the extra staff.

The 'Les Grande Dames' are so looking forward to the wedding. So I do hope the ship arrives in time, but I fear it will not be there until mid-February. If they have not yet set a date. . . and there is no hurry, maybe they could delay it until our return. Your mother would be very disappointed if she too missed it.

Please extend our warmest congratulations to Wills and Cathy. It seems that your mother is not at all surprised. Women apparently notice things that we men miss.

I have heard of a new route being opened. I will attempt to direct this letter via the Suez Peninsula and see if it is quicker. It should be transported by ship to Aden, then overland, then picked up by another ship to Sydney. I hope it reaches you in good time. At least before we arrive with the news of us descending on you, if this is so, we might see if we can do this ourselves one day. I plan that there will be more trips, so please don't think this is the only one. I want my children to truly understand the meaning of Life from all perspectives. Here, they will only see the luxurious side of life, where everyone will bow down to them. There, they will know they are human and part of mankind. We are all equal. They must learn this. I am determined they will have a balanced view of their positions. Chip, especially in his future role as Duke. We may have to swap children at some stage. Send your children to school here, Ed. They will always have a home with us.

One thing you might find interesting. It pertains to Harry. I know you have not met Annabella, but her maiden name and Phil should have known this, was Watkins-Harlow. If this is 'the' Harry Harlow from Tunbridge, as you say, then he certainly is possibly related to Phil at least. If so, Harry's older brother is Viscount Anthony Winchester (not a pleasant chap, from what I hear). The family name is Harlow. I think it was his Great-Great-Aunt (or possibly just his great-aunt) who married Annabella's great-great-uncle. Hence hyphenated the name.

Harry sounds like me. Harry will be "The Hon. too. His wife would be Mrs Henry Harlow. I'm sure he knows, but like me will not tell. I'll speak to him when I arrive. I'll bring my Debretts, and we can see who fits where. By the way, I have ensured that your father will be included in the next edition.

Eddie, I was thinking that we can bring the first load of foundry items. You will be able to store them until required. I know the sort of digging tools required, as I had to order them for the chain gangs. This will be a start for your stock. We know the kinds of things you can make, but I also thought we could buy and send you a load of 'Pig Iron' to make some of your own items. I presume they have the ballast arranged for this ship, but I will search out the options and sort something out. I will also bring some moulds for said items. Even if these are used as templates, it's a start. I will do my homework and bring something that is hopefully useful.

Ed, these are not the sort of issues that come across a Duke's desk often. It's why I love doing this for you. So much nicer than working out who owns which ram or sow, or decisions to which Ball invitation to accept. Give me a road to build any day.

Ed, another reasonably new product I will endeavour to either bring or send is a product called Correlated Galvanised Iron. These are sheets of wiggly iron used for roofing. As you have sent drawings of the Parramatta Emporium, I have been able to calculate the extent of the roofing - I will multiply this by four and add more. If you don't use it all, then sell it. I will include all the necessary items. It will mean no shingles or slate roofing. This material comes in big 8-foot sheets. Very easy and quick to install, but it will be hot to work under. There might be a way to insulate it with planks, bark, or something similar. It's designed to fit over shingles, so that should work. I'll leave that to your ingenuity.

I had better post this missive. I shall see you just after Christmas.

Please extend my love to Jenna and the children, as well as to the rest of the clan.

Uncle Ned

Chapter 8   Fun Things

Sunday dinner was a joyous event. Cara had cooked a special meal for Eddie and Jenna's fourth wedding anniversary. The house was full, as was the dining room. Eddie, Jenna, Wills, and Luke were, of course, there. The Turner girls had arrived with their parents, and the six English gentlemen were all there, as well. Charlie and Gracie, came with their twins for the meal. Then, after the meal, Eddie's sisters, Liza and Anna and their husbands arrived to celebrate with the family. Moira and Shauna had set up a special children's table and sat with them, feeding the little ones and keeping them all quiet. Paddy waited on the table like a butler, with Cara assisting, and then both joined the family in the sitting room.

Wills had explained to his friends that Paddy and Cara were 'lifers'. They could never be free. Their children, however, were. The family were included in as many things as possible. They had five other children, but the girls lived at the house with their parents.

In the sitting room, and during the conversation, Luke produced a newspaper. He took it to Aidan, to whom he had grown close.

"Aidan, did you see this?" Luke handed over the article that had caught his eye.

Aidan read it, "Ho. Are you going to offer, lad?" Luke shook his head.

Lew and Edmund were sitting close by and said, "Offer what, Aidan?"

Luke was looking awkward and almost hopping from one foot to the other. "Read it out, Aidan."

He did…

"The Dandy Horse Match 6th December 1845

MONDAY next is the day appointed for this long talked of and singular exploit. Our readers may remember that a wager of £50 to £20 was made that a Mr.— — could not, within one month, find any person to ride the ordinary two-wheeled velocipede one standard mile, during which transit the rider was not to allow either foot or hand to touch the ground. It was purposed to make the last deposit at Parramatta, but at the request of several Sydneyites, the parties interested have resolved to run as near the metropolis as possible, and the Woolpack, opposite Petersham, has been named as the place of rendezvous. The final sum will consequently be made good at the above Inn, at 11 o'clock in the forenoon, when the ground will be named and the effort made for the accomplishment of this novel, and, as far as we can learn unexampled feat. The betting can, with difficulty, be quoted, as persons are offering 5, 6, and 10 to 1 against its being accomplished.

Aidan read further on and discovered another was to be held in Parramatta on the Monday following. Meeting at "The Rear Admiral Duncan Inn" in Church Street at ten o'clock, contestants were to register their interest.

The conversation had stopped as he read, and everyone listened.

"Why, lad, that's tomorrow. Are you interested?" Harry asked.

Luke nodded. "I saw one once, and wondered how hard it was to ride."

Harry and John looked at each other. Harry knew John had one of these contraptions at home. Both had ridden it often, but on a smooth "Macadam" road surface. On the bumpy dirt roads of the colony, it would be more difficult, but certainly possible.

Luke looked at Eddie. "Can I go, please, Ed, Charlie? The school has finished for the year, and, oh, I'd love to see one." He looked over to his two older brothers.

Charlie turned to Eddie. "Don't you just love how he always asks you first? Am I that much of a strict disciplinarian?" he chuckled. "I have a suggestion. Why don't we all go?

Luke jumped and punched the air. "You mean it, Charlie? I can go, we can all go and watch. Really?" The lad was so excited.

Harry turned to Vicky, who, of course, was standing next to him. "John has one, you know," he said quietly.

She looked up, surprised. "John, is this so? You have one and can ride it?"

John smiled, "Yes, I have one; I ride it often. Harry can, too, you know. He's ridden it often as well."

She gave him a gentle push. "You could have said."

Harry chuckled.

Luke looked at these two men, whom he already idolised. They were learnéd gentlemen and were just what Luke aspired to emulate. "Oh, coo, really you can both ride one?" He looked down at the paper on Aidan's lap. "Why don't you both apply?

All turned and looked at these two reluctant participants.

Harry volunteered a reply first. "Well, why not? It could be fun. They are not to know we can both ride. This should be interesting. John, are you in? Or do I have to do it alone?" He looked over to John.

John grinned. "It's taking money from a baby. Oh, of course, I'm in. Remember to tie up your trousers this time, though, Harry."

Eddie was watching his youngest brother's face. "Luke, it looks like we are all having a family outing tomorrow. I want you to promise me something. You are absolutely not to ride in the competition. You may, however, have a try afterwards, but only on level ground. Is that understood?"

Luke nodded. He gave a delighted grin.

Eddie had never told his family that he had tried to ride these contraptions a few times when he lived in Sydney. Each time had been a massive fail. Once he skinned both elbows and a knee, also nearly knocking himself out. No wonder he never said anything. Riding an unbroken horse was easy compared to this horrible two-wheeled contraption. His favourite horse, the black stallion he had named James, was one such mount. He had the temper of a devil when he was frisky but gentle as a lamb at other times. He would rather ride this black charger on his friskiest day than try to mount another bicycle. "Promise, Luke? I mean this. I will allow you to ride one after the competition is over," Eddie said seriously.

"Thanks, Eddie, thanks so much," Luke said. He turned to his new idol, John. "Can we go and register early? Please? I don't want you to miss out. Please, John?" he pleaded.

"Oh, to be seventeen again. Not a care in the world and totally regardless of danger, especially if it's not your own," John laughed. "Yes, lad, we shall all go down and register early. If we win, we'll give the money to the girls' orphanage. They need it."

The following morning, the entire family group of around twenty persons lined the street to see the first, then the second, of their friends ride the one-mile length of Church Street in Parramatta. Both had a trial run, turning a quick circle, making their efforts look amateur. They needed to get the feel of the apparatus on the bumpy road.

Betting was rife on the sidelines, and of course, the friends could not resist some easy money.

The start was at the top of Church Street on the southern end of town. They were to ride past the "Rear Admiral Duncan Inn" and finish just past the Emporium. The road was bumpy, but was not in too bad a condition, especially if they stuck to the centre of the track.

Both grinned at the other. The road would do.

Several others had registered. A few had already tried and failed by the time John's turn came. There were jeers and chortling as he stood the apparatus up. It was still in a reasonable condition even after a few mishaps with the previous riders.

The coordinator called for final bets. Then yelled, "Ready? Go."

John turned the large front wheel to point downhill and took off. By the time he settled on the seat, he had gathered quite some speed. He dodged some of the larger holes in the road and finally steered it to the centre of the road, where it was smoothest. He careered down the road, being encouraged by the cheers of the community who had turned out to watch. He flew past the halfway mark and was approaching the finish line. He could see his friends, Edmund and Lew, waiting for him, and he screeched to a stop just past the Emporium at the finish line. A huge cheer went up from the entire street. He'd done it. The organisers weren't happy. That lost them money.

The contraption was loaded onto the back of the waiting cart, and it was trundled back up the hill for the next daredevil to use. John was elated, as were his friends. Now for Harry's turn. They stayed down at the finish line and waited.

A few more attempted it; now they knew it could be done. Word had got back to the start that John owned one in England. The organisers had not considered asking that before. Each contestant was now queried, "Did they own one?" Harry honestly answered, "No, and I never have." They were satisfied. Thankfully, they never asked if he'd ridden one. A few had seen his wobbly attempt at riding before the start. Betting was heavy. Only John had completed the distance so far.

Vicky was waiting at the Emporium Tea Rooms with the other ladies. It was too rough and noisy on the street. From here, she could see when they were getting close, and they could, of course, hear the roar of the crowd.

Five more failed attempts, and then it was Harry's turn. He had watched how John had found it hard to catch the spinning peddle if he started downhill, so he turned the bike sideways and was able to be seated before the velocipede gained speed. He had also noticed how John had stuck to the middle of the dirt road. He took off.

Wave after wave of cheering followed him down the road. He flew past the Inns and then the Emporium, stopping at the finish line with Vicky waiting for him.

She had flown out of the Tea Rooms when she heard the crowd noises following the rider. She knew it would be Harry. She ran, totally disregarding her mother's pleas for decorum. She arrived at the finish line just before Harry. Everyone stood applauding. He had done it, too.

Vicky stood waiting for him. Pride was shining from her.

He passed the bike to the waiting cart driver and walked over to her. He reached out his arms and embraced her.

"I'm so proud of you, Harry," she said simply as she walked into his arms.

He was so overwhelmed that she was ignoring the propriety of showing public affection for a male person she was not betrothed to that he gathered her to him, her hands resting on his chest.

She lifted her face to his and whispered, "Kiss me, Harry, please."

He did, for the very first time. He kissed her, totally disregarding propriety. He savoured the taste of her sweet lips, the lemony scent of her hair, the softness of her kiss, and the warmth of her body as it was wrapped in his arms. He wanted it to go on forever. It was so much better than even he imagined. She responded to his ardour with hidden passion. The depth of their kiss staggered him.

Behind him, he heard John cough. Reluctantly, he released her. Her red lips beckoned him to do it again. He said, "Later."

She nodded, then blushed.

Jack appeared in moments and had thankfully seen nothing. "Congratulations, lad, to you both, actually," as he spied John. "Of course, I had money on you both." He shook their hands. He looked to Vicky and noticed her glowing and her lips reddened. "Hmm," he thought to himself, then looked to Harry, who had the courtesy to blush before looking away.

Edmund offered Vicky his arm. They walked back the short distance to the Tea Rooms. "You're brave," he whispered. "You could have been in real trouble there if your father had seen."

"I don't care, Edmund. I love him," she said quietly in reply.

"He knows, and trust me, it's returned," he said. He patted the hand on his arm as he walked through the door. "You can trust him, too."

She could only reply, "I do." She did trust Harry totally.

Jack, John, Harry, and Lew followed. Harry's eyes did not leave the figure in front, Vicky on his friend's arm. Edmund realised he had to remove her quickly before they gave their actions away. Harry was still in awe of that kiss. He remained silent.

Eddie and Charlie had two bottles of champagne and a pile of glasses waiting. Eddie knew that at least one of them would win. To have both was a double bonus. He admired these six new friends of Wills'. It was also nice for him and Charlie to have friends who believed in God, lived clean lives, and were not inclined to associate with the town's loose women. Also, they were only about six years older than he and Charlie.

Something Wills had encouraged since their return was regular Bible discussions. These often occurred in Eddie's sitting room and were normally informal and sometimes even impromptu.

They could hear cheers followed by groans as more contestants tried and failed. One managed to make it to halfway before hitting a hole and falling. John and Harry were the only two to complete the course. They would receive their reward later that afternoon at the "Rear Admiral Duncan Inn." In the meantime, they were all assembled now in the Tea Room.

Harry felt he had already had his reward. All doubt of his emotions was gone. He wishes he could return with the Turners when they departed the following morning.

~

A week later, at the breakfast table at Bramblemere Close, Eddie was sitting at the head of the table with a folded letter in front of him.

Eddie asked while eating porridge and toast. "Wills, how set are you on getting married in January?"

"Why, Eddie? That's the first month Jack said we could marry."

"I was wondering if you would be interested in postponing for a few weeks, like about five weeks, possibly even six," said Eddie between mouthfuls of toast.

Jenna was trying hard not to look up at him. She knew what the latest letter from Uncle Ned said.

Luke piped up. "Oh, Ed, you can't make them wait any longer. They are always touching each other anyway." He looked at Jenna, who was trying not to giggle. He asked, "There's more to this, isn't there?"

"He's quick, Ed," Jenna chuckled.

"I was wondering if you'd like Mama and Dar to be at your wedding, that's all?" he replied before taking another bite of his toast, his eyes smiling at Wills.

"Oh, Ed. Seriously? They are coming home? When?" said Luke. He'd just folded half of his boiled egg into a slice of toast.

"Are they? Really?" said Wills. "Yes, of course. When did Uncle Ned say they were coming?" He took a bite of his toast.

"In February, Wills." Eddie looked at Luke. "There's more: Grandmama is coming too, as well as Uncle Ned, Christina, his Mama and the children, plus servants."

"Oh, how fabulous. That's wonderful," said Wills. "Cathy won't mind for that reason. I'll go and write to her. May I use your desk, please, Ed?"

"Yes, of course, Wills, stationery is top right. You have only twenty minutes before the mail coach passes through, so you'd better hurry," he said.

Wills gobbled down the rest of his breakfast and went into Ed's office. He quickly penned a letter to Cathy and finished it with much professing of his undying love. He checked the time, just after half six, and the mail was due through at seven.

That done, he took off up the street to wait until Jim, who drove the mail coach, passed. He walked toward the Post Office just to make sure he didn't miss him. He arrived in plenty of time and was able to have a quick word with Jim.

"Lad, I promise to deliver your love note," he said and shoved it in his top pocket. "I have an order for Jack, so I won't forget to give it to him."

"Thanks, Jim, it's important. It's not exactly a love note. We have to delay the wedding as Dar and Mama are coming home a few weeks later. Could you please ensure she receives it? Thanks so much, Jim." Wills went from there up to O'Connell Street to see John and the men to tell them too. The tall Yorkshireman, Jim, had often stopped the night with them at the Jolly Sailor Inn, especially if the road had been blocked or impassable.

He walked off up the main street and turned past the decrepit-looking church, then into O'Connell Street to see his friends.

He knocked on the door. The Portuguese maid answered. She didn't speak much English, and Wills found her difficult to understand. He asked if his friends were there.

"Non, sir, all gone." She then made a riding action.

"Darn," thought Wills

"Can you tell them I called?" he motioned to himself. "Tell them to see me. Yes? *Sim? Por favor?*"

He'd learnt 'Yes' was *Sim* and 'please' was *Por favor'* but not much else. He'd also heard her finish with *eu digo* and had worked out that it meant, *I say.* It was the closest he could translate. She was just rude.

She replied, "*Sim, Sim. Eu digo*" She closed the door in his face.

Wills hoped that meant she would tell them. Wills stood looking at the Roseneath door. Yes, she had done it again. The girl was rude. He turned away. He had always loved the house since he was a young child. He knew the family who used to live there, the Templeton family. It was perfect for his friends, as it had six bedrooms, a large drawing room, and a dining room. It also had stables, which were now full, a coach house, and it even came with servants. The rental included two servants, an Irish girl and this Portuguese female. He didn't know how they communicated with her, but they had not yet sacked her. Maybe they spoke her language. It wouldn't surprise him.

The more he found out about these men, the more he admired them. God certainly provided for them. They had only stayed with them for seven weeks before this came up for rent. He remembered the night they sat around the dining room table at Eddie's place. They had held hands, and John had prayed. "Dear Lord, you know our plans and that we want to work this for you. We ask that you provide us with somewhere we can live for a year or more. Somewhere, you have already prepared for us. Somewhere close to our friends and family, and Dear Lord, somewhere big enough for us all, Amen."

Wills had heard that there might be a few cottages available, but none with six bedrooms.

About a week later, Harry had romped in one morning in August, holding the Sydney Morning Herald. Eddie and Wills leaned over him and read the advertisement.

TO BE LET OR SOLD,

ROSENEATH COTTAGE, Parramatta; at present occupied by Mrs Anderson, contains six rooms, with attics, has an excellent verandah all round, a garden attached; also kitchen and servants' rooms detached. The whole is to be sold on liberal terms, or, if let, possession can be given in a short time. Apply to Messrs. Tingcombe and Watkins, Parramatta, or to GILCHRIST AND ALEXANDER, 2454 Sydney. SALE BY AUCTION.

"Oh, Roseneath would be perfect, Harry," Eddie said. "We know it well. It's perfect."

Harry had gone straight down to the agent, and a lease was agreed upon. He would even be able to put an offer in on the place, and he notified the agent of this possibility. It could be a place he could take Vicky to live, too. He wanted the very best for her. Now, he could ask her to marry him. His Victoria. He sighed. How nice that sounded. He'd already told her his older brother was a Viscount, but that he'd rejected the stuffiness of the English society. He just wanted to be plain old Mr Harry Harlow.

He and his friends had arrived with a lot more than they had taken on their journey, and they had it stored at The King's Arms in Sydney. John and Edmund had taken the ferry to town and bought a classy Town Carriage while there, with two rideable carriage horses to pull it. It was smaller than a travelling chaise but was enclosed so the ladies could travel with some warmth. They arrived back a week later, having stocked up on various items they would need, as well as all the stored items. There was so much luggage in the new carriage that there had not been room for either of them inside. The weather was cold, but their overcoats had kept them warm enough. They had purchased a sealskin wrap for their knees. This proved very effective for both warmth and weatherproofing.

Wills' friends had been living in Roseneath for four months now and had made it a home. Aidan blustered about the Irish lass Maureen and often spoke to her in Irish Gaelic, telling her not to be rude. Sadly, this did not work. Sophia, the Portuguese girl, would giggle each time she was reprimanded. Both girls knew that these men could not sack them, and they exploited that position with sassiness and wilful disobedience.

Today, Wills had no idea where his friends had gone, but now realised he should have brought a note. Frustrated, he turned and walked back down the street towards the Emporium. "Humph," I'd better go and warn Reverend Bobart, too." He called at the church, but no one was there; it was too early. He would need to call back later. The building had still not been repaired after the 1841 tornado nearly five years earlier. The roof beams were now rotting, and the seats inside were deteriorating badly. It was in a sad state, and the rectory was even worse. Repairs for this, however, were slowly progressing. The Bobart family had moved in with another family member, and Reverend Mr Bobart was still ministering at St John's. Reverend Bobart had been head of The King's School the entire time he was there. He liked him immensely. He was a youngish man who made teaching and learning fun. So much nicer than his father-in-law, Reverend Marsden, who had scared him silly. He remembered him and Luke mimicking him, blowing out their cheeks to try to make them look fat.

The building of the new church would start soon, but not before his wedding. Wills knew that an architect, John Heuison, had offered some land to Reverend Marsden, and it was on this land that the new church was to be built. Wills sat on the St John's church fence, looking at the sadly neglected building. The stonework was still intact, the roof half gone, the remainder rotting. He remembered the day after the storm. He and Luke had organised all the boys in town to collect the shingles that had been blown off. They had been placed in piles ready for re-applying, but those piles were now covered in moss and rotting. It was so sad. It had happened only a few days before Christmas. Years later, services were still held on the wide church lawn, and weddings were held inside at the Sanctuary. He still wanted to be married, where Eddie, Charlie and the Duke, or the Major, as he still thought of him, were married.

The plans for the new church in Sorrel Street were nearly ready. Charlie had shown him where it was to be built. Hopefully, it will start next year. Reverend Marsden had negotiated the purchase of this land and left £200 for its construction; it was to be called 'All Saints.' Some of the sandstone was already arriving on site. Beautiful chiselled blocks, all done by convict labour. Wills still hated seeing the convict work gangs being marched through the town. True, there were now fewer of them, but they had a horrible life. His run-in with the two escapees at Hartley gave him the shivers. It jogged him back to reality. He had headed down to the Emporium and written a note, then dropped it back to the Roseneath to make sure they got the message. At least the Emporium should be open. He would wait for them there.

~

John had suggested an early morning ride to Harry and the last few days had been spent sitting and planning. They needed some activity.

Harry and Wills were heading out to Emu Plains on Friday. They had a small delivery to make at Orchard Hills on the way to Doctor Gerry's sister Genevieve Sheridan, but decided to do it on the return trip instead, as they really wanted to see their girls.

Harry's heart turned over with just the thought of seeing Vicky again. He had been courting her for a bit over six months and had decided that it was long enough to ask Jack if he could marry her. He had put in an offer to buy Roseneath and should hear back before the weekend. Either way, he would buy the house and the land in Emu Plains. He planned to build a beautiful home for Vicky near her folks.

John and he had long walks, discussing the pros and cons of the relationship. Harry asked John to play Devil's Advocate and try to talk him out of proposing. None of the cons outweighed the pros.

Harry had finally decided to take that final step. He'd make New South Wales his home. He knew Vicky was his destiny. He wanted to be with her more than anything. The kiss after the race had sealed it for him, but he no longer wanted John to try to talk him out of his decision. None of his arguments, if you could call them such, were even considered.

Vicky had the grace of a queen. She was everything he had dreamed of in a wife. Good, pure, and God-fearing, too. She was the sort of person who people would turn and look at as she walked into a room. Not just for her beauty, although he considered it great, her mere carriage was regal. She glowed with warmth and love. However, even beyond her stately carriage and the way she walked, she had an aura of love. He had yet to meet anyone who did not have a good word to say about her. He loved her totally, completely, and unconditionally. She cared for the less fortunate around her.

Harry knew that, as convicts, her parents had a fairly tough life. They were looked down upon by any man who arrived from the Motherland. She understood poverty. She gave her only cloak to a child who had none, only saying she could borrow her sister's spare one. Harry knew that neither Jenna nor Cathy had a spare coat. Harry bought Vicky a new one but handed it to Jenna to give to her. Wills had also bought one for Cathy. Both new overcoats were really thick and warm. Jenna had handed them over when she saw her sisters together.

Harry smiled. Vicky's entire way of life showed her love for her fellow man. She inspired him. His initial judgement of her far underestimated her quality. She could hold her own in a room full of Duchesses. She was always unflustered. Little did she know that this would soon be put to the test, with two Duchesses and two Countesses.

~

The morning after the seven wanderers had returned from their trip west, Eddie sent Paddy away on the excuse he needed him to buy something, but it had been to get him out of the way. Cara and the girls were both at the women's house, Coxheath, helping with the craft and sewing group. Jenna, along with her sisters-in-law Liza and Anna and Grace, would be with the children there too. John, Harry and the others helped Wills and Edmund unload the hundreds of pounds of quartz rocks from under the mattresses. Cathy and Vicky were asked to stand guard to make sure they were not to be disturbed. They would keep the finds secret for as long as possible. Jenna knew of the gold but had to accompany the others to avoid suspicion. She had thought the first delivery was huge, it filled an entire wine cask, but this.

Wills had given Cathy a glimpse of the rocks before the others had appeared. She marvelled at the volume of rock. All three wagons now had an eight-inch or more layer of rock under the mattresses as the rocks had cut through the hessian bags they had originally been stowed in.

Cathy gasped, "Wills, there must be hundreds of pounds here."

"Yes, Cathy, and there's more out there, but we couldn't carry it back. This is ample for us, but I've bought the land at Hartley and will return to bring more back next autumn if we can."

She looked stunned. "Wills, that is wonderful. Just wonderful." He may only have just turned eighteen. but he was now a man. The man of her dreams.

The seven friends had estimated the volumes. Edmund and John had guessed there could be about one hundred pounds of gold in this load of rocks, possibly more. There was a shade over ten pounds in the bag of gold dust. About another forty pounds or so in the rocks from the first find at Hartley. They knew the set value of gold was £10 per ounce —a guess of over one hundred pounds of gold in all. £20,000, and that was only a rough estimate. Wills knew the money for the new church was £200, and it was going to be huge. Eddie had said when he left school that his yearly wage at the forge the next year was to be £15 per year. He still loved the work and would often help out, but he did not have to return full-time, ever.

Once it was crushed, the final weigh-in was significantly higher than the original estimate. There were one hundred and sixty-two pounds of gold and smelted. Valued at £25,920 and half of this, £12,960, was Wills alone. The others would get over £2000 each. Wills had insisted that smelting costs were to be covered by his share and would brook no argument with his friends. This was less than £50. However, Wills eventually gave Mr Tindale £100 as a 'thank you.' Other places received some money, as well.

One place that needed an instant injection of funds was The Female Orphan School. Mr Richard Childs would get an anonymous £50 donation immediately. The Charity School in Parramatta was another.

Eddie had suggested that they crush the rock in their basement, where it was virtually soundproof. Even Cara upstairs couldn't hear them. They had tried this, but eventually had to bring Mr Tindale into the discovery as it was just taking far too long. Then, they had to work out a way to crush the huge volume of rock they had. Eventually, Eddie and Wills put their heads together and invented their rock-crushing machine. It was still slow, but it worked more quickly than by hand and required significantly less manpower and skill.

Eddie had cast a huge solid weight of pig iron, This was made with a hole in it. It fitted into a solid but hollowed-out base of a similar shape. The handle would be wound up, and the weight dropped onto the rock.

It took over six weeks, but most of the ore was finally crushed. They each kept a specimen chunk to show their family. Eddie and the seven explorers worked after hours for those weeks. Once the ore was crushed, work at the forge was stopped early each day, with the young apprentices sent home.

Eddie and Wills made some rough ingot moulds. They intended to pour most of the gold as small ingots, but on realising they would need two thousand five hundred of them or more. Therefore, they made various large ones and about sixty small ones. More small ingots could then be poured as required.

Wills needed some medium-sized ones, too, to pay for the land. Plans for his buildings had yet to be drawn up, but no work started until all the gold was 'dealt with'. The final weight of smelted gold was one hundred and sixty-two pounds and a few odd ounces. If they included the specimen bits, another pound could be added. However, these seven chunks were excluded from the total weight. Wills wanted to give his friends more, but they assured him they needed nothing.

The money from the gold would mean they need not apply home for funds. They had pooled resources for the new carriage and horses, for rent and other group purchases. Each already had ample funds for a year or more in the Antipodes.

Wills was determined he would not to be greedy with this bounteous gift from God. He was using it to benefit the community, much as Eddie had done with the £1000 gift from the Duke on his wedding.

The physical activity of crushing the rocks had a revitalising effect on the six Englishmen. They worked hard at the forge with Wills, Eddie, and Mr Tindale and learned to appreciate the effort that went into making a thing as small as a horseshoe. They retired home each evening, energy absolutely sapped, but they were happy. They'd fall into bed exhausted each evening, but each also felt wonderful. Their muscles ached for the first few days; however, by the end of the six weeks, each of them felt rejuvenated.

Thankfully, all the ore had been processed before the heat of summer hit. The many ingots were now safe in Eddie's hidden strongbox.

These were divided into seven parcels. Once done, this gave them time to explore the area. They were seen on daily walks or rides if they wished to go further afield.

Each Friday, Wills and Harry rode westward. Often, one or more of the others joined them. If there were no deliveries, they would ride the twenty-four miles and spend time with their girls. Both had purchased new thoroughbred horses and they would give them their heads for the first few miles until they had worn off their friskiness. They would then walk them for a while, then let them canter over the undulating roadway. They stopped at the various waterholes and rested.

Harry was anxious. For on the trip this weekend, he planned to ask for Vicky's hand. After that kiss, his body still burned when he thought of it. He was nervous but also excited. He was sure Jack would approve, but you never could tell. He had the right to say no. Harry had bought a ring in Sydney, the best he could find. It was a beautiful diamond solitaire. He and Wills shopped together as Wills had not been able to buy one until they had smelted the gold.

Cathy had told him what she would like. She said a small blue sapphire. Wills, however, bought a large blue one surrounded by diamonds. He thought later it may have been too large for her. When he gave it to her, she looked stunned. It was huge on her hand and far too large for her finger, so they decided to go to Sydney and swap it for one she liked. At least she had a ring.

The one she chose had two smaller, lighter blue sapphires and three diamonds, but as it was much cheaper, the jeweller added matching earrings, a collar necklace and a brooch. Then Wills thought about a wedding ring, and the jeweller added that too. She was overwhelmed. He asked Wills if he was interested in also wearing a wedding ring, and it was something that Wills actually wanted to do. So while Cathy was admiring some pearls, he added the two wedding rings and the pearls she was admiring with matching ear-bobs and brooch. The pearls were to be wrapped separately.

Cathy stayed with Caroline Evans and her now-retired seafaring husband, Captain Douglas. She was Mr Tindale's sister, and Eddie had lived with them for five years when they were at school. They were like family. Wills and Harry stayed at The King's Arms hotel.

Wills and Harry were determined to get both girls to do some shopping. They both needed clothing. Jenna was able to persuade her mother to accept money from Eddie and her, although it had been supplied by Wills and Harry. They didn't tell her that. The five travelled to Sydney, and Martha took both girls shopping. Jenna also instructed Martha to buy herself a new dress for the wedding. Martha found two gowns she loved, so brought both; just in case, she said. She had never had a bought dress since arriving in the colony years earlier. Martha had always made their frocks. Cathy, being the youngest, inherited the hand-me-downs. Hence, she had only the thin overcoat. They purchased some beautiful lawn underclothing with lacy trim, such as they had never seen before, and each purchased a new bonnet. They felt like queens when returning on the ferry the next day. They, too, had all stayed with Captain and Mrs Evans.

Wills and Harry had accompanied them to town but left the ladies to shop alone.

Caroline often accompanied them to advise on their choices. She also knew the best shops to patronise. Wills had arranged this and left extra money to cover costs. Mr Iles, the bootmaker, had supplied new ankle boots with laces as well as dancing shoes. They were made from soft kangaroo leather and were beautiful.

~

Keen to see the girls, Wills and Harry left at dawn on Friday morning. They had a delivery. It was small and could be carried in Wills' saddlebags. It was two boxes of special roofing nails for some new sheets of corrugated iron brought out from England. The nails needed to have lead flanges on them and were fiddly to make. It was not a regular stock item, so these had to be first designed, then made. Harry had helped with cutting out the lead washers so they could get away on time.

Only Wills and John knew how important this particular visit was going to be. Harry was keen to be gone. He was on Ginger Mick, his new chestnut gelding, and Wills was on Felix, a dappled grey gelding. They were well matched for weight and speed. Both were thoroughbreds. They were frisky in the cool of the December day. Cara had made tucker bags for them both, and they added these to their saddlebags. Boiled eggs, bread, fruit of some sort and a bottle of ginger ale each. Knowing Cara, there would be more than she told them was in the packets; neither of them cared much.

They walked the horses out of the stable yard, and once mounted, they had to hold them back until they were off Church Street and onto the Western Road. A convict chain gang was already heading out. Others were also up and about; the roads were otherwise quiet. It would be another very hot day. Both wished to cover as much ground as quickly as possible. Once on Church Street, the horses broke into a trot. They were as eager to run as their riders were to let them.

On reaching the top of the hill where the bike race had started, they turned west. Neither wore spurs; both thought they were cruel, but they heeled the horses and took off.

They were neck and neck and covered about two and a half miles in an amazingly short time. The edge off the horse's stamina, they reined in and walked them for a while. Ginger Mick was itching to go, and soon, they settled into a comfortable canter. Both riders enjoyed seeing the distance pass quickly. They had twenty-four miles to cover, and it often took a full day, but they could cover the miles faster at a canter. They rest the horses often, at least at each creek and let them get their breath back.

Oh, the wait was so frustrating for Harry. He wished he had wings. He had not had a chance to see Vicky alone since the race on Monday. They had left early Tuesday morning. He was only able to kiss her hand politely. He groaned. Oh, how he wanted her. Over their early lunch stop at the shady tree with the trough, he broke into the conversation they had been having. "Wills, I have an apology to make to you," he started.

"Huh? Why Harry?" asked Wills

"When you first mentioned Cathy and how you felt, I teased you. I didn't understand. I've never felt like this before. Wills, I'm sorry. Truly, I am," he said.

"Oh, Harry, forget it. I'd seen Eddie when he met Jenna. I know how fast it can hit. I've known Cathy for four years, and she has only treated me the same way as her little brothers. Laughing and teasing with me, but not at all romantic, I was worried. I had fallen for her when I was just fourteen. I was still at school." He swallowed, remembering those feelings of insecurity that he'd felt. "Harry, this was also part of the reason I needed to get away from her. To be near her and not be able to say anything. Oh, Harry, it was agony. There is absolutely no need to apologise."

Harry said, "Thanks, Wills," and then he fell silent for a while. "Wills, you know it is tradition that the older daughters are married first, does that go for here too?"

Wills nodded, "Yes, Harry, that's normal here too."

Harry said, "Oh," then fell silent again.

Wills could see he was thinking, and something was bugging him. Wills said, "Harry, if she says yes, which I'm sure she will, well, let me put it this way: the last family wedding was a triple wedding. We could always pull a double one. If you marry first, then Cathy and I second, well, that is one problem solved. How about it?" He looked over to Harry.

Harry looked amazed. "Seriously, Wills? You'd let us do that? Oh, that would be wonderful. I wonder if Martha and Jack would be okay with that?"

Wills laughed. "I don't see why not, considering Marc was one of the ones in the triple wedding. I don't think have much money, and this was one way we could shield them with them not having to pay," Wills explained. "I think we can spin it so that we can do the same. And I know I'd be honoured to share my wedding day with my brother-in-law."

Harry chuckled, "Two for one. Sounds great. February, eh? So not long to wait. At least if we're engaged, I can kiss her again."

Wills looked over. "You've kissed her? When?"

Harry flushed. "Well, she kissed me, really, after the race on Monday. Oh, Wills, it was the most wonderful feeling," Harry said dreamily. "I've kissed plenty of girls before, but this was so different. Pure. I wasn't always the nice gentleman you think I am. I have had much confessing to do to God." He looked at Wills, shame-face. "Hmm, maybe I shouldn't have admitted that to you." He chuckled. "I didn't always believe as strongly as I do now, Wills."

"Ahh. I believe that changes things." Wills looked at him. "Kissing your loved one is nice, isn't it? Very nice."

"Having said that, let's be gone. I really want another one from her." Harry jumped up and onto Ginger Mick.

Wills was hard on his heels. Again, they let the horses have their heads, and they both took off. They only lasted about a mile this time before the horses dropped to a brisk walk, but it wasn't long before they again settled into the comfortable canter. They arrived at the last creek stop by early afternoon. If they could changed horses a few times, they could have made it in a few hours as a full gallop.

They would only take another hour from there, but the horses needed another rest and a drink. Neither wanted them blown.

Harry kept checking his pocket to make sure the ring was still there.

Felix came over and nuzzled Wills. "I think they are itching to go, too, Harry. We'll take them easy, but let's go."

They were on their steeds and into the final furlong in no time at all. They slowed the horses to a walk as they crossed the bridge. They certainly did not want a strained fetlock this close to their destination. The last few hundred yards felt like miles.

As they turned into the street and saw the inn, then, they saw both girls waiting for them. The horses were stirred into a trot, and they covered the distance quickly.

They were both off their horses and had dropped the reins, leaving the horses to wander. Neither man particularly cared. The girls were each swept into the arms of their lovers. Vicky reached up and drew Harry's head to hers. "Harry, oh Harry, kiss me again," she pleaded.

He lost himself in her deliciousness. She had melted into his arms. After a few moments, she wiggled. "Harry, what's in your pocket? It's digging in."

"Something I have to show your Papa, love." He took it out and placed it in the pocket at the back of his trousers. "Now, where were we?"

She was just about to step back into his arms when Martha appeared. "Why, hello, you two. You're early." She looked at the faces of Vicky and Harry and shook her head. "Just don't let her father catch you," she said quietly and knowingly.

"Sorry, Mama," Vicky replied softly.

"Harry, take the horses to the stables; Jack is out there. Marc's away today. Wills, carry the bags inside." That should do it, thought Martha. Give him a chance to talk if that's what he's planning. They unhitched the saddlebags with clothing and food, and Wills and Cathy carried them inside. Vicky hung back.

"Sorry, Harry, I didn't mean to get you into trouble," she said.

Harry stroked her cheek, "Anything for you, my love, anything. Now let me get rid of these two brutes." Ginger Mick nuzzled him as he was speaking.

She giggled.

Harry walked the two horses to the back of the house. Her welcome kisses were still warm on his lips. Lost in thought, he didn't hear Jack's welcome.

"Something on your mind, lad?"Jackhe asked. "You didn't hear when I spoke, did you?"

"No, sir. Sorry, I was deep in thought," Harry mumbled. Groan, not how I wanted to start, he thought.

"Harry, relax. I won't bite. But I believe after a certain kiss, you may have wanted to speak to me about something, am I correct?" Jack laughed and perched himself on a railing.

"Oh, sir, you saw? I'm so sorry. Can you put it down to the excitement of the moment?" Harry looked apologetic. There was no way he would blame Vicky. He would protect her until his death now.

Jack chuckled. "If you have to think of an excuse, maybe you'd better think of a better one."

Harry looked at the twinkle in his eye. He swallowed. Here goes. Jack was making this easy after all. "Sir, I'd like to ask for Victoria's hand in marriage. If you'll allow me?"

"I know, lad. I could not be more glad. Do you know the reason I made Wills wait at least six months before his marriage? I was hoping that maybe Vicky would be married before Cathy, being the older daughter, and all. Then I saw on that first night how you two both looked at each other. I could tell you were hard hit, but she was the same, lad. She had never even looked at a boy, let alone the way she looked at you. Like it or not, you've met your match, lad. I told you, as did Martha, that once she sets her mind to something, nothing would change it. You're her 'something', lad." Jack smiled.

"Sir, Wills and I were talking about this on the way here. We have a solution. He told me of Marc's triple wedding. Would you consider a double with Vicky and me marrying first, then Wills and Cathy? It's still eight weeks, but I'm not going to change my mind; after what you've said, I don't think she will either." Harry looked at Jack and hoped he'd agree.

"Grand idea! It's what I was hoping. Martha's idea, actually, and I dare not cross her - you'll find out just how strong their ideas can be. Be wise and bend to their wishes, unless it's a matter of life or death. Makes life easier," he chuckled. "Now go find my girl."

"Before I do, sir, I want to say I have come prepared. This isn't a spur-of-the-moment thing. Look." He flicked open the ring box and showed Jack the large diamond ring.

Jack gasped. "Cor. That's some gewgaw. I think she'll like it too. Not too showy but impressive at the same time."

"I found out her size when I asked her to hold my signet ring once. I saw it fitted neatly on her finger." He grinned.

"Off you go, I'll fix the horses. Take her for a walk or something. Wills and Cathy can accompany you." Jack waved him away.

Harry washed his face at the well, then wiped it on the clean towel that was always left for this purpose.

Vicky was waiting for him in the kitchen.

Harry breezed in. "Anyone for a walk? I need to stretch my legs." He'd smiled at her with an eyebrow raised, but walked into the other room. "Vicks, would you like to come? Cathy, Wills?" he bent and stretched, pretending to be stiff.

The girls grabbed their bonnets and were ready in a moment. He'd winked at Wills and knew they'd either take off or drop behind. Either way, he'd be alone with Vicky to propose. They wandered off to the riverbank, headed north towards the ford.

There was a sand flat where they could wander to the edge of the water. There was a stand of she-oaks; they provided some sparse shade in the heat of the December afternoon. He had sat there before today. Harry planned to sit there and watch the birdlife. At least, that is what he said. They crossed the wide dirt road near the bridge and meandered down the grassy edge.

Wills and Cathy walked much faster and had disappeared from sight by the time Harry and Vicky crossed the road. They walked on until he reached the spot he had chosen, and she could sit comfortably in the shade. It also happened to hide them from the bridge and road, so no passing vehicles could see them.

He was wracking his brain to think of some romantic way to propose. He just wanted to take her in his arms and claim her lips again. Being a gentleman can be hard when it goes against all human feelings.

In the end, he held her hand as she sat. She had removed her bonnet and set it aside. She had turned to clear a space, and when she turned back, he was on one knee and held the ring box open in his hand.

"My darling Victoria, would you do me the honour of becoming my wife?" His heart was beating a tattoo. He was sure she would hear it.

"Oh, Henry. Harry, *yes,* of course I will. But if you call me Victoria again…" She sat down and chuckled. She stretched out her arms to him.

He slipped into them and claimed her lips.

They fell back onto the ground.

Her passion contained in the kiss after the race was a taste of heaven. Today was pure joy. They kissed until both were breathless. She lay entwined in his arms. "Oh, Harry, I never want to move again. I'm so very happy." She looked up at him. "Are you sure, though?" she asked. "I am a convict's daughter."

"All I know is that I love you, and I don't care what you are. All I know is now you will be my wife. That alone is enough." He had not yet put the ring on her finger. He sat up and found the dropped box. The ring had fallen out and lay on the grass under them.

After a brief panic, they found it. He kissed her finger before sliding it on.

"It's a perfect fit," she said, looking at the diamond. "How did you know?"

"Remember when you once held this?" He held up his hand with the signet ring.

"Ahh, yes. I put it on because I felt it would be the only time I would wear your ring."

"Not so, my love. I knew from the moment I met you." He sat with his arm around her. She had hers wrapped around his waist. "My love, there is one thing I should mention. Your father requests that we marry before Wills and Cathy." He paused, watching her reaction.

"Oh! Seriously? But that's weeks away," she said.

"Eight, Wills and I were talking about it at the lunch stop today. I had a feeling your father would want the older daughter settled first. However, we think we have a solution."

She looked up at him adoringly. He lowered his head and, again, lovingly kissed her rose-red lips before continuing. "What do you think about a double wedding?" He adored watching the emotions flick across her face.

The realisation they were to be married finally hit. "Could we? Really? Harry, that would be perfect. Oh, Harry." A tear of happiness trickled down her cheek. He kissed it away. Her salty giggle stirred him, and he reached over her and brushed his lips against hers. Hers opened expectantly, and he took possession of them again. She wrapped her arms around his neck and lay back, drawing him down beside her. "I think I'm going to enjoy being married to you," she murmured against his lips. She ran her tongue over his perfectly straight white teeth. It sent shock waves of desire through him.

"Oh, Vicky. Don't." He was finding it hard enough to control himself. "Hold that thought for eight weeks, love. I'm only mortal. If I weren't, I'd drag you off and marry you today." She had no idea what she was doing to him. No idea at all. He groaned and lay back on the grass. "Give me a moment, love."

She curled up next to him, her head resting on his outstretched arm. "Eight weeks. Could we make it sooner, Harry? Do we really have to wait eight whole weeks?" She pleaded with him. She half sat up and leaned on his chest. "Harry, I'm serious. Do we have to wait? What about next month?" She bent down and brushed her lips over his. "I'm serious, Harry."

"As I said, I wish I had a special licence. I could make you mine today. I suggest we wait and talk with your parents. We'll let them know we don't want to wait, but I feel they may not budge. We do not want to be seen to have a hasty marriage. It's not done. Mind you, neither is lying here like this." He rolled her over and flipped her onto her back. He punished her by kissing first her throat and her cheek, working up to her ears and forehead.

She giggled before finally drawing his head down to her own mouth. Her tongue ran again over his teeth and then found his tongue. His hands were now roaming over her bodice. He started to unbutton it. This time, he released his passion, and she responded in kind. Her bodice was open, and his hands were on her breasts. Her groan of desire finally stopped him.

"Oh, Harry, I feel all tingly inside. I want you close, so very close," she said huskily. Her hair was mussed, and her eyes languid with desire. He had nearly forgotten the hold on himself.

He rolled off her and lay face down in the grass. "No," he exclaimed. He would not, could not do that to her. Groaning with desire and willing his body to behave. His breathing was ragged.

"Have I done something wrong, Harry?" she asked as he still had his head resting on the cool grass.

"No, love, I'm just fighting the desire to make you mine fully. Just give me a minute or so. I'm so sorry. Re-button your top, my beloved. I dare not even look again." He was slowly gaining control of his passion. "I won't do that again, my sweet, at least not until we're married. Then watch out." He'd sufficiently gained control. "Darling, I will hug you and kiss you, but I cannot risk being alone with you like this. It only makes it hard for us both."

"I'm sorry, Harry," she looked at him coyly, "Well, I'm not really. Because I look forward to being close to you, if that's how it makes me feel, I look forward to it a lot. Especially that tingly all-over feeling."

He sat up and took her face in his hands. "So do I, my love, so do I." He pulled her up and plonked on her bonnet with a laugh.

They stood embracing, but he did not kiss her again.

Wills and Cathy reappeared further downstream. They had their shoes off and had obviously been paddling. He waved, and they walked towards them. They stopped at the edge of the grass.

Wills helped her clean her feet before they each put on their shoes.

They walked quickly up the embankment.

Harry greeted them with a grin and a thumbs-up.

Cathy and Vicky embraced.

Cathy admired her ring and they hugged again, both joyous for each other that they had found their loves.

Each couple walked back hand in hand.

Harry was overwhelmed with emotion. Just the thought of her sent desire spiralling through him. No, he would not find himself in that position again. He loved her so much. He sighed. He was like a lovesick schoolboy; he grinned at himself. Realising for the first time in ages, he was happy. Really, really happy.

The look on her beaming face melted his heart. She lifted her hand from his arm and took his hand. He rubbed his thumb along the back of hers. Showing her his love with his action. He picked a tuft of grass from her hair, then realised that both girls looked a little grassy. He suggested that they adjust themselves before presenting themselves to their parents. The girls each tucked away wisps of hair from each other's faces and tidied themselves, giggling coyly. They each tied the other's bonnets. Wills brushed Harry's coat and vice versa.

Each was blushing, and looking embarrassed.

This done, they offered their arms to their chosen ladies and walked the remaining distance to the Inn. Each received a final, gentle kiss before entering the inn.

Nick and Calum were the only ones inside. Harry asked them where their parents were. Twelve-year-old Callum pointed towards outside with his thumb.

Fourteen-year-old Nick told him he was being rude and that's not how you treat someone. He then vocalised Callum's reply. "They are out in the stable yard, Harry. Papa is sharpening a scythe, and Maa is putting water on the block for him."

He liked these two lads and could see that he and Wills would be able to assist greatly with their education, amongst other things. Nick was a fabulous mimic. He could copy the sounds of most birds and many people, too. Callum was a fabulous actor, but also loved sport. Both were characters and often had the family laughing at their combined antics.

Harry left the four talking as he ushered Vicky out to the stable yard. He stole a quick kiss in the kitchen. He was seen by Nick, whose jaw dropped. "Did you see that?" Nick asked Wills.

"What?" said Wills innocently.

"He kissed her," he whispered.

"Men do that sometimes, lad. One day, you'll understand," smiled Wills.

"Oh yuck," said Callum. "Well, I'm never going to want girl germs."

Cathy laughed and went to kiss her little brother. "How about mine?" she giggled.

"No! Go away! Yours are worse; they are sister girl germs." He fled into his bedroom, laughing.

Harry opened the door for Vicky. They walked into the courtyard in front of his future parents-in-law. They had walked quietly, not by intention but by happenstance. Harry saw them break apart from an embrace as he crunched over the gravel.

Jack grinned. "Benefits of marriage, lad."

"And one I am looking forward to, sir," he replied as he held up Vicky's hand, showing them the ring.

Martha, showing no sign of embarrassment, hugged Vicky and even kissed Harry on the cheek. "I knew you were the one the moment I saw you. I never even mentioned it to her, either. I just knew." Martha smiled lovingly at her daughter. Smoothing her hair and petting her cheek, she said, "Congratulations to you both!"

"While we're alone, would you mind if we discussed wedding dates?" He looked down at Vicky and smiled. "Sir," he said as he turned to Jack, "We were wondering about marrying in a month rather than waiting for the eight weeks until Cathy and Wills marry."

Martha looked surprised and raised a questioning eyebrow at Vicky.

"No, Maa," she said. "No need to be married that fast, but why do we need to wait?" She looked at her father. "Pa, you said once the mind is made up, act. Well, we've decided. And we decided we didn't want to wait until Wills' parents got home. Harry is thirty-two, and I'm twenty, both much older than they are. It's not like we don't know our own minds."

Harry stood there grinning. "She's taken the words out of his mouth. Summed up my feelings too, sir, ma'am."

Martha stood with her hands on her hips. "Let's get one thing straight, my boy. We're Jack and Martha or Pa and Maa, none of this high-faluting sir and ma'am stuff." She stood like a crewman on a ship.

Harry was abashed, but laughed, "Yes, Maa."

"Good," she said. "Now, weddings, I'd say go for it. Marry as soon as you can. It's hard holding off, but it's worth the wait. Better if you don't have to, though. There, I've said my piece." She bustled off, heading back into the kitchen.

"See, lad, never argue with them once they have made up their minds. Looks like we have a wedding in a month or so then." Jack hugged his favourite middle daughter, as he always called her. "I think you have a good one there, love. A man after my own heart." Then he turned to Harry. "Mind you, do the right thing by her. She's special, is my Vicky."

"Very special, sir, I mean Jack." Harry drew Vicky to him. "Very special indeed. How about it, love? I wonder if a parson could marry us out here? I believe Reverend Mr Clarke sometimes takes services. I'm sure we'll arrange something. I'll ask around tomorrow."

"Oh, Harry, I'd love that. I'd love that so much." She melted into his arms.

"Nuff of that," Jack said with a laugh. "You'll find it hard enough to keep your hands off each other until the knot is tied. Trust me in this: we have seven children. Don't make it harder for yourselves than it already is. Harry, it's as well you're a man of faith too, as you are honouring not just her but God too. Don't put yourselves in situations where your emotions run away with you. It can be hard to stop. Vicks, don't push him. Do you understand what I mean?" He looked directly into her eyes.

"Yes, Papa, just kissing him makes my head spin. Indeed, we have come to the same decision. I love him, Papa, it's why we want to marry as soon as we can." She drew Harry's arm that was around her, and lifted his hand and kissed his palm. "We'll wait. Won't we, Harry?"

"Yes, love, we will," Harry had the courtesy to look embarrassed when Vicky said they had already kissed. He smiled adoringly at her. Yes, she'd have the Duchesses eating out of her hands. Her golden eyes danced with joy and shone with love. She still had a wisp of hair out of place; he gently lifted the light brown curl and tucked it behind her ear. Jack stood watching the gentle act and knew his girl would be loved and cared for by this man.

Jack was content. She had made a wise choice. He smiled realising all three girls would have titles of sorts.

~

Wills and Harry finally made the delivery to Guy and Martha Manning at Orchard Hills on the return trip, then rode quickly back to Parramatta. Harry called into the church on his way back from the Inn and left a message for Reverend Bobart that he wished to make an appointment.

On Monday morning, Bessie, Reverend Bobart's maid, arrived with a letter to ask him to come at ten o'clock.

At precisely ten o'clock, Harry was at the door knocking. Bessie showed him into the Minister's office. They were well known to each other, as Harry and his friends often did the Bible readings in church on Sunday mornings. Their voices carried, and the congregation could hear them clearly. John's especially.

He was greeted and invited to sit. Harry explained his quest and wanted to know if it were possible for someone to marry them at Emu Plains. "Sir, we'd like the Banns read as soon as possible and be married in a month or whenever possible." He watched as Mr Bobart checked his diary.

Harry went on to explain, "Mr and Mrs Turner then have to

prepare for a second larger wedding, here, for William and Cathy's nuptials. We would like to have a small family service, but some of their friends would like to come. They want Vicky to be married before Cathy. We thought that we could have it out at Emu Plains, where the new church is to be built. We could wait and have a double wedding, but we'd rather marry sooner. Her parents are also in favour of this."

Reverend Bobart was friends with Reverend Mr Clarke and was sure he'd be honoured to do the service out there. He would book it in. He could manage three weeks rather than four if they wanted to, as he had a Mattins service soon.

Reverend Bobart sat musing and thinking aloud. "I could do the first reading tomorrow, with the next one Sunday..." He was not addressing his comments to Harry. He finally looked at Harry. "Today's the 15th, Mattins. Tomorrow is week one; they could be read again on the 21st, then the 28th, so the wedding could be anytime after the 28th of December. Even that afternoon, but the next day would be better. I'm seeing Clarke tomorrow, so I'll talk to him then. I'll have already done the banns once by then. It's stretching it a bit, but it's how we fitted Gracemere in. Shh." He lay back in his chair. The law says for four weeks. He grinned. "It should be Sundays, but I know you both. Now, where's Bessie with my tea and cookies? Wait until you try them."

At that moment, Bessie knocked and brought in a tea tray and a plate of freshly baked biscuits. "You must try them," he said as he handed the plate to Harry. "Wattle seed and honey. I don't know where she gets the stuff from, but it's delicious."

Harry took one and, like Eddie, some three years before, exclaimed how delicious it was. Harry took his leave and hurried home to pen a letter to Vicky. Then he went to bed.

Roseneath
O'Connell St,
Parramatta
15 Dec 1845

Arms of Australia Inn
Emu Plains
My Darling Vicky,

I have seen Reverend Bobart; by the time you receive this, the Banns will have already been read once. We are to be married on Monday, 29 December at Emu Plains, hopefully by Reverend Clarke, who had directed Wills to his mineral find, or if not by Reverend Bobart himself.

The day cannot come fast enough for my liking.

I was thinking about a honeymoon. You mentioned you had not spent much time in Sydney. There is much to see, and I thought mayhap you would like a week or more in the metropolis? If this is not your desire, your wish is my command. If you wish to change the date, please notify me as soon as possible. The rider will await a reply.

> *Your loving, future husband,*
> *Harry.*

Harry had failed to announce his return. He had eaten with Wills at the big house, Eddie's place, as they called it. He arrived home, washed and went to bed. He was drained, both emotionally and physically, but happy. He was still asleep when the others went riding the next morning, and he would gone when they returned.

John was on tenterhooks. Had Harry been refused? Did he actually even ask?

When Harry emerged, the smile he had on his face said it all. The stress and frown lines had gone. He had shed the years of turmoil in India, the death of his parents and the rejection by his brother. John again thought back to that meeting at White's in London. Harry had said to him, "John, I have to go. I need to go. I feel I'm being called." He would not been able to settle after his experiences. Looking back, John could see that each of them was traumatised. Losing a close friend through a betrayal of identity. It was why they all had to leave India.

Sitting in the kitchen, John also thought of the meeting with Wills that fateful day in Parramatta. Was it already over a year ago? It, too, was God-ordained. They arrived as six hurting souls. He knew the day in Hartley when they had been led to the quartz outcrop that the first cracks in their armour appeared. The first night around the campfire, again at Hartley, when they talked. The baring of souls occurred more and more each night, chipped away a little at a time, and then there were the weeks in the outback. The first time they saw the brolgas dance, the final cracks broke the souls wide open. Chunks of their self-imposed armour had fallen. They stood in awe, their mouths agape. They had been woken before dawn by a cacophony of birds. They had struggled out from under their blankets. They watched as wave after wave of birds took off for the daily foraging. Then it happened. Wills was standing on the seat of the cart, and he just pointed. They all turned to see two grey, velvety birds dancing and pirouetting to each other.

Just thinking back to it now, his heart soared. It was like setting the worries of their world free. Each slowly released their burdens. No, they would not ever forget those experiences, but they knew now that they could cope. They surrender their burdens to God. John thought about how important Wills was to them. His simple question of, 'But what do you do for others?' had challenged each one. They had ignored his original question, but when he asked again, they all knew they must answer. By turning their problems to God and deciding to work for good rather than gratification, each had their entire attitude to life changed. All this flashed through his mind as he waited for Harry. He emerged from his room, letter in hand.

"Hi, John, sleep well? I did. I'm on top of the world. Oh, and by the way, we're getting married on December 29th." He turned to walk away and then returned. "Oh, and John, as my cousin, I'd be honoured if you would stand up with me. You know, best man and all."

"What? Of course. Wait… what?" John was stunned. "In December? It's December already. How?" He was flabbergasted.

Harry chuckled. "She doesn't want to wait, John, and neither do I. Wills and I had discussed a double wedding, and I was happy enough with that, but it wasn't quick enough for Vicky. First, Banns are being called today, so that's week one. Then again, on Sunday, and the week after, is the 28th. So Monday, the 29th, is the earliest we can marry. Reverend Mr Clarke is going to be asked to do it. How appropriate, eh?" He waved the letter. "And this is to let Vicky know. We're planning to have it at Emu Plains, on the site where the new church is to be built, up on the hill. I might even consider making a donation towards its construction. We'll probably be living nearby in the fullness of time. So I'd like to start as I mean to go on." He turned to walk to the door. "You know, that's something my mother always used to say to me. I'd forgotten."

The Harry he'd known all his life was back, full of confidence and life, and oh so happy, oh so very happy. "Harry, Harry, slow down," John said.

"No, John, I can't. Grab your hat; we have to catch the mail. I'll tell you as we walk." Harry slapped his hat on his head and opened the door.

John knew that if he didn't hurry, he would go without him. He grabbed a hat, but he didn't think it was even his and walked out with his cousin.

"Harry, tell me what happened." John was having a bit of a hard time keeping up. Harry was certainly in a hurry.

"Well, we arrived. I asked Jack; he said yes. Then we talked about dates. We initially agreed on a double in February. Jack and I didn't take Vicky and her wishes into consideration. Well, Vicks and I went for a walk down the riverbank, and I asked her, John. After she said yes, I kissed her. Oh, how I kissed her." He paused, remembering the desire from them both. "Anyway, we talked about dates too, and she was a bit non-committal. I was surprised, but thought I'd wait however long she needed. That apparently wasn't the problem. She couldn't work out why we should have to wait, as we're thirty-two and twenty when the others are only seventeen and eighteen, well, both eighteen now. She, um, well … after this time, she kissed me; well, it was mutual, and we got a tad carried away." He paused when John coughed. "No, not that far. She decided that she wanted to get married as soon as possible and very quietly. Suits me down to the ground. I never liked the society St George's Church weddings in London; they were far too big. Too much *hoo-ha*. So I saw Reverend Bobart this morning; he's making all the arrangements for Monday, 29th December, at Emu. End of the story, but the beginning of my new life." Harry finally took a breath. "Oh, John, I'm so happy. I can't describe it to you. Do you remember the feeling of watching the birds out there? Do you remember how you felt? How your heart drained of impurity and the soul felt again? It felt, well, clean, fresh, new. Well, I'm whole again now, too. I have a purpose in life. I'll have a home, this wonderful new country, and I have Vicky. A reason to live, and Vicky is only part of it."

John stole a look at his cousin's face. His eyebrow cocked.

Harry chuckled. "Okay, she's a big part, but you should hear some of the things she wants us to do. A new school or two, the church, of course, and then there's Wills' Emporiums and warehouse and the jobs that will bring. Then, when the gold comes, that will mean many more needs, accommodation, in particular, so more inns and accommodation houses. She wants to build a new accommodation block for Marc at the back of their inn. Might have to fight with Wills for that one. We might go half-half for that."

He had not let John get a word in edgeways. Harry's excitement was tangible.

They made it to the Post Office. He asked, "Could you have a rider send this? The letter is important. Could they please await a reply?" He paid a lot extra, but the letter was on the way.

Only now did he turn to John. "What do you think, John?"

Finally, John was to get a word in. "I'm thrilled, Harry, truly. If you're happy, that's all I want." John slapped his cousin on the back. "Harry, I was thinking back to White's. Do you remember what you told me? God was calling you here."

Harry nodded. "I did say that, didn't I? I had felt I needed to come. It's as simple as that. The fact that the others joined us was a blessing. It wouldn't have been half as fun without them. But, John, we each needed to come. Think back a year. We were mere hollow shells. We're each God-fearing men. But we were each seeking our own pleasure and not much of the God-fearing. I look back to myself of last year. I see how shallow I was. Mind you, I feel that all is not yet washed clean for some of us."

John agreed. "Yes, I can see I've changed too. I'll certainly live a different life when I return. If I return, Harry."

It was Harry's turn to be surprised. "What's this? Are you thinking of staying, too?"

John stopped. "Harry, I think I'll stay for a while, possibly a few years, before I go home. I want to see these buildings done, too. I think I can help here, as well as keep learning. Will you let me?"

"Let you? Oh, John, that would be fabulous." Harry did a jump for joy. "Not very gentlemanly," he chuckled. "Oh, John, Vicky and I will love having you around too. Pity she doesn't have another sister," he laughed. "That's made my day." He slapped him on the back, and nearly sent him flying.

John laughed.

At four o'clock in the afternoon the following day, Harry was sitting outside the post office. He expected the rider to return with a confirmation of the date. Harry was sitting in the hot sun, but he wasn't going to leave until they closed at five. After three-quarters of an hour, he had to wait until the rider arrived and handed him a letter. He tore open the seal.

Arms of Australia Inn

Emu Plains

Tuesday 16 December 1845

7 pm

My Dearest, Darling Harry,

You will make me the happiest woman in the colony on 29 December. Maa and Papa both agree the date is suitable. So, on that day, I will become your wife. Oh, how wonderful that sounds. I do not care who marries us as long as it is legal. As to your idea of a honeymoon in Sydney, again, as long as I'm with you, I do not care. Just keep me close. Send my love to all your friends. I hope they won't mind sharing the house with a female.

I wish I could send myself in this missive, but be assured you are in my heart (which is nearly bursting with happiness).

Until Friday, my love,

Yours forever,

Vicky

Harry took the letter directly to Reverend Bobart's office. He said hew would be there until five o'clock. Hopefully, he would have time to speak to Reverend Clarke.

Reverend Bobart was waiting. A plate of his favourite biscuits sat on his desk. Harry knocked and walked in.

"Good evening, sir. The answer is in the affirmative. The family is very happy with the date." He showed him the letter, then pocketed it. He no longer stood on ceremony with this man. He respected him for all he was achieving; from teaching, ministering to convicts and free alike and equally, arranging for the waifs and orphans to be educated. He stood as a beacon of faith in this un-Godly town. For such a young man, he had already achieved a lot. Harry stood in awe of his untiring work, and he had waited for him. Harry worked out that he would only be ten years younger than the Reverend gentleman and had as yet achieved nothing. But that would change. "Sir, I am honoured for the time you have spared me," Harry said.

"I waited because I want a word with you." He paused before continuing. "Harry, in the time I have known you, nearly six months, I have seen a change in you and your heart. All for the good, lad." Reverend Bobart looked at the concerned man seated across from him. "I don't know that it has just been Vicky Turner's influence, but I just wanted you to know I have noticed. You now seem to have shed the stresses you had when you arrived."

Harry looked at the man sitting across from him. A puzzled look sat on Harry's face.

Reverend Bobart continued, "Yes, I saw you all here that first Sunday you came. I didn't get to speak to you, but I did notice you all. Haunted was the word that comes to mind. Now you seem at peace." He didn't wait for a reply. "I never ask a person's story. They will tell if they want me to know." He took a biscuit and just waited. He sat back in his chair and nibbled on his treat.

Harry bit into one and, for a moment or two, sat thinking of the past months. He recounted the reason for the six of them coming. "Sir, our time in India and the trauma we had encountered, the poverty and horrific things we had experienced over there. It had haunted us all. None of us could settle; we tried, oh how we tried." Harry paused. "While I was away, my parents died. On my return, my brother informed me I no longer had a home with him. It had been a year since my return, and although all of us had tried to settle, none had. God had manoeuvred us all to be at the one spot in the one night in London."

He told Reverend Bobart everything. Then he added Wills' part, and the challenge he issued. "Sir, the scales have finally fallen off our eyes when we saw the beauty and freedom of the dance of those brolgas. Who would have thought that something so simple would tear away the last vestiges of armour we had built around ourselves?" It was a question that needed no answer.

Mr Hobart smiled. God, however, performed these miracles daily, all of which went unnoticed by any human.

Harry continued. "Sir, we felt like eavesdroppers on a private conversation the first time we saw those dancing birds. We stayed for days to get the high from each performance." Harry did not elaborate to him about the gold, but added, "God blessed us more."

They had all decided that they would, reveal all to Reverend Clarke. They would tell him everything. Wills said he was going to give £1000 ingot to Reverend Bobart, for whatever he wanted to use it for. He was going to drop it in the collection plate with an anonymous note to for him to take it to Harry Moffatt to cash it in. He chuckled at the thought. Reverend Clarke was to get the same from Wills as a thank you.

Harry then got to meeting Vicky. He paused and thought back to the initial look. He had sobbed before John came out. Overwhelmed and gutted at the feelings of inadequacy and unworthiness. He was stunned that a woman could bring him to his knees with a single look. She did, but while on his knees, he rededicated his life to God. He repented of his past sins and lusts. Now, he knew they could and would walk the next road together.

Mentally, he had cut ties with England when his brother cast him off. It took until this conversation with John before he realised how final that was. This was now home. No turning back, no regrets.

He took out his watch. Half past five. He gasped. "Oh, sir, I'm so sorry I have kept you far too long," Harry said with regret.

"Harry Harlow, time getting to know yourself is never wasted time. Now you can move on with a clear conscience." Reverend Bobart spoke gently and with love. "Go with confidence, my boy. I'll see you on the 29th as I doubt you'll be here for the next two weeks. I've missed you over the last couple of months when you have not been here, but I understand, absolutely. Never hesitate to talk. I'm always here if you need me." He stood to shake Harry's hand. "Even if Clarke can do the service, Elizabeth and I are both coming. We wouldn't miss this for anything. We'll leave after service on Sunday and camp on the way. We need a break, and this will be like a mini holiday for us too. I feel there may be a caravan of wagons heading west that weekend."

The Journey from London

"Make sure those harnesses are tied up tightly, please. I don't want the children falling overboard," Ned said to Nanny.

"Yes, sir, I have double-checked each one," she said.

The weather on the ship had been inclement. Foul would be more apt for some sections. The children had been confined to the tiny cabin for weeks. How they managed, they didn't know, but they had, with each taking turns to entertain them. Even the *Les Grande Dames* assisted. It turned out the twins loved the made-up stories the two older ladies told about their toys coming to life. The children would sit still for hours listening to the adventures their toys were supposedly having while the children slept. To add to the story, the toys were in unusual places when the children woke.

They called them Suze, Ned's Mother, Granny One, and, Elle, Charles' mother, was Granny Two. The ladies would take turns in weaving the stories and adventures the toys would take in travelling overland to get to New South Wales to be with the children. Both ladies had this planned well before they left and hidden said unseen favourite toys in their luggage. They would be sitting on the children's beds, awaiting the children on their arrival. All they now had to do was occupy them. Day after day, the adventure continued. It was kept for when the children had driven everyone else crazy. Ned would then arrive apologetically with said angelic-looking monsters. Their large blue eyes and blonde curls gave them an ethereal appearance, which belied the behaviour. Liam, another fair-haired angel, had started crawling. He had not yet managed to climb up on anything. However, it would not be long now.

Finally, the weather had improved enough for an outdoor expedition. Ned had Chip tightly in hand; for being an absconder, he trusted no one else with his son. Sarah was in Nanny's arms, and Christina had Liam. Ned checked each child's leather harness and made sure the handle loop was on the wrist of the carer. He paused and offered a prayer of safety for his offspring. They left the cabin.

Christina asked for the cabins to be fully aired in their absence. The portholes were thrown open, as were doors, communicating doors and the stewardess and their maids went in and gave the cabins a complete clean. They had not been able to air them for weeks, and the air was stale.

They had seen very little of the two young ladies travelling in one of the two other first-class cabins. An older lady was travelling in the second cabin but was obviously with them. Christina had been introduced to them by the captain on boarding. However, she missed their names, such as Liam, at that moment. She had expected to see more of them, but the weather worsened soon after leaving port. Because the family group ate in their own cabin, they did not meet at meals. It was not until the sun emerged and the sea quieted that they emerged white and unwell.

Christina's compassion took over. She introduced her family and waited, hoping they would realise she had not heard their names. Mrs Browne was still prostrated with sickness. She had been as soon as she stepped on board, the ship was still tied to the wharf.

Miss Amelia Stather and Miss Fiona Moreton. "We're travelling with our chaperone, Mrs Browne, to a place called Parramatta. We're visiting our aunt, Mrs William Clarke."

The girls, cousins in their twenties, were considered 'on the shelf' as they had both reached the age of twenty-five and did not want to venture to London for another season. Being adventurous, they hit upon a scheme of visiting their Aunt Maria Clarke in the Antipodes. Both were of independent means.

Charles' ears pricked up. He knew Reverend Clarke well and had occasion to meet Mrs Maria Clarke as well. "I know this gentleman well. He has been teaching our sons at The King's School."

Christina took both young ladies under her wing. They recovered quickly from their seasickness and were soon playing with the children in the cabins. This gave the others a wonderful respite, and for the first time in weeks, Ned and Christina were able to spend some quality time together. Thus diverted, the young ladies also were not ill again.

Most days were now spent together in the group sitting room, discussing life in the colony.

The final weeks on board were a direct trip across the Indian Ocean. They had rounded the Cape of Africa and were now on a continuous Eastward passage with the wind behind them. The seas were kind, and everyone now had their sea legs. Even the apologetic chaperone, Mrs Browne, finally emerged from her cabin.

Amelia and Fiona were often on the floor playing with the three cherubs. Christmas was still a few days away. It would now be celebrated with their new friends.

Emu Plains Wedding

Christmas Day was a Thursday. Everyone was torn about where to spend Christmas. Finally, Martha declared they would have Christmas in Parramatta. Harry and Wills greeted the family on their arrival. They were staying in various places, but mostly with Eddie and Jenna. The boys would be with the men at Roseneath. Harry decided to give them some time away from being the young brothers, and it also gave him some more time to get to know his future brothers-in-law. They were interesting young men, and he wanted to see if he could discover their interests. He planned to help them into a better life. How exactly he had not yet worked out, education certainly, if not full apprenticeships.

The Turners' covered cart rolled in at eight pm the night before Christmas. Harry and Wills were waiting on the fence for them to arrive. Both were anxious that the Turners would arrive safely. They wished the family were already there.

Finally, they heard the rumble of wheels slowing and turning into Phillip Street. The final minutes of waiting were almost the worst. They both laughed that Jack was intentionally driving slower than normal, only to find out later that it's exactly what he did. Vicky and Cathy told them on arrival. "Harry, Pa slowed right down when he turned into Church Street. He's so mean," Vicky explained mournfully.

"I kept asking him to hurry," said Cathy plaintively. She was already in Wills' arms.

Harry greeted everyone and handed Martha down from her front seat. Then turned to assist Vicky. He reached up for Vicky, and she leaned down to him. She slid into his embrace with her arms wrapping around his neck. He drank in her delicious, clean, lemony scent and bent to claim her lips.

The two couples stood entwined for some minutes until Calum's exclamation of "Oh yuck" broke them both apart. The four stood laughing.

Eddie and Jenna looked at each other, remembering the sadness of parting and the joy of reunion. It was four years ago. Their love and bond were still as strong. Lily sat on her mother's hip. She gurgled and bounced as she waved. Her fair baby hair had darkened a little, as had her eyes, which now looked like they could eventually be the amber colour of her mother; at the moment, they were dark blue but were changing.

Martha and Jack went up to their room, and the boys went to Luke's for a wash. Ed and Jenna waited for both other couples to finish their greeting and say hello. Eddie bent towards Jenna, "I haven't said a proper hello since I arrived home from work." He lifted Jenna's chin and gently kissed her.

Lily stroked his cheek as he did so. "Da da da," she said.

He gasped.

Their daughter had not made any word noises before this. Her doing so at such a time brought joy to them both. Eddie kissed her forehead, too. He gathered them both into his arms and gently cradled them both to his muscular chest. Jenna snuggled closely, as did Lily.

Eventually, all three couples joined Cara in the sitting room. Rather than a full sit-down meal, there were plates full of tiny pies, bacon and egg slice squares, and other food where they could help themselves. There were also platters full of sandwiches and biscuits, followed by a Christmas fruit cake. Most of this was devoured by the three boys, but not before the others had eaten their fill. Luke was un-fillable.

Marc and Milly had decided at the last minute not to come, as they had very little time on their own since their marriage. They asked if they could be excused, and they planned a mini holiday with no one there but them. Jenna was initially upset as she loved her big brothers. Alex had gone to the Parkers as Mary had invited him weeks ago. They had finally become engaged in November when she had turned eighteen. It seemed they had been together forever, as Alex had declared his intentions when she was only fourteen. He was only her father's apprentice back then. Now, he co-owned the saddlery with Mr Parker. He was the son they never had.

Sometime earlier, Eddie had spoken to Alex about Wills's plans for him to supply goods for the Emporium out that way. Eddie, Alex and Ben Parker had sat and gleaned through the list of local tradesmen they knew working in the area who they could invite to sell their items in-store. Some may refuse due to the percentage taken, but the price increase of those same items covered any losses that would otherwise be made. Alex had encouraged many of the locals to participate in this venture. He was integral for the Emu Plains Emporium to work. Mr Parker also did his bit. He knew that if he gave a glowing report to others, they would join in.

The payment of the various land claims and purchases had finally been completed, paperwork was signed and titles registered. Building plans that had been prepared, and could now be started. Wills had been so impatient. He had already commissioned the felling of trees and sawing of the timbers required. More importantly, the purchase of the large area of land on the Western Road just out of Parramatta had finally been processed. Wills had paid for it with his share of the fine gold dust. His one sixth share of the dust had been twenty five ounces of gold. This was also £10 per ounce.

The Emporium Warehouse would have a small Tea Room for those purchasing goods and a shop-front for wholesale purchases. This would become the main stock room or warehouse for all three Emporiums. It was on this land that Wills had been stockpiling some of the sandstone building materials. Other building material, like the timber, were at Eddie's in the back yard, along with the assorted huge logs for beams, crates of shingles, sawn planks, and sand-stock convict-made bricks.

It all stood in readiness for transport to the new building site. Wills and Harry had planned to get started on the building after their honeymoons. Wills had planned to stay in Gracemere Cottage for the first few days and then head into Sydney. However, the arrival of his parents would have meant they would not be alone. So they would now go directly to Sydney on the afternoon ferry. Harry and Vicky had planned for a week in Sydney but were going to spend the first few days in a wagon down by the river, then slowly head mosey towards town. Neither was in a rush to cut the time short. Both just wanted the weddings to be over. If things changed, none of them were too stressed. They had all learned to "let go and let God," and it had become a sort of motto for them all.

The Christmas service was help on the lawn of the church, as it had been for some years. The ladies were sitting under their new Christmas parasols and sharing the shade with their loved ones. Reverend Bobart gave a brief children's talk about Jesus loving them, followed by a full sermon on the meaning of the coming of the Christ Child. The service over, the two families and the six English friends returned to the inn, rather than to Bramblemere Close for drinks. Cara had given instructions that no one was to appear until she sent Moira for them.

Soon after noon, Moira walked sedately down the hill to the Inn and calmly announced. "Mam has sent me down for ye all. Christmas is now ready."

Charlie hoisted the eldest of his two-year-old twins, Teddy, on his shoulders, then John picked up his namesake, and they walked off. The three five-year-old cousins, Bertie and Liza's son, Albie; and the twins, Ned and Tina also wanted "up-up" rides, so Eddie lifted his son and Harry lifted Tina, and Bertie took his son Albie for a piggy back ride. Tim and Anna's two-year-old son, Billy wanted to walk. As it was hot, he'd tired quickly so Tim hoisted him for a ride as well. Amongst much giggling the children's shouts of glee brought smiles to everyone's lips. The merry party all headed to Bramblemere Close for Christmas luncheon.

Cara and the girls had added a long trestle table to the side of the room. They had decorated both tables the same.

Charlie, as the eldest family member, sat at the head of one with his wife and twins. Eddie sat at the foot with Jenna and had one of their twins either side of her. Liza and Tim with Billy between them. Anna and Bertie sat opposite them, with Albie wedged between them. Wills sat at the head of the other table with Luke and Cathy, either side of him. The rest of the Turners and Wills' friends fitted in where they could. Cara, Paddy, and the girls served them and then joined in the festivities.

They had just sat down when a scuffle and voices were heard in the kitchen. Paddy jumped up and went to investigate. He walked back in closely, followed by two recently washed lads of youthful age. It was Shéamus, aged thirteen, and the Connors youngest child, Liam, eleven. Everyone wiggled up on the bench seats and made room. The boys could rarely get away from milking duties at the government dairy where they worked, but they had risen early and worked quickly, doing all the preparations before milking rather than after it. They only had a few hours before the afternoon milking. They thought they would surprise their parents.

"Oi, we didn't expect a bang-up feast like this tho'," said Shéamus.

"We'd come to see Mam and Pop," chipped in Liam.

"Boys, you know you are always welcome," said Eddie. "That was part of the deal I made with your folks. There is always room at our table for more."

"Thankee, Mr Ed, dats real kind o' you. We love comin' too, cos the food good, in't it, Liam? We knows the cook." Shéamus winked at his mother.

Cara blushed. "Mr Eddie, Mrs Jenna I jus' wanna thankee so much for letting us even eat wiv your fambily. We did fall on our feet when Major Grace, sorry the Duke, hires our Maryanne as his maid." She stopped talking and took a bite of her home-cooked meal.

Paddy just sat beaming. "Its went through my's head I'm a convict sitting sharing Christmas with a Viscount and his fambily."

Luke laughed. He thought, Paddy would probably have died and gone straight to heaven if he knew who Wills' English friends were. Eddie quickly rectified that.

"Two actually, Paddy, Edmund is one as well," Eddie chuckled. "Wait until the next lot arrives. You'll have another one, plus two Countesses and two Duchesses, an Earl and Duke."

Paddy's face drained of colour. "Cor blimey," was all he managed to say. His eyes were so large, Ed wondered if they'd fall out.

On Board

Christmas on board the *Eagle* was a joyous affair.

Food was a little different, as the captain had extra rations and had stocked up with fresh fruit and vegetables in Cape Town.

These were brought out and shared among the group. Little Liam had his first taste of solid food.

Nanny had pureed everything up until now. The onboard cook, though certainly not a chef, had managed to bake some potatoes in dripping and Liam grabbed some from Ned's plate and stuffed it in his mouth. His eyes flew open as he reached out again. He liked it and wanted more.

Nanny tried to remove it from his hands, but he was too quick for her, shoving two more lumps in his mouth at the same time. He grinned with squishy potato oozing down his chin.

Ned chuckled. Solid food was now to be added to Liam's diet.

The weather held fine.

After their joyous Christmas meal, they went for a constitutional walk or two around the poop deck.

The children had all fallen asleep, and they were left in the care of a ship's maid.

This freed up the adults, including Nanny and the two Gracemere maids.

Ned and Charles walked together behind all the ladies.

Amelia and Fiona set the pace, followed by Suze and Elle, *Les Grande Dames*, and then Sal and Christina walked close to their husbands.

Chapter 9 Shipmates

*T*he Turners returned home early the morning after Christmas.

They had much to get ready, even for a small wedding.

Charlie sent some cider, ale and glasses back with them.

They had two days to prepare for the new arrivals for the wedding. Everyone was bringing food.

Harry was paying for everything else. He had left some money with Jack.

Sunday morning, after the church service in Parramatta, a caravan of wagons departed town and headed west. The Bobarts were in one. The three English wagons were filled. Charlie and the family in the Lockleys wagons, Eddie and Jenna had their shop wagon as well as a large pile of sails to use as awnings for the wedding.

Tim's parents had lent their wagon to Liza and Bertie. Each wagon was loaded with food, drinks and bedding.

Jack told them they had scythed a section of grass in the holding yard behind the barn. So all the wagons could stay together. It was a full moon, so even though they would arrive late, there would be enough moonlight to see the road.

They watered all the horses at the usual trough stop at Rooty Hill. They didn't stop long, as they were already running late. Harry wanted to mount up on Ginger Mick and take off. However, he knew he would not be allowed to see Vicky anyway, so he made himself be patient. Instead, Ginger Mick hadn't even come, as he didn't like pulling a vehicle of any sort. Only the slow wagon horses were in harness. Harry was sitting next to John on their dawdling wagon.

Martha had told him even when he arrived, she would not let

Vicky out to greet him. He was so impatient for the wedding.

The slow-moving caravan finally crossed the bridge to Emu Plains. It was sunset, but the moon was so bright the cavalcade of wagons proceeded without hindrance.

The noise made by the wagons on the bridge gave the family enough notice they had finally arrived. The yelling and cheering brought all of the family outside except Vicky. However, she had told Harry to watch for her hand in the window. She made a heart with her fingers and pointed to him. He could not see her face, she was behind the curtains. He placed his hand on the glass and she matched it with hers from inside.

They were finally to be married on the morrow.

Martha saw their action and shooed him away. He went around the back with the wagons and readied himself for the night.

After a long day on the road, everyone went to bed soon after arrival. They had stopped and eaten on the road. A few slept in the barn in hammocks and the rest, slept in their wagons. The children were used to camping out. It was the only breaks anyone took.

Eddie and Jenna returned frequently to the site of their honeymoon on the banks of the river at Windsor. They often took the children, therefore the three children were asleep before they had even arrived at Emu Plains. This, however, probably meant they would be up early.

Sure enough, Lily woke when the dawn chorus started. She then woke everyone else.

The day dawned bright and sunny. However, that meant it was going to be another hot one.

Reverend Clarke and his wife were the only ones yet to arrive. They had to come the furthest.

Wills was itching to talk to him about the gold and introduce him to his friends. Reverend Clarke had been placed at Dural for the Christmas Services but they were on the way to a new area of work in Campbelltown. Wills had not been able to meet up with him since his return in June. Any spare time Reverend Clarke had was spent at the new Museum in Sydney with Dr Holmes and John Evans.

John Evans, Mr Tindale's nephew, worked assistant curator, although Doctor Holmes oversaw his work. Occasionally when he remembered, John would put pen to paper and write to Eddie.

Wills was, therefore, able to sort of track Reverend Clarke's movements. Harry had yet to meet him, but when Reverend Bobart suggested he do the wedding, he grabbed the offer. He was instrumental in how all this had happened.

By mid-morning, the Clarkes wagon was spotted crossing the bridge. He was greeted by a group of happy people. He recognised Eddie, Wills and Luke, having taught them at The King's School. Wills particularly was a favourite of his as he listened to his stories and was a good student. Luke was studious but had never seemed inspired by the clergyman's interest in minerals.

Reverend Clarke was always looking for more mineral deposits. He had discovered there were traces of tin in some local areas in the Sydney basin. He walked with his eyes fixed on the ground. Every rock and pebble spelled out a history of something for him.

Wills greeted them on arrival and led their horses around to the back. Their wagon would join the rest from the earlier cavalcade. Some would leave straight after the wedding; some would stay another night.

One wagon that would leave after the wedding was the one the bride and groom would travel in. Vicky had decided to go to Sydney but only after their first few days in a wagon. Harry was stunned. No other lady he knew wanted to spend time roughing it in a wagon.

The wedding was to be just before noon in the back yard rather than on the church hill. It was too hot to be out in the open. Many of the Turners friends and the rest of the family had arrived early, just after morning chores.

Everyone was busy setting up the shade sails that Eddie had brought with him. They did this before it got too hot, and hot it got.

Martha came out of the house giggling, "Look, Jen. You know it's hot when the wax candles melt. I'm used to the tallow one's flopping, but look." She held up a wax candle that had flopped into the holder. She lay them down and straightened them. Hopefully, they'd still be usable when they cooled down.

The mothers had all taken the children down to the river and sat them in the shade on the edge of the water. Lily loved it and splashed with glee. Jenna looked around, lifted her skirts, and sat in the cool water with the children. Her dress was around her waist. "Oh, nice," she said to Milly, who had done the same.

"Marc would be horrified if he knew. Still, he doesn't have to wear long dresses and petticoats," Milly said. Her cheeks were nearly as red as her hair. "My drawers were wet with perspiration anyway," she chuckled.

The children were all soaked. They had all been told to keep their clothing and hats on, but they were cool. They would be dry by the time they walked back. The children wanted to stay and were only tempted out of the water by the promise of a return trip later.

It was time. Harry was champing at the bit.

Vicky was nervous. She had not even been able to sit outside in the cool. Jack had let her wait in the cellar as it was much cooler than even outside. There was just time for Jenna to change Neddie's dirty shorts and Lily's nappy.

Jenna arrived back from the wagon as everyone was gathering. The sails provided a blessing of shade.

The barometer inside the inn read over one hundred degrees.

A cider keg had been tapped. However, it was the sweet lemon water from the cellar that everyone was aiming for. Callum, Nick, Cathy and Wills continued to bring around jug after jug. Vicky kept refilling the jugs as they came down for refills. Thus keeping her occupied.

On his arrival, Reverend Clarke had been taken aside to meet the couple individually. He spoke to Harry first.

After their conversation, Harry waved Wills over to join them. They told him of their gold finds. "Are you serious? This is wonderful news. I told Gipps it was there, and he didn't believe me. Well, he did but told me to be quiet about it." He slapped his leg with joy. "Wonderful news, absolutely wonderful! And you say in most creeks around Bathurst, eh? Amazing!"

Wills nodded and handed him a little wrapped parcel. "You should be able to tell by the weight what it is. This is a *Thank you* for everything, sir. Reverend Clarke, you have no idea what this find has done for us all, and for what it will do for the communities." He placed the small parcel in his hand. "Sir, it's heavy, careful."

Reverend Clarke's hand dropped as Wills placed it on his hand. "Oh, my lad. That much?" he asked. "It was worth coming just to hear your news, lad, but this. I am overwhelmed."

"Sir, this is a mere sample. That is your share. Use it as you will. There should be about £1000 worth there. The church got the same. This is for you and Mrs Clarke's personal use." Wills smiled at him.

Reverend Clarke stood stunned. He put out his hand to shake Wills' but instead drew him into an embrace.

Wills turned and left his mentor, both still grinning.

Harry was still with him. "I would get Jack to lock this up for you, sir. You don't want it going for a walk without you."

Harry called Jack over and said very softly, "Jack, can you lock up a packet for the Reverend, please? We don't want it to go missing."

Jack nodded and walked into the kitchen. Harry smiled when noticed Jack didn't even ask what it was. He smiled at the man's trust.

Reverend Clarke had yet to meet the bride. Jack pointed for him to go into the kitchen. Vicky had left the cellar and returned to the busy kitchen. The minister met with Vicky and ascertained that she was willing to marry without due pressure. She assured him she desired to do so, even admitting she wanted the early date.

Charlie started getting everyone settled, the children were put together in the shade of the barn. They sat still because it was too hot to move. Jack had planned for the service to be on the hill where the church was to be built, but it was too hot to walk up there. So Reverend Clarke asked if they would mind if they stayed in the shade in the yard.

Therefore, less than fifteen minutes later, Eddie came outside and, in his booming voice, said, "Please give your attention to this door."

Jack came out with Vicky on his arm, and they walked to stand next to Harry. The service started. Harry gently squeezed her hand. Soon, they would be husband and wife.

"Who gives this woman?" Reverend Clarke asked.

"I do," said Jack, "and you take good care of her."

Everyone laughed, though Harry had already promised him he certainly would, and he grinned in reply.

Reverend Clarke continued with the well-known words of the marriage service. When he pronounced them husband and wife, Harry didn't wait for permission. He took her in his arms, and she wrapped hers around his neck and pulled him down. Their kiss was deep and intense, causing oohs and ahhs from their family.

Callum and Nick both said, "Yuck," again, and there were chuckles from some of the others.

Reverend Clarke finally coughed, and Harry lifted his head and smiled down at her. She was his wife. She had been kissed senseless in front of all their friends and family, and she loved it.

Harry lifted her, spun her around, and then kissed her again. Everyone laughed.

Soon, they were showered with flower petals.

Harry pulled her into his arms again.

She threw her head back and laughed with joy. Her joyous laugh was effervescent.

Harry could not believe she was finally his. He was so happy a tear slid down his cheek. He raised his head and thanked God. Eventually, they turned back to Reverend Clarke, and he blessed them, then turned and introduced them to the crowd: The Honourable Henry Harlow and The Honourable Mrs Henry Harlow.

They had yet to sign the register that Reverend Bobart had brought with him. This they did, with John and Jack signing as witnesses. Thus done, everyone cheered.

"I love you so much, my darling wife." And in front of everyone, he kissed her so sincerely and passionately that she could do nothing but cling to him.

"Oh, Harry! I love you too," she had whispered, still weak at the knees, then responded in kind.

His senses were reeling.

John went over and congratulated them both, kissing Vicky on the cheek. "Welcome to the family, Vicky."

Everyone else crowded around them, all giving their congratulations and blessings.

Jack brought another keg, this time of ale, and it, too, was tapped. In the heat and with the movement of bringing it up, it fizzed everywhere and caught the nearby folk unawares.

Many squealed, and all laughed.

Reverend Clarke went inside to take off his robes. He was drenched in perspiration.

Martha brought him a glass and jug of cool lemon water as he changed. He drank most of it. "My, it's hot," he exclaimed.

Martha and her friends started bringing out food from the cellar and kitchen. There was some hot food but most preprepared cold finger food. Everyone was milling around.

Cathy and Wills passed frequently throughout the afternoon and would take the opportunity for a quick kiss as they passed.

Jack chastised her a few times.

Cathy passed him and whispered, "Meet me in the cellar. Come in about ten minutes." She went to fetch some jugs of cool water but waited for him.

Wills meandered in the direction of the kitchen. Everyone was hopefully occupied. He opened the cellar door and scooted down the narrow stairs into Cathy's waiting arms. He gathered her to him and stood looking down into her beautiful face.

"Cathy, we're not staying here long, but I just wanted to do this." He lowered his head and brushed her lips with his. She reached up and threaded her fingers through his thick locks. As his passion deepened, her tongue slid over his. He crushed her into his arms. They broke apart when they heard someone open the cellar door. Thankfully, it was Marc.

"Out, you two. Not until you're married," he chuckled. "Yeah, yeah, I know. Thank goodness, it was me, not Pa or Maa."

"Sorry, Marc," Wills said. "It was just a kiss." He turned to look at Cathy, and muttered "And what a kiss."

Marc pulled himself up onto a barrel. "Look, I know how hard it is, especially as you two have been betrothed for so long. I'll always give you some space, but you also have to protect her, Wills. If you had been found down here by anyone else, Cath would have been in trouble, not you."

Wills still had his arms around her. She was leaning against him. "Thanks, Marc, I know. I'm sorry. It was me who asked him here." She looked apologetic. She turned in his arms and looked at her beloved. "Sorry, Wills."

He bent and gave her a quick kiss, then pushed her towards Marc. "Take her upstairs, please, Marc; I'll follow in a bit." Please, God, give me strength, he said to himself. He was glad Marc came when he did. He blew Cathy a kiss as she turned for the stairs. He walked upstairs some ten minutes later. Jugs of cool lemon water in his hands. He heard the wagon being brought around. The party was in full swing. However, it was time for the bride and groom to hit the road.

Wills, Eddie, and Charlie had decorated the wagon earlier. Marc was in the seat, bringing it around for the bridal couple's departure.

Eddie and Charlie had a bundle of noisy old tins and things to be hooked under it when it arrived in the yard. They had also written a sign that said, "Just Married" and put it on the back.

They each stood looking at their handiwork and smiled.

As best man, John made a speech, and Jack replied. Toasts were drunk, and cheers surrounded the couple.

Phil, Lew, and Aidan hoisted Harry on their shoulders and heaved him onto the wagon. Marc, Wills and Eddie carried Vicky and deposited her next to him.

Harry bent and gave his wife a quick kiss, then flicked the reins. The wagon started moving out of the yard.

Charlie bent and hooked the tins on the back of the wagon. The horses gave a start at the unaccustomed noise.

Harry laughed but soon settled them. Everyone followed them to the front of the inn and stayed watching until they were out of sight. The cans made a heck of a lot of noise as they crossed the bridge. Then fell silent.

Edmund figured that they'd stopped and removed them.

As they crossed the bridge, Harry stopped to remove the tins. He left them hanging on the bridge with the just married sign on the same hook. Harry hopped back into the wagon, and he then bent down and kissed his wife. "My wife! Oh, how wonderful that sounds."

They soon turned down to Castlereagh Road. They were spending the first night close by, camping at Birds Eye Corner on Colless' Farm near the old ford.

Vicky didn't care as long as she was with him. She sat holding his arm, and he steered the horses along the road.

"Do we have to go far, Harry?" she asked, looking at him provocatively. He had not told her where he'd planned to spend the first night.

"No, love, just down to the crossing. Not far, my sweeting."

"Oh, good," she said. Even though it was hot, she lifted his arm and wrapped it around her and snuggled next to him.

He said, "You smell so good."

Vicky was thinking just the same. "So do you. Sandalwood or Pine?"

"Both, sweeting, it's a special blend." Just as well, the horses could see where they were going; he was otherwise occupied.

They arrived about fifteen minutes later.

Vicky hopped down and chocked the wheels.

Harry was surprised she knew what to do, but forgot she was a colonial lass, not an English lady. Oh, how he was going to enjoy working with her on all their plans. He chuckled.

"Anything wrong, love?" she asked. "What's so funny?"

"Nothing, Vicks, nothing at all," he smiled. "I'm going to enjoy having a capable wife, that's all. Not a stuffy, prim English miss who would do nothing for herself."

Soon, the horses were unharnessed and hobbled.

The cart was readied for the night.

Vicky revealed a basket of food Martha had provided. She was sitting under the canopy after clearing various items off the mattress. "Harry," she called.

He stuck his head in through the back of the canopy. She was sitting provocatively with her bodice unbuttoned and beckoned for him to join her. "Now?" he asked enquiringly.

"Yes, now we don't *have* to wait until tonight, do we?" she said coyly. "I've waited long enough, and I liked those tingly feelings. I want you, Harry."

He hopped up and took her in his arms. She fell back on the mattress, taking him with her.

The wagon had a cool breeze from the water blowing through it. This was the first time for her and he knew he had to take it slowly. Give her time. He knew she was as pure as he had always hoped his wife would be. This is not what he had planned, but he was happy to oblige. Life with her was going to be an exciting, passionate adventure.

Onboard the Eagle

January passed with a week of wet weather.

By the middle of the month, they were overjoyed to see birds landing on the masts. Land was not far away, which meant the journey's end was close.

They restocked with fresh food at Fremantle, then headed south for the final legs of their journey.

~

Portland was the next stop, then Melbourne was the last stop until Sydney. Home.

Charles and Sal stood at the railing as they left Melbourne. "Nearly home, love," he said. They didn't stay long, as by the time they reached the end of the bay, the wind was up.

They had left Melbourne in the middle of a blustery day on the first day of February. The wind was coming from the northeast, and the seas were rough. It was going to be an indoor trip, by the looks of it. They passed some points and islands that the Captain pointed out to them. They had to tack up the coast.

After days of rough weather, early one morning, the Captain

knocked on the Duke's door. "Sir, I'm pleased to tell you we're approaching the heads. We'll be there by nightfall."

Liam reached for his captain's hat.

"It's a pity the breeze wasn't from the south; we would have arrived four days ago."

The children were, of course, already up, and Ned was in a long velvet robe, with his youngest son on his hip.

The captain smiled, reaching out to touch the child's tiny hand. He had grown to admire this intrepid family. Initially, he was fearful when he heard that his passengers included a Duke, two Duchesses, an Earl, and two Countesses, not to mention children. He hated travelling with small children. However, they had been fabulous passengers, all of them even taking under their wing the two young females in one of the other first-class cabins. He would miss them all.

He walked back up to the wheelhouse. The ship was tacking into the heads as the family emerged, the children all in arms, each attached by harness to an adult. Ned was pointing out the two big headlands to the small children. Chip was plying him with question after question. Sarah sat on Sal's hip, sucking her thumb, listening to all Chip's questions. Christina had Liam in her arms, and he was wiggling and itching to get down. Christina was having a hard time holding him still.

Charles offered his stronger arms. He relieved her of her precious bundle and held him tight. Liam stopped wiggling, knowing his chance of escape was nil. He, too, popped a thumb in his mouth and rested against Charles's chest.

As the ship tacked and the wind caught the sails. The waves were behind them and carried them swiftly into the safety of the beautiful harbour.

With the wind behind them, there was no scent of eucalyptus. However, they could see the blue haze hanging over the mountains.

Sal walked up to Charles, each with a child in their arms. "We're home, love, home to our own children," she said.

"And my great-grandchildren, too," Elle piped up from behind her. She walked to Charles and stood beside him. "Oh, Charles, what a wondrous harbour!"

Charles dared not admit the first time he saw it. He and Jack had watched beside Ned at they arrived as convicts. He caught Ned's eye and smiled. With Liam snuggled against his shoulder, he drew Sal to him with his other arm. "Yes, isn't it, Mother?" He said to his wife quietly, "Yes, we're home." They'd had a wonderful time, but nearly two years was a long time to be away. This time, he was bringing his mother to meet her grandchildren and great-grandchildren too. His heart was full. He was finally at peace with his life. Here, he could be himself. Yes, this was home.

It took a further two hours to sail into the wharf. They had to proceed under less than half sail for the last mile of the trip.

The captain dropped to just one sail at Bradley's Head.

The wind took them swiftly along the remaining mile.

The final sail was furled as they rounded Mrs Macquarie's Chair. There, the barque was met by a small steam tug.

Ropes were thrown aboard, and the ships tethered together. From there, it was only minutes before docking.

The three staff members had finished the packing.

All was in readiness for disembarkation.

Mrs Browne's chaperonage of Amelia and Fiona was officially handed to the *Les Grande Dames*. She would head straight to her husband.

The young ladies thanked her graciously. They would travel to Parramatta with the family until they could find their aunt. Reverend Clarke was not one to ever stay in one place; his loving and ever-patient wife, Maria, was forever travelling with him. He may yet take some tracking down. In the meantime, Sally had invited them to stay.

Ned sent word from the dock for rooms to be reserved at The King's Arms Hotel. He had let Eddie know of their planned arrival sometime in February so that they would be half-expected.

Ned received a note back to say their rooms awaited them. They were ready to head down the gangplank when shouts and cheers met their ears. A ferry was also pulling into the wharf.

Eddie, Jenna, and Lily greeted them. They had hoped to be there before the ship docked, but had only missed it by a whisper.

Captain Roberts was still at the helm and joined the shouts of welcome. Eddie had told him they were coming home. He pulled on the steam whistle with a *toot toot* in greeting. He had seen the big ship tacking down the harbour.

The new arrivals stood on the dock waiting to greet their travelling family. The joyous reunion was merely a sample of what was yet to come.

As the first round of hugs drew to a close and the children met their cousins, another small group arrived.

Harry and Vicky arrived mere seconds before Caroline and Douglas Evans. Both couples had left word at the hotel for them to be informed when the ship arrived. Harry and Vicky had no reason to return to Parramatta and were enjoying a six-week honeymoon. She was holding his arm tightly.

Sal looked at her enquiringly. As yet, they had not received the news of their relationship, let alone their marriage.

Vicky greeted her with a hug. "Aunt Sally, oh, I'm so happy you're home. You too, Uncle Charles. May I introduce my husband, Henry Harlow, known as Harry?" She smiled at him dreamily.

Fiona made a quick intake of breath. Sal heard but said nothing.

"Husband? Oh, Vicky, really?" Sally exclaimed.

Vicky introduced him to everyone, but she did it in her own style. "I know I should do this properly, but I'm not. Harry, this is Aunt Sal and Uncle Charles, Eddie and Wills' parents, and this is Major Ned and Christina. They are absolutely no relation to me, but they are really the Duke and Duchess of Gracemere, and this is my wonderful husband of six weeks, The Honourable Henry Harlow."

Ned bowed and greeted him, then introduced the rest of the group. "My mother, Dowager Duchess of Gracemere, and Charles' mother, Dowager Countess of Coxheath. Miss Amelia Stather and Miss Fiona Moreton. The younger ladies are Reverend Clarke's wife's nieces."

Harry started. "Oh really? He married us."

Amelia exclaimed with surprise, "Oh, wonderful. Do you know where they are?"

"Yes, actually, we do," Harry said. "They were heading to Dural and then hopefully back here to the museum. We can send him a message at the museum. They always seem to know where he's heading."

She turned to Fiona. "Fi, did you hear that?"

Fiona smiled in reply. She stood looking at Harry, then turned away, sheet-white.

Harry noticed and wondered, puzzled at her actions. He didn't even know her.

Fiona's heart was pounding so hard that she was sure others could hear it. No! It could not be so. If Henry Harlow were here, then Lewis would be somewhere near. She knew they were friends. Lewis said in his letter to his parents that he was travelling with a party of friends and that Harry Harlow was one of them. She had never met Harry but knew he served with Lew in India and that they were friends. He did not, however, say where he was going. She had presumed it was Europe. She had come here to leave her memories behind. She blanched, and a tear came to her eye. She brushed it away angrily.

Amelia had never asked why Fiona had agreed to come; she had just been happy to have company.

Only Amelia, Sal, and Harry had seen her action. Amelia walked to her. "Are you all right, Fi?"

Fiona replied with a slight nod.

Amelia saw her eyes flood with unshed tears. Amelia looked at Sal and shrugged.

The group turned to walk up the hill. It was a nice day; not too hot, and after so many months at sea it was lovely to stretch their legs finally. The children were also revelling in being able to walk and even run a bit. The twins were on their harnesses but were gleefully trotting beside one or other of the adults. Even the *Les Grande Dames* were enjoying a walk in the warm sunshine.

Sally took Fiona's arm. "Are you all right?" she whispered.

Fiona could not answer for a few moments. Eventually, she said, "No, no, I'm not, Sal. If Harry Harlow is here, then Lewis will be too. Oh, what am I to do, Sal? How did this happen? Sally, Father turned him down, but I love him so." She sniffed. "Sal, I have been forbidden to talk to him or even see him." Tears now trickled freely down her pale cheeks.

Sally squeezed her hand. "Now, love, remember what we were talking about, trusting God? I think this is a perfect case in point, don't you?"

Fiona glanced at her, "Sally, my heart is already broken. I thought I was all right, but at the thought of him and look at me? A blubbering fool." She wiped her face with a scrap of a lace handkerchief.

"Not a fool, love, just someone still hurting. Dry your eyes; we'll be here for you. Come to me if you're worried. I could have prepared you if I had known. However, let's not cry over spilled milk. Fi, I must tell you Lewis is Ned's cousin. I'm not sure if you know. If it's meant to be, it will happen. Please trust God." Sal patted her hand.

She nodded. She had discovered that. "I'll try, Sally," Fiona said miserably. "I miss him so much. And no - I didn't know." She sniffed in a very un-ladylike manner.

Lily and Liam were eyeing each other off over the shoulders of their respective fathers as they walked beside each other.

"Sir, sorry, Uncle Ned, I'm so pleased you have come. With both you and Dar here, things will get moving along quickly." Eddie said. Lily curled up into his neck and went to sleep. Her arms were tightly wrapped around his neck. He looked at Liam, and he was doing the same. "Isn't parenthood grand? I love them so much."

"Yes, lad, you're right there. I thought I was a strong, disciplined, and mature man, but then those two scamps came along. I'm mere putty in their hands." He laughed. "Now, this one. When I think back to being stationed here as a Major. Alone, but for your family, no prospects, and having rejected my own family, even my family name. You, lad, were my light." Ned looked at this wonderful young man. "Eddie, I lived for the times I could see you and Charlie. To see you happily married to a wonderful and Godly woman and now blessed with the beginnings of your quiver, I am content." Ned walked musing. "Do you know, If I *had* used my name, for I am Edward Lockley too, I think we would have worked it out years before?" He fell silent again. "You were my namesake because we share a birthdate; I just never let on how much."

Eddie had no words. He looked to the kind figure who had been so instrumental in his life, taking the direction that it had.

Ned continued. "Then Gerry arrived with news that I was now the Duke, which, of course, opened the door for Christina, and now look at me. No. Look at us. I thank God daily." Ned looked at his friend and cousin Charles. "Eddie, these last eighteen months spent with your parents has been heaven-sent. Having them beside me in my new role and seeing Charles fit into his life as an Earl, we grew even closer together."

Ned paused and dropped his voice. "Now look over at those two. *Les Grande Dames*," he chuckled. "Can you imagine how Sydney is going to cope with them? They have me in stitches so often. Mother is playing the Dowager Duchess to the hilt, and Elle, sorry, your grandmother is following in her shadow. This is going to be such fun, Eddie. Exceptionally fun." Ned chuckled again as he watched the two agile ladies manage the harnesses of the boisterous five-year-old twins.

The arrival at the hotel caused a great stir. The twins immediately made their presence heard.

The manager was at the front to meet everyone. He had expected them to arrive in the carriages he'd sent and was surprised to find they had walked up from the dock. When he saw the harnessed children, he groaned softly. He looked up and realised his groan had been heard by the older lady. This time, he groaned inwardly. He bowed as low as possible.

"My good man, of course, the children are rambunctious. They have been cooped up indoors for some four months. This is the first chance they have had to stretch their legs outdoors since we left Cape Town." The Duchess has not even yet introduced herself.

Ned came to the rescue. "Good afternoon, Mr Stewart; as you can see, we have arrived. Let me introduce you, Mother, The Dowager Duchess of Gracemere, The Earl and Countess of Coxheath, and the Dowager Countess of Coxheath, Miss Stather and Miss Moreton, who travelled with us are here to stay with Reverend Mr Clarke as they are his wife's nieces. These noisy ones are Charles, Earl Lockley, and the Lady Sarah, and this young one is William."

As Ned finished saying their names, the two older children each bowed and curtsied. They performed with some prompting but with the perfection of practice and at their grandmother's instruction. They astounded even their parents. Suze and Elle looked at each other and smiled. They now stood silently as the adults talked. They were hot and thirsty.

Ned continued, "You, of course, know Mr Edward Lockley and his wife, Jennifer. This sleeping angel is their youngest, Lily. Captain and Mrs Evans you also know. I have just met this young man and his lovely wife, who I believe are already your guests."

Mr Stewart acknowledged Harry and Vicky.

Sarah yanked on her mother's gown and just said, "Up." Christina shook her head. "No, Sarah, you can walk to our rooms. It's not far, sweetie. There will be a cool drink waiting for you there." Sarah nodded.

The manager got the hint and personally ushered them upstairs.

He had the entire floor booked for them and the best suites, too. Each room had fresh roses and a tray of cool lemon drinks, as well as the usual grog trays.

The luggage carriages arrived as they left the foyer. The porters and their maids appeared. Ned and Charles advised on which cases were to go where.

Chip leaned against the wall in the sitting room. "Dada, the room is moving," he said quietly.

Eddie had followed them in and knelt beside the lad. "Do you remember when you got onto the ship and you found it hard to stand up?"

The boy nodded.

"Then, after a while, it wasn't that hard?" Ed continued.

He nodded again.

"Well, that's called 'getting your sea legs', and now you're back on land after so much time at sea, now you have to get your 'land legs' again," Eddie explained. He had heard Captain Evans say the same each time he arrived back in port after a long trip. Eddie had never been at sea.

"Fank you, Eddie, I fink I understand. So I'se not sick?" Chip asked.

Sarah sat on the floor listening. She, too, was giddy.

"No, lad, but it will take a day or so, so be careful. Still, hold the rails and don't run unless you are on grass, and you can't hurt yourself if you fall," Eddie explained.

He nodded. "Okay, Eddie." Then he flung his arms around his neck. "Fank you."

Ned watched the conversation and laughed quietly to himself. This boy, who had been named after him, was now a man, a husband and a great father, too. Eddie had named his son after Ned. Jenna was as besotted with him as he was with her.

After nearly six years of marriage, Ned felt the same as he did for his Christina. The couples had married only weeks apart in Parramatta. Both had conceived twins within the first month of marriage. A rough start for both ladies, but each coped with the rigours of a double birth well. The two sets of twins were born only two weeks apart. He was itching to meet them. Their third children were only ten days apart. At ten months old, they were both crawling and very active. Lily was able to stand unaided but had not taken a step alone yet. Liam scooted around on his bottom and then pulled himself up. He was going to be a handful. It would be fun to see them walk and even talk over the next year.

Eddie offered to take them outside while they settled in. Sarah eyed him suspiciously, but when Chip ran to his side, she, of course, followed. "I know somewhere they can run and play and not annoy anyone. I think everyone will settle better after they have let off steam.

Nanny can then get their room sorted in peace."

Christina took the sleeping Lily from Jenna and laid her in the cot with Liam. The children's room was in the room between theirs and Sal's. She shooed her off with Eddie. "I'll watch her, dear, as will Sal and Elle. She has more carers than she needs."

Jenna took Sarah's lead in her hand and followed Chip and Eddie out the door.

Rather than allow Jenna to go with him, Eddie kissed her and sent her to lie down for a while. He took both leads and took the two children downstairs.

There was a lovely walled park down the street where the children could run, scream, and play until exhausted.

For the first time in four months, Christina could relax. She fell backwards on the bed. "Oh, Edward, there's so much room. And Edward... the bed is so soft."

He bent over her and kissed her. "Don't tempt me, love... yet."

"Why not?" she chuckled. She reached up and wrapped her arms around his neck. "Meanie, I want another baby, my love. I'm just warning you. I want to go home with four, at least."

"Tonight," he smiled and brushed his lips over hers. He tried to stand up.

She gently took hold of his lapels. "You'll keep," she chuckled. Christina adored her wonderful husband. He was everything to her. Ned had stood up to her father on her return to England and was very matter-of-fact when answering his probing questions about their whirlwind courtship and subsequent hasty marriage.

Ned explained that they had known each other for some time, but due to her being in mourning, they had been unable to announce their understanding before she was out of mourning. The hasty marriage was to stop tongues wagging. Ned had slightly twisted the story, however, as their marriage was *'fait accompli'* and she was expecting twins, there was not much her father could do. After all, Ned was a Duke. Surely her father could not complain that this time, her choice was as perfect... or could he? Her father never seemed satisfied.

Suze sat in her hotel room, alone and resting. Her mind flitted from one thought to another. Susanna fell to musing over the past years. She was joyful to be here with her son and his beloved wife, let alone Elle's family. She thought back to the long-awaited meeting with Christina's father, Edmund Snr, the Earl of Riverdell. When they arrived home, Christina was already married and expecting twins, yet he still wanted nothing to do with her family. Edmund felt as though he had been cut all those years before; overlooked for a Duke. Yes, a conversation was long overdue. He had finally come around after she pinned him down They were now all on good terms. She knew he still had feelings for her, though.

The animosity, or now the lack of it, arose after her conversation with him. Unbeknownst to all their children, Suze had once refused Edmund's offer for her hand when she was young. She had instead married Charles, the much older Duke of Gracemere. He was some twenty-five years her senior. No one had believed it was a love match, but it was very much so. She adored her husband. She had done so since she was nearly eighteen. He had never married, and at forty-three, he considered himself a confirmed bachelor. Then he saw Susanna. She was still only seventeen, vivacious, confident, and self-assured, with twinkling blue eyes and a wicked sense of humour. Her Scottish lilt had captivated him. He loved to hear her talk.

He was over twice her age. However, she was as smitten as he was. Within the month, they announced their betrothal and married three weeks later. David was born ten months later. Neither she or Charles had looked at any other person from the day they met. She thought it funny that Ned had met Christina at forty-three as well.

Susanna had tried to explain to Edmund, then Viscount Eames, that she was already spoken for. They could not announce it until she was eighteen. He had not believed her and had carried a grudge ever since. They had not spoken again until their children married. He tried to avoid her, even then. At the twins Baptism she had a chance to take him aside and speak to him. This time, she put her foot down firmly. She remembered saying to him. "You will listen to me, Edmund. You need to hear what I say. You never gave me a chance to explain. Surely, after so long, you must believe me."

And yes, after all these years, Edmund finally realised that she had been telling the truth. If she had met him even a month earlier, things might have been different. She had already given her promise to Charles before Edmund had met her. However, because their betrothal had not been announced, she could not mention his name. Now, he was gone.

Edmund had begged her forgiveness. She gave it willingly. Edmund had called his wife, Catherine, to them. She came, and they sat with the Duchess for some time. Making up for lost years. Catherine and she had become friends, each unburdening to the other.

Susanna had become almost a recluse on the death of her beloved husband. He had been in his late eighties, and she was just in her sixties. They had five sons, one of whom, a twin, died at birth. However, they also had a daughter, and she was stillborn. This had happened th year after Douglas, her youngest son, was born. Suze had been crushed at the stillbirth of her daughter. She sat thinking of little Sarah Joy and bit on her knuckle at the memories, her eyes pooling in sadness.

One day, she would tell them. One day, Neddie should know that he had a sister. She was to have been named Sarah, too. It's why his little cherub was so special to her. Suze never conceived again. It was only on Neddie's return with Christina that her heart started to heal.

When Neddie came home, everything for her changed, too. Elouise had gone. She had been a thorn in her side for all those twenty-five years. And although Suze adored seeing her son again, it was the birth of the twins, and little Sarah in particular, that changed her life. Yes, she had two other sons, though they too had only sons, and she craved a granddaughter.

Then there was Elizabeth, her dear Elle, her best friend. Guilt washed over her. All those wasted years. If she had thought her life was hard for her, then Elle had been given a rotten deal. She was married to a wonderful husband, John Lockley. They had only seven years together before he died of an illness he had contracted during the war. Thankfully, he had been able to die at home. Elle was with him at the end. It was only weeks after their second child was born.

She remembered when Elle had told her, "Suze, my John died when Lilabet, our daughter, was only a few weeks old. He had come home from the war so sick. At least he got to see her and hold her." Elle had struggled on a minimum income. She had known it was from her husband's family, but had no way of knowing where it came from. It arrived monthly in an envelope with no contact details.

The cottage was hers for life; she knew that. She had so much to cope with bringing up two small children alone, on a pittance that she asked no questions. Their day-to-day living took all her time and energy.

John had told her little of his family except that they had fallen out. She did not ask, as she did not want the risk the small amount she was given. Elle certainly never spoke about her family, and as a matter of fact, she still hadn't, Suze thought. It had never occurred to Elle that there was a reason someone gave her a monthly income or that she could turn to them for help. She needed that money. It's all they had to live on. Then Charles was arrested. Her world collapsed. Lilabet was only fourteen. Then they were alone.

Susanna wiped a tear away just thinking about her. They lived on the meagre pittance with a vegetable garden and some hens. For over twenty lonely years, they had managed to survive.

Elle and Lilabet were malnourished, alone, and unhappy. How they still were gracious, loving, and forgiving astounded Suze. They welcomed the help when it came, Elle with tears, Lilabet with a hug.

Elle had sobbed with relief when she heard about Charles and that he was still alive, married and had children.

Suze's heart broke. Then, when the rest of the story unfolded, she sat sobbing in Suze's arms. Lilabet has sat silently, watching it all unfold.

Ned sat watching the meeting, grief-stricken. All these years…

He had explained to his mother later that he had always wondered about Charles. He wondered if he was actually a by-blow of his father's, and he did not want to tread that path. There was only a year between them. That would have meant... No, he did not want to think about that. He had never admitted his thoughts to Charles when he arrived in England.

Neither Elle nor Lilabet were angry or vindictive. Both were grateful that time had come to a close. Ned had arrived with a carriage full of food, a maid and gardener.

Suze caught herself with a sob and a lump in her throat each time she thought about that week. Elle needed her as much as she needed Elle.

Suze was horrified by how close she lived, and she never realised. Ned took her to visit that very week, and they became instant friends. They were less than a year apart in age. Suze claimed her as a cousin as soon as they knew. This too had been divulged to all in that very first week as was Elle's nearness to the Castle. The income she was receiving was a family minimum pension automatically paid to family members. Elle's husband, John, was a grandson to Neddie's great-grandfather. They, therefore, were third cousins. Ned had called the Estate manager to his office the night he arrived and asked about Bramblemere Cottage. Who lived there, and who were they? All the information about Charles Lockley senior had been recorded in the Estate Files. Ned had checked within hours of his return.

He had the butler show him where the books were, and soon, he was on the hunt for the entire story. Sadly, it had taken two full days. On the fourth day home, they went for a visit.

Oh, to think all this time she had been in need. To think she could have done something about it if only she had known or cared, for that matter. Suze wiped another tear away. Her guilt was eased when Elle decided to accept her offer and share the Dower house with her. She could no longer live alone. Lilabet was finally getting married at thirty-eight. Her new husband was Viscount Ellison's son, Matthew. He was Annabella's brother. They had met during one of his frequent visits to his sister at the Castle.

It had not taken long before they announced their plan to marry. At such an advanced age, she did not expect to have children, but God had other plans.

The Honourable Matthew Edward Charles John was born on the 9 September, just the month before they sailed to Sydney and just nine months after their wedding. He was the apple of their eye, heir to the title and adored by his grandfather. Sadly, they no longer lived close enough to see him regularly. Elle had managed to have a few visits, but they were moving to London for Matthew's work for a few years. Hence, Elle had decided to come and meet the other grandchildren and great-grandchildren now, too — all seven of them.

Gerry Winslow-Smythe still resided at the Castle and had started a medical clinic to keep him occupied.

Suze smiled, and now she was in the Antipodes with her friend, and son, on a fabulous adventure.

She sat up straight. "Stop being morose, woman. Wallowing in self-pity will get me nowhere," she said to herself. She sniffed in a very un-duchess-like way. She then smiled to herself. Yes, they would have fun. Make up some more lost time. She knew her maid would soon enter.

The luggage was sorted according to what was required for a few days' stay in Sydney.

There was a knock on Ned's door. He was handed an invitation to Government House for Thursday, 12th Feb at ten am if they arrived in time. They had, so they would attend, as it was tomorrow. He wrote to inform the Governor that their party would again include some extras.

Jenna had brought their best clothes, just in case.

Suze had chuckled when Jenna had said to Sal, "GH is a regular haunt for us these days. We almost have a standing arrangement. Tea with the Governor and his good Lady wife." No wonder Ned loved these people and their informality. She chuckled as Jenna said to Christina, "Do you remember taking us there the week you left? I had absolutely nothing to wear, and you gave me one of your new gowns. I still have it. I'll never part with it."

Christina thought that after six years of marriage and motherhood she would have rounded out a little. Jenna was still the same beautiful, bubbly lady. She had grown into a wonderful, confident mother.

Ned replied that their party of twelve would accept their kind invitation. He sent a list of who would be included.

Jenna looked over to Vicky and saw the panic on her face. "Government House? No, Jen, I can't," she whispered.

Jenna took her sister into her room and assured her, "I was thrown in the deep end when I was first taken there. Don't stress; wait and watch. Vicky, you have more grace and elegance in your little finger than I ever will have, and I survived. If you love Harry, you will stay calm. You *can* do this. Remember what Pa and Maa taught us."

Christina knocked, and Jenna answered the door. Sally was hard on her heels.

Vicky stood in the middle of the room and burst into tears.

Christina took her in her arms. "Oh, Vicky, you think tea with the Governor is bad. After Edward proposed, only then did he tell me he was a Duke. Sweetie, you will be fine. We will all be there with you."

"Seriously, Vicky, don't panic," Jenna said. "Christina, Sal and I will show you exactly what to do. We'll even do a run-through after dinner tonight. Thankfully, Maa taught us manners, and we learned a lot from you before Uncle Ned took you away." She looked at Christina and smiled. "Tea there is just like we've done at home. Only there will not be any children crawling over us," she giggled.

Sal said, "Harry said he had frocked you out beautifully, but let's see what else there is. Something that will knock their socks off." She went to the wardrobe. She opened it and gasped. "Vicky, these are superb."

Christina walked over, and one caught her eye, "This one, Vicky."

It was a pale emerald-green tea gown with cream netted lace on the neck, cuffs and collar, with gathered puffs on the sleeves. The full skirt of the gown was caught up with tiny bows made from the same fabric, and there was a ruffle of netted lace at the hem. The waist was tiny, dropping to a point at the front. She would look magnificent.

"Vicky, in this, you could do somersaults down the hall and get away with it. Just sit there and drink the tea. You do not have to do more than make polite conversation. You can do this; do it for Harry."

Christina hung the gown on the wardrobe door.

"It's glorious," said Sally.

"Harry made me buy it, Aunt Sal. I never thought I'd wear it," she hiccupped. Her tears had stopped.

Another knock on the door, and Harry entered.

She fled into his arms. "Oh, Harry," she said and proceeded to burst into tears again.

The older ladies departed. Jenna, however, stayed.

"Harry, she's just frightened. I know exactly how she feels; only I didn't have a gown like that to wear. Aunt Christina lent me one of hers."

"Sweetheart, it's just tea. Honestly, it's no fancier than we've had a few times in the last week. Only the building is more formal." Harry thought he was helping. It didn't seem to.

She looked up at him, her eyes swimming in tears. "I don't want to shame you, Harry; I should never have married you. I'm not good enough. I'm not usually a tear-pot like this," She sobbed again.

Jenna reached out, took her from his arms, and shook her.

Harry was horrified; he wanted to comfort and cuddle her, but her oldest sister shook her. "Victoria Mary Turner Harlow, look at me. Are you going to shame your husband, or are you going to stand tall and make us proud as you always do?" Jenna said firmly.

Vicky swallowed. "I want you all to be proud of me. You both know that." She hiccoughed again.

Jenna giggled. It broke the ice.

"Do you really think I can do this, Jen?"

"Yes, I had to, and I'm as graceful as a farm pig. You truly will be fine," she replied. "For you, my beloved sister, have the grace and deportment of a queen."

Jenna turned to Harry. "Harry, don't pander to her; she'll crumble. Challenge her, and she'll fly through this." She said this quietly to her new brother-in-law. She then turned and looked at her sister.

Jenna took her aside and asked her something.

Harry could not hear what it was.

Vicky shook her head, and then her eyes flew open. She looked at Harry and then back at Jenna. She beamed.

Jenna kissed her and walked out, closing the door quietly behind her.

Harry watched his wife with a puzzled frown.

She blanched, then sat down fast.

He went to her and knelt beside her. "Darling, what did she say?" he asked pensively.

"Harry, we've been married for six weeks," she said.

"Yes. Six wonderful weeks." He smiled knowingly.

"Darling, do you know how a woman's body works, you know mensuration; monthly menses or courses or whatever you call them and stuff?" she asked tentatively.

"Errr, yes, sort of." Nodding his head, then changing to shaking it instead. "Err, no actually. Not really, I never had a sister, you see. I have heard of them, though," he said somewhat bashfully, alternately shaking and nodding his head.

"Harry, my menses, like Jenna's, come on the dot of every twenty-eight days. It's a woman's monthly cycle. Always have, never late." She smiled. "I've been having such a wonderful time with you and, I you know, being married and what we enjoy, the tingly feeling stuff, that it never occurred to me. Harry, I have not had them. I should have had them twice since we got married." She took his hand and placed it on her stomach.

He looked stunned. "Are you serious? Really? A baby." His face broke into a beaming smile. He lay his head on her lap. "Sweeting, I thought I was happy before. This is marvellous news."

She stroked his hair.

He lifted his head and looked at her. "What, er, how did Jenna know?"

"I got emotional, and I rarely do. She has not seen me like this since I got my first ones at twelve. I just cried and cried. I thought I was dying." She giggled. "Now I know why I've been feeling a bit sick too." She blushed. "I threw up this morning. I thought I'd eaten something last night that upset me." She took a deep breath. "I'm going to be fine, love. We all are. All of us." She gulped. "Harry, we're going to have a baby."

Still on his knees, he wrapped his arms around her and hugged her.

"I'll never love it as much as I love you, my dearest," he said. He lifted her and carried her to the bed. He lay with her wrapped in his arms. She cried and laughed and finally fell asleep on his chest, emotionally exhausted.

His heart was whole. However, he now had to think about where they would live. They could not stay just renting the front room at Roseneath. He wanted to get her settled before the baby came. Or... he could buy Roseneath. He would have to look around quickly. He would certainly put an offer in for the house, though. He drew her close to him.

She snuggled up, laying a hand on his chest as though taking possession of him.

He let her snooze in his arms for about twenty minutes. She woke when he moved his arm. She woke and looked at her husband. "Harry, am I dreaming? I am, aren't I? I can't be with child already?" she asked, concerned.

"Well, love, you know your body. I think that while we're here, you may need to speak with a doctor. However, maybe we should talk to Sally as Jenna suggested. Do you want me to see if she can come in now?" He bent and caressed her lips with his.

She nodded. "I think I'd like that, Harry. Do you mind?"

"No sweets, whatever you need." He rose and straightened his clothing. He pulled on his coat. She was sitting on the side of the bed as he left. He closed the door quietly and walked along the corridor to Sal and Charles' room. He hated disturbing them, but Jenna said she could help, so he'd ask her. Vicky needed assurance, and according to Jenna, Sal was the one to ask.

He knocked gently.

Charles opened the door. He had his jacket off, but greeted him warmly.

Harry quietly asked, "Sir, I was wondering if Lady Sally could come and talk to Vicky, please?" He didn't explain.

Charles looked at him in a concerned manner and then turned to Sal. "Love, Harry is here and wondering if you'd go to Vicky. She needs you," he said.

She was on her feet instantly from the settee in their room. "Of course I'll go. Wait a moment." She slipped on some shoes and followed Harry.

He knocked on the door before entering, and Vicky was standing at the window looking out. She turned slowly.

Sal saw her face and went straight to her.

"Oh, Vicks, what's wrong?" Sally asked.

"Well, that's just it, Aunty Sal; I'm not sure anything is. I'm not sure of anything." She gently put her hand on her stomach and looked down. "I need to ask you things. Like, how do I know? And stuff like that."

"Oh, love, that's wonderful." She looked at Harry, "It is, isn't it?"

"Oh yes, it's wonderful. That's not the problem; it's, well, how are we sure? I don't have sisters, so I don't understand how women's things work." He blushed.

"Ahh," said Sal. "What put you in mind of this? If I may ask...?"

"It was something Jenna asked me. You see, I was crying and moody, and she knew that was not like me." She beamed. "Then she asked me if I'd had my menses since I was married." She blushed. "We've been enjoying ourselves. I had forgotten about them. It sounds crazy, but he's, err, well diverting," she giggled.

"Perfectly understandable. I know exactly what you mean. Remember, I have been married for thirty years and have six children." She looked at Vicky and whispered, "Fun, too."

Vicky gasped, blushed, and nodded. Her mother had said something similar. She merely nodded again, then smiled.

Harry came and put his arm around her waist.

"Please be seated, Harry." Sal pointed to the settee, and he ushered Vicky to the other end. He sat on the floor at Vicky's feet. His arm rested on her knees.

Sally smiled. The last time she had this conversation was with Eddie and Jenna on the verandah at home. They, too, had been married a very short time. She took her hand. "Now first, Harry, listen, but don't ask anything at this stage. I'll get to your questions later."

He nodded. He felt like a child at his mother's knee again.

"Vicky, first, before your marriage, were your menses regular?"

"Yes, Aunt Sal. Like Jenna's, on the day."

"Have you missed before?"

"No."

"Did you, err, preempt your vows?" She looked at Harry.

"No. Absolutely not," they both said adamantly.

Harry added, "It's why we married so quickly, so we would not be tempted." He looked earnest and concerned.

"Good," she smiled. "Then you could easily be, and probably are, expecting, and about, um, September." She smiled at them both. "Now, what I'm going to say are things you both need to know and won't ask."

They looked surprised.

"Vicky, I know you would not even ask your mother these things. Harry, I don't know you well yet, but you're like my Eddie, and I will treat you as such. First, yes, you can still keep, um, 'having fun'." She smiled as they both blushed. "As your condition advances, you have to be more careful and, let's say, accommodating for your bundle. Harry, she will be very emotional. Good days and bad days, her emotions are going to spiral. They will rise and crash often all in the one day. There will be days when all she wants to do is to cry. Some she will laugh, and others flip between the two, or you may not even notice, as she may not change. Each woman is different, and often each confinement is different as well." She paused, looking at these two young people. The adventure before them would be great.

They waited, hanging on her every word.

"Harry, hug her, touch her and love her. She will need this, especially as she gets bigger. Care for her. Charles used the word 'cherish.' Look it up. She will be uncomfortable and even get angry at her size, especially when her feet swell towards the end. Mine did every time. I felt like one of those whales in the harbour." Again, she paused. "Charles used to rub my feet. Oh, it was wonderful; they hurt so much."

Charles had done the man talk for Eddie, but I bet Eddie said nothing to Harry. "One more thing, and this goes for all through your marriage. It is very personal, but let me say, you both know lye burns. You both know that?"

"Yes," they agreed, nodding.

"Well, all soap has lye in it, Harry. Don't use it on delicate parts of your anatomy. Only hot water below the waist. This is especially vital for men, and, well, certain bits end up inside her." She blushed, as did they.

"Oh," they both said, nodding and blushing at the same time.

"Eddie said something along those lines before the wedding. It had never occurred to me," Harry said.

"It stops a woman from a lot of pain and discomfort. And the cheaper the soap, the worse it is," Sal said.

Harry asked a few questions. If they could discuss lye, they could discuss nearly anything.

Finally, Sal asked, "Are you coming back to Parramatta or staying on here for a while more?" Sal stood to leave.

"We haven't talked about it, but Harry, I think I'd like to go back now. Is that all right?" Vicky asked. "I want to stay at Roseneath with you."

"Yes, love, whatever you want," he replied.

"Please don't hesitate to ask me anything. Jenna and Christina will also help. Once you have had a child, you learn a lot." She smiled. "Is there anything else for the moment? You will have more questions later, I assure you. Harry, I'd talk to Eddie if I were you."

He nodded and grinned. "Thank you, Lady Sally."

"Enough of the Lady bit, Harry. You're now family. I'm either Sal, Sally or Aunt Sal." She smiled at Harry. "So now, young lady, you have a stunning gown. Would you like to show it to me again? I believe Jenna told you of the first time she went to Government House. Well, I didn't have someone to copy. I muddled through. Lady Gipps is lovely, and you will like her. She does not care about status either. I came out as a convict, yet we're on first-name terms. I like her, and I'm sure you will too. I'll be there with you, so stay near me, copy us. You'll be fine. Governor Gipps will probably take the men away, so stick with me," Sally said.

Vicky gave a huge sigh. "Thank you, Aunt Sal. I feel better now. I think I was just frightened. So much, so soon. Now, this." She gently placed her hands on her stomach. "Aunt Sal, I'm still frightened." Tears welled again in her eyes.

"Don't be, sweetheart, I'll be with you all the way through," Harry said.

"Don't get up; I'll see myself out." Sal stood to walk out. "Oh, are you going to tell everyone?" she asked.

Vicky nodded. "Yes, I think so," she looked at Harry.

"Yes, why not?" he agreed. "Feel free to tell Charles; we'll let everyone else know at dinner time," he grinned. "Thanks, Sally."

She let herself out and walked along the hall to her own room.

Charles was waiting anxiously for her return. He went to her and took her in his arms. "Is everything all right?" he asked, concerned.

Sal laughed. "Yes, love, looks like we'll be having another birth."

"Oh," said Charles, "is that all?" He bent and gently kissed her. "Aunty Sal, in demand again."

"The joys of young love." She reached up and mussed his hair. "I love you, Charles Lockley; always have, always will." She drew his head down to hers. "And to not so young love too."

An hour later, they walked downstairs to prearranged pre-dinner drinks.

Ned and Eddie were already waiting, as were Caroline and Douglas Evans. All the others appeared soon afterwards.

Nanny and the two maids were with the children. They were able to enjoy a child-free meal, the first one in four months.

Jenna watched Vicky and met her eyes for a smile.

Sal had told her they had spoken, and she was happier. Now she understood why she was emotional; she could handle it better.

Vicky was glad her sister was with her. They had always been close, and to have her near at this time was special.

Drinks were brought in. The stewards left them alone with their meal.

Harry stood and took a glass. He cleared his throat. "I know some of you saw Vicky a little upset this afternoon. I thought you might like to know, um, some information. We're expecting a happy event, about September, I believe," he grinned. "As you can imagine, we're a little overwhelmed with the news."

Congratulations came from all around.

Christina and Jenna both confided that the same occurred to them on their honeymoons.

Charles turned to Eddie, "I forgot to ask you, son. When is Wills getting married?"

"Cripes, Dar, I forgot all about that. It's this Saturday if that's all right. We had it all ready to postpone for a week if you weren't here. Do you think we can do it?"

Charles said, "I think we can make it. Tomorrow is this Government House, which should finish by about noon. We could even go tomorrow afternoon, but I'd like to do our bit of shopping and have things to arrange, and Ned wants to catch up with Major Downs at Hyde Park Barracks and Major Tom Turner, too."

They chatted about it for a while and agreed to head to Parramatta on Friday.

"We'll check the ferry time for Friday, but the luggage can go by road tomorrow. Nanny can come with us. The maids can go with the luggage and get it all sorted," Ned said.

"Fabulous. I'll send a note back on the morning ferry. Charlie will pass the word around," Eddie replied.

Suze and Elle put their heads together, whispering. "We'll have to get the children's toys out of our bags and on their beds before we arrive. We'll send them with the maids in the carriage."

Elle chuckled and nodded. Tonight, the bed time stories would draw the toys adventure to a close.

Chapter 10   Tea with the Governor

$\mathcal{A}$rrangements were made for the return to Parramatta.

The excess luggage had gone by road with the two maids that morning. Nanny was left with the children at the hotel. Two of the hotel maids would assist her until they left on Friday.

Two Government Town Coaches called for the group at 9.45 am. Six piled into each vehicle, and they leisurely moved along the streets to Government House. The vehicles pulled in under the portico and the party alighted; waiting to enter until all were together.

They entered in order of priority, with Ned and Christina in the lead, then the *Les Grande Dames*, Charles and Sal, Eddie and Jenna, Harry and Vicky, and Caroline and Douglas, with the two single ladies walking in together. Vicky's eyes grew large, and she clutched Harry's arm tightly.

He patted her hand and gave her fingers a gentle squeeze. They were greeted warmly. "Smile; and hold it." She did.

Eddie and Jenna had regular contact with the viceregal couple and were on friendly terms. Jenna introduced her sister and Harry, and Lady Elizabeth Gipps broke with protocol and hugged her.

Vicky relaxed. Harry smiled.

Everyone else was seated, but Lady Elizabeth took Vicky to sit next to her. "My dear," she said, "if you are anything like your dear sister, then you will be a wonderful helpmate for your dear husband. We all have to learn new roles after marriage; yours will be no different. Please know that while I am here, I will always be here to help you in any way I can." She sat holding her hand for a while. "Remember, I was not always a Governor's wife, so relax; I can see you are unsettled."

This is not what she expected from such an exalted lady. Vicky did relax, and the time passed quickly.

Soon, they were being ushered into the official function to which they had been invited. After the informality of the earlier group, this was a very formal function.

Many were in uniform; others wore medals and decorations. Vicky clung to Harry. She was no longer as stressed as she was before.

The governor, who did not look well, greeted everyone. He announced that due to his ill health, a replacement was being sent from England. It took everyone by complete surprise.

Lady Gipps walked to his side as he spoke. "We shall hopefully stay until they arrive, then step aside. I expect this to be the mid-year this year. I have achieved most of what I wished for the settlement. My dearest good Lady here has been my help and support."

Gasps were heard all around. Vicky leaned into her husband. "Oh, Harry, they are so nice; that's so sad."

The Duke walked up to the governor, followed closely by Charles. They shook his hand. "Sir, I am grieved," said Ned

"We all get old, Major. Sorry, Your Grace," replied the Governor. "I'm glad you're back, Charles, as in my absence, you will need to put on your Viceroy hat. You both may need to fill in for me. I do not think I will see the middle of the year. We may have to leave earlier. I feel my facade is see-through; I am not as well as I look." He was beginning to look grey around the mouth.

Ned turned. He called for some chairs.

The staff placed them under the shade of a tree.

Ned ushered them into the chairs. "Please, Ned will do fine, sir, or Major if you wish. We've known each other long enough not to stand on ceremony. We may have irritated each other somewhat, but we have always been friends." Ned looked concerned.

Charles replied, "Anything I or we can do, you only have to ask. I shall be staying home now. However, the duke will be here for only a year or so." They sat with them for a while so others would know they could join them after they had taken their leave.

The chairs meant the governor did not stand while saying all his farewells. If it were diplomatic enough for the Duke to sit with the governor, then others would follow.

Ned and Charles called over their wives, who took seats. Both shared their sadness at the news. Ned promised to call back within the next week or two with Charles and sort out any necessary paperwork.

The large group mingled for some time.

Formal introductions were made to a few of the better-known dignitaries. *Les Grande Dames,* as well as Amelia and Fiona, stood with Sally and Christina. Eddie had done the same for Harry. This would set them on the right path with the appropriate persons in the colony. "The Honourable" was still a title to the folk of Sydney. Any relation of His Grace the Duke or to any of the Lockley family was now considered titled. They did not need to know more.

Vicky could hold her head high. She was born free – not that anyone asked.

They returned to their hotel in the same Government Town Carriages. All the ladies went to lie down. Ned and Charles said they needed to sort out some business.

Eddie and Harry needed to stretch their legs, and decided to walk to the harbour. The twins were giving Nanny a headache, and Eddie offered to take them for a run. They could play on the grassy headland while the men talked. Eddie had been pleasantly surprised by how similar these two were to their cousins, his own twins. It would be interesting to see how they all got on together. Uncle Ned would be staying with them for the year so that they would hopefully become friends. Each child would particularly like having a friend the same age. Not to mention sharing the nursery.

The men had much to discuss.

Harry had questions he needed to ask someone. He liked Eddie; he was friendly and open to talking to. He was also in the best position to supply the information he needed. He was pleased that they were now brothers-in-law. Someone he could be close to and to whom he could confide. Something he never was with his blood brother. He shivered at the thought. There was no way he would ever be able to have a friendly chat with Anthony. He shuddered again. His brother was dictatorial, cruel and abusive, and thankfully, he was on the other side of the world. So different to when they were boys when they had been close.

Harry wanted Eddie's views on which building to start on and the priority of a new home for Vicky. Eddie and Harry, were married to the most amazing sisters and Wills would be soon as well. He had new brothers, related by marriage. Not only the four Lockley brothers, but also Vicky's brothers. He smiled. All these things were churning through Harry's mind. He admitted to Eddie, "It never occurred to me that parenthood could be thrust upon one so soon after marriage. Children, wow, we had not even really had a chance to discuss them with her. Now to find her with child and so early in our marriage." Harry shook his head in wonderment. "Eddie, I am still dumbfounded."

"Harry, I know exactly what you mean. Only in our case, Jenna realised on the return from our eight-day honeymoon her monthly courses had not come. So, for us, the realisation struck even earlier. We had twins, as you know." He looked to the two blonde cherubs rolling down the grassy hill. "They are only a few weeks older than these two. We four found out on the same day of the…" he chuckled, pausing "…the impending doom before us all. Oh, but what a blessing they have been."

"Eddie, is it normal for a stomach-turning fear to dwell in you?" Harry asked. "I know to trust God, that's easy on the whole, but I, for some reason, am worried. I cannot explain it." He shook his head as if to chase the thoughts away. "Eddie, my soul is disquieted. I don't understand it." Harry looked worried. "Eddie, it's more than fearful. I felt this way before we set out from England. Yet, I knew I had to come here." Harry fell silent. "Eddie, I look forward to having children. I can't wait. But, I am, well, ill at ease. I feel something is just not right."

"I know. I was fearful, too. Thankfully, we had family close, though." Eddie tried to sound comforting but knew he'd failed. "I believe Mama talked with you both. Do not hesitate to consult her. Many do, as she is a great source of knowledge on these things. You should have seen me blush." He paused, chuckled, then asked, "Did she give you the soap talk? I did warn you before you married."

Harry nodded, smirking, "Yes, that one threw me a bit. Somewhat personal," he chuckled.

"Imagine hearing it from your parents. However, I discovered how true. One night, I forgot, and my poor Jenna burned and was in pain for days. It's one worth remembering. I have tried to buy a more gentle soap, but it's not worth the risk." He chuckled, "Not the usual topic of conversation for two gents, eh?" He looked flustered, but both roared with laughter. Each man remembering the severe embarrassment during the initial discussions with Sal.

"At least you didn't get *The Talk* from Dar. Thankfully, we were sitting in a darkened cellar for that one," Eddie said.

"No thanks, Eddie." Harry was still disquieted. "But Eddie, this is more. It's not fear. This is not the fear of the unknown; this is deeper. I'm not worried about Vicky having children, but for Vicky herself. I can't put my finger on it."

"All I can say is pray. You will not be in this without help. We are family now, Harry. Whatever happens, we will be there for you both."

"Thanks, Eddie. That helps. I've not had that sort of relationship with my brother," Harry said quietly.

"Now, to dwellings for you and Vicky," Eddie paused and thought, "There are a few vacant houses. I believe Adderton is also coming up for sale later, but you could do no better than buy Roseneath. Sadly, our house looks as though we will be packed to the rafters for the year. Grandmama may move to the cottage with Dar and Mama, but I think she would rather stay in the larger, newer room at our place. Plus, we have an indoor privy and help in the house, not to mention private commodes. Grandma Suze's staff will have to stay in the spare room with the Connors out the back, and Nanny will be in with the six children, poor dear." He looked pensive. "And you think you have problems." He laughed, thinking of poor Nanny. "We'll have to lock our door to get any privacy," he chuckled.

"I certainly don't envy you. I think you may need a few trips away and leave the *Les Grande Dames* in Grandmother mode for a while," Harry said.

"Oh, now that's a grand idea," Eddie replied.

"At least you also have your parents. Mine are both dead." Harry said. Thinking back to Anthony's behaviour after their death, Harry swallowed his anger. Anthony could not get rid of him from the house fast enough. No wonder he could not settle in England; he had nowhere to go, no home.

Eddie put his hand on Harry's shoulder. "We are your brothers now, too, Harry. You're no longer alone." Harry nodded, and tried to smile. Anthony's rejection hurt.

Chip was getting a little boisterous, he pushed Sarah over. Her wails brought Eddie back to his guardian duties. He picked her up and comforted her. Thumb in mouth, she wrapped the other arm around his neck and hid her head on his shoulder. Harry took Chip aside and gave gentle chastisement about pushing a girl and he was never to do it again. Harry said, "Gentlemen never hurt someone weaker than them. Certainly not a girl and especially someone you love, like your sister."

Chip's lip trembled. His big blue eyes held his own honestly and trustingly.

It was the first time he'd had much to do with children. He'd have to learn. If theirs were like these two, they were so sweet.

Suitably chastened, he went to his beloved sister and apologised. "I'se sorry, Sarah. I didn't mean it. Wreally." he said in his funny baby talk.

She lifted her head and wiggled to be released. "Dat's alright, Chippy." She hugged him, and they ran off to play again.

"If only the adult world could be so simple and forgiving," Harry said.

Eddie pulled out his fob watch and realised they should be heading back. He called the children. They rolled down the hillock towards him. Laughing gleefully, they'd had a fabulous time. They did admittedly now have some grass stains on their clothing, but they were happy. They wanted to be carried, though he knew if they walked, they would be tired enough to have an afternoon nap, and all the adults needed one, too. They clipped the harness straps back on and walked back to the hotel. On arrival, they walked into the foyer just after Charles and Ned. Eddie handed over the harness straps to Ned. They were looking surprisingly pleased with themselves.

Nonetheless, they carried no parcels. Eddie did not think about it as they walked up the grand curving staircase to their rooms. Each returned to their rooms and would all meet downstairs at six pm for the evening meal. The evening passed uneventfully.

The next morning, the large group gathered in the foyer. The remaining luggage was loaded into a cart and taken to the ferry. The two older children were again on their leading reins, Liam in Nanny's arms.

Dowager Duchess Suze said as it was downhill, they would all walk.

No one argued.

Four months of enforced inactivity still needed to be counteracted. Ned bowed in acquiescence to his mother with a broad smile on his face.

The Hotel Manager, Mr Stewart, had never come across a grand lady like this one. He stood in awe of her. He waved the passenger carriage away. The group proceeded out the door.

Amelia and Fiona were to accompany them. They had found out yesterday that Reverend Clarke and his good wife were not going to be ensconced in Sydney after all. The Clarkes were currently believed to be somewhere between Campbelltown and Dural. The girls would stay with Eddie and Jenna until they could be found. There was one spare room at the big house. They would have to share it if they did not mind.

She looked over to Sally. A flash of fear shot across her face.

Sally laughed. "Fi, dear, we know where he'll be on Saturday. He's doing Wills' wedding."

Fiona said, "We are most appreciative. We were fearing we would be left alone in Sydney." Amelia missed it, but she knew something was amiss.

Sal fell into step beside her as they walked down to the boat. She took her arm. "Fiona, dear, please don't worry. We must trust that God knows best," she whispered to her.

Fiona nodded and squeezed Sally's hand. "I do want to see him, but I'm so afraid he will turn from me," she spoke quietly so only Sally could catch her words. "It's not so much that I am willing to go against Father's wishes, but Lewis is good and honourable and will accept his no as a 'No, not ever'. If that is the case, then so must I." She lifted her chin as she spoke. "I do trust God. Now, I must put that into action, mustn't I?"

Sally nodded. "Remember, dear, your Uncle William Clarke is your guardian while you are here, and he is a Minister," Sal whispered.

Fiona's eyes flew to her face. A smile spread on her face. It spread from there to her eyes, too.

As they walked down Pitt Street, Caroline and Douglas Evans joined the group. They considered the Evans family as extended family since Eddie lived with them for his years at school in Sydney. Caroline's brother, Thomas, was Eddie's mentor and now business partner.

Captain Roberts, the ferry captain, greeted the large group on arrival and winked at Charles. Eddie knew something was going on. He knew his father well enough to know he would say nothing until the time was right. As he had done as a child, he helped cast off the ropes. The ferry pulled out from the wharf. They all stood waving to the Evans's. Ned had Chip on a short lead, and Sarah, no worse for her tumble yesterday, was standing holding her brother's hand. Eddie was on his knee between them, pointing out the various points of interest.

Soon, a dolphin appeared near the bow waves. It stayed with them for a few minutes, then swam off. Ed pointed out birds and headlands. They stayed quiet for the entire trip, knowing that their father would not allow them to move from his side. He had used his stern army voice and told them to stay still. They knew not to move. They adored their kind and gentle father but knew he was not to be crossed. Especially if Chip had hurt his sister or upset his mother.

Once they settled, Eddie returned to Jenna and relieved her of Lily. He stood with her until they could see the entrance to the river. He returned to Ned and the children.

The children were beginning to fidget again.

Eddie again knelt. "Hello, you two, I thought you'd like to know that we're nearly there. You will soon meet your cousins. See that clump of trees; we head up the river on the other side and should arrive shortly." He looked down at these two blonde-haired, blue-eyed-cherubs and thought again how much their cousins looked alike. Lily was certainly following her mother's colouring, with her light brown hair and her eyes darkening blue. Their twins were fair-haired and blue-eyed like him. Ned would be very surprised when he saw his ragamuffins.

A crowd was waiting for the ferry. Some were under the trees nearby, and some on the wharf. The little boat pulled in. Charles threw the ropes to Charlie and tied up the ferry.

Captain Roberts slid over the gangplank.

Eddie was first to disembark. He handed his sleeping bundle to Gracie and returned to help the others disembark.

Ned handed his mother off the wobbly ramp, and then the rest of the passengers followed her down.

Eddie introduced his grandmother to her grandchildren, then great-grandchildren.

Charles stood on the wharf and received their hands as they were halfway down the gangplank. He introduced each of them as they stepped on dry land.

Elle turned to Suze, "Look, Suze, I'm responsible for all these people. I thought I had no one but Lilabet and both Matthews."

Charles walked to his mother and drew her into an embrace. "I'm so glad you finally get to meet my brood, Mother. However..." he pointed to the wagon, "...We have no fancy carriages here. It's the wagon or walking. It's far closer than the walk this morning." Pointing out to the two older ladies both the inn and Eddie's house.

When they saw the facade of Bramblemere Close, they both gasped, as did Ned and Christina. Ned turned to Eddie, "Oh, lad, it's wondrous."

"And it's thanks to you we have it, sir," Eddie replied. "That was part of your wedding gift. Wait until you see the rest." Eddie's grin said it all. "Your room is waiting, as I promised."

Another meeting was taking place behind the departing group. Fiona was the last to walk down the gangplank.

Standing with the group under the trees was Lewis Bland. He had greeted Ned, whom he had met at various family functions when a lad, and Great-Aunt Suze, he greeted with a kiss. Then he stood as if frozen to the spot.

Sal walked up to him. She had asked Harry to point him out. "Good afternoon; I believe you to be Lewis."

He nodded, not removing his eyes from the girl leaving the ferry.

"Lad, she is as anxious as you. What happens next will be your call. She did not come knowing you were here and only found on her arrival that you were not in Europe with Harry as she had been led to believe."

Lewis looked down at the lady speaking to him, and he realised it was Eddie's mother, for she could be no other. He shook his head to shake the vision away.

"Lewis, I suggest you talk to her. Together, you must work this out. Lad, her feelings have not changed." She patted his arm, and with that, she walked off, leaving the two anxious people alone.

He walked down the last few yards and, without words, offered her his arm. She took it, and he placed his hand over hers, interweaving his fingers around hers and gently squeezing.

She looked up at him, her eyes swimming. She saw the love he felt for her almost written on his face. Still, neither had spoken. Yet, moments later, she was in his arms, weeping on his chest. He stroked her hair until her sobs subsided. They had time enough to talk later.

John walked back up the hill with his friends, but noticed Lew was not amongst them. He turned to look back at the boat and saw him embrace a lady. She was holding him tight, and her arms wrapped around his chest. He said nothing, but raised his eyebrow. He turned and rejoined the group. One of the older ladies had taken his breath away. She was the image of his mother. She was so alike, it could be her. He had yet to be introduced.

Vicky looked pale. Was she now well?

Harry was concerned. By the time she arrived at Eddie's house, Vicky was faint. Harry carried her the last few yards to Eddie's house. He placed her on the settee and knelt beside her. She said, "I'm just dizzy, love. I hope it's just my body getting used to its new condition." She lay back and closed her eyes.

One happy reunion at the ferry was between Edmund and Christina. She had not seen her little brother for some time. He had gone to London, and her father had not deemed it necessary to inform her of her brother's whereabouts. She loved him, but wondered about his faith. His life since his return from India had been nothing but frivolity and aimless pursuits.

Edmund hugged his big sister as she disembarked. He swung her around and gave her a big kiss on the cheek. "Hello, big sister. I've missed you." He greeted Ned, then grabbed both children as they ran off the jetty.

"Hwllo, Uncle Edmund," they chorused. They had not forgotten him in the intervening year since his visit to the Castle.

He took them both in his arms at once and hoisted them up. "Hello, you rascals. Have you been good?"

They looked at each other. One said yes, the other no. Then they giggled and wiggled to get down.

He laughed and released them. "Typical," he said to his sister. The twins took off, their leather harness straps following like tails.

As the group walked up to the house, Aidan had introduced himself to Charles and Sal. Pointing out the relationship between Sal and himself. Sal was overjoyed to meet him. Aidan offered to tell her more about his 'Aunt Shannon', Sal's mother. Sal was sad that she had so little time with her mother, and Aidan, who had known her for many years, had now offered to talk with her. Sal, who had resigned herself to knowing very little about her family, was delighted. Finally, some questions could be answered.

Aidan said, "I will catch up with you later if I may. I shall leave you to your reunions." He bowed and walked back to Edmund.

Charles and Sal left the group at their cottage. Wills and Luke followed them inside. There, the four had a warm reunion.

Wills had been standing silently in the background with Luke. Charles finally greeted them warmly. Wills had expected a reprimand from his parents, but this had not occurred.

Luke was also hopping from one foot to the other. He may be seventeen, but he had missed his parents so much.

After they entered the cottage, Sal turned to her two "baby boys", who now both towered over her. "I have missed you both so much." She held out her arms, and they shared a group hug, much like they had when they were small children.

Moira was there waiting for the arrival. She had the kettle on the stove and was making tea.

Sal removed her shawl, and Charles placed it on their bed.

They were about to walk into the kitchen when there was a knock at the front door. Luke answered it. Liza, Anna and the children all bounced in. More hugs, as Nana had come back.

Luke stood leaning against the kitchen door. How he had missed this.

Charles stood looking at him. He had grown. He was only just fifteen on their departure, and now he was nearly a man.

"Dar, would you mind if I moved back here?" Luke asked quietly. "I think I'd like that. At least until I go to University."

Charles, stunned, looked at his son. "University? What's this about, lad? No, don't start telling me now, we'll sit and talk about that later. Of course, we would love to have you home with us again. It would be a delight." Charles patted his son's shoulder, then embraced him.

After the girls departed for their homes, Sal, Charles, and the two boys sat in the kitchen.

Moira headed back to the big house for the night. Cara had sent over a meal. Moira served it, did the dishes, and then departed.

Only when Moira closed the door did Sally relax. "Oh, Charles, we are home. I can take off the false smile and put on my faded clothes. Don't get me wrong, I have loved every moment of it. Especially being with Mother in her last days." She looked at her husband. "Charles, Aidan is going to tell me more about her."

He reached out and gently took her hand. "Yes, Sal." He knew she was sad. He also released a long, happy sigh. He was home.

With a lift of her head, she said, "It's just, well, this is home now. This is where our family is, and I have missed them all so much." She gave a teary chuckle. "Can you imagine us sitting in the kitchen at the Castle with the maid, having tea or dinner? No, this is the home I want, Charles."

Both boys sat looking at their parents in wonderment.

"You're not the only one, Sal. I may be an Earl in title, but I have a convict soul, I think." He smiled at the boys. "Yes, yes, I know I had the conviction quashed, but there is something in me that was not settled until we left Sydney on that little ferry. When we pulled into the unsteady wharf, I realised this was the life I wanted. My life was... no, my life is my family. Nothing but our faith is more important." He looked at his wife and two youngest sons. "You are my life, you all, and God." Charles cleared his throat. "Here are we prattling on about us and Wills, you're getting married tomorrow," he said, "I'm so glad you delayed it."

Sal said, "Now tell us what's happening. I'm guessing they are staying with the Millers again?"

Wills nodded, "Yes, and they won't let me see her," he said almost sulkily.

Charles laughed. "I think Martha is a bit superstitious—only one more day to go. I can't believe you are both grown up enough to get married. Well, nearly. You were all still children when we left."

Luke grinned.

Will shuffled his feet. He knew what was coming.

"Wills, we have to talk before you head back."

"All right, Dar," said Wills. Eddie had warned him about this. He knew what was coming, and his heart was in his mouth.

Cara and Paddy welcomed everyone. Cara led them all upstairs. She showed everyone which rooms belonged to which people.

Paddy and Cara had placed an enormous bouquet of roses in Ned and Christina's room. They exclaimed their beauty, and Christina thanked her profusely. Cara said, "Only the best for you, Your Grace. My Maryanne is now happily married to Robbie, with a kiddie, all because of the Major, sorry, the Juke and you, m'Lady." She gave a mini curtsy and departed.

"Oh, Edward, I didn't realise Cara and Paddy were Maryanne's parents," Christina said. "Nor that she is now married." She smiled, thinking about how Maryanne had come into her life. It was the week she had become engaged to the Major, as he was back then. Now, he was her beloved husband and father of three. He had arranged things so she would be protected from gossip, hence Maryanne's arrival. It had come full circle.

"I wonder if her Robbie is Gracie's brother-in-law Robert?" Ned pondered.

They all settled into their rooms. There was a lot of noise emanating from the large nursery at the back. Three sets of parents responded to the multiple howls. Charlie, Gracie, Ned, Christina, Eddie, and Jenna all appeared at the nursery door at once. Liam and Lily had knocked over a tower of blocks that the three sets of twins had built. No one was hurt, although there was enough noise to warrant mess time at Battalion Headquarters.

The six stood laughing at the multiple responses. "I think we had better get used to this," Ned said. "Eddie, I cannot get used to how much our four look alike. Lily and Liam, not so much, but these four could all be mistaken for the other. Amazing!"

Charlie said, "Have a look at our two and compare them to Liam; it seems the Lockleys have some variations."

Ned looked at Charlie's twins and then at Liam and saw that there was undoubtedly a similarity. "Not surprising, I suppose, considering they are all cousins, and we are all fair. Except our dear Jenna, of course." He gave her a nod. "I can't wait until they are grown. They will take London by storm. That's if you will still bring them, Eddie. You did promise, and I'm sure that Sarah and Tina will leave the Gunning sisters for dead."

Christina saw Jenna and Gracie's blank looks. "The Gunning sisters were from about one hundred years ago. They were poor Irish beauties who captivated the London court. Both married titled gentlemen, a Duke and an Earl, I think and became the toast of London. No one has ever rivalled their elegance, beauty and fame. However, these two might do so in a dozen or so years. Yes, we shall hold you to that promise,

Eddie, Jenna. My namesake will have her come-out ball with Sarah in London. 1858 or '59 will not know what has hit it." She chuckled. "Lily can have her own a few years later. Or better still, bring her cousins. I'm hoping she may have another cousin or three by then. I'm trying to persuade Edward."

"Gracie, Charlie, I'm not asking, I'm telling. We're covering all the children's education. All the boys can go to whatever school you choose, either here or in London. King's, Eton, then Oxford, wherever they or you want." Christina looked at them.

The children were now quiet, and the parents retired to the sitting room downstairs.

Vicky and Harry were still there; she was sitting up and looking much better.

John and Phil had returned directly to Roseneath to take their luggage from their honeymoon.

Harry had initially intended to travel to Sydney in the covered wagon, but they decided to leave the wagon at home and travel by ferry. They had done this the week after their wedding. They had each taken one bag. Harry had taken Vicky shopping, and they returned with five suitcases of clothing for Vicky and numerous new shirts and linen undergarments for him. Other items ordered but not finished will be sent later.

~

Finally, nearly everyone had headed off to bed.

Between Fiona and Lewis, they had left everything unsaid. Time enough when they had recovered from the shock. It was enough to know the other was close. Their feelings were unchanged. Maybe, while here, they could work things out. Lewis would seek counsel when his heart stopped pounding. "How could she be here?" He had not even mentioned her to his friends, nor the crushing rejection by her father.

His time with his friends had taught him a great deal about his own character. Lew had belittled her work with the poor and the crofters on her father's land. Her father wanted a man for her who would care for the people, not just any people, but her people. Eventually, she would lead her Clan as chieftain. His time in this land had shown how shallow he and his behaviour had been. He would return a different person. He wanted to be a responsible person, one who was willing to put others first. He had yet to prove this to himself. Tomorrow, they would talk, yes, tomorrow—but only with Reverend Clarke's approval.

Marc arrived at Eddie's place at dusk to say they had arrived safely. He didn't stay long and returned to Miller's inn. He had not waited to see Wills.

Luke arrived at the big house; Wills followed about half an hour later. Eddie let him know the Turners had safely arrived. Relieved, he said,

"Thanks," and headed to bed.

Eddie thought, "Something is definitely wrong." He tried to shrug it off, but couldn't.

Fiona and Amelia disappeared after dinner and had not returned downstairs. Nanny, Ned, and Christina had to try to settle the three children down in strange sleeping quarters. Having never shared with other children before, they were all unsettled. Neddie, Tina, and Lily had all been worn out earlier in the day and were already asleep.

Eddie felt unsettled in spirit and didn't know why. Something felt just not right.

Harry had finally accepted the offer of a carriage to take Vicky home to Roseneath. She was not looking too well.

Suze and Elle had sat talking with Eddie and Jenna until they, too, pleaded tiredness and headed upstairs to bed.

Eddie walked into his office, looking for peace. He did not find it. He turned to look out the window and could see the silhouette of the trees in the veiled moonlight. He fell to his knees. "Lord God, my soul is depressed. Fill me with peace, Your Peace." He was still on his knees when Jenna joined him.

"Do you feel it too, love?" she asked. "Some sense of disquiet?"

He nodded, then stood up. "I don't know what it is, but Wills is not happy. That I know." He was still looking out the window, then turned to her. Drawing her into his arms, he said, "Jen, I think I need to talk to him. I think I know what it is. I need to be sure. It could take a bit of time, so go to bed. I'll be in as soon as I can."

She reached up and pulled his golden head down to hers. "It's why I love you, my dear; you care." She quietly left him alone.

He prayed some more. He turned out the lamps as he went, leaving the house in darkness. He left to ascend the stairs to Wills' room quietly. He knocked, but there was no answer. He could hear his muffled sobs. He opened the door quietly and entered.

"Go away!" said Wills.

"No, Wills, we need to talk. You need to talk, but I'll start. Wills, you haven't been the same since two weeks ago, when you returned from Emu. I've never seen you look so, well, haunted." He sat on the end of his brother's bed. Eddie continued talking, keeping his voice peaceful and quiet so it could not be heard in the next room. "Tonight, I saw your face when you came in from Dar."

Wills groaned.

Ed didn't stop. "I know what that talk was. I had it too, but from your reaction, I have a feeling things might have gone too far last week?" Ed knew he had hit the nail on the head by Wills' reaction.

Wills gave a huge sob. "Oh, Ed, what have I done?"

"I thought so," thought Eddie. Dear Lord, what do I say? "Wills, did you force her? I need you to answer me honestly."

Wills flipped over and looked directly at his brother. "Oh, no, Ed! No way, I would not have done that. No, we both wanted it... But now, I wish we hadn't. No, I wish I'd had the strength to have waited. Dar's words tonight just reinforced the guilt, that is all. I feel horrible."

Wills slowly sat up. He was dejected, unhappy and sorrowful. "I feel I have disrespected her, dishonoured her. I love her so much. I have hurt her. It nearly happened once before, but we stopped in time. It was fine while Harry was there, as we decided that neither of us would go off alone. I think something similar must have nearly happened to them, too, the day they became engaged. The past few weeks have been incredibly challenging. We were alone so often. Well, we got carried away. So now, here I am, sobbing like a baby, and I'm supposed to be grown up and married tomorrow," he hiccupped.

"Have you spoken to her since it happened?" Eddie asked.

"Yes! Oh yes, Ed and I have begged her forgiveness as she did mine," he said sadly. "But I have betrayed her trust in me, and I cannot forgive myself."

Ed hurt for his little brother."You must, Wills! You must now use this as a stepping stone in your marriage, allowing both of you to grow from it. Or it could become a stumbling block, and then you will trip yourselves up," Eddie said. "You *must* talk it over with her and not bottle things up. I want you to go to your wedding tomorrow with joy, not regret. You are making an honest woman of her; that was never in doubt. Make sure that you never find yourself in a situation again where lust has taken over. It's not worth it, Wills." Eddie stopped, thinking hard. "Wills, if you feel like this with the girl you love and are to marry just because you preempted your marriage vows, imagine how you would feel if you strayed with someone else?"

Wills gasped. "I would never!" He was absolutely horrified at the thought.

Ed continued in his gentle, loving voice, "Over the coming years, you will be travelling a lot. She will not always be with you. The desires of the flesh, I'm talking of lust, Wills. It is strong. You have discovered that. Use this lesson and never be tempted away from her. That is a decision only you can make. You may think this is a long way from taking your betrothed to bed, but it's not, and the consequences are vast. It could even end your marriage."

Wills sniffed. "Okay, Ed."

"Wills, Cathy loves you; you love her. I think Charlie and I were hard for insisting you wait. If we had not, then you would already have been married. Did you think of that?" Eddie said, looking at his little brother. "Yes, it's nice that our parents are here, but I should have made it easier for you to marry without them. Trust me, when I say I know the temptations you went through. It nearly happened to us, but James, yes, my horse… came over and stopped us. He nuzzled me as I was finding my emotions were, shall I say, getting the better of both of us. That was also the day I asked her to marry me, too." Eddie laughed, thinking of his beautiful black stallion. "Wills, if it were not for him, I'm not sure we would have stopped either. Brother, it's not like you're going to clear off and never see her again. You're marrying her tomorrow."

Wills looked at his older brother. "Really, you don't condemn me? I feel I have let everyone down, Cathy, most of all."

Ed was stunned at the question, "Are you kidding? Oh, Wills, I could not be prouder of you. Look at what you have planned for this town, Emu and Bathurst. How could I not be proud of you? You could have sat on the money and not shared it. But *no!* You look around and see what's needed and how you can supply it. I am so proud of you. More than you will ever realise." He tousled his brother's hair, as he had done a thousand times before.

Wills laughed. "Are you sure, Eddie? Really?" he sat up straight. "I will never fail her again. I will be the kind of husband she deserves. I will make her proud of me, too, Eddie. I love her."

"Make sure you tell her every day. When you're away from her, write her every day and tell her of that love. It keeps it fresh in *your* mind. By staying honest with yourself, you will be honest with her," Eddie exclaimed. "Oh, and Wills, we are all human; we all fail. Just make sure it's *not* this way with someone else."

Eddie looked at his brother in the dim moonlight. "Wills, I want you to take it to God in prayer, then go to sleep. God can turn this into joy. Let him. Remember the Bible says, '*Cast your burdens on Him?*' It's what you now have to do. I'm going now, but I want you to pray, then sleep, all right? Remember, God does not just forgive us once, but every time we ask. The fact that you're in here sobbing your heart out shows you are remorseful. God knows that. Confess all to Him, ask His forgiveness."

Wills nodded.

Eddie left, closing the door softly behind him. He walked downstairs to his office, deep in thought. How easily that could have been after that day on the riverbank. The passion that so nearly overtook all reason for them both. He thought back to his honeymoon, the wonder and the discovery of each other's bodies. It was aptly called 'the joys of marriage,' and yet, it could have been so easily destroyed by breaking that delicate tie of trust. He had never let himself get into a situation where that could ever occur. Jenna held his heart and only her.

Dar had said that in marriage, the union of two bodies was not just for procreation, but recreation and relaxation too. And how they had found it so in the last five-plus years. They still delighted in their physical union. They had decided never to use it as a means of making up after a fight, and although they had a few crossed words and differences, they had never really fought.

Jenna was strong-willed, yes, but was always willing to talk things through. Cathy was the same. Ed knew that they often disagreed about things, but had never really fought. Their lovemaking was always mutual and still passionate, to the point that she never ceased to surprise him in some way. Just thinking about her upstairs in bed was enough to stir his body. He stood again at the window in the dark and thanked God for giving him the right words.

He turned to seek the privacy of their room. Hopefully, she would still be awake. He needed her so much. If she was asleep, he would not wake her, as he also loved her so. He opened their door quietly, walked in.

As he closed it, he was greeted with "Hello, love, come to bed."

He did.

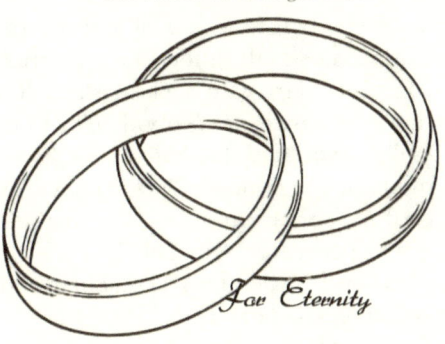

Chapter 11   For Eternity

*E*ddie knocked on Wills' door early the next morning and found him standing at his window.

"Hi, Eddie, thanks so much for last night. I did what you said, I took it to God. We shall use this as a stepping stone. Together we shall grow strong," he smiled.

Eddie did not realise the knot in his own stomach was still there. "Oh, Wills, I'm so glad. Whatever happens now is only between you, Cathy and God. You *can* make it right, and I know you will." They now stood eye to eye. Ed was surprised; when did his little brother grow so tall?

Wills walked over to his older brother and hugged him. Wills said, "Thank you again, Eddie. I really do appreciate that you were there for me last night. You cared enough to come. You cared enough *not* to go when I told you to. That and everything you have done for me. Even to Luke and I living here with you for the last two years." He paused, "Well, just, thanks, Ed." He turned away and picked something up. "I want to show you something. You know how we give our wives a wedding ring when we marry? Well, I was thinking, even before this happened, I wanted one too. When we chose her ring in Sydney, I ordered this, unbeknownst to her. These are made with some of the gold we found. See, there is one for me as well. They are a matched set. I've had them engraved." He handed the small box to Eddie. Two gold rings sat in it, one larger, one smaller.

Eddie picked up the larger one. On the inside read *For Eternity*. "Wow, Wills, that's beautiful."

"I mean it, Ed, I will always be there for her," he smiled.

"Chin up, lad. Big day ahead," he messed up his hair. "Glad it's you and not me. I hate being the centre of attention. Mine was bad enough. At least you shouldn't be accused of horse theft in the middle of the service. Nah, your turn now." Ed turned to leave, then hesitated.

"Wills, just a thought. Maybe before you, well, before the first time, well, you know the 'Joy of Marriage' stuff, after you're married, pray first, and ask for forgiveness together. Start with a clean slate. Just a thought, it's really only God you have to answer to. Nobody else's business but yours and His, just saying! Wills - *only Him.*" He left.

Wills stood thinking. He nodded, "Yes! Yes, we will."

It was a beautiful February morning. Even the children weren't fighting. By chance, it was February 14th. This had not been planned, but they were getting married on St Valentine's Day. The wedding should have been late December or even early January.

The inn yard was once again prepared for a party. Everyone had been invited. Not as many people as at Eddie and Jenna's wedding, yet it would be an open invitation affair, so many more would come to the party. Drinks were on the house, so many would turn up for the free ale.

Over the past two years, Charlie, as Assistant Viceroy, had cleaned up the drinking in some inns. The Union and the Woolpack were still a little rough, but the rest of the town was a little safer now. The Red Cow and what once had been the Bird in the Hand inn were now combined and it was a family run inn.

Charlie had the dray, cart and wagon all readied for the festivities.

Some still chose to walk, but John Saunders had brought the Town Carriage for the ladies who wished to drive. Suze and Elle both took this option. Harry and Vicky were already inside. Christina and Jenna joined them with the two babies. Walking would burn off some of the stored-up energy from the three sets of twins. At least they knew they could move around. However, they were not to make a sound. They were all accustomed to church and knew that they had to sit quietly, if possible. Chip and Sarah had never been in a church with no roof.

The church roof had been torn off in a tornado the week Ned and Christina married some years before. It happened only four days before the wedding. That had been 21st December 1841. What a horrible experience that was.

As Ned walked up to the church, he saw the piles of shingles that Wills, Luke, and the other boys in town had collected. They were now rotting, still sitting in the piles from that traumatic day years ago. The timber beams, too, were now weather-damaged and rotting. A roof of sorts, made from old sails, had hastily covered the rotting beams. These had been only meant to be temporary. However, they had now aged and disintegrated. Ned was horrified that no other permanent repairs had been done. Nothing at all. A sour taste in his mouth and a flash of anger crossed his face. He shook his head. Project number one, he thought. At least I can pay for a new roof. He shook off his anger. Today was not the time to discuss it.

Tim and Anna arrived in a flash new phaeton.

Jack and Cathy were assisted of the carriage by Bertie. She stood looking around, trying to see Wills.

Charles and Eddie had hurried Wills in through the Vestry door. He was out of sight. Charlie stuck his head in the vestry, saying, "She's here and grinning like you wouldn't believe."

Charles left to join Sal. Eddie would stand with Wills as best man. "Ready, lad? Don't you pass out on me?"

Wills was standing with his back to the inside Vestry door. His head bowed. He chuckled, "No, Eddie, just praying. I'm asking God to bless this day, as well as us. I'm good. Well, you know."

"Yes, I know. Just trying to lighten the mood, lad." Eddie walked to the inner vestry door. He could see the ministers, both Reverend Bobart and Reverend Clarke were waiting for them.

Reverend Bobart beckoned them to enter.

Eddie grabbed Wills' arm. "Time's up," he chuckled. They walked into the church and stood facing the Ministers. The piano started playing. Ned was amazed it still worked, but it sounded sweet and pure. They must keep it covered. He thought.

Eddie whispered to Wills, "Look."

Wills did. He turned to see her haloed in the glare of the doorway. She was dressed in a fabulous cream, lacy gown, pinched to a pointed waist with hundreds of tiny gathers of netting over the skirt, dropping down to a flounce at the bottom. He gasped. She looked like an angel. His angel, he beamed.

Jenna preceded her up the aisle.

Eddie watched the emotions flash across his face. Finishing with a beaming smile. Wills would be all right, as would they both. Eddie smiled, contented.

Cathy walked to Wills and stood beside him. He took her hand and kissed the palm.

Jack stood beside her, but Wills did not even notice him. His eyes were fixed on her.

Her gaze, locked onto his.

Reverend Clarke coughed. They turned to face him. He started the service. He greeted them with a smile. This was one wedding he had no intention of missing. He lifted his eyes to the congregation and said, "Dearly beloved, we are gathered here today to join William, Wills, and Catherine, Cathy, in Holy Matrimony...

...the service continued.

Eddie held his breath when it got to the words where their wedding halted. He had been accused of being a horse thief in the middle of the service. "Is there any reason why these two should not be joined in Holy Matrimony?" He looked at Jenna, remembering their own wedding.

They both swallowed, eyes fixed on each other. When Reverend

Clarke continued, and they both released their breath.

Jack did his usual spiel when asked, "Who gives this woman?" He replied, "I do, and make sure you don't hurt her."

Wills grinned, and said, "No, sir, not likely." He had heard this twice before.

Jack chuckled. Wills caught the words of the service. "Love, Honour and Cherish," that's funny, he thought it was "obey"? His eyes flew to Reverend Clarke with an eyebrow raised.

Reverend Clarke then softly added, "Obey," too. He glanced at Maria and smiled.

Wills and Cathy smiled at each other and both replied, "I will," firmly at the appropriate times.

Reverend Clarke sighed, thinking that he always loved this bit. With a deep breath, "I now pronounce you man and wife. You may kiss your wife."

And Wills did. He first lifted her short veil, gently brushed his lips against hers. He looked into her eyes, then gathered her into his arms, kissing her passionately. She wrapped her arms around his neck, closed the remaining space between them and clung to him. Everyone laughed. A few called out. Their kiss deepened.

Some time passed before Reverend Clarke coughed again. Finally, Wills released her, grinning broadly again.

"You can sit over there for the homily," Reverend Clarke pointed to the two chairs off to the side.

Wills led Cathy to the seats, then shuffled his chair closer to hers so he could hold her hand. Reverend Bobart delivered the sermon. He started, "1 Corinthians verse 13 is the Bible reading normally read at Marriages, but The Song of Solomon is all about the Joys of Marriage. However, we have to go back to the Book of Genesis, and we discover that woman was made from man's rib to be his helpmate. It was taken from his side. Not his foot nor his head. God meant man and woman to walk beside each other, as one strong unit. Each with their individual roles, equal but different. I'm sure that this young couple, still in their teen years, will grow old together."

Wills would remember that bit, equal, but different. From then on all he could think of was the prayer together they must have. He meant to start the way he wanted them to go on. They sat listening.

Cathy clung to his hand, their fingers interwoven.

The sermon over, they signed the Marriage Register. Harry and Vicky were the signatures in the Register before them.

Wills and Cathy stood before their friends and family. He was clutching her hand. She was his wife, for eternity. They each wore rings saying so.

Reverend Clarke turned to the congregation. "Please, everyone, to be upstanding. May I present to you, The Honourable William and Mrs William Lockley." He started clapping. Everyone else joined in.

Harry caught his breath. He had completely forgotten that Wills was also the son of an Earl. He laughed. Jenna and Cathy would take precedence over him. He was only the younger son of a Viscount. He chuckled, "Well, that puts me firmly in my place." He smiled to himself, another thing to remember in this new country of his. His title meant nothing or virtually nothing. Here he was just Harry. He was what he made himself to be. Work hard and do good, and you succeed. He smiled again and took Vicky's hand and kissed it. They walked down the aisle, Jenna and Eddie following them, then Ned, Christina, *Les Grande Dames*, Charles and Sal, then finally the rest of the family. The children had been wonderfully quiet during the service.

Mrs Jenkins stood just outside and showered them with rose petals. Jenna greeted her with a kiss. Mrs Jenkins was a changed woman from the bitter, busy body Jenna had first spoken to some four years ago. She now ran the Women's Social group and was popular in her care of single and abused women in the town. They knew she could be approached when they were in need. She understood being ostracised. Convict or free, they all knew she'd help.

Wills and Cathy moved to the shady trees, and everyone gathered around them, congratulating them both.

Charles sought out Reverend Clarke and his wife. "I have a bit of a surprise for you, Sir, Ma'am," Charles said before beckoning the girls to their side.

Amelia and Fiona were escorted to them by Phil and Edmund.

Mrs Clarke greeted them with joy. "Oh, my dears, when did you arrive? I did not know you were coming. William, did you know?" She turned to him.

Reverend William looked confused, then she could see he remembered something. "Wait a moment." He was patting his pockets. "I was handed this moments before the service." A crushed, dirty letter was pulled from his pocket. "This has been chasing us around for some time. Eventually, the postman knew we were doing today's wedding, so he decided to hand it to my learnéd colleague here," motioning to Reverend Bobart. "Is this it?" he handed over the unopened, crumpled letter to his wife.

Amelia giggled, "Yes, Uncle William, that's it." She turned to her cousin, "Fi, it seems we are not expected after all."

Their aunt said, "You're always welcome, lass, both of you. When I wrote, I thought we'd be stationed in Sydney, but these last few months we have been floating around various parishes. We're heading to Campbelltown after this with the children." She added softly so Reverend Clarke couldn't hear. I admit, "I do grow weary of this life style." She sighed. "We've also been in Dural, Castle Hill and I believe we're to soon be at North Sydney. Uncle William also has his duties at The King's School, which is where he got to know young William, whom he has just married."

"Oh," both the girls said.

"How are you here and with this wonderful family?" Aunt Maria asked.

"We were on the same ship as them, Aunt Maria," said Fiona.

"Ahh, well, my dears, we are going to have to work something out. We won't be able to get into the new rectory until August. This is the one at North Sydney." She looked from face to face. "Until then, we are living in the wagon, with three children." She looked so apologetic.

"Oh, Aunt Maria, I'm sure we can stay with the Lockleys," said Amelia happily.

Maria noticed the panicked look on Fiona's face. "We'll sort it out later, let's enjoy this wedding first." She patted Amelia's hand, and she walked off. She had not let Fiona's hand go. "Spit it out, lass, I know that look, I've seen it on many a lovelorn face." She looked Fiona in the eye.

"It's Lewis. He's here." A tear spilled down her cheek. "Father refused his offer, and he went away. So did I. Thinking he went to Europe, I came here." She turned and met his eyes across the lawn. "What are we to do?"

Aunt Maria laughed. "You come halfway around the world and find that the love of your life is here already waiting for you?"

Fiona nodded. Another tear escaped; her eyes had not left Lewis' face. "Yes."

"Has he been here since he was rejected, sweetheart?" her aunt asked.

"Yes, well, mostly, I think, that was over a year ago," she whispered meekly. "Very soon after papa said, *no*. Lew said he met his friends in London, where he was going to drown his sorrows. Only weeks later, his parents told me he had left the country. I have not had a chance to ask him more. Lew's sister said he was with Harry."

Lewis was walking towards her. She drew her breath, "What will I do, Aunty? Papa forbade me even speaking to him. Aunt Maria, help me."

"Err, darling Fi, I don't see your Papa here, do you?" She smiled at her niece. She knew her brother, and she knew his reasons for the refusal. Maria also knew of the radical change in Lewis since he had arrived. "Talk to him, lass, just talk to him. Then send him to Uncle William."

Her face brightened. "Really, Aunt Maria? May I?"

"Go, Fi, but do not be alone with him." Her aunt gave her a gentle pat. "Come and see us together tomorrow."

Lewis arrived beside her. He greeted her aunt, "Good morning,

Mrs Clarke. I did not know you knew Miss Moreton?" Lewis' eyes devoured Fiona.

Maria watched him, "Lad, she's my niece. Both of the girls are. My William is their guardian while they are here." She patted his arm while looking him in the eyes, "Lewis, you may talk to her, but only in public. You do have my permission for that, and no more. No walks, and no alone time. I will talk to William."

"You are too kind, Mrs Clarke. I will not disappoint you." He offered his arm to Fiona. She placed her hand on it, and he covered it with his. They wandered off and sat under a tree with the children playing around them.

Family surrounded Wills and Cathy. Martha walked up to her daughter. She took her face and cupped it in her hands. "Oh, my baby girl, you are married. My baby girl is married. I'm sad, but happy too." She turned to Wills, "And now I have another son." She kissed them both and went away in happy-tears in her eyes. She walked into Jack's arms.

Jack pulled her close. "Come on, love, it's a happy day," he spoke softly to her.

Martha nodded, "Cathy is our last daughter, Jack. Thank God for Milly. At least I won't be totally alone in a house full of men," she blubbered. "I'm all right, Jack, honestly. Just happy-sad,"

She gave him a very teary smile, then chuckled. "Jack, do you realise that they are all The Honourables? Harry tells me Jenna and Cathy, Wills and Eddie have higher precedence than they do. It took me a while to work out what he meant. I was racking my brain back to our time in London." She giggled. "I think this means more for Harry than us. Jack, I just love them all. Our girls are all so happy. The boys are good, Godly men. We can ask for no more."

Jack smiled at her. "See. Who knows where our children will end up in this place. I wonder who'll turn up for the boys?" He chuckled again. He slid his hand down her arm and took her hand, interlacing his fingers with hers. He had been bowled over by her before his first job placement at Camden. That had been in 1820. However, they had met once in London a year earlier. They married soon after meeting out here. Neither spoke of their past lives. Both knew each other's story and that was enough. Ned knew some of him, but little of Martha's. Martha had had a rough time as a convict, especially on the trip out, she was sent to Hetty Walker to recuperate before assignment. She was malnourished and well underweight, yet she was still beautiful, so much so, he recognised Harry's look when he first saw Vicky. He knew that feeling too.

Charlie, Eddie, and Harry brought round the carriage, carts and wagons. Everyone possible climbed on board, including the bride and groom. Charles loaded the *Les Grande Dames* into the carriage with Vicky, Sal, and Christina. They slowly proceeded down the main street back to the Inn. Once again, a flat wagon was used for the musicians. Kegs were tapped, and the food started appearing. Every guest who came brought more. Soon, the tables were laden and the party in full swing. People came and went all afternoon.

Fiona and Amelia sat near their aunt with Lewis attending to their every need through the afternoon. He was constantly on the lookout for something, though. Reverend Clarke had taken Wills aside and told him what he planned to do with his share of the gold. "Wills, I have had some weeks to think. I want to conduct a thorough mineral survey. This would truly benefit the entire country to know what minerals are out in this amazing place. What do you think, lad?"

Wills was ecstatic. "That's fabulous, sir, but I also want you to spend some on your good self and Mrs Clarke. She deserves something, sir." He looked to her and smiled.

"The only catch is that I promised to say nothing about the gold until Gipps goes." The minister looked crestfallen. "We do also have to send the children to England for education."

Wills chuckled. "Then you might be pleased to know he has announced that he's returning to England mid-year. So, you'd better get cracking on that idea." Wills shook his hand a congratulated his mentor.

"Is that really true, lad? Oh, that does inspire me." Reverend Clarke's eyebrows danced with joy. His moustache wiggled into a broad smile. "Wonderful news, lad, truly wonderful, God is working his mysterious ways again. I must away and tell Maria."

"Oh, sir, can you possibly wait until you are alone? We don't want the news out just yet, but do start working on the submission. We'll help where we can," Wills pleaded.

"Oh, lad, that does make sense. Yes I will tell her later. Good idea, good idea," he walked off muttering.

Wills laughed. It was hard to believe this scruffy clergyman was the same age as the Duke and Dar. He had certainly travelled far more. He was wise beyond his years. Wills both loved and admired him. He watched the minister walk to his long-suffering, loving wife. Poor Maria.

Cathy walked up to him as he was now standing alone. She slid her arm along his. "Hello, husband. I think it must be time for speeches, don't you? Then we can leave." It was by now getting on for dark.

Wills went and spoke to his father.

Charles nodded and moved to the cart. The musicians were on a break, and dancing had stopped. Charles climbed up so everyone could see and hear him. "Friends, greetings and welcome. As you can see, we're just back in time to see our runaway son commit himself to this delightful young lady for the rest of their lives...."

He continued for some time, often making Wills groan, but on the whole, good-hearted banter.

Wills also spoke, and this time it was Cathy's time to be embarrassed. He called her up beside him, and after a few calls, they willingly obliged and kissed.

Whistles and cheers eventually dying down, they would head off soon. Toasts were made, then Cara produced a beautiful cake.

Once it was cut and shared, it was time for the couple to depart. They didn't have far to go as they were spending the first night in 'Gracemere Cottage,' just a few doors up from the inn. From there, they would spend a week or so in Sydney.

Upon their return, they would get down to work and begin building. Even Cathy was excited and had asked if she could listen in on the planning discussions. She had asked if they only needed to stay away for the week. They could always go back later. Wills agreed.

As yet, few outside of the family knew of the building projects, and fewer knew the reason for them. They had managed to divert speculation. Wills had done all the transactions directly through Mr Moffatt, the Clerk of the Peace at the Courthouse. He had been told not only of their plans, but of the extent of the gold finds. He had even helped with future planning advice on behalf of the government. The Emporium Warehouse was to be built and set back a little from the main western road, but close enough to it for access by a range of large vehicles and wagons. The large site had room to grow.

Mr Tindale also knew, as he had helped smelter the gold. He knew it was a lot, but not the final amount. Reverend Clarke, was told how much they had found, but not that there was more in Hartley. Others in town knew of the plans of extending the Emporium, but it was rumoured that Major Grace, now the Duke, was behind it all. The Duke played along, knowing it was vital that the word not yet get out. He said it was why he had returned. Reverend Clarke had given his word, nothing would be said to Maria until their departure from the wedding. Hopefully, by then the buildings would be started, if not some nearly finished.

Wills and Cathy were receiving many congratulations of many townsfolk before their departure. Ned and Charles called them over. They went hand in hand. Ned took them aside, and the four stood with heads together, talking quietly.

Eddie heard Wills and Cathy exclaim, "Really?"

"Oh, thank you, Uncle Ned," from Wills.

"Thank you, sir," from Cathy. She gave them both a huge hug and Wills shook their hands, then hugged them too.

"I can't believe it. Thank you so much," Wills said, totally overwhelmed.

Ned laughed and said to Charles, "Who would have believed that a boatload of Pig Iron and corrugated galvanised roof sheets would have evoked such a reaction. Not the most usual wedding gift, but perfect for this young couple."

Ned knew they had ample funds, but these items were not yet available in this country. He and Charles had purchased as much stock as could be carried in the ship's hold, both as ballast and cargo.

Charles and Ned's mystery shopping trip while in Sydney, was to make arrangements to transport it to Parramatta. The cargo would be arriving by road in the next week. The hired carts would have to park in Eddie's yard until they could be unloaded at the warehouse.

Final plans for the warehouse had been completed. All they needed was the convict labour to arrive. They would arrive during the week.

Ned had already spoken to the "powers that be" in Hyde Park Barracks in Sydney, and a gang of labourers were being sent out with the carts of iron. The reason for these felons being allowed to come was that most were being transferred to Hobart. Some were still being considered for their Tickets of Leave, and this project would be one of the last before final transportation.

Wills had already stockpiled a lot of building supplies. Piles of rough-hewn stone was already on-site and being shaped, and the building timbers were at Eddie's. It was all ready for the foundation to be laid.

Cathy dragged Wills away. He would stay talking work all night if she let him. He chuckled. "I'm coming, love. Truly, I am." Groaning and saying to himself, "What a time to leave?"

Everyone parted, cheering loudly. They walked through them and up the hill. Luke stood looking until they were out of sight. Eddie saw him and realised this was how Wills had felt too, alone in a crowd. Ed went to Luke and drew him into a group of his friends. Eddie had learnt the hard way, parenting was more than just supplying a roof over their head, food, and a warm bed. He may not be, Wills' parent but he had been responsible for his care. He had failed him. Thankfully, it had worked out well, but it could have gone very wrong. Last night's conversation didn't help him either. Hopefully, it had helped Wills.

Thankfully, Mama and Dar were back. He expected Luke would want to move back in with them. He would wait and watch. But watch him, he would.

Wills and Cathy had reached the cottage. Wills opened the door, turned, and carried her over the threshold. He kicked the door closed.

She giggled but was surprised that he carried her into the sitting room, and not the bedroom.

Wills gently set her down and led her to the settee. "Cathy, we need to talk. Do you mind?" he asked.

"No, love of course, what's wrong?" she said lovingly.

"It's about the last time I went to Emu, my love. I have been wracked with guilt all week. Last night, Eddie heard me crying."

She gasped.

"Yeah, like a baby. It was with regret, Cathy. I betrayed you by not being able to control myself. I should have stopped us. I didn't. I want to apologise again, Cathy. I'm so sorry." He was on his knees before her.

"Oh, Wills, it was not just you. I wanted it as much. I know if I had said, 'No' or 'Stop,' you would have. You did ask, remember? There is no way you forced me. We did this together. I love you, Wills. I wanted to be married much earlier." She bent and kissed him quickly. "Yes, we should have waited, but we didn't. Now we're married." She looked at his sad face. "Wills, what do you want to do?"

"Cathy, Eddie suggested that before we're together again, that we pray together, and ask forgiveness; from each other and God?" He looked pleadingly.

"Oh yes, that would be wonderful. Yes," Rather than pull him onto the settee beside her, she slipped onto her knees and they knelt together in prayer.

They knelt, heads bowed, as they both confessed their lust and lack of self-control. A sin that was only between themselves and God. Wills asked for him to be a strong and faithful leader in their new family and lead it as a Godly figurehead. They prayed together for some time, then he said, *Amen*. Then he reached over and kissed her cheek.

She leaned towards him and wrapped her arms around his neck. "Wills, we will be strong in this marriage. If the first thing we do as a couple is pray, then that's what I want to do every day. Yes, we should have a prayer time together every day we can." She got to her feet and took his hand.

He followed her lead as they walked to their bedroom. Now they were married. He turned her to face him. "I will try my hardest to be the very best husband ever, Cathy. I will do everything I can to be everything you want." He bent and brushed her lips with his. He kissed her nose, then her eyes. "I love you so much. I've waited so long to call you mine. No guilt, only love."

She twisted her arms around his neck. "Only love. I like that my dearest and only love." She stood on tiptoe and kissed him. "We will go where God leads, but we go together. Always together, all right? And I will be the best helpmate and wife I can be."

He nodded, then pulled her close to him, kissing her with passion. He started to undo the buttons of her gown. He paused, puzzled.

She giggled. "Every third button, love, the other two are fake, Maa's idea."

He blushed, "I've, um, well, never undone a gown before, Cathy."

"Good, I would hope not," she said, giggling. She turned so he could undo all the rest, which, knowing the trick, he managed quickly.

Then as she turned back, her gown slid down her arms and pooled on the floor. She undid his jacket, then vest and shirt. She was easing each item off and sending them fluttering to join her gown in a pile on the floor.

Her new lacy undergarments did not even get a glance. They joined the rest of the divested clothing.

He lifted her and placed her on the bed, then turned down the lamp, but not off, and joined her. "I love you, Cathy, so very much. Tonight we start anew. Together." He'd never seen the female form unclad before. Their previous time together was almost fully dressed. His hand shook as he touched her. He groaned with desire. "No guilt, just love," he murmured.

Cathy lifted her arms behind her and let him look and touch. In the soft lamplight, her skin glowed warm, smooth and silky.

After a minute or so, she ran her fingers along his forehead and into his fair hair. With her hand around his neck, she slowly drew him to her. "Together forever, love."

She whispered while his lips rested on hers. "Wills, I want you."

They fell asleep in each other's arms sometime later.

The wedding party broke up soon after they departed. There was much to clean up. Most of it could be done tomorrow. Suze, Elle, and Christina had headed back to Eddie's house just up the street. They were all tired and would wash, then head to bed before the others arrived.

Cara and her girls had the hot water ready on the stove. Moira arrived from the party and took the hot water from the kitchen up to the two grandmothers' rooms.

Christina had already learned the run of the house. She fell back into her old ways of doing things for herself. She preferred having no personal maid. Christina thought, "Edward was perfectly capable of fastening or unfastening my gowns. Admittedly, it sometimes took longer, but it was far more fun." Her hair, she did herself, and had done for years.

Suze and Elle were still in the sitting room. Moira let them know the hot water was waiting for them both. They both thanked her.

As she left, she shut the door. Suze turned to watch her leave. "Elle, have you noticed how out here everyone is treated equally?" Suze looked over to her friend. "We sit down to a meal with convicts. They are treated as friends. My Neddie is on first-name terms with Paddy and vice versa. Although, I found out that Moria's sister, Maryanne, is married to Robert, and he's Albert's brother. So, in a way, they are all related."

Elle looked blank. "Albert?"

"Bertie is married to your Liza," Suze explained.

"Oh, that Albert. Suze, Charles, warned me of this," Elle replied. "I still feel a bit like this with your friendship. I felt worthless. I had nothing, and then you and Ned came and rescued us. We had no food in the house at all." Elle remembered the sad, hungry years.

"No, Elle. Oh no. You were never a convict," Suze said.

"No, I wasn't, Suze, but at the time Charles was. I was the mother of one. I did not know, well, anything else but poverty. Certainly, I had no idea that my John had been an Earl. I'm sure he never knew either," She shook her head. "I'm sure he would have told me." She wiped a tear from her cheek, thinking of her beloved John. There had never been anyone else for her.

"We had so little time together before he died. Seven short years. Some of that, John was away in the army. At least he got to see and hold Lilabet before he died. The last time he came home, he was so ill. I was not coping with Charles. At five, he was already rebelling. He had no father figure, except for the fathers of the other village children. They were all bad examples for him. I failed him, Suze. I felt I failed them all. I had no way to introduce Lilabet to any prospective husbands." Elle sat thinking about the life they had led.

Suze looked at her friend. "I have always wondered. How did you meet John?"

Elle sat looking at her hands; her wedding ring had worn thin from the gardening. The calluses had now gone, but the scars on her heart remained. She smiled at the memory. "It was at a county ball in Kent, Suze. I was staying with my grandparents, my mother's parents. My father was away somewhere with my sister. I was a wallflower and so shy. I stood looking at my shoes all evening because I knew no one there. I was petrified someone might actually talk to me." She laughed at the memory. "John walked up to me and stood beside me. There was a large floral display next to me, and he started talking to it. I giggled. I looked up at him, and oh, Suze, he was so handsome in his uniform. He looked like my Charles but in a red uniform." She sighed. "He asked me to dance. Suze, it was a waltz. I knew how to do it, but never danced it in public. He drew me onto the dance floor. He pressed me close to him as the dance floor was crowded. We swirled and twirled, and I fell in love. That night, he asked my grandfather if he could court me. Grandpapa said, 'Yes'."

Elle relaxed. "We married six months later. My father disowned me, Suze. I had married a mere soldier. I was a disappointment to him. Charles was born ten months after that. John was still enlisted, so he had to report for duty daily, but for our first four years, he was home nearly every night as he was stationed locally. It was only when I was expecting Lilabet that he had to go overseas."

Her voice shook. "John was so sick when he returned five months later. I was so big with child, and Charles was continually being naughty. Then, before I knew it, I had a tiny baby, and John was gone. I think it was his lungs. We did not have enough money for a doctor, so I don't truly know." She did not cry. She had done that long ago. The sad memories remained, but the pain had softened. Sharing the story eased the burden.

Suze looked at her dear friend. "Elle, I feel so guilty. I *had* known about the Earldom, my Charles told me. I should have sought you out. I got tied up with my own children." Suze felt guilt wash over her again. "Elle, I look at Wills and Cathy and realise I was only that age when Charles both married. He was Ned's age. I never once thought about you. I had the boys to keep my eye on and... no. That's no excuse. It was my job as a duchess, I failed you. I'm sorry, Elle. I, too, failed in my duty of care for our family. I should have enquired, I should have searched for all the family. I didn't."

They sat holding hands, Suze gently patting Elle's.

Their bond of friendship did not need words. Old hurts had been shared and forgiven long since.

Elle smiled. "Suze, have you noticed how everyone in this family also has one thing in common? All of them have a strong faith? Maybe it's the challenges this country gives them," Elle said in awe. "Suze, in some of them, they just glow. Charles said that he and Ned listed to Jack Turner on the voyage out here."

"Yes, I've noticed that too." Suze paused, thinking. "If this country can draw out the goodness in people and bring them closer to God, then I think we can trust our family that the friends they have made are worth having. I'm all for embracing whatever happens on this trip."

"So am I, Suze, but for now, I'm so tired. I'm for bed. Goodnight, dear friend, and Suze..." Their eyes met. "Thank you, for just everything. You came in the end, and that's what matters. You are here with me now." She squeezed her hand as they stood up. Her friend followed, and they walked upstairs together.

Chapter 12   Loss and Gain

*U*icky was still not well. She felt sick, with hot and cold flushes and the pain. Pain that doubled her over.

Harry wanted to call the doctor. He had carried her in from the carriage and placed her gently on their bed. She was in tears from the pain.

Maureen had already turned the bed down for them. She helped her undress and quickly washed Vicky as Harry went to see his friends.

John, Phil, and Aidan were in the sitting room waiting for him. All were concerned with Vicky's illness. They handed Harry a whiskey as he walked in. "Thanks. I need it." He tossed it back in one hit.

When he informed them she was expecting, they sat back relieved, and they all congratulated him.

Harry shook his head. "I think that maybe things aren't going too well," Harry didn't sound happy.

Lew had not yet returned from the wedding.

Harry said that Edmund was still with Ned and Christina.

John asked if anyone else had noticed Lewis and his lady friend.

All shook their heads.

John went on to explain, "Lew was standing hugging her at the wharf yesterday. He went straight to bed last night and was gone before I woke this morning."

"Sorry, John, I've been too worried about Vicky to notice much else. Any spare time we've had has been with her parents. We had to let them know her condition. I can tell Martha is worried." Harry sounded concerned.

Phil and Aidan had gone off for a ride first thing and only had time to dress for the wedding. Neither went to the reception, and therefore neither had seen Harry all day except at a distance. "Sorry, John," both replied. Neither had seen Lewis, nor whoever he hugged.

At Sally's suggestion, Harry went to the kitchen and searched for a basin for Vicky. She also had Cara make up some of her magic medicine, as Christina called it. It was a mixture of baking soda and powdered sugar, combined with lemon. "Take a small spoonful when required," Christina explained.

Harry just hoped it worked. He took the basin, water, and the powder to Vicky. He said goodnight as he passed his friends. He knocked on his door and entered.

Vicky was sitting on the bed, still in tears. Harry dumped the things down and went to her, drawing her into his arms. She relaxed against him. His sandalwood and pine scent comforted her. "Oh, Harry, I'm not supposed to feel like this. I expected a bit of sickness, but not this agony." She turned her head into his chest and cried quietly.

Harry sat, wracking his brain about what to do. Sally's words came back to him. 'Hold her, love her and comfort her.' So he did. He lifted her feet and laid her down. He divested himself of his clothing, donned his nightshirt, turned off the lamp and crept in beside her, gathering her gently into his arms.

"I'm not a teary person, Harry, but I just don't feel right," she said wearily.

"I know love. We'll talk to a doctor, all right?" He stroked her cheek. "Stay in bed tomorrow. I'll get your Mother to come up and see you. Thankfully, she's still here. All right?"

She nodded. She snuggled against him. His heart warmed, but he was worried. He pulled her closer and kissed her lovely, lemony-smelling hair. Soon her breathing was deep and rhythmical. Now he could relax and sleep. It must have been after midnight when he heard the front door open and close again. He didn't know if it was Edmund or Lewis, possibly even both. She was still asleep, so he didn't move.

Sunday dawned bright and sunny.

Vicky was still asleep. Harry eased out of bed and grabbed his dressing gown and his clothes. He snuck out of the room and went to the kitchen. He was first up, stoked the fire and put the kettle on to heat. He walked outside to the privy. It was already hot. How could it be so hot so early in the morning? By the time he padded back into the kitchen, John was up too. They sat in the kitchen drinking tea.

Harry admitted he was worried about Vicky. Very worried. "John, can you stay here while I go and get Martha? Vicky is still asleep, but I need someone listening for her," Harry asked.

"No, Harry, I can't, not my *forté*. She's your wife, you stay here. I'll go get Martha," he said.

"Thank you, John, that would be better." He dropped his head into his hands. "I didn't expect marriage to be... well, this hard. Seeing her sick and in pain is horrible."

They finished their tea. Harry made another black and sweet cup and took it to Vicky in their bedroom.

John shaved and pulled on his trousers.

As Harry opened the door, he saw Vicky on the side of the bed, heaving her stomach out.

He put the tea next to her bed. "Oh, sweetheart, what have I done to you?" he asked lovingly.

She turned to him and smiled, "Only seven more months of this." She reached for the tea. "Just as I love it, Harry."

He left her sitting on the bed and went to empty the basin. He had better get used to this. He emptied it, washed and dried it, then returned to their room. He decided to fully dress as Martha was coming. When he explained that and told her she was not to get up. Vicky sank back against the pillows. "Thank you, darling husband. No arguments from me," she replied weakly.

"Hmm, no, not like Vicky," Harry thought.

Sophia knocked and came to empty the chamber pot, swapping it for a clean one. He knew little Portuguese but did say *por favor* as she left.

She looked concerned. "*Que?*" and pointed to Vicky.

Harry looked puzzled, then worked out she wanted to know what was wrong. He made the action of a rounded stomach.

Sophia said, "Ohhh, *bom.*" She smiled and walked out giggling.

Harry groaned but smiled.

Vicky smiled and said, "Just as well no one speaks Portuguese, eh, love."

He finished dressing. Vicky was lying back watching him adoringly. "Oh, I do wish that I was not feeling so ill, Harry," she said somewhat sulkily.

He walked to her side of the bed and leaned over and kissed her good morning. He asked if she wanted some more tea. She nodded. He took her cup out. He asked Sophia to make more "Tea, *cha*; sweet, with honey. Yes? *Sim?*"

The girl looked confused.

He gently took her arm and showed her what he wanted. He made a cup and then pointed to Vicky's room. "*Sim*, yes?"

"*Sim, Sim.* Yesss sirrr." She made a play of rolling her 'r's. She made the tea and took the cup to Vicky.

Surely she could get that right, Harry thought. He left shaking his head. He washed his face in the warm water from the stove and a kitchen basin. Then he shaved. He would miss church today. Vicky was far more important. He was sure she would be better soon.

John arrived back with Martha, then left to get the doctor.

Harry greeted his mother-in-law and took her straight to Vicky. She sent him out. He left them alone.

They were sitting in the kitchen when Aidan and Phil joined them. They sat drinking tea and catching up. Martha called for Harry. He followed her in the sitting room.

"Harry, I'm worried," Martha stated.

"John's gone for the doctor, Martha. This isn't normal, is it?" he asked.

"No son, not like this. At least not that I have ever seen." Martha had a frown on her brow.

When he looked at her, he could see she was worried. "Martha, is there anything I can do?" Harry felt perspiration bead on his forehead. He was holding himself together until he saw her reaction.

"I don't think so, Harry. Other than keeping her calm. She must not realise there is a problem. Do you understand she could well lose this child? It happens often. Many women lose one at some stage, but won't realise they have. We just have a heavier... um...'" she nearly had started talking about courses with him.

"She told me about her courses, Martha. I don't have sisters, so I don't quite understand. I looked it up while we were in Sydney." Harry said, "I felt I needed to understand." He shrugged.

She looked surprised.

"I have made friends with a doctor there," he explained, embarrassed. "It was, err, eye-opening reading. Martha, I only want her well."

Harry jumped up when there was a knock at the front door. It was the doctor. Harry showed him into the sitting room first and introduced him to Martha.

Martha asked Harry to stay here, and she took the doctor in to see Vicky. Martha returned in a few minutes. She sat with him, anxiously awaiting the medic's return.

Harry was up and down, walking around and worried. At one stage, he walked out and down the corridor. On his return, he said, "Martha, I have done the only thing I can. I have asked my friends to pray, as I have been doing." He sat again, head in hands.

They heard the door open. He stood as the doctor joined them. The doctor looked sad. "She is with child, but as you expected, I don't think she will keep it." He paused, looking at them both. "She is already showing signs, back pain, some slight bleeding and cramps."

"Is there anything we can do for her?" Harry pleaded. "Anything to help with her pain?"

"No," said the doctor, "I do not want to lessen the difficulty of the loss; however, sometimes I have found that if a child may not, um, be formed as it should, it um, naturally passes as a miscarriage."

Martha gulped.

The doctor went on to say, "Hug her, comfort her and let her tell you what she wants and feels like. I know this sounds harsh, but I'm thankful that this is so early in the confinement. The pain of the child passing will not be so bad, physically. Emotionally, however, each person is different. I feel she is strong."

Martha nodded, "She is."

"And does she have faith?" the doctor asked.

"Yes," Harry replied, "A very strong one."

"Good, that will help. You must let her know the child will be in Heaven in its perfection." He looked at Harry. "This will help you as well. If the condition were further along, I often recommend that you name the child. That is your decision. You can discuss this later. Though you would not know the gender of the child, it being so small."

Harry nodded; his head was spinning. This was all too much for him. He needed time to think, but that was not going to happen. There was no time. "Breathe, Harry, Breathe," he said to himself. "Okay, I can do this. I *have* to do this." If this is the worse, in the 'for better or worse', then so be it. "Does she know, doctor?" he said when he finally had control of his voice.

"Yes, I told her. Let her get up and walk. Let her express what she feels. However, I would not leave her alone or even leave the house for a few minutes. Call you if you need me. I'll come as soon as I can." He sat thinking. "Hot water bottles will help. Do not give her alcohol, nor Willow Bark, though. They thin her blood, and will make her bleed. Talk to her about what is going to happen. Talking about it will help you both. She will feel the loss more than you."

Unable to speak, he shook his head, "Lad, there is no reason why she can't carry more children." The doctor patted his arm.

Martha was sitting with tears pooling in her eyes. "Oh, my darling, gentle Vicky," she thought.

"Doctor, we've been married only a couple of months. Well, nearly eight weeks. And this happens," Harry's voice cracked.

"Go to her, lad," the doctor said.

Harry didn't need a second suggestion. He left.

The doctor sat with Martha and explained in far more detail what would occur. She sat listening. Her abdomen was churning; it was turning over and over. Yesterday she had been at her youngest daughter's wedding, now this.

The doctor soon took his leave.

Martha sat stunned. Poor Vicky, poor Harry. She prayed, "God, what should I do? Help me. I can't do this alone." As soon as she said it, the words, "Send for Sally!" came to mind. "I will." She stood and went to find one of Harry's friends. She heard voices coming from the back of the house. She walked towards the kitchen, wondering what she would say. She need not have worried.

John stood as soon as she walked in. "Oh, Martha, I can see by your face it's not good news. What can I, we, do? We are here for you."

She looked at these fine men. All but Lewis were there. "John, I'd like Sally to know, and to come. This could take a few days, or the child may pass today. Either way, I will need to stay here. I'm sorry."

Edmund stood. "Martha, we guessed this could be the case. I have already moved John's things in with mine and Lew's possessions with Aidan. We have two rooms ready."

She looked puzzled. "Two?"

"In case Sally needs to stay overnight too," Phil explained.

Her eyes were swimming again. How kind they all were. She nodded her thanks, unable to speak.

"I'll go now, Martha." John was up and heading down the corridor. She brushed a tear away as she returned to Vicky. She knocked quietly.

Harry called, "Come in."

Vicky was sitting up in bed, "Come in, Maa," she said.

Martha walked to her daughter. "Oh, love," was all she could say. She stood beside her daughter and hugged her.

"Maa, I know this sounds crazy, but I understand. I said to Harry when I found out I was in an 'interesting' condition, that I felt immediately that something wasn't right."

Harry was sitting on the bed next to Vicky. He looked at her, amazed. "But, love, how did you know?" He had not yet admitted he felt the same. He had said much the same to Eddie.

Vicky, although in a bit of pain, leaned against him. "Harry, I did not have peace. I know this sounds strange, but I was not at ease. I can't explain it. I just knew. Don't get me wrong, I am sad, very sad, but not crushed. I know I will lose this one, but there will be more."

He drew her to his chest. "My love, I too felt disquieted but did not know why. I said as much to Eddie in Sydney." Resting his head on her hair and breathing in the scent of her delicious-smelling hair. Her strength was incredible.

"Vicks, the doctor said you do not have to stay in bed. You are free to do as you please. However, you are not to be alone," Martha said. "The boys have shuffled the rooms. I'll be staying for a few days at least."

"Oh, thank you, Maa," she said. "Can you thank your friends for me, Harry? This is not the way we planned to start our marriage, is it, love?" He sat with her resting on him still.

"No, my sweet, but I got you into this; we'll go through it together," he said softly.

Martha sat at the end of the bed. "Love, John has gone for Sal. I have told them what's happening. Well, they had guessed. Harry, your friends are wonderful. I wish I had some more daughters for each of them," she laughed.

"I'm glad I saw her first, Martha. She makes my life complete. I'm in awe at her strength." Harry chuckled. The first bit of relief in a tense morning. How could she be so brave?

"Maa, could I have some tea, please? Black and sweet?" Vicky asked. She squeezed Harry's hand, holding him back.

"Yes, love," Martha got up and kissed her, then left.

When she closed the door, Vicky said, "I have to use the unmentionable, Harry, can you help me up?"

He sprang off the bed and stood at her side. One of the things he had bought for their room was a commode chair with a lid. He did not want her walking through the house full of men to use the outdoor privy.

He helped her to the chair. He said he would wait outside.

She nodded, "Thank you, sweeting."

He walked to the door, glancing back, he saw her smile at him and blew a kiss as he left.

He walked out and closed the door gently behind him.

Martha was walking up the corridor with the tea. "Harry, what are you doing here? She should not be alone."

"She needed to use the unmentionable, Martha. I haven't left the door," he said. At that moment, he heard a scream of pain and a thump. He had the door open in an instant. They both went in. She had crumpled on the floor, twisted and writhing in pain. The lid was up, and Martha noticed blood in the bowl. Vicky was contorted in pain; fear was etched on her face. She reached for Harry.

"Get her into bed, Harry. It's happening, if it hasn't already." Martha pulled back the sheet.

He lifted Vicky and placed her gently in the bed. He wiped her hair from her face.

Another groan of pain. She curled into a ball. "Don't leave me, Harry." Vicky reached out for him.

His stomach churned as he held her.

"Sorry, Harry, but leave. Give us a minute, Harry. I'll clean her up," Martha said.

Vicky clung to him.

He unwrapped her arms and gently kissed her. "I'll be back, I promise." He left the room, haunted and agonising over what she was going through.

John entered the main door. He was followed by Sal and the Duke's mother. Harry wondered what she was doing here; he wasn't even going to think about that. Sally was here, and that's who Martha needed and wanted. Martha heard her voice and stuck her head out, asking her to come in. Martha was equally surprised when she saw the Dowager Duchess. Sal went with her friend.

Harry took Sally's wrap. He stood in the hallway, holding it, just looking at it, unsure of what to do.

John ushered the Duchess into the sitting room. He took Sally's wrap from Harry's hands, then pushed him to follow her.

Suze flicked her hand for John to leave them alone. As he shut the door, she turned to Harry. "Son, I'm here for a reason. A good reason. I'm going to tell you what I have never even told my Neddie." She looked sad. "I'm one person who knows what's happening and how she'll feel. I lost two babies. One was Paul's twin, the other...," she took a breath as though having trouble voicing the words, "The other was my daughter as a stillbirth."

Harry looked aghast. It shocked him back to reality. He looked at her in earnest. Seeing her in a new light. "Oh, I'm so sorry, Your Grace."

"Let me get something straight. Forget the 'Your Grace' stuff. How about Aunt Suze, or Great-Aunt if you prefer? Do you think you can get your tongue around that lad?" the grand lady said.

"I, um, I could, Your Gr... um, Aunt Suze," Harry mumbled. He was still dazed over Vicky. He wanted to be with her, but knew he would be in the way.

"I'm here to let you know about what she'll probably go through. I asked, and neither Martha nor Sally has lost a child. I have. Two! I want to tell you what *you* will need to do to support her through this, and I want you to know you can talk to me. You will both need to."

Harry drew a quick breath, his eyes pooling with unshed tears.

"Yes, lad. Me," she said. She was sitting ramrod straight in a chair, obviously uncomfortable. "Oh, bother, Harry, help me to the settee and come and sit with me."

Harry helped her to her feet from the chair, and they walked to the settee near the window. As they sat down, she asked, "Has she lost it yet?"

"I think so. I heard her collapse as I stood outside the door. She wanted to use the unmentionable. I left the room so she could have some privacy. I heard her fall. Her yell of pain was horrific." He blanched at the memory. "This happened moments before you arrived." He groaned. "The doctor had said not to leave her alone, and I did, barely ten minutes after he left. When I picked her up, her nightgown was covered in blood. Martha sent me out as you arrived."

She took his hand, "Harry, you *will* both get through this, together. You have to do it together, you *must* talk about it." She patted his hand. Still holding it as she said, "You must open up to her. If you don't, she won't. She will be strong for you, but will be crying inside. She will draw away from you, and a wedge will occur. I've seen it happen too often." She paused.

Looking him in the eye, she said, "Harry, it's what happened to my son David and his wife Elouise. They went their separate ways. She lost a child early in their marriage, and they both bottled it up. She did not think she could have children, but..." She shook her head. "That's another story. They would not listen to me. The stiff upper lip and all that. Elouise went off the tracks... but I won't go into that."

Suze sat thinking, the best thing that ever happened to her, Neddie, was escaping the clutches of that sh. It was a pity that the shrew had settled her sights on David instead. She said nothing of this to Harry.

Harry was astonished at her openness and honesty.

Suze continued. "Harry, I learnt when I lost Paul's twin, his name was Charles, after my husband, our doctor said that the best thing was to talk about the child. We talked often about our Charlie. But when I lost my Sarah Joy...," her voice broke. "Harry, I bottled it up. We never spoke about her again, but I never forgot her. Harry, you must not let this happen to you. I have never mentioned her aloud until today. Harry, Ned doesn't even know."

She looked at the wet spots dripping onto her lap. She looked up at him, her eyes sad and filled with the grief of her loss so long ago, and smiled wanly. "Sarah Joy never breathed, but she never left my heart. Let some good come from her passing. Harry, do this for me." She lifted her head and raised her eyes to him. They were brimming with more unshed tears.

He swallowed. "I thank you, Aunt Suze. Thank you for sharing this with me. I will talk to Vicky, I promise. I do know what we shall call a daughter one day, though." He smiled at her and patted her hand.

Sally came in, teary. She sent Harry to Vicky. "Go, Harry, she wants you." He was still holding Suze's hand. He squeezed it and smiled his thanks. Then he left. Sal sat in the seat he had just vacated. Still raw with her own grief, Suze drew Sal into her arms, and they both wept. "It's not fair, Grandmama Suze."

"Life is not fair, my dear, but God knows best. We do not have to understand, we only have to trust." Suze was emotionally drained after her conversation with Harry.

Suze drew a deep breath and said, "Sally, they will come through this. I've just had a long talk with Harry. You know I lost Paul's twin. I never told you that his name was Charles, did I?"

Sally shook her head. "No, you didn't."

Suze took a deep breath, "Well... I also never told you or anyone else that I lost our only daughter at birth. Her name was Sarah Joy, my princess. Sal, she would have been only a little younger than you." The older lady pushed Sal away slightly but laid a gentle hand on her cheek. "Sarah Lockley, you even share the same name."

Sally gasped, "Oh, Suze. No..., it wasn't your fault, you didn't lose her, she didn't die because of you, Aunt Suze. She was taken before her time. Then something dawned on Sal. So that's why you wanted to come today. You know."

Suze nodded. "Sal, your Charles was born the same year as mine. Now, can you see why you're both so special to me?" She had more tears in her eyes, but they did not fall.

"Oh, Suze," Sal took her hand and held it comfortingly.

"I told Harry what I needed my Charles to do for me after our baby's death. He was wonderful. If I thought I was sad, he bottled it up for days. The child named after him had died. For a while, something in him died too. He was strong, so as not to upset me. That was wrong. Finally, when we did talk, the floodgates burst for us both. However, it drew us together rather than pulling us apart. But with Sarah Joy, she never breathed, and maybe because she was a girl, I don't know, but somehow she was my grief alone." Suze lay back on the settee—more at peace than she had been for decades. "Sal, the funny thing is, I finally decided to tell Neddie the night before we arrived. Ironic, eh? I haven't had a chance yet, but I will today."

Martha entered and sat on the chair. "Harry is with her now." Martha looked at the older lady. "Have I interrupted something?" she asked.

"No, dear," Suze said, "I had finished."

Martha said to Sally, "I was wondering if you would stay here for an hour or so. I need to tell Jack and get some clothes for the week. The boys here have sorted a bed for me. I feel I need to be handy."

"Oh, course, Martha. John will walk with you. We'll stay as long as we're required." She turned to Suze. "Won't we?"

Suze was elated, "Of course, my dear, of course." It had been so long since she felt needed. Her heart sang.

John walked with her down to the Rear Admiral Duncan Inn, where they were staying.

Jack was anxiously waiting for her. He, too, had stayed back from church, just in case. When she walked into his arms without saying anything, he knew the news was not good. They walked into their room, and she told him everything.

John walked on down to the Jolly Sailor Inn again. He was greeted warmly. He asked them all to pray for Harry and Vicky. He added that she had lost the baby.

Murmurs of condolences swept across the room. He still had yet to be officially introduced to the Earl's Mother and to both the young ladies who arrived with them.

Ned did the introductions.

John looked hard at Elle. "Ma'am, you are the Countess of Coxheath?"

"Dowager, but yes. May I ask why, sir?' Elle enquired.

John smiled. "Ma'am, you are so like my mother you could be her twin," he said.

Elle drew a quick breath. "Who's your mother, lad?" she asked. "I don't know the name Saunders." Her heart was in her mouth.

"Mother was the daughter of George and Esther Staverly. She married Mark Saunders somewhat late in her life," John stated.

Elle's hand flew to her mouth, and she gasped. "No, that's my parents' names. Father disowned me when I married John, because he was only a soldier. As I presume you know, Father was the local Squire in Laddingford. He had dreams of us marrying 'up'. He told me that if I married John, I was not to contact him again. Well, my maternal Grandfather gave me away at the wedding, so I never did contact Father. John, you say 'your mother'. So that would be Emily?"

"Why, yes, but how? Huh?" John could not stop staring at her.

She chuckled, "John, Emily is my twin." Elle said with a smile. "She said she would never marry. She hated me for leaving her alone with our father. She hated Father even more for not letting her come to my wedding. If Mother had been alive, things might have been different. Sadly, she died when we were young." She reached out for him. "John, so Emily still lives?"

"Yes, as does my Father." John sat down next to her. "You are my aunt?" He was dazed.

"If you are Emily's son, then yes," she lay back in the chair. "My nephew, well, goodness, gracious me. Imagine that. I come halfway around the world and find a nephew." She laughed. She sat bolt upright, "Then Charles and Lilabet are your first cousins. Oh, this is so entertaining. Wills and all the rest of their children as well. You said you were the only one in the group not related, funny to find you are now the closest." She chuckled.

John was bewildered. "Mother never said she had a sister, let alone a twin." He sat pondering. "I often wondered why I was named John. I think I know who now. She told me it was after the husband of her best friend. I am actually John Mark, like in the Bible." John smiled, "Father also had a brother named John, but I never knew him. He came here some time ago."

"John, I never left the area either. We lived in Coxheath. Where do you live?" Elle asked him.

"Just outside Tunbridge Wells, Aunt Elle," he smiled.

She grinned back, "I like that, equal distances from Laddingford in opposite directions," she chuckled. "Why, you must live less than twenty miles from me." She laughed heartily. She told him the rest of her story while Charles, Ned and the others sat listening in awe. Christina and Jenna were up with the children.

"Won't Wills be amazed when he finds out?" said Eddie.

"Cousins, eh? Welcome to the Colonial Clan, John," Eddie laughed.

"Grandfather would be livid, you know," John chuckled. "He was a cruel man sometimes. I was petrified of him." He smirked. "To think you became a Countess and my Mother was only a Baron's wife. Pity he'll never know. I would have loved to rub that in. He would come crawling to you. Believe me, I had no respect for him, Aunt Elle."

"Seems we have that in common, as well." Elle smiled. "John, unbeknownst to me, my John was an Earl when we met. I had no idea until recently. How different life could have been for us all."

"Grandfather did set one good example for me, though, Aunt Elle, what sort of person *not* to be." John gave her an impish smile.

She hugged him to her, "My nephew!" She sighed with happiness.

Christina joined them. After some discussion, she realised she knew John's parents. Christina knew Elle looked familiar, but had never put one and one together.

Three hours passed before Edmund, Sal, and the Dowager Duchess arrived in the carriage from Roseneath.

Paddy took it around to the shade at the back as they walked indoors. They followed the voices and joined the family in the sitting room.

Suze stood staring towards her son. With a look and a nod, she called him to her. Ned leaned forward and asked Eddie quietly if he could use his office.

Eddie said, "Of course."

Ned walked to his Mother and escorted her out. "Mother, what's up?" he asked when he was out of earshot.

"We need to talk. Something I can't put off any longer, son. Take us somewhere we won't be interrupted." His mother's voice had a catch to it.

Ned opened the door to Eddie's office and ushered her in, then closed it quietly behind her. There was a small settee near the front window. She sat there and patted the seat next to her. "Neddie, I had decided to tell you something on the ship out. Well, actually, I only decided to tell you the day of our arrival, but we've not had a moment alone." He opened his mouth to speak. She put up her hand. "No, let me speak while I'm brave enough. It's no big secret, just something I need to tell you about. Neddie, I told you about Paul's twin brother dying. I didn't tell you that he was a day old when he died. His name was Charles, after your father. I know you knew about him."

Ned nodded, then took her hand and gently stroked it.

Suze swallowed. "I should have spoken about this earlier, Neddie. But I couldn't." She paused and swallowed again. "What you don't know is that after Douglas was born, I had a daughter. Ned, she was stillborn. Her name, her name was..." She took a deep breath. "... was Sarah Joy.

My little princess," Her voice broke. She bit her lip but could not hold back her grief. The years past came flooding back.

"What? Oh, Mother," he drew her into his arms and gently hugged her as she wept.

She stayed like this for a while, then sat up and continued her story. "Yes, my little Sarah Joy. Now, do you know why your child is so special to me? She is my Sarah all over again. You sometimes even call her your Sarah Joy. I catch my breath each time. I should have told you when she was born. I should have told you all of this much earlier. But it will come out now as I have told them up there. I wanted you to hear it from me." Her voice broke. "I told Sal, too."

He drew her into his arms again. "Oh, Mother! I do wish I'd known. I do now understand why our Sarah is so special. Thank you for telling me," Ned sat still, holding her against him. He smiled. "I'm never going to be able to stop you spoiling her now, am I?" He stifled a laugh.

He felt her shake her head against his chest. "Oh, Neddie, no," she chuckled, "But she must have discipline. If she is to take the town by storm as I intend, she will become an 'Incomparable'. She must not only have a personality, but also the ability to cope in any society, and that includes discipline. I love her too much to let her become truly spoiled. Spoil her with love, but not things. I think some time out here will be good for them all. They shall see and experience society from all sides, and life should bring them some balance. So far, she's my only granddaughter. I have had enough of boys." She kissed his cheek. "Thank you, son," she said, looking at him and smiling. "Christina told me she wants more. I do hope so. You two do make beautiful babies, Neddie."

She stood and took a deep breath, then a very un-Duchess-like sniff. "Let us return to the others."

"Much is happening in there, too. Elle is John's Aunt." Ned said quietly.

"What? Elle has a sister?" she asked. "She never said. Oh, wait. Yes, she did, but only last night. I must admit I didn't think more on that."

Ned smiled. "And an identical twin, too, Emily. John thought he was seeing things when she arrived. No wonder both Charlie and Eddie had twins. It's on both sides of their family." He presented his arm to her. She reached up and stroked his cheek. Then she grasped his arm, and they walked to the door. Just before he opened it, she said, "Neddie, I do love you so, my boy. I should never play favourites, but my heart broke when Elouise destroyed our family. She was a viper, and I'm glad you saw through her before she destroyed you. I'm glad she's gone. David was always your father's favourite, you were always mine. Shh, never tell the others. I love them too, but they were 'spares'. You never were. You were mine." She chuckled. "Look what God had planned for you. I love Christina so much. She is everything a Duchess should be, but more than that, she loves you for who you are, not what you are." She patted his hand again, then walked out.

Ned nodded in full agreement.

They met Luke as he came down the staircase. Two large bags in hand. "I'm moving back to Dar and Mama's place, Uncle Ned; Your Grace." He gave a bow to Suze.

"Fiddlesticks, boy, I'm Great Aunt Suze to you, lad. We're all related, remember." She giggled softly as she walked into the sitting room to join the others.

"You've been told, lad," Ned said over his shoulder as he watched her leave. He smirked at her ability to rebound. "Your Dar mentioned this to me after church this morning. It's somewhat noisy here for your study now, too."

Luke nodded, "Yes, but I'll be sad to go. I do love it here, but I want to be home with my folks."

Ned looked outside. "Ask Paddy to take the carriage with your things. He's only just taken it around the back. It's not too far, but it will save you some trips."

"Oh, thanks, Uncle Ned, I will," he grinned. "I'll go and get him to wait. I'm all packed. There are still a few of my books upstairs; the rest belong to Eddie. I'll put those away later." He dumped his bags down and went into the kitchen. Paddy and Cara were in there talking. He could hear their voices carrying along the corridor.

Ned joined the others in the sitting room. The murmur of various conversations buzzed around the room. He stood looking at all these. All were family or related to them in some way, even John. He shouldn't be surprised. The Tunbridge Wells area was not huge. Neither was the pool of Aristocracy. They socialised together; intermarriage was normal for most of the nobility. Why should he be surprised to find so many cross-connections? Most family trees in the area are related somehow. Even Harry. Ned knew he must tell him about that connection if he hadn't already realised. He laughed to himself. He didn't expect it to occur halfway around the world. The six were best friends, and yet their link to Wills was the lunch-pin.

Cara knocked and entered, "Luncheon is nearly ready, Mr Eddie. It's only a light luncheon as we're having a large Sunday roast tonight if that's all right." She bustled out.

Eddie nodded.

Suze and Elle looked at each other and laughed. Not how the servants in England would announce a meal at home.

John and Edmund made their farewells.

John met Luke and discovered he was moving back to his parents' place. With Wills and Cathy, moving into Gracemere Close, he realised there could be a couple of spare rooms here for the few days that Martha would be at Roseneath.

Luke loaded up the carriage with his bags and books.

John stuck his head in the dining room door and beckoned Eddie.

"Hey, Eddie, can Edmund and I stay here for the next few nights? Martha and Jack will need the beds at our place. Luke is loading up the last of his things now," John said.

"Sure, John, it will give us more time to talk too. Bring your things before dinner. Better still, bring everything, stay here. Leave Harry and Vicky in some peace and quiet for a few weeks. That will only leave Lew, Phil and Aidan up there, but bring them for dinner too."

"Great, thank you, Ed. See you later then," John said.

Eddie returned to the dining room table.

Moira came in with some food, and he called her over, asking her to make the two boys' rooms ready for tonight. She nodded and went to get the next lot of food.

Sunday night dinner at Bramblemere Close was always a flexible feast. Five more bodies would join the already full table. Fortunately, it was a large one.

Martha had returned to Roseneath with Jack. They had put their bags in the sitting room. They would stay there until they worked out what was happening. Martha knocked gently on Harry's door. She opened it enough to see them both asleep, curled up in each other's arms. She closed the door and drew Jack to the kitchen. "They are asleep, love. They need it too. I don't think Harry slept much last night."

Phil, Aidan, and Lew greeted Jack and Martha as they entered. Aidan stood to make the tea.

Lew said, "Jack, Martha, we're so sorry this has happened. Please let us know if there is anything we can do."

"Thanks, lad. No, not much anyone can do, but be here for them, other than of course, pray." Jack looked sad. "She lost it, you know."

They all nodded. Yes, they knew.

Martha and Jack went back to the sitting room to collect their bags, and Phil showed them their room. John's room had a double bed, so he took them in there. They decided they too needed a lie-down.

Sophia and Maureen had already changed the bed linens and cleaned the room.

Lewis was still in the kitchen when John and Edmund returned, bringing an invitation to dinner. He greeted them with a beaming smile. "Hello, friends."

John looked at him, "Lew, what's happened?"

Lew said, "Grab a tea and I'll tell you."

They each made tea and sat down.

Aidan and Phil came and joined them.

Lew stood and closed the kitchen door, then joined his four

friends. "Mmm, where do I start? Okay, London. Let me get this off my chest before you all pump me with questions, eh?"

"All right," they each replied.

"Good, in all this last year, not one of you has asked why I was not in Scotland, but was sitting in the club that wonderful, fateful night," he grinned at them.

Guilt flickered across the faces of each of the others.

"Oh, don't feel bad, even if you had asked, I would not have told you. I couldn't, until now. I can't believe how God has teased and pulled the threads of all our lives. Remember, I have not asked any of you either," his eyes glinting with happiness.

John swallowed. He had not yet had time to tell them of another thread being woven by God's almighty hand. A smile crossed his lips.

Lew continued, "I was there to drown my sorrows. I had offered for a girl and been flatly and rudely refused by her father. I was told in no uncertain terms that I was a self-centred, lazy, pleasure-seeking fellow who had no other idea in life but myself." He looked crestfallen.

The others shuffled uncomfortably in their seats. All felt the words could have applied to each of them.

Lew continued, "He was so right. I was oblivious to anything but myself. I was lazy and completely self-oriented. I thought the work she was doing was beneath her and told him so. She was working in a small school helping children to read." He sighed regretfully, "That first night around the fire at Hartley, Wills challenged each of us with a simple question. 'What do you do for others?' Oh, chaps, that tore into my heart. I had to walk away. Do you remember, I left the fire? I needed to be alone. Just me and God. I had her father's words thrown at me again from across the other side of the world. Her father called me selfish and useless, amongst other things." He wiped his hand across his eyes. The heels of his hands dug deep into them. "Convicted with my own pride and idleness, I could not go home and do the work Wills challenged me to do. Fiona was there, too close. She worked at the school, helping the poor, and she and her friends made clothing for them. She and her mother gave them food. She did everything Wills hoped we would all do. No, I could not go back. I had thrown all that in her face." Lew sat silent, deep in thought.

So were his friends. Each remembered Wills' unanswered question.

With a shake of his head, Lew continued, "I was going to re-enlist on my return, go back to India or somewhere and see what I could do there. I was just going to disappear. I was so miserable. I had loved her for so long. Her father forbade her from even speaking to me. I wrote after I met you and said I would leave. My sisters were her good friends. If I were at home, I would be thrown with her constantly. After that, I wrote daily until my departure. She never received them. Apparently, he returned my letters unopened, so they did not know where I had actually gone, only that I was with Harry, and that information was from my sisters. I had no other option but to leave. So I did. I went to London. I wanted to get drunk and die. Yes, to die. I had ordered the waiter to keep my glass full with the strongest drink he had. Some vile Russian vodka, I believe. Kick like a mule, he told me. Perfect." He paused, thinking back to that time. "I'd just tossed back the first one when you arrived with Phil. Edmund, you saw me. I groaned. I didn't want company. I wanted to be alone and drown my sorrows. I smiled when you saw me. You both sat without invitation. I wished you both to blazes. However, I now know God sent you because then the others came. He had placed around me the only five fellows on the face of this earth I could possibly tolerate. They were, one crazy Irishman and four Sassenachs and a grieving, pitiful Scotsman." He gave a wan, lopsided grin.

He looked at each face, "Then Harry came up with his harebrained scheme of coming here." His voice wavered, "It was the straw I needed to grasp. I could leave the country. At least on the other side of the world, I could try to forget." He rubbed his eyes again. "Oh, God, how I wanted to forget. It was way more than just pride. No, in hindsight, it was my pride. I had been rejected, found wanting. I did not measure up. Oh, that hurt!" He groaned softly. "That first night at Hartley, when Wills asked his question, I discovered I was like Jonah. I could not run from God. There was nowhere on this Earth I could go. So I did not want to *be* on Earth. That night, I went off alone, my soul shredded. I begged, I pleaded for God to take me then. Knowing I was not worthy, I did not want to live." He got up and walked around the room. "Then, I looked up. Do you know what I saw?"

His friends were still silent. All shook their heads. Lew sat.

"I saw a shooting star. It went from one side of the sky to the other. I knew God *was* still with me. So I fell on my knees and confessed. I confessed everything, from my immorality, my selfishness, greed, lust, drunkenness, self-centredness, everything. I just let everything go." He drew a quick breath, like a silent sob. "Each time I looked at Wills, that damn question haunted me, challenged me." He was thinking of that question. He stood and walked around the kitchen again.

His friends did not interrupt the silence. Each was remembering their own challenges posed by the same question.

Leaning against the kitchen bench, Lew continued, "Wills asked it again before we got to that damned swamp. And then there were those confounded birds. That haunting dance of love. It crushed my heart with a final blow. Their love was so pure; mine was not. That was the final straw. I needed to leave. I walked and walked, and sobbed, and walked some more. I wanted a snake to bite me so I could die. To be sucked into a swamp and drown. Something to take away the pain. I had no idea that such misery could be caused by love... Until I realised it wasn't... The pain was *my* guilt. My sin! No snake came, and I had to return to camp. I put on a brave face and a false smile. Slowly, I noticed I began to enjoy things again. The pain and hurt were easing, the guilt not so much, but it was now acknowledged and confessed."

Listening heads nodded.

"It was, of course, Wills again and those damned ducks. When I grabbed the two I caught, I was laughing for the very first time in ages. It was a real laugh, not something pretend. And then we found more gold in Hartley on the return trip. I caught myself laughing about it. Who would have thought gold could be found like that?"

He returned to the table again. "Do you remember I was alone at the wagons loading the bags of gold rock when those two escaped convicts arrived? When, later, we discovered who they were and knew how easily they could have killed me, I realised for the first time in ages, I didn't want to die. I had something to live for. Something I could do and prove myself changed. I realised I could be the person Fiona's father wanted me to be. The person he challenged me to be. I didn't know how to change myself. I'd learnt to trust Him. But now I was ready to try. I still needed time to think, and God gave it to me. However, not enough, because the ferry had arrived. I saw a ghost. How could she be there? How could she still want me? Had I changed enough to be worthy of her?" He swallowed.

"I did not want to approach her. I stood frozen to the spot as did she. When they disembarked in Sydney and met Harry, she realised I must be somewhere nearby. The only thing she knew after he rejected my offer was that I had left the country with Harry and his friends. I think my sisters or parents must have told her that much, as I do not remember writing anything like that. She had presumed Europe." He took a deep breath. "Fiona had poured her heart out to Sally on the ship, then again in Sydney. Sally took me aside as she walked up the hill. She told me to go to her. That she still cared for me."

John opened his mouth to speak, then closed it again. Time for that revelation later.

Lew saw but didn't stop, "When Amelia asked her to come here, she jumped at the chance. Here's another thread that God was pulling. They are Reverend Clarke's wife's nieces, and so we were destined to meet here. God had not even left that to chance. Friends, I have been in regular correspondence with him in the last month, since Harry's wedding. Wills said that I could trust him implicitly. So I did. I had poured my heart out to him. I told him absolutely everything. Yes, absolutely everything, I held nothing back. I confessed all. Maybe it was because of Wills' trust, and that I trusted Wills' judgement. Whatever the reason, he knew all. How was I to know his wife's relationship to Fiona? He did not know mine to her. I never mentioned any names."

"That day on the wharf, we didn't speak. She just walked into my arms. I didn't kiss her, I just held her." He lifted his head and sat straighter. "Reverend Clarke knows I've changed. I know I've changed. He has permitted me to pay my addresses to her, and I will." He beamed. "Without my soul-pouring confession to him before she came, he may have treated me differently. Again, God has played His hand perfectly. I am seeing them for dinner tonight. Please pray for me."

Finally, they spoke. Great joy for him, and they each assured him of their prayers.

John spoke softly, "Lew, we each are running away from something. I had been jilted, but now I'm glad. I'm also glad you have let God continue to pull his strings." He waited for a while before he told them to get another cup of tea, as he was going to tell them of another cord God had pulled.

Once the new pot of tea was made, he began his story. He started his tale, "Thankfully, I was only running from boredom post the jilt, I was in reality glad that occurred. But let me tell you my story."

Again, they refilled their mugs and sat at the table. John's telling would not take so long. "As Lew said, God has been pulling strings, or really, He's been weaving them. He did another one that day at the Ferry. Lew, the reason I stood watching you is that you are not the only one who saw a ghost that day. Was it really only three days ago? I had caught a glimpse of someone whom I knew to be half a world away. She walked the same and looked the same, but I knew it was not her. I was bewildered into silence by the similarity, but definitely knew her not to be the same person." John shook his head. He still had not let the idea fully sink in. "I was born to Mark and Emily Saunders, their only child. Mother was, to my knowledge, the only daughter of George and Esther Staverly. Evidently, this was not so. Although I think back now, she never actually said so. I found out this morning that she has a twin sister. An identical twin, as it happens. This girl, Elizabeth, ran away and married a man named John, one John Lockley, Lord Charles' father." John grinned. "What's more, I believe I am named after him. Mother said I was named after her best friend's husband. This would have greatly irritated my grandfather. I will ask her on my return home."

There were gasps all around.

"What?" Asked Phil.

"The Dowager Countess is your aunt?" chipped in Edmund. "So we are all related, after all."

"Really?" whistled Lewis. "I told you God is still pulling strings. We're all His puppets. I love it."

"I had no idea there were any more children in the family. Mother rarely even spoke of her parents. Father has a brother, but no one knows what happened to him once he arrived in this fair land. I hoped I would come across him. I knew Mother's mother had died when she was young, and I disliked my grandfather intensely, so we never saw him unless it was unavoidable. He was a cruel and vindictive man. I suppose by the time he died, he was old and cantankerous. Alone, and miserable as both daughters had now ostracised him because of his behaviour to them," mused John. "To think Mother named me John after her sister's husband, just to annoy Grandfather. This way, Grandpapa was reminded every day of his cruelty and the loss of his daughter. To his knowledge, I was his only grandchild."

"Yeah, well, some of God's twists I don't like," said Phil.

His friends turned to look at him as he stood and walked out.

He pushed his chair out with a bang, and it toppled over. He let the door slam behind him as he left.

Edmund was just about to join him when Lew stopped him. "Edmund, leave him."

Aidan watched him leave, "He'll tell us when he's ready. Something has been eating him for the last few days. He's not hurt; he's angry. Extraordinarily angry," Aidan said. "He came in seething yesterday."

They finished their tea and opened the internal kitchen door to find that Martha and Jack had gone into the sitting room.

Edmund went and made them some tea. As he took the tray into the sitting room, they heard a horse on the driveway. It was being ridden at speed. Edmund looked out and saw it was Phil heading along the road past the prison. "He's probably going to ride out his anger," he thought.

They all sat in the sitting room, drinking more tea with the Turners.

Harry heard their voices and opened his door, joining them. He looked at peace. His clothing was crushed, but he did not care. Harry explained. "We have been talking, but she's asleep again now. I made her some tea earlier. She didn't want anything more. Do you mind if I make myself something to eat?"

John walked out with him. "Sorry, Harry, this is not a happy start to your marriage." John was somewhat at a loss as to what to say to him. "How are you coping? Anything we can do?"

"No thanks, John. Just keep praying. Knowing that you are doing that helps." Harry lowered himself into a kitchen chair. "We only found out a week ago she was expecting, so the loss of the child is quite honestly something I'll deal with later. It's seeing her in pain. The actual excruciating pains she has suffered were horrible to see. Her forbearance is amazing. How she copes with it is beyond me," Harry rubbed his hands over his prickly face. He groaned. "I'm sure God will reveal His will to us eventually, but oh, it's so hard walking this day-to-day path. At least she is alive and will recover. That is all I can ask."

John let him talk for a while. Then he quickly filled him in on the other developments of the day. Lew was going to dinner with the Clarkes and, hopefully, propose to Fiona again, sometime soon. Then he told him of his discovery that the Dowager Countess was truly his aunt.

Harry laughed, "God doesn't seem to understand human barriers, does He?"

"No," John paused and then asked Harry, "Do you know Phil's story?"

"No, except that his parents wanted him to meet someone, and he refused. He didn't elaborate," Harry said. "I dare say he will tell us when he's ready, he will."

"It's just that he's ridden off, seething. Something has happened," John said. "I'm a bit concerned."

Harry shrugged, "Sorry, don't know."

"I hope and pray Vicky will be up and on her feet soon," John said. "Oh, and the other thing I must tell you, Martha and Jack will be staying on here in my room. Edmund and I are heading to Eddie's for a few days. Luke has moved back with his parents, and Wills, of course, will be staying in the other cottage…err, Gracemere Cottage, I think he called it."

"Okay. Thanks, John. It will be good to have them nearby," Harry said.

Sophia and Maureen had been wandering around the rooms, cleaning and tidying them. Maureen answered a knock at the door.

It was the doctor, he'd come to check on Vicky. She showed him into the sitting room, where Harry, Martha and Jack joined him. Martha said that she'd lost the babe soon after the doctor left. She'd been asleep for most of the day.

Martha and the doctor went into her room.

Vicky had woken at their entry.

The doctor said he wished to examine her. Vicky turned and asked her mother, "Can you wait with Harry, please, Maa?"

Martha nodded and left them alone. She went back to the sitting room where Jack and Harry waited. The three sat anxiously.

The doctor thoroughly examined Vicky and, after much gentle poking, was sad but pleased that things seemed to have passed completely. At only two months, he couldn't feel the child, only the inflamed abdomen. Her bleeding was already easing. He comforted her, then said that in a day or so, she would be able to get up. She was to let her body tell her how much she could do, but to limit all heavy activity for a week, at least.

The doctor went to the door and called Harry in.

The newlyweds sat together on the bed as the doctor spoke to them both. Assuring them that the worst was now over. He said, "She must now get her strength back. Her emotions will be in turmoil for some time, but talk it all over with each other."

The doctor then called both Martha and Jack. He outlined the next week and suggested they stay that long so that they could ease the burden on the others. "Mrs Harlow should be out of all danger, but complications could occur. Send for me if she becomes feverish at all. I will come as soon as I can." He turned to Vicky and said, "Mrs Harlow, you must say something if you are feeling unwell. Do not keep it to yourself." He patted her hand and assured her she would be fine. "You are supported by a fine family, Mrs Harlow, and good friends too. Do not underestimate your faith at this time. I want you all not to be afeared of talking about your loss. It will help you all." The doctor was so sympathetic.

"Mr Harlow, may I please have a word?" They walked out together and returned to the now-empty sitting room. "I believe you said you are reasonably newly married?"

Harry nodded.

"Your conjugal rights are something that must be withheld for at least the next weeks. At least until she has had her courses once, this will reset her body." The doctor went on to explain in detail to Harry, especially the complications that would arise if this were not adhered to, including infections and other issues.

Harry promised, and the doctor, pleased with his reply, departed. Harry stood looking out the window, deep in thought. He was searching for feelings but did not yet understand. He was confused and very heart-sore for Vicky. More than anything, He was in shock. Yes, Vicky was strong, but this loss of a child was hard. Even so early on.

Harry had decided to talk to Vicky about naming it, for they could not keep referring to their lost child as *it*. He bowed his head in a prayer of thanks for the support of a loving family and good friends. Family, yes, they were his family. He felt the first breath of peace flow over him for days. He felt God's strength.

They would get through this.

Chapter 13   The Building Begins

$\mathcal{N}$ed, Eddie, and Charles met with Major David Bond. He had replaced Major Carter, who had taken over from Ned on his retirement. It seemed like another life. Ned knew the procedure, and they went fully prepared.

As yet, Charlie did not know the full extent of the gold find. Wills had told him they had enough to build and stock the Emporiums, and he was spending it on the town. Wills would make sure Charlie would benefit in his way, but for the moment, Wills was still keeping the size of their discovery quiet. If he gave too much away, word would get out. He didn't want that.

Digging the foundations of the new warehouse would not start until Wills returned from his honeymoon. The immense timber beams could certainly be transported to the building site from Eddie's house. The unskilled convict labourers could move them. It would take them at least a week to do this.

Two gangs were to prepare the site for the week, and then one would be returned to road building. The more skilled labourers would then be brought in.

Harry Moffatt, Clerk of the Courts at the Courthouse and Justice of the Peace, knew the plans. He had met them in Major Bond's office to make sure they were all of the same mind as per the construction plans.

The five, Harry Moffatt, Ned, Eddie, Charles, and David Bond, stood around the desk, pointing and discussing. Wills had made his ideas and desires clear to both Mr Moffatt and Eddie. They had been the only ones to whom he could confide. Well, both of them and Harry, but Harry was otherwise occupied; Eddie and Mr Moffatt would speak for him.

Wills would make the final decisions on his return. Thus decided, Major Bond went off to arrange a group of soldiers to accompany the convicts to the stockpiled building materials in Eddie's yard. The sheeting would remain at his house until the roof was nearly ready for installation.

Eddie already had plans for some of Wills' wedding gift of pig iron. His brother had already suggested picks, hammers and bolsters, amongst other tools. He knew he'd have to make more moulds for ingots. His brain was trying to get around the volume of work needed to stock three stores, as well as more at the warehouse. More apprentices definitely need to be hired and trained.

~

In Sydney, Wills and Cathy were having a wonderful time. Neither of them had spent much time there. Wills asked, "How about a night at the theatre, Cathy?"

"Ooh, could we? I've never seen a play," she cooed.

"I'll ask Mr Stewart what he recommends. I believe there are three this week. Then there's a concert on Wednesday." He asked Mr Stewart to recommend some interesting events for them over the week and was handed a list of things. They entered into all the joyous activities presented to them with the exuberance, flamboyance, and passion only youth can exhibit.

Mr Stewart was surprised at the young couple. Most bridegrooms were at least twenty-one, but this lad seemed to be not long from school, and the lass even younger. This came up in conversation once, and he found them both to be eighteen. However, they had known each other for many years. Mr Stewart knew Eddie and Jenna well, as they were regular visitors. When he discovered that this young couple were actually both their siblings, but newly married. Wills was therefore an earl's son. His attitude to them changed remarkably. The staff's demeanour as well. Then, they received an invitation from Government House to meet with Governor Gipps and his wife.

Wills had expected this, as he had sent him a note. He had warned Cathy and both had bought suitable clothing.

They had giggled at Mr Stewart's reaction when he personally delivered the invitation.

Wills and Cathy had listened to accounts of such a situation from Eddie and Jenna.

The governor sent his Town Carriage for them. It was to be a meeting, rather than tea. Cathy was a little nervous, but now that she was an Earl's daughter-in-law, she could hold her head high. She did. They were shown into the Governor's study.

Cathy's hand was lightly resting on Will's arm. She was not nervous at all. More excited.

Lady Gipps was there to greet them, too. She asked Cathy to tea with her while the men discussed their work.

Wills had warned her of this. He also told Cathy that Lady Gipps was no fool. She was able to see through a person and discover their worth.

Cathy was looking forward to meeting her.

Lady Gipps took Cathy into the garden. Tea was brought out to them and served under the shade of a tree.

Wills was introduced to Governor Gipps by the Aide and asked about his health. All the appropriate words were spoken. The Governor then asked, "What's this all about, sir?"

"Here goes," thought Wills. "Sir, first, may I ask, does your Aide know about Reverend Clarke's last visit to you?"

"Yes, lad, he does. So it's about that? His name, by the way, is a mouthful, Edward Christopher Merewether. So I call him Merewether or Merry when we're alone." He chuckled.

"Yes, sir, it is, about that I mean. What I'm about to tell you is going to be a surprise. Let me start with some background." Wills filled the Governor in about his connections with Reverend Clarke. It was the gold he had come to report. "Sir, I have come to make a verbal report as I do not want the information to leak out. We are here on our honeymoon, and I thought it would be a good cover for my visit, Father being an Earl and all."

Wills swallowed. This was so much easier in his mind. He found he was nervous. He outlined the trip. "Well, sir, six friends and I have recently returned from an inland trip. In the space of a few months, we easily collected one-hundred-and-sixty-two pounds of purified gold. This included some alluvial dust, about ten pounds of golf dust, but most of the reef, or quartz gold. All the reef gold we found was where Reverend Clarke told me it would be, in Hartley. I know he wants to conduct a mineral survey, and I would like to place on record that he is familiar with his minerals. Sir, he should be listened to."

Governor Gipps sat up abruptly. "How much did you say? Do you mean £162 in value, don't you, not weight?"

"No, sir, one hundred and sixty-two pounds in weight and some odd ounces, yes, in weight, Sir. At the set price of £10 per ounce, and sixteen ounces in a pound, times the one-hundred and sixty-two pounds of gold in weight, we figured that's about £26,000 worth in value, Sir. We've divided it among the seven of us. We had to pay for crushing, smelting and even gave some to Reverend Clarke, and the church got an anonymous donation too." He chuckled, waiting for that to sink in. "£26,000 worth, you say? Are you kidding? In how long? In just six months?" He nearly choked again.

The governor nearly choked when Wills said the value. "£26,000 worth, you say? Are you kidding? In how long? In just six months?" He nearly choked again.

"Well, not exactly, sir, we did a week collecting at Hartley on the way out west; then a week in the creek north of Bathurst, collecting the dust; then another week or so at Hartley on the way back." Wills again let that be absorbed.

Governor Gipps spluttered on the sip of tea he'd just taken, sitting upright quickly, "You found all that in three weeks? Damn! I said we'd be murdered in our beds to Clarke. We're going to have every criminal in the world and every gold seeker rushing to our shores."

His Aide, Lieutenant Merewether, was stunned.

Wills had a wicked thought, grinning, he said mischievously, "We have a fair few criminals here already, sir."

Governor Gipps groaned as he mopped his brow. "Don't remind me, lad," the Governor chuckled.

Wills smiled. "Sir, the bulk of it at Hartley was a freak find. I own that land myself. I think we have collected the majority of that site. I do not think more will be found there. The dust, however, is also plentiful in most creeks around the Bathurst area. We checked many of them. We seven men collected ten pounds of dust in a week."

Wills waited again for that to sink in.

The governor rolled his hand, signalling for Wills to continue.

He did. "We checked most of the creeks we passed on our journey. Many had gold flecks. Only one creek had a bounteous amount. A reef will be able to be there somewhere." Wills continued. He realised he should also buy that land. "Governor, I'd like to tell you what I have planned. Sir, I realise this is a shock, and you'll need time to mull it over. You know that Eddie has the big Emporium at Parramatta? Well, he and Mr Tindale own it. Eddie is joining me in a partnership. We are going to build two more, one at Emu Plains and one in Bathurst. However, before we do, we are building a warehouse in Parramatta. From there, we can stock the three shops." He pulled out his watch. "The family should have the first of the building materials on site about now."

Wills put his watch back in his fob pocket. It was not a big flashy one, but silver, neat, and in very good taste. Everything about him was actually in good taste. He was, in essence, the epitome of the young Victorian English Gentleman. Slightly sparse sideburns, but his fair hair curled over his ears, and his waistcoat pinched in his trim waist. He needed no shoulder padding as his physique was above average due to his Smithing skills. His clothing was immaculate, understated. Nothing showy to give away his wealth, but he was just so young.

The governor reclined in his chair. "Lad, you have totally floored me. What do you want me to do then? You seem to have everything well in hand. How old are you anyway?"

Wills smiled, "I'm nineteen in two months, Sir."

"So, eighteen, married already to a lovely lady I believe. Rich as

Croesus and a head on your shoulders. You will go far," he rubbed his jaw. "I leave in a few months. I presume your Papa will have told you."

"Yes, sir, he did," Wills replied politely "I'm very sorry to hear about your ill health."

"That is as may be, but what do you wish me to do with this astounding information? I presume you have nutted that out as well?" Governor Gipps enquired.

Wills nodded in understanding. "I want you to *do* nothing yet, sir, at least nothing for me." Wills paused, looking at the older man. "I wish it to go on record that the Government *needs* to do a Mineral Survey of this land, and Reverend Clarke may just be the person to both arrange and lead it. Feel free to keep a record of today's conversation. However, if you write down any quantities or even mention the 'G' word, someone will see it and the word *will* leak out. It's your call, but I would prefer at least two years to get our buildings completed before the rush starts. Roads, gold stores, more soldiers, barracks, gaols, all this must be built by the Government."

"I agree; nothing in writing accessible to prying eyes. However, I will make a record in the private governor's diary, lad. I can leave this for my successor. What do you think? Even better still, I will leave a command that he calls you and Eddie in for a meeting. Then nothing will be in writing. I shall say it had to do with large mineral deposits. As you are blacksmiths, they will presume iron or coal. Yes, that's what I shall do." He chuckled, smiling at his thought. "I shall word it carefully."

"I think that Reverend Clarke may be interested in some more work at the Museum. As I said, he wants to do a mineral survey of all the minerals in the colony. Just a thought, do you know he has also found tin traces now? Ed hopes he can grin iron deposits." Wills stood. "I must be going, sir. Thank you so much for your time."

Governor Gipps rang a bell, and the door was opened by a footman. "Anytime you're in town, lad, you or that brother of yours, please update me, won't you? Nice meeting you!"

Cathy was waiting. She looked delightful in her emerald green tea gown with cherry-coloured bows around the cream lace bodice insert. Her honey-golden ringlets peeped from under her bonnet. She looked exquisite, and she oozed confidence. Her deportment was graceful and elegant.

Lady Elizabeth stood watching her departure.

As the door opened, the governor caught a glimpse of her waiting for Wills. As the door closed behind the lad, he sat thinking; for lad is what he was. Eighteen, married to a beautiful girl and rich. Such confidence, no quaking, absolutely self-assured, knows just what he wants and how to go about it. He chuckled to himself, "I wonder what my Elizabeth will say about the lass?"

He did not have to wait long.

His wife entered as the door opened for her. She waited for it to be closed again before speaking. "George, I have just had the most amazing time talking to one of the most self-assured young ladies I have ever met." She sat opposite him, in the chair recently vacated by Wills. "I see a great future for her, if her new husband is anything like she says."

George Gipps was reclining in his chair. His fingers arched together, deep in thought. "Elizabeth, if she's half the person he is, this colony is going to go a long way. What an amazing young couple! What an astounding family!"

He proceeded to tell her about the finds. He could not write it down, nor discuss it with anyone else. He knew Elizabeth, and he could discuss it without fear of it going further. "Trust me, we shall hear much more of this mineral, and I am sure of this lad, too. What astounds me is what he plans to do with his share. He's looking to help the towns with his bounty rather than going and getting more. I do know, however, he bought the Hartley land. I saw that six months ago when it passed over my desk. Clarke told me about that find last April, and I was wondering if there was a link." He frowned. "Do you know that the lad gave the Reverend £1000 as a mere thank you. Elizabeth, £1000, would you believe? Well, he gave him the gold, not the money." He sat thinking for a moment. "Elizabeth, his share of the find was over £13,000 in value. With what he's already given away, and that's over £2000, he still is one of the richest men in the colony, and he's only eighteen."

Elizabeth Gipps sat also in thought. "George, what sort of gold was it?" she asked.

"Both reef and alluvial, dear," he replied. "Do you know they crushed and smelted it themselves. Benefits of being blacksmiths, I suppose, then they poured it into ingots. I'm going to have to build a Government strongroom. A big one I think, and a mint." He muttered something unintelligible. "Do you know what he wanted? Other than to let me know about the find, he wants William Clarke to do a Mineral Survey. He says it needs doing. They want iron and coal for the forge, and if we found it here, think of all the other things we could bring from England rather than pig iron as the ballast."

Elizabeth's brow cocked. Would he listen to the lad?

He rubbed his chin again. "Yes, yes, I'll do it. I'll write a recommendation to London, and for a post at the Museum for Clarke, too. He's been on at me about this, and I refused."

Elizabeth Gipps knew that the conversation was over for the moment. She smiled at her ailing husband. "Dear, don't overwork yourself."

"No, my dear; I must pen this now." He started writing.

Wills and Cathy caught the Governor's carriage back to the Hotel and went to change. With the coachman and footman within earshot, he motioned for Cathy to sit silently. She nodded and sat holding his hand and tracking circles on his palm.

"Cathy, please, don't. Yet," he groaned with desire. "I have to walk inside soon."

She smiled and stopped, knowing the effect she had on his body, but did not release his hand. They arrived, he alighted and handed her down.

Mr Stewart greeted them with a bow.

Wills asked for luncheon to be sent to their room in an hour. He tried to give nothing away about the visit. Let them wonder. Wills smiled. One day, they would discover what that visit was about.

~

By Friday afternoon, all the building timbers from Eddie's house were onsite. Wills would turn the first sod on Monday. Only he would be given that privilege.

Wills and Cathy were due back on the ferry tomorrow morning.

Harry and Vicky were sitting outside in the back garden. He had barely left her side all week. The one surprisingly regular visitor was The Dowager Duchess, now known by all as Great Aunt Suze. Harry knew she was the one person Vicky wanted to speak to alone. Each time she came, Vicky was happier. They spent much time talking.

Harry and Vicky had decided to name their child Alexis, as it could be either a boy or a girl. The doctor was right, a name made the child more real. Once they had chosen a name, it became much easier to discuss the loss. Vicky thought it was appropriate as her name was Victoria, and the Queen's first name was Alexandrina. Vicky also loved her brother Alex. They were two of a kind, the quiet ones of the family. Vicky said, "I feel it was a girl, so that's how I'll refer to it, as her. Only God knows Harry, and she's now with Him. And she's perfect."

After that decision, Harry could see she relaxed. He took the advice from the duchess and the doctor. They both spoke about her often. When they both found themselves laughing at the possible future antics of their children, a lump formed in both their throats, and they both felt the raw emotion of their loss. However, knew they had taken a step forward. They reached for each other and knew that together they would be strong. Aunt Suze was right, again, by showing his feelings to her, Vicky could do the same.

Vicky wanted a walk, so they walked around the back garden and out to the stables. Ginger Mick greeted them with a whinny. Aidan and Edmund had been exercising him, but he greeted his owner with a whinny. Vicky fed him some apples and carrots. She wandered along the rest of the horses and fed them as well. The activity brought a slight flush to her face. Harry stayed within arm's reach to make sure she was all right.

She'd had a lovely time, diverted from their grief and her pain of loss.

Harry learnt a new depth to his feelings for her. He remembered what Eddie once told him. His feelings for Jenna increased a hundredfold after he'd been with her through the delivery of Lily. For the twins, he had not been allowed to be with her. Eddie had said, "I actually helped hold her during the delivery, Harry. I thought my heart would break with what I put her through. Within half an hour, she turns to me and says she wants more. Our women are so strong. I will *never* underestimate her again. I could not bear that sort of pain, and I am a strong man." Harry now understood what Ed meant. However, their pain was from loss, not a birth. The physical pain she coped with herself. That scream of pain, the look of fear. His heart twisted even remembering. They had made it this far. One day at a time, just one. He could do that. They could do that together. No, they *would* do that.

The midday Saturday ferry was met by most of the family. Charlie had the cart harnessed, and he drove it to the ferry.

Luke laughed. "They won't need that, Charlie," he teased. "They have been gone only six days."

As the ferry docked, Eddie grabbed the ropes and secured them. Captain Roberts slid over the gangplank, and Wills and Cathy disembarked.

He looked up and saw that Charlie had brought the wagon. "Thanks, brother. You know us too well."

"No, I just know what you told me you were intending to bring." Charlie chuckled. His eyes flicked to Luke.

Wills subtly nodded in reply.

Captain Roberts started bringing off the forty bags, cases and hat boxes that were now their luggage.

Luke stood gazing at the boxes. Some were very heavy, and most contained clothing and hats. "What have you got in these?" he asked as he struggled with one especially large box. He was told to put it carefully on the back of the cart.

"Furnishings and stock, Lukie," was all Wills said.

Luke had settled back into his old room with his parents. In the 'down-time' from the building project, Eddie, Charlie and Charles had knocked up a new desk in his room under the window. It was sanded and now shellacked, and was awaiting a chair before he could use it. Wills used to have his bed there, but now Luke no longer had to share a room; they had moved out the second bed and added the new desk. This was done while he was at school on Thursday. He was overwhelmed when he walked back in. And, wonder of wonders, he had a bookshelf.

He had twelve mismatched books of his own, but this shelf would allow for many, many more. Sadly, he had to leave most of the books he was using at Eddie's place, as they were part of his library. He had the most important ones, but he would love to buy more. As yet, he had no income and little cash. One day. He had to sort something out to make some money. Something that would not significantly interrupt his studies.

Charlie drove the full cart up to the cottages.

Wills pointed to four of the heavy cartons. Charlie grabbed them and pushed them out of the way. Once the majority of the boxes were taken into Wills and Cathy's cottage, he gave instructions for some very large ones to be unloaded into his parents' cottage rather than his. Six boxes were to be carried into his parents' cottage. Luke picked up one heavy one.

Wills took it from him, and they followed Eddie inside.

Luke was surprised when Wills, Charlie and Eddie dumped them on his bed. They called him in. His father followed with another. His three brothers and father stood just inside his room.

Wills came and put his hand on his shoulder. "Lukie, I wasn't here to help change your room, so I brought you something to decorate it with."

Ned and Edmund arrived with the last two cartons, including a huge one.

Luke was astounded. "But, Wills, why? I'm overwhelmed."

"Don't say that until you open the boxes, you may not like our choice." He chuckled. Wills handed him a knife. "Open them, Lukie."

Luke didn't need a second suggestion. He cut the string tying the boxes closed. As he opened the first one, all he saw were books. "Books, loads and loads of books." He moved to the second one, "More books," and the third, the same. "Wills! Oh, Wills!" His eyes misted. Luke ran his hand over the soft green leather covers. He picked one up, "Gold-leafed edges, too. Oh, wow!" He swallowed. "Oh, Wills, these are the set of geology books, same as in the library in Sydney. Oh, there is also a selection of journals from the Geological Society of London. Are these all Reverend Clarke's ones?"

Wills nodded, "Plus others." He smiled at his brother's joy.

The fourth box was a different shape. "Careful with this one, Lukie, it's breakable."

Luke slit the string and opened it. "A desk lamp of the latest fashion. It's fabulous. Oh, Wills, I've been trying to study by a tallow candle."

"I know, Luke. Keep digging. There's more in that box," Wills said.

Luke did. There were desk organisers, quills, ink, an ink well, not to mention reams of lined paper and assorted study things like metal-edged rulers, charcoal, and folders. All the stationery he had ever dreamed about. Luke was now on the verge of

letting the pooled tears flow. Not usually a demonstrative person, he hugged each of his brothers and his father, then went back and gave Wills another one. "Thank you so much, Wills. This means the world to me, but you know that," he sniffed.

John arrived to watch the proceedings. John, Ned, and Edmund were standing just inside the door.

Ned had been watching his reaction. "Luke, don't forget these two boxes." The first one was huge and the second, odd-shaped.

Luke walked to him in a daze. "Uncle Ned, you too?"

"Yes, Luke, this one is from me. With all this stuff you have here. You will need this. Cut here, very carefully."

Luke did, and the packaging popped open. He pulled off the wrapping. There was the most beautiful swivel desk chair on wheels, padded on the back and seat with buttoned green leather. He was lost for words. All he could do was to look from it to Ned and back again. The lump in his throat now made it hard for him to say anything at all.

Edmund cleared his throat. "Luke, you have one more, this one is from all of us. It's in two parts, so be careful when you open this one."

He ripped open the wrapping. Everyone gasped except Wills. Inside was the most magnificent, exquisitely made, deep mahogany, brass-inlaid, travelling writing desk. He placed it on his homemade desk and opened it. It had a burgundy leather writing slope, with a removable lid that revealed a hidden drawer and a small travelling ink bottle, more quills and even some ink pen nibs and holders. He noticed a tiny handle and discovered a small secret drawer at the bottom. He had a lump in his throat.

Ned brought over the last parcel.

Luke shook his head. Tears slid down his cheeks. "No more. Please. I don't deserve it."

Charles placed this one on the desk next to the other. He pushed Luke to the desk and said, "Open it, son. This is from Mama and me, for your seventeenth birthday next month, but getting it early makes it a surprise."

Sal had joined the group. "Happy Birthday, son," she said.

Luke turned to the last parcel. He laid his hand on it. Still unopened. He said a silent prayer of thanks. He cut the string when the wrapping was pulled aside there was a matching deep mahogany box. Again, with brass fittings, only this one was larger. He flipped open the lid, and when he lifted the lid, the front also hinged down.

It was a stationary carrier. Pre-loaded with monogrammed LL stationery. There were ivory desk items slid into leather loops on the lid. It contained letter openers, nib handles and an ivory nib holder box for the nibs in the other box. There were also two small drawers; he gingerly opened one. It was full of sealing wax in three different colours, red, gold and green. He took a deep breath before he gingerly drew open the lower drawer. He saw an ivory-handled seal with the same LL monogram on it. He gasped, his own seal. He wiped away a wayward tear.

He turned and walked to his parents, gathering them both into a hug. "Thank you! Thank you all so much. I don't deserve all this. It's too much."

Wills said, "Luke, trust me, you are going to earn all this. Not that you have even looked at the books in that box."

Wills chuckled, knowing how many times Luke had told him about the books he'd love to have from the library in town. "Oh, these last two and the chair are made by a chap named Andrew Lenehan. Good stuff!" "Now, I'd like to make an announcement. Everyone, I'd like to introduce you to our first bookkeeper. The Honourable Luke John Lockley," Wills chuckled. "Take a bow, lad. You have just landed your first paid job."

Luke's knees finally gave way. He sank onto the desk. "What?"

"You are the only one I can trust, who knows what we're actually doing. You are good at figures. I'm not. I thought this would give you a way to help without disrupting your studies too much. How about it? You can get us started until you go to university. I believe that is your goal?" Wills looked at him and raised one eyebrow enquiringly.

"Yes, yes, of course, I'd love to. Of course, I would. You mean it?" This was even better than all the gifts. "I'm just so overwhelmed. As I walked in here last night, I put my few books on the shelves and thought I'd better get a job so I could buy more. Now, look at me." He was beaming. Thank you all so very much." He sniffed, but a huge grin spread across his face.

Wills mussed up his hair, "I love you, little brother. Never change. Mind you, we'll work you hard." He chuckled, "Now, I have a new wife to return to." He left. The others left soon after.

Soon, only Sal and Luke were left in his room. "Happy early birthday, Lukie! We wanted you to have something that, for once, wasn't handed down from three older brothers. Something only *you* wanted. I'll go and get some oil for your lamp." She walked off, leaving him with his bounteous gifts.

Luke turned to the books, lovingly caressing the leather binding on each one. In awe that each title was one he'd at some time or other mentioned to Wills in their shared room. They were bound in matching leather bindings. One by one, he placed them on the shelves, sighing with contentment. Not from the possessions themselves, but the symbol of his family's love for him.

Lewis's dinner with the Clarkes and Fiona had gone well. Both girls were still staying with Eddie, but soon the Clarkes would have to leave. They were heading down to Campbelltown.

Lew couldn't even offer to go. He wanted to go if Fiona went, but he couldn't travel with them as they weren't married, and she'd have to share his wagon. What a quandary. What to do? In the place of her guardian, Reverend Clarke permitted Lew to court Fiona. He said Lew had to wait before he asked for more. At least she was close ,and he could see her. He would bide his time.

Lew stopped on the way back to Roseneath and prayed for a way to be made clear. He lifted his eyes heavenward and asked for guidance.

The evening before Wills and Cathy's return, Harry had helped Vicky to bed and returned to the group.

Martha and Jack were sitting, talking to her and spending some time with her without Harry.

Phil made himself scarce most days, gone before they had risen, and back after they had retired. Tonight, he came in and dragged out the kitchen chair he'd knocked over only days before. He sat on it backwards. "I can't run any more," he said quietly. His head sank onto his arms. He was emotionally drained. Looking gaunt and haggard.

Harry had no idea what had happened before, but knew they had all had a heart-to-heart and Phil had stormed out. That had been Monday.

John and Edmund were still at Eddie's place, but the remaining friends were in the kitchen when Phil joined them.

Phil still had his forehead on the chair back. "Lew, you weren't the only one running away. Only I was running for the opposite reason."

They could hardly hear him as he was still speaking with his head down.

Phil said, "I was told I *had* to marry my mother's best friend's daughter. Hell, I had not even met the girl. Why should I have to get married just because Mother said so?"

"But Phil, why now? What has happened?" asked Harry.

"The ferry, that's what damn well happened; that's what. That damned Ferry brought her here." Phil said in absolute horror tinged with anger.

"Do you mean Amelia?" asked Lew.

Phil nodded and groaned. "Eddie introduced us as he handed her off the boat. I heard her name and froze. She obviously missed mine. I presume she knew of the plan. Now I'm stuck. I still do not want to marry someone chosen for me. Do I run?" Phil looked haunted. "I can't marry, not now... not yet."

Harry said, "Cor, Phil. That's enough to make any sane man bolt. I certainly would have done so."

Aidan saw his friend's face. A thought occurred to him. "Umm, Phil, it occurs to me that maybe she's here for the same reason? She doesn't want to be pushed into a marriage with someone she doesn't know, either." A note crept into his voice, one of joy. "Ahh, um, are you sure you're not interested?" he asked. A smile spread across his grinning face. Even his eyes were smiling.

Lew and Harry noticed.

Phil heard the tone change and looked up, puzzled. "No way. Gosh. No, no way at all!" replied Phil adamantly.

"Good! The coast is clear for me then." Aidan said. His three friends stared in surprise. "Well, someone has had to sit talking to her. No one else has even been saying, 'boo' to the poor *cailín*. So, well, we've been thrown together a bit. She does have the most adorable dimples, you know." He looked embarrassed.

"*Cailín*? What's that?" Harry asked.

"Irish for a girl, Harry. Hopefully, my girl," Aidan smirked.

Phil threw his head back and laughed. "Good riddance to her. I shouldn't say that, should I, considering I have not even spoken to her? Have you ever been called an angel before, Aidan?" Phil finally smiled at him. "Aidan, I have an idea. I need to know, and so do you. You have my total blessing, believe me." He moaned, but with relief. "You realise I have been seething at her for following me. Absolutely livid she was here." He looked sheepish. "If I had told you on Monday, I could have saved myself a lot of heartache, couldn't I?"

His friends nodded in unison.

Lew said, "We've been worried about you, but knew you would tell us in time. It's something that each of us has learned this year: patience and trust."

"And forgiveness, too," Aidan said. "Phil, I think that's a great idea. However, I was thinking that maybe Lew could ask her why she came first? She might open up to him."

Harry sat looking at his friend Phil. There was something more. Harry's eyes burned into Phil. "I'm not ready for it, Harry, not since *she* died. I can't even think of anyone else." Phil could not tear his eyes from Harry's. "We became engaged, then she died less than two hours later. We were unable even to announce it. She was thrown from her horse, soon after I asked her." He said softly, explaining to his other friends, "It was Christopher's sister, Charlotte. I still miss her so much. I'm still wracked by nightmares about her accident. I'm certainly not interested in anyone else. I'm still heartsore. After it happened, only my neighbour, the Norfolks, and Lucy, their daughter, were told. No one else but Harry and Lucy knew. Lucy and Charlotte had been best friends."

His friends gasped. All but Harry looked bewildered. Harry reached out and touched his friend's hand. "After what we have been through this week, I can understand some of the pain you have felt, Phil." He smiled. "I do understand even better."

"Harry, I'm so sorry," Phil said quietly.

Harry stood and left them talking in the kitchen as he returned to Vicky. Oh yes, now he understood. And now he understood Aunt Suze, too.

Sunday morning, Lewis, Fiona, Aidan, and Amelia walked back to Eddie's house after the service.

Aidan, walking with Amelia on his arm, broached the subject of why she came.

She gave him a horrified look. "Mr O'Keefe, I should not say, but I feel I can reveal all to you. Mother had arranged for me to meet the son of some friend of hers with a view to..." she hesitated "...more," she finally added. "Even though I'm five and twenty, I refused. To put it mildly, Mother was not pleased with me. I did not even ask who it was."

They fell a little behind the other two. Aidan fell to wondering how to proceed. "Miss Moreton, I have something to confess. I know the identity of the person."

She looked horrified.

He chuckled. "No, it was not I," he said softly. "May I explain before I reveal all?"

She nodded. Her eyes flew to his face. She blanched. "He's here? Oh, no," she exclaimed.

"My dear Miss Moreton, do not fret, yes, he's here." He began telling of the saga. "A dear friend became betrothed to the sister of another of our brother soldiers. He was killed in India. Her brother was the seventh of our close group. His death was the reason we all had to resign our commissions. Christopher's secret identity had been revealed, therefore ours too. We were all in danger. Not that it worried any of us. For various reasons, we had all volunteered for this dangerous mission. I have told you a little about what we did. More I cannot say. Charlotte was his sister. Our dear friend lived near enough to be able to care for the family. He and Charlotte courted and, as I only found out last night, became betrothed. They were out riding, she took a hedge, and the horse fell. She died instantly. Amelia, it is Phil. He is still, um, heartsore was his word. It was not you that he was rejecting, but every female his mother threw at him. There had been many."

Aidan had placed his hand over hers as they walked slowly. "He, too, ran away. He came here with us. He is still not over her loss. Both your mothers were very inconsiderate and insensitive to push this on either of you, but that is mothers' for you."

They walked in silence for a few minutes.

"But how did he know? We have not met. When?" she paused, thinking, "Oh, he must have been told my name."

Aidan was still silent. He had to give her time to think.

Then it suddenly dawned on her, "Oh, the Ferry. Eddie introduced us."

Aidan nodded, "Yes, the ferry. He has not been the same since your arrival. He's been quite, how shall I say this, angry. You see, he thought you had been sent after him. To catch him."

"Oh," she said and flushed. "I never knew his name."

"It was only on Friday night, he revealed the story to us," he explained gently.

"Oh no. I had no idea. As I said, I did not even know his name," she said again. Then she giggled. "Here we are both running away from the same thing only to find ourselves thrown together on the other side of the world."

When she smiled, two impish dimples appeared on her cheeks. When she laughed, they deepened. She had an elfin beauty.

He turned and looked at her face. "Is it all men whom you despise?" His heart in his mouth, he took a breath.

Her head shook. She blushed delightfully.

Aidan's heart sang. "Miss Moreton, Amelia, would you do me the honour of consenting to walking out with me?"

She looked up at him adoringly. "Oh, Mr O'Keefe, Aidan, I do not despise men at all, only being forced into marrying one that I have not met. Sir, I would be honoured, but you will have to ask my uncle. He stands guardian to me while here."

"I shall, of course, but I wished to ascertain your feelings first," he looked at her with a smile. "I shall seek him out this week before his departure to Campbelltown."

"Mr O'Keefe, Aidan." She looked embarrassed. "They dine with the Bobarts tonight. Fiona and I have been invited. May I ask for an invitation for you? I believe Lewis is coming." She glanced at him.

"My heart would be glad if you possibly could," was all he could reply. Unexpectedly, his heart was certainly singing.

The invitation was forthcoming, and the men escorted the ladies to the rectory.

Before the meal, Aidan had the opportunity to request an audience with Reverend Clarke. A suitable opportunity arose after the meal, when Reverend Bobart was called away for a short time, leaving the three men alone. Lewis made himself scarce, and Aidan made his request.

Reverend Clarke's moustache wiggled, and he laughed. "I believe they are both here escaping their parents' interference and machinations. God seems to have other ideas." He chuckled. "You have my blessing, boy. I have watched all six of you. What you may have been before you came is not who you all are now. Yes, you have my blessing. Come. Let us join the ladies."

Aidan opened the door for the reverend and followed him into the room. He was attracted to her, but love? He certainly liked her. He wasn't quite sure. He was sure he could love. Did he have it in his heart to love anyone? She was someone he already admired. Amelia's eyes met his on entry, and he gave her the nod of approval. Her dimples appeared, her eyes smiled back at him. His heart somersaulted. "Oh, now that was unexpected," he thought. He had been emotionally almost dead since leaving India. Mayhap he could give her the love she desired. He remembered the last time he felt any emotion. It was while watching Wills' dancing birds. A lump had formed in his throat that day. That was the first time he felt any flutter of emotion. Yes, that was when the healing started. He smiled. He now found it hard to keep his eyes from following her through the evening, but the night ended, giving them no chance to talk alone.

Mrs Clarke was concerned about leaving the girls at Eddie's and asked Mrs Bobart about ideas.

Lewis and Aidan, however, had discussed an idea while they were shaving in the kitchen, as they prepared for the evening visit. They were hoping the Clarkes would approve their suggestion. If they each drove a wagon with one girl, then the girls could share one at night and they, the other. The Clarkes would be there to chaperone them. They would each get to spend time helping both the Clarkes in their new parish and have time with their lady friends.

Lewis took the opening from Mrs Clarke. "Mrs Clarke, Mr O'Keefe and I were discussing our plans for our stay. We wish to see more of this land. We may have hit upon a plan that may benefit us all."

Mrs Bobart smiled. She had come to know of Lewis's interest in Fiona. She had much time for these six English friends of young Wills. Each had proven their worth.

Aidan spoke. "Mrs Clarke, as you know, we have ventured out to the far west as you have. We loved it. We have three wagons sitting in our stables unused." He swallowed. This wasn't coming out right. "I was wondering if you might allow us to accompany you on your journey south. We can each drive a wagon during the day, and the young ladies could then have one at night, and we the other." Phew. His heart in his mouth. "Your daughter might even share with them."

Mrs Bobart said, "Maria, I know these two young men quite well now. I will vouch for them. They are true gentlemen. I trust them too. I don't say that about many young men these days." She paused. "Yes, I trust them."

All eyes turned to Reverend Clarke. He had been standing silently, listening. "Maria, it looks like we have us a caravan." He gave her a cheesy grin. "However, I don't think they will be able to ready themselves before tomorrow. Elizabeth, may we presume on your hospitality for three more days? I think Wednesday should give these four ample time to prepare. We only have a few more months down in Campbelltown until we move to North Sydney. The building there will be ready by August, I'm told. The children will be pleased to have real beds, as will we."

"By all means, William, Maria. We would be honoured." She smiled at him, then at Maria. Reverend Bobart joined them, the new plans discussed. He called for their small buggy to be brought around. Bess was asked to ready herself to accompany them, and the four departed. They escorted the two ladies to Eddie's. Then rather than get them dropped off at Roseneath, they alighted at the Rectory and walked home. Aidan told Lew he'd been given permission to court Amelia, and they congratulated each other. Both were happier than they had been for years. Now, to tell their friends they were leaving, and to relieve Phil's anxiety.

Martha and Jack had left for Emu after church that morning, and the house was quiet when they returned. Only Phil was in the kitchen. He was awaiting Aidan.

Harry heard their return and joined them in the kitchen.

Vicky was feeling much more 'the thing' as she said. All pain now passed, only exceptional tiredness remained. She only wanted a snack and then more sleep. Harry was certainly more relaxed. He took her in a light meal, then rejoined his friends.

They sat at the table as they talked. This time, their moods were vastly different.

Aidan had explained over luncheon that Amelia did not know the name of the mystery suitor. He was now able to tell Phil that he had been permitted by Reverend Clarke to 'walk out with her,' and she was in full agreement.

Phil released a deep sigh, relief sweeping through his body. His head sank onto the table. "Thank you, Aidan. Thank you so much. Now she is safely out of my reach, and I from hers." Another huge sigh escaped him. "I think I would like to talk with her now. Would you mind?"

"No, of course, I don't mind. I was actually going to suggest it," Aidan replied. "Clear the air for you both." He chuckled, "and make my path clear too."

"Harry, Phil," started Lew. He looked pensive.

"Oh, we're in for it, Phil," laughed Harry

"No, you're not. Shut up and listen," chuckled Aidan.

"We're, um, leaving," Lewis said at a rush.

"What?" Phil and Harry asked in unison.

"Reverend and Mrs Clarke have invited us to join them on their trip south. They have been trying to work out how to get the girls to go with them. Their wagon won't fit any more, as they also have three children. If we go with two of our wagons, we can share one and the girls the other."

Harry looked across at the faces of his two friends. He smiled, they seemed so different from the haunted, hollow, hurt faces from over eighteen months ago in London. "Go with my blessing, lads. If you find the happiness I have, you will not regret it."

"Mine too," said Phil. "But I'll miss you."

They heard a noise at the front door. Harry went to open it.

John and Edmund had arrived back home. Maureen and Sophia had their rooms ready. They dumped their bags and joined the others. They all sat discussing the wagons for a while, working out which ones to take and which horses would be best.

Phil was especially glad his two other friends had returned. Being alone with his thoughts was still hard. His friends said good night and departed for bed.

Harry sat in the kitchen with Phil. Something Aunt Suze said resonated deeply within his thoughts. Her words weighed on his mind. Now he understood what she meant, as he did not when she spoke them. He wished to say this to Phil, and now seems like a good time.

The two men were left in the kitchen.

Harry said, "Phil, Aunt Suze said something to me. It hit home earlier today. She said, 'You do not grieve what you do not love.' Phil, without your love for Charlotte, you would not feel as you do. Never regret that grief, nor that love for her. Find a way to make her proud of who you are today. Find a way to be the man she loved." Harry gently placed a hand on his shoulder, gave it a gentle squeeze and left him to his thoughts and memories.

Phil gazed at his friend in the dim candlelight as though he had been slapped. He understood. For the first time since Charlotte's death, he felt at peace. She would wish that for him. Eventually, he nodded to Harry.

Harry left Phil alone with his thoughts.

The candle had nearly burnt to the stub.

Phil was left in the silent kitchen. The warm core of companionship permeated its walls. This had become a place of refuge, companionship, and care for them all.

Over the past six months, they had fallen into the habit of meeting at the kitchen table once the staff had retired for the night. They would talk until a candle guttered, then they would head to bed. It was as close as they could get their fireside discussions. What was it about a live flame that opened the soul? He missed those nights around the campfire. No luxuries, but surrounded by God and his created order.

Phil sighed, then snuffed the stub of the candle. "No secrets, no barriers, I can breathe again," he thought. He too went to bed.

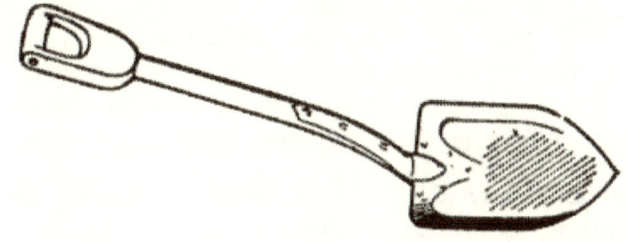

Chapter 14   Turning the First Sod

*J*t was nine o'clock on Monday morning, 23rd February 1846.
The family and significant friends gathered on the new warehouse site.

Eddie had made a new shovel, and Wills was to turn the first sod.
He burnished it until it shone. Wills decided the final building placement.
He gave the instructions for which direction it would face. Surprisingly,
the original building was moved forward slightly and closer to the road.
This plan allowed for an expansion of the building at the rear without
compromising accessibility during construction. A circular driveway was
to be added around the back.

Eddie chuckled; Wills was already thinking about extending, even
before he'd started building. He knew he had met with the Governor and
now had his approval for his plans. He was genuinely amazed at what his
little brother had achieved in the past twelve months. Wills had left a
schoolboy and returned an engaged man, and Ed stood in full admiration
of his abilities. Wills was still only nineteen.

The Reverends Clarke and Bobart both joined the family and
prayed for blessings on these projects. Even Vicky was well enough to
attend; however, she stayed in the carriage with Aunt Suze and Aunt Elle,
as she also now called them.

Harry was able to join his friends and knew this would be the last
time they would be together for some time, maybe even ever. He was
both sad and happy. They had each changed, each having met and chased
away their blue devils. This meant that now each had a purpose, whereas
before they had all been drifting. Harry knew that God had healed them.
He knew he had been healed. Ego had always been a problem for him. He
called it the 'younger son syndrome.' Now he had a purpose and a new
family.

Harry's mind drifted back to a conversation with John and
Edmund. One of the plans they decided to implement was not actually
for the poor, but for the rich. Those who, like them, had drifted from the
path. They saw that time after time, the "poor little rich boys" would hit

the clubs in London and almost come to ruin. They knew others who could help them and, even more importantly, *how* to help them. Giving them a purpose was what they really needed. They had decided to enlist Matthew's help as he now lived there. Aunt Elle had mentioned a little of what Matthew and Lilabet were doing in London. This seemed to fit in nicely.

Matthew was working with one of Ned's friends, Sam Garney, and helping young gentlemen who had partied a little too hard. Yes, they could still let their hair down, shake off the harnesses and traces of responsibility, but do it in a way they would not hurt anyone, their prospects, or even themselves. This was the first idea they would put into action on their return. They had already written to a few friends, including Matthew, asking them to help. They were sure Phil would be keen to join them, but it wasn't the right time yet to ask him. They knew of others of faith who they could enlist in this project.

After the sod turning, word spread that Aidan and Lew would be leaving with the Clarkes and the ladies on Wednesday.

Harry assured them that they would always have room for them at home. He let them all into the secret that he had made an offer on Roseneath, and he was awaiting the final paperwork until it was theirs.

The Clarkes were also overjoyed, as he gave them an open invitation to stay whenever they wished.

Vicky wanted to join everyone at Eddie's house for the celebration party. She was absolutely determined. Harry was hesitant.

Suze overruled Harry and said, "She's coming and you're carrying her."

Harry meekly smiled and said saucily, "Yes, Great Aunt Suze."

"Drop the 'great' bit, Harry. Makes me feel older than I am. Mind you, it's not that I'm not great. For I am." Her head lifted as though in defiance, should anyone contradict her. As their eyes met, he saw the twinkle in her eyes.

Harry did. His mother would have been of a similar age. He had learnt quickly to love this wonderful, compassionate lady.

Her brusque attitude was sheer bravado. She had a heart of gold.

Harry said, "I am honoured to call you anything you wish." He gave her cheek a quick kiss and returned her smile.

The kiss threw her and she blushed, then chuckled. "Be off with you, lad." Harry chuckled and left her side.

Wills arrived back at the house, having instructed the foreman on the initial stage. Major Bond had found a very skilled team.

Wills returned after lunch to check the footings before the first layer of stone was placed in the trenches.

He was no builder, but had studied one of Francis Greenway's plans in detail, as well as the detailed instructions for construction. He had decided to use this as the template for the warehouse. Insisting on the final say in everything, so he would only be to blame if anything went wrong.

Harry, Eddie, and he had pored over the internal dimensions and layout. What needed to be structural and what could be added later. Finally, they decided on a two-story stone building with a mezzanine timber floor. There was also a geared, dual rope lift, like he had seen in haylofts, but much bigger, where heavy loads could be lowered directly from the top floor onto carts on the roadway. Similarly, they could unload directly onto the upper floor from a wagon. No steps for loading. He'd planned a kitchen, a privy, even a small onsite caretaker's room.

Wills was thinking of asking Paddy's eldest son, Patrick, if he would like that job.

There were to be two strong-rooms built under the floor. These were to be stone-lined. They needed to be the first things built, and Wills had decided to increase the size of these to make them walk-in with built-in steps. They would be ten-foot square. One for storing more valuable items, and the other for explosives and other hazardous materials.

He's seen and heard of explosives now being used to move rocks in road building. This would be needed for removing the gold-bearing quartz. Yes, he needed two strong-rooms, one for valuables and one for explosives. Cara had made a special cake in the shape of a shovel.

Wills and Cathy cut it together. Then they all, glasses in hand, turned and toasted Reverend Clarke. He looked utterly embarrassed but grinned a big thanks.

Thomas and Margaret Tindale, Eddie's mentor, partner, and boss, said their farewells to the two departing men, then left as they had to return to the smithy's forge.

Luke had stayed until the blessing was over and had headed back to school. He had stayed in his old room on Saturday night, still overawed at his gifts. He now had the chance of working with his brothers. His foot was now on the first rung of his ladder. He would take far more notes in the Mathematics classes with Mr Fishbon, now he had a practical use for them. He was sure they would make sense now. He would start by determining the most effective system for bookkeeping work. He would do his very best.

Wednesday morning came all too soon for everyone.

Lew and Aidan had their two wagons harnessed up, and the four horses were champing at their bits. The men had placed a lot of their things in storage at Roseneath and planned that they would return at least by August to collect them, if not before. They both kissed Vicky, then shook hands and hugged their friends farewell. Lew led off. They were to meet the girls and Clarke's wagon at Eddie's house.

Vicky stood wrapped in Harry's arms. She was feeling well,

although she was still quite weepy.

The doctor visited on Monday afternoon and given her the all clear, no infection. They had again been told not to resume marital relations until after her next monthly flow had passed.

Harry had been her rock. Any feelings that she may have had about his acceptance of her convict's child status had totally evaporated over the past week. The entire experience and loss had drawn them closer than ever before, bonding them. She needed him, she knew that, but he needed her now. She said something earlier that brought his thoughts about their status to mind.

She lay on his chest on their bed as he told her. "Love, I know you were worried about me, about that my brother is a Viscount and all that." He drew himself up, leaned over her and looked her in the eyes. "Do you realise that we have to take lower precedence at places like Government House and Official functions, for both Jenna and Cathy? They are married to Earl's sons." He chuckled. "So, put that out of your mind forever, my sweet."

She gasped, then smiled. Vicky giggled and relaxed. "I forgot about that." That final hurdle kicked was over. She chuckled and said, "Harry, in my precedence list, you will always be number one." She drew him down to her. Cradled in his arms, they slept.

~

The Sunday before the caravan of wagons left, Phil finally had a chance to talk with Amelia. The three had gone to the riverbank to talk after church, as they knew they would not be interrupted. He apologised to her and explained that it had been nothing personal. She was a kind, gentle, and understanding person, as Aidan said. She also apologised.

They ended up laughing at how God had pulled His strings with them as mere puppets, only this time they were to be friends, not partners.

They agreed that this was good. The three walked back past the Lockleys Inn. Charlie and Gracie were standing on the verandah of the inn. Grace waved them over.

The two girls had become friends over the past week. Each felt somewhat out of things and had drifted together. Grace would miss her.

The mantle of Viscount and Viscountess still did not sit well with either of them. Neither did being called My Lord and My Lady. Charlie and Gracie fulfilled their civic duties with the poise and dignity that was required. For a couple with minimal education, it was a trial they had to bear. Each time they returned home, they shrugged off the clothing they abhorred and donned the faded, comfortable clothing they loved.

Charlie still felt like a convict's son, Assistant Viceroy or not. They were happier living at the Inn than in the cottage and were delighted when they were able to move back again. They had made it into a real home.

Charles had handed over the reins of the inn when he'd departed for England with Mama. They had not had a chance to talk since his return.

Gracie felt much the same. She was the daughter of a convict who'd married a convict's son. Now she was a titled lady; Lady Lockley. Life wasn't supposed to happen like this. She loved Charlie, had adored him most of her life and trusted him implicitly. This path they had thrust upon them both; they walked it together. Charlie had little education, and she virtually none. Mrs Bobart, then Miss Marsden, had taught her to read and write at the Charity school. Yet, their children had been promised the most prestigious education that money and title could buy. The King's School in either rParramatta or England, or even Eton, and their choice of Oxford or Cambridge or anywhere else in the world they chose. Their eldest son would be an Earl. He must have the training to fulfil that role. Would he wish to live in England? Time would tell.

Charlie understood there was something more to Wills' gold finds, but again, this was something between him and Eddie. He had felt terrible that he, and he alone, was heir to Dar's title. He was thrilled for his younger brothers, who now each had something that was theirs alone. He had never been the jealous type.

Eddie had supported him in tough times as boys. He would always support him in anything he wanted to do. He didn't really mind that their youngest brothers turned to Eddie rather than to him. He would use his position to ease their paths where possible. He and Eddie had been through much as children, not least of all, the trauma of the abuse they had suffered as children, at the hands of a cruel soldier. He'd still shudder when he thought of him, Lieutenant Simmons. Felled by an act of God, when lightning struck the tree under which he had been standing. Eddie had seen the lightning strike happen and then saw him dead. Not a dream nor a nightmare, but certainly a finish, only then could he tell his father all. Years later, he told Gracie everything shortly before they became engaged. However, just the man's name and the thought of him would still make him shiver.

They watched as their three new friends drew closer. He and Grace had taken a moment together as she had just told him she was expecting again.

She had a difficult time with the twins and had not wanted to worry him unduly, so held off telling him until she was at least two months along. She wanted Amelia to know before they left on Wednesday. She whispered to Charlie, "Do you mind if I tell her, even before the family knows?"

"Of course not, love," Charlie replied. He bent and kissed her gently. "When do you think it's due?" he asked quietly.

"September again or thereabouts, love," she replied softly.

They were joined on the verandah by their three visitors.

Amelia and Gracie greeted each other with a kiss. Grace drew her aside and left the men talking. Arm in arm, they walked around the side of the inn and out of sight. Gracie then told her.

Amelia was excited. She had fallen in love with the adorable twin boys. At twins they were a delightful handful. Amelia and Gracie had spent much time in the nursery at 'Bramblemere Close' with all the children. As similar as they were, little John would run to her and snuggle into her lap. He couldn't say Amelia, so he called her "Aunty Milla." So, Aunty Milla she had become to all the children. She was going to miss them all so.

The next day, the two wagons pulled into the new wide circular driveway at Bramblemere Close.

Everyone was up waiting for them.

The Clarkes wagon already packed, and loaded. It had moved far enough forward to leave room for the others.

Cara was piling them up with food for their travels; fruit cakes, biscuits, tea, flour and all sorts of other goodies.

Eddie had a cask of not-too-potent cider for the back of the men's cart. Not all water was safe to drink.

Neither Fiona nor Amelia had even seen a wagon like this, let alone expected to live in one. They had gasped when their uncle and aunt had arrived.

It really *was* just a covered wagon. So different to the grey stone castle in Scotland that Fiona had grown up in. The girls had spent many hours over the past months sharing a room. For four months on the ship out, and also on arrival here, and both decided to enjoy this new venture. They had arrived as two spinsters, considering themselves on the shelf.

Fiona was running from heartache; Amelia, looking for adventure. Now they were off into only God knew, and they had met two wonderful men to accompany them. Fiona already knew her destiny. It was always meant to be with Lewis. He was all she had ever wanted. Hopefully, Amelia and Aidan would find the happiness that they now had.

They stood holding each other's hands. Waiting in anticipation for the two wagons to arrive. They each had two bags and some coats. They sat on the verandah next to other items to be loaded.

They could hear the slow rumble of the wheels on the dirt as they turned into Phillip Street. Now they saw the vehicles, they wondered if this trip was so wise.

Jenna had advised them to pack their heaviest overcoats, even though it was summer. She helped sort through their luggage to work out what would be best to take. Their remaining luggage would be held in storage until their return, or it could be sent on if required.

Eddie and Charles took the reins of the horses. Lew and Aidan greeted everyone.

Suze and Elle were sitting against the wall on a long bench seat. They sat sewing. Both had decided to finally discard the black they had each worn for so long.

Elle dressed in mauve and Suze in royal purple.

Charlie and Gracie had also arrived with their boys. There seemed to be small, fair-haired children running everywhere on the side lawn. Moira and Shauna were keeping their eyes on them. John, Edmund, and Phil jumped off the wagons. They had leapt on as they were brought round from the stables at Roseneath.

Lew went and wished his Great Aunt Suze a fond farewell. Most had forgotten the distant relationship. It had been nice seeing her again. Lewis missed his grandmother a lot.

Suze was as kind and loving as always. She did not really like public displays of affection; however, she presented her cheek to him and, with an impish smile on her face, said quite loudly, "Get it over with, lad."

He bent and kissed her cheek, then gave her a big bear hug.

She smiled as she hugged him back. She cupped his face, saying, "Don't be a stranger when we all finally arrive home, boy." She also gave him her approval to Fiona, kissing both her cheeks and farewelled her too with a hug. She whispered to her, "I'll be praying for you all."

Fi looked her in the eye and smiled and said softly, "Thank you." Fiona's lilt made a lump form in Suze's throat; memories of her own childhood.

Aidan farewelled his cousin, Elle. They had agreed to him referring to her as Aunt Elle, the same as John, even though the relationship was more distant. They all started saying their goodbyes.

A new chapter was starting for them both. One that only a year ago none could have imagined. This entire trip had been an unplanned adventure into the unknown, both physically and spiritually. From here, they would all trust God. More than that, they could not ask.

Loading did not take long.

Lew placed the bags carefully in the back of the cart.

The girls were surprised by how comfortable their wagon was. They looked inside and saw it even had a lamp.

Lew was to drive the girl's wagon and Aidan the men's one.

They said their last goodbyes.

Lew lifted Fiona onto the seat of his wagon. Aidan did the same with Amelia next to him. With such a late start, they would be on the road for a night at least, possibly two, before they set up camp.

Reverend and Mrs Clarke gave Cathy and Wills an extra hug and thanked them again.

Reverend Clarke told Wills that the ingot was safe with the Communion Wine he always carried. It would pay for many more adventures for both of them.

Wills suggested that they bank it as soon as possible, and Harry Moffatt could arrange to cash it.

Eddie and Charles had taken the opportunity of the extra days to refurbish the wagon for them. They added new shelving and storage, as well as greased the axles and performed general servicing on the wagon. Their work was quite rough, but it would do. They also added a set of triple hammock bunks at the front for the children. These had a canvas base, and the poles slipped in slots in the wagon's frame.

Wills felt guilty, considering his share was half of the £26,000 haul. The £1000 he gave them was a pittance. Without Reverend Clarke, none of the gold would have been found. There would be more if required. Still, it was worth about five or ten years' worth of wages in value. Wills had said that to Mrs Clarke, and he hoped she would tell him if she needed any more. Wills knew that the majority of his share would be put to good use in the community.

Finally, they waved off the three wagons. "Until August," they all called, and they departed.

As they drove out of town, they passed the building site. The first two rows of stone were already in place. By the time they returned in a few months, they would not be surprised to see the entire site tidy and the building finished.

Both Lew and Aidan had been feeling a little left out with the building plans. That was not for them to plan. They knew God had a different path for them. This next stage was theirs alone. Hopefully, they would both not have to walk it alone for too long.

By the end of the week, the first floor stonework at the Warehouse was ready for the lintels for the big barn doors. The stone corbels for the wooden top floor were also now in place. The entire building was huge. Wills had added strength to various beams. As it was a Warehouse, he wanted it strong. Preferably as fire-proof as possible too.

One night, a few months before, he had taken his sketchbook along to Eddie, and they sat in his office poring over the plans. Wills sat pondering. "Eddie, if the wagons unload here, how do we get the goods upstairs without having to man-handle everything twice?" They had sat thinking for a while. Neither could sort out an answer.

Luke poked his head in the door to say goodnight and that he'd finally finished replacing the library books he had borrowed.

Wills called him in. He explained what they were discussing and advised him to think it through.

Luke picked up the pad, flicked over a few pages, then said, "You'll need a dual cantilever pulley system with gears: one to lift it and one to draw it in. I'm sure you could make something like that. I was thinking about that a few nights ago. I had a dream of how it worked." He handed the pad back and walked out.

His older brothers watched him as he left, their mouths agape. He'd taken one look at the issue and summed it up in an instant. But they had no idea *how* to make one. That was something they could work out later. Over the next month, the two doodled, drew, and thought. Finally, Eddie hit upon an idea. "We could make a big iron rail, maybe even a steel bridge girder or even a large pig iron girder. At the end of that would be a large pulley system that could be raised and lowered from the ground, but it could run along the track to pull it inside. The mechanism could then be released either from the ground or inside. If we tied two ropes to that lever, then it could pull along the track into the loft. This could all be done using the ropes and gears."

Wills grasped exactly what he meant as he described his idea. Once they had the basic idea, making it proved more difficult. Eventually, they made a working model and tried it out. It worked. So, they upscaled it and made it at the forge. The tricky bit was the unlocking mechanism. In the end, they hit upon a spring-loaded release lever with two ropes attached.

Once the stone corbels were in place, the final preparation of the floor beams could begin. A team of skilled adze men trimmed and shaped the beams. They insisted on chamfered edges, and they were placed in set grooves on the support beams of the corbels. This meant that each beam had to be positioned in the exact spot. Fortunately, they had a lot of manpower. The ironbark beams were extremely heavy, but they would be strong.

February passed, then March, April, and the gabled roof was ready for its timbers. For this, they had chosen red cedar beams. It was light and strong, and the white ants didn't seem to eat it. It did not have to bear the weight of slate tiles.

The ridge beam was finally in place. Now, only the new corrugated roofing had to be installed. Again, they had puzzled over how to insulate it. As corrugated sheeting could be installed over normal shingles, Wills decided to try to modify that idea. They would line the entire roof first with long, narrow cedar shingles. Thin planks of cedar off-cuts with the bark still on them, overlapping, then place the sheets of iron on top. Termites didn't like eating this wood, so hopefully that would also keep bugs away. If this worked, they would duplicate it for the other two buildings. Either way, with the rolls of lead as flashing, it would be far more waterproof than thatch. They had seen how many thatched roofs burned in bushfires. Wills knew that any exposed dry vegetation was a fire danger.

Wills had been intrigued with shingles. He had to pick up enough, five years ago, when the tornado had hit the church. Luke and he had to collect all the old ones, hundreds of them. He thought that exceptionally light cedar planks might do the trick for the roofing. Typically, the outside thin slices of sawn timber were thrown away or used for firewood. They'd try a few and see if they'd work. They did.

Cathy suggested they whitewash the underside before placing them up. It would add more light to the interior.

Before they placed the first sheet of iron sheeting, he sat and read the instructions Uncle Ned brought back with him. "It says nail on the topside of the curves, Eddie. That sounds strange." It didn't take long to figure out why. Leaks.

Eddie had the apprentices make a lot more of the nails with the lead disk at the top. He'd had to make the first lot for an Orchard Hills order some months ago. Guy Manning wanted tin sheeting over this jam factory. Now the nails made sense. The lead circle washer prevented water from getting in, as it was nailed from the top of the corrugations, not the bottom of the channels. Eddie had made a punch for the washers, and Harry had cut them out. They no longer had to be hand-cut.

The instruction sheet showed them which order to place the sheets, how to hammer them off, and then how to "flash" the roof to waterproof it. The top row of sheeting needed to have each dip folded up so water could not run up the sheet and under the flashing. Once they had worked out the mechanics, most of the roof was up in one day. They decided to use lead flashing as ridge capping. According to the instructions, you could also buy ridge capping. But as they didn't have that, they'd make do with what they did have. There were unlimited quantities of lead sheeting in the colony, as it was used as ballast for ships.

Word had spread around town, "Lockleys' warehouse building is using a new leak-proof roof." Over a hundred townsfolk, including many of his own family, stood watching the way these strange sheets of tin needed to be hammered on. Roof installation usually took over a week to complete. This took a day.

Wills spent his nineteenth birthday watching the roof go on.

Cathy stood or sat with Wills. She was often onsite to oversee, if he or Eddie could not attend. She was as much "boss" as he was.

The foreman had learnt that early on with the building. Cathy had seen a problem and called him over. They had missed a bit on the plans, and she had picked it up. He would not listen to her, Cathy finally had to send someone to get Eddie, as Wills had gone to Emu Plains.

Ed had not been impressed and had severely reprimanded the foreman. The man never made the same mistake.

Sadly, Cathy had no reason to stop her work. Each month that passed, her monthly flow came. No baby again. She and Vicky commiserated with each other when alone.

The doctor has told Vicky not to worry, as it sometimes takes a while for her body to adjust.

Cathy and Wills had discussed their problem. Once she'd been late, and she had a very heavy flow that month and wondered if the same thing had happened to her, only earlier than Vicky's loss.

Vicky confided in Cathy but not Harry. Both girls put on a happy face. Both felt the pain. They were already thin, but both lost more weight.

Phil, John, and Edmund were all at a loose end. None were required to assist with either the business or the building. The three sat discussing what they should do one night and decided to pray. They asked God for some way to help.

It was after church one Sunday that Mrs Bobart spoke to them and asked if they may perhaps be interested in trying their hand at teaching. She explained that before her marriage, she taught at the Charity school. Mr Childs at the Orphans' School needed some help. He was short-staffed at the moment. It was now a church run orphanage, rather than the government institution it once had been. Mrs Bobart refused to allow them to answer straight away but sent them home to think about it. It didn't take any thinking. Both girls were ecstatic, but the Englishmen wished to join in with the project. This idea was perfect and would give them both some experience for when they returned home. They all went along with her on Tuesday that same week. She introduced them to Mr Childs.

They discovered that there were only females in the classes. She had not mentioned that it was the 'Female Orphans' school. That threw the men for some time, but John said as they had been called to serve God, they had to trust Him that this was where He needed them. So it was the Female Orphans' School that gained new teachers.

"John, I've never seen so many little girls." Edmund shivered.

"Neither have I, Edmund, but I'm prepared to help where I can. How about we really give this a go? Learn what we can. This is what we had planned to do at home. Let's learn what we can while we're here," John said pragmatically. "I agree, though, so many little girls." He shivered.

The children needed to learn basic writing. Specifically, how to write their names. The more they could learn here, the better their lives would turn out. She encouraged them to sit in on lessons and learn how to teach.

John and Edmund sat in on the first lessons together.

Phil had missed out as he had a meeting arranged. They didn't question him further.

The fact that all the children were female was enough to instil fear in them. However, this worked out as a benefit. Within a week, both were teaching. Each started with a small group of ten students together. They both loved it. By the end of the month, they were each teaching a whole class each day. They made a rule of always working together, especially when working with the older students.

Phil only came occasionally and sat in on their classes, listening and watching. He always arrived late and freshly scrubbed with his hair still wet. He started by helping individual students and floating from one class to another.

This was actually very beneficial. If one student were having a problem, Phil would take them aside and quietly help them. He loved this; he felt useful and became a favourite with the little girls.

The students in both classes were soon able to write their names. Mr Childs made up a song that taught the children the alphabet. They then taught them the sounds each letter made, and then easy reading. Some caught on very quickly; as they progressed, Phil would also take these students aside and read with them.

The only book they could access multiple copies of was The Bible. Ruth or Esther was always the first choice in stories. Soon his "story time" became more popular than classes. Only those who reached their weekly goal could sit and read with "Mr Phil".

The teachers were Mr Childs, the headmaster; John and Edmund, who were known as "Mr Saunders" and "Mr Hunt"; and "Mr Phil". Phil had wormed his way into their hearts. "Mr Phil" was their favourite. They all laughed over this, considering Phil was the most reluctant of the teachers. However, each of them learnt how children craved almost individual attention. If a child were to succeed, it needed love and attention.

They decided to try something. Once a week, the classes joined. Mr Child was taking the majority, as he had done before they came. The six best students would have a choice of story and reading time. Two old, leather armchairs had been placed in the back corners of the room. The third pair sat with Phil on a pile of pillows on the floor. They would supervise the story time. Their goal was to eventually get the older ones to read to the younger ones.

Mr Child would have special lessons on these days. Geography, History, Mathematics or even Celestial navigation, depending on the age of the group.

By the time the roof was on the new building, the three men were attending the school daily. They would be up and out and "off to school". The more they worked there, the more they came to love it.

If Wills were at the building site, which was often, then Vicky and Cathy would sometimes join the men at the school. Harry also headed along and helped where he could. With the ladies there, the children were able to sit in small groups and have a real story time.

They had been able to source some children's picture storybooks. These times were great fun for them all. Vicky and Cathy had taught the girls about health and cleanliness. Each child had to wash their hands and face before entering class. If they left a dirty mark on a clean towel, they would not be permitted to join the reading circle. It inspired them to do a good job scrubbing.

The children ranged from three to thirteen. About one-fifth were orphans, but the rest had one parent living; many of the mothers were still at the Female Workhouse or Factory. The friends had all been horrified when they learnt that all the girls lived on site—boarding at the school. Many never saw their parents again. Some of the mothers were still living and working at the Female Factory. The babies would be removed from their mothers as soon as they were weaned.

As the group got to know the students, they learnt to love them. Cathy and Vicky enlisted Mrs Jenkins and Sally and began getting them to come and teach the girls to sew. Suze and Elle occasionally put in an appearance.

Sal also took the older girls aside and explained menstruation and how babies were conceived and born. She taught them to value themselves and their chastity. They were not to lie with a man before marriage.

The requirement for cleanliness was foremost, as none wished to get the lice. Many, if not most, of the children had lice. They discovered that all the children were infected with the itching critters.

Harry remembered a Scottish soldier in India told them to pour strong alcohol into their hair and wrap it in a damp towel for an hour. It killed everything, including eggs and lice. It certainly worked. It was also an excellent use for the overproof illicit rum brewed locally. They all became less hands-on after the lice incident. There were one hundred girls, but as they covered a ten-year range, the class the men had chosen to teach was the six to ten-year-olds. They also refused to be alone with any of the children. The smaller ones they couldn't handle as they wanted to be touched and cuddled all the time, and the three men felt uncomfortable with this. Vicky and Cathy relished the cuddles from the love-starved children.

Any of the older girls who wished to study further they certainly would help, but the men discovered that they were often not that interested. The men changed that by making the study both fun and relevant, so the children wished to learn to cook. Cooking involved reading a recipe. So did knitting from a pattern. Both required reading. Shopping involved mathematics, so did cooking. However, it was the touch, love and compassion that these children craved. If they had to learn and behave in class to receive affection, then that's what they would do. The more the children learned and the more effort they put into the lessons, the more reward time they received.

The special teaching time with Mr Phil, Mrs Sal, and, as a super treat, with Great Aunt Elle. The very little ones adored her.

Mr Phil's Bible stories or the ladies' special classes became a huge motivation for all the girls.

~

By the end of May, the new building was nearly complete. This meant phase two was about to start, the next building. Wills and Cathy planned to either rent or buy a house around Emu Plains for this next stage.

They said farewell and headed west. They would return often, as they needed to sort out building materials for the first shop. Harry took control of sourcing items locally. Excess building materials were already stored there. There would be ample roofing tin for all three buildings, and then some to spare for sale.

Phil and Harry put their heads together and implemented Vicky's idea of colour-coding the stock.

Eddie and his new junior apprentices were madly making more roofing nails and other stock for the Emporiums.

Phil was also working with Eddie quite often now. The regular meetings that he often had were working as a blacksmith's apprentice. They had kept it quiet for as long as they could. However, one day, as he was washing up at home, John and Edmund had arrived early and discovered him covered in smithy soot! He was filthy, but he was smiling broadly. He had been having a wonderful time. John and Edmund were stunned. They had not guessed for nearly three months.

Phil was always one to keep things close to his chest.

Phil and Wills had also put their heads together and had to try to make a small drop hammer that ran without steam or a water mill. He had tried two different ideas, the first one based on a bicycle like the one his friends had ridden. He had removed a buckled front wheel of a discarded velocipede he had found. Then he added another idea, which he gleaned from watching a spinning wheel on Sal's verandah, a bent axle. He scavenged the bike pedals from the broken machine.

Wills, Luke, and Phil had fiddled and played with these two and finally designed a form of trim hammer. A semi-automated Smithy hammer, like a person standing there, hand hammering all day, only with this idea, he could sit on the seat of the contraption and peddle. The hammer weights could be changed easily, from a small half-pounder to a five-pounder or even bigger. He had developed it as a smithy hammer, but it crushed the quartz quickly and with little effort. For this alone, it would be fabulous. The various apprentices were none the wiser.

Phil had been working with Eddie and Mr Tindale as a 'striker'. The muscles behind the smithy hammer. Very cathartic. Mr Tindale told them that the term 'Smythe' was actually the striker for a blacksmith. He loved belting the living daylights out of a chunk of hot metal.

For Phil, a person who had lived a sedentary, posh life, it was the most fun he'd had in years. He was a thinker, not a doer. He thought this is how he decided he could help.

Reading to lots of little girls was also beneficial, in a different way. For that, he had to learn to be calm and at peace.

Luke, too, had been busy. He had a plan in place for his future as a bookkeeper. He had even sourced some books on a bookkeeping system. Mr Fishbon at The King's School had helped him, but then he'd tweaked the books.

Captain Roberts, the Ferry captain, had been charged with asking where to buy one for him. He had done better than that. Eddie had given him £1 and asked him to have a good hunt if possible, or if not, ask Caroline Evans.

Luke and Douglas Evans had become friends. Douglas often accompanied Stephen Roberts on the ferry to catch the scent of the sea spray again. They had gone together to the stationer. On explaining their quest, the storekeeper was very helpful. Comparing Luke's request to what the man had, they chose four sets of books. One for the warehouse, a thick one for overall inventory; one for Parramatta, as Eddie had not sorted out a bookkeeping system; one for Emu, and the last for the Bathurst store. There were different sorts, too. Journal books for inventory IN sales, and OUT, payments to the various artisans supplying goods to the store. A double-entry accounts book and a payroll book for each, as well. Up until now, Eddie had done it all in a single notebook, and not very neatly.

Each man was falling into their allotted role, but working together as a whole.

By August, Wills and Harry were both feeling guilty that they had not been able to spend as much time with their wives as they had wanted to. They hatched a scheme to take a week off and a mini-break.

Wills and Cathy had returned from the two months at Emu. It had been work, day in, day out.

Wills was exhausted.

Harry had taken a few trips to Emu Plains himself since the work on the Warehouse had finished, and to finalise the Emu Plains building plans. Vicky always went with him. They suggested to the girls that they might like a slightly longer break. Both were ecstatic.

Cathy had been able to have her husband to herself when he was home. However, he was often working until bedtime. It's not that they had drawn apart; Wills was just busy.

Cathy was fretting; she had not yet conceived. They had been married for six months and… nothing.

She and Vicky were both troubled.

Vicky had not conceived since the loss of Alexis. It was always the first question they asked each other when alone. Now it was only asked with a raised eyebrow and answered with a shake of their head. Yes, a holiday would be good.

When Harry suggested they go to Hartley for a week at least, Vicky was over the moon.

This came about because Harry had received a letter from Lew. The wagons were returning.

The Wagons
Campbelltown Parish
28 July 1846

Roseneath
O'Connell Street
Parramatta

Dear Harry,

I thought you would congratulate me. Fi and I are getting married the last week in August. Reverend Clarke, aka Uncle William, has arranged to marry us at St John's, so all our friends can join us.

The best news is that Aidan and Amelia will also be married with us, in a double ceremony. From there, we will both honeymoon in Sydney before returning to England whenever there's a ship. We're really in no hurry, so we will come and visit after our honeymoons. Maybe, even a stay for a bit.

It would be delightful if Fi could be 'with child' before we arrive home. We feel her father might be somewhat less angry. I dare say that is in God's hands.

Aidan and Amelia are also pleased to be heading homeward bound. They will live in Ireland with Aidan's family. We both have many plans for how we can help our communities. However, we know God will lead us down the path He has already prepared for us.

Our hearts are now well and truly open, after living and working with these two amazing people and seeing how the Clarkes identify the needs of their people and provide the necessary aid. The four of us have been teaching children to both read and write. I have discovered that I love this work. It is real, genuine, honest, loving work.

My eyes are now well open. Oh, Harry, Fi's father was right. I WAS a selfish, pleasure-loving creature. But no more. I try now not just to be worthy of her, but of our Lord and Saviour. Please continue to pray for us.

Living in the wagons has been a trial for the girls. They look forward to having a house somewhere. We will be pleased to return the wagons to you. We have modified them again, so they are now more homely and comfortable, but we shall all be glad to have a solid roof finally over our heads again.

Please let everyone know about our upcoming nuptials and keep August 22nd free. Everyone is to be invited.

Your blessed and ever-loving friend
Lewis.
PS You can keep the wagons, we won't ever want to see them again.
   Lewis   *(A very happy Lewis.)*

Harry could not read it fast enough. "Yes," he yelled as he punched the air. He told Vicky immediately, and as soon as he heard the others return from their day's activities. He took the letter out and let them read it as well.

It had taken ten days to reach them, so they only had a couple of weeks to arrange both a wedding and a party.

Easy! Charlie was good for that. The inn was a perfect venue for a wedding party.

Ned was thrilled when he heard; this was the excuse he was looking for. The church needed some urgent work. They had at least covered the gaping hole with some new canvas sails. They had sourced some huge ones in good condition. They were oiled before being lifted into position.

Ned, Charles and Harry organised a town working bee. Ned enlisted Major David Bond's help. He asked the various battalions for volunteers, as well as some convicts usually in chain gangs, who offered to assist.

By Saturday, fifty strong men were at St John's ready to cover the missing roof.

They used a harpoon gun to shoot numerous ropes over the roofline. With six ropes attached to the top of the canvas sheet and two more on the edges, the sail slid into place with ease. A second sail was slid over the top, making it entirely weatherproof. They tied them down firmly and secured the ends to huge rocks on the ground. This mammoth effort meant that, at last, they could worship inside the church during the winter. When the last rope was finally secured, everyone cheered.

Wills and Cathy returned from Emu Plains that night.

Vicky told Cathy the next day about the proposed holiday. They went directly to Cara and informed her.

After a long, cold winter, this is just what they needed to brighten their spirits. They planned their trip for early spring.

Cathy had let on to Vicky that Wills and Harry had been waiting for the wagons to return. They were hoping to borrow them for a week. With Lew and Aidan no longer wanting them, they could have longer than just one week. John and Phil would help Eddie while they took time off.

All they had to do was clear their schedules. This was not that easy.

Cathy and Wills had only had a six-day honeymoon, and even then, Wills had worked. Not that she minded, but having some time together would be nice. They knew Hartley was the planned destination, and both were keen to see the place they had heard so much about. Wills had spoken of one day building a small cottage for them there. He had an idea of a pre-fabricated building and set about constructing the panels. It would then be taken by wagon and erected on site.

Cathy said, "Vicks, I would love to see the fish trap they built, to see the outcrop and, oh, just to be part of things again." Cathy added, "One day, I would also love to see Duck Creek."

Vicky looked pensive. "Since I lost the baby, Harry is all love, care and attention, but we've lost the 'joy of living' we first had. We too need a change. Also, it's hard living in a house full of men."

Cathy looked at her older sister coyly. "Who knows, Hartley might put more than heart into us. I think it's because they have been so busy that, well, Wills' attentions have, um, err, not what they used to be."

"You too?" she said, "Yes. Some nights Harry is so tired he's asleep before I turn off the lamp."

They giggled. "I think we might have a lot more than fun up there, and I believe nights are much colder in the wagons, more excuses for snuggling."

Cathy smirked. "Want to go shopping before we leave? I believe there's a new shipment of lacy undergarments for sale in Sydney. Mr Smith is bringing some stock up from his Park Street store to Parramatta."

They giggled and planned. Both decided that some lacy underclothing may well do the trick. They set about procuring some and planning a camping ambush. They timed the holiday to coincide with the middle of their monthly cycles.

The double wedding drew closer. The Clarkes and the girls would stay with Eddie; the men would be back with Harry and Vicky. They arrived five days before the wedding and were surprised at what had been planned for them.

~

The wedding day dawned bright and sunny. The two groomsmen had each enjoyed a long soak in the hip baths, along with haircuts, shaves, and the general luxury of the space. They had managed to stay reasonably clean, unlike the west trip, where baths consisted of waterholes; often with leeches and snakes. Mrs Clarke had cut their hair, and Fi had learnt how to do this. She did Lew's the last time. Amelia was not game to try her hand on Aidan's more curly hair. The men had shaved each other as neither had thought to pack a mirror.

Phil congratulated Aidan privately, and Aidan thanked him for not being interested.

Their good-hearted banter eased the topic.

Harry and Vicky took the carriage with everyone from their house and left them at the church on the way down to get the *Les Grande Dames* and brides. On arrival, they discovered *Les Grande Dames* had seconded the dray. Luke had decorated it with greenery and flowers. It looked so pretty that they decided to go up in this and to leave the carriage to Mrs Clarke and the brides. She was to walk each bride up the aisle and give them away. Reverend Clarke was then to marry each couple.

The decorated dray also fitted Ned, Christina, and Sal, as well as Charles, who drove it. Bobbs was in harness; he was getting older but still loved to pull a load.

Charlie had the cart loaded with a very expectant Gracie and all the younger family members and staff.

Eddie and Jenna had their larger cart, filled with all the little children. Moira and Shauna were with them. The houses and inn were shut up for the hour. Everyone went to see four more of God's threads drawn together and tied into two neat knots.

Lew's wedding speech later that afternoon echoed Aidan's thoughts exactly. It was not exactly a wedding speech.

Lew spoke clearly, his voice tinged with a slight Scottish burr. "Friends, old and new. We six jaded British soldiers arrived in this country, heartsore, after a long and weary war. We served together in India and had lost our seventh friend. Actually, we lost many more than that; however, Christopher was special. None of us could settle. A year after our return, we all found ourselves sitting in White's, a very fancy Men's Club in London. What had drawn us each there, we didn't know. Only Harry and John had planned to meet; the presence of the rest of us, I'd say, was by chance; however, we know that with God, there *is* no chance, only God-incidence. Harry asked John to come here with him. He had agreed, then called us over to join them for a drink. Aidan, first, I believe. As I say, we had not planned to meet. Soon the six of us were packing for a bigger adventure than we could have dreamed."

Some of his audience were shuffling.

"You'd all better make yourselves comfortable, for I'm going to tell you the entire story," Lew said happily.

There was some more shuffling and moving as everyone found somewhere to sit. They all listened. What was he going to reveal?

Lew continued. "As we had no idea what we were to find here. Our letters home were severely devoid of information. We merely stated our plan to leave the country; some of our family did not even know our destination. None of us mentioned a duration, nor the mode of transport we planned to take. In fact, we were all to some extent we were all running away."

Gasps echoed around the courtyard.

Lew waved for them to be quiet. "We came, I don't even remember the name of the ship." He looked to each of his friends, and they all shook their heads too. "We hit Sydney and we were amazed at what we found. We expected tents and chained convicts. We found a mini London. I have since heard that Governor Lachlan Macquarie was responsible for the many magnificent edifices I saw. Then, after a week or so, we heard about Parramatta, so one day we packed some duffel bags and stored the remainder of our possessions. We came by ferry and met Captain Roberts. Stephen Roberts is pivotal to our story, as it was he who first mentioned the road across the mountains and then Lockleys Emporium. This piqued our interest. What was over there? We had not met anyone who had been. Why not go and look for ourselves?" Lew gave a nod to Stephen Roberts, who was standing at the side beside Douglas Evans.

"We wandered around town, and finally bought three covered wagons of sorts and six sturdy horses. Our quest for equipment brought us to Lockleys Emporium. A place where we discovered you could buy almost everything we needed, *sans* the wagons and horses, which we already had. In the store, we were served by a lad who had just finished school. There, John fell into conversation with Wills, again a God-incidence. For it was through Wills our lives were to change, and to heal." Lew gave Wills a nod of thanks.

"Wills ran away from home and joined our motley crew. I will cut a long story short. After leaving Emu Plains, we stopped the first night at an inn on the range. We had the wagons rifled. The second night, and up until today, the most significant one of my life occurred. Without that night, we would not be here today. We seven sat around a campfire for the first night, sleeping rough. We were getting to know each other better. We had not even done this in India as our work did not involve us working closely together. Wills asked us two simple questions that had far-reaching consequences. "What do we do?" and "How do we help others?"

The six men's gazes fell on Wills.

"Friends, we six were stunned into silence. We each admitted to our selfishness, self-centredness and pleasure-seeking ways to ourselves but dared not voice them. We *did* nothing that was not our will. Fiona's father refused my request for her hand due to my attitude and selfish ways. I'm not even sure she should have accepted me back then, either. I certainly was not worthy of her." His eyes flicked over to his new wife.

Fiona blew him a kiss.

"I wander from the plot, as our wedding is at the end of this saga. Our journey west continued, for Wills was the only one amongst us with a plan or a direction of sorts. He wished to see the brolgas dance. I used to think, 'Why watch a bird dance?' Reverend Clarke, here, had told Wills of the birds in class, and obviously, they caught his imagination. Much of what Reverend Clarke told sank deep within this lad's soul. Ahh, the words of a teacher, how important they can be."

He looked at Wills, who was nodding.

"We finally made it. It had taken months, but worth every single night. Each day, another scale was loosed. That first night, when the flocks of birds descended on the waterways was, I thought, the most awe-inspiring sight I could ever have imagined. Cloud after cloud of every colour and size of bird imaginable. And the noise. A cacophony of bird calls; screeching so loud you had your fingers in your ears. Have you ever heard the chirping of a million budgerigars or galahs? A pen of crowing roosters compares as quiet to that noise. I wondered *why* Wills wished to come to a swamp filled with wild birds? I thought it was horrible. We lit our fire and talked again, as we had done each night. With each new campfire, we opened our hearts a little more. The loosened scales of our stress started falling off. However, the souls of each of us were still tightly locked. Then came dawn." A lump rose in his throat, and his voice broke.

Everyone could see him struggling for the words.

"Ah, dawn…" Lew paused. "This was the first dawn of a new day that unlocked our souls and threw away the keys. Wills, of course, was first awake. He slept on the front seat of the wagon. Uncomfortable and uncovered, and not a single word of complaint for the seven entire months."

He again looked to Wills. "No, not once." He swallowed. "That morning, I woke to see him standing on the seat. The dawn was still some way off, but there was enough light to see his silhouette. 'The dawn chorus', he called it, was just beginning, but something had caught his ear. A different sound. We all must have heard something. Soon, without a word to each other, we were all sitting or standing on the seats of the wagons. In absolute awe at what we saw. Millions upon millions of birds in a myriad of colours and sizes. The cacophony of horrible noise from the night before had magically settled into divine singing. What did you call it, Wills? A conference of choirs?"

Wills nodded.

"What a perfect phrase? We sat spellbound for over an hour. The chill permeated our bones, but we still didn't move. Another scale fell off."

Lew paused, rubbing his eyes. "Then, in the early morning light, we saw him point. 'Look,' he said softly. One simple word, and the walls so carefully built around our lives tumbled like Jericho. We each stood, struck dumb in amazement. Two pale grey, velvety cranes started to dance. They rose, they pranced, they jumped, they bowed, they danced. Each graceful movement was magnificent. I looked at Wills, and his face glowed, but I noticed that each of the others' faces looked similar. Strong, manly men we all may be, but God spoke to each of us that day and softened our hearts. More than one tear was shed, I assure you. I know I wept. More importantly, I was at last at peace. I had no idea what had happened to us, but it was something special. That night, Wills asked his darned question again. This time, we answered, or at least most of us did. I fled. I fought the challenge. I wasn't ready. But God dealt with that later."

His mouth was dry, and he took a drink.

"We stayed for the rest of the week as we had planned. I wish it had been a year, but we were running out of food. The scales had ceased to fall individually, as they now fell as entire bricks. Each day, more bricks in our walls fell. By the time we tore ourselves away, as we were short of supplies, we were all different, changed. We each knew the healing had begun. Some of us still had things left unsaid, but they, too, slowly healed. The return trip, which took us more months on the road, forged the future paths for us. Each, now with a purpose. Each of us was in touch with God and our souls. Our Bibles were given a regular workout around the campfire each night. We all believed; however, we six had done nothing with our faith. Wills' simple question challenged us, and each knew we must change our way of living. I know that on our return, our families will not recognise our new selves. I know that only now can I look Fiona's father in the face and say, 'I'm sorry you were right.' I now have a new purpose in life. We will walk this path together. Won't we, my love?" He looked at his new wife. "I'd now like to make the toast I was supposed to make fifteen minutes ago." He reached down for a refill. Wills poured it, champagne.

Lew lifted his glass, "To my wife, may I live to be the best husband I can be, for she deserves no less."

They all cheered and toasted her.

Then he added, "A second toast, 'To Wills and my friends'. The miles may keep us apart, but our souls will always be together when we remember those brolgas dancing. To a new beginning!"

Again, everyone cheered.

Aidan also spoke, his deep Irish brogue carrying across the assembled multitude. He endorsed everything that Lew had said. Adding that he had not known Amelia before her arrival. He had not mentioned why the girls had come, only that they had come to join their aunt in helping her for some time. He, too, thanked Wills by saying, "Thank you, Wills, for helping remove some bricks that had blocked the path of two Gaelic lads. We plan to build or work in some schools on our return home, or whichever path God leads us to, and to help His people become the best they could be. I have seen the benefits of education, and we have also learnt *how* to teach. Thanks to our new aunt and uncle, the Clarkes. Our input in our communities will now be hands-on. The lessons learnt here have reached into my soul. This country has a hold on me. One day we will return. I look forward to that day, but only when things there are settled. I previously followed the path of least resistance. Now I will follow God's path. I, too, propose a toast. To Amelia, my wife and partner on this new path. Please, charge your glasses."

They all did, and drank the toast to the two brides.

Aidan added, "And now... Wills, thank you for challenging us and letting God use you to light our path. Also to Eddie and Charlie for not blasting him on his return after running away."

Everyone laughed, but still drank the toast.

Aidan finished with, "You are all so lucky you *can* stay here. We will for a while yet, then we must return, as we have new jobs to do." He jumped down and took Amelia in his arms. He looked into her face, now cupped in his hands, devouring her adoration of him, then bent his head and kissed her.

They were still locked in an embrace when the Irish fiddlers climbed up onto the cart and played an Irish tune. It was in 3/4 time, and Aidan's eyes flew open. He leaned over and whispered something to Lew, who nodded in return. As he did so, Aidan swung his new wife into his arms and asked her to waltz.

A whispered gasp circled the courtyard when Lew and Fiona took the floor with them. They circled gracefully.

Many had still not seen this dance performed in public. These four performed it with grace and dignity.

Ned swung Christina onto the dirt floor, too, closely followed by Charles and Sal. Once the Duke and Earl began dancing, others who knew the steps joined them. There were many missed steps, but everyone had fun.

Suze and Elle sat together enjoying the festivities. It was nothing like any other wedding they had attended. Wills and Cathy's had been a reasonably small affair. Word had spread at the school, the forge, and also the church that two of the Englishmen were getting married. Everyone came as it was an open invitation. The two Reverends were up dancing with their wives. Elle's feet were tapping. She so wished someone would ask her. She heard Suze take a slight breath.

Captain Roberts and Mr Childs were walking to them with determined intent. They both offered the regal ladies the chance "to show them how it was done properly."

With a grin at each other, they accepted, gratefully and gracefully. As they swung onto the dance floor, the crowd parted. Both men danced exceptionally well, and the ladies in their gaily coloured, sparkly London evening gowns were stunning.

Elle's gown was a dark electric blue brocade satin with tiny, floral insert and cream lace trim. It swayed as she danced. Suze's gown was shiny, deep purple silk with an inset of Honiton lace with real pearls, and even more lace frills around the skirt. They were pure elegance. The two older couples held the crowd spellbound with their display.

The two dowagers still had fair hair, although both heads were flecked with silver white. Both were young at heart. Both felt young again and as giddy as schoolgirls at their first dance.

The crowd was hushed. All stood and watched these two amazing women who had won every heart in the watching multitude. Ned led Christina onto the floor again and motioned for the fiddlers to up the tempo. After a while, they did, but not before the two ladies had finished their majestic display. George and Bertie Ellis stowed their violins and danced with their wives. The Irish fiddlers kept up the music.

Everyone needed to warm up, as the chill of the August evening settled in. Many were able to see the waltz done so gracefully for the very first time. The Captain and Mr Childs asked the ladies for a couple of the more sedate dances, this time swapping partners.

The ladies had not had so much fun in decades. The two-dance rule was non-existent in this town.

Charles had never seen his mother so happy. Neither had Ned. They just grinned at each other. Ned whispered, "They couldn't do this at home." Charles nodded.

Cara once again produced a cake. Only this time it was two interlocking ones, befitting a double wedding of friends and cousins. She had even made fondant icing in two different colours and decorated it with a satin ribbon and hearts.

The four newlyweds cut the cake together.

Soon, the children needed to head to bed, as did some of those who needed to rise early the next morning.

The two couples were staying with Harry and Vicky in their old rooms. It was only for one night, then they planned to head to Sydney the next day, but plans, of course, could change.

Reverend and Mrs Clarke retired to their new room at Eddie's house. They were looking forward to moving into their new rectory in North Sydney. They yet had a few days to wait and would spend them here.

~

Eddie and Harry brought their buggies around. Each was decorated with garlands of flowers and had tins and ribbons tied to the back.

Lew and Aidan handed their wives in and climbed beside them.

As they departed, the crowd dissipated quickly, their breath now clouding as each spoke; the chill of the evening set in.

The food was put away. Everything else was left for the morrow.

Before the last lamp in the shed was snuffed by Charlie as a waddling Gracie awaited him. She loved dancing, but at such an advanced stage in her confinement that it did not happen at this wedding. He knew how she felt. Charlie took her in his arms and gently waltzed a turn or two around the yard. Then he extinguished the last lamp on the verandah, and they went inside.

Chapter 15   Then There Were Four

*B*oth couples stayed until Monday. Neither rose early so they missed the morning ferry. They wished to see their friends, and they were all at church. They occupied themselves contentedly in their rooms.

Both Lew and Aidan emerged in brocade dressing gowns to bring food and drink. Each gave the other a wide grin.

Sophia giggled as she saw their tousled appearance.

Maureen told her to mind her own business. She handed them a plate full of food each that they could nibble at will, mini pork pies, sandwiches on fresh bread, boiled eggs and assorted sweet treats.

Aidan asked for more Portuguese custard tarts to be added to their plates.

Lew wanted more pork pies.

They retired to their rooms again.

Maureen knocked on each door.

They found a flagon of cider and glasses placed outside each room.

Maureen said, "When you want more food, just leave out the plates." She swung away saucily, swinging her hips, a wicked grin on her face.

Sophia ducked in and swapped over the chamber pots while the men were talking to Maureen. "*Perdão*, um, pardon," she said as she saw both young ladies still in bed, each attired only with a sheet. She did her job and departed giggling again.

Mortified, Fiona tried to hide under the sheet.

Lew came in and saw her face. He smiled and dumped the tray on the dresser. Lew locked their door so as not to be disturbed again. Then he crawled over the end of the narrow bed to her, divesting himself of various items of clothing as he came. By now, Fiona was trying hard to be quiet. She could not help giggling.

Similar noises emanated from the next-door room. Then all went quiet.

By noon both couples realised that no one else had returned and made the decision to rise and dress.

They all needed some outdoor exercise and were getting sick of hearing Sophia's snickers each time she walked the corridor.

"Grr, she has to go. Now that Harry owns the place, I hope he finds her somewhere else to work." He moaned into Fiona's shoulder.

She traced her fingers through the gingery hair at the base of his neck.

He propped himself up on his elbow. He looked at her adorable cupid-like lips. "We have to dress, love. They are waiting for us already," he said as her fingers reached his nipples and then ran down his stomach. He groaned with desire again.

"Sure?" she said saucily. "Five minutes?"

She lay naked on the sheets in the warmth of the heated room.

"After so long, what are five minutes between friends." She murmured against his lips.

He thought. "Just five then, you're insatiable."

She nodded and pulled him down to her.

~

Next door Amelia had discovered the thick curls on her husband's muscular chest. She, too, was languidly moving on the bed. Aidan had managed to at least don a shirt and trousers but had not yet managed to get any buttons done up.

Amelia lay back with her arms stretched above her head. Her nightgown still lay unused on the end of the bed where Maureen had unpacked it last night.

"Aidan…" with a lithe movement, she flipped her legs around him and rubbed his back with one foot. "Love, just ten minutes?"

He turned and looked at her feminine perfection, all in full view. His for the taking, guilt-free. He moaned with desire. Over the past months, he had discovered that this wonderful woman had reached deep into his heart. They had waited until their marriage. Now they could not get enough of each other's bodies. She resided in his heart, in a way no-one had ever done before. A place he thought no longer would ever be accessible. A place he didn't even know existed. The physical side of marriage with her dissolved away the remnants of any hurts and loneliness he had felt.

"What's ten minutes?" he said quietly.

All thoughts of dressing were forgotten.

At two o'clock, both couples finally dressed and leisurely strolled down to Phillip Street. The walk would warm them. Everyone would be there; they would invite themselves to dinner.

Everyone cheered as both couples entered through the kitchen.

The girls looked embarrassed but clung tightly to their new husbands' hands.

Maria Clarke hugged both her nieces. Whispering to each to which they replied only with a nod, a blush and a smile.

They joined the happy throng and were made welcome.

It seemed that the Clarkes, too, had delayed their departure, enjoying the company and friendship of this warm family. They had been welcomed as honoured guests. Now, however, they were more than friends and were treated like family.

Everyone now called them Reverend and Maria. They were delighted.

They were good, honest, trustworthy, Godly friends, through both Aidan and Lewis' wives, they were now fully claimed as part of the family.

It was yet, only afternoon teatime and so not all the family had arrived. Those there were familiar to the knowledge of the gold. All except both new wives, both knew the scant outline, but not the details.

Lew had neatly skirted any mention of that in his speech. All congratulated him on that oratory explanation. They each agreed they felt the same. Even Phil.

It was an open house for the family at Eddie's every Sunday night. It used to be at Charlie's Inn but since the return of Ned and Christina with *Les Grande Dames*, it moved to Eddie's more fancy and larger dining room.

Cara had long since given up on setting the table as she never knew how many would come. With the wedding on last night there was an abundance of food leftover. She expected everyone to come. She made a stew and the obligatory pot of boiled potatoes. Paddy and Mr Eddie would have her head if there were not enough of those.

Charles stood and address the group. "Friends, I have a letter that arrived on the morning ferry run. As you know the new Governor arrived four weeks ago. We have all, yes all, present here, as well as Mr Moffatt, and the Tindale's, been invited to meet Governor Fitzroy and his wife for tea tomorrow afternoon. He wished us to be a private party. He lists us, I won't read the full titles, well not all of them, Ned and Christina, Aunt Suze, Sal and I of course and Mother, you too. Charlie and Gracie; Eddie and Jenna; Wills and Cathy; and Luke, then he adds," he perused the list. "Viscount Eames; The Honourable, Sir John Saunders; Sir Phillip Corsairs; The Honourable Henry Harlow and The Honourable Mrs

Henry Harlow; Mr Aidan O'Keefe, Mrs Aidan O'Keefe, The Honourable Lewis Bland, The Honourable Mrs Lewis Bland; Reverend William and Mrs William Clarke, Mr and Mrs Thomas Tindale and Mr Henry and Mrs Henry Moffatt, all were included."

"Gracie dear, we do understand if you do not wish to attend, but it would be lovely to have you with us," Charles said.

"Actually, Dar, I still have a month to go, I think I would like to come. If I can leave the twins with Cara and Paddy, I think I could do with a rest before the next one arrives." She giggled. At least I can still walk with this one."

Christina and Jenna both agreed.

"What I'd like to know is how he knows exactly who is who?" Charles asked.

"Ahh, blame me," piped up Wills. "We went to tea on our honeymoon. Well, not exactly. I wrote and asked for a half-hour of the Governor's time and arrived with my new wife. I filled in Governor Gipps on the sequel to the Reverend's find two years ago. I told him everything. I need the Colony and Government to be fully prepared, and this means gold storerooms and cash on hand for cashing it in. I need access to soldiers, plans for gold stagecoaches, even more soldiers as guards, better roads, well everything that no one else had thought about. We all saw how much is there. We know what is going to happen. When word finally does get out it's going to really go crazy. I knew Governor Gipps was the person to talk to as Reverend Clarke here had already informed him of his find. So I did not need to have that part of the story corroborated."

"Thank you, lad," Reverend Clarke said quietly.

Wills continued. "I advised him not to write anything down but to call us in once the new Governor had settled into his office. So now he has." He grinned cheekily. He turned to his friend's new wives, "He's up on everything. Must have been written moments after you two said yes."

Ned laughed. "Looks like you four will have to share your honeymoon hotel with a hoard of us," he chuckled.

They chattered about it more until Liza and Anna arrived with their husbands and more children.

Wills had not told his sisters about the gold. They had not asked about it. Rumour had circulated through town, that both The Duke and The Earl were paying for all the new developments. Both men were often seen on-site, therefore, no one had guessed. They had decided to keep it that way.

Charlie too had not been told the full extent of the find, only that it was a lot. How much was 'a lot'?

Charles discussed the tides and Ferry times. He asked everyone to meet at the ferry wharf just before ten o'clock.

Cara and her girls were called in and asked if they would mind having all the children for the night. There were eight children, with three of them, two maids and Nanny.

"Yes, no problem," Cara replied.

Liza, Anna and their families arrived in time for dinner and left directly after the meal. They said farewell to the four departing newlyweds. All their children had the sniffles and had been fretful all evening.

After dinner, Lew and Aidan presented Wills with the wagons in thanks for a healing adventure.

Lew added, "You'll need them for all the travel you'll have to do. At least they are in somewhat better condition than they were on our trip. We met some master craftsmen down at Campbelltown. They showed us what could be changed inside a wagon. Sorry, but all three have been redone. The Clarkes are thrilled with theirs. It has even got built-in drawers and a special compartment for his Communion wines and things."

Fiona and Amelia joined Vicky and Cathy.

Amelia said, "If you travel in the wagons, just remember that you have to turn the lamps down when you change."

Fiona giggled, "I had no idea I gave a wonderful silhouette show at night. Lew eventually told me. We have now double-lined both canopies. Now it doesn't show as much, and it's also warmer."

As Vicky and Cathy had grown up camping, the shadows were something they learnt about early in their lives. As children, they used to play shadow games.

Harry had joined the other three men during the conversation.

Eddie caught the phrase 'soap talk' directed to the two new husbands. He chuckled. This would be interesting. He sidled closer to overhear the chat. He heard them both gasp. He chuckled. They didn't know he was so close. He leaned back and said, "It's the lye; it burns them." He chuckled again. "Trust me, just don't use it." As Eddie joined them.

Wills caught Charlie's eye, and beckoned him over then left the others talking.

They stood off to the side. "Charlie, before we get there tomorrow, I have to talk. Actually no, come with me now." Wills walked to Eddie and whispered something. He received a nod in reply.

Wills led Charlie into the office and shut the door, then walked to the desk and sat on it. He got straight to the point. "Charlie, tomorrow we will be discussing things you need to know about now. We have, no I have, intentionally kept from you the amount of gold we found. When I said a lot, how much do you think?" he asked.

Charlie was puzzled. "Oh, I don't know, about ten pounds of the stuff? That's a lot isn't?" Charlie was used to being the brother in the know, not the one in the dark.

Wills choked, "Well, we did get ten pounds of alluvial gold. That's the pure fine stuff that was about £1600 worth, we split that."

"Yes, that's what I thought, Wills." Charlie felt a tinge of jealousy.

"But, Charlie, we found reef gold, too. A mother load of reef gold, Charlie," Wills said quietly.

"Like another ten pounds or more?" Charlie asked.

Wills was reluctant to reveal the full extent, but he would rather Charlie heard it from him. "Charlie, sit down, you'll need to."

He stood and pushed his eldest brother into the chair. "Charlie, altogether we found, once crushed, one hundred and sixty-two pounds of gold, that's just shy of £26,000 in value."

He heard Charlie choke. "What? How much?"

"Yes, you heard right." Wills perched himself on the desk again. "But there's more. As I was the one who actually insisted we go there and then found the reef, they insisted we go half, half." He stood up and looked out the window. "So my share was shy of £13,000. I've already given Reverend Clarke £1000 for telling us of it and also a similar donation to the church." He heard Charlie make a guttural sound.

"But, Wills, what? Eh, where? Oh hell, Wills, why you're rich. Rich as Midas!" Charlie was still digesting the information. "No wonder Cathy wanted to marry you."

Wills rounded on his oldest brother. "Charlie, that's unfair, and you know it. Yes, I told Jack and Martha about the gold, but only about the bag of alluvial stuff. They think I got one-seventh of that, less than £200. They still don't know about the rest, other than we found some more in rocks. But I'd already asked Jack if I could marry her before that. Before he knew Charlie, yes, *before*, he had already said *yes*. It was only after I asked him to lock up the bag. He had no idea there were over five hundred pounds or more of gold-bearing quartz in the base of the three wagons. Not to mention what we had already sent to Eddie." He paused.

"Go on," said Charlie.

"Well, when he said yes, I asked her outside and asked her to marry me. At the time, there was no way she could ever have known. I had to be sure she was marrying me for *me*, and not for that." Wills looked at his eldest brother. "Charlie, she said *yes*, thinking I had just left school and that I was going to work with Eddie as a blacksmith." He paused, remembering how his heart sang. "Charlie, she wanted me, just me. No money, no wealth, just as I am."

"Oh, gosh, Wills, I'm sorry. I should have trusted you both," he said remorsefully.

"I didn't tell her the full extent of the find until after we were married. Even so, she doesn't care about it. To her, it's just some pretty rocks. You know she's never even asked me what it's worth or what our share is. She knows it's enough that we can build all this without going into debt. More than that, she doesn't care," Wills explained. "Charlie, she's one in a million."

They sat silently for a while.

Charlie was still digesting the information.

Wills said, "Charlie, one more thing, other than the seven of us who found it, only Luke, Eddie, Dar, Uncle Ned and Reverend Clarke know exactly the amount of the haul was, and now you too. Mr Tindale doesn't even know the final figure, but as he helped crush and smelt it, it was hard not to tell him. We had to tell Luke, as he's been doing the books. Mr Moffatt knows there's a hell of a lot, well, more than a lot. We have to tell the new Governor, hence the invitation. Everyone else in town thinks Uncle Ned and Dar are financing everything. We're letting them think that. I wanted to tell you before, but you've been so distant. I'm sorry."

"Oh, Wills, I'm the one with the monkey on my back. I'm the one who should be apologising to you, but to tell the truth, I was damned jealous of how you and Eddie have shut me out. Even all your letters were to him. I didn't get one. I was hurt. I am your eldest brother. And I also was your guardian while Mama and Dar were away, not Ed." He still sounded hurt.

"I know. I'm sorry, Charlie. Do you know why I couldn't write to you? Guilt. It's also *why* I wrote to him. It was his house I ran away from. I had the physical luxury of everything I could want. I had gone from sharing a squashy room and one bed with my three brothers, where I was teased mercilessly by you all, but, oh, I love you all so much. I would do anything for any of you. Then I was given my dream room. River views, comfy bed I didn't have to share, maids, a cook, and Charlie. I was so lonely."

"Oh, Wills, I didn't know." Charlie was filled with remorse.

"No, Charlie, no one noticed me anymore, not even Luke. He always has his head in some book or other. I had nothing and no one. I was lonely. I so wished for that squashy room again, with four of us sharing one bed." Wills saw the guilt on his brother's face.

"As you heard in Lew's speech, I met John. I felt a rapport with him. I was accepted by him for being me. He asked me if I would be interested in coming along with them. He didn't know I was one of 'the' family. I was just a staff member who could read and write. George Allan and I both went. We snuck out. They collected us at the cemetery gates. George only stayed the one night at Emu and then came home. Pity, they could do with the money. The sad thing is, if I gave them some now, word will be all over town in a day. I got Dar to put in a good word for George at the newspaper." He smiled, then sat upright. "Oh, I put £1000 in the church plate and gave the same to Reverend Clarke as a thank-you. So by the time I give Lew and Aidan £1000 to buy stock in England, I will still have £9000 plus."

He continued, "Anyway, George piked at Emu and came home. He has taken the job Dar arranged and is working with the printer. Well, we went on. The first night after Emu, we stayed at an inn just before Major Mitchell's new bridge, the next night at Hartley, where Reverend Clarke found a trace of gold. I asked everyone if we could stay a day or so."

Wills related the story of the find to Charlie. "It took us three days just to get that down. We needed to use two horses as pack horses. We had nothing to put them in, so we just put the rocks flat under the mattresses. That lot must have been about one hundred pounds of rock. We sent that back in a locked keg from Lithgow to Eddie. I told Ed what was in it, but as I had the key, well, he couldn't see it. He hid it in his cellar. I knew it would be safe."

"Cor," was all Charlie added.

"Well, you know about the birds and stuff, you heard it all from Lew. On our return through the mountains, I needed to find out about Cathy. I have loved her since I met her when they first visited. We were fourteen. When we arrived at the inn, she just walked into my arms. No words, no explanations. Charlie, I knew she just wanted me as I am." He chuckled. "She's going to have the best and biggest house money can buy. It will be near Emu by the way, as it's halfway along the road. I've chosen the block already. Mr Moffatt is processing the sale this week. It's near the bridge."

"Damn, Wills, I'm sorry. Here I was jealous because I had been left out. Oh, lad, I'm so sorry," Charlie said.

Wills said, "Charlie, this money is in my name, but I believe God let me find it because He knew what I would do with it. Oh, none of us will go without, but we're going to build the foundations of a great town. Tim and Anna will get a new office. Bertie and Liza will get a new saddlery barn and a beautiful house too, with a music room and good acoustics. All of our children will have the best education possible. However, this entire town will also benefit. When the word finally leaks out, and I give it only a few years, I want us all to be ready for a gold boom. So I hope you don't mind, but that includes a new floor on the inn. If they can build an entire church for £200, a single floor is pennies."

Charlie gasped. "Are you kidding? Wills, you can't."

"Why? Don't you want a nice home for Gracie?" he asked cheekily.

"Of course I do. But I won't be beholden to you," he said.

"Suffer, brother. How do you think I've felt all these years? You may have the title, but I have the money. No, you're part of the big picture. You see, you are going to be the most popular inn in town. I *need* you to have lots of nice rooms. You want a new house too? May I build one for you, please? One worthy of your title? How about just down the street from the stand of willows? I know, 'Willow Grove.' That's a nice name." He bit his lip, trying to hold back his mirth. "A twin to Eddie's, but a lovely big double story bay window on the front."

Charlie was sitting open-mouthed, speechless. He swallowed.

Wills smiled, his eyes twinkling. "Come on, Viscount brother, let's join the others. Pick up your chin, will you?" He laughed, "Oh, and remember, you can't let on. Tell Gracie, but I'd prefer you didn't do it while you are here."

Eddie was watching for them.

Charlie was ghost-white when he first walked in.

Eddie went to his side.

Wills walked up to Cathy and cradled her. "Ready to go, wifie?" he asked.

She chuckled and nodded, then said her goodbyes to her sisters, then to everyone else.

They walked out through the kitchen door and down the few houses to their cottage.

They reached their door and he opened it for her, but then swept her up in his arms. He gently kicked the door shut. "I've just 'bested' my biggest brother, and now it's your turn."

She giggled and drew him down to the bed where he'd placed her. "That sounds fun," she murmured against his lips.

About half an hour later, he sat up in bed and turned off the lamp. "You know, love, a weight has been lifted off me tonight. I've hated keeping anything from Charlie. Tonight I told him everything. Including that, he's getting a new house and a new floor on the inn."

He kicked all the clothing onto the floor as he half shut the door and built up the fire in their room.

He came back and sat on the bed. "Cathy, you've never said much about the gold. You do understand what it means for us?"

"Wills, for me, it means I don't see you as often as I want; that you're always thinking of something else and how to spend the stuff. Love, it's just money. I said I would marry you without any. It's just not important to me. *You* are. You are all I could ever want, Wills, all I have ever wanted. I don't want to know about it or how much there is. Just don't go into debt, it's the only thing I ask."

She could see his naked silhouette in the firelight. "Wills, it has always only ever been just you since we were fourteen. I fell in love with you while I was laughing about Eddie kissing Jenna. Then I saw you. Wills, if all we ever have is each other and no children, I'm well content. Now come back to bed and see if we can add to my happiness."

"Again? Yes, ma'am, willing to oblige." He chuckled as he crawled under the blankets. He ran his hand over her flat stomach, and his own turned somersaults. His hand kept exploring her soft curves. He had the same glorious feeling he had the night of their marriage.

Maybe one day it would be like Gracie's. However, like her, he too was content. More than content. That thread was in God's hands as well.

~

The next morning, everyone was in panic mode.

Most had overslept.

They were usually up at dawn or soon after.

This morning, of all mornings, each had slept in. The bird chorus had not woken them.

By half nine, the Roseneath group had left the house and were already on the way down to Phillip Street.

Harry was going to leave the carriage at Eddie's place. Paddy could look after the horses.

Charles had suggested they pack for two nights, just in case.

By ten, the entire group of family and friends were on the wharf.

Thankfully, the ferry was running a little late.

Wills said his hat had become mouldy and he needed to buy a new one. Hopefully, they would have enough time. If not, he'd have to see if Mr Stewart at the hotel had a spare he could borrow, or he could have to send someone out to buy one. He chuckled.

Charlie looked at him with an eyebrow cocked. His brother was bareheaded.

Wills leaned over and whispered back, "I'm probably the richest nineteen-year-old in the colony, and I don't even have a hat that I can wear." He tried to hide his smirk.

Charlie laughed. He was the same old Wills.

Cathy came over to him. "Hi, Charlie, are you all right?" She put a caring hand on his arm.

"Yes, Cathy, I am now, thanks to your husband. I'm fine, and I want to say, Cathy, he's so lucky to have you." He walked back to Gracie.

Cathy stood looking at him, then turned to Wills. "What brought that on?" she asked.

"Our conversation last night, love. He found out you accepted my offer before you knew about the find." He put his arms around her as she leaned near the railing. He whispered, "I think you'll find him somewhat more respectful from now on. It had never occurred to me that was the reason for his attitude, my love." He bent and kissed her neck. "Hmm, how long to the hotel again?" he whispered.

Her eyes dancing with anticipation, "Way too long, husband mine."

"Sorry, I've been preoccupied. I've had a lot on my mind leading up to today. You'll get sick of me from now on. I was thinking, maybe you'd even like to come with me on some of my trips? Do more together?" He was speaking softly into her ear as he stood behind her.

"I'd love that, my dearest," she tilted her head back and quickly kissed him.

The ferry covered the distance to Sydney Cove quickly.

They were met by three Government Town Carriages.

"Ohh, this is nice," Fiona said.

Grace was handed in first, then Ned and Charles each handed in their mothers. Charlie, Eddie and Jenna went with them in the first carriage. It would take them directly to the Hotel and be sent back again to collect them for their appointment.

Within half an hour, everyone and their luggage had arrived.

The carriages would return for them at quarter to three.

The Governor had already booked rooms for them all. They were welcomed by Mr Stewart again.

Wills asked him about obtaining a new hat and stated his size.

Half an hour later, a hatbox was delivered to their room.

Wills tipped the bellboy and later Mr Stewart. Wills was greatly relieved, and now they could head to their afternoon appointment with a happy heart. It was a top-quality silk top hat. He must find out which store it came from.

Wills noted that on this visit, the staff at the hotel went out of their way to make everything possible. One was even left hovering in the corridor, so that their every wish could be attended to instantly. "Nice travelling with a Duke," he commented to Cathy. He still did not understand his own importance.

They settled into their rooms.

Ned ordered luncheon to be delivered to each room so the ladies could rest.

Wills again whispered to Cathy. "Not too much rest," as he drew her to him, as the door finally closed.

At half past one, Christina and Suze checked over each of the ladies' outfits before heading downstairs.

Poor Gracie found going downstairs a lot harder than up. Thankfully, it was cold out, and she could cover up with a large redingote to hide her shape.

Her high-waisted gown of dark green hid the growing bundle. It was only her gait that gave away something a little different about her.

All the other ladies were garbed in a fabulous array of incredible colours. The men in their light-coloured trousers of various shades and patterned waistcoats and top hats all looked impressive.

Mr Stewart opened the front door for them himself and handed them into the various carriages.

Five shiny Government Town Carriages now awaited them. One was the Governor's personal Carriage. Suze, Elle, Ned, Christina, Charles, and Sal were loaded into this one.

The carriage moved up to make some room for another.

Charlie, Gracie, Wills, Cathy and Luke departed next, and everyone else filled the remaining two.

As it filled, they moved off at walking pace to cover the short distance to Government House. By the time they had unloaded the precious passengers, the other two carriages were already pulling up.

Charlie almost had to lift Gracie down as she could not reach the step. When her condition was revealed, a set of steps was provided, and she was able to alight easily.

This had taken a little time, allowing the arrival of the other carriages. The Governor's *Aide de Camp*, Lieutenant Master, greeted them.

The Duke and Christina were shown into the formal sitting room. The large group followed.

When everyone was assembled, the Governor asked the Duke, "Which one of these gentlemen is William?"

Wills came forward from the back of the group and introduced himself.

Ned stood watching with a smile hovering on his lips.

The fifty-year-old governor was stunned to discover that the teenage lad was the person he needed to talk to. He was even more surprised to discover the confidence of this young man was astounding. Gipps was correct; this was going to be the most interesting afternoon.

Gipps had not written why he had to see him, just that he *must* and that this was *not* negotiable. He had definitely inferred that this was a vital meeting for the future of the Colony. No one was to be left out if possible. When a very expectant lady was ushered in, his eyes grew large. He discovered this was The Viscountess Lockley. He swallowed and tugged at his collar. He hoped her time was not close. He had to work out how best to arrange the discussion. He had chosen the Red Drawing Room as it was larger.

He was still wondering how this would proceed when Wills suggested some of the ladies retire with Lady Fitzroy. All but Jenna, Vicky, and Cathy departed with her.

The Governor soon discovered that Wills knew precisely what he wanted to say and do.

Sally was itching to stay but knew that if she did, others would want to as well. Charles would have to fill her in.

Wills arranged everyone and led the gathering. At the end of the hour, the Governor's head was spinning. This lad was worth over £10,000. "Amazing story, lad. Amazing! Can you now tell me again, how each of these gentlemen and ladies fits in, please? The names meant nothing before. Now I think I have my head around the situation."

One by one, Wills reintroduced the party and their place in the story. When he reached the ladies, "This, Sir Charles, is Jennifer, known as Jenna, who is my brother Edward's wife. Her younger sister, Victoria, is married to my friend, Harry. He is the new Warehouse Foreman and Second-in-Charge, The Honourable Henry Harlow."

Everyone gasped, even Vicky. Harry reached for her hand.

Finally, Wills drew Cathy to him. Wills continued, "And this, Sir Charles, is Catherine, my wife. She is their youngest sister. These three women are fully aware of all that this find involves. More than that, they are not swayed by the passion and lust for gold. Without their support, our projects would not be possible. I cannot speak highly enough of them all. Cathy has my full authority to make any decisions on my behalf in my absence. We are full partners in this project."

Charles, Earl of Coxheath, stood looking at his young son. His face was full of admiration. God had indeed chosen the right person. Yet where had his little boy gone?

There was one more in attendance who had not yet been mentioned. Wills turned and looked at Luke. "Sir, there is one more member of the family. Our youngest brother, Luke. He is still at The King's School. His passion is Science, particularly Geology. However, he is so skilled with the books and figures that he is our new Financial Officer. He must and will be involved in all financial transactions. He has wisdom beyond his years and a knowledgeable head on his shoulders. Do not underestimate him because of his lack of years."

Luke gasped and smiled at his older brother. 'Financial Officer.' He thought he'd just be doing the books.

The governor was flabbergasted. "Well! I don't know what to say, other than I foresee more meetings between us, young man." He turned to his Aide who had been standing silently behind his chair. "Schedule regular meetings with this gentleman, please, Lieutenant Master!"

"Yes, Sir Charles," replied the Lieutenant.

"With pleasure," said Wills. "May I please have a moment of your Aide's time now? I wish to review some key points that we will need to discuss before our next meeting. Things the Colony will need to have in place before the gold rush begins."

Wills turned to Harry. "Harry, can you please join us?"

Governor Fitzroy spluttered a reply, "Why, of course." Watching the lad lead his fearsome Lieutenant Aide to the other side of the room. He chuckled. He walked to the Earl. "This young son of yours is an amazing man, sir. He knows exactly what he wants and is not afraid of anything, nor anyone."

Charles laughed. "Welcome to my world, Sir. I have four boys with the same dogged determination. I am proud of them all. Our daughters, too, have a strength of their own."

Charles looked at Ned. They had discussed if they should tell him his history. He decided he would. "The youngest has yet to grow. I feel he may outshine the rest. Of all of them, he is the one who loves to study. The academic, if you will."

The Governor turned to look at the youngest Lockley.

Charles spoke quietly to the Governor. "Sir, if I may, I have a little of our history to impart. It pertains to the knowledge of our area and life in the Colony."

"If it's about your convict history, I had heard about this before my arrival. Gipps filled in the gaps in his diary that he left for me." Fitzroy stated. "Also, that he's appointed you Viceroy and your oldest son, Assistant Viceroy. That will continue if you're agreeable?"

"You know?" A stunned Charles swallowed. "Yes, sir, of course."

"Excellent," said the Governor

"Sir, then you know about the man I was transported with, John Turner. He, too, was given a Ticket of Leave. These three ladies are his daughters," Charles said.

"Ahh," The Governor exclaimed. "Now that I didn't know. I shall make that a Full Pardon. That will solve that problem." He already knew Jack had one, but had been told to keep that quiet. He turned and looked at the three beautiful and gracious ladies. The thought went through his mind, "If only all convicts' children were like this." He had driven through the streets of Sydney and seen the dirty waifs and gutter children. The Governor heard from John Landon at church in Sydney about a young lad he was helping. The young man had apparently been a street waif himself. Ricky English, born free but orphaned. He might seek him out and see what ideas he had.

The Lieutenant, having concluded his conversation with Wills, received a nod from the Governor and left. He returned shortly, followed by Lady Fitzroy and the other ladies. He had Gracie on his arm. She was ushered directly to a straight-backed chair.

Les Grande Dames came in with Lady Fitzroy.

Ned and Charles each raised an eyebrow. They could tell by their demeanour that their afternoon was enjoyable. When Ned heard his mother call Lady Fitzroy 'Mary,' he smiled.

A second afternoon tea was brought in. The governor's staff hovered until he dismissed them. He was unsure how much he could say in the presence of the others, but Wills again led the conversation. Although it was formal, everyone remained relaxed.

By the time they were ready to depart, the governor, his wife and Aide were fully aware they were mere puppets in this young man's hands. They each smiled. Half an hour later, they were leaving Government House for the hotel.

After they departed, Sir Charles, Lady Mary, and Lieutenant Charles Master sat and discussed the incredible conversations that had just occurred.

"I think this time in the colony is going to keep us on our toes. Mary, we have to prepare for a gold rush. When young William comes for our next meeting, ensure you are free. You will want to meet this young man."

"Charles, I wish you had been able to speak to the ladies, each wonderful in their way. What about the other three?" she asked. "And did you see Mrs Harlow? She is astoundingly beautiful and so graceful."

"Let me say that young William has a mate who is his equal." He spoke in great admiration. "Mary, the three are sisters, and daughters of a ticketed convict."

"What?" she gasped. "First blacksmiths, then convicts, now gold. Oh, the time here will be interesting. Did you know that, in their spare time, they have all been teaching at the Female Orphans' school? The men, too. It was they who started teaching first."

"Mary, I must tell you about the find. Charles heard. Yet I find that I, the Governor, have been sworn to secrecy. The find, which came in just over three weeks, amounted to just under £26,000 worth of gold. Hence, their fear that we will not be ready when *it* happens." He rubbed his brow. "We must prepare."

Lady Mary and Charles Masters agreed.

~

Back at the hotel, Ned booked a private sitting room, as the one attached to his room was too small for the group. The men sat and discussed the meeting.

Each felt that Governor Fitzroy was the man for the job.

Harry laughed, "Did you see the look on his face when Wills stepped out from behind you, Eddie, and took over the meeting? He was obviously impressed with this young man. As we all are." Harry chuckled again. "You could have given me a bit of a warning that you were going to announce giving me a job."

Vicky squeezed his hand.

Wills explained to all listening, "Well, Eddie and I have been talking. He's busy enough with the forge and extra work there, as well as concentrating on his own Emporium. His contribution will be a 20% share of the Warehouse profits. Harry will have 20% of the Emu Plains Store and... Phil 20% of the Bathurst one, and that in itself needs explaining.

Wills looked at Phil with an eyebrow raised.

Phil nodded.

"Well, here's another surprise for you. You won't be working alone, Harry. I've been in negotiation with the new Store Manager for the Emporium in Bathurst. I would like to introduce him to you." He paused and smiled. "Phil, take a bow."

"What?" his friends said.

"Yes," Phil grinned. "We've been talking for some time. Remember that meeting I said I had, while you were teaching? You all presumed later that it was with Eddie. It wasn't. Harry, I'm staying, at least for the foreseeable future. You see, I can be useful here. The good Lord brought me here, I thought I would hang around and see what else He has in store for me."

They mingled around him, congratulating him.

"I'll stay here until you get everything going, and the boom starts anyway," said Phil. "I would like to see it happen, hands-on, though, hence, Bathurst."

"Aargh! I'm so jealous, lads. I, too, would have loved to stay. However, I have responsibilities at home and must return," said Ned. "Be assured. We shall come back. The boats are getting faster all the time. Soon it will be only eight weeks instead of twice that long." Ned looked at his brother-in-law, Edmund, with an enquiring glance and cocked his head.

Edmund smiled. "While we're talking about returning and horrible thoughts like that. John and I will only be staying until this lot departs. We shall accompany them home," pointing to his sister. Edmund said quietly. "I thought I could help with the young ones on the return trip."

"Ah, yes, well, we may have to stay a little longer than we planned," said Ned. "You see, we do not want our child born on a ship." He chuckled and walked over to Christina, and lovingly placed a hand on her shoulder. "It seems our dearest wish will come true. We will have our own little Australian after all." He smiled as everyone started congratulating them.

"When?" asked Sal.

"January, we think, well, we hope," Christina told her. "We are over the moon."

Eddie walked to Ned and congratulated him. "Uncle Ned, this is wonderful news." He looked around and seeing no one was near, said, "We're about a month earlier than you again. We're not quite sure of the dates. I told you she wanted a quiver full." he grinned.

"Oh, wonderful news, lad," Ned congratulated Eddie.

John saw this and asked, "What's this? You two as well?"

Eddie looked slightly embarrassed but nodded.

John turned and looked at Jenna.

She greeted his glance with a grin, too, and nodded.

"Folks, it seems we've got one more baby on the way. Eddie and Jen too." John chuckled.

"We didn't want to announce it quite so publicly," Eddie said.

Vicky and Cathy were the first to congratulate their sister.

Jenna knew how they would feel. She was trying to delay the news as long as possible.

It was during Vicky's last visit here that she discovered she was expecting a child. A tear pooled in her eye, and Harry walked to her and took her hand. Sometimes good news is hard to take.

He lifted her palm to his lips. Words were not necessary.

Wills looked at Cathy.

She blew him a kiss.

His heart swole with pride. He could not do this without her. He loved her so. If God blessed them, so be it. If not, then they would be wonderful uncle and aunt to their family.

Aidan and Lewis were asked to consider staying for a few weeks until the Governor had all the information he needed.

Lew replied, "We asked Mr Stewart and he said that the next suitable one was due in October sometime. The *Rajah* is that time enough?" he asked.

Harry and Wills had their heads together. "Yes, that would be perfect, Lew," said Harry.

Aunt Suze spoke, "Lewis, Aidan, you are all on your honeymoon. I think we should leave you four to your own if you wish it."

"No, time for all that later, Aunt Suze. You're only here for today." Amelia interjected. "Once we leave, we won't get to see much of you at home. We will come and stay for your first winter you are at home. We'll bring Lew's sisters if we can."

Suze glanced at John, then at Edmund. "That would be delightful."

Ned noticed an almost wicked grin on her lips.

Aidan asked Harry if they would mind if they spent some more time with them at Roseneath before departure.

Vicky overheard and replied, "Oh, please, I need some female company. I would love to have you two with me for a while."

Everything was falling into place a little too comfortably for Phil. Not that he wasn't happy. He still felt the spirit of disquiet. He was not as unsettled as he used to be, but the discontent was still there. He would still wake at night in a cold sweat with Charlotte's name on his lips. He saw her fall over and over. There was nothing he could do to save her. He understood Wills and how one could feel so utterly alone in a crowd of people. His thoughts of Charlotte still haunted him. He had never told his friends that not only was he with her as she died, but that he encouraged her to take the hedge. She had fallen. He was racked with a guilt that he would take to his grave.

The group departed for Parramatta on the morning ferry, leaving only the honeymooners in town.

The newlyweds stayed for two more weeks, enjoying the luxury of a service hotel with staff to do all the work. The four returned relaxed and looking forward to seeing their friends.

~

At Government House, Governor Fitzroy and his Aide started poring over the list Wills had handed to Master.

It listed the things Wills felt needed to be built before the rush happened. As some were major expenditures, they would need to be included in the next budget. The list read:-

1/ A good road; coach-worthy. Widen the road all the way to Bathurst.

2/ Build New Barracks in Bathurst.

3/ A gold store and/or strong room, both in Bathurst and either Sydney or Parramatta or all of the above.

4/ Training staff for Claim Registration, etc.

They started listing the jobs in order of priority and ability to implement. The 'G' word had not to be written. All the new work needed to be done quietly. All too had to both "flow and grow" with the town. The Governor knew a trip across the mountain would be beneficial to the entire community. They had to work out how to accomplish it. The work would be done correctly and on time. All would be in readiness for when the news leaked. The official opening of the new Bathurst town allotments would suffice.

Lady Mary wanted to know everything that was going on so she could discuss it with the three ladies when they arrived, and therefore was included in all the private discussions between her husband and his Aide.

October came all too quickly.

The *Rajah* docked and was unloaded.

Mr Stewart sent a note to Bramblemere Close. It read,

October 1846
The King's Arms Hotel
Sydney

William Lockley
c/- Bamblemere Close
Parramatta

The sailing date is towards the end of the month, probably around the 18th. I have reserved six rooms for a week, as I am sure friends would accompany you to say Farewell. If more are available, do not hesitate to contact me.

Stewart

Captain Roberts delivered the reply.

The King's Arms Hotel
Sydney
3 October 1846

Mr Frederick Stewart
Thank you, sir,
Please add one more suite to the reserved rooms.
William Lockley.

Wills and Cathy wished to come, too.

All other farewells would be at a large party at the 'big house'.

The first round of farewells occurred. Tears shed and friends and family parting.

Fiona was looking unwell.

Sal guessed her condition. It was as with Jenna, conceiving a child on her honeymoon. It had been six weeks since their wedding.

Sal took her aside. "Are you all right, love?" she asked gently.

"I think so, Sal. I'm just tired and feeling off all the time," Fiona replied. "Lew's soft eggs nearly made me lose my breakfast this morning."

"Come with me, we need to have a little chat, dear." Sally took her for a walk in the garden. When they returned, Fiona walked to Lew, and they too left for a turn around the garden.

Sally stood watching them from the window. The joy of finding a new life growing was incredible. She turned and looked at some of the six children she bore. With each new babe God gave them, more room was found in her heart. Each time she thought it full. Each time, God had made room for more. The physical similarities of many of the room's occupants indicated that they were related. Yet each was unique. They had been blessed with six perfect babes. All fair-haired and blue-eyed. All now grown and settled, save her last—what a wonderful, blessed, handsome family.

Charles was leaning on the mantlepiece, watching her.

She felt his eyes on her and met them.

A smile of understanding passed between them.

The room may as well have been empty, for the notice they had of others.

Unbeknownst to them, they, too, were being watched by both Ned and Elle. Each was in awe of these two dear people they loved.

Lewis was aglow on their return, as was Fiona.

Amelia noticed, as did Jenna. She had guessed. She walked over and hugged her. Amelia whispered something to them both, and both girls nodded in response.

It seemed she, too, may have a secret.

Time would tell.

Christina had also been watching from her seat across the room. At six months, she was as large as she was in her first confinement. She wondered if it was because this was her third child or if she was carrying twins again. She hoped not, or did she? This would probably be their last baby, as she was fast approaching forty. Ned would be forty-eight by the time of the birth of this one. She turned thirty-seven on Christmas Day.

She caught Fiona's eye and patted the seat next to her. "Something tells me you are in an interesting condition, my dear. The joy on your face is readable, but the hands on your stomach are a giveaway. You must be careful if you do not want the world to know," she said, smiling.

"Yes, I've been feeling unwell for a few mornings now. Lew's soft egg this morning... well, I had to leave the room," Fi said.

"It was the same with me, Fi, only it was meat. Ask Sally for some of her magic powder. It helps with morning sickness and won't harm the baby. It's only powdered sugar and baking soda with lemon." She patted her hand. "I'm overjoyed for both of you and Amelia."

"You know about her, as well?" Fiona asked.

"It's to be expected, my dear," Christina laughed. "Sal and I have been watching you both. Does Aidan know yet?"

"I don't think so, but he soon will have to, won't he?" Fiona asked with a secretive smile on her lips.

"Yes, and the sooner the better, especially before you travel." Christina looked over to Amelia and caught her eye. "Tell her that she needs a walk around the garden with him."

Fiona nodded and walked to her cousin.

Amelia looked to Christina. She nodded and looked outside, then smiled. Amelia's eyes flicked from her to Aidan and back again.

Christina nodded.

Amelia tapped his hand and whispered.

They too left for a turn in the garden.

The absolute joy on their faces when they both returned was delightful.

~

On Sunday morning, they all attended church.

Reverend Bobart was to give them a travelling blessing and farewells from their church friends.

The group planned to catch the afternoon ferry and would be in town before dinner at the hotel.

The family met the seven friends and four ladies on the wharf for their last farewells.

They loaded the remaining luggage on the little boat, most of which had been sent days before by cart. Farewells and hugs abounded.

Promises of regular contact and visits after their return.

The ropes were cast off. The ferry left the wharf.

If this parting were hard, the next one would be worse. From this point, all the lives were to take different paths.

On arrival, Mr Stewart met them as usual at the door. "Mr Bland, Mr O'Keefe, departure for the *Rajah* has been moved forward to Wednesday. I have reserved a sitting and dining room for your use." He bowed and left them to be taken to their rooms.

Cathy and Vicky stood by each other, hands grasped.

Their two friends were leaving.

They would make the most of the time together, "No tears," they said, only joy.

The sisters were overjoyed for Fiona and Amelia when they were told their news. Both swallowed their sadness.

Harry and Wills knew both disappointments as well as joy. Wills had said to Harry some time ago, "God in his infinite wisdom knows better, Harry. We have to all trust Him and Him alone. It will even be harder if one falls, and the other doesn't."

Harry agreed. At least he knew Vicky could conceive. Cathy had not. He shook off his melancholy feelings. Time for that later. No! Correction, no time for that at all. Like Wills, he would trust God.

~

The final day arrived, and the hotel supplied transport for the luggage. The group walked down to the wharf. They were met there by Captain and Mrs Evans.

They, too, said their farewells and stood back. The group walked through the small cabins and found that Ned had arranged a third central one for them for use as a sitting room. This meant they could also store the excess cases in there.

"Trust Uncle Ned," Wills said.

Captain Ferguson came and introduced himself. He then informed them, "Departure in one hour."

The group walked around the ship looking into all the pubic rooms. There were not many, as the vessel was not that large. They all met some of the other passengers. Then the Sydney visitors departed down the gangplank.

Mid-morning, the ropes were cast off and pulled on board.

Rowboats towed the ship into the channel.

Sails unfurled, and they were off. The ship jumped to life as the sails filled with the gentle westerly breeze.

Then they were gone.

~

The emptiness of parting was felt by all.

The adventure first planned on that August day in London a little more than two years ago, had drawn to a close. Aidan and Lewis had new lives before them.

Well, nearly. The job was not yet finished, it was, however, in hand.

A note awaited Wills their return to the hotel.

Addressed to Wills, it was an invitation to Government House for tomorrow morning, for Wills, Harry, and their wives to attend a meeting. "It seems the Governor knows our every movement," Cathy chuckled.

"Phil, I'll need you too if that's all right?" Wills said.

Phil agreed. He would need to know the lay of things if he were to take over running the Bathurst Emporium, as well as assisting Harry with the Warehouse.

Wills had promoted Harry to overall manager, with Wills still as boss. Nothing happened without him or Cathy knowing.

He penned a reply, adding Phil's name to the list coming. He turned to John and Edmund. "Sorry, but it looks like we have an appointment tomorrow, so we won't be returning with you this afternoon after all."

The two friends nodded and went to their rooms to pack. They both had commitments at the School the next day. Mr Childs now counted on them.

They shared an unhurried lunch in the grand dining room, then walked to Mrs Macquarie's chair along the foreshore.

Mr Stewart arranged for John and Edmund's bags to be delivered to the Ferry. They wandered around the grassy headland until it was time to leave.

The departing friends also waved farewell.

Harry suggested that the girls rest. The three men sat in the empty hotel's morning room and plotted their ideas. They had to be on the same page with thoughts and ideas before tomorrow morning's meeting. They were well into discussions when the girls joined them.

"If we're your backstops, don't you think we too should know what's going on?" Cathy said.

Wills and Harry looked guiltily at each other, then at the girls again. "Yes," they said in unison.

"We'd look pretty silly tomorrow if we are asked something to which we did not know the answer," said Vicky.

Wills gave them an outline of their discussions to date.

Vicky suggested to Phil, "Phil, when placing all the items in the warehouse, how are you planning to sort them? I've had an idea."

They all turned and looked at her. They had been pondering over this same issue.

"When I was at the school last month, I was asked to help with some filing. I was amazed at how easy everything was to find. Alphabetical, but in age groupings. We could do similar." Vicky continued, "Divide the building into various sections: building, carpentry, ironwork, leather goods, camping, etc. You will need to maintain a card file of what's in stock and the quantity of each item. Also, all will need to be colour-coded." She looked at their blank faces. "Well, if each section were also sorted alphabetically, anvils, hammers, mallets, mattocks, picks, etc, wouldn't this make it easier to pick and pack for orders?"

The simplicity of her idea should have been evident. They loved it. They heard a noise and looked up.

A group of strangers came into the room.

Phil had been wondering how they could compile a list of some of the items they planned to stock. He could use a page for each section.

Wills suggested they all go for a walk. "Bring your notebook, Phil." They needed to stretch their legs, so they agreed. The idea had come a little out of the blue, but they had learnt to trust him.

Harry chuckled to himself. What would Wills come up with next?

They walked, but not down to the waterfront as they usually did. Wills guided them to Bent Street and showed them the new library.

Luke had taken him there on one of their visits together.

They entered, and he asked for an encyclopaedia and reference books.

"Ahh," thought Phil.

The librarian directed them to the latest edition of the Encyclopaedia Britannica. The leather-bound books looked very similar to the ones they had seen in Luke's boxes.

Wills slid his finger along the row to G. He pulled it out. "See Physical Resources" was written under the "Gold" entry. "Humph!" he exclaimed, then walked back to the shelf and took P from the shelf. He licked through until he reached Physical Resources. "Gee! You would think that there would be something." He stood scratching his head.

Cathy whispered, "Try under Mining."

So he placed these two back on the shelf and tried M. Still no luck.

Phil had wandered off. He stood looking at the other books. "Hey, look," He held up a thin, tattered book. "It's a picture in the book for children about mining, but look, it gives a list of what is required," he laughed.

"Pans, picks, shovels, a cradle. Huh? What's that? And something for 'puddling'. I wonder what that is, too." Phil read out the list quietly.

Wills nodded. "Can you write them all down? We know those, well, not about the puddling, but then we also know the next stage, the crushing. We can't stock that stuff yet. So let's go with the alluvial stuff in the store for the moment," Wills whispered. "I think we can add some graded sieves as well." He stood thinking. "We might stock the makings of the other large items."

Harry asked, "Do you remember the story of Jason and the

Argonauts?"

Wills looked excited. Luke had told him that one.

The girls looked blank.

Harry looked at his friend and the girls.

"Vaguely, what's that got to do with this?" they asked.

Harry explained. "He stole the 'golden fleece'."

They both shook their heads.

"So?" Phil said.

A librarian started stacking books next to them. She frowned at their conversation.

"Let's go," said Harry.

They put the books back and left. It was nearly closing time anyway.

Cathy suggested they sit in the garden.

They walked across the road and into the Botanic Gardens.

Harry continued his story. "If you know your Greek history, Jason stole the sheep fleece that had alluvial gold in it."

Phil and the girls still looked confounded.

Harry continued. "In days of old, they used to peg fleeces in the fast-running creek beds and hold them down with rocks. Then they'd sluice the dirt over them. After some time, it could even be months, they would lift them, dry them and shake out the gold. It was one of these that Jason and the Argonauts stole." Harry simplified the story, but it explained what he meant.

"So you want us to stock fleeces?" said Phil.

"No, not fleeces, but certainly some new gold mats. I read about these being used in other places, like California. Like big rugs with rows of high and low ridges on them. They called them 'riffles', but I think that is what they meant. A special mat, with ridges on it."

A gardener was walking by.

"And don't forget creature comforts," he said loud enough for the gardener to hear. "Sleeping beds, blankets, pillows, tents, and tent pegs, canvas sheets, sailcloth, not to mention pots, pans and utensils. Think of what we used, that's what we should start with: camp ovens, tri-frame, billy. That sort of stuff," Harry continued.

"Wash-basins, even chamber-pots," added Vicky. "And also something to store their finds in, like jars."

The gardener left them in peace. He probably thought they were planning a camping trip.

"Lamps and oil drums," Phil said. He sat writing. They had soon filled more than one page. "Great, I'll sort these and leave room for more. Vicky, your idea of categories is great. It certainly will make finding things easier. I was also thinking of colour-coding the sections. Camping-blue; panning-red; digging-green; that sort of thing. Then if the main inventory stays limited to say six or eight categories, each with a different colour, it again would make filling orders quicker."

"Fabulous," said Wills. "One thing I do have to tell you is I have sent Aidan and Lew home with jobs. They are our new 'resourcing officers'." He chuckled. "I gave them each a £500 gold ingot and asked them to send out a shipment, or five, straight away. I've left it to them to buy what they can. They know what we need. The first load is expected to arrive around mid-next year. That allows for four months at home, two months for shopping and arrangements, and four months back. I've suggested including more roofing. The building in Bathurst will need a thickly insulated roof. We've discovered how quick the corrugated tin is to erect, too, and also that the slabs work brilliantly as a lining. Up there, we will need to thicken the lining, due to the extreme condition."

Harry chuckled. "Trust you. Not one to miss an opportunity, are you?"

Wills grinned. "Nope, why should I? They know what we want. And why not? We don't then have to explain to anyone else." Wills smiled to himself. "It's coming together nicely, isn't it?"

"Let's head back," Vicky said, shivering.

Harry offered his arm to her, as Wills did to Cathy. They wandered back to their rooms.

~

The meeting the next day was very productive.

Rather than separate, Lady Mary and the Aide Charles Master joined in.

The eight sat in the Governor's office.

Phil had been deep in thought overnight and proposed some brilliant ideas.

Phil and Charles Master drew aside and talked together for some time.

The group was invited for lunch, but they declined, as they needed to catch the Ferry. Wills said, "Sir, would you kindly permit us to postpone that kind offer until next time?"

The Governor smirked. "Not many would have the audacity to say that, lad, but we have much to discuss and few who know the topic." He turned to his Aide. "Charles, make a note, luncheon next visit."

The Aide nodded, penning a note. He again called Phil aside. They sat writing and discussing the plans.

Wills looked over at the Governor. "Sir, I do not mean to be rude, but when one is born of convict parents, grows up in an inn and then finds one's Father is an Earl and cousin to a Duke, nothing much phases me anymore."

Again, the Governor chuckled. He liked this lad.

Wills, the Governor and Harry were deep in conversation at his desk.

The Governor turned to Wills and asked for his suggestion on what should be done first.

Without hesitation, Wills said, "Yes, sir, the road should be done first, and it needs to be wide enough for two fast carriages to pass all along the route at some speed. Following that, I suggest adding a Government gold strongroom somewhere. Then Bathurst Barracks with a large lock-up. Also training for some Claim Processing Staff. Mr Harry Moffatt in Parramatta has that sorted for the moment, but he will need help, so I'd call him in for an interview. Once trained, set up a claims office in Bathurst. I'd also deploy more troops in Bathurst, so you had better order more from England. That will take a year in itself. I know from Uncle Ned, that most of the troops once serving here have been redeployed overseas." Wills looked at Harry and asked if he had any suggestions.

"No, lad, you have it all in hand." Harry grinned at the Governor, knowing just what was going through his mind. He had known Wills for over a year now, and the lad never ceased to astound him. He was pleased to be able to call him brother.

Lady Mary turned to the girls. "You two, of course, are always included in all the invitations." She smiled at them. "I have much to learn about living in this colony. I feel you can help me."

Both were overwhelmed. Without answering, they bowed their heads in graceful acquiescence.

Chapter 16   And Baby Makes More

*T*heir return to Parramatta was accomplished without mishap, this time.

Two months earlier, Gracie had gone into labour on the ferry home. Thankfully, she held on long enough to have her daughter at the Inn.

Emily, to be known as Emma, entered the world only two hours after they arrived.

Eddie had carried her to the inn. They had to stop twice as her contractions were close together.

Wills had run to the Rear Admiral Duncan and told Molly. They made it back in time.

Sal and Molly delivered the healthy baby girl.

Gracie was exhausted. Charlie was a mess, but the baby was healthy.

~

Christmas came and went.

January brought two more confinements.

Christina and Jenna went into labour within hours of each other. The house was in chaos.

Cara, Sal, Molly, and Martha were all in attendance.

The poor doctor was moving from one room to another.

Eddie took Ned aside, "Uncle Ned, you have to go and help her. Go in. You'll never regret it. I did with Lily, I feel so close to her. She feels more like mine. Listen to Martha, she's great."

Ned looked aghast. "You don't mean I see the birth?"

"Oh yes, Uncle Ned, trust me, Christina needs you. Remember, you got her into this. It's only fair you know what she's going through.

You won't regret this. I'm just about to go in now. Just make sure you are in comfortable and clean clothes. Scrub your hands and use the privy before you go. It could be hours before you get another chance."

Ed smiled, remembering the last time. "Martha had me kneeling on the bed with my arms around Jenna. She could brace against me, and it really helped her. Also, rub her lower back, that helps too. Try it."

Ed walked off and into their room, where his wife needed him and was in pain. He was about to witness the miracle of birth again.

Ned did as Eddie said. When he was dressed comfortably and in clean clothes, he knocked and walked in.

Christina was trying hard not to scream. Ned's heart turned over. He went to her and took her in his arms.

She turned to him and just said, "Thank you, Edward."

Sal and Molly told him what to do.

Her contractions were only two minutes apart. Now that he was there, she was not holding back. She let out a bloodcurdling yell.

The doctor took a look, "We're nearly there," he said.

Christina threw up.

Molly was ready for it. She said to Ned, "Get in position. The baby is coming."

Kneeling on the bed as Eddie had said he had needed to do, she leaned back against him. Ned wrapped his arms around his beloved wife. He kissed her hair and gave her encouragement. Thinking all the time, "How can she want to do this again and again?"

The doctor had him kneel back on his heels so she could lie back a little. Ned's hands were locked around her, and she grabbed his arms and screamed. "Oh dear God, help her," he prayed silently, all the while whispering lovingly to her.

She pushed, took a few quick, deep breaths and pushed again.

"It's coming," Molly said.

"One more, push Your Grace," the doctor said.

She pushed and then gasped. Her nails dug into Ned's arms and drew blood. She took a deep breath and pushed again, then groaned. She almost collapsed against him.

Molly said, "Come on, Christina. You can do this. The head is out. One more big push."

Ned kissed her cheek. "Come on, love. I'm here with you."

A scream of pain from down the corridor sounded through the closed door.

"One big push, love," said Ned. He kissed her cheek.

An exhausted Christina nodded. "Okay, let's get this over." She took a huge breath and braced against Ned. She pushed, another breath, and pushed again. She gave a gasp, then a final push, and relaxed against him.

The doctor held the child upside down and gave it a gentle smack.

It took a breath, and Ned saw it change colour, from blue-grey to pink. It hiccupped and let out a bellow. Ned released a long breath of relief.

Molly wrapped the still-attached child in a linen cloth. "You have a daughter and she's beautiful."

The doctor turned to Molly and Cara. "Okay? Can you do it from here? I'll be back as soon as I can."

He walked out quickly. "At least they are close," he thought to himself.

Cara had a bowl outside and some lye soap. He scrubbed his hands and went into Eddie and Jenna's room.

Martha had Eddie in the same position on the bed.

The doctor walked in just as Jenna threw up. "Perfect timing," he thought.

Sal was ready with a basin.

Martha relinquished her position to the doctor. He inspected her and agreed she, too, was ready to deliver.

Martha relaxed back against Eddie. He too relaxed and comforted her. "Nearly done, love."

Sal mopped her face "Ready to push? Deep breath."

Jenna nodded, groaning. She pushed.

Martha said, "The head is out, another one, Jenza love."

The doctor contradicted. "Hang on, don't push yet." He fiddled around and gently eased the cord from around the baby's neck. "Okay, push now."

Eddie counted "One, two, three, deep breath, and push. Okay."

Jenna nodded.

Ed counted, "On three." He braced her tightly, and she pushed and yelled. "Good girl, once more," he said gently.

Jenna nodded again, took a breath, and pushed again. She felt the rush, the baby was born, and it screamed. She smiled and relaxed against Eddie.

"Welcome to the world, Master Lockley," the doctor said. "Look at the size of this one, he's certainly your son, Eddie." The doctor took the large baby and passed him to Sal.

Sal wrapped the child in another length of clean linen. She stood waiting for the last stage. Until then, the baby remained attached.

The doctor left, returning to Christina. Again, he washed his hands in the clean water. He smiled, wishing every house would do similar. Clean water and a new towel every time he passed.

Moira was changing it after every person washed.

Cara had done enough birthing to know cleanliness was vital.

The doctor walked into Christina's room in time as she writhed in pain.

She grabbed Ned's arm again.

Ned looked horrified. "What's happening? Why is she in pain?" he asked.

"The afterbirth, Mr Ned, often hurts more. Mine certainly did," Cara said. She smiled at Martha as she entered.

"No, it's not that," Christina said. She gasped as another contraction hit. "Nooo! Not again!" She grabbed Ned's arm again.

"What love?" he asked.

"Another baby," she gasped.

The doctor had her lie back on the bed. He gently probed her stomach.

Ned stared at him. "Is it?" He stroked her cheek. "We had twins the first time."

The doctor finished his examination. He looked up, amazed, "Yes, twins. Don't know how I missed it. Better deal with baby number one first." He tied the cord with a string twice and cut between the ties.

Cara took the little girl and wrapped her properly, wiping her face.

"Do you think you can stand up, Your Grace?" the doctor asked.

Ned looked surprised "Why?" he asked.

"The baby needs turning. Now that the other one is out, it will have room, but walking around helps," the doctor said.

"Yes, if you think it will help," Christina said.

Ned hopped off the bed and supported her as she stood.

Martha had come in and quickly cleaned up the area, preparing for the next one.

Ned and Christina walked around the room.

She clung to him when the next contraction hit. Her fingers dug into his arms. After three of these, her knees finally gave way. She was exhausted.

Ned lifted her back onto the bed again.

"So tired, Edward, I want to sleep." She turned to him and snuggled close. "Oh, love," she cried as another one hit. Her fingernails bit into his arm.

"Good girl, they have started," Molly said. "Sleep between them if you can."

The doctor had returned to Jenna and told them of what was happening. He cleaned her up after the afterbirth, then left again.

"Oh, no," said Jenna, then giggled. "Been there!" She looked to Eddie and stroked his face. She was lying against him with the new baby in her arms.

The doctor had no words. He had forgotten that they, too, had a set of twins. He had not delivered them. They had been born in Sydney.

Sal had cleaned up the room and left them together.

The doctor scrubbed again and re-entered Christina's room. As he walked in, Cara said, "One minute apart, doctor."

"Stations people, for round two." He laughed. "Three in twenty minutes. That's a record even for me." He took her pulse. "Steady, good. Can I feel, please?"

Christina nodded, and Ned moved so she could lie back again.

The doctor's hands gently probed her stomach. "Oh, good. It's turned. Head is down." He stood up.

She relaxed with her head in Ned's lap.

Cara came in and brought a basin of cool water. She sponged her face.

It gave Christina the boost she needed. "So tired, Edward. So very tired." She closed her eyes for a minute, relaxing. She was gripped by another contraction. "Thank you, darling one, for being with me this time. It makes such a difference."

Ned stroked her cheek. "I wish I'd known. I would have forced my way in the last two times."

Molly had a basin handy again; she wasn't sure she'd need it, but it saved a lot of cleaning up.

Christina was still lying in his lap. She was dozing.

Ned traced his finger down her forehead and moved a lock of damp blonde hair. "She's asleep, exhausted, poor love," he whispered.

"Not for long," said Cara, "More's the pity."

As she spoke, another contraction woke Christina.

Molly passed the basin to Cara, and from then on, things moved fast. Christina was so exhausted that Ned had to pull her up against him as he moved forward on the bed. He whispered a prayer in her ear and prayed for her strength.

She nodded and whispered, "Thank you." Christina felt another contraction starting. "Now," she yelled. She groaned in pain. "I need to sit up properly."

Ned eased her up and moved them both to the end of the bed again. "Better, love?"

She nodded. "Yes, I can do this!"

"Yes, *we* can love. I'm here with you. Lean on me and we'll push together," he said lovingly.

Three more pushes, and their second baby was out.

Christina collapsed back against Ned. She was too tired to stay awake. She was asleep on his chest. Absolutely exhausted.

The baby gave a healthy cry.

Ned didn't even look. His love for this woman nearly broke his heart. She had made his life complete. Finally, he took a glance at the baby. Red, wet, and squealing. It was another girl.

Christina woke with a groan of pain. She delivered the afterbirth.

The doctor said, "Look." He pointed to the ugly mass—one afterbirth with two cords. "Your Graces, these two are identical. I'll bet they will twist you and turn your life around," chuckled the doctor. The doctor looked at the exhausted parents. Fine-looking people. These girls will be as beautiful.

"Thank you, doctor," Ned uttered, his stomach heaving. "How's Jenna?" he asked quietly

"She has a fine, healthy boy, born between these two. I've never been so busy," he chuckled. The doctor checked Christina and was satisfied.

Christina was still asleep. She had been for fifteen minutes. She stirred when she heard a babe cry. The mother instinct in her responded.

The doctor smiled as she woke. "She'll be fine, Your Grace. She can get up when she feels well enough. How she feels will guide you. You've had children before. You know the 'six-week minimum' rule afterwards?"

Ned nodded.

The doctor bowed to them both and departed. He checked Jenna before leaving the house. Satisfied with both patients, he said he would return tomorrow and check on them.

Jenna had already fed their new son. He was a hefty nine-pound babe with a healthy pair of lungs.

Martha came back in and checked on her new grandson.

Eddie had not left Jenna, but he had cradled his new son, Christopher William, to be known as Kit. They had decided on this name some time ago. The recent events were all due to these two men. Christopher, whom neither knew, but who was responsible for the six new family members they now had. The name meant 'Christ Bearer' and named William after Wills.

Cara clucked lovingly over the twins. "This be the first one, sir. See, she has a small 'stork mark'." Cara pointed to a small v shape on the nose bridge." Cara handed the first baby to Christina.

Molly said to Ned when he handed him the second one. "This one is the younger one. She has a tiny heart birthmark on her foot. So at least you will be able to tell them apart."

Ned took the tiny bundle in his one free arm. Not one to ever to shed a tear, he felt them pool in his eyes. They were beautiful, absolutely, stunningly, beautiful. No longer blue and wrinkled but pink and sleeping. He looked at the two departing women and softly said. "Thank you. Thank you both so much."

Ned and Christina were finally left alone. Cara had given Christina's hair a quick brush and handed her a damp cloth to wipe her face.

He was still sitting, leaning against the bedhead, Christina resting between his legs, now feeding both babies, reclining against his chest. He was just cradling her, in awe of her strength. Her short rest had revived her. Each babe swaddled in their linen wraps.

Ned was overwhelmed with the experience he'd shared with Christina. Eddie was right. He would not have missed that for anything. He would not have been allowed in at home. Gerry would have had a fit if he'd even asked. Yet he saw the miracle of birth often. Ned would have words with him about letting the fathers in.

Christina was an old hand at feeding two at once and soon had both babes suckling. They were tiny, at only five pounds each they had a lot of growing to do. They were perfect though.

His leg started cramping. He moved slightly and Christina leaned forward so he could stand. After a turn around the room, he sat on the side of the bed and watched her in amazement.

She glowed. "Two again, Edward," she said looking at her daughters. "What are we going to name them? We'd chosen Charlotte Isabella for a girl. We could split for first names, but what about middle names?

"How about Grace and Jennifer? Or even Catherine and Victoria?" he suggested. After trying a few variants, Charlotte Jennifer Victoria for the elder and Isabella Catherine Grace for the younger baby.

Cara knocked on the door. Ned called "enter" and she poked her head around the door. "Chip and Sarah want to see the babies. May they come in?"

Ned nodded and two boisterous five-year-old's bounced in.

"Oh, Mummy, two. Can we have one each?" Sarah asked.

Ned took her in his arms "Actually, poppet, we can keep both. Is that all right?"

She nodded. Blonde curls bobbing as she did so.

"Do you like them?" she asked.

Again she nodded.

Ned asked, "Chip, what do you think?"

"All right, I 'spose. I still get to keep Liam, don't I?" he said.

"Yes, Chip, we get to keep Liam too," Ned said

"That's fine then," he said, "You can have both, Sarah. I'll have Liam you have Charl and Izzy." He turned and walked out.

Ned chuckled. "Boys! It looks like these two have nicknames already."

Cara came to remove Sarah and asked if they were up to some visitors.

Christina said, "Yes." She had just finished feeding the babes for the first time. Both were asleep and they each held one.

The door opened and Jenna, Eddie and Kit entered.

"You're up already?" Ned exclaimed.

"Yes, sore but fine," Jenna said breezily.

Eddie carried their huge bundle. "We thought we'd introduce Christopher William to his cousins. Ned, this is Kit."

"According to Chip, our two are 'Charl' and 'Izzy,' in reality, Charlotte and Isabella," Ned chuckled. "We're still trying to get our heads around twins again. They are the same size. Six pounds each, I believe."

Christina piped up, "I felt it was a possibility as I had far more movement than last time. Kicks in different places at the same time. The first time, I was as big as a wagon, though. Sorry, love. I should have said something. I think I was in denial." She smiled at her precious bundle. "The doctor showed us the afterbirth. They are identical."

Jenna was sitting on the bed holding Izzy. "She's so tiny. But perfect."

"Kit will be up and out playing with his brother in no time," Eddie said. "Makings of a fine blacksmith," he chuckled. "Nine pounds, Uncle Ned."

A month later, all three babies were baptised together at St John's.

~

The building programme was paused for a time due to the extremely hot weather. Many nights there was a late thunderstorm. To keep the convict building team occupied, Wills had them sitting under shade sails, making shingles and cutting the lead circles for roofing nails. These items would later be sold in the Emporiums. However, these occupations kept the majority of the convicts occupied until the building restarted. One or two men were shaping stone blocks, while the rest enjoyed a brief respite from the heat. They were, on the whole, a good bunch. All would receive their Tickets of Leave upon completion of this job.

Wills had discussed this with Major Bond early on in the project. He didn't want any troublemakers on site. The major had chosen twenty excellent workers. If they misbehaved, they would be sent back to the chain gangs. It worked as a halfway between the Ticket of Leave and the chain gangs. The reward system was working well. They were guarded, but not shackled.

On the last visit to Government House, Sir Charles mentioned that the gangs were to be transferred to Hobart.

Wills had told the Major about this.

Together, they worked out who in this final team deserved their Tickets and who would be sent.

Wills had already returned two men who didn't wish to work. Both were bad-tempered workers and cantankerous. They caused trouble with the other workers. The others liked being without them. He had no further trouble with the remaining crew. These were the final team and worked well.

The warehouse in Parramatta was already complete and now was filling fast. Once finished, the Parramatta team started on Charlie's house. The system Vicky and Phil discussed was working brilliantly. The new Emporium at Emu Plains was taking shape fast, and building materials were also now being sent out to Bathurst. By the middle of the year, Wills was also planning to start building their house on the banks of the Nepean River. He had not yet told Cathy about that. It was to be a birthday surprise in June for her turning twenty. He would have the outline of the building in by then and the internal walls too. He had had her sketch a floor plan of her dream home. Unbeknownst to her, he'd kept it, and it was now under construction. It was a two-story house, but with a difference. It was to have a side-gabled roof with a steep pitch. It was something she had seen once in a drawing and had fallen in love with. The ground-floor verandah would be surrounded with wrought-iron lacework. And there would be an expansive back porch so they could sit and watch the river. He was also building a special ground-floor room, like a flat, for Jack and Martha. It was walking distance from their inn, but Marc and Milly were itching to take over, and Jack wanted to take it a bit easier.

Finally, after Easter, Harry suggested they take the girls on the long-promised Hartley holiday, just the four of them. They planned it for Wills' twentieth birthday in April.

A week in the wagons sounded lovely. The prefabricated shack was awaiting erection, as the wall panels had already been delivered to the site. They arranged that it would be done as soon as they could spare a builder. Sheets of the roofing were to be taken up next week. The summer heat had passed, but the winter chill had not fully set in. They had booked for at least a week.

~

On arrival, they noted that the old fish trap would be easily repaired and closed. This was one of the first jobs the men did.

This time, they had brought tools to get some more gold. They also had empty bags. Hopefully, the cliff would produce more of the vein. The girls were keen to help. The horses would once again be used to transport the excavated mineral.

Wills and Harry dug and hammered the reef gold. Another small rockfall had occurred, exposing a thick vein of gold. They filled the bowl-shaped ledge with rocks, then crawled down. Cathy carefully climbed up and started throwing them down to the waiting men. They filled the bags as Vicky held them. It took three half days, but they had finally emptied the remaining visible gold.

The girls now had gold fever to a degree. The creek bed was checked for rocks that had fallen over the cliff. Each collected a few more quartz chunks with gold traces. The girls had both found some and were thrilled with their discoveries. The four large bags took both men to lift. Until they were ready to return, they used them as seats and covered them with blankets.

Harry and Wills compared it to the last haul and estimated that it would be another fifty or so pounds of gold in the rocks, maybe even more. The girls had their swimming smocks, so the four of them went swimming in the water hole. The water was cool but not too cold. They took it in turns swimming as couples, then warmed each other afterwards in their wagons. All used it as a mini second honeymoon.

They sat around the fire at night, talking about the possibility of neither couple having children. The girls had already cried over this. All four wanted children, but it seemed not to be in God's plan for them. They had been married for over a year. Vicky especially was feeling it. They sat cuddling in the firelight.

Harry said, "You know, we've all talked, we've done the physical requirements, but one thing we have not done together is to pray."

"Oh, Harry, that's so true," said Cathy. "And you can add cry to that list as well. I've done a lot of that." She turned into Wills's shoulder and sobbed.

Vicky too wrapped her arms around Harry and turned her head to his neck, and he enfolded her, drawing her close to him. His heart hurt too.

A little later, they sat under the stars, lifting their eyes heavenward and praying. Harry started, and each joined in petitioning God for His help just like Samuel's mother did in the Bible.

They all felt drained, but they could do no more.

They went to bed in their wagons.

Once alone, Cathy and Wills added another prayer for forgiveness, as it still hankered with them.

Vicky and Harry prayed for her healing.

Then all slept. A deep restorative sleep. They knew it was in God's hands. They would accept His decision.

They returned from their holiday much refreshed and happy. It had done them all good to have the time together.

Jack and Martha were overseeing the new Emu Emporium building site and the construction of the new house.

Phil was a regular visitor to the inn. He shared the boys' room and went to work from there each day.

~

Mid June, Wills came home from the warehouse and asked, "Cathy, would you like to see the Emu shop? It's going up quickly, and you can see your parents for your birthday too." He tried to act calm, but he was anything but. You don't usually give your wife a house for her birthday. It was not exactly something you could wrap. Eddie had made a beautiful key and padlock for their front door. Wills wrapped the gold-dipped key and would give it to her. Harry and Vicky were coming, and they were taking the wagons.

Being winter, they had arranged to sleep in the living room on the floor in front of the fire.

They arrived on Friday evening, and Martha greeted them. Jack was busy and would catch them later. He arrived just before the evening meal and greeted them warmly. He winked at Wills and nodded.

Cathy, who was totally oblivious to anything other than the joy of seeing her parents, sat talking with her mother in the kitchen, accompanied by Vicky. It was like old times.

They were having a delicious roast dinner, and Martha had just removed it from the oven and looked at Vicky's face.

Vicky excused herself and walked sedately out of the room. Martha smiled to herself. "Finally." She continued talking to Cathy. The next morning, with so many around, she cooked fried eggs for everyone to eat after their barley porridge. She served them on toast for everyone.

Wills took two. He loved Martha's fresh eggs. He dug his fork into the soft, gooey top and let the yolk soak into the bread.

Cathy took a look and departed quickly. Vicky was hard on her heels.

Wills looked a bit concerned but took a bite before it got cold. "Think I should go?" he asked.

Martha laughed, "I think you both should. Then come and see me afterwards."

Harry and Wills quickly chomped their toast and followed the girls outside.

Squeals of joy emanated from the yard area. When Vicky followed her outside, Cathy thought it was from concern. Until she, too, threw up in the garden. They stood staring at each other.

Cathy just asked, "Are you?"

Vicky could only nod.

When moments later they were joined by their husbands, they were still digesting the information.

The four stood looking at each other, not sure what to say. Cathy finally said, "I think God has finally answered our prayers from Hartley that week"

Harry was the first to react, carefully embracing Vicky. "Are you sure?"

She again nodded. "Yes, and this time I feel fine. Well, all but for the morning sickness."

Harry gave a whoop of joy and swung her around.

Wills took Cathy in his arms but asked nothing. Just holding her, and she could feel his shoulders shaking. He whispered, "Are you really?"

She replied, "Yes, love, I am with child. I didn't want to say anything because of Vicky, and I wanted to be sure."

He had confessed to her earlier that he was sure they were being punished because of their precipitous activities before the wedding.

She had comforted him. "Wills, God doesn't work that way. I feel it's more than He wanted Vicks and me to be able to share this with each other. Imagine how she would feel if I had fallen and she didn't. No, this way we can all be joyful together."

Wills was so proud of her. "Oh, Cathy, trust you to feel that way. Now we can all rejoice together."

Their haul of quartz in April had yielded fifty-three and a half more pounds of gold. They were sure the seam had finally run out as the last half-bag only had traces in it. As they only had to split this between the two of them, they added another £4280 each to their tally.

Wills had arranged for the cabin to be erected, and the family could use it as a holiday cabin. It was so lovely and peaceful there. Hartley now had a double meaning for them all. They both now jokingly call the town 'Heart-ly'.

Martha finally came outside and saw her two youngest daughters cradled lovingly in their husband's arms. Time enough for conversations later. She returned to the kitchen.

At morning tea, Martha produced a cake for Cathy's twentieth birthday. They had a small celebration, and Wills suggested they all go for a walk as he had eaten so much. A stand of she-oaks hid the building site from the road and bridge. So even when they crossed the bridge the day before, she had not noticed the new building. He had neatly distracted her to look down the river in the direction they had walked on that fateful day.

As they turned onto River Road, she looked up and saw the construction. "Oh, look, Wills. Someone is building right on the river. What a beautiful spot."

"Let's go and look, love," he suggested.

The family walked towards the building site. As they drew near, Wills reached into his coat pocket and drew out the wrapped key. "Cathy, did you wonder if I'd forgotten a gift for you? I haven't, you know. Happy Birthday, love. You are my world, but hopefully, this will be ours." He handed her the awkwardly wrapped gift.

She took it and looked puzzled.

"Open it, love," he encouraged.

She tore off the paper, which he pocketed. A large, ornate gold-plated key fell into her hand. She looked at it. Then it dawned. She swung around to the house. "This is ours?" she asked.

"Yes, sweetheart, ours. You need to tell us how you want the rooms inside before we can proceed. But we've designed it for a Cape

Cod roof as you've always wanted," Wills said. "I couldn't exactly wrap the entire house," he chortled.

"Oh, William Lockley. I should be so angry, but I'm not. Our own house. Will it be finished in time for the baby?" she said.

"It had better be. The Inn is getting crowded. By the way, your parents are also moving in, as are the boys until they marry."

At seventeen and fifteen, this could be a few years until Nick and Calum found life partners.. "We can fit up to six bedrooms plus a few rooms for the help."

"Really, Wills? Oh, that's wonderful." She hugged him.

Martha kissed her daughter. "Colleen Murphy has asked if she can be your housemaid. You might score a few more of them if you want them. They are all good workers and we know them too." Cathy burst into tears and turned to Wills.

Wills cradled her to him. "Why, love, what's wrong?"

"Nothing, Wills, absolutely nothing. Everything is just perfect!" she muttered into his neck. "I'd love to have Colleen here as well. She's my best friend, and it's one way I can help her."

He looked to Martha, puzzled.

She grinned back. "Welcome to the world of an expectant mother. Never mind, lad, she will be very emotional off and on from now on."

The joy over the new house multiplied the next day as Harry and Vicky returned from a long walk and announced they too had found a site to build on. Their new building block was about half a mile further down the road. It was set back from the river and backed onto the forty-acre farm that Harry had bought some time ago. They could now finally build. He had wanted to show Vicky before he said anything to the family. "We also want a farm and a citrus orchard," he explained.

They would start after Wills and Cathy's house was finished. "We want to live nearby, and Vicky would also have her family close too."

After their-four day sojourn at Emu Plains, they returned to Parramatta to find the English family had finally decided to return home.

John, Edmund would accompany them. They would depart in July. A pall of sadness descended on the family.

Life must go on, and duty calls.

Gerry had kept in regular contact with Ned, detailing the happenings of the Estate and Castle in full. He was handling all issues. He kept thanking Ned for the opportunity to learn to run an Estate by necessity. Paul and Douglas had been fabulous teachers.

Ned could no longer forestall his return. The twins were well and thriving. By the time they returned home, Chip would need to start his education. They had agreed on a tutor for him and a governess for Sarah, at least until they were eight. However, after spending time teaching at the

Orphans' School, they began to think of making some changes. If the tutor also taught at the village school, then Gerry's children could not only benefit, but all the village children, too. It would be good for them all to get to know the local children. He smiled. Yes, he would stir things up a little. He was jolted back to reality. Liam was running everywhere and cannonballed into his legs. Depart, they must. He would talk to Christina about his idea.

Elle and Charles were particularly sad. She, too, had to leave. They had only a month to share the love that had to last a lifetime.

That month passed all too fast. He discussed his idea with Christina.

Captain Roberts took the sad group to Sydney three days before departure.

They needed to find lots to occupy the children. They loved seeing their beloved toys waiting for them on their new beds upon arrival. Suze had the maid arrange them on their beds before they arrived. They were packed, and now the two babies were sitting up; they, too, needed toys and books.

Boarding day came in the pouring rain. A storm was brewing. Ned and Charles had spoken with Captain Papps about delaying departure, but he assured them that his ship was safe and watertight.

Charles said on the way back to the hotel, "That was an odd comment, don't you think?"

Ned agreed, but said nothing to the ladies.

Final loading packed and cabins inspected. The family parted. *The Harpooner* cast off and was towed into the channel by a small steam tug boat. She unfurled her sails, and they filled with the strengthening breeze, taking them away.

Charles was silent. He had pleaded with his mother to stay. Even Mr Childs, the headmaster, had asked Elle to stay.

"Please, mother," Charles begged. Alas no! Now his mother was gone. Charles needed time.

They would stay in town for a few days. He had to see the Governor tomorrow anyway. Sal knew the pain of parting. The farewells to her own mother were hard; and she had been ill and in great pain until she died.

Charles remained silent at the departure of the younger family members. Only Cathy and Wills remained with them. They too were part of tomorrow's meeting.

The storm blew relentlessly all night and all the next day. Their visit to Government House was nearly cancelled due to the ferocity of the wind. However, around mid-afternoon, the wind died down.

The meeting proceeded and extended well past the allotted time. All other appointments at Government House had been cancelled, so the

Governor and Lady Mary enjoyed some informal time with the Earl and his wife.

Charles still had not grown used to the title. It still did not sit well after all this time. He requested the Governor call him Charles. "Please, sir, if you are to work so closely with me as almost an assistant, then I feel in private at least I can be Charles."

The Governor chuckled. "It goes both ways, then. For I, too, am Charles, as is my right-hand man here. Only he's Charles Chester Master."

"At least I'm a William," said Wills chuckled.

"Then how about Lord Charles, Sir Charles, and Charles M?" the Aide asked. He smiled before adding, "I'd suggest calling me by my surname, only that would be more confusing."

After Charles Lockley chortled, they settled on the Aide's suggestion.

The storm was still blowing after dinner when they finally left Government House. They returned to the hotel and sat talking in their private suite. Cathy was feeling well, and her morning sickness was abating.

The gale blew all night, and it continued to rain the next morning. The weather was so bad that they decided to delay their return to Parramatta until the storm cleared.

Charles and Wills ventured out mid-afternoon and surveyed the damage. They needed to stretch their legs. Charles's leg still hurts in weather like this. His limp was barely noticeable on sunny days. He had broken it nearly two decades earlier. Sal and Cathy walked around the sitting room. Neither felt like braving the elements.

The rain eased, but the wind continued to blow. The danger of being hit by flying debris finally drove the men back inside. They sat reading the much read, newspapers that had arrived from London by ship three weeks earlier with the arrival of *The Harpooner*.

They retired early, hoping the storm would finally die overnight.

They woke to find the day sunny but still windy. The hotel was in turmoil as an incident had occurred.

Mr Stewart himself came and knocked on Charles's door. "Sir, I regret to inform you, but the ship has returned. No one is injured, but all must alight. We are making their rooms ready."

Charles told Sal, then went next door to let Wills and Cathy know. They all rugged up against the bitterly cold and climbed into the carriage that Mr Stewart had waiting for them. Two more had already been sent to the ship.

Their family were already disembarked when they arrived.

Elle opened her arms to Charles. "It's all right, son, we're unharmed. Not so the ship. It leaks like a sieve."

Ned explained the hull had started taking on water. "We may have hit something, but it also might explain the Captain's comment. We're not getting back on that one. We'll find another better, newer ship."

Edmund and Christina had the babies, Nanny had the older twins, and John had Liam. The three older ones were all crying and white.

Sal and Cathy rescued the two men. The children soon calmed.

Ned and Charles saw another sleek ship standing at anchor. Since their departure, the *Princess Royal* had arrived in port. Captained by Von Zuileron, it was waiting again for a berth before unloading its cargo. The passengers from the other ship had alighted some days before. The storm had delayed unloading her cargo. She moved to allow the passengers on the *Harpooner* to disembark. Once the *Harpooner* was towed to the slips for repair, it would unload its cargo before undergoing repairs.

By the next day, they ascertained that the new sailing date would be some four weeks hence. They decided to return to Parramatta.

Charles relished the fact that he had more time with his beloved mother. He did not look forward to a second parting.

Captain Roberts carried word to Eddie on the morning Ferry to expect their return the next day. The party that greeted them in Parramatta was larger than the one that had farewelled them only days before.

Mr Childs had also joined the throng. He was at the gangplank and helping everyone.

When Elle alighted, he held her hand a little longer than was expected. "We need to talk." He whispered, then offered her his arm to walk back to Eddie's house. She clung to him, almost leaning on him.

Sal pointed all this out to Charles.

Charles stood looking, amazed. "Mayhap she would stay after all, my love."

Thanks to John and Edmund, Richard Childs had become a regular visitor. Everyone both liked and admired him. There were not many who could cope with the rigours of caring for up to one hundred little girls at the Female Orphans' School. Some had the calling for this and Richard was one such man. He had dedicated his life to the education and nurture of those less fortunate.

The days passed quickly. Mr Childs would arrive every afternoon after school. He often stayed for dinner before walking home. Word finally came from Captain Roberts that departure was set for August 5th.

Elle, Dowager Countess of Coxheath, knew it was decision time. She sought out her friend. "Suze, what do I do?"

"Oh, my dear, do not ask me to advise you, for I am a selfish old lady. I want our friendship to last forever." She patted her hand. "However, you have had so little happiness in your life so far, and deserve more. Charles wants you here. You have far more family here than there and more coming. Anyway, Matthew and Lilabet are young enough to come and visit. They can bring young Matty too. Here you are surrounded by family. You will get to see this town grow."

Her words didn't comfort Elle greatly, yet she knew their wisdom. Richard had not yet declared himself. He may never do so. His friendship was enough.

Suze added. "I will miss you, Elle. I still regret those wasted years, but those we had were grand" Suze embraced her friend. "Stay with my blessing, not that you need it."

Elle could say nothing. She nodded and went to tell Charles. His house was so close. She grabbed her cloak, walked out the front door, and was greeted at the front door by Mr Childs. He had arrived early.

"Are you going for a walk? I was coming to ask if you would accompany me on such a jaunt." He presented his arm to her. They strolled down to the waterfront, then along to the bridge. They found a seat, and he laid his handkerchief for her to sit down upon.

He stood looking at the river with his back to her. "My heart is torn asunder, my dear." He turned to face her and then knelt at her feet. "I had word of your imminent departure, and my heart broke. Would that I could throw my job and come with you." He looked forlorn. "Lady Coxheath, Elizabeth, my Elle, would you look upon this lowly teacher and give me your hand in marriage?" He paused and looked into her blue, blue eyes. "If you feel you cannot, then please, stay here with your son, and at least I can be close. I am a mere Baronet's second son, but would you consider my offer? Do not answer now, but please consider it." He was still on one knee.

"Mr Childs, Richard, I was walking out the door to find my son to tell him I was staying. I cannot lose them all again." She paused.

He started to say something, but she put her fingers on his lips. "Let me finish, my dear."

His heart soared at those words.

"Another big part of my decision was you. I do not have to wait to know my mind. I know it now. Yes, I will marry you, dear heart, and soon." She looked him in the eye. "You see, I love you."

"As I love you. I am called to teach. I did not seek to find a wife. I have never looked before. My heart has never been stirred that way until I met you. Our years together may be short, but they will be sweet and golden years. This I vow." He sat beside her now and took her in his arms, gently kissing her. They did not care who watched. Oblivious of all who saw.

As Sal looked through her kitchen window, she saw them on the riverbank. "Charles here is a sight to behold. You must see this for yourself."

Charles looked and saw his mother being embraced and kissed in public. He was thrilled. Now, he knew she would stay. However, his mind was swirling. He could cope with his children in a relationship, but his mother? He laughed to himself.

They watched for a while.

Charles embraced Sal and swung her around. "Now she'll stay, Sal."

Elle and Richard sat for some time before they continued their walk. They walked along the riverbank for some way and then returned, calling in at Christina's Cottage, where Charles and Sal lived.

Richard asked her, "Should I ask Charles for your hand in marriage? Does the Earl need to provide consent?"

"Fiddlesticks, Richard! He has no say in it at all," Elle said.

Charles saw their approach and opened the door with a smile and a greeting, but hands-on-hips. "So, I'm to have you as a Father, am I, sir?"

Richard swallowed. "Err, if you allow me to, then yes."

"There is no allowing. I saw you kissing her in public. She is compromised." He roared with laughter at the look on their faces. "Congratulations to you both! I am delighted!" He shook Richard's hand and kissed his mother's cheek. "Just don't take her away from me, ever again."

Richard shook his head. Now he knew how the children felt when sent to the headmaster.

Charles turned to look at her. "Mother, I truly am delighted," he said and hugged her. "Now you have another reason to stay."

~

The trip to Sydney went as planned, except for Elle. She would miss seeing her sister, but she had Richard and her family here to support her.

She waved them off with Richard at her side, she clinging to his arm. They had an engagement party the night before. Only family, the Bobarts and the Tindales, attended.

The Banns were to be first read that Sunday.

Elle said her goodbyes to Suze in the privacy of Eddie's sitting room. They stood together, both in tears.

Suze was sad, but happy too.

Elle would not go to Sydney; that would be just too hard.

As the group departed, Richard stood with her to comfort her. A shoulder for her to cry on. She needed it, and she needed him. After so many years alone, God had given her another helpmate. A good and Godly man.

Chapter 17   *A Melancholy Day*

*T*he heat of summer would soon be upon them. The Fitzroys'
were coming to Parramatta in December and would catch up with the
family and visit the new Warehouse improvements. Wills had added an all-
weather lean-to addition, so the stock could now be loaded in all weather
conditions. Governor Fitzroy wanted a tour of the Warehouse's hidden
stock.

Wills had various locked sections internally, as well as the two
underground strong rooms. Phil, Harry, and he knew what was in there,
but not many others. Currently, it had five hundred gold pans, assorted
sieves of various mesh sizes in cartons of one hundred, and numerous
picks, shovels, scales, and some sluices of various designs. There were also
small screw-top glass jars for the gold itself. If the last of these were seen,
the word may leak out. For you need only scales to weigh gold, the same
with pans and sieves.

Lew and Aidan ensured the external cartons were incorrectly
labelled to waylay suspicions, and then well sealed.

When Wills saw eighteen cartons marked with 'bedsprings' being
unloaded, he thought, "What?" So, he opened them.

"Hey, Phil, look at this. See what Lew has marked these as,
'bedsprings,' when packing them for shipping. Have a look inside." Wills
laughed.

"Trust Lew," he chuckled. "Parts for sluices."

The Emu Emporium was now complete. The local tradesmen
were all now keen to sell their goods from the central store.

Alex married Mary Parker as soon as she turned eighteen.

Ben Parker, her father, was first tradesman to place his leather
goods in the store, and sales had taken off. George Ellis and Ben had

arrived soon after the Rum Rebellion occurred. They had worked together for years before Ben and Kath moved to the Nepean River.

These days, Milly and Mary worked together in Milly's leather carving workshop at the inn. With Jack and Martha moving to the new house, the inn had room for the newlyweds.

Milly was still carving for her father, George Ellis, but she taught Mary how to emboss the leather. Mary was as clever and just as skilled as Milly. Together, they turned out the most fantastic work. Their fathers were delighted that their daughters were sisters-in-law, just as Ben and George were. They had both married Rosedale girls.

Marc had hired two of the young Murphy girls as babysitters cum maids. This freed up Mary and Milly to continue their work. They would stop to feed their babies; otherwise, the Murphy girls did everything for the two young couples.

Ben Parker and Alex had employed Nicky and Calum Turner in the saddlery to keep stock flowing. Both boys had often worked with Alex. They did the easy jobs, such as cutting out and hole punching, then Mr Parker and Alex would finish off the items. It gave the boys some pocket money, which they loved. As they grew older, their work became increasingly skilled, but they also watched Milly and absorbed the lessons she taught them. They worked there whenever they were not at school.

Ben Parker set the precedent when he was the first to sell only from there. He moved all his stock from the saddlery and sold exclusively from the Emporium. Soon, others followed suit as tradesmen realised the passing trade would catch more sales than their individual shops. The prices were increased by 20% to offset the percentage charged for the sale. Most items that Eddie couldn't make, they would source locally. Wills also insisted on product control and would only allow top-quality stock.

Ben Parker, the saddler; Richard Davies, the local blacksmith, with his one-man forge; Mrs Walker and her basket-making friends were also encouraged to sell from the Emporium. All did and encouraged others to do the same.

Once Harry's orchard started producing, He built a Fresh food section next door. Finn Murphy added his spuds that weren't market quality. Mrs Walker also added eggs and honey to her products. Harry also enquired of Wills if he intended to sell hay. The answer was yes, so Harry added a lean-to shed to the Emu Plains Emporium. They had yet to find a supplier.

~

In September, Vicky and Harry moved to Bathurst for two months to oversee the construction there.

They had sent a message to Mr Barry, the squatter on Condobolin and asked if he had anything that he wanted to sell from the Bathurst store. It was one way they could help him. He had gone out of his way to help them, and they could not even tell him how that had helped them.

Mr Barry had written back, "I'd love to sell some stock feed bundles, and I also have bags of grain if they are of any use. Are they of any use?"

They wrote back saying they would love to stock his products permanently. Harry invited him to drop in when he was next in town.

He did, and they discussed terms and signed an agreement. Both were happy. He was the first of several farmers who wished to sell through the Emporium.

Wills and Harry had jointly bought a caravan of carts and wagons. They planned to have a constant trail of vehicles carrying goods to and from the stores. They could also collect back loads of produce from Bathurst and beyond. One large wagon was for Western collections from farmers. This also meant more jobs for two-man teams as drivers.

They figured this way, stock and produce could be transported more conveniently than if they only used the three small covered wagons. This vehicle was a large, flatbed wagon that had a team of twelve draft horses and a three-man crew.

Now that the Bathurst Emporium was nearly complete, they had to consider stocking it with building materials. Until the stock supply was complete, the large wagon would bring up a whole load of items from the central warehouse. The smaller wagons would have to make various trips. The big wagon could carry all the big and bulky items, like some of the seven hundred sheets of corrugated iron that Lewis and Aidan had sent. The first part of the shipment, worth £1000, had arrived as ballast. It had, therefore, not been charged shipping costs.

Now that they had the contract with Mr Barry, they could also bring back loads of stock feed to Emu and Parramatta. He was ecstatic, as were they. He had never had a guaranteed sale for his crops before.

As Wills read the accompanying letter from Lewis, he kept exclaiming, "Good job, Lew," and "Oh, Lew, you trooper," and the like.

Phil was in stitches with the labelling of various other boxes. On the cartons of glass jars for gold dust, he had written "Clock parts. FRAGILE!" Another crate six contained flat-packed, gold washing cradles, and he had written "baby cots."

All the items Wills had wanted were included in bulk. Both Lew and Aidan had a wonderful time shopping in London, Manchester and Belfast.

They had hunted for everything they could think might be useful, and added it too. The more they dug, the more unusual items they found.

Lew had included a costings sheet. The total was only £330. Wills whistled. All this for that little? He would get as much as soon as he could. This first load included two long section of rail track for use as the cantilever beam.

Wills had sent Uncle Ned home with £3000 and asked if he would do the same. The new corrugated roofing sheets would undoubtedly be in significant demand, but Wills ordered the proper ridge capping. Nails could be made here. Other things were what was not available here. Pig iron was always good, as were gold pans and sieves by the crateful. Lew had included a few different small sluices, marked as baby cots. He wished there were some way of communicating their needs. Maybe, one day, someone will invent something and eliminate the nine-month turnaround for orders.

Phil and Wills had the warehouse nearly ready for the inspection by Governor Fitzroy next week. Wills heard wheels on the gravel outside. He went to investigate as he wasn't expecting anyone. "Harry! Vicks! Hello, how are you? Welcome back," Wills greeted them.

Harry hopped off and lifted Vicky down.

She and Cathy were now in their seventh month. "Wills, the place out there is beautiful, but it's time to get my girl home. No more travelling for her for a while," Harry said with a laugh.

"Oh, Harry, you're mean." She giggled. "I'm not that big yet. Jenna was always huge at seven months. How are you, Wills? How is Cathy?" She kissed Wills on the cheek.

"Enough of that, my girl, I'm jealous." Harry laughed and kissed her himself. "Hello, Phil. How are things in the warehouse? All going smoothly? The Bathurst Emporium is nearly done. Not much else we can do there until the stock arrives. Mr Barry grabbed a group of farmers and built a lean-to shack out the back. He has somehow worked out that it was Wills who organised the land transfer into his name, so he's no longer a squatter, but a landowner. He can't do enough for him now. So now there is a place to stay at the Emporium. We can park the big wagon right next to our covered one. I told him he can use it when he wants to."

The men had wandered around the building. Vicky sat on a carton at the bottom of the staircase and waited. Nearly home. She bowed her head, as she often did, and laid her hand on her growing stomach. "Lord, be with this child I carry. Bless it, keep it healthy, and give me the strength to deliver it safely, Amen." As her hand rested on her gown, she could feel the little one moving. Sometimes the child even put a hand or foot where her hand rested. It was moving constantly, sometimes to the point of disturbing her rest.

Harry would laugh when it kicked him when he would cuddle her. Yes, she was pleased to be home.

"How are you going, love? Can you hang on for a few more minutes?" Harry called from above her.

"Yes, Harry, but I do look forward to being home. I could do with a lie down soon." She sounded tired. They had been travelling slowly for a few days. She got up and wandered around. Her idea of sorting the stock alphabetically worked beautifully. The divisions had been colour-coded, and all the signs made things easy to find. The store was divided into the sections that she'd suggested.

Eddie was working hard at keeping the shelves full.

Mr Tindale now employed five full-time apprentices. They were busy making the building materials and various sorts of nails. Nothing gold-related could be made at the smithy yet. Time for that later.

The Parramatta Emporium had needed another extension, and it was done as Wills built the warehouse.

Luke was now able to keep track of everything easily. Anyone could now look and see if an item was in stock.

It was all working smoothly.

Vicky ran her hand over the old kegs that held pick handles, rakes, hoes, spades, or vegetable posts. Everything was here.

She heard the footsteps on the stairs and dawdled back to her husband. She took the arm he offered.

"Let's go home, love," he said.

"Home. Oh, that sounds so good," she said. "I think I'll spend tomorrow in bed." She waved as they left.

Harry laughed as she was always on the go. He lifted her onto the wagon. He wanted her well-rested before the Governor arrived the next day or so. Lady Mary had asked them to tea.

~

It was five days later that they all gathered for Tea at Government House in Parramatta.

Charles Master and Phil were sitting at the back chatting quietly. "Phil," he said quietly, "I haven't had a chance to tell you, I became engaged last week. Lucy has finally accepted my offer. Sir Charles knows, but I need to get my CO's paperwork completed before we announce anything. I can't see him until Saturday."

"Charles, that's wonderful. Congratulations." Phil shook his hand and patted him on the shoulder.

Phil and the governor's aide have become close. Charles said, "Thanks for introducing us, Phil."

From the first meeting over six months ago, Phil and Charles had become friends. They often worked together on what they referred to as "our project." This was preparing the colony for the onslaught. Phil had introduced his childhood neighbour, Lucy Norfolk, to Charles some months earlier when she had arrived from England with friends. Phil never had asked her what she was doing out here, but she'd arrived with friends rather than family.

Governor Fitzroy, his Aide Charles, Harry, Wills and Phil and Eddie left the ladies and went to view the warehouse. They could also talk without others listening.

The Governor walked in and looked at the aisles. "Oh, this is wonderful, Wills. I am vastly impressed!" he exclaimed when he saw both the quality and extent of the building. Like Vicky had just days before, he walked around running his hand over everything. Wills showed him the locked sections, including the two strongrooms.

The governor returned to them and said they had his full support. Was there anything he could do to assist?

Wills laughed and replied, "Well, the road to Bathurst still needs a lot of work, and while you're at it, some safe campgrounds on the route, preferably with a privy too. The bush is already smelling at some stops." He stated the practical needs with a smile. A well or two would be ideal, or a tank, near the creeks.

Harry and Wills returned to Government House with the Governor, collected their wives, and then returned home.

Eddie invited the Governor to tea at 10:15 a.m. on December 7th, so they could finally meet the children. They were bringing their son, George. They had not yet met him. He was to assist his father in his official duties. A second Aide to Charles Master, as they knew he would need help once work spread.

Cara was waiting. Paddy, too, was ready to take the carriage.

By half after ten, they still had not arrived.

Eddie walked outside the kitchen door as he could hear a lot of noise of people shouting.

Then Anna arrived. She had run down the hill in tears, no hat and distraught. She threw herself into Eddie's arms. "She's dead, Eddie. There was an accident. She's dead."

"Who is Anna?" Eddie asked. He had never seen his sister so distraught.

"L-lady M-mary. She's dead." She sobbed into his shoulder.

Charles had seen her fly by their house. He was running late for tea. He knew something was up, so he followed her. When he arrived and saw her so upset, he asked, "What's happened, love?"

She turned to her father and clung to him, sobbing, unable to speak.

Eddie went into the sitting room where everyone else had gathered. "They are not coming. There's been an accident." His voice broke. "Anna said Lady Mary is dead."

There was a collective gasp.

Harry, Eddie, Wills, and Phil told the ladies to stay at home.

Charles brought Anna in, and Jenna came and took her arm.

Jenna led her to the settee.

Charles followed the other men and went to see what had happened.

Phil ran the three blocks to Government House while the others walked as fast as they could.

As the Lockleys and Harry approached, they saw a huge crowd milling around.

Phil was nowhere in sight.

They probed the crowd for information.

When the crowd realised who was asking, they slowly parted to allow them through.

The soldiers keeping back the people also recognised them, and they allowed them in.

The sight of the wrecked carriage and carnage that met them was horrific.

The injured horses were whinnying in agony.

The governor was sitting on the ground holding his dead wife. Lady Mary lay in his lap. She was covered in blood and was obviously dead. Her face had blood from her mouth and nose. Governor Fitzroy was distraught, holding her and not allowing anyone near.

Their son George was sitting off to their side, also injured, but not severely. He was in deep shock.

Wills went to him. He could do no more than sit with him.

The injured horses were still thrashing on the ground and in pain. Both unable to be released.

The scene was chaotic.

All were in shock.

Tim had sent Anna to get to her brothers. He had told her not to return; he would wait with Charles Master until his brother Robert arrived.

Eddie saw a soldier, Phil and a lady at the side of Charles Master. The girl was distraught, and Phil was trying to comfort her. Eddie heard Phil's words of comfort, then Phil said, "Lucy, we must get him to the house." He realised this was Phil's friend Lucy Norfolk, from home.

Eddie came over with his father.

They ordered that someone go to Government House and get shutters, doors or something to carry Charles Master up there.

Phil called Harry over. "Harry, this is Robert, Charles' brother, and Lucy, Charles' fiancée."

Phil took Harry aside. "It's not good, Harry. He's still alive but insensible. Oh, Harry, it's Charlotte all over again. They have just become engaged, but have not announced it." His eyes glistened with unshed tears.

Harry comforted his friend as best he could. All he could do was place a hand on his shoulder. "I'm so sorry, Phil." He could see a group coming downhill from Government House. They carried the shutters from the front of the house. He touched Phil's shoulder and pointed to

Lucy, motioning him to pull her away. "She needs you, Phil. She'll listen to you."

Phil nodded.

She did. Lucy stood and turned to him. He took her in his arms, and as they lifted Charles, she finally broke. She sobbed against Phil's shoulder.

Robert held Charles's hands as he was carefully rolled onto the shutters.

Harry saw the side of his friend, Charles's, head—bloodied and with gore dripping from his ear. The entire side of his head was smashed and badly injured. He had seen less damage than this, and the patient died. He knew there was no hope. It was just a matter of time.

Eddie, Charles, and Charlie, who had just arrived, along with another of the Governor's Aides, helped carry Lady Mary's body. They, too, had rolled her onto a shutter and reverently carried her home. Her face was now covered with a kerchief.

The Governor and George hobbled beside them. The Governor would not release her cold, limp hand.

As they left, they heard two shots. Both horses had broken legs and were put down.

Each shot jarred them all.

The procession's arrival at the door saw all the staff standing in disbelief.

Anna's husband, Tim, emerged from the office and called them to place her on the desk. He had cleared it off. There was nothing more they could do for her, so there was no point in carrying her upstairs. She would lie in state here until her burial.

Minutes earlier, Anna and Tim had seen them off. Tim had an early morning meeting with the Governor at Government House. They had taken Lucy with them as she had been staying at his parents' inn, Royal Admiral Duncan, with her friends. As they had gone, Lucy was to stay at Government House with Lady Mary. Her luggage was to follow.

Tim and Anna had watched the entire accident and could do nothing to stop it. The horses bolted from the moment they were released. Anna knew where they were heading. They went straight down to help and saw Lady Mary and the extent of her injuries, then saw she had died instantly.

The Charles Master was still breathing. George crawled out of the crumpled vehicle and attended to his mother. As did the Governor had been driving and was thrown clear.

Lieutenant Robert Master had been on duty nearby; he was called to attend his brother. The staff did not want to allow Lucy in to see Charles. Robert waved them aside and asked Phil to bring her in. She stayed until the medic arrived.

Sadly, their betrothal had not been announced, Phil knew, therefore, her loss would never be acknowledged. It was what had happened to him. The horrible day Charlotte died returned to him afresh. The grief washed over him once again.

Lucy clung to him outside the bedroom while the doctor was with Charles. The doctor finally emerged from the room, white and in shock himself. He shook his head. Lucy nearly collapsed.

Phil escorted her back into the bedroom and placed a chair next to the bed. Robert sat on the other side. There was nothing they could do but wait for his passing. There was no hope. Charles did not rally. There was no miracle. He lingered until seven that night, then slipped away. He was gone.

Lucy struggled to breathe. Prostrated with grief, Lucy finally collapsed. She had remained as strong as she could. She was unable to hold it together any longer.

Robert was in no condition to assist; he, too, was deep in grief.

Wills stayed with him to make sure he had some support.

Phil assisted Lucy from the room. Now unable to stand, he carried her downstairs. Her arms were tightly clasped around his neck. He knew she was staying at Tim's father's inn, the Rear Admiral Duncan, but that was no place for her now. Her chaperones had left that morning. He decided to take her to Eddie's.

He was met by the family who was waiting for him downstairs. Paddy had sent up the trap in case it was needed. "Eddie, I have to get her out of here," Phil said. She was still in his arms. "She has been staying at the Rear Admiral Duncan. Even though it's owned by Tim's parents, but I don't want her there alone. Can I take her to your place? I'll ask Molly to send down her things."

Eddie said, "Of course."

Tim went to help her into the trap. Paddy was in the driver's seat. Phil lifted her in and sat beside her. She leaned sobbing on his chest.

Phil knew exactly how she felt.

Even Robert could not change the timing. No announcement had been made, so the engagement could not be acknowledged. The governor knew, but he was in no condition to be approached.

Phil needed to be there for her. She needed him.

Jenna and Cara saw them coming. They were outside the front door, waiting. They knew that at some time they would be needed. They swung into action. Cara already had the rooms ready in case they were needed. Jenna saw Phil with Lucy again in his arms and led him to a bedroom. He gently laid her on the bed and left her with Cara.

She tried to stop him from leaving her. He promised he'd return later. She nodded.

Cara would stay with her. She was numb with grief.

Phil did not want her left alone.

Both still had blood on them. Cara would clean her up. He knew he must do likewise. Harry and Vicky had been at Eddie's for the proposed tea. Phil had to let Cathy know what was happening.

Paddy would take Phil home. They stopped to ask Molly to send Lucy's things to Eddie's place. His heart was twisted with grief. Vicky would remain with Cathy at the cottage. She knew Cathy would not want to be alone. Vicky and Cathy wept. Paddy drove home to Roseneath. He walked to his room to change.

Paddy was waiting for him when he came out again. He took him back to Eddie's place to be with Lucy.

Now that John and Edmund had returned to England, the house was too quiet. Vicky would often spend the day alone in the large, empty house. Not now; she wanted Cathy.

~

The following days passed in a haze of stress, turmoil and inquests. The Governor had been ruled as innocent. The incident had been ruled accidental with the horses bolting. The Governor, who had played down his injury, was later found to have badly injured his leg. Possibly even fractured it. George escaped with minor cuts, scratches and bruises. He was still in shock as he saw his mother die.

On the day of the funeral, Parramatta fell quiet. The shops shut, and the community lined the streets. The funeral cortège was so long that it extended almost halfway along Church Street. Two ferry loads of dignitaries had arrived from Sydney. All accommodation was full. Lucy, as expected, was not invited to join the mourners.

Robert and George would walk behind the coffin carriages with the Governor in a carriage behind. One only had to mention Lady Mary, and tears would form in their eyes. She had been so loved.

The shops remained closed all day. The town was still and quiet.

~

Lucy remained in bed for the week. Once up, she would sit on the window seat in her room, gazing at nothing.

Ten days after the funeral, Jenna asked Lucy if she could help her dress. She had a visitor.

Phil had come daily, but today would be special. He had discussed with Harry and Eddie what he should do.

There was an obvious answer for both of them.

Lucy saw who awaited her and ran to him, falling into his arms and weeping. "What am I to do, Phil? Lady Mary was my chaperone. I have no one," she cried softly. "I loved her so much. I loved Charles, too."

She was no longer the little sister he had grown up with. Her dark curls tickled his chin. Her green eyes melted his heart. Why had it taken him so long to realise his feeling had changed?

Chapter 18 A Letter Arrives

"Come, my dear, we need to talk." Phil took her to the garden, away from prying eyes. "Lucy, I know how you feel, I know exactly how you feel. You are one of the few who know of my secret engagement to Charlotte."

She nodded.

"Lucy, I know the grief is raw." He paused, remembering. "I have a suggestion. This way I can be close, and we can grieve together." Phil said the words he declared he'd never say again. "Lucy Norfolk, I'd be honoured if you would marry me."

She looked at him aghast, mouthing the word, "No!" Tears slid down her cheeks. Her eyes locked on his. "Phil, you are my friend, my best friend, his friend too. How could you ask me that?"

"It's for exactly that reason, Lucy. You also knew Charlotte; I knew Charles. We each admired them. No, we loved them. Marriages have been formed from a lot less. I know we do not share a grand passion, but we like each other; we always have. We are already friends. However, it is grief that has drawn us together, instead of love. We each know that loss. We can be open with each other and talk about our feelings as with no other."

He looked away. He could not face her for a while, lest his true feelings be revealed. "I feel that in time our marriage could be more, a full marriage, but initially it would give you security. A marriage of convenience, if you like." Phil still felt his loss; until recently, he had woken most mornings with thoughts of Charlotte. The trip west, then Charles' death, had made a change. One he could not forget. But one does not have to forget. He realised that there is room for more than one in his heart. Yes, he knew exactly how she was feeling, but that led to hope.

A wave of grief washed over them both.

She turned to him, and he took her gently in his arms. "I miss him so, Phil." She sobbed into his shoulder.

He laid his cheek against her dark hair. He too had tears of pain in his eyes. He realised the emotion he experienced when Charles told him of their joy was one of jealousy. They could heal together and grow together.

Lucy was a woman of faith. Somehow, they would make it work.

Finally, she looked at him through tear-filled eyes. She held his eyes to make sure he was serious. "Are you sure, Phil? Really sure?

He did not look away. "I'm sure, Lucy." He kissed her forehead. "Very sure!"

"Then, yes, Phil, I will. We both need time, but yes, I'll marry you. Though I need to tell Robert myself, I need to tell him everything. Can you come with me?" she asked.

He nodded. "Of course, my dear. Outwardly, no one will know it was ever Charles, do you understand? Only Robert, the family, and the Governor knew of your engagement. All will understand."

She nodded. She knew the situation was dire. She was an unaccompanied woman in a convict town. She had travelled with a friend and her family, and she stayed with them at the inn for weeks. Her family, the Norfolks, lived next door to Phil's estate in England. Her parents were friends with some of Lady Mary's family. So she had been left in the care of Lady Mary, who was also a friend of her family, and she was to have moved that afternoon to Government House to be with her. Now she was dead. Lucy was unable to stay at the inn alone as Tim's mother was not an adequate chaperone. She had no other place to stay other than Eddie's. She couldn't ask that for long. Her plans were awry, her world shattered.

Yes, she would marry Phil. She had always liked him, more than liked him. However, it was he who had introduced her to Charles. Charlotte had been her childhood friend. She had seen Charlotte and Phil leave for their ride on that fateful day, and she had supported him in his grief.

~

A month after the horrific accident, Robert Master accompanied Eddie, Phil, and Lucy to Sydney. They were married in St Phillip's Church by a Special Licence issued by Bishop Broughton.

While not exactly a love match, Eddie knew they would support each other and grow together.

It was enough.

They waved farewell to Eddie and Robert at the wharf and stood watching until the ferry was out of sight.

Phil asked if she would like to go for a stroll before returning to the hotel.

Lucy suggested they walk to the point. "Phil, I need to say something. Can we find somewhere we can be private?"

They walked along the foreshore into the shade of a large tree.

She turned and took both his hands. "Phillip, have you never wondered why I came?"

He shook his head. The thought had never occurred to him. He had been so wallowing in his own grief he had not thought of why.

"It wasn't to see Lady Mary. It was to find you," she admitted softly.

"What? Why me?" he asked, searching her face for answers. Hope bloomed.

Lucy met his eyes, holding them with her own. "I'm six and twenty, Phil, you know that. No one had offered for me. I think my brother saw to that. His love of gambling ate money. I was a confirmed spinster, or so I thought. Then you introduced me to Charles. I fell in love. No, we fell in love." She was trying to find the right words. "Phil, I never expected that to happen."

Phil smiled, "That's why I introduced you. I thought you would be perfect for each other, and I was correct," he said. He thought of his friend; they were a good match. Charles was a year older than her. Stable, handsome and a lovely person. He had not expected the jealousy he had felt.

Lucy took a deep breath and continued. "Phil, I know he was, and you were right. I adored him."

A flash of grief washed over her face. She lifted her head and looked Phil in the face again. "But, Phil, I came to offer myself to you as a wife. Someone to fill the lonely nights. Someone to talk to about Charlotte. I had always respected you, liked you, and even loved you. When Charles died, I just wanted you." She held his eyes. "Phil, you are my rock, my best friend. You have always been there for me, as I was for you when Charlotte died. You have always had a special place in my heart. Far more than a brother, more like the unattainable goal."

He gasped but let her continue. Searching her face, she still held his hands. His heart was now racing.

Lucy pushed on, "Don't get me wrong, I love... no, I loved, Charles; with my whole being. I would have been a loving and faithful wife. However, as a mother loves all her children, there has always been a place in my heart for you. Even if I had married Charles, you would still have been there." She had been holding his gaze the entire time. She dropped his hands and looked away, letting the words she had just said sink in.

A minute or so later, she turned back and looked at him again. She took a half step backwards. "Phil, I wanted to say this before we go back to the hotel. Today is our wedding day, and I am willing to make it a truly special night. If we wait to choose when the time would be right, it may never come." She blushed and turned aside again, embarrassed.

He laid a hand gently on her shoulder and turned her back to face him. He took her chin and lifted it with his fingers. He took a step and closed the gap. He brushed her cheek with the back of his fingers. So soft, her face so sweet and dear to him. He had known her all his life and spent many happy hours playing as children. She was far more than a sister to him. It had been her dark ringlets and green eyes that had haunted his dreams for a month. His voice was soft and gentle. "Lucy, last night I dreamed as I do most nights. Recently, they have been different. I have not woken to call Charlotte's name in a panic, as I've done for years." He moved his fingers, gently tracing her lips. "Lucy, I woke dreaming of you in my arms as I carried you."

It was her turn to gasp. Her eyes locked with his again, only this time they were pooled with unshed tears.

Phil's hand paused on her cheek, "My heart restarted that day a month ago. As I held you in my arms, my heart skipped a beat. You clung to me. You needed me. Lucy, it's your name I have been crying in my sleep for the past month; your face I keep seeing. I did not want to tell you, as I thought it was too soon. When Charles told me of your engagement, I realised I had been stupid. A wave of jealousy washed over me. I'm willing to commit to this marriage in any way you wish."

A look of astonishment settled on her face. A tear slid from her eye.

He brushed it away with his fingertip. Another rolled down her cheek and settled on her lip. Her eyes were still locked with his.

He again traced the outline of her lips with his thumb. Then he bent to claim them with his lips. He kissed her tenderly and drew her once more into his arms.

She reached up and drew him close. Their newly discovered love, still raw with pain, would bind them close.

~

Captain Roberts let Eddie steer the ferry down the harbour as he'd often done as a child returning home from school.

On arrival at the small wharf in Parramatta, a note awaited Eddie. Paddy handed it to him. It contained three words.

"Birth Imminent. Wills"

Ed wondered where everyone was. Vicky had delivered a healthy girl last week. A perfect gurgling bundle of joy, they named Sarah Joy. Now it was Cathy's turn.

Eddie handed his bag to Paddy and walked up the street to his brother's cottage. Wills was in the sitting room, pacing. He looked anxious. "Hello, Wills, everything all right? Why are you out here?" Eddie asked.

Wills was wiping his clammy hands on his trousers. "I can't go in there, Ed. Why it's just not done!" Wills said, aghast.

"I did, even Uncle Ned did. You won't regret it, trust me. Go. Use the privy then, scrub up." Eddie dragged him to the privy. "You won't have time to go later." He led him into the kitchen and made him scrub his hands. They walked to the bedroom.

Eddie opened the door. He was greeted by his mother. "All okay? How close?" he asked.

Sal said, "Yes, two minutes."

"Good, I've told Wills to go in," he grinned.

"Excellent," said Sal

She took her younger son aside and told him what to expect.

White with fear, Wills followed his mother. He looked back at Eddie for reassurance.

Wills's glance was met by a broad grin and a nod from his older brother.

Cathy was walking around the room. She stood in her nightgown. When she saw him, and reached out for her husband, he took her in his arms. Another contraction hit as he embraced her.

She grasped him tightly. "You got me into this; it's only fair you help me through it."

Her nails bit into his back as the pain increased. She groaned in pain. Her grasp was strong, and it hurt.

He didn't mind. He would do whatever she needed. His heart was in turmoil; how could he do this to her? Why did women willingly go through this pain?

It only took an hour before Luke Henry William Lockley entered the world—a healthy eight-pound bouncing baby.

When Eddie and Jenna joined them, Wills mouthed, "Thank you" to Eddie. He was sitting, holding her still.

She was wearing a brocade bed jacket. The smile on her face said it all. Finally, they were a family.

Wills sat silently, in awe of what he had just experienced.

Luke and young Neddie arrived home from school an hour later.

Luke was ecstatic to find a new nephew named after him. His reaction said it all. "Are you serious?" The smile spread across his face like quicksilver.

~

Captain Stephen Roberts had brought up a letter and parcel. He walked along to the top cottage and handed it to Charles.

"Mail," the Captain called as he knocked. "Charles, it's from Ned. Hopefully, they are home and safe, and all is well with them."

Charles read it.

He would take it along to Eddie. He unwrapped the accompanying parcel: two books and a bundle of newspapers. 'Old News' Ned used to call these. Charles chuckled.

Captain Roberts finished his tea and headed back to the river.

Charles went down the street to Eddie's house. He had devoured the letter and would pass it on.

Gracemere Castle,
Maidstone England
15 December 1847

"Christina's Cottage"
Phillip Street
Parramatta

My Very Dear Charles,

Greetings to all, from cold and blustery England. I already miss the permeating heat of an Australian summer. We arrived after four months at sea. This trip, we came via Cape Horn. Oh, how I wish for an alternate route. I have never seen such seas and winds. Mother and the children stayed abed for days as it was far too rough to stand.

Nanny broke her leg and the maids were prostrated with seasickness. Oh, how we thanked the good Lord that Edmund and John were with us. They were our saving sanity. Five under five is a trial at the best of times.

Now, where to start? Some Good News! Gerry and Annabella have a second son. I didn't even know another child was on the way. So now they have an heir and a spare. Matthew Henry arrived the week before we did. Gerry did not write to tell us, as he thought we might be home before he was born. So, we have eight under seven living in the Castle.

You may think a Castle with over two hundred rooms has plenty of space, but when there are eight children here. Well, life is never dull. Especially, now both girls are walking. Charlotte, or Charl is the boss and Izzy her shadow, but they are always together. They are mini versions of Sarah and follow her everywhere. She adores them. Oh, they will certainly, take London by storm, especially if we add some of your grandchildren.

On our arrival, we heard that the "Harpooner" had run aground and was stuck fast. No loss of life, but we are so pleased we were not on board.

Do you remember our conversation that day? We were both hesitant.

We're so pleased we refused the second passage on the repaired vessel. God certainly unsettled our hearts.

We had an 'interesting' passenger with us on board. We met another Lieutenant Simmons who looked uncannily like the other one. He was travelling with Major Smythe from the 58th. This Simmons claimed that the other one (his much older brother, I'm guessing) was disinherited by his family due to his predilection, or should I say, proclivity for young boys. When I informed him of his demise, which had occurred some twelve years before, he seemed overjoyed. He never owned up to the actual relationship but was relieved to be able to finally report to the family of his permanent absence from this world. He had been fearful of meeting him on his placement in the Colony. He admitted that he refused to ask about him. He received some odd looks, but no one had mentioned the other one.

Smythe and Simmons are returning from the Governor's protection detail. I believe Smythe is a friend of Phil's and the new Aide, Charles Master. Say hello to them both for us.

Other news is that Edmund and John are to start a new school here near Yalding on Vicarage Road. Their experience in Parramatta has inspired them. They are building it from scratch as soon as they return from visiting their families. We have offered them Bramblemere Cottage as a home base, as we feel it should be lived in. This is only until they get settled. Only God knows what's in the future after that.

John told his mother about Elle, and she said she was sad she never knew she was so close. However, they will come and visit soon. She said if Elle could do the trip, then she could too. She has met with Lilabet and Matthew.

We had word from both Lew and Aidan. Both are now fathers. Their ladies are well, as are their children. Lew and Fiona were surprisingly greeted with a warm welcome by her family. It seemed Fiona's father had no real animosity for Lew, but instead wanted to prod him to change his lifestyle. This he has done incredibly. He also now runs the local school as a sort of manager rather than headmaster. He has implemented some amazing changes in their community. They had a son in May, named after both their fathers, Colin Fergus Bland. Fiona's father, Colin. He is, of course, chuffed. They are coming for a visit with Lew's sisters in tow (At Mother's invitation). We expect them in February, after the snow has melted. Brrr. Did I say I do not like the cold?

Do you remember the December day last year when all the candles melted? Oh, I do miss it so much.

Aidan and Amelia also had an 'interesting' welcome—certainly not the one they expected. Ireland is in the middle of a horrific potato famine. Rather than start a school, they have begun many food kitchens. Amelia also had a boy, Eamon Liam. Named for Sal's Grandfather and Wills. The English translation of his name is Edward William. Nice, eh?

Charles, we have to pray for Ireland. The situation there is dire. Absolutely dire! There is no food. Their staple crop, potatoes, are rotting in the ground from 'blight'. No matter how much food we send, it is not enough. We have never grown potatoes here, but we do now. It's a new learning curve! We have sent much food and will continue to do so. (We have been sending it directly to a church on the west side of the island.) Gerry and I have put all our fallow land to crop and ship it all to Ireland. I have brought Sal's family, the O'Shanes, here for the duration; some of the older O'Keefes have come too. They initially objected, but there is no food to buy over there. Money is not the issue. Aidan insisted that his own parents escort them, so they are here for the duration as well. They are advising us on how to tend the new crop.

I have not waited for the Government to supply Aid. We have mobilised the local landholders, and every available acre is now under cultivation, with many fields planted with potatoes. As it is in Southern Ireland, no help will be forthcoming from our Government. We will do everything we can for them. Thankfully, we had a bumper harvest last year, and Gerry had all the barns full. We have a personal contact with the minister of a Catholic church and can send our crops to him. He is the half-brother of my own chaplain. We have sent much of the food on hand to them immediately. He runs a food kitchen for the starving. I have ordered quick crops to be planted. Hopefully, what we have sent will sustain them until more food is grown locally. Earl Grey and I are in talks at how we can assist further.

On a lighter note, I am enclosing two new Novels. They are written by the "Bell" siblings.

Christina said Sal would like them. There are rumours that the authors of both are female. They are 'Wuthering Heights' and 'Jane Eyre'. The accents are a bit thick, but the storylines are good. (Mother made me read them. They are quite good.) There is also a bundle of 'recent' newspapers. So you may enjoy reading all the 'old news'.

I hope that by now, all the buildings for 'Wills' project are nearing completion. I have purchased goods and have sent them on three ships as ballast, splitting the load. Hopefully, they will all arrive intact. If a ship founders, then we have not lost all. I have added more items to the order that I think could be good and a few for templates for Eddie. Something called sluices, also ingot moulds and crucibles for melting the mineral.

I send my greetings to the Fitzroys. I'm so glad they are so much easier to work with than Gipps.

I hope your mother and her new husband are well. Have you settled to the idea of a new father? (I chuckle- for I could not!) I hope so, for her sake. I know I shall love my Christina for as long as I live.

I hear all the children are descending upon me! I must away.

I shall sign off for now. I look forward to your news.

Ned

Gracemere

PS Your Aunt Emily and Uncle Mark plan to visit as soon as John is settled. They have noted he is much changed and far more settled. Expect them to stay for some time. Lilabet and Matthew may travel with them.

Ned

Charles quickly replied.

Christina's Cottage
Phillip Street
Parramatta
15 December 1847

Gracemere Castle,
Maidstone England

Dear Ned,

I hope you have arrived home safely—no more leaky boats.

I pour out sad tidings in this epistle. We have just returned from the double funeral of Lady Mary Fitzroy and Lieutenant Charles Master. The town stopped. The accident occurred on December 7th.

Oh, Ned, we are all grieving. They were on their way to Eddie's for Morning Tea to meet the children and have private discussions. Lady Mary wanted to meet all the babies, so they had made arrangements for a 10.15 a.m. tea.

Sometime after that, Anna arrived in tears, informing us of her demise. Suffice it to say, we are shocked.

We hot-footed it up to GH. We found to our dismay the remnants of their carriage. And as the newspapers have reported 'A Melancholy Accident'. The horses bolted on Sir Charles. They were too fresh. Lady Mary was killed instantly.

Charles Master died at 7 p.m. that night. Phil, too, is in shock as he and Charles had grown close. Phil had introduced him to one of his Charlotte's friends, Charles and Lucy had only become engaged the day before. Sadly, they had not inserted the notice, and she is receiving no condolences at all. Lady Mary was to have been her chaperone. Lucy, therefore, moved in with Eddie and Jenna as she had nowhere else to go. She was, as you can imagine, prostrated with grief. The entire Colony is in shock, with some three thousand mourners turning out for their joint funeral. Charles Master's entire Battalion (58th), lined Church Street.

The Governor was injured (his leg), and their son George, working as his second Aide, had cuts and bruises. George and Charles' brother Robert Master (also in the 58th) led the mourners with Sir Charles following in a carriage. Oh, Ned, Lady Mary was so loved. She is already missed, as is Charles.

At least Lucy was allowed to be by Charles' side as he died. Robert, Phil and the Gov insisted she was allowed to stay with him until he died. She has no one here but Phil, a childhood neighbour and friend.

Now about Mother - I should now say, Mrs Childs. They married by Banns just three weeks after you left. My mind is still not used to her being with a man, any man, as I barely remember my father. He died when I was five. However, it's nice to see her so happy. She works with Richard daily at school and is relishing the joy and love she can show the little girls. She is giving 'Grooming and Deportment' classes to the older students and also gardening classes for all ages. Well, Paddy does all the actual digging, but she does the teaching. She grew all our food for years, so she does know what she's talking about. Paddy is her slave.

Vicky and Cathy's interesting conditions are advancing well. Both are in good health. The buildings are progressing, including Charlie's new house, 'Willow Grove'. Wills and Cathy's house in Emu is now nearing completion. Harry's will follow. The foundations are in for that.

The Bathurst Emporium is complete. Buildings in Bathurst are being constructed at a faster rate than we can deliver the materials. New, larger wagons have been purchased. One has a team of twelve draught horses and three drivers. Wagon trains of building supplies and tools are delivered on a weekly basis. They backload with fodder and grain. I cannot imagine what it will be like when the word finally leaks out. It will be all hands on deck. The stock continues to build.

I will write again after the babies are born.
Charles

~

Christina's Cottage

Phillip Street
Parramatta
20 January 1848

Gracemere Castle,
Maidstone England
Dear Ned,

A quick note to let you know both babes have been born safely. Vicky and Harry's 'Sarah Joy' arrived on 7th January. They ask that you please make sure you tell your mother. They said you would know why. Eddie made Harry attend the birth. He's pleased he did.

I was involved with our Luke's birth by default. Sal had not told me she was having pains all day. He came so fast. Molly and I were the only ones near for some time. I have always felt somewhat closer to him than the others. We take our pleasure with our wives; they pay with pain. I have learnt to never underestimate what our women can bear. The next week (14th Jan) Eddie had been in Sydney (more about that later) and Paddy met him at the wharf to let him know that the next birth was imminent. Ed arrived in time to prep Wills and send him in to Cathy. An hour later Luke Henry William was born. All parents survived and no complications. Both babes are beautiful and are thriving.

As I wrote in my letter last month of the horrific accident, poor Lucy Norfolk was at a standstill. The short version is Phil and Lucy are married.

They went to Sydney last week with Eddie and Robert Master (Charles' brother) and were married by Special Licence from the Bishop Broughton himself. Phil, as we know, is, or was, grief-stricken from the loss of his fiancée, Charlotte, some years ago. He consulted me soon after the accident, as to what he should do. He planned to propose to Lucy to give her some security. On his return from Sydney, he again spoke to me, unbeknownst to him, Lucy had come to seek out Phil and to offer a 'marriage of convenience'. Lucy was a close friend of Charlotte and of his from childhood.

However, she fell in love with Charles instead. Phil and Lucy had always been close, closer than we knew, or they ever acknowledged to each other. They arrived back from their honeymoon yesterday smelling of April and May. So, not so 'Marriage of convenience' after all. Phil no longer has that haunted look of grief. He is happy, as is Lucy. They can talk about their losses to the other. Though it may have started through grief, this marriage will work, of that I'm sure.

Mother and Richard are going from strength to strength. The school is thriving as are the girls. Some of the programs John and Edmund started have now been fully integrated into their curriculum. 'Mr Phil' and Mrs Corsairs (Lucy) regularly join the others in the classes, they are a bit of a loose end.

Some of the literate women from the workhouses have been released to help both teach and learn. It's certainly wonderful to have their help. Harry sometimes attends to assist with 'story time' with Mother.

Wills is busy with his two new Emporiums and the Warehouse, but manages to pop into our Emporium or the Smithy whenever they are in town. Cathy and baby Lukie travel with him wherever he goes. They have a special cradle built into their carriage, and their baby travels well.

Harry has finally found someone willing to take Sophia off his hands. A Spanish sailor and his wife have moved into town, and they can make themselves understood. They are pleased to see her leave. Harry and Vicky can now hire some decent staff. I wonder if you could find some staff for us?

In the meantime, Mother has sent two of the older girls from the school and Vicky is training them. This will be another avenue for the students. Surprisingly, Maureen has been an exceptional teacher for them.

Phil and Lucy are still staying with the Harry and Vicky. The girls get along well and are good company for each other. As Roseneath is so large, there is plenty of room for them all. Phil and Harry head to work together most days. They have the Warehouse humming.

Phil and Lucy are considering moving to Bathurst, but will wait until things are a little more settled with them. They are, however, very happy together. It is a love match now. They are more surprised than us.

Even with all the new buildings, the 'news' has not leaked out yet. Hopefully, the road will need to be vastly improved before it does. The governor has used this project to channel his grief. I visit him regularly to ensure he is coping. Their son is still in shock. This is to happen soon. I will keep this short, just one sheet.

Stay well, and I send our love to all.

Charles

Gracemere Castle,
Maidstone England
20 April 1848

c/-Christina's Cottage
Phillip Street

Parramatta

Dear Charles, although this is addressed to you all!

I have just received your December letter, Charles. I am, no, we, are all shattered! I had heard a whisper last week of some tragic accident in Sydney. I did not know how closely you were all involved. My heart bleeds for Lucy, Sir Charles and George. Please send our sincere condolences to both Lucy and Phil. I have to digest the implications, but it's a tragedy. Somehow, I feel that God will have a plan in this, even though we cannot see it yet. I am glad George is sticking close to his father. Replacing Sir Charles would be extremely hard. George is known to be very capable. I'm sure he will excel in the role.

Charles, there have been the first few whispers of the possibility of 'certain' finds being found in New South Wales since the California Rush. People are now looking or speaking out where they have previously kept silent. Someone produced a small smelted ingot in 1845. They kept the information quiet for over two years. Word says it's from somewhere around Berry or Goulburn. If this is so, then the mineral could be further spread than we imagine. I feel it is not long now. The fever has hit here. So far, all with the fever are heading to California. Few ships are going elsewhere. It's just as well that I bought the goods I did last year, as there are none left now. All mining tools are sold out. Even pig iron is in short supply. Smithy's and Foundries are working non-stop here, making tools.

Now to a more disheartening topic.

Charles, I must tell you about the famine. Numbers of over 400,000 have died. We will never know the exact numbers. Living skeletons sleep in graves, knowing they will never awaken. Death is everywhere. Our Government is still doing little. If you can believe it food is now being grown in Ireland; however, it is all being exported by the government. There is no money for the poor to buy food even if it were available. Potatoes will still not grow. This blight is still in the soil. Hundreds of pounds of food, butter, grain and livestock leave Ireland monthly. We are still sneaking in our shipments through the back door.

Somehow, we need to find a way for the Irish poor to earn a living. It's a vicious circle. I feel many will emigrate. Many will follow the gold too, as at least there they can obtain money for food. Canada and California are already reaping the rewards of that. I am considering chartering a ship and offering passage to Australia. The O'Shanes and O'Keefes could sort out the passengers as they know which group is the most needy. (They, by the way, have all now returned home.) It may well be some of the older orphans. Some of these young people could be trained to work as house staff, others as gardeners or drivers, and they are also skilled in leatherwork and other cottage crafts. Eddie could do with some qualified help at the forge and his new foundry, and Wills needs drivers. Earl Grey and I are collaborating and working on a plan.

Many are skilled at building rock walls, and others are carpenters. I will start asking around for a suitable ship. Aidan can be my liaison. I believe he's just sent his third shipment to Wills. The Irish are great smiths, and this is one thing they can make at this time.

My mind is made up. I shall endeavour to do this. I will fill the hull with a cargo of Irish made goods for Wills, especially with roofing and meshes for sieves. These flat-pack and transport easily.

On to brighter things. Mother sends her greetings and her congratulations to Elle and Richard. To ease her loneliness, she, too, is now inspired to start a 'story-time' for the little girls at John and Edmund's school. We finally decided to rebuild the local schools in both Maidstone and Coxheath. Christina and Annabella both attend with her. Lilabet, too, if she is around, which sadly, is not often. Her little Matty is so cute, he loves following the others. All children of school age at Castle are attending the local school, with our Governess in charge of the junior class. Chip's Tutor is in charge of the senior class. Why we had never thought of this before, I do not know; however, now that we have Chip's tutor working there and the older children in the village do not often miss classes. If they do, often one of their family is ill. Gerry keeps a close eye on the health of the villagers. Our children, of course, love learning as they have many new playmates to enjoy. This will bode well in the future, I'm sure. As Christina and Annabella take our children with them, the village children follow their example. The kudos of being at school with the future duke inspire all the students not to skip school, as you used to do, Charles. Chip and Sarah encourage all the other students and are inspiring their friends to work hard. At just six, they each understand their roles in inspiring their friends, and they lead by example. Both have come to me at different times, stating the need for one friend or another. Gerry has started a free Medical Clinic, and the health of the area is slowly improving. I may find a cottage for him to work from in the village. He wishes to start a proper hospital, and this could be a way to ease into that.

Charles, Wills is responsible for all of this. His simple question that night so long ago has had far-reaching effects. Sewing lessons are next for the girls. Mother has sourced ten bolts of fabric in bright colours, and her seamstress has cut out some dress patterns. They are teaching the village women how to sew them. The older girls also join the adult class. Some of the Castle laundry staff are showing the village wives how to wash their clothing, generally and adequately, to stay healthy. Teaching gardening and carpentry will follow for the boys (as well as where not to use the lye soap). Something as simple as changing the straw in the mattresses regularly is unknown to them. From now onwards, at the beginning of Spring and Autumn, I will ensure that there is sufficient straw is available for their use.

I asked more of my staff and they suggested training more foresters, hunters, hedge-makers and other 'cottage craft skills' like thatching. Therefore, more apprentices are being added daily. It is beginning to show in the pride they are all now taking in the various villages. Even the grass road edges are being kept trimmed regularly and tidy. The cut grass is dried and used a stock feed. How did we, no I, never see these problems before? How did I miss the basics? These are my people, and I failed them.

Everyone here is well. I do, however, have some interesting news. I told you in my last letter that Lew and Fiona were coming to visit. Lew is playing on the relationship big time. And we love it. Scotland is very, very cold this year, and the snow has not yet melted. They came by sea. They were accompanied by Lew's sisters, Catriona and Elspeth. They have been here for three months already. I think the ladies will at least stay... IF (wait for it...) John and Edmund come up to scratch. Yes, amazing, isn't it, and more connections of the family trees. The men seem to be here frequently. The four are constantly together with Lew, Fiona and little cute red-headed Colin.

Cat and Else (as they like to be called) are at the school in Yalding daily with John and Edmund. They have been teaching Grooming, Deportment and Cleanliness, as well as assisting with sewing. The two ladies (in their mid-twenties) have thrown themselves into the school.

I found an unused baby grand piano in one of the rooms I had never been into, so I had it moved to their school, along with another upright one to be sent to each of the other schools. We are also building a hall for our Maidstone one so the children can run around in the cold and wet weather. A piano will be moved into that when it's finally completed. Already, some children have shown promise on the piano. Even if they can pick a tune to play in the church, it will be worthwhile. Both ladies too, have grown in their faith since they have been here. Our church has never been so full. My chaplain, Hugh James, is ecstatic.

On my return here I visited our Reverend. He had written and requested an interview. He, Reverend Hector James, wished to retire. His nephew was newly ordained and was looking for a living before he married. Would I consider allowing him to take over the Parish? I insisted on meeting the young man and his fiancé.

Reverend Hugh James is an inspiring young man. I gave the living to him willingly. He is truly a man of strong faith and full of the joy of our Lord, and Isabel is a loving, capable woman who will be a wonderful helpmate for him. I suggested that Reverend Hector marry them and then allow a fortnight honeymoon before they took up the role of Rector. This has all happened, and Hugh and Isabel have become deeply involved in the growth of the towns.

They are amazed that in private we are all on first-name terms. I asked him to call me 'Ned', but he finds he cannot. So I am Duke. But as their friendship grows with our younger ones this may change. He is Hugh to us all. Their youth, passion and involvement have filled a void that Reverend Hector was too old to do. They are of an age to Lew's sisters and they have become firm friends. At Hugh's instigation, I now lead a weekly Bible Study group. Oh, Charles, this is so rewarding. We all learn so much from each other. Even children are welcome. Their questions cut through our preconceived beliefs. Just like Wills' question to his six friends. Their faith is so pure. We hold them at the church in Maidstone, so all can attend. Our group is getting so large that Gerry is preparing to split our group and lead the other one. Hugh to lead a third in the Church Hall. Then we are to join together for supper afterwards.

One child summed up our life last study. With large innocent eyes, this little four-year-old looked lovingly at me after prayers one day and simply stated: "Ain't God grand." I totally agree. I leave to start my new project.

When a shipload of starving Irish immigrants comes knocking on your door one day, they come with our blessing and references! They will be accompanied by more Irish goods for sale at the Emporiums.

Ha ha- Enjoy! Just hope you can find them some honest work.

Again, our sincere condolences to all.

With love to all.

Ned

Chapter 19   It's Time

*F*our years had passed since Harry bought Roseneath.

Dressed in his brocade dressing gown, he stood at the door of his children's bedroom. His heart flipped. What was it about this room that brought a tear to his eye? Their three beautiful cherubs were peacefully asleep.

Vicky walked up to him and slipped her hand into his. He drew her to him and kissed her hair. Still smelling deliciously of lemon. She wrapped her arms around her beloved husband's waist. She laid her hair against his chest. They stood in awe of the blessings God had given them. "Harry, I want more," she said looking up at him. "As many more as God will bless us with."

He looked down to her smiling face. He bent his head and brushed his lips over hers. "I am at your command, my love," he murmured, then took possession of her mouth. His passion building, he bent and picked her up, carrying her to their bedroom.

Wills and Cathy had come in from their house at Emu Plains, known as Emu Hall, to celebrate Kit's 4th birthday.

Gracemere Cottage, the Duke's old cottage, was kept in readiness for any family visitors who needed a bed. This was the first family gathering since Charles' Aunt Emily and Uncle Mark had returned to England. Lilabet and the two Matthews had come with them, but not stayed as long.

John was right; Aunt Emily was so like his mother. No wonder he was surprised. Gracemere Close was also Wills and Cathy's second home. Their three children settled quickly. After the initial difficulties conceiving, the next two children came without any problems. Lukie was quickly followed by Phillip, called Pip, in September '48 and Tilda, Catherine Victoria Matilda, in March last year. Cathy had fallen again in October while feeding Tilda, which was a big surprise. She had bad morning sickness this time, something that had previously passed by three months, but in the last week, things were settling down. She had gone to bed early, claiming tiredness. Wills still had only to think of her, and his heart skipped. Mother to three, expecting another and still finding time to teach at the orphan school. Their nocturnal activities were not confined to just nighttime. One thing he had discovered about Cathy was that her expectant condition raised, rather than lessened, her desire for him. He crept into their room and drew off his dressing gown. He carefully sat on the bed, planning to slip in beside her and sleep. As he lay down her hand reached for him.

"Wills," she said softly, "I can't sleep." She traced her fingers over the neckline of his chest. She pulled him to her. "Wills, are you tired?"

"You should be asleep, love," he chuckled. He divested himself of his nightshirt and pulled her into his arms, "And, no, I'm not that tired." In the moonlight, he could see her smile. He pushed a lock of hair from her face, then leaned over and gently kissed her. She wrapped her arms around him, and there was no more conversation for some time.

Half an hour later, she lay in his arms, content and sated. "Wills, can you believe we've been married for nearly six years?"

"I know, my love. I still break into a cold sweat when I think of my feelings for you and how uncertain I was about you returning them, and that's getting on for seven years ago."

She was snuggled into his neck, one arm thrown across his chest. He lay thinking. They had only been teenagers, he eighteen and she seventeen, when they became engaged. Jack had made them wait before marrying, which occurred on 14th February 1845.

Cathy murmured, "Wills, do you remember that trip to Hartley? The week we four sat around the campfire and prayed. Beseeching God to bless us both with children?"

He thought she was asleep. "Yes, love. I remember it well. I also remember your response to not falling. The love you showed to Vicky still astounds me."

She didn't move, but continued to speak softly against his neck. "Wills, I want to go back, but this time also to your Duck Creek, or whatever they call it now. Oppif, Phiro, what is it? Something to do with King Solomon and the Bible, though."

"Ophir, love," he corrected her lovingly. "Why, love?"

"I had a dream that we were going to have to show someone where to look." She fell silent.

"Cathy, have you had another one of those dreams?" he asked.

She didn't reply, but he could feel her nodding.

Over the last six years, he had learnt that God had blessed her with another extraordinary gift. She had normal dreams like everyone.

Occasionally, though, she had ones that were different. Some good, some bad. The worst was the day of Lady Mary Fitzroy's death.

That day, she had woken in a cold sweat, crying, and she was inconsolable for some time. When the news finally came with Vicky, it was almost with relief. For she had seen Charles, Phil, and Eddie in her dream but not Wills and had not confided this to him. She had sat in bed rocking for some time. Her eyes closed, and she was praying. When the horrific news finally came, as soon as he arrived home, she ran to Wills and poured out all her fears. She was no less sad, but it was not one of her family. She had fallen to her knees and thanked God that her family was all safe.

They finally fell asleep. All was at peace.

~

Early 1851

One night, after a midnight feed for Tilda, but a few month before their fourth baby was due, Cathy sleepily said, "Wills, we are ready. I dreamed the Governor will send a letter with someone, and we need to accompany him. It will be soon." She snuggled closer. "If this is so, we have to be ready."

"Oh, all right, Cathy, sure?" Wills asked.

She reached up and kissed his cheek. "Yes, night, love."

Her steady breathing against his neck told him she was already asleep. He lay in the dark, his heart racing. He too closed his eyes, but to pray. "Thank you, God, for giving us the time we needed. We hand the reins to you again and ask that you lead us on this new venture. Bless the colony and bless us. Amen."

Having handed the journey over to God, he relaxed and slept.

On waking the next morning, Cathy greeted him with a long, loving kiss. "Wills, I had that dream again. We have to get ready. Today, Wills. Did I say something last night? I can't remember."

"Yes, you did, but you didn't mention when. I have already thought of the plan, love. I'll call around to Harry and get him prepared. You start organising what we'll need, and we'll call in at Emu to get anything else. All the children can come too. It may be the last break we get for some time, maybe even years." His heart was pounding. They had been preparing for this day for what seemed like an eon. Now the time was here. Wills heard Tilda cry and knew the day had started. He bent and kissed Cathy, grabbed his dressing gown and went to change Tilda and bring her to be fed. At ten months old, she now received her morning and evening comfort feeds. Occasionally, Cathy gave her a midnight feed, as she was teething.

Cathy still wanted that precious time alone with her before the other children woke. Lukie and Pip were full-on from the moment they woke. Wills chuckled, thinking back to what he and his little brother were like. By the time he returned with Tilda, Cathy had slipped on her nightgown and was sitting in bed waiting for her daughter. This had been their routine since Lukie arrived. As she fed the baby, Wills would make her a cup of tea. He would then bring it to her after she finished feeding. He would have his first cuddle of the day with their child while burping her. It was bonding time for them all. This way, he too was involved, but he did it because he loved Cathy. He had been with her during each confinement and supported her through them. He sat playing gently with Tilda after her feed. He had learnt very early on with Lukie not to bounce or be too rough, as more than once he would be covered with milk spit.

It was nice being the boss. He had no one to report to if you're late to work. He chuckled to himself.

Cathy finished her tea, and sounds were coming from the other room. The boys were awake. The day had started for everyone.

An hour later, Wills harnessed Felix at the stables down at the inn. It was too hot to walk to the Roseneath, and he had to see Harry before heading to the warehouse to work. There was much to do, and now a holiday of sorts to plan. The rush was about to begin. He trusted God, and he trusted Cathy. The last time Harry and he had met with Governor Fitzroy, some two months ago, the Governor had been able to whisper, "Soon. All is ready!"

Wills' reply had been a look and a nod. "Soon" had been a long time coming. That was weeks ago.

Harry met Wills on the front verandah of Roseneath. He was leaning against one of the fancy pillars, drinking a mug of tea. He saw Wills' massive, dappled grey stallion before he saw Wills. Together, they looked nearly as magnificent as his older brother Eddie on his now ageing black stallion James. Wills and Felix were a sight to behold.

The bond between these two men went well beyond mere friendship—encompassing best friend, mentor, partner, family, and even brother-in-law. Harry had nothing but admiration for Wills, and it was reciprocated. The fifteen years separating them were as nothing.

"Morning, Wills, to what do we owe this pleasure?" greeted Harry.

"Morning, Harry, got some more tea?" asked Wills.

It was not that he needed it, but more of a code they had developed for "I need to talk."

"Sure, Boss," Harry chuckled as he tied Felix's reins to the hitching post under the tree. It was cooler there, and there was a small water trough.

Wills smiled each time Harry referred to him thus.

He made tea for Wills and carried it out to the back garden where they could talk without prying eyes or ears.

"Cathy had another dream, Harry. Officially, we're all going on 'holiday'. You are both to come with the children, and we're to take someone else. We don't know who yet. If Sir Charles' hint last November was anything to go by…" he paused, thinking. "Harry, send the first load of panning stuff to Bathurst. Just a small load this time, but have a selection for prospectors."

Harry smiled. "Funny thing, I've had a feeling it was getting close, too. It's sorted, packed and ready to go. It just needs loading. It seems God has been prepping us all."

Wills grinned. The faith they shared was part of their bond. They were both now part of Charles Lockley's Bible Study group. Reverend Bobart came as often as he could, but Charles led the group. There were so many men in it that they split into three smaller groups for study—one in the sitting room, one in the office and one in the dining room. Then join together for supper and discussion. Ned had inspired this four years before. He had been inspired by Wills and their campfires.

Between Harry and Wills, nothing was out of bounds, including strange dreams. "Harry, we're going to Duck Creek first, then Hartley on the way back. Makes me wonder if there's been another rockfall after all the rain. Cathy's dream said we have to show someone. We need a break anyway. This will be the last break we get once this takes off. So, pack for an adventure, a week at least, hopefully two. It's a great time for the children, too. I just hope the dingoes are gone. We'll collect Phil and Lucy on the way. Hope she's up to it after the birth of Charles. I heard he was a big baby. Little Charlotte should be fine, though; she's three." Wills fell silent, thinking about Phil and Lucy. After a while, he said, "Isn't God amazing how He brought Lucy and Phil together? Their love for each other and naming their children after their lost loves. I am in awe of their strength."

"So true, Wills. Phil is a changed man. He opened right up the last time I saw him." Harry thought back to their conversation. "He truly loves her. I wondered at first. However, it was sad that it took Charles Master's death to reveal how he felt. We all need to be needed."

"I would love to have them with us," Wills admitted.

"Oh, that would be nice. Sort of like old times," Harry said. "Deal. I'll get packing. For how long? Two weeks? Three?" he asked. "Can we stretch it out a bit, Boss?" He grinned.

Wills shrugged. "Plan for three, two at Duck Creek. But who knows?" He turned to go, then turned back. "Harry, these things, Cathy's dreams, seem to occur within a few days. So we don't have long. The letter may even come today."

"Okay, Wills. I'm on to it." Yet, Harry still didn't move.

Wills walked back through the house, greeting Vicky and his nephews and niece along the way. "Hi, Vicky." He gave her a brotherly kiss in greeting. The new maids were tidying the room. He whispered,

"Go talk to Harry." Then he quickly left.

Vicky watched him go. She asked her lovely Irish maids to look after the children and walked out the back to find Harry. She found him in the stables. "Wills sent me, love," she said as she walked into his arms. "What's up?" she whispered.

"Nothing, love, at least not yet. Cathy had a dream to prepare," he said simply.

Vicky knew Cathy's dreams of old.

"Oh!" She stood looking him in the eye. "And...?"

"We're going on a holiday and apparently taking someone whom we have yet to meet." He bent and intended to brush her lips. She pulled him to her and opened her lips to meet his.

A long time later, he lifted his head, and she murmured against his lips, "Oh, love," she finally said. "Remember the first time we went to Hartley together?"

His senses still reeling from her passion, holidays were not on his mind; his body was fighting his thoughts, but he pulled himself together. "We're not going there until the return trip, but out beyond Bathurst. We'll meet Phil and Lucy and take them as well. We're finally taking you to our Duck Creek."

"I don't care where you take me - just take me." She once more drew his head down to hers.

They walked to the back of the stables out of the sight of the kitchen. There was a convenient pile of straw placed for such romantic trysts. It was hard to be alone with a house full of staff and children. A little bit naughty, but a lot nice.

She was insatiable.

He didn't mind at all.

~

Captain Roberts pulled the ferry into the wharf. Today was his last day. There were only four passengers on board, and they had asked directions to Wills' house. He wanted to see the family he had grown so close to over the last twenty years, and let them know of his retirement. They knew he was thinking of retirement, but not when it would occur. At sixty-seven, he should have retired ages ago. However, it was an easy job and he loved it. He thought back to the first day he'd taken Eddie to Sydney with Tim and Thomas Tindale, the small blonde lad in awe of everything he saw. It was hard to believe twenty years had passed. Eddie was now thirty. He had seen each milestone, been invited to each Wedding, Baptism party, and he and his wife stayed with them as guests for the funeral four years ago. Yes, he wanted to say farewell.

When Edward Hargraves had boarded, he had been handed a note in a crested envelope from Governor Fitzroy.

𝓕

It was instructions from the Governor.

"Captain Roberts, can you please direct these men to meet William Lockley.

C F."

This man, Hargreaves, did not travel alone. Others were with him: brothers William and James Tom. Something didn't sit well with him, but he couldn't put his finger on it. The Tom brothers sounded as though they had hired Hargreaves as a guide. He had no idea why. He had never met him before. They didn't seem really friendly with each other either.

Parramatta now had a permanent deckhand on the wharves. The Captain left the Ferry in his care. No one else used the Ferry wharf. It had been built when river traffic became so much that the Ferry had often had to wait to dock.

Wills was rarely in Parramatta these days. He and Cathy had moved to Emu Hall some time ago. Maybe the governor knew something he didn't. He knew they could be in town this week, as there was a party. Kit was turning four. Hopefully, their timing was good. If there, Wills should be leaving for work about now. He knew, however, that if he were meant to find him, he would.

Captain Roberts also trusted God, and if the meeting was meant to be, then God could sort that out, too. He had a simple faith and firm trust. He did not need to understand, only believe, and he did.

The men followed behind the ferry captain.

Wills answered the door to his friend. "Welcome, Captain Roberts. We've been expecting you." He gave a cheeky smile and then looked over his shoulder. "Cathy, our guests have arrived, love."

She emerged from the kitchen, baby on her hip and two small children at her heels. "Welcome, the cake is just out of the oven. The kettle is on. Please come in."

Captain Roberts did the introductions.

Edward Hargraves looked puzzled. He muttered, "How can you be expecting us? We didn't even know we were coming."

Wills and Cathy looked at each other, smiled and then Wills replied, "No, we didn't, but God did."

This puzzled the visitors even more.

Captain Robert's merely chuckled and shook his head.

Mr Hargraves handed Wills a letter.

Wills turned to look at Cathy and showed it to her, flipping it in the air. "Right on time, love."

She merely nodded.

Wills smiled and slit open the Governor's personal stationery. It message contained just five words.

$\mathcal{F}$

5th January 1851
It's time! Show them where.
Sir Charles Fitzroy

"Ready, love?" Wills asked Cathy.

"Nearly, sweets, the last batch of biscuits is in now," she replied. "You take them to the sitting room. Can you take the boys too, please? They'll eat the middle from the fresh loaves if I let them go," she said. She'd caught Wills doing this more than once. Thick with fresh butter and sweet clover honey.

Captain Roberts made his excuses and went to find Charles, Eddie and Charlie. He said his farewells to Wills, who promised to catch up with him in Sydney on his next visit.

Wills took the visitors into the sitting room, one young boy in each hand.

Mr Hargraves sat on the edge of his seat. "Sir, I'm puzzled. Are you expecting us?" he asked enquiringly.

Wills gave a half-laugh, "Yes, and not exactly." Wills thought, "How do I explain without giving too much away?" After smiling at them, he said, "Suffice it to say I have been expecting the letter, but did not know the bearer of it." He swallowed, tugging at his collar. Knowing what was ahead of them and how one of these men would be famous, he didn't really envy whichever man it was. Wills could have taken that path, but it was not the one God wanted for him. Wills and his friends could well have kept the glory for themselves. Now the entire colony, no, the entire state could grow and benefit, he thought.

"Sir," Wills explained, "We are preparing for a holiday west. We shall accompany you for some distance and then point you in the right direction. From there, you will be on your own. We are going for a break. You will not wish to stay with us as we shall have eight small children with us, possibly even more." He thought that would be the best explanation.

Hargraves said, "But we have not even told you what we need? Or even asked for help."

The four looked confounded.

"No, you haven't, have you?" Wills chuckled. "The letter said all I needed to know." He smiled as he picked up his youngest son.

Mr Hargraves saw the letter sitting on the table; it had two lines and no directions.

Pip wanted a cuddle.

Wills explained, "The Governor and I have had various

discussions as to exploration of the western area. He said I am to help who he sends. I am friends with Reverend Clarke." His statement had the desired effect. He noted the eyes of the mens' lit up.

"Ahh, I see you know his name. He was my teacher and mentor. He taught me much," Wills said. "Now, down to business. Do you have wagons? Or anything?"

They said no, and all sat talking for half an hour. Wills then gave them a prepared list of what they would need. They took themselves off to rejoin the ferry. Hargraves knew he would need to cash in the bits of gold he had found on his failed trip to California. He needed a wagon, beasts and equipment. They could buy their own transport and stock up on supplies in Sydney, then meet them two days hence at the Warehouse. They would overnight there in the new holding yards and depart on the third morning.

Wills sent word to Phil and Lucy as soon as they had departed. This would give them a few days' notice. He called a meeting that night for all the family men to meet at Eddie's house.

"It's time. Dar, would you run the inn, please? Robert, would you oversee the store, while Eddie and Charlie could attack the Warehouse and start arranging the goods in stock? Harry has the list ready of what to send to the two Western Emporiums." He handed it to them. "All will be needed to help out where required. We need a load for them to buy from Bathurst in two weeks. Do you think Uncle Thomas could man the forge with the help of the lads?"

Eddie nodded, smiling to himself. This young brother of his could have had everything, but instead, he chose to share with everyone.

Wills paused, thinking. "We still have some months' grace for the bulk of the stuff, but I'd like a shipment to go up now. We have to stock both the Emu and Bathurst Emporiums in secret. Transport is still slow. We need to start now before the word spreads, or others will become suspicious. Remember, we don't know if these fellows will stay quiet, and if they do, for how long. Bathurst is currently set up only for building products. Phil does have a few items in his house, but not in commercial quantities. At least we've now got a manager up there, too. We will inform James King upon arrival that we expect the onslaught to begin. That Emporium there will take the biggest conversion."

The new lockable stockroom had been completed only last month. Some stock was in readiness. Many of the special items had been carefully stored at Phil's house in a spare room. This now had to be surreptitiously moved into the storeroom under the cover of mislabelled cartons. Their staff had no idea what was in them, only that they were in the way. A few gold scales, sieve sets, and gold pans were in readiness. The sluices, washboards and larger equipment would be sent up over the next month.

Cathy suggested that on their return, the mattresses be stripped from the wagons, more obvious items be sent up in the covered wagons under the mattresses. The bedding would cover the items.

Wills had two other visits to make. The first was to Major Bond. Governor Fitzroy would surely send more troops, but he wanted David to be let in on the secret. There would explain much to him.

The second visit would be to Mr Moffatt. He, too, needed to prepare. Once the miners started to arrive, the rabble and trouble would follow. The government printer had already printed the mine leases. These sat in his personal safe. Mr Moffatt had also built a gold storage vault under the courthouse. It already had some ingots in it, some of Wills' gold. Much was still held in the false-bottomed cask in Eddie's cellar.

One item that the forge had been busy making was gold ingot moulds. Eddie had even added a seal-type mark on the bottom of each new mould; *Au NSW*. Uncle Ned had included some ceramic crucibles for smelting gold; these were already well used, but the ingot moulds could be made from the pig iron. These were made after the apprentices had gone home for the evening. They had a good stockpile and these were now in the cupboard in the back visitor's bedroom of Mr Tindale's house.

Mr Moffatt took Wills by the shoulders. "All right, lad. Now the hard work is going to start. Are you ready?" He had looked Wills in the eyes. As a friend of Uncle Ned, he was the one person Wills had confided in. Harry Moffatt not only knew all the people involved, but more importantly, he knew Wills and his anxieties about the entire project. Wills confided his inability actually to do what God asked of him. To everyone else, Wills presented a brave face. Mr Moffatt had also prayed with him and been a guide. Everyone needed that one person who could be their sounding board. Harry Moffatt became Wills' confidante.

The three days blew out as Hargreaves was slow in sourcing the necessary items. He didn't bother asking Wills, or he could have bought everything except the wagons and horses at the warehouse. Wills was pleased he hadn't, as it would have let the cat out of the bag. The delay meant that many wagon loads of equipment had been sent west. The Bathurst warehouse basement was now half full.

~

On the morning of 27 January 1851, a caravan of wagons departed from the Warehouse, heading west. Eddie and Charlie saw them off. The children were settled inside the wagons, and lattice barricades had been built across the back to prevent them from falling out. They could bounce and play. More often, they sat and watched as new things passed. When tired, they lay down and slept. The pace was slow; the trip was not rushed.

Harry and Wills had always intended to take the girls to the Duckpond but had never got around to it. Soon it would be obliterated under the diggings. Now would be the last time to see it in its pristine state. He had bought the land at the headwaters of the creek. Above this land, no gold was found. For the moment, Wills ran stock on it. One day, he would mine this and try to find the motherlode.

In their chat with the men, Wills had said that the pond was where the family would camp, and the others could head further up the creek. They were not staying with them. The track extended some miles further on. They had ridden it years ago, but found no better camping spot than near to a pond, so they stayed put, as there was gold all the way along the creek.

Phil and Lucy were packed and ready for their visitors when they arrived. Phil had built a house with some of his share of the gold. It was to one side of Wills' Emporium. Their manager, James King, would live on the other side. Phil had purchased three blocks of land next to Wills triple allotment. Their house was sandstone with a green iron roof. A large stable and coachhouse were at the back. The third block was a holding yard for their cow. Eddie had made a balustrade of iron lacework for their verandah. These were wide and allowed the air to cool before blowing down the long, straight corridors. The veranda caught all the breezes as Lucy had wanted a double corridor, in a cross. So a central door on each verandah carried both cool air in summer and warm air in winter into all the rooms in the house. Summer in Bathurst was hot. Very, very hot and very cold in winter as it often snowed.

Phil stood in the shade with Lucy under his arm. He held Charlotte's hand, and Lucy had Charles on her hip.

The children greeted Charlotte warmly, and Phil's Nanny hustled all the children into the fenced back yard to run, yell, and play. She was not coming; she was having a break at home by herself. Only the three families, comprising six adults and eight children, would be on this trip, other than the men who were showing them the area. No staff would accompany them.

The day before departing, Hargraves informed them that a fourth man was to join them. They had stayed at an inn in town and met a man named Lister. It seems Hargraves had been to Bathurst before and hunted around the Macquarie river, but found nothing. In California, he honed his gold hunting technique. Wills smiled. It wouldn't take much to find this gold.

The children had been cooped up for two days in the wagons and needed to let off steam.

Phil had hired a trustworthy assistant manager, James King. He, too, had a wife, Eva, and three children. They rented a house in town and so were likely to stay. But Wills was building a manager's residence on the other side of the Emporium. It was nearly finished. Phil had made arrangements for at least a week off.

James King walked to the front of the store,

"Hello, James," greeted Wills.

"Hello, Sir," his manager replied cheekily. "I believe you're stealing Phil."

James was twice Wills's age, and it was always a bit of a joke between them. "I may keep him for a bit longer than the week, so don't send out a rescue party until the third week," Wills chuckled.

Phil's wagon was also packed and nearly ready to go. When he saw the lattice of the back that Wills and Harry had put on their wagons, they delayed their departure as they added something similar.

They departed Bathurst on the last day of January. They were finally on the last leg of their trip to Duck Creek. They hoped to arrive by nightfall on the second day after leaving, but this depended on the children. Had it been just them, they could have made it in a day.

The four men wished to stop and pan each creek; however, they were using an enamel basin. Therefore, the caravan stopped frequently.

Finally, Wills led the caravan of wagons into their campsite on the morning of the third day. He directed Hargraves to head further along the track. He looked forward to reading their reports to the Governor. Wills handed Hargraves a large paper-wrapped parcel and left them to unwrap its contents after they had camped. It contained proper sieves and a gold pan. After travelling with eight rambunctious children, the four men were content to leave the three families as fast as they could.

On the second morning, Wills, Phil and Harry pulled their wagons into a triangle. They would build a fire in the middle and set up camp. The first thing Wills wanted to do was to scythe the grass short in the central area. He had the evil-looking contraption ready. Wills said to Cathy, Vicky, and Lucy that the children were not to get down until it was completed, or they could get covered in ticks, or worse, there could be snakes in the grass.

It took about half an hour; Phil and Harry removed the cut grass with the rake that Wills had also added to their wagon. The horses were hobbled, and the stack of fresh grass was placed for them to eat.

They were left with a lovely clearing and a safe area for the children. They also cut paths to the creek and pond. The three girls took the children into the shade by the creek's edge and stripped them off so they could paddle in the cool, shaded area.

Knowing what they had found when they camped there years ago, they were not surprised when Vicky came and asked for a pan. Phil had put in eight of them so they could each learn how to pan properly. They could then instruct others how to do it. They had taken nothing with them on that first trip.

By the time the fireplace was rebuilt and the camp fully set up, the men were ready for a dunking, too. They took a bucket and the other gold pans to the creek. The rest of the morning was spent playing with the children in the shallows and panning. The older children had mastered the art by lunchtime, and the bucket had a nice layer of gold-rich wash in it. This would need to be panned again, as the children were not that fussy about how clean they washed their pans. As soon as they saw some sparkle, it was tipped into the bucket. Lucy, Vicky, and Cathy each had a baby and were itching to have a go. Finally, Cathy splashed Wills. "You're mean, love. Can't we try?" After a cooling water fight, they finally handed their precious bundles to their husbands while they went hunting for precious metals instead.

With a baby on each hip, the men understood how limited their ability to work was. The other children needed watching as well, but they each managed to show the girls where to find the richest deposits. They rolled over rocks with one hand and showed them how to sift the dirt underneath. They scooped the deposits from the water-worn rock platforms and panned them as well. By early noon, the sun was overhead, and the creek was in the full sun. Harry and Wills had reminded the girls about the sunburn that Lew and Aidan suffered.

Cathy noticed that the children were now in the full sun and suggested they return for something to eat and a snooze. Lucy had made a lot of food for the journey, but it had been mostly eaten over the past three days. The fire had burnt down to coals, and the billy was hot. Cathy put on a camp oven and placed about two dozen eggs in it. Boiled eggs were easy finger food, as her mother called it.

Wills made the billy tea, while Phil and Harry made a damper and placed it in another camp oven and then into the coals, with more on top.

Lucy had never seen this done and watched her husband with awe. Phil had not forgotten the lessons he learned from their camping trip years ago. The eggs now done, the pot was reused for a stew. Harry had helped Vicky and Cathy chop vegetables, and they had a stew cooking while the bread was still in the oven. The children were all asleep, exhausted after the unusual activities of the morning.

In the quiet of the afternoon, the adults took the chance to erect a shade sail with an old triangular sail that Wills had bought with him. Three ropes tied to the corners were thrown across the canopies of the wagons and tied to the axles. This caused some of the smoke from the fire to swirl, but at least it was shady. They placed some blankets on the short grass, and they all lay down for a rest.

They waited until the afternoon, when the creek was once again in the shade, before they returned. The children had never had so much fun. Although they had been there in winter last visit, they were hoping the ducks would still come in at dusk. They had seen flocks of them in other creeks and hoped to catch some.

Wills had a large basin of clay ready. All they needed were the ducks, ideally seven, but preferably eight.

By five o'clock, the bread was cooked, the stew was sizzling, and the children's mouths were watering. They all ate their meal, and after cleaning the area and storing the rest of the food, just in case there were dingoes, they wandered down to a swimming hole further down the creek.

During the afternoon, each couple was given an hour or so off from parenting and went for a swim and some quality time together. Harry and Vicky had gone first. They had checked that the deepest area of the pool was still cleared and accessible. When they reappeared wet and cool, Harry reported that it was still beautiful. He had his arm draped around her lovingly.

"Next," Harry called laughingly.

Phil and Lucy went next.

Cathy waited until they had gone before she said to Vicky, "Hmm and didn't even get your swimming smock wet. Clever!"

Vicky blushed, "Why not? It's beautiful down there. Not much privacy when sharing a wagon with three children," she whispered to her sister.

"Trust me, there's a reason we're going last," Cathy said quietly. "You get the children when they are hungry," she chuckled. "And, as I'm expecting, I want my husband," winking to Vicky. She giggled. "Often," she thought.

They were relaxed and clean, the children too. The girls' hair had now dried. They all wandered down to the waterhole, or the 'duckpond' as Wills called it. The children had been told to sit still and not make a sound, just as they would in church. If they did, they would see something special. The three men were wearing their swim shorts again and had a bag with them.

The girls were sitting on the bank watching. The three men were already neck-deep in the water. The children were amazingly quiet. The ducks flew in, and one by one the men's heads disappeared. Two ducks disappeared underwater as each took turns at catching dinner. Wills then went back for two more.

They surfaced, not far from where they had gone under, each showing its bountiful gifts.

Wills showed Lucy and the girls how to cover them in clay, then to place them under the coals.

They kept the children up as long as possible so that they would sleep until dawn. Not long past dusk, they were all in bed. The wagons were still hot inside.

Wills and Cathy had pulled their mattress out onto the clearing. "Wills, shh, you'll wake everyone," Cathy whispered, not so quietly. He dumped it on the ground.

Vicky heard giggles. She was still awake and so hot. "Harry, are you awake?" she whispered.

"No, I'm asleep," he said as he reached for her. Sarah muttered as he bumped her.

"Shh," said Vicky. "Wills and Cathy have just put their mattress on the ground. It's too hot in here. Can we too?"

"What? There are snakes," he said.

"They shouldn't come near the fire. Honestly, it's safe. Wills wouldn't risk her. Trust me," she said.

"Sure?" he said very unsurely.

"As I can be. I'm certainly not going to sleep in here. I've stripped off everything I can already. And look, my lawn nightgown is wet." She grabbed her nightgown and flapped it. Trying to cool herself.

"Take it off," he murmured against her neck.

"No!" She giggled as his hands wandered under it. "Ohh," his hands kept wandering. "Oh, Harry," she cooed softly. "Only if we can sleep outside afterwards."

"Deal!" he pulled her on top of him and helped lift her nightgown up.

Wills and Cathy were quiet by the time they eventually pulled their mattress out onto their rug. Once settled, they too slept.

~

Each day, they caught ducks or fish.

The next day, Phil and Lucy placed their mattress on the ground too, leaving the wagons for the children.

Harry had a couple of leeches bite him in the creek.

Vicky removed them with salt, but they had become itchy. Very itchy. "Here, love, rub a tiny bit of this into them." She picked a milk thistle, broke it and rubbed the sap on his skin.

He complained that it was always him. "It's not fair. They like my English blood."

Phil and Lucy laughed. "No, they just like you. We don't get eaten alive."

Vicky said it was because he tasted so good. She reached over and nibbled his neck.

Three-year-old Henry was in his arms and said, "Mummy, don't eat Pappa. I want to keep him."

"Oh, so do I, sweetheart. Forever," she replied with a saucy chuckle.

Some hours later, Harry said the itching had eased. Even the redness was much less. He dabbed on some more thistle juice.

The week passed in a state of bliss for them all. The children had friends to play with, and the three couples enjoyed the closeness of both good friends and the intimacy of marriage. Phil, Lucy, and Harry were happy as the only snake they saw was heading in the other direction. They were all relaxed, and each couple was given free time each day. They knew the next few years would be hectic. Soon it would start, very soon.

Their supplies were running low after ten days, and they still had to reach Bathurst. They finally decided it was time to return. They had lost track of days. After the decision had been made, they put the children to bed. They started to break camp by removing the shade sail in the cool of the night.

The next morning, they all walked down to the duck pond and took a final look. It would never look like this again, destroyed by mining. One day they would return as Wills still had his farm further up the valley.

Wills took the bucket of fine gold and went to wash the muck out. "Another pound or two. Nice," he thought. "That's a split three ways, another £50 each. Over two years' worth of wages, found in the dirt. Very nice." He lifted his eyes and gave thanks to God again.

Harry and Phil joined him at the creek.

"Ready?" said Harry. Not meaning the panning, nor the camping, but rather the onslaught that was about to occur. They would stay a few days at Phil's and get things organised there, then head home.

"No," said Wills, "but it's what we're called it to do. Come on. Pandemonium awaits."

~

By June, the news had spread. They had used those four months to stock the Emporiums totally.

As Wills expected, the four men found gold, but it was Hargraves who snuck away and reported the find. The Tom brothers were livid as they were the ones paying him. Wills was sure this would one day be acknowledged. His name was kept out of the papers, and of this, he was pleased.

Hargraves' discovery quickly made the newspapers in London.

By the end of the year, the gold hunters were arriving by the boatload. Blackman's Creek, now known as Ophir, originally had about thirty people living in the area when they visited in February. By the end of that year, there were over two thousand. The duck pond and creek were destroyed, and the country was raped. Wills was pleased he had purchased the farm further up the valley. It was a patch of verdant green in a stripped landscape.

On the 6th July, Aurelia Lucy Lockley was born to Wills and Cathy. AS before, Wills was with Cathy from the beginning. Aurelia, meaning gold, and Lucy, meaning light. The new baby had a mop of white-blonde hair. So the names were perfect. Pip called her 'Goldie', and 'Goldie' she stayed.

~

And so began the New South Wales gold rush.

The fighting, greed, and lust that accompanied the miners transformed the colony.

More and more towns and waterways were panned, dug, raped, and destroyed. The lure of the gold attracted every sort of person imaginable. The crooks, poor, greedy and hopeful all came. The settlement of Bathurst was no longer just a farming town. Brawls were frequent, so more police and soldiers arrived.

The Emporiums could hardly keep up with supplies, but at least they had access to stock. Eddie mobilised the apprentices, and they often worked long and late. They had never been so busy. A new store opened close to the diggings. Mattie Saunders was a new widow whose husband had been shot en route to a new future. Her husband Jim had wished to open a shop, and Mattie decided she would do it anyway. She and her three small children bravely forged a new life for themselves. When trouble hit, Mattie turned to Lucy and Phil. The two ladies became firm friends. Faith and grief forged the bond.

Mr Tindale and Eddie built a special gold smelting forge. They had planned this many years before. They started building it after Wills' Duck Creek trip. It had been completed just before the main rush. The week the word hit the newspapers in Sydney, the local rush started. First with a dribble, then a flood, finally, the tidal wave of miners began to arrive. The flow of unwashed, filthy miners seemed never-ending. By then, the apprentices were let into the secret. Gold was found.

The back bedroom at Tindale's house was finally emptied of the crate of precious ingot moulds and crucibles that Ned had sent.

Eddie taught the young smiths how to crush the rocks with Phil's bicycle machine, but only Eddie and Mr Tindale would smelt the final gold. They, too, were ready for the onslaught.

Eddie was also excited as he now had a mini foundry too. He had always wanted one. He had financed the building of the site next to the old forge. The foundry was only small, making tool heads and the like, but it was a start. It would grow as more coke and coal were brought to town.

The three Emporiums were restocked from the warehouse daily. The money was flowing in, including payments in gold dust. The price was set in London at £10 an ounce; however, they bought it at £9, 19/- shillings. Outside each store was the fixed price for how much an ounce of gold was worth. The sign acknowledged that more could be obtained if they wished to travel to Sydney, but no one was prepared to travel that far for just one shilling per ounce. The cost difference was attributed to transportation costs. Everyone was content with the prices. Wills knew the official rate was £10/oz, but they needed to make a little profit.

Wills's £4,000 expenditure for stock was easily covered in the first month. Uncle Ned's last shipment arrived with a boatload of miners. Lew and Aidan's £1,000 had been well spent on building products. It gave the Bathurst store the cash flow it needed. Every shipment arrived on time and undamaged.

Phil and Lucy's share of twenty per cent of the profits of the Bathurst store meant that they were becoming very wealthy. The £100 of sales a month of the past year turned into that per day; sometimes they made that much in a morning. Phil and James King were run off their feet. Harry received twenty per cent of the Emu Plains store, and Eddie earned twenty per cent of the warehouse.

Wills and Cathy had the means to have anything they wished, yet they lived a simple life, nothing ostentatious. Martha and Jack were more than happy to help them with the children. Two of the Murphy girls lived with them: Colleen, Cathy's best friend, and Deidre. They had indeed called in to Hartley on their return in February. Another rockfall had occurred, and more gold was visible.

Harry and Wills dug out all they could and once again covered the seam. One day they would return, but there was no hurry. Neither needed more. They now had the small shack finished. They stocked it with dry food products and left bedding there.

They were content.

~

On a Sunday night in June, the family gathered at Eddie's for dinner. This evening, everyone in the family was there.

Even Luke, who had returned for a mid-year break from the new University in Sydney, where he was one of the very first students enrolled. He was in his second year of Science. The Tindales, Moffatt, and Clarkes were there too.

Wills stood and made a speech. "I want to say thank you to each and every one of you. Each one has been instrumental in where I am today. More importantly, is where this country is heading. The gold will slowly remove the convict beginnings of the settlement. Dar, you came as a convict and ended as an Earl. Tim, look at you, a member of Parliament and yet a convict's son. Bert, you have the Government contract for all saddlery and leather goods. How many do you employ now? Twenty?"

Bertie nodded. "And then some." He smiled. More orphan apprentices had arrived from Howard Marlow at the boys' orphanage that week.

Wills looked at his family, smiling. "In this country, nothing is impossible for anyone who puts their mind to something. However, we must also remember that we do not own what we have. We are but caretakers for God." He paused, looking at each beloved member of his family. His five siblings and their families, his parents, grandmother, and step-grandfather, along with all his wonderful in-laws, all hung on to what he was saying. "I am certainly blessed. I don't know why I was, but I am. I can't believe I ran away because I was lonely in a house full of loving family, but God used that as well. Without that find in Hartley, this may have ended very differently."

Everyone sat in silence listening to Wills's powerful words.

He swallowed, then continued. "Friends, dear ones, we did not seek what we have. I know that together we will work for the good of those who have little. Grandmother, Pa Richard, you have both been an inspiration to us all. Your continuing work at the school is fabulous. Those girls found love and acceptance they never would have otherwise. You supply them with a start in life that would not have been possible."

"Dar, Mama, just where would any of us be without you and your faith and stamina. You both taught us of God and his forgiveness and love. You set us all on the path to Him. For that, we will all be forever thankful, but more than that, you gave us all a great example of *how* to live."

"Reverend William Clarke, sir, how I do respect you! I soaked up everything I could from you when at school, and my thanks will never be enough." His eyes rested on his teacher lovingly.

He went through each of the others until he got to Harry. "Harry. Where do I start?" His eyes misted. "As close as I am to my brothers, we are soul-brothers. We married two of the best women God ever made. We are friends, confidants and business partners as well as now my Chief Manager." He paused, looking his brother-in-law in the face. "Harry, I remember watching your face on the day we saw the brolgas dance. We all stood transfixed. But I saw something else that day. Peace. I know that pair of dancing birds changed me. I didn't know why. I still don't, but it did. Harry, thanks for being my friend through all of this."

Harry was embarrassed but acknowledged this adulation. He had nothing but awe for this young man.

Wills stood looking around at his family. His eyes finally rested on Cathy. "My darling, Cathy! Do you know that Catherine means 'each of the two' and also 'pure'? You, my darling love, *are* the other half of me. Without you, I am not complete. After over six wonderful years of marriage, I still catch my breath when I see you. Each day, I love you more and more. You are my heart, and I thank God for you every single day." He bent and gently kissed her and whispered, "I love you."

The family sat silently.

Thoughts flowed through each, some wiping tears away. What would they have done, given a windfall of so much money? Surely, they would not have been so generous, knowing how differently this could have turned out had they been the ones to discover a treasure trove of gold. God blessed a young boy of seventeen with a fantastic discovery. Knowing that this lad would use the "talents of gold" for all, and not for himself. Other than a few new suits, the house for Cathy, and of course, his top hat, which he needed to do his work, he had not purchased a single thing for himself alone. His silver fob, he bought with his pay from the forge. Everything Wills had done was to benefit others.

Many had received anonymous gifts and bequests. Liza and Charlie were both living in their new houses, and Tim was in a new office with a house attached.

Luke was at University and now living in Wills's own cottage with a Scottish friend who helped care for him in exchange for food and a bed.

Wills knew that Luke would forget to eat unless food was placed in front of him. He looked at Eddie. "Ahh, Eddie, we are now in business together and both so wealthy we would struggle to spend the money. If we were inclined to spend it on ourselves."

He chuckled. Both of them donated anonymously to numerous worthy causes. Not all were charities, or even the churches.

Eddie nodded and dropped his chin. His emporium was a thriving business, but Wills's stores were making as much in a week as his store did in a month. His percentage from the warehouse equalled the takings of his store.

Charles looked at his second youngest child and smiled lovingly. All the things the family received to ease their lives were well thought out; however, none were extravagant. If wills gave them a new coat, they were encouraged to donate their old coat to someone in need.

Each of the nephews, as well as male cousins, was promised the best education that money could buy. If they wished, this could also be in England. Each niece or female cousin would take a trip to London, where Uncle Ned and Aunt Christina would sponsor their presentation at court.

Wills was about to sit down when he thought of one more thing. "I have a verse that spoke to me years ago, and I shall always try to live up to it. It's from the Gospel of Luke 12v 48b."

For unto whomsoever much is given,
of him shall be much required. (KJV)

Wills took his seat and lifted his mug of tea toward Cathy as a silent toast. He lifted his eyes heavenward and also gave thanks.

~

One more letter would be sent to England. This missive required no answer, but the author hoped it would be received well.

Wills' words had challenged Harry to extend an olive branch to his brother. If nothing else, Harry would write to Anthony and let him know he was not returning. Only time would tell if Anthony returned it unopened.

HVH

Yodalla
Emu Plains
29 December 1857

The Right Hon. The Viscount Winchester
Chester Castle
Nettlestead,
England

Dear Anthony, no, Tony, as that's how I think of you again.

I do hope you are well. I thought it was about time I wrote and let you know that I am still alive and well. I have married and settled in Emu Plains in New South Wales.

My wife's name was Victoria Turner. We married on 29th December 1844. We now have five beautiful children. We currently have Sarah Joy, Henry, Marcus, Elizabeth, and James Anthony.

I thought here I could leave behind the formality of 'home,' however, I find not so. We are all frequently invited to Government House as Vicky's sisters are both married to the Earl of Coxheath's sons, Edward and William. Wills and I are now in a business partnership, and it's doing well.

I have written to Mr Pence, the Estate Solicitor, and informed him to please bank the allowance due to me. I do not need it out here as my income is ample for our needs. We have built a beautiful home with river views named 'Yodalla.' We are surrounded by an orchard.

Tony, I want to tell you, I hold no hard feelings now. I left in anger and was hurt. Because of that, I found my feet and my Victoria. She is a queen amongst women. One day, I hope you will be as happy with Maud. She deserves it, she adores you, you know.

We shall be visiting in some six years or so. I should give you notice. Sarah Joy had been promised a come-out Ball along with her cousins and the Duke of Gracemere's (Uncle Ned) twin daughters. Do not fear, for we shall stay with them. They will be presented at court together. There are seven cousins all due to come out at once, possibly an eighth. All but three are fair with blue eyes. Our Sarah Joy is as beautiful as her mother; both she and her cousin Lily have honey gold hair with amber eyes. Phillip's daughter, Charlotte, who is known as Charly, is dark with green eyes, like her mother, Lucy (Norfolk).

So that year, the Duke's twins, Earl Coxheath's granddaughters, Viscount Winchester's niece and Sir Phillip Corsairs' daughter Charlotte, will be presented together. What a year that will be. Something for everyone's taste. Uncle Ned is also asking Lewis and Fiona's daughter, as well as Aidan and Amelia's daughter, so there could be more presentations a year or so later. He is giving presentation balls for them all in London, not to mention the boy's Levée's.

Tony, as I mentioned above, I have made arrangements for my allowance now to be banked in England and to await my return home. This is now done. Uncle Ned's man of finance has arranged this for me with your solicitor. I have fallen on my feet here. I am both happy and useful. Life here is good, so very good.

Although we may visit over the years, we shall never move back. This is now home and we love it so. A half a world between us may not be so bad either, but know our door is always open to you. You will be made welcome, should you ever decide to come for a visit.

One day I shall tell you all, but I shall never write it down. You will, I'm sure, have heard of the new finds in the area, suffice it to say I am instrumental in its set up, along with Wills and the rest of my new family. Therefore, I am surprisingly flush for funds.

I have no hard feelings brother. I have learnt to forgive from the heart. Take care brother.

Harry.

P.S. No need to reply, just come.

HH

Post Script

In time, Eddie and Jenna went on to have ten children. Harry and Vicky, six, plus Alexis, whom they lost by miscarriage. Wills and Cathy also had six.

In 1858, two ravishing seventeen-year-old blonde cousins, Ned's daughter, Sarah, and Eddie's daughter, Christina (Tina) Lockley, took London by storm. One a Duke's daughter, the other an Earl's granddaughter.

Due to the Death of Prince Albert in December 1861, Drawing Room Presentations at court were delayed until 1864. (Fact)

Six years later, eight more of the extended family were presented. Identical twins Charl and Izzy, and Lockley cousins Emma, Lily; Sarah Joy Harlow, Charlotte Saunders, Charlotte Corsairs and Elizabeth (Betty) Watkins-Harlow. Five were fair with blue eyes, one dark with green eyes like her mother and Sarah Joy and Lily were breathtaking with honey-gold like their mothers; all beautiful, stately, gracious ladies.

Ned's daughter, Sarah married Harry Harlow's nephew, Ant, and the healing of that family was completed.

Tina did indeed marry Charles (Chip), who in time became the 11th Duke of Gracemere.

Ed's son, Neddie Jnr, built the first full foundry in the Colony. He married Miriam Evans and they lived with her Great Uncle Thomas, at the forge.

Charlie's son Earl Edward (Teddy, the older twin) married Annabella (Bella) Jennifer Winslow-Smythe and eventually took his place as Earl, they lived in Bramblemere House in Coxheath. His twin brother, John Lockley, married Sarah-Joy Harlow and took over the inn in Parramatta.

Wills' sons, Lukie and Pip, took over the large Emporium chain their father built, and Rick eventually ran the Warehouse.

Harry's boys sold the Emu and Bathurst Emporiums to Wills, and each stayed on the land, farming and breeding horses.

All their stories are continued in **"Diamonds in the Dirt"** and **"The Earl's Shadow."** (You will also discover who Mattie Saunders is.)

And then there was Luke, the youngest Lockley sibling. His adventures involved another incredible journey of exploration, but that is an entirely different story.

Also, to, find out if Harry and Vicky get an unexpected visitor.

Read **Diamonds in the Dirt** *now*
to follow Luke's adventures

~

*The prequel, "**Unshackled Lives**" is Ned's story and is free when you sign up for my newsletter.*

The Lockleys of Parramatta
is the name of the 100-year, six-book family saga.
Available in one click from Amazon.

Mitchell's1st Expedition - 1839 map

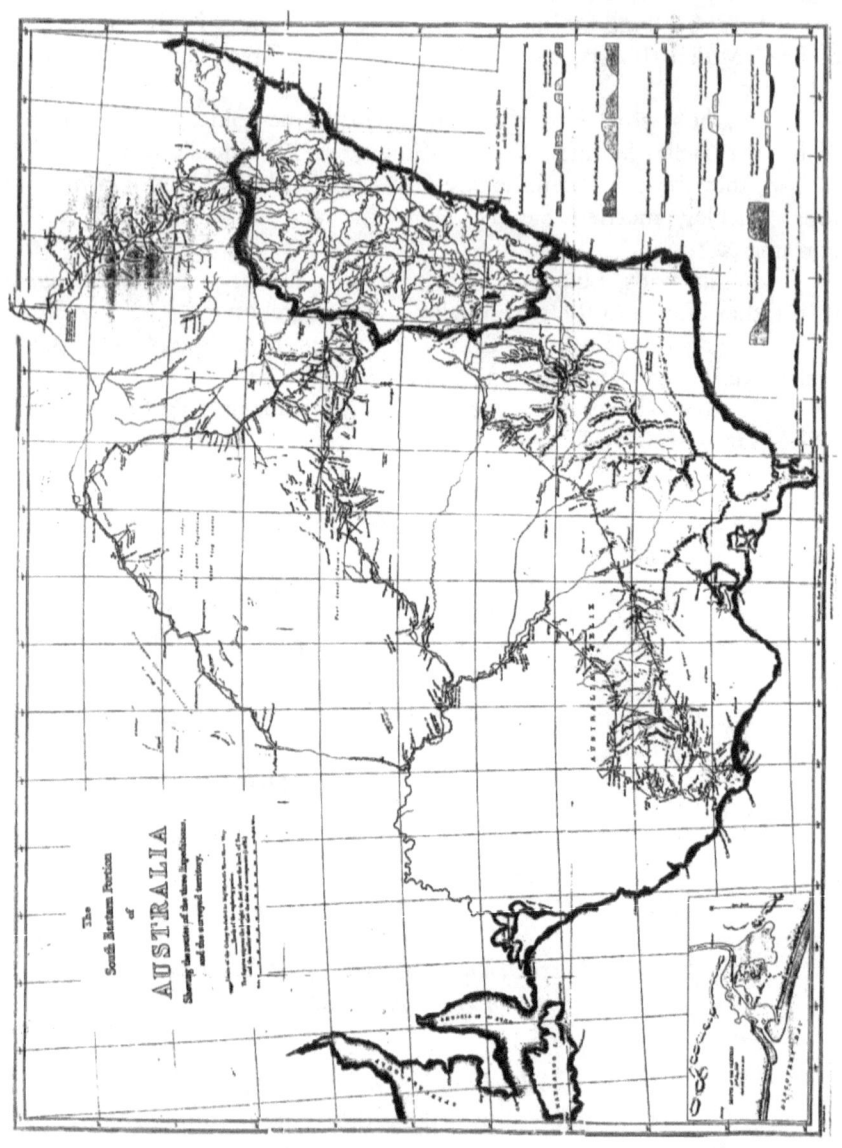

The Duke/Earl Tree

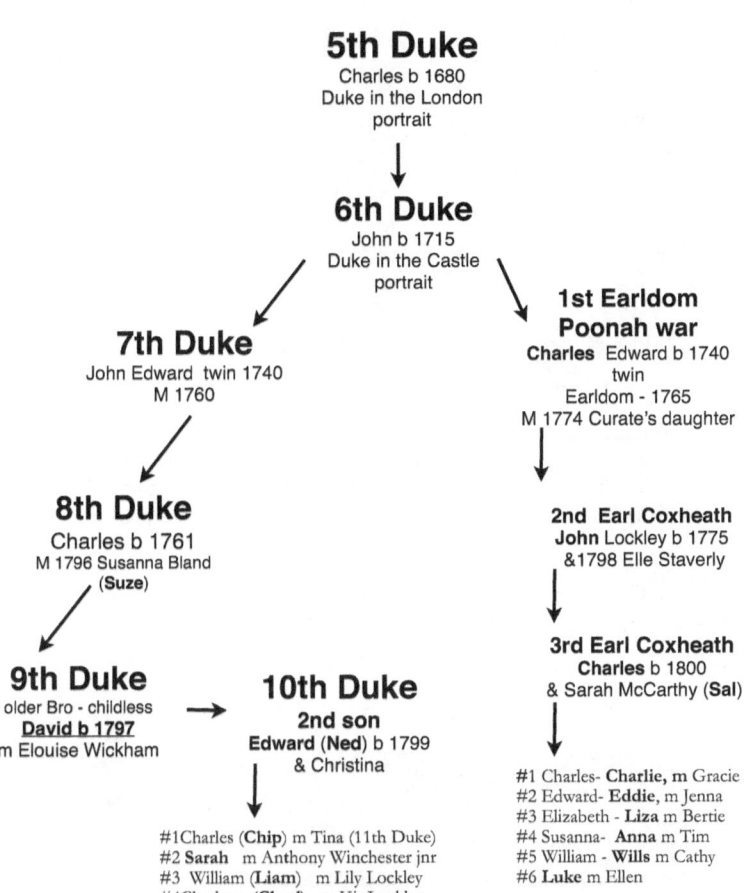

5th Duke
Charles b 1680
Duke in the London
portrait

6th Duke
John b 1715
Duke in the Castle
portrait

7th Duke
John Edward twin 1740
M 1760

**1st Earldom
Poonah war**
Charles Edward b 1740
twin
Earldom - 1765
M 1774 Curate's daughter

8th Duke
Charles b 1761
M 1796 Susanna Bland
(Suze)

2nd Earl Coxheath
John Lockley b 1775
&1798 Elle Staverly

3rd Earl Coxheath
Charles b 1800
& Sarah McCarthy **(Sal)**

9th Duke
older Bro - childless
David b 1797
m Elouise Wickham

10th Duke
2nd son
Edward (Ned) b 1799
& Christina

#1Charles (**Chip**) m Tina (11th Duke)
#2 **Sarah** m Anthony Winchester jnr
#3 William (**Liam**) m Lily Lockley
#4Charlotte (**Charl**) m Kit Lockley
#5 Isabella (**Izzy**) m Ned Winslow Smythe

#1 Charles- **Charlie, m** Gracie
#2 Edward- **Eddie,** m Jenna
#3 Elizabeth - **Liza** m Bertie
#4 Susanna- **Anna** m Tim
#5 William - **Wills** m Cathy
#6 **Luke** m Ellen

Main Characters

Charles Lockley b 1800 the Earl. To Elle and John Lockley 'Jolly Sailor'
Sarah (Sal) McCarthy b1800 (Dar and Mama) Sally's mother:-   Shannon McCarthy
    parents Eamon (Edward) and Nioiclín(Nicola) O'Shane. Ireland
Charlie b 1820   m **Gracie** Miller Dec 1842
        #1 Edward (**Teddie**) William 26/9/44; twin
        #2 **John** Charles 26/9/44; twin
        #3Emily (called **Emma**); b 25 Aug 46
        #4 **Molly Grace** b1850
Eddie b 1821   m **Jenna** Jennifer Martha Turner m 4 Dec 1841
        #1 Edward (**Neddie**)Charles John b 15th Aug 1842 twin
        #2 Christina (**Tina**) Sarah Martha. b 15 Aug 1842 twin
        #3 Jennifer Annabella Elizabeth (**Lily**) b 13/4/45
        #4 Christopher William (**Kit**)   b 26/1/47
        #5 Nicholas **Nick** Calum   b 2/3/49
        #6 **Shannon** Mary   b 1/10/50
        #7 Victoria (**Toria**)   b1852
        #8 **Henry** Charles   b 1853
         #9 Phillip John (**Pip**)   b 6th Dec 1856 twin
         #10 Ruth Alexandra (**Ruthie**) b 6th Dec 1856 twin
Liza b1823 m 11/41 **Bertie Ellis** (saddler)called #1 **Albie** 15/8/1842. + others
Anna b 1824 m 11/42 **Tim Miller**   b 6/9/43 #1 William (**Billy**)Charles + others
Wills -William Lockley b 20/4 1826 (Wills) m **Cathy** Turner 14/2/1845
        #1 Luke Henry William, **Lukie** b14 Jan 47
        #2 Phillip(**Pip**)Charles;   b Sept 48,
        #3 Catherine Victoria Matilda(**Tilda**) b 3/3/50
        #4 Aurelia Lucy (**Goldie**) b 6July 51
        #5 Richard(**Rick**) Edward b 26 Oct 1855 twin
        #6 Elizabeth(**Bette**) Martha b 26 Oct 1855 twin
Luke b 1828 16 in (March 44)   m '56 Ellen

SIX ENGLISHMEN

John Saunders, b 1811 The Hon, leader (Sir John, Baron's son) CO Harry's cousin John's
    mother was Elle's twin Charles 1st cous. and Elle's nephew. m48 Catriona - Lew's sister

Edmund Hunt b 1811 (Lord) Christina's brother Viscount Eames 3yrs younger
    m 48 **Elspeth** Bland (Lew's sister)
Phillip Corsairs (Sir) b 1811 Annabella's Cousin. dead fiancé Charlotte
m **Lucy** Norfolk m7th Jan 1848 - dead fiancé - Charles Master
        #1 Charlotte b Oct 48
        #2 Charles b 7th Jan 1850(2nd wedding anniv)
        #3 Matilda Victoria 2/1864 (when Lucy was 41) in UK
Harry Harlow b 1811 the Hon. 2IC - bro Viscount Anthony Winchester.
m **Vicky** Turner Dec 44
        #1 miscarriage d mid 45 **Alexis**;
        #2 **Sarah Joy**; b 7 Jan 47
        #3 **Henry** William; b Oct 16, 48
        #4 **Marcus** Edward b 2/2/50;
        #5 Elizabeth Susanna; (**Sanna**) May 52
        #6 James (**Jimmy Ant**)Anthony; 13 Dec 1856 in UK
        #7 Harriet Margaret (**Maggie**) 5th Feb 1864
Lewis Bland, b 1811 Dukes mother's cousin also the Hon m 22 August. 1846
m **Fiona** Moreton
        #1 b Colin Fergus (**Ferdie**)Bland May 47
        #2 b **Susanna** Fiona Elspeth Dec 48
Two **sisters Catriona and Elspeth**. m **John and Edmund**
Aidan O'Keefe b 1811 cousins O'Shanes, Cork Ire *Shéamus O'Keefe, Erin O'Shane.*
m **Amelia** Stather 22/8/46
        #1 b **Eamon** Liam 7 May 1847
        #2 b **Shannon** Amelia Dec 1848

Major Edward 'Ned' Grace b 1799- Parramatta (10th **Duke of Gracemere.**
Edward John Charles Lockley of Gracemere) at Maidstone 48th Battalion
Mother Susanna Bland - Dowager Duchess
m Dec 25 1841 **Christina** Meadows b 1808
        #1 Charles Edward John (**Chip**) Viscount Lockley b 1 Sept 42 twin
        #2 **Sarah** Christina, The Lady Sarah Lockley b 1 Sept 42 twin
        #3 William Edmund(**Liam**) April 1854
        #4 Charlotte (**Charl**) Jennifer Victoria 26 Jan 47 twin
        #5 Isabella (**Izzy**) Catherine Grace 26 Jan 47 twin

Brother 9th Duke **David** (b1798 d 1839) of Gracemere and wife Elouise
;-young bros **Paul** b 1800 Twin died at birth -**Charles** b & d 1800
Douglas b 1802
Sarah Joy - still born b & d 1804
Doctor Gerald Winslow-Smythe (Gerry) b 1800

m 1842 **Annabella** Derbyshire (nee Watkins-Harlow)
  1 Annabella Jennifer - **Bella** b 5th Dec 42 to marry Teddy Lockley(Charlies son)
  2 Edward Gerald Charles - **Neddie** July 46 to marry Lady **Izzy** Lockley
  3 Matthew **Matty** Henry Dec 47
  4 Susanna (**Sanna**) Elizabeth Sarah Joy b 49

John (**Jack**) **Turner** convict
Martha Turner (Pa & Maa) - Australian Arms Emu Plains,
  #1Marcus (**Marc**)   m **Milly** Ellis Dec 1843
      #1Charlotte Amelia, Sept 4 1844
  #2 Alexander (**Alex**) works for saddler Mr Ben Parker m **Mary** Parker,
  #3 Jennifer Martha (**Jenna**) met in 1840   m **Eddie** Lockley
  #4 Victoria (**Vicky**) b July 1825,   m 29/12/44 **Harry** Harlow
  #5 Catherine (**Cathy**), b 24 June 1827   m 14/2/1845 **Wills** Lockley
  #6 Nicholas (**Nick**) b 1830
  #7 Malcolm (**Calum**) b 1833

Bill (Bill) b 1800 **Miller** convict
Molly Miller b 1800 (Par and Ma Rear Admiral Duncan convict
  Timmy b 1822 (lawyer)   m 42 **Anna** Lockley
  Gracie b 1824   m 11/41 **Charlie's** Lockley wife
  Samuel b 1828 (**Sammy**)   m 51 Isabella '**Belle**' Ellis 2 children in 56
  Ellen b 1830   m 2/Aug 1856 **Luke Lockley**

Real People and Places

Sir James Martin ; Martin Place, politician and Chief Justice. (inspired Tim).
Hon George Thornton - politician in the NSW Legislative Council (also Tim).
The **Governors** and their stories are real, as is the accident about **Lady Mary Fitzroy, George, The Gov & Aide Charles Masters.**
The Memorial is at the gates of **Old Government House Parramatta.**

Revd William Branwhite Clarke
the Father of Australian Geology
(1798-1878), geologist and Anglican clergyman, was b 2 June 1798 at East Bergholt, Suffolk, England.
M Maria Moreton in England - four children. A son and three daughters. The youngest girls was born in Australia
Reverend Clarke's find of gold at Hartley was certainly true, a few specks were found in the creek in April 1844. He reported his finds to Gov Gipps. Wills' find of an escarpment is totally from my imagination. I have not even been to Hartley. The gold finds at Ophir were also genuine but certainly not in the quantities that I have here. I believe there is still some there.
Miss Amelia Stather and Miss Fiona Moreton are fictitious nieces of Reverend William Clarke's wife Maria Moreton.
Plain Statements and Practical Hints Respecting the Discovery and Working of Gold in Australia and in 1860 *Researches in the Southern Gold Fields of New South Wales*
https://adb.anu.edu.au/biography/clarke-william-branwhite-3228
In 1988, William Clarke College opened in Dural. Rev'd William B. Clarke is one of Australia's real heroes.

NB - Correcting some facts.
I have invented a fiancé for Lieutenant Charles Chester Master who died in the carriage accident that also killed Lady Mary Fitzroy. He did however, have a brother Lieutenant F Robert Chester Master, who with Gov Fitzroy followed the coffin. They both served in the 58th Foot. They were two of ten children. The accident occurred on 7 Dec 1847 at Parramatta.

Emu Hall at Emu Plains is the building I have modelled Wills and Cathys' house from. It however was not built until 1851 and was remodelled in the 1880s.
Harry and Vicky's house I have modelled from my own grandparents9Norman A and Ellie Hunter) house, **Yodalla** in Emu Plains (built in 1880's). Normans parents, James and Sara Hunter lived at **The Arms of Australia Inn**, in Emu Plains today as a Museum. I was named after her.
    Sara Powter

Author's Historical Note

The original story in the series was inspired by my own Great, Great Grandfather Thomas Ellison. He was the third son of convict John Ellison and Sarah Watkins. Thomas was born at The Jolly Sailor Inn in George Street Parramatta. John had helped 'put down a mutiny' on the Albermarle in 1791. He was given a Ticket of Leave as a reward. He did indeed become the Innkeeper of the Jolly Sailor and also government Stores Keeper in Parramatta. However, from there, the story becomes fiction.

Thomas Ellison
1902

John's second biological son however (William was not his son, he was Sarah's) John Thomas Ellison was Educated at Cape's Academy in Sydney and Attended the School with Sir James Martin and Hon George Thornton. Thomas' father, John Ellison, often took the boys to school in his boat. But according to oral family history, they also sometimes stayed in town (probably during the week). We do not know where. They may have occasionally walked home on weekends. We do know that John Ellison or one of the other boat owners could have collected them. The witnesses at John and Sara's wedding were John and Martha Bishop. They inspired Jack and Martha Turner. Martha Bishop was actually a convict on the Neptune in 1789.

Thomas' eldest biological brother, John, married Amelia Huff (daughter of Joseph Huff, a convict who 'stole' a sheep, after it wandered into his yard). Thomas married Elizabeth (Betsy) Huff, Amelia's sister.

John and Sara's second son, Henry, married a Julia McCarthy, an Irish lady who for some reason is buried with a Catholic priest named Charles McCarthy, possibly her brother, in the Catholic Cemetery on Pennant Hills Road, Parramatta. The grave is clearly visible from the road, as a 'Table' grave.

Thomas was born at The Jolly Sailor Inn in George Street, Parramatta, where his parents ran the Inn and also the Government stores. He trained as a blacksmith in town. Betsy's parents, Joseph and Mary Amelia Huff, ran one of the other Inns in town. Thomas and Betsy later owned and ran the Arms Of Australia in Emu Plains as well as Ellison's Pinch at Linden.

Sir James Martin ; Martin Place, politician and Chief Justice. (inspired Tim).
Hon George Thornton - politician in the NSW Legislative Council (also Tim).

Reverend Clarke's find of gold at Hartley was certainly true, a few specks were found in the creek in April 1844. He reported his finds to Gov Gipps. Wills' find of an escarpment is totally from my imagination. I have not even been to Hartley. The gold finds at Ophir were also genuine but certainly not in the quantities that I have here. I believe there is still some there.

Miss Amelia Stather and Miss Fiona Moreton are fictitious nieces of Reverend William Clarke's wife Maria Moreton.

I have invented a fiancé for Lieutenant Charles Chester Master who died in the carriage accident that also killed Lady Mary Fitzroy. He did however, have a brother Lieutenant F Robert Chester Master, who with Gov Fitzroy followed the coffin. They both served in the 58th Foot. They were two of ten children. The accident occurred on 7 Dec 1847 at Parramatta.

Emu Hall at Emu Plains is the building I have modelled Wills and Cathys' house from. It however was not built until 1851 and was remodelled in the 1880s.

Harry and Vicky's house I have modelled from my own grandparents house, Yodalla in Emu Plains (built in 1880's). James and Sara Hunter lived at The Arms of Australia Inn, Still in Emu Plains today as a Museum.

I was named after her.

James Hunter
1902

Another Landmark Gone

Mr Thomas Ellison, a resident of this district for a number of years, passed away at his daughter's (Mrs James Hunter's) residence, Emu Plains, about 4 o'clock on Friday morning. The old gentleman, who was 88 years of age, was a native of Parramatta, and was born at the "Jolly Sailor," an old George-street hotel. This hotel and the adjoining store was built by Mr Ellison's father, who had at the time a contract for the provisioning of convicts. The deceased was a schoolmate of the late Sir James Martin, the late Hon George Thornton, and many other old colonists. In 1840 he was married to his late wife, then a Miss Hough, the late Rev Mr Bobart officiating. During Mr Ellison's long life he kept an important hotel at Linden, then called Ellison's Pinch, where he had any amount of strange adventures with bushrangers and other desperadoes. He at first, so it is stated, kept the old Pilgrim Inn at the top of Lapstone, which the late Mr Wascoe carried on until the iron horse crippled the traffic and he had to shut up shop. The late Mr Ellison has been unwell for some time, and his death was not unexpected. He leaves a family as follows: Mr J T Ellison, Springwood; Mr James Ellison, Emu Plains; Mrs J King and Mrs James Hunter, Emu Plains; and Mrs F B M Coogan, Parramatta; besides a number of grandchildren and some great grandchildren. The funeral takes place this Saturday afternoon. Some further particulars will appear next week.

Bibliography

Reverend'd William Clarke
http://adb.anu.edu.au/biography/Clarke-william-branwhite-3228

The Great Game:- added Poonah connection
https://en.wikipedia.org/wiki/The_Great_Game

Gov George Gipps
http://adb.anu.edu.au/biography/gipps-sir-george-2098

Squatters rules
https://en.wikipedia.org/wiki/Squatting_(Australian_history)

Tolls
https://en.wikipedia.org/wiki/Mount_Victoria,_New_South_Wales

Ghost story
https://mountvictoria.nsw.au/our-great-places/victoria-pass/
From: The Ghost Guide to Australia by Richard Davis. Bantam, 1988.

Brolga story
https://www.abc.net.au/science/articles/2001/06/01/2614588.htm
Brolga - by John Gould - Image Right
https://en.wikipedia.org/wiki/Brolga#/media/
File:John_Gould_Australian_brolga.jpg

Roseneath advert
https://en.wikipedia.org/wiki/Roseneath_Cottage
for rent again 22 Aug 1844

The Dandy Horse Match. 6 Dec 1845 - bycicle ride
https://trove.nla.gov.au/newspaper/article/59765340?
searchTerm=parramatta%2C%20%20%22

Female Orphan school
https://www.westernsydney.edu.au/femaleorphanschool/home/
the_female_orphan_school_1813_to_1850

FirzRoy accident
https://trove.nla.gov.au/newspaper/article/12893742?searchTerm=charles%20chester%20Masters
https://trove.nla.gov.au/newspaper/article/65979501?searchTerm=charles%20chester%20Masters
Shipping
http://marinersandships.com.au/1847/07/027joh.htm

Gold discovery- Bathurst 12 February 1851
https://en.wikipedia.org/wiki/Edward_Hargraves

Roads across mountains
https://australianfoodtimeline.com.au/road-across-blue-mountains/

founding of Sydney Uni
https://www.nma.gov.au/defining-moments/resources/sydney-university

Parramatta map 1812
https://historyandheritage.cityofparramatta.nsw.gov.au/sites/phh/files/wp-images/2014/10/
Parramatta-Town-Map-1812_Meehan_LSP00431.jpg

Mitchells 1839 Map 1st Expedition
https://sp.lyellcollection.org/content/287/1/343/tab-figures-data
Hargraves
https://en.wikipedia.org/wiki/Edward_Hargraves

Revd William Branwhite Clarke
the Father of Australian Geology

(1798-1878), geologist and Anglican clergyman, was b 2 June
1798 at East Bergholt, Suffolk, England.

*Plain Statements and Practical Hints Respecting the Discovery and Working of Gold in
Australia* and in 1860 *Researches in the Southern Gold Fields of New South Wales*
https://adb.anu.edu.au/biography/clarke-william-branwhite-3228
**In 1988 William Clarke College open In Dural.
Reverend William B. Clarke is one of Australia's real heroes.**

If you loved this book, you may also enjoy these similar titles.
(All are stand-alone stories)

First Fleet Convict Era Trilogy 1788-1800

Gentle Annie Soames

Her dreams lead to unexpected outcomes. An Australian First Fleet story.

A First Fleet story with the descriptions taken directly from the Journal of Doctor Arthur Bowes Smith was the doctor on board the Lady Penrhyn.

Annie Soames is a girl beloved by the community but not afraid to voice her desires. That leads to trouble, illicit love, and a world turned upside down.

Oliver Quilpie, the newly married Marquess, finds his arranged marriage unsatisfactory; he is irresistibly drawn to his wife's companion. Unfortunately, he can't keep his hands off her. In retaliation, Annie copies his every move while riding, dressed as a highwayman. However, she has now fallen in love with him. This ultimately leads to her arrest and banishment to a distant land.

After some years, Oliver's wife dies, and his thoughts turn to Annie. He seeks to find her, but she has vanished. He is horrified to discover she was transported to New South Wales as a convict on the *Lady Penrhyn.* Will Annie want to see him?

ISBN 9780645441574   ISBN ebook 9781923097063   LP ISBN 978-1923097346
https://mybook.to/GentleAnnieSoames

Long-listed in the Historical Fiction Company Competition 2024

The Emancipated Potter

Sydney Cove 1788 to Parramatta 1795

Not all felons are convicts, and not all convicts are felons.

Colin Osborne's serene life as a talented potter is crushed by a self-important peer. A single punch sends Colin across to the other side of the globe.

Aggie Gibbs is a young convict girl being hunted by a wayward soldier. The two find themselves in a town of criminals and lecherous men.

Captain John Hunter is Colin's mentor, and he paves the way for a new life for his young friends. Then disaster strikes, and he must leave.

Can Colin keep Aggie safe? Will they fulfil Captain Hunter's wishes to build a decent life for the convicts destined to live out their lives in the penal town? Will John ever return to New South Wales? Paperback ISBN 9781923097476   ISBN ebook 9781923097483

Paternity Unknown

Sydney 1788 - 1800 The Aftermath of the First Fleet landing.

Can forgiveness be that easy?

Connie Waterson is traumatised after she became one of the victims of the attack when the convict women were landed on February 6th, 1788. She finds herself expecting an unwanted child. Along with her friends, she must learn to cope with the challenges of their new environment while protecting the life growing within her.

Nigel Bray is a young convict who almost instantly regrets his carnal actions on the day the prisoners from the *Lady Penrhyn* landed. Knowing that Connie is the unwilling recipient of his base desires, Nigel does what he can to ease her path. He is racked with questions: is the child his? Will she ever forgive him? What must Nigel do to win Connie's trust?

ISBN 9781923097438   ISBN ebook 9781923097445   LP ISBN 978-1923097452

The Hunter to Macquarie Collection 1795-1822

When Upon Life's Billows

Sydney 1795-1821 - Governor John Hunter

Keep your friends close, and your enemies closer.

John Hunter loved his life at sea. The wind blows where no man knows, and John is caught in a storm. His ship, the *HMS Sirius,* was wrecked in 1790. Five years later, he became the second governor of the rough and filthy penal settlement of New South Wales. From a place he once loved, he now seems to be in the wrong place at the wrong time, trusting the wrong people.

Helena Rosedale is not your typical female convict. She fiercely battles to prevent the men from abusing her, earning her the nickname "*Helena the Hellcat.*"

Crispin Milroy, alone in the world, serves on the new governor's security detail. Can he win the fair lady's heart? Life in 1795 in Sydney Cove was harsh at best. Food is scarce, and disease often ravages the settlement. Life throws everything at these three, yet somehow, they manage to survive. Why does John trust this young couple when others betray him? What trials must Helena and Crispin endure to make their new lives in this unforgiving town bearable? How can John ease their path?

ISBN: 9780645783339   ebook ISBN: 9780645783346

The Saddler's Song
London 1790s to Parramatta 1840s
The Strains of Starting Again.

George Ellis is the son of a tanner, living on the outskirts of London. Alone and hurting after a disease takes his family, he seeks a new life, setting up a business in New South Wales. His beloved violin is his most treasured possession, and his talent for making music is hidden from all but a select few.

Ben Parker, a saddler, is also heading to the colony. Combining their skills to start afresh in a new world, the young men find accommodation with a family. Two of the daughters steal their hearts — but how will the business survive in a stock-starved land where access to leather is limited? What is the saddler's song, and why is it so special?

ISBN: 9780645783353   eISBN: 9780645783360

Tuppence to Pass
London 1800s to Parramatta 1820s
An Unlikely Partnership

Josh Callan is a London lad making the best of the life dealt to him. Stealing from the man who killed his father, Josh gets arrested. The judge belittles him, saying he is not worth tuppence. Transported to the penal colony of Sydney, Josh arrives at the commencement of Governor Lachlan Macquarie's term.

Life in the Colonial town opens opportunities Josh could never have dreamed about and soon proves his worth to the Governor, becoming his confidante.

Can Josh find his niche? Where will this strange friendship take Josh and his family?

ISBN : 9781923097070   eISBN: 9781923097087

His Majesty's Pageboy
London to Emu Plains, Australia, in the 1800s

Jack Turner was born into a life of pomp and privilege that was not rightfully his. He was brought to the royal court for his protection. By the age of ten, he served as King George III's pageboy and was known as Lord John. For years, he struggled against society's immorality and people's shallowness; then, he met an unspoiled young girl whose purity stood out amidst the mire of humanity. He is unable to pursue her before his life hits a wall.

Martha Alexander is the daughter of a wealthy shipping merchant. She has been presented to London's second tier of society, where she meets the young man of her dreams. She is expected to marry well, and Lord John sets her heart fluttering. However, her father's drinking shatters her future. He was made to sign all his possessions away while drunk, unknowingly including his daughter. Refusing a forced marriage changes her life. How did these two young people end up as convicts in Australia?

Paperback ISBN 9781923097308   eISBN 978192309792

Coming 2026
A Fist Full of Holey Dollars
Sydney Cove 1810+

Captain **Rudi Greenwood** is a solitary man trapped in a job without a purpose in a land where alcohol is the currency and rules are frequently ignored in the pursuit of wealth.

Bethany Edwards is a grieving widow expecting her late husband's child. Rudi's attraction to the lovely widow compels him to reassess his views and contemplate someone new. She seeks Rudi's help and support, but is that all she truly feels?

When **Governor Lachlan Macquarie** asks Rudi for help improving the roads, a casual remark alters Rudi's life and affects the entire colony. To tackle the alcohol issue, he proposes creating a new currency. With Bethany by his side, will he rise to the governor's challenges? What actions led to him being despised by the exclusives and free settlers in the colony?   Paperback ISBN 9781923097407   eISBN 9781923097414

Coming 2026
Far From the Whispering Sheoaks
Set in Australia in 1817+

Fanny Little was in the wrong place doing something she thought was legal. Her actions led to her arrest, trial, and banishment. She was assigned from the female prison to ex-soldier Gordon McKenzie and soon found herself in the despicable and humiliating situation of being sold in the public marketplace.

Phil Bentley is a man running from his jealous uncle. He is seeking safety on a secluded farm half a world away. With the community backing them, can Phil save Fanny from Gordon's vile abuse? Why is their relationship destined to spark controversy? And who is Jas? Why does Gordon wish to harm the child? Will they ever escape the shadows pursuing them?   Paperback ISBN 9781923097315   eISBN9781923097322

Coming 2026

Bound Down in Iron Chains

An Australian Historical Tale, set in the Boys' Orphanage in Sydney in 1818+

Smuggling, Rum and Ructions

Howard Marlow is a studious and honest London bookkeeper. When asked to help a friend's brother with his bookkeeping, he unknowingly helps a crime gang. He is arrested, convicted, and transported. On arrival, Howard is assigned to the boy's orphanage, where a possibly crooked soldier is in charge. He is asked to use his skills to decipher bookkeeping entries that make no sense. He discovers his love for the affection-starved boys at the orphanage.

Naomi Buckingham, a convict girl, is thrust into the harsh reality of the orphanage alongside Howard. She is assigned to the orphanage, but it is far from the refuge she had hoped for. The supervisor is a man who does not respect women. With no one to rely on but the new accountant, she grapples with the question of trust.

Naomi is the key to breaking the bookkeeping code and cracking the case wide open. Can Howard use his brains to save them both? How do they become involved with some of the worst criminals in the New South Wales penal colony?

Paperback ISBN 9781923097353   eISBN9781923097360

Coming 2026

Unlikely Convict Ladies Trilogy 1792-1840s

Dancing to Her Own Tune

Co-authored by Sheila Hunter and Sara Powter

Sydney 1790s to England 1830s

Annie White is released after serving seven years as a convict in Sydney. She has a visitor who helps her start a baking business. Annie is then asked to assist another ailing man, **Sam Corbett**. She nurses him back to health, and a relationship blossoms between them. They settle into a life together, barely making ends meet, when she realises she's expecting a child. Sam's past is laid bare, and he must come to terms with the revelations. They both must confront their accusers and discover that the answers to their questions are not what they anticipated. Their life experiences seem to cling to them, and unable to shake them off, they end up back in England. They must face their ghosts and recognise they are not who they think they are. How can they transform their anger and spite into love and forgiveness? The Dance of Life goes on.

ISBN 9780645110715   ISBN9780645110722

Long-listed for the Historical Fiction Company Competition 2022

Amelia's Tears

Parramatta 1828 – England 1840s

From Tears of Sadness to Tears of Joy.

Amelia Westaweller awaits her assignment in the Parramatta Female Prison. Forced to leave the relative safety of gaol, she is assigned and now faces her worst nightmare. A foul man claims her and makes her life a living hell. Then, her world goes black. A glimmer of hope arises when she hears from her brother, Jim, who has enlisted a friend to help her. She writes to Jim, pouring out her heart and telling him of the horrors of her new life. He encourages her to stay firm in her faith. All she can do is pray. When Major **Ned** Grace, her brother's friend, enters her life in Parramatta, he starts to ease her path. Things have changed, as now she has a child in tow. How can Amelia forge a new life for herself? What man could want her with her background and a child at her side? Who is the gentleman who turns her tears of sadness into tears of great joy?

ISBN: 9780645110739   eISBN: 9780645110746 Hard Cover ISBN 9798420617953

A Lady in Irons

England 1800s - Parramatta 1808+

Katy Harrington is mourning the death of her husband after he died in a shooting accident. Barely coping, she awaits the birth of their child. If it's a girl, she must hand the family home to her husband's brother. The day after giving birth to a daughter, she and her daughter are left on the side of a road. She collapses and is found by someone she thought had died in a fire ten years before. **Perry White**, badly scarred himself, nurses her back to health. They marry and move in with his widowed friend, Mary.

After some years, she discovers her husband and friend in each other's arms. Now living in a love triangle, she flees. Grasping the only straw available, she intentionally gets arrested and is sent to a colony far away. By doing this, her marriage can be annulled.

What happens in the Colony is different from what she expects. Governor Macquarie comes to her rescue, but what of Perry and her children?

ISBN: 9780645110784   eISBN:9780645441505

NO MORE, MY *Love*

Hunter Valley, NSW, 1820s

Jess Elkin is distraught when tragedy ravages her family. Now widowed, she becomes the victim of a carriage accident and is nursed back to health by the driver.

Marcus Ryan, a hard-headed woollen mill owner, was not expecting to fall in love. Yet, when Jess's fortunes suddenly turn for the worse, Marcus must decide how far he will go to pursue her. Years after following her to Newcastle, Australia, Marcus vanishes. Jess is left wondering if he will keep his promise to return to her… Will she ever see him again?

ISBN: 9780645441536   eISBN 9780645441581

Long-listed in the Historical Fiction Company Competition 2023

The Vine Weaver

Hawkesbury River area 1820s+

New Beginnings and Old Threats

In the 1820s, **Joel and Hetty Walker** lived on a secluded farm on the Hawkesbury River, which became a haven for the protection of young convict women. A series of events brings **Fran Rea** to Hetty's attention, and she is taken to the farm. Fran and Hetty develop a cottage industry under the compassionate eye of farmhand **Hector Macdougal;** Hector's loving words change lives. It is to him that Fran turns when threatened.

The vines now must draw them close to survive the future revelations, and of those, there are many.

ISBN: 9780645441512   eISBN: 9780645441529

Long-listed in the Historical Fiction Company Competition 2023

https://amazon.com/dp/0645441511   https://amazon.com/dp/B0C6Z552Y2

The story continues in "Scotch at The Rocks"…

Scotch at The Rocks

Glasgow, Scotland, early 1800s to The Rocks, Sydney 1830s

Orphaned children Brodie Stewart and Heather Anderson live on Glasgow's streets. Although hungry, they somehow manage to survive and stay out of trouble. Heather finds a job and looks to be settled; things go pear-shaped for them both. Eventually, they marry by declaration, but even that gets complicated, and they are both arrested soon after exchanging their vows. In 1838, they were transported to Sydney as convicts. Heather arrives within weeks of Brodie, and they are assigned close to each other. They are now living in the docklands of Sydney, known as The Rocks. They now have to forge a new life halfway across the world from their homeland.

Adventures abound, and Brodie gets press-ganged. While he's away, Heather's life changes and soon, she's officially selling Scotch Whisky at a shop in The Rocks.

You can take a Scot out of Scotland, but where did the Scotch come from?

ISBN 9780645441550 ebook 9781923097001 Large Print 9781923097254

https://mybook.to/ScotchatTheRocks

Waiting at the Sliprails

The Bathurst Road 1830s

A Convict's Tale

Bea Dawes's term of conviction nears an end, and she has few options other than marriage to a stranger or going on the street.

Jack Barnes, the hired drover, wants a wife. Bea accepts his offer; then, she discovers that he could be gone for months, leaving her alone with **Billy and Netty**, part of the tribe of an Aboriginal tribe who live on his secluded farm. Bea learns to love her husband and also this wonderful Aboriginal couple. Drought ravages the farm, and Jack must hit the long paddock with the flock. In his absence, a visitor arrives, threatening to destroy everything she has worked so hard for. Can Bea touch her heart? Can she cope? Will the drought ever end? And when will Jack return?

ISBN: 9780645441543   eISBN: 9781923097032

https://mybook.to/WaitingattheSliprails

August 2023

PenCraft Award Winner for Literary Excellence
Christian Historical Fiction 2024

Convict Shadows of the Past
Two Jennifers, two hundred years apart

When she discovers her convict family history, eight-year-old Jenny Kellow learns that she was named after a convict from nearly two hundred years ago. Inspired by her grandfather's stories, she delves into her ancestors' convict past. From him, she hears tales of bushrangers, convicts, and life in the early colony of Parramatta. She embarks on a journey to retrace the footsteps of her convict great-great-great-grandmother to honour her. Jenny's quest begins with microfiche in the 1960s, where she discovers a small tin mining town in Cornwall and the production of a cheese that set London alight. She uncovers that her ancestor, **Jennifer Kellow,** brought her cheese-making skills to Parramatta, where she taught others the craft. Echoes of the past can still be heard if you know where to listen. Who was the first Jennifer, and what does she have to do with cheese? Why is she so elusive? Did Jenny's ancestor, Jennifer, ever see those two small crosses carved into the bricks of the Female Factory? Would Jenny ever uncover her ancestor's story?   ISBN: 9780645783315   ISBN ebook 9780645783322
A NaNoWriMo 2022 book winner

In Defence of Her Honour
London 1800s to Parramatta 1819
Will the real man of quality please stand up?

Bill Miller was raised and educated with the sons of the family. The youngest, Bert Edison-Browne, had been his best friend. However, jealousy intervenes when Bill's excellent schoolwork begins to curtail their friendship. He wins a scholarship and enters Oxford University. When Bill's father dies unexpectedly, Bert insists that Bill take over as butler, but it's more to oppress him. Bert's jealousy grows and festers. He is now looking for a way to rid themselves of their new butler. A ruckus ensues, and Bill is arrested for assaulting Bert.

Molly Ross, the housekeeper's daughter, will vouch for him. It's too late; Bill has been arrested and is soon to be sentenced and transported. With Bill gone, Molly now fights to defend herself from Bert. After hitting him with a pan, she, too, is arrested and sent to Sydney. Bill and Molly arrive with letters of introduction and compensation from Bert's father. Soon, they will be running the best inn in Parramatta with an endorsement from the governor.
                ISBN 9780645441567   ISBN ebook 9781923097049
Long-listed in the Historical Fiction Company Competition 2024

I Can't Stop Tomorrow
Irish Famine 1840s to Avoca Beach, Australia

Escaping bigotry and prejudice in Ireland, the O'Shane family lives on a secluded farm on the west coast of Ireland. The potato blight soon decimated their farm. It's always darkest before dawn, and the two remaining girls cling to the hope of a new life. With the kindness of strangers, the eldest girls, **Clare** and **Kerry O'Shane,** head to their cousin, Sal Lockley, in Parramatta, Australia.   A new, wonderful life awaits them both. **Shéamus Connor** is the annoying teenage boy who reluctantly draws Clare's affection. However, living in a convict town means ruffians abound.

John Moore is a bad-tempered and troubled Irishman who is content to live alone on another secluded farm until he discovers Clare and two other lads need rescuing.
Can John protect her from the pain inflicted by an evil world?
Can Shéamus find his lost love, who has fled?
                ISBN: 9780645441598   ISBN ebook 9781923097056

Madeline's Boy
England 1830s to New South Wales 1840
The race to protect an Orphaned Boy
All is not straightforward when money and titles are involved.

Orphaned, afraid and on the run, Chip must flee.
Madeline was his mother's best friend. Maddie now needs to keep her charge safe and alive. She must give up her life to protect the boy she has loved since birth.
Months after Chip's parents' demise, Maddie sets out to deliver Chip to his Uncle Humphrey, who lives in Sydney. Through him, she meets Chip's uncle's friend, Tim, who falls for Maddie—but will they find happiness?
The menacing presence soon finds Chip, and Maddie needs to hide him again. They are relocated from hidden farms to secret valleys, ultimately ending up in an Aboriginal encampment.
Can Tim find a way to be with Maddie? And if so… Will Chip ever be safe?
                ISBN: 9780645783308   ISBN ebook 9781923097094
Long-listed in the Historical Fiction Company Competition 2024
https://mybook.to/MadelinesBoy

Jam or Marmalade for Tea

England 1820s to New South Wales 1825 (Governor Brisbane Era)

Martha Hamilton is the eldest of four orphans struggling to survive on their own. She is caught stealing, tried, convicted, and transported to New South Wales. With her family gone, she becomes despondent. Life holds no meaning for her, and the ocean waves look inviting.

Captain Guy Manning is a frustrated and injured redcoat soldier returning to Sydney for a new assignment. He notices Martha trying to jump overboard and rescues her. How do two cats bring them together?

A convict ship is no place for romance, and she's far too young anyway, isn't she?

Can Guy save her and forge a life together for them? What connections does he have to try to save her siblings? Why is marmalade important for their future?

Paperback ISBN 9781923097933   eISBN9781923097285

A NaNoWriMo 2023 book winner

A prequel to 'The Lockleys Parramatta' series
(Free novella with newsletter signup)

Unshackled Lives

Set in England & Australia in the 1800s
Australian historical fiction of early colonial days

Ned Lockley is the second of four sons of the Duke and Duchess of Gracemere. As his mother's favourite, his childhood years were blissful, but he needed to grow up, and quickly.

A whirlwind romance is followed by a loved one's betrayal. The following emotional turmoil is particularly challenging for Ned to cope with, especially amid a collapsing and immoral society.

Ned can't stay as his family is falling apart. His mother's words to remain true to himself and his faith make him leave everything he knows. How did Ned end up in New South Wales in charge of placing female convicts? Will he ever find happiness or discover who Charles is?

ISBN 9781923097377   eISBN 9781923097384   LP ISBN: 9781923097391

A 100-year, six-part Australian Colonial series

The Lockleys of Parramatta 1800-1900

Hands upon the Anvil

A blacksmith's life and love are more than work
Parramatta 1830s

Eddie Lockley's parents were transported for their crimes. Can a steadfast lad rise above his origins and guide others to succeed in a land of opportunity?

Ten-year-old Eddie longs to help his mum and dad. Living in a convict town with his family, the keen youngster has been working with the local blacksmith since his sixth birthday. But when a lieutenant doesn't stop abusing his older brother, the young boy yearns for the day when he can stand up and end the torment. Though he's thrilled when his mentor offers to send him off to learn his letters, Eddie fears he won't be around to watch his siblings' backs. But as he takes on the biggest adventure of his life, the brave believer soon discovers that God is looking out for everyone he loves. Does this young man in the making have what it takes to change everything for the better?

ISBN 9780994578235   Ebook ISBN 978-0-9945782-5-9   Hardcover 9798496177368

Out Where The Brolgas Dance

Gold is found, and so is love
Parramatta 1840s
How can a question change so many people?

It's the 1840s, and discoveries across the Blue Mountains continue. Major Mitchell's new road is complete, and towns are planned and being built. Abundant land is available for those who want it. Eighteen-year-old **William "Wills" Lockley** has laid a solid foundation for a respectable career as a blacksmith, but the Lockley lust for adventure flows deeply within his veins. He dreads the monotony of work at the blacksmith's forge and yearns for adventure in a new frontier. Wills meets six Englishmen (*Coping with what is now known as PTSD*) who have the means to make his dreams come true. What they discover changes the Colony and their lives forever. Gold fever ensues. While in the West, Wills must deal with an uncertain romance. Does Cathy even want him?

ISBN 9780994578242 Ebook ISBN 978-0-9945782-6-6 Hardcover ISBN 9798755445504
LP ISBN 9781923097155

Diamonds in the Dirt
Diamonds, love and money… but there is much more to life.
Parramatta 1850s

The youngest Lockley son, **Luke Lockley**, has completed his university education, and his life lacks direction. No job, no money, and no love. Desperately alone, he prays for guidance. How can Luke trust that God has a plan for him if he can't even find a job? He does the only thing he can … he prays. Within a week, life has changed … oh, how it has changed as his brother Wills turns up with a suggestion. Would Luke be interested in joining the expedition with John Evans? **Reverend William Clarke** needs assistance with a government mineral survey. The challenges, adventures and finds are life-changing for many. However, it gives Luke meaning, purpose and direction. The condition of his heart problems also takes a turn. Can he walk away? Will she wait for him?

ISBN: 9780994578273 Ebook ISBN: 978-0-9945782-8-0 Hard cover ISBN 979-8788011141
https://mybook.to/DiamondsintheDirt

The Earl's Shadow
Who or what is the 'shadow'? How does it affect so many?
Parramatta 1860s

Charles Lockley is the Earl of Coxheath. He spent his youth as a convict in Parramatta and had no idea he was an Earl. He had minimal education and few social skills; his eldest son, **Charlie,** is no different.

Now faced with mortality, Charles has to work out how to live the remainder of his life after a near-death experience. He is called to step way out of his comfort zone in London. His action will change the world for many. The echoes from the past still haunt Charlie. London is calling the family, and they can't postpone the trip. How does the Cobb and Co. coach driver **Jim Leslie** fit in? And precisely what is *'The Earl's Shadow'* that he speaks about? What happens if the 'Shadow' is gone?

ISBN: 9780645110708 Ebook ISBN 978-0-9945782-9-7
Released June 2022
https://mybook.to/TheEarlsShadow

Once a Jolly Swagman
An old black Billy Can contains the secrets of an incredible life
An Australian Historical Novel Inspired by the songs of The Seekers
Set in 1870s Parramatta and Kent, UK

Rick Lockley, struggling to escape his family's expectations, runs away to find himself. **Jack,** a jolly swagman, takes him under his care. Even after years together, Rick knows little about the old man.

On his death, Jack leaves Rick his precious billy can; the contents reveal Jack's identity. Stunned, Rick must travel to England to finalise Jack's wishes. There, he uncovers Jack's life of love, betrayal and a link to his own family. Rick also discovers there is much more to learn about this enigmatic man.

ISBN 9780645110753   Ebook ISBN 978-0-6451107-6-0
Released Sept 2022
https://mybook.to/OnceaJollySwagman

Jonty's Journey
Gems, Love, Artists and a Golden Lion
Australia and South Africa 1880-1902

Sydney Jeweller Jonty Evans's passion for gems takes him to Africa at a volatile time. There, he finds the diamonds he wants and is given a lion cub. However, Jonty is all but kidnapped. His experiences in the Transvaal plunge him into questioning everything he knows about life. Soon, nightmares haunt him. (This is now known as PTSD.)

Upon returning home, he nearly ruins his chance with **Lottie** before it even begins, and he finds adjusting hard. Lottie's father, **Luke** Lockley from Parramatta, takes him under his wing and directs him to someone who can assist.

Jonty is then called back to Africa as a liaison and reunites with his lion, Chimbu, after saving the life of his security detail. His life journey introduces him to remarkable artists, politicians, poets, rebels, and the scapegoat soldier Harry Breaker Morant. Can Jonty lay the past to rest and find his lost peace?

ISBN 9780645110777 HC ISBN 9781923097124   Ebook ISBN: 978-0-6451107-9-1
Released Feb 2023
https://mybook.to/JontysJourney

Mattie

The Story of an Australian Convict Child
An Australian Historical Story inspired by real Life.

An orphaned child, Mattie, is convicted of petty theft, sentenced to seven years, and sent to Australia. She meets another convict woman who, at her death, gives Mattie a chance for a new life. She makes the most of everything that comes her way, earning her freedom, falling in love, marrying, and becoming a mother. But life is not kind to her.

She meets bushrangers, moves to the gold fields in Bathurst, and starts a store. Yet, she is the kind of woman who made Australia what it is today. Can she survive alone in a man's world? She is a remarkable woman who breaks down all her barriers.

(Mattie's story continues in The Lockleys of Parramatta - bk 4 & 6)

ISBN 9781503252370 & ebook AISN BOOTTEDBTO

(The story continues in The Earl's Shadow & Once a Jolly Swagman)
Released 2015
https://mybook.to/Mattie_sh

Ricky

A boy in Colonial Australia

Ricky English and his mother immigrated from England to join his father in the new Colony of Sydney. Upon arrival, there was no sign of his father. Ricky's mum uses the tiny amount of money they brought to get lodgings in a run-down building. Things go from bad to worse when his mother dies; he is thrown out of the hired rooms, and the caretakers confiscate all their possessions.

Ricky lives on the streets of Sydney Town as a street waif. Ricky finds safe places to sleep and befriends freed convicts who can help him survive. One day, he encounters a lost child and helps reunite her with her family. These people try to help him, but he insists on doing things his way because of his stubbornness. However, he has found a mentor and confidante. The story follows him through his life. He survives and turns his life around, helping others along the way. ***(Will's story continues in Jonty's Journey)***

Paperback ISBN 9780994578211   Kindle ASIN: B00MLYN6IG
Released 2014
https://mybook.to/Ricky_sh

The Heather to The Hawkesbury

Four Scottish families brave a new life in a strange land.

Mary Macdonald and husband **Murd** and family; her brother **Fergus** MacKenzie; sister-in-law **Caro** MacLeod; cousin **Alex** Fraser and all their families who have had to emigrate from the Isle of Skye during the "Clearances."

The story follows the four families from Scotland as they sail to the NSW colony in the 1850s. Mary does not cope with the changes and losses that occur in the first months in the colony. The other women in the family rely on her, and she nearly crumbles. The families struggle together through accidents, losses, trials, floods, and hard work, forging a strong bond with their new country. Trials, tribulations and triumphs see the four families make a firm mark in their new homeland. The immigrants from Scotland helped make Australia what it is today.

ISBN 978994578228   ebook AISN B01A21JYWQ   Large Print ISBN1533473641

Available on Amazon/Kindle & Large Print
Released 2016
https://mybook.to/TheHeathertTHawkesbury

Sara's Author Bio

Sheila Hunter and Sara Powter were a passionate mother-and-daughter team of amateur genealogists. While working together on their family tree, they made many captivating discoveries. Our most significant discovery was finding four convicts who held very different perspectives on life in the colony from the military. These four felons were transported to Australia between 1792 and 1814, during the height of convict transportation. Before her passing in 2002, Sheila adapted some of these histories into enchanting stories, known as her Australian Colonial Trilogy. Sara later had these published. Sheila left a fourth unfinished story, inspiring Sara to complete it. However, before she did, **The Lockleys of Parramatta** were created to see if she could do justice to her mother's work. The first two in the series were completed before attempting to finish **Dancing to Her Own Tune** for her mother. (*Sheila wrote the first 30k words*)

Vividly living through the Colonial Era, these books delve further into the theme of overcoming adversity in Colonial Australia, and how it developed, the demise of the Convict system and the discovery of mineral wealth.

Sara skilfully intertwines precise archival data with a captivating narrative to craft a collection of stories about faith, love, loss, and redemption.

Two hundred years after her family arrived in Australia, Sara continues the Australian Colonial stories that start with **Gentle Annie Soames**, a saga about the First Fleet. Her **First Fleet Trilogy** is now complete. Following this chronologically are **The Hunter to Macquarie Collection,** the **Unlikely Convict Ladies Trilogy**, and The **Lockleys of Parramatta. The Convict Birthstain Collection**, set in the mid-1800s, follows. All the stories are stand-alone novels. There is a chronological list of her books on her web page.

See Sara's web page to keep up to date with more stories.
An online store is available for a signed copy of Sara's books.
https://www.sarapowter.com.au/ (*Australian Postage only*)

Feel free to email her at
saragpowter@gmail.com

BOOK BUB
https://partners.bookbub.com/authors/6273615/edit

FACEBOOK   https://www.facebook.com/profile.php?
id=100063887262514

Do you want the book *"Unshackled Lives"* *for free?*
Download from Book Funnel after you sign up.

FREE Newsletter signup
From my web page.